A Whisper of Chaos & Crowns

Jordan A. Day

<u>**CONTENT WARNING**</u>

PRONUNCIATION GUIDE

PLACES

DISPARYA:	DIS - PAR - YUH
CAELUM:	KAY - LOOM
MINISTRO:	MIN - EE - STROW
AGNITIO:	AGNEE - SHE - OH
VENATOR:	VEN - AH - TOUR
TENEBRAE:	TEH - KNEE - BRAY
VORSUTOS:	VOR - SUE - TOWS
PRAVUS:	PRA - VUS

MAGIC

UNDA:	OO - N - DA
IGNISIAN:	IG - NISS - EE - AN
AERIAN:	AIR - EE - AN
MEDICUS:	MED - EE - CUSS
EMPATHI:	EM - PATH - EE
IMPERIUM:	IHM - PEER - IUM
TREMO:	TREM - OH
ILLUSIO:	ILL - OO - SEE - OH
MAGUSIER:	MAG - OO - SEER
VERUS:	VER - US
SEER:	SEE - ER
OCULI:	OC - YOU - LIE
SONOR:	SO - NOR
VENARI:	VEN - AIRY

PRONUNCIATION GUIDE

CHARACTERS

AINSLEY:	AYNZ - LEE
FELIX:	FEE - LICKS
DASHIELL:	DASH - EEL
EVANDER:	EH - VAN - DER
OLIVIER:	AH - LIH - VEER
MARCELINE:	MARSA - LEAN
LIA:	LEE - UH
CALIDORE:	CAL - EH - DOOR
TALLIS:	TAL - LIS
JAHIER:	JUH - HEAR
SIRONA:	SIH - RONA
IMOGEN:	IH - MUH - GIN
PERCEVAL:	PUR - SUH - VL
BRANDLE:	BRAN - DLE
ELENORA:	ELL - EH - NORA
OBERON:	OH - BER - ON

KINGDOMS OF DISPARYA

CAELUM
ELEMENTAL MAGIC
UNDA: WATER AND ICE
IGNISIAN: FIRE AND HEAT
AERIAN: WEATHER MANIPULATION

MINISTRO
ANATOMICAL MAGIC
MEDICUS: HEALER
EMPATHI: EMOTION MANIPULATION
IMPERIUM: ANATOMICAL MANIPULATION

AGNITIO
INTELLECTUAL MAGIC
SEER: CLAIRVOYANCE
VERUS: TRUTH TELLER
MAGUSIER: MAGIC AND BOND DETECTION

VENATOR
STEALTH MAGIC
OCULI: PRETERNATURAL VISION
SONOR: PRETERNATURAL HEARING
VENARI: PRETERNATURAL TRACKING

TENEBRAE
DARK MAGIC
TREMO: FEAR INDUCER
SHADOW SHIFTER: DARKNESS MANIPULATION
ILLUSIO: ILLUSIONISTS

DISPARYA 
VORSUTOS
TENEBRAE
AGNITIO
VENATOR
ARCANUS
MINISTRO
CAELUM
THE SOUTHERN SEA
N
E
S
W

Shade Recap

*A*nother book, another recap. I don't know about you, but I can't remember half the stuff that happened in the last installment...and I'm the one who wrote it. But do you know who probably does remember everything from the last book? Felix. So, I've once again asked him to do this very important recap for you all. Take it away, Felix!

....

......

.........*Felix?*

I'm not doing it.

What do you mean you're not doing it? The people need a recap.

Sorry, but I'm too busy BEING DEAD!

**eye roll* You're not seriously still pissed about that.*

....

Felix, the plot—

Sucks without me? I know. You only have yourself to blame for that one.

**mumbles* Dear Gods...*

I'm the fan-favorite—or at least I was. I know it. You know it. THEY *points figuratively* know it.

long sigh *I'm sorry. I did what needed to be done.*

Whatever.

Are you seriously not going to do the recap?

Nope.

Fine. I'll just go ask Brandle inst—

So Shade opens up with my best friend, Ainsley, who is heartbroken and betrayed by her ex-fiancé, Dash—the Crowned Prince of Caelum. You see, during her time with us, both Dash and I learned that she was a product of Conjoining. That meant that magic from two different kingdoms ran through her veins. It also meant that her mere existence was against our laws.

Dash learned the truth first when his father told him one evening. King Perceval instructed his son that the only way to keep Ainsley safe was to take all of her power from her during a ceremony known as Entwining. I was firmly against the idea, but Dash didn't see another way to save her from her fate if others learned what she possessed.

So he lied. We both did. Eventually, I kidnapped Ainsley and brought her to the Kingdom of Tenebrae—her *home*. And that's where our story picks up.

We discover that Ainsley not only possesses the magic of shadows but also illusions, making her Heir to Tenebrae. She wasn't thrilled at the news, knowing it meant she was tied to King Evander of Tenebrae—a man she loathed (and a complete prick).

Despite her opposition to her Gifts and Evander, Ainsley slowly started to come into herself, trusting her magic and her intuition. She began to heal from her past hurt and learn from her mistakes. She continued to bloom and flourish in her role as heir. That was never more evident than when she developed a fourth Gift, making her also the Heir to Ministro, just as her late father had once been.

The more time passed, the more confident Ainsley became in herself and her decisions. She followed Evander's lead but was never afraid to take it from him when she had an idea. He seemed to thoroughly enjoy that fact about her.

Ainsley learned a lot regarding her world and the pending war with the continent of Pravus. Evander shared his concerns and his hunt for a mythical kingdom known as Inmuto. He was hopeful that their numbers and magical abilities could help us in the war he was certain would grace the content of Disparya sooner rather than later.

We also had a theory that the soldiers from Pravus possessed magical stones that granted them the ability to stay hidden and disappear into thin air. Ainsley was hellbent on finding them.

Eventually, she grew closer to Evander, her hatred for him turning into respect, then friendship, and then finally, love. But just as Ainsley had cast aside her apprehension and fear of trusting someone who could hurt her, a secret was revealed.

Evander and Ainsley were split from the same soul, bonded in this life like no one had ever been before. He knew this fact and chose to keep it from her. She was rightfully upset, but the love they felt for each other was too much for her to cast away without a conversation. Evander shared the story of what they were and why he kept it hidden, and she had found it in her heart to forgive him.

One night, they decided to get married, but before we could conduct the ceremony, an attack on Disparya occurred. The enemy made it look like the Kingdom of Tenebrae was behind it, but we were being set up.

Ainsley decided to go back to Caelum to learn Perceval's secrets and find the stones we were after. It didn't go very well. Not only did she try to stab her ex-fiancé, Dash, every chance she could, but Perceval didn't trust her, which made her sleuthing that much more difficult.

On our last night in Caelum, she took it upon herself to enact revenge on King Perceval for his hand in both her and Evander's parents' deaths, as well as for stealing her away as an infant. She cast an illusion on him, making him believe he had the upper hand during their fight, only to stab him through the chest in the end. After killing the King of Caelum, she fled and encountered Dash on the way out.

Their battle was quick, and Ainsley was able to get away. But it didn't last for long. Shortly after we met in the woods for our escape back to Tenebrae, soldiers surrounded us after Dash had given the order. They fired at my best friend, and I dove in front of her, taking an arrow to the chest. She brutally killed them all before holding me in her arms as I died. Our tentative allies, Elenora and Brandle, showed up to help, but after exhausting his Imperium Gift, Brandle declared there was nothing he could do.

More soldiers came, and Ainsley barely made it back into Tenebrae.

She vowed to end Dash's life after I lost mine.

Prologue

Julian

"We're so close, Uriel. I can feel it," I argued as I stepped toward the wooden desk in the private library of the palace. "We can't give up the search—not yet."

The King of Tenebrae released a heavy breath as he shook his head. "I'm not saying we give up altogether, Julian," he began. He rose from his seat and discarded his pen amongst the scattered parchment on the surface. "But we've been hunting for Inmuto for centuries now and have found ourselves no closer to discovering it than we were two hundred years ago."

"But—"

"I want to find that kingdom as much as you do, especially after learning of Lord Oberon's recent visit to Perceval." My lip pulled back in a sneer at the mention of the man who had betrayed me all those centuries ago—a man whom I had once called my best friend. "But we should focus on ensuring our army is prepared for the magnitude of combat before we request aid from a kingdom that has remained hidden for eons."

He had a point. I just didn't like it.

"Have you received word on Perceval and Oberon's meeting?" I asked. Uriel nodded as he shuffled papers around in search of the small slip he eventually handed me describing the details of their encounter. "Perceval turned him down?" I said in disbelief as I read.

"According to my inside sources, Queen Calida of Caelum isn't fond of Pravus's ruler. She convinced her husband to refuse him. I'm still trying to gather what exactly was offered in the first place, though."

My lips quirked upward as I remembered the beautiful brunette with deep teal-blue eyes, a warm smile, and a kind heart who had always been too good for her husband. I tossed the paper back onto the desk before meeting Uriel's gaze once more.

"That meeting is all the more reason to ensure we have the numbers should a war occur. Venator and Ministro don't believe us, and Agnitio and Vorsutos aren't enough to claim victory," I told him.

"I know, and I'm not saying we don't eventually pick the search back up, but right now isn't the time."

I shook my head as I took another step closer, desperate for him to heed my advice. "Think about your son, Uriel."

"I *am* thinking about Evander, Julian," the King of Tenebrae said as he released a defeated sigh. He stepped around the desk and moved toward me, placing a comforting hand on my shoulder as I held his gaze. "Just as you should think about your daughter."

"Are you saying I'm not?" The accusation came out harsher than I intended.

"I'm saying, Viv is going to give birth any day now," he said with a soft smile, bringing my own to my lips. "I'm saying that before we know it, we will have two children running through this palace. Two children who deserve to have their fathers present and not traipsing through the land in search of a lost kingdom."

I wanted to argue, but I could tell by the stern look in his eye that his mind had been made up. I nodded shallowly, conceding the fight.

"I may be the King of Tenebrae and your best friend, but more than anything, I'm terrified of your wife. Viv would have both of our balls hanging over that mantle if we left at any point within the next few years," he said as he pointed to the roaring fire across the room. "And Dahlia wouldn't even try to stop her."

"Your wife would probably hand mine the blade."

"A dull one, too. Just to make it hurt worse."

I laughed and shook my head, picturing the enigmatic storm that was our wives.

"They're insanely stubborn," I pointed out.

"Argumentative," he added with a nod of agreement.

"Competitive."

"Refuse to listen to reason."

"Always have to be right."

"Even when they're *very* clearly wrong."

"Not to mention difficult," I said.

"And uncompromising."

A throat cleared at the back of the room a second before the scent of lavender and rain hit me. *Shit.*

"And beautiful," I replied.

"Gracious."

"Loving."

"Selfless."

"Forgiving."

"Definitely, forgiving. In fact, that's my favorite quality of theirs," Uriel added.

I twisted my head to peer over my shoulder, letting a look of surprise flood over my features as I took in the two women standing on the threshold of the library—One with hair as black as a starless sky, the other with auburn waves that flowed down to the swollen belly her hands rested upon.

"Oh, hello my darling," I said with a loving smile. "I didn't see you both there."

"Were we interrupting?" my wife asked innocently, her eyes narrowing into slits.

Both Uriel and I shook our heads at once before moving toward our wives and guiding them to the large couch near the fireplace, the crackling sounds of the flames adding tension to their skeptical silence.

"I love you," I told Viv as she settled herself against the cushions and propped her feet onto my lap.

"Mmhm," she replied with an arch of her brow and that defiant look I fell in love with. If our daughter possessed even a fraction of her mother's temper, may the Gods help whoever she ended up with.

I leaned forward and pressed my lips to Viv's stomach, feeling our daughter's soft kick beneath my touch. Any day now, she'd be brought into this world and bring with her as much joy and light into my life as her mother has.

I looked up through lowered lashes, meeting my wife's stare. She pressed her index finger to her lips in a silent demand. Immediately, I obliged, scooting higher until my face hovered about hers.

"I love you desperately, fervently, endlessly," I told her, emphasizing my point with a kiss between each word. She smiled against my lips and I basked in the taste of her happiness.

"Eww," a small voice called from the opposite end of the room, pulling my attention away from Viv.

"Why are you not asleep, Evander?" Dahlia scolded as she raised a brow at her son.

"I'm not tired," he replied through a yawn as he clutched a black stuffed wolf in his hand—a near-perfect replica of the small pup currently nipping at his shirt.

"Clearly," the King of Tenebrae responded with a smile. "Come say goodnight to everyone and then it's off to bed."

Evander stuck out his bottom lip and his eyes appeared to grow twice as large as he pouted. I stifled my smile as I turned away, knowing I would have given in to any request from the three-year-old if I had met his adorable stare.

"That's not going to work on me," his father said.

With a huff of agitation, tiny stomps pattered through the room until they neared the couch. I twisted again, watching him hug and kiss his mother before he hurried to me.

"Can you take me swimming tomorrow?" he whispered conspiratorially as he threw his arms around my neck.

Dahlia had already turned down the request four times this evening, but the kid was clever enough to know how to get his way. He learned early on that the easiest path to get what he wanted was to go through Olivier or myself, as we were the only two incapable of telling him *no*.

"Only if you keep it a secret," I whispered back.

Evander attempted to wink but, as usual, shut both eyelids instead of one. He moved over to Viv next, careful not to climb over her the way he did to me. He kissed her cheek before moving his little hands to her belly and hugging gently.

"Why doesn't Little Love have to go to sleep, too?" he asked as he pressed his ear to her stomach.

"She's sleeping now," Viv answered. "Which is something *you* should be doing." She ruffled his black hair, and he playfully batted her hand away before climbing down from the couch where the small wolf was waiting for him.

Evander cast his gaze over us, his brow furrowing as if he were thinking hard of a plan. Slowly, he took one deliberate step backward and then sprinted from the room and down the hall as he yelled, "No!"

We all exchanged glances for a short moment before the room filled with declarations of, "Not it!"

"Dammit," Uriel swore after finishing last in our little game. With a grunt of frustration, he got up and chased after his son who was still currently yelling his refusal down the palace corridors.

"How are we going to survive two of them?" Viv joked as her hand slid across our daughter.

"We start by asking how anyone survived the both of you," I jabbed. Both women smacked my shoulders for reasons unclear.

"She's not sleeping! She kicked me!" Evander yelled as he passed the door's opening, now running in the opposite direction down the hall. "If Little Love doesn't have to go to bed, then neither do I!"

Onyx was seen next, his floppy ears entirely too big for his head as he hurried after his owner.

"You know," Dahlia began, capturing my focus just as Uriel ran passed the door with shadows swirling around him, "Little Love is starting to stick. We could prevent that if you'd just tell me her name."

"No," I said before Viv could get the chance to reply. Dahlia had been relentless in her desire to know the name we had decided on for our daughter, but I was determined to uphold the Tenebraen tradition. "You refused to tell us Evander's name before his birth, so you're just going to have to wait for her to be born to know it."

"That's stupid. Viv, tell your husband that's stupid," she said.

"What if we only told *her*? No one else would have to know," my wife tried.

I shook my head. "She'd tell Uriel."

"I wouldn't. I don't even like my husband all that much," she lied.

I laughed at her ridiculous and, quite frankly, unbelievable response. Before I came to Tenebrae, I didn't know that love like the kind Dahlia and Uriel shared could exist. Through the centuries, they only seemed to grow closer and their love stronger.

I arched a brow, calling her out. "Fine," she grumbled. "If you're not going to tell me her name, at least let me give you a present."

The Queen of Tenebrae hurried over to the wooden desk across the room and rummaged through it until she found what she was looking for. She walked back to the couch with an excited smile on her face as she held a rectangular black velvet box between her hands.

"It's something for you to give to her," Dahlia explained.

Viviette sat up and took the box from her best friend as she stared at her skeptically. The queen squeezed onto the couch, positioning herself on Viv's right side as we both impatiently waited for my wife to open the present.

Slowly, Viv removed the lid and pulled out a delicate silver chain with a small hanging pendant. I reached out and carefully ran my fingers over the symbol of Tenebrae etched into it—a species of bird said to always lead you home no matter how lost you are.

"It matches Evander's bracelet," Dahlia explained as Viv set the necklace back into the box. "I wish I could take credit for the idea, but it was Uriel's." She threw her back against the cushions as if that fact pissed her off. I'm sure it did. The two of them were always playing games and trying to outmaneuver each other.

"It's perfect," Viv told her as she wrapped her arms around her dearest friend. "But if it was Uriel's idea, wouldn't he want to be here when we opened it?"

"Probably. But he should have thought about that before he called me argumentative and uncompromising."

The two women shot pointed glares in my direction which I narrowly avoided as I dropped my gaze to the box I took from Viv. I didn't pay much attention to the conversation as my wife explained to Dahlia that she wanted to have our weekly family dinner at a restaurant tomorrow night rather than at the palace like we usually did. Instead, my focus was on the small necklace, picturing our daughter wearing it as Evander flaunted his matching cuff.

"Do you think we made the right choice?" I asked, my eyes flicking up to meet theirs. "Having them share a soul."

Sirona had conducted a ceremony and cast the magic on Dahlia and Viviette decades ago, but I hadn't thought much about it until recently. With my daughter due any day, I couldn't help but question what we chose to do.

The room grew quiet, the smile on Viv's face faltering slightly as her hands drifted across her belly on instinct. I didn't want to upset her, but the four of us were in this together and I needed to know if they had any regrets.

"Yes," Uriel answered from the doorway, holding a small grey wolf—our daughter's wolf, Nova—named for the bright star that represented the Solum bond we tried to replicate in Evander and our daughter, though our magic failed to compare to its intensity.

He set the animal on the ground and she patted over to the couch, trying and failing miserably to jump onto it. I leaned down and gently picked her up, letting her snuggle into me as she closed her eyes in my arms.

"Onyx wouldn't stop trying to sleep on top of her and she was getting annoyed," Uriel explained as he joined us on the couch. I smiled and scratched behind her ears as her quiet snores quickly filled the space.

"You don't think they'll hate us?" I asked, referencing our earlier topic. Uriel's eyes darted across my face as a crease formed between his brows. He didn't have an answer.

"I think," Dahlia said, slicing through the growing unease, "That our children will have a bond like no other. They'll be there for one another through dark and difficult times. No matter the uncertainties they'll face, they'll always have each other."

Viv's hazel eyes met mine as she reached for my hand and squeezed gently. "That alone makes it the greatest gift we could have given them."

1

Ainsley

The sounds of shattering glass and sharp breaths filled the space, but they were nothing compared to the roaring in my head. Evander's eyes closed, and his jaw tightened as he tried to hold back his anger or maybe gather his patience. I didn't know which, and I didn't care.

"This is fucking bullshit," I yelled as I lowered my raised hand. I shifted my focus to Evander as I took a step towards him, forgetting about the vase I had just thrown. "I have *every* right to lead—"

"You have *no* right, Ainsley. None," Evander interjected abruptly. His eyes fluttered open to reveal a deep gray storm billowing within. He was furious. Good, because so was I. There was no way in hell I was going to sit back and do nothing while our kingdom was in danger.

"I sure as hell do," I growled, hitting the wooden surface of his desk with my open palms.

Out of my periphery, I could see the generals in the room flinch at not only the sound but the shadows that pooled from my hands as violent as my fury. Van remained still. He stayed tall and regal, the King of Tenebrae and owner of my heart—though right now it held nothing but contempt for him and his decisions.

"Our kingdom is under attack from all sides—"

"Because of the decisions *you* made," he said, stealing the words from my lungs and making me relive that fateful night all over again. The night I murdered King Perceval. The night I fought Dashiell. And the night I held Felix in my arms as he died. The words hit me as hard as any physical blow, causing me to rear back.

He couldn't possibly have been serious. Did he want me to let the king responsible for our parents' death go unpunished and free? Would he rather I not have sought vengeance for that man stealing me away and keeping me hidden for nearly my entire life? And Felix... Felix's death wasn't *my* fault. It was Dashiell's. *He* gave the order to come after us. *His* men shot an arrow through my best friend's heart.

"Perceval stole everything from me! He deserved worse than what I did," I argued.

Though his eyes softened, Evander's face remained rigid, never relaxing into the man I loved. The face he wore was that of the ruler of our kingdom. With a deep breath, he took a tentative step around the desk.

"I know he did, Ainsley. And as your Soul Bonded and your Claimed, I love you even more for what you did to that piece of shit. But…" He placed a reassuring hand over mine. Despite the part of me that longed for him, I quickly withdrew from his touch. He swallowed the sting of my actions before continuing. "But as the King of Tenebrae, I can't overlook what your choice caused our kingdom—our *people*. You went against my orders and because of that, you put us at war." I was going to argue, but he spoke before I could get a word in. "Because of that, your friend is dead."

My shadows swirled around my hands, and my skin burned with the flames that rose higher within me. I clenched my teeth while struggling to hold back the tears that were welling in my eyes. My anger kept climbing as my chest rose and fell with each suffocating breath. Evander didn't move. He remained steadfast in his belief, staring at me with unwavering resilience. I took a step back and shook my head, creating an even larger divide between us.

Evander's voice softened as he said, "The sooner you accept it, the sooner you can move forward."

"You can't do this to me," I whispered, not knowing exactly what I was referring to. Was it about being told to sit on the side as my family fought for our kingdom or about having to face his accusations of causing the death of my best friend?

"I'm sorry, love, I truly am. But I don't trust you to lead right now and I won't put our people at risk." He moved forward, reaching out his hand to comfort me. I moved back, rejecting him. My stomach was twisted into knots, and bile was rising in my throat. He didn't trust me.

"Go fuck yourself," I spat back before turning on my heel and storming out of the room.

My pace quickened as my anger intensified, causing my shadows to rush around me. If I couldn't calm down soon, there would be more destruction. But how could I? Evander didn't trust me and that fissure of knowledge had cut so deep it was now bleeding me dry.

I had only taken two steps into the hallway when someone grabbed my arm. Despite my efforts to break free from Evander's grasp, he held me firmly in place, denying me any further retreat. I spun around, ready to spit more venom, when deep golden eyes met mine. Calidore.

"I'm not in the mood, Cal," I told him, trying again to pull away, but to no avail.

"I don't care, Ainsley," he said flatly, and my eyes widened a fraction at his tone. I was taken aback by Calidore's cold and distant demeanor because he had never been anything but kind to me. "You've been acting like this nonstop, and it needs to end."

"I'm sorry my attitude hasn't lived up to your standards for the past two weeks. I'll make sure my best friend doesn't die in my arms next time to avoid making you uncomfortable." Did everyone think it was easy for me to forget about Felix and pretend like nothing happened?

"Cut the shit," he ground out, holding onto my arm just a bit tighter. "You know I loved Felix. Maybe not to the same extent as you and Oli did, but he was family. I'm mourning him too, Ainsley. We all are."

I averted my gaze, not wanting to see the truth in his eyes I knew was there. Lia had barely spoken these past two weeks, and Olivier was nowhere to be found. Once his injuries from Caelum had healed, he said he had to inspect the camps on our southern border. Evander refused to let Olivier leave, citing his concern over his well-being. However, the following morning, Oli was gone.

"I know," I said, feeling remorseful for implying that Calidore wasn't affected by Felix's death, but not enough to apologize.

I relaxed my stance to be less combative and Cal loosened his grip, realizing that I wasn't going to verbally attack him once more. He was not the target of my anger; that was the asshole in the other room who I claimed to love.

"He doesn't get to treat me like that," I said. The sound of Evander's muffled voice beyond the closed door drew my gaze towards it.

"Like what?" Cal responded. It wasn't a question meant for me to answer. "Like someone who needs to be held accountable for their actions?" I ground my teeth together as I worked through my rage. I didn't want to lash out at Cal but the tension within me was coiled and poised to strike. "Like it or not, the only person responsible for what happened that night, Ainsley, is you."

A tear escaped, but I wiped it away before more could follow. The constant sense of dread consumed me, but I refused to show my pain and heartbreak. Despite the urge to break down and cry, I remained strong over the past few weeks, never once giving in. I wanted to, though. Countless times my legs would tremble and my knees would start to buckle as I fought against gravity and grief. But I always won. Everyone had always claimed I used anger as a weapon, but this time, I wielded it as a shield. An impenetrable force that kept me whole and alive.

Just barely.

"I know you're hurting, Ainsley," Calidore said. He spoke in a gentle and soothing tone as if I were a child who needed comfort after a nightmare. "But that doesn't excuse your actions in there."

I stared at him in disbelief.

"So he gets to act like a dick when—"

"Yes," he interjected. "Yes, he does." My mouth fell open and my blood boiled as I readied myself to fight. "You may hate him at the moment, but that doesn't alter the fact that he's king. Your behavior in there was immature and unacceptable."

I clamped my lips shut because what the hell could I say? He wasn't wrong and I hated it.

At a time like this, it was crucial for Evander to exude strength and confidence in front of our generals. Yet my lack of self-control made us appear weak and divided instead of presenting a united front. I had no doubt the only reason I was able to get away with my behavior was because of who I was—*what* I was—to him. His Soul Bonded, his Claimed, and the woman he loved above all else.

"The bottom line is that you fucked up," Cal added. "You went against the orders of your king, and in doing so, it cost us one of our own. You'll have to live with that agonizing guilt for the rest of your life, but that doesn't change the reality of what happened." Watery silhouettes flooded my vision, and I forced myself to look away. "You're young, and because of that you made a rash decision without thinking the outcome through. That's a situation we've all been in. We've all made mistakes due to inexperience and faced the outcomes, but the important thing is to keep pushing forward. You refuse to."

I couldn't.

If I were to relinquish my anger and let go of the past, I would have to come to terms with the fact that Felix was no longer here. I would have to come to terms with the fact that it was because of me. I wasn't prepared to do that, nor did I think I ever would be. The longer I stood in the flames of my wrath, the longer I could prolong the inevitable.

"If you want to lead, you'll need to show him that you're capable of doing so," he added.

"How, Calidore? He doesn't trust me." My voice broke slightly, giving away the pain I felt.

Evander had pushed me to claim my role as Heir to Tenebrae and the moment I messed up, it seemed he had withdrawn his support. My heart squeezed at the thought of disappointing him—of him realizing that maybe he had been wrong about me all along.

"What am I supposed to do?" I whispered, finally meeting his gaze.

After taking a deep breath, Cal released my arm and stepped back. He maintained a rigid posture that conveyed an air of authority that dared to be challenged. I wasn't his friend at that moment, but rather a rogue soldier who stepped too far out of line. Someone who needed to be disciplined—or dismissed.

"You need to go in there and receive your orders from your king. You accept the probation and do everything that is asked of you without objections. Whatever you're feeling or going through with Van, leave it at the door—it's exactly what he's doing, too. In that room, you are king and heir. You fulfill your duties and leave your personal shit out of it. As soon as that meeting is over, you can mourn how you see fit, but not a moment sooner."

Holding Cal's stare, I swallowed hard and thought about my options. He was right. My people deserved more than what I was giving them. I may have been lost to my anger, but it wasn't fair for my kingdom to suffer as a result. I could do what Cal was requesting. I could go in there and accept my punishment willingly.

I steeled my resolve and sliced away the dark vines that were gradually encroaching within me. They were persistent in their attempts to pull me down and force me to confront my grief, but I didn't have time for that. I gave a brief nod, and Cal opened the door to the meeting room, motioning for me to enter ahead of him.

Evander was leaning over a map on his desk and pointing to various places as he spoke to our generals. His eyes met mine as I made my way through the room, but he didn't falter in his instruction. I decided to stay back while Calidore took up his position beside the king. He shifted his focus back to the task at hand, freeing my gaze from his grey eyes and allowing me to breathe a sigh of relief that I wouldn't be reprimanded yet. I had caused a scene earlier and wasn't sure how pissed Van was at me for it.

"How extensive is the damage in the southernmost camp?" Van asked General Roshard.

"Not as bad as it could be," he answered.

"Injuries?" Van questioned.

"Several, but no casualties. It seems that King Dashiell is more focused on attacking our resources and means of survival than taking lives."

Evander nodded along in agreement as if he had already realized the same thing. Dashiell had been relentlessly attacking Tenebrae since I returned from Caelum. Every day seemed to bring news of another one of our camps being targeted. There was, at the very least, silence from Oberon, the Pravus leader. Now that Disparya appeared to be at war with itself, it looked as though he was getting exactly what he wanted—unrest.

"Although what's happening within the camps is worrisome, Your Majesty," Roshard continued, "It's not our biggest concern." All eyes turned towards him. "King Dashiell's soldiers have started cutting off our trade routes. There's no way to get supplies in or out of Tenebrae."

Shit.

Evander dragged a hand through his black hair and shook his head in frustration. "We'll have to go through Agnitio's routes then."

"Unfortunately, that is appearing less like a possibility," he countered. Van looked at his general quizzically. "King Dashiell has sent word to the other Kings of Disparya and all have agreed to cease trading with Tenebrae until…" Roshard trailed off as he glanced my way.

"Until what?" Evander's voice was deadly as he spoke. We were all aware of what was being demanded.

"Until the Heir to Tenebrae is handed over to Caelum for crimes against the Crown."

With a shuddering breath slipping between my lips, I tilted my head towards the ceiling and closed my eyes. I knew there wasn't a chance in hell that Van would turn me over, but it didn't make me any less afraid. What would keeping me in Tenebrae cost our people? What kind of heir would I be if I willingly let them suffer because of a decision I made?

"Evander—" I started, my focus dipping back down to him. He lifted a finger to silence me.

"Don't even think about suggesting it," he growled, his face full of rage and frustration. Though he spoke to the generals next, his eyes were firmly on me. "Under no circumstances are we turning over our princess. Is that understood?"

Van's order went unopposed.

⇥†↤

For the next hour, everyone discussed different scenarios that could help grant us an advantage over Dashiell's men, including utilizing old trade routes that had long since been forgotten. As the generals received their orders, I couldn't help but feel anxious about what mine would be.

"We'll conduct these meetings away from the palace from now on, so you'll return home," Evander instructed me.

My heart sank but I didn't let my body sag with the blow of his order. Without looking at him, I gave a small nod, accepting his command.

"You're all dismissed," the king announced. Just as I was moving to leave, his voice broke out over the crowd. "Except for you, Ainsley."

People cleared the room quicker than expected, giving me worried looks, probably due to their king's upcoming punishment for breaking the vase. As soon as the massive oak doors slammed shut, I inhaled sharply and turned to face Evander. He had his arms folded across his chest and was staring fixedly at a point on the ground. This wasn't going to be an easy conversation for either of us.

"The reason I'm keeping you at home—"

"I know the reason," I interrupted, my tone harsher than intended. I couldn't pretend I wasn't furious about being sent to sit in our house instead of helping rebuild the damage I had unintentionally caused.

Van lifted his head and tilted it to the side as he observed me through narrowed eyes and scrunched brows.

"Do you?" It didn't sound like a question when he asked.

"You said it yourself, you don't trust me."

"And you believe that's the reason I'm keeping you home…"

I took a step back and ran my hand through my hair, needing more space between us. The anger was resurfacing, and I could feel the heat in my blood. I was going to explode on him if I didn't get out of that room quickly.

"I think you're trying hard not to admit what we both know," I countered.

"And what's that?"

"That I have no business ever being queen." The words burned like flames on the way out, but they needed to be said.

He had lost faith in me, and our love for one another wasn't going to change that. It wasn't going to fix the simple truth that I wasn't fit to rule. Evander advanced with a cold and calculated step.

"Are you under the assumption that being queen means you won't fuck up?" he bit out angrily. I had never seen his rage directed at me like this before and it wasn't something I ever wanted to get used to. "Because I have news for you, Ainsley, you absolutely will. A crown on your head doesn't make you exempt. You *will* make decisions that will cost lives. You *will* feel like you're failing more often than not. You *will* make mistakes. And you *will* have to move forward."

His silhouette blurred momentarily before I blinked the tears away. Evander reduced the distance between us but kept a healthy space, realizing that I wasn't comfortable with him closing it completely just yet. My magic extended its claws, reaching for him, longing to be near the other half of my soul. I tightened my hold on my power; I was too set in my anger for now.

"I love you, Ainsley," he said softly, and my gaze met his. His face had fallen and I could see the pain written on it—the complete loss he was at while trying to reach me. "And I have no doubt you will be a fierce, merciful, and beautiful queen, but you have to believe that too. My decision to keep you home has nothing to do with me doubting your capabilities."

I greedily accepted his words but couldn't make the move to seek his comfort, no matter how much I longed for it. I didn't deserve to feel an ounce of it after how I had treated him and everyone else these past few weeks. Nor was I ready to give in to my guilt.

I wasn't ready to let go of the anger I felt coursing through my veins. It was easier to be mad at him for putting me on probation than it was to let him hold me as I crumbled. I didn't want to break. So instead, I closed my eyes and pictured the arrow going through Felix's heart again and again. Every time it was fired, the soldier's face transformed into Dashiell's.

Evander's hands cupped my cheeks as he sensed me retreating back into my pit of wrath and vengeance. I immediately broke free from his grip.

"Is there anything you need from me as Heir to Tenebrae?" I said before he had a chance to comment. Evander's stare lingered on me for too long, as if he was searching for a way to pull me back from the brink. In the end, he shook his head in surrender. "Then we're done here."

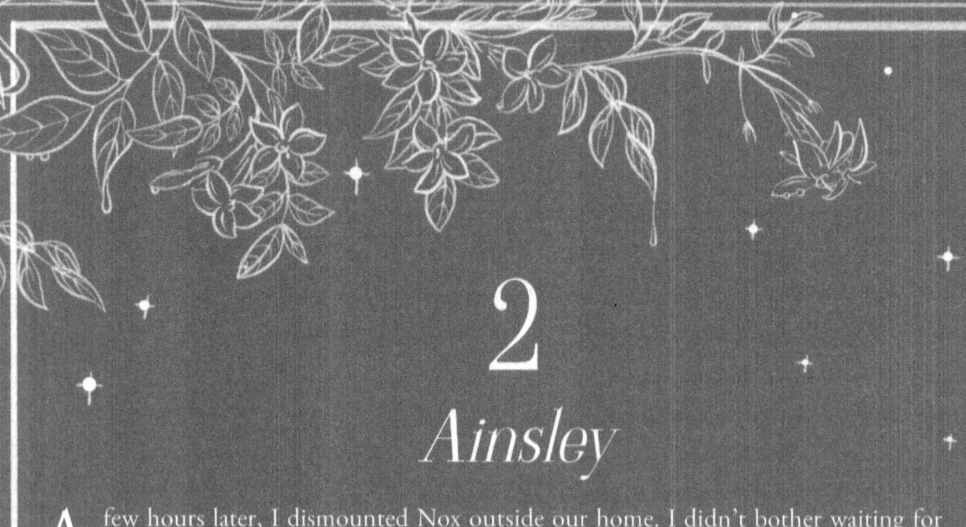

2

Ainsley

A few hours later, I dismounted Nox outside our home. I didn't bother waiting for Calidore to lead me back or for Van to traverse us. I needed the crisp air and winter chill to flood my head and empty the worrying thoughts.

The house was quiet when I entered, though I knew my family was present. I could feel them—feel *him*. My stomach twisted as I wrapped myself in our Soul Bond, feeling the warmth and love it provided and wishing so much that I could go back and change the events that led us here.

Ever since the night I came back bloody and clinging to life, things between Evander and I had been tense. Our tender reunion came to an abrupt end once I recovered from my injuries and was forced to confront the aftermath of my actions and what it caused not only our family but also our people.

I walked through the house on soft feet, not wanting to give any indication that I was home. I didn't want to see or speak to anyone, but I should have known Evander would have sensed me the moment I crossed the threshold. As I ascended the stairs, I saw him at the end of the hallway, standing tall and gorgeous with his back firmly pressed against our bedroom door, as if he had been waiting for me.

He observed me intently, tilting his head. His brows were furrowed and his hair disheveled as if he had been running a hand through it incessantly. Was he angry or just exhausted with me?

"You didn't wait for me," he said softly—sadly.

"I didn't know I needed to," I responded as I made my way down the hall. His shoulders sagged ever so slightly and the light in his eyes dimmed, sending an ache through my chest.

"You didn't. I just…" His throat bobbed and he looked away as he spoke again. "I just thought you would have."

Seeing him in so much pain made my knees tremble, but I couldn't do anything to help. I couldn't even erase it for myself, though it wasn't like I wanted to. The pain gave me a reason to live and kept Felix alive in my heart. It gave me a purpose. Without the agony, I would have to face my loss and accept it—something I wasn't about to do. Not yet.

But seeing Evander looking at me as if his entire world was just out of reach was far too much to bear. I couldn't go to him, couldn't stay in our room. I would suffocate under the weight of the crushing guilt.

So I grabbed the handle of the door to my left and twisted.

Evander traversed to the doorway the second I stepped inside, grabbing my wrist and spinning me around to face him. His eyes were wide and filled with panic as he reached up to hold my face between his hands.

His touch was *everything.* It was firm and unyielding, passionate and desperate, tender and loving. It was my home, my sanctuary. He was everything I wanted and needed yet couldn't allow myself to take. He deserved so much more than I was able or willing to give.

"No," he begged, his voice cracking. "Please, love. Don't do this. Don't push me away." A single tear slipped free from my eye and Evander swept it away with his thumb. His face shifted slightly and his charcoal eyes filled with something that looked like hope for the first time since Felix died. I didn't understand why.

"Please, Evander. Just let me be," I whispered.

"I can't." Meeting my gaze at eye level, he held my attention with his piercing stare. "I won't abandon you. You're not alone, so please let me help you through this. Let me be there for you."

"I can't—"

"—You can," he countered. "You've let me in before; you can do it again. You shouldn't have to feel this pain all on your own."

"Evander—"

"Blame the world. Blame *me.* Hate *me.* Do whatever you need to. Throw everything at me. I can take it. I can be whatever you need. You can be angry and vengeful, sad and empty, broken and brutal. Be whatever you need to. But please, love... Just be those things in my arms."

My hands shook, and my throat tightened as I struggled to keep the pieces of me from shattering completely at his declaration. My entire being urged me to take him up on his offer and fall into his chest. To let him hold me and kiss me and carry me to bed as I wept over the loss of my best friend. But something inside me prevented me from doing so. I wasn't ready.

I stepped out of his hold and shut the door in his face.

The next morning, I awoke to the sound of near-silent footfalls across the floor. I rolled over to find my door cracked open and Nova and Onyx padding over to me.

"No," I said firmly.

My wolves halted their advance at my command and then looked at one another curiously. I had never shooed them away before, but I couldn't deal with them now. When they didn't move, I spoke again, this time raising my voice.

"Leave."

After a brief hesitation, Onyx was the first to retreat, whimpering as he backed out. Nova held my gaze for a moment as if she could somehow communicate her thoughts. Her ears drooped and her brown eyes tried desperately to convey words she couldn't. I turned away.

"I said get out!" I yelled.

Nova turned and rushed through the door, past Evander, who stood there with sorrow-filled eyes and a breakfast tray in his hands.

He looked in the direction of our wolves as if contemplating whether to go after them or stay with me. I wanted him to go. Not only because I desired to be alone, but because I knew he would comfort Onyx and Nova after I snapped at them for no fucking reason other than the anger I had at myself. Evander took a deep breath and fully entered the room, closing the door behind him.

"What would you like to do today, love?" he asked as if our conversation last night had never happened. As if I didn't shut the damn door in his face like the undeserving asshole I was. He set the tray of food down and sat at the edge of the bed, waiting patiently for me to answer.

I didn't.

I rolled over, pulled the blankets over my head, and went back to sleep.

The floors creaked beneath my feet as I shifted my weight, trying to get more comfortable while in the meeting from hell. Evander had decided that every debrief with our generals would take place in the study of our home rather than the council room of the palace. It was most likely because he wanted to babysit me, but I couldn't bring myself to fight it, let alone care.

This meeting, in particular, had been going on for over two hours as Evander, Cal, Marce, and our generals worked out the best paths to safely deliver supplies to and from our kingdom.

Van was confident that the old trade routes were our best option for now until we could push Dashiell's soldiers farther back from our territory.

This morning, I awoke to Van quietly entering my room with a breakfast I wouldn't touch and a question regarding what I wanted to do, just like he had yesterday. And just like then, I didn't respond. I wasn't purposefully trying to hurt him, but I didn't know what to say or how to react. I didn't know how to be anything but angry without losing myself completely. The only difference was today, I got out of bed.

"And I want a full report at the next meeting," Evander was saying as my attention was focused on a small speck of dust drifting through the air.

"You're not coming with us?" someone inquired.

"No," Evander responded. "I have important matters to tend to here. I trust you can handle this without me."

"Of course, Your Majesty."

"Good. You will all return in a week and we'll go from there," he finished.

Shuffling sounded around the space, an obvious indicator that the meeting was over and I was free to retreat back to my room. I pushed off the wall I had been leaning against and made to leave when Evander stopped me with a gentle hold on my wrist. I fought the urge to aggressively yank my arm away.

"We have work to do." I opened my mouth to argue, but he spoke again. "Royal duties," he explained. There was something about the way he said the words that made it seem like he was happy about whatever it was we needed to do. I nodded cautiously and followed him through the house.

Leave my personal shit out of it, I told myself. If this task pertained to my job as the Heir to Tenebrae, then I could put my struggles aside and do this for my kingdom. And when I was done, I could get back to the solitude of my shattered self.

Evander led us out back to the training ring, which was now covered in a thick sheet of snow. Though spring loomed around the corner, winter was still in full force. He stopped in the center and turned around, waiting for me to approach. I glanced over the space, not understanding what the hell we were doing. Shadows filled Van's hand until a long, wide shovel formed and solidified. He looked pointedly at me, clearly expecting me to do the same.

"What are we doing out here?" I asked, crossing my arms over my chest—partly out of defiance and partly because I was freezing. I felt a small spark of anger directed at Evander. He knew how much I hated the cold, yet had no qualms about dragging me out in the snow for seemingly no reason.

"Was the shovel not obvious enough?" he quipped. My heart involuntarily skipped a beat at the lightness in his tone. "I know they didn't teach you much in Caelum, but generally, shovels are used to... well, shovel things." I knew what he was trying to do, but my sullen expression didn't change.

Once upon a time, he had used humor and my own temper against me in order to break me out of my shell. Of course he would try that tactic again. But this was different. I wasn't recovering from a broken heart—I was mourning the loss of someone who was my family.

Evander subtly nodded to himself, the movement barely perceivable. "We're going to clear the ring free of snow," he answered when he realized I wasn't going to play with him.

"How is this a royal duty?" I asked flatly, feeling tricked. Evander sighed and began shoveling the snow.

"Because," he drawled while focusing on his task, "Spring is around the corner, and during the warmer months, we teach the children from the orphanage how to defend themselves." I perked up, slightly more interested now. "It's a lot of work to get this place ready, so we need to start now."

"Why wouldn't you just conduct the lessons at the palace? It has a far larger training area."

"Because our home is closer, and I enjoy spending time with the children."

He removed a large heap of snow from the ring. I thought about that briefly but didn't find a flaw in his logic. My fingers twirled around until shadows spooled from them and formed a shovel... slightly larger than Evander's. I noted that the corner of his lips twitched in response, but he didn't comment on it.

For hours, we worked in silence until the entirety of the ring was nothing but frozen dirt and worn paint in a shape resembling a circle. When we were finished, I let my shadows dissipate and returned inside without a word to Van, though I heard his soft goodbye from a distance. I had done what was asked of me as heir and could now retrieve my personal shit from where I left it and stew in my misery.

"Are you fucking kidding me?" I demanded.

"A storm must have rolled in overnight," Evander commented. His cavalier tone only pissed me off even more.

"No shit."

All of the work we had accomplished with the training ring yesterday was for nothing, as it was filled with snow once more. I gritted my teeth and formed a shovel again, muttering under my breath about how stupid the weather in Tenebrae was.

My shoulders burned and my lungs ached as I tirelessly cleared the snow from the ring for the second time. I had to admit, it was nice to channel my anger into something other than lashing out at the people I loved.

For just a moment, I could mask the pain of my heart with the pain of my muscles. I could pretend that the only agony I felt was because of my overworked body and not my incompetence. I could continue to lie to myself for as long as it took to complete my task and ignore the grief that was a constant weight in my chest, increasing in mass the longer it went unattended.

Soon, the sharp bite of the winter air was like a welcomed kiss. I lost myself in the harsh sting of cold and my tired limbs. I breathed in so deep that the frost filled my lungs and doused the persistent flames living inside me. For a split second, I was me again.

But then Felix's lifeless eyes flashed across my mind, and my facade came crashing down.

When the training area was once again solid dirt, I rested my hands on my knees and surveyed the space. There wasn't a single pile of snow within the circle. I nodded in satisfaction at my work.

I felt a sense of fulfillment for the first time in weeks and stifled the smile that wanted to form as I pictured the young children practicing their techniques come spring. Evander would be there front and center, wielding his weapons like the cocky asshole he was. Knowing him, he'd probably implement some rule that the children would have to admit he was better than everyone else before they were allowed to step into the ring.

A sudden flash of black caught the corner of my eye, and I twisted automatically to find Onyx cowering behind a tree as he observed me from a distance. Nova was at his side, and the second our eyes locked, she turned away and sauntered off into the woods. My heart fractured a bit, knowing that I had hurt her the other day. She didn't deserve my wrath, and neither did Onyx.

"Are we finished?" I asked as an idea occurred to me. Evander's brows furrowed as he watched me with curious interest before finally nodding. I quickly made my way into the kitchen without another word.

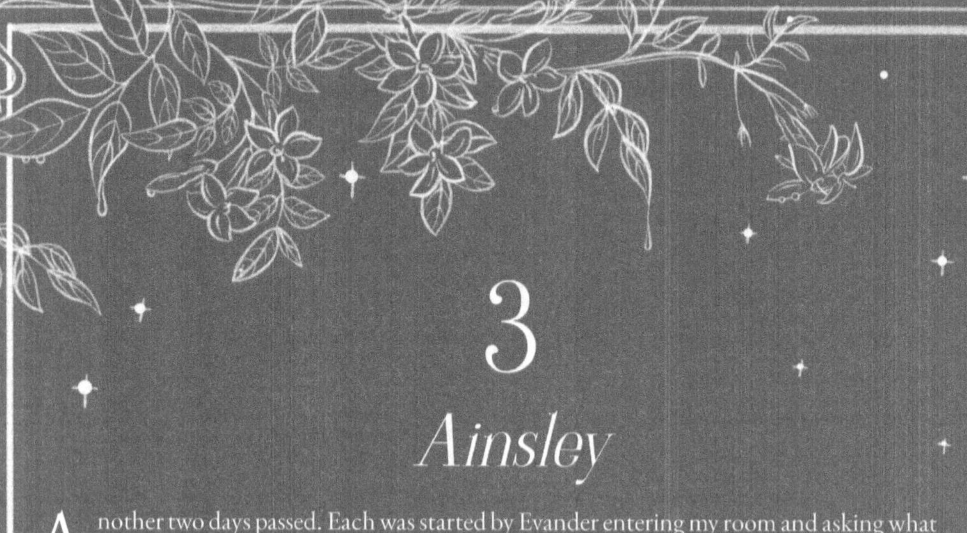

3

Ainsley

Another two days passed. Each was started by Evander entering my room and asking what I wanted to do that day, directly followed by me heading outside to check on the training ring. It was always piled high with snow. The thick coat seemed to only be within the circle, as if the storm had targeted it for its destruction. Maybe the Gods were laughing from above, content to watch me grow more and more frustrated by the day,

"We're crafting a tent to cover it!" I ordered through gritted teeth as I began shoveling away the remnants of snow yet again.

"I think that's a great idea, love," Van replied as he worked alongside me.

"Why the hell is it only gathering in the training ring? Nothing along the rest of the grounds seems to have accumulated anything."

I aggressively began shoveling faster. The longer I was outside, the more irritated I became with the situation. I had to remind myself that this would all be worth it in the end when the children had a safe space to learn and grow.

"I think the snow is filling the ring until it levels out with the rest of the lawn. Then the wind picks up most of it, so it doesn't seem like much has fallen," Evander explained. "Look how smooth the snow is over there. The wind removed any trace of footsteps from yesterday."

I turned and glanced in the direction he was pointing. He was right, of course.

"It's still fucking stupid," I mumbled, going back to my task.

"Indeed." I could hear the smirk in his voice.

Once everything was cleared yet again, we crafted sturdy polls and a thick tarp to stretch across the top and shield the ring from the next storm. It may not have kept everything out, but it would definitely prevent the amount of snow that had been piling up this past week from accumulating again. I dusted my hands after surveying our work, pleased with what I saw.

"Are we finished?" I asked as I did at the end of every day. Van nodded, and I headed to the kitchen in hopes of continuing my success today.

The first few batches I had baked came out more burnt than the toast Van had made me for breakfast the morning of his birthday, but I was determined to get it right. I pulled the sheet of oatmeal cookies from the hot oven and breathed a sigh of relief once I saw they were a perfect golden hue.

My lips curved as I plated the warm cookies and brought them up to my room. Nova and Onyx had stayed away after our encounter days ago. After how I behaved, I couldn't blame them for that, but I hoped the smell of my fuzzy black wolf's favorite treats would help lure them out of hiding.

Once the sun had long been set, and I was sure everyone had gone to sleep, I cracked my door open before crawling onto my bed and sitting crosslegged with the cookies in my lap. I waited and waited and waited some more, refusing to give in to sleep until I saw my plan through.

Finally, when I thought it wasn't going to work, I heard the soft padding of paws outside my room, followed by quiet whimpers. Onyx wanted the cookies but was trying to obey my order to stay away. I bit back my smile at his adorable struggle.

Slowly, the door pushed wider and a snout appeared, sniffing the open air. He stayed there for a few minutes like he was testing the waters to ensure I was asleep and he wouldn't get yelled at again. I chewed on a cookie as I waited.

Once he deemed it safe, he poked his head through. His dark eyes widened as they locked onto mine, and then the full plate of treats in my lap. He didn't push his way into my room, still obedient despite the temptation. I smiled before placing my hand on the bed next to me and patted twice—a white flag and peace offering.

Onyx bolted into the room and jumped onto the mattress, knocking me and the cookies over as he threw his weight over me, licking and nuzzling into my neck.

A small laugh bubbled over as I scratched behind his ears before apologizing for my outburst. "I made you cookies," I told him and jerked my chin to the treats scattered upon the floor. "Save some for Nova too." Onyx shifted his weight and pushed off me before jumping down.

I watched him happily scarf down nearly every piece when Nova's grey fur caught my attention. She sat at my room's entrance, watching the scene play out. I patted the bed to indicate for her to come, but she sat uncertainly on the threshold.

There was a twist in my heart and a lump in my throat at the sight of her so conflicted, and knowing it was because of the pain I had caused her. Nova had always been there for me, even choosing to leave her Solum to be at my side when I was heartbroken by Van's lies. And I had been horrible to her.

Sliding from the bed, I made my way slowly across the room and knelt down in front of my wolf. Her ears were drooped and her eyes lowered like she couldn't bear to look at me. She didn't seem angry at my outburst, just sad. And that made it so much fucking worse. I could deal with anger. I *deserved* anger. What I couldn't handle was seeing her upset for something that wasn't her fault. What I couldn't handle was her being afraid to be near me.

I reached up and cupped her face, forcing her to look at me. "I'm so sorry, girl," I whispered before kissing her lightly on her head the way Evander always had. She nuzzled into my neck and I threw my arms around my wolf as a gentle tear trickled down my cheek.

The next morning, Evander didn't comment on the fact that both Nova and Onyx had slept in my bed, but I didn't miss the twinkle in his eye as he took in the scene. After he asked me his usual question about what I wanted to do that day, I dressed and headed outside to see if the covering we secured over the training ring had held up. There was a thin layer of snow over the dirt that was most likely brought in from the wind, but for the most part, the area was clear.

"It looks like your idea worked," Evander said, and I nodded absentmindedly. I should have been happy; should have been beyond thrilled that I wouldn't have to spend another day shoveling cold, wet snow. But instead of satisfaction, I felt a pang of something else. Disappointment?

"Good," I told him with no real conviction. "I finally don't have to be stuck out here all day long."

My eyes drifted over the space, searching for any part of the ring that needed more work. I told myself I was just trying to be thorough—that the children deserved the best. No matter what I tried to convince myself, I knew the truth.

Sure, my body was happy for the break from physical labor, but my mind was a dark place, and if I had nothing to keep it busy, I wasn't sure where it would go.

"Are we done here?" I asked weakly. I didn't want to be.

Evander eyed me for a moment before indicating that we were. My stomach dropped as I nodded and swallowed hard. I gave the area one more glance over before backing up toward the house.

"You know," Evander began. My feet halted before my brain had the chance to catch up to the movement. His lips twitched at my eager curiosity. "I was thinking a new target practice area could be beneficial. If we had more space, we could probably train more children at the same time." I studied the ring, trying to envision what he was suggesting. "Unless you don't think—"

"No, I do," I said immediately and fluttered back to his side. "I mean, if *you* think it's something we should do." Evander's mouth formed fully into the crooked grin I loved so fiercely.

"I do." His voice was light and full of hope.

"Then where do we start?"

⚬

"Good morning, love. What would you like to do today?" Evander asked, just as he did every single morning.

With some difficulty, I scooted from beneath Onyx and made my way to the large window in my room, which overlooked the grounds and the work Evander and I had done.

We had devoted a week to improving the space. We added a new target area, a larger hydration station, and built a shed to store the practice weapons we made for the children. All that needed to be done was add fresh paint to outline the border of the sparring ring and a few finishing touches to the practice targets. As soon as spring arrived, the space would be filled with smiling children.

I headed to the dresser to change so I could start on the work that needed to be done as soon as possible. After each day, I felt more and more accomplished. Though I wasn't on the frontline with our soldiers as they defended our borders, I still felt a sense of fulfillment here. As if my contribution was just as important to the future of Tenebrae as what was happening in our camps.

"Are you sure you don't want breakfast?" Evander asked—again, just as he did every single morning. I shook my head.

I wasn't intentionally starving myself, but food had lost its flavor and I hardly felt hungry. It was difficult to keep anything down, and I only stomached it when my body was on the verge of falling over or passing out from how weak I'd become. The muscle I had spent months building was slowly starting to atrophy, but it was hard to care. It was difficult to find joy in something as simple as a good meal.

Without permission, my mind wandered to the picnics Felix had always planned for us and how much he cherished those moments together. Had I known they'd be cut short so soon, I would have done it more often.

Once dressed, I immediately got to work, and before the lunch hour came around, everything was completed. The sparring ring had a new border around the edge and each target had different marks painted into the wood for the children to aim at. A slight smile curved my lips at what we had done. Everything was perfect and ready to go. But that also meant that there was nothing else for me to do; no task to give my hands or project to keep my mind focused on something but my loss.

"It looks amazing," Evander whispered at my side before leaning down to press a kiss to my temple.

"Yeah," I breathed quietly, trying to hold in the fear of now being forced to go back to my anger.

"Would you like to have lunch?"

"I'm not hungry."

Van gave me a gentle smile before nodding and escorting me back into the house.

As we reached the entrance to the kitchen I stopped in my tracks, eyes going wide at what I saw. Evander paid me no mind and instead ventured into the room and took a seat at the long table now piled with dozens of baked dishes. The aroma was decadent, smelling of spices and herbs and warm crust. My mouth watered...just a little. Taking a few steps into the space, I gestured to the table.

"What is all of this?"

Evander looked up from unfolding a napkin and getting his place setting situated. "Oh, this?" he asked as if all of this food wasn't out of the ordinary. It most certainly was. "The spring festival will be coming up soon, and there will be a baking competition. These dishes here are the submissions. It's our job to select the best ten to be served at the festival, where our people will vote on the winner."

I eyed the spread and the baked dish consisting of chicken, carrots, diced potatoes, and some sort of gravy that Van was serving himself. The options looked similar in size and shape but there were subtle differences like the coloring and designs baked into the crust. Everything looked almost too pretty to eat.

"But don't worry," Evander continued, pulling my attention from the rows of food before me, "I know it's technically a royal duty, but I can handle this on my own. I know you aren't hungry."

He piled a small bite onto his fork and placed it into his mouth, sighing contently as he did. Then, he scribbled something down on a piece of parchment—most likely his rating—before looking over the table to decide which dish to go with next.

"I don't mind," I told him. Van peered up at me curiously as I moved to sit next to him at the table. "I mean, I'm the heir, so I should help. It's my job." I unrolled the napkin and glanced over our choices. "Can we try this one next?" I pointed to a large dish with the shape of a bird baked into the top.

"As you wish, love," Van said before kissing my cheek and serving me a portion of the food.

⚮

"More?!" I exclaimed when I entered the kitchen to find the table filled once again with baked goods, though this time they were desserts. It had taken us five days to go through all of the casseroles and savory pies, and now we had to start again. I let out a deep huff of air as I looked everything over.

"You can sit out if you'd like," Van offered as he sliced into one of the desserts, "but this one's chocolate." My stomach rumbled involuntarily, and I practically sprinted to him to rip the plate from his hands. He simply held it high above his head and snickered at my attempts to reach it.

I couldn't help but return the smile.

The desserts took another four days to get through, the homemade jams and wines took three days each, and we were on day five of the baked loaves of bread. In between the tastings, more meetings with the generals occurred, and occasionally, I would offer an opinion or thought on how we could improve our tactics. Our secret trade routes had been discovered a week ago and had since been cut off. Caelum's only demand to stop the battles and continue our trading was to turn me over.

Anytime I spoke up, Evander never prevented me from making suggestions. I think he was mostly just happy I was finally involving myself in a less violent way. Though I was never assigned to one of the camps like Cal and Marce had been over the weeks, it still felt like I was being put to use, and that was enough for now.

Slowly, with each passing day, I began to feel a little more like myself.

"Absolutely not!" Evander exclaimed.

"You're completely out of line!" I fired back, placing my hands on my hips. I was going to kill this man.

"I'm not the one who's making the wrong choice."

I snorted and shook my head. "Yes, you are! And it's *my* choice to make—not yours." I poked my finger into his chest to punctuate my point. Evander grabbed my wrist to halt my assault, his fingers curling around my skin, gentle but firm. His touch only fed my anger.

"The last time I checked, I'm the king," he growled and leaned closer to me. "The answer is no."

I pushed forward, closing the distance even more. I wasn't going to let him use his higher rank to shove aside my opinion—not with this.

"The answer is *yes*," I snarled, baring my teeth at him. I wasn't going to back down. He was being unreasonable and an asshole.

"What's going on?" Lia called as she entered from the other side of the room.

I hadn't spent much time with her since Felix had died, and I felt guilty for it. But I didn't know what she thought of me anymore. The two of them were close, and as everyone had pointed out, *I* was the reason he was gone. For all I knew, she hated me for what had happened, but I was too scared to find out the truth. I was barely holding myself together as it was, and there was no way I wouldn't crumble if I knew I had lost her, too.

"Van is being unreasonable and an asshole," I responded, never taking my eyes off of him.

"And Ainsley is trying to poison the people of Tenebrae," he added.

I rolled my eyes at his dramatics and pointed to the bread loaf I had selected. "We have one spot left and this is the clear winner."

"Trust me, love, it most definitely is not. As King of Tenebrae, I will not subject my people to this monstrosity," he said, picking the bread up between his thumb and forefinger like it was the most disgusting thing he'd ever touched.

I crossed my arms over my chest and groaned while throwing my head back. We had been going in circles for the past hour.

"What are the options?" Lia drawled as she fluttered closer, evidently annoyed by our bickering.

"We're between these two," Van answered, dropping the bread he was holding onto the table. It made a loud thud as it bounced, and I winced a little. Was bread supposed to do that?

He slid his chosen winner forward and Lia eyed both of our selections before taking a bite of Van's first. She hummed as she chewed, clearly enjoying his choice. "It's really good," she said with a full mouth. Van beamed down at me in smug victory. I wanted to punch that arrogant, gorgeous face of his.

"Yeah, yeah. It's fine, but try this one," I told her, pushing mine closer.

Lia forced a smile before picking up my loaf and eyeing it suspiciously as if she was certain it was going to explode in her hands. She ripped a small piece off slowly—mostly because it was an extremely difficult task, for some reason—and brought the bread to her trembling lips. After inhaling deeply in preparation, Lia took a bite... and then immediately spit it out and grabbed Van's glass of wine to drain the contents.

"Ainsley, that was... Just no. Dear Gods, please don't serve that to our people."

I stared at her unblinking as Evander pulled me into his chest and padded my head placatingly. There was no way my choice was *that* bad. It was warm and full of flavor and... wait, did one of the olives in it just crawl away? Oh Gods.

"It's okay," Evander said, still being dramatic in his attempt to comfort me. "I still love you, even if your taste in bread is complete shit."

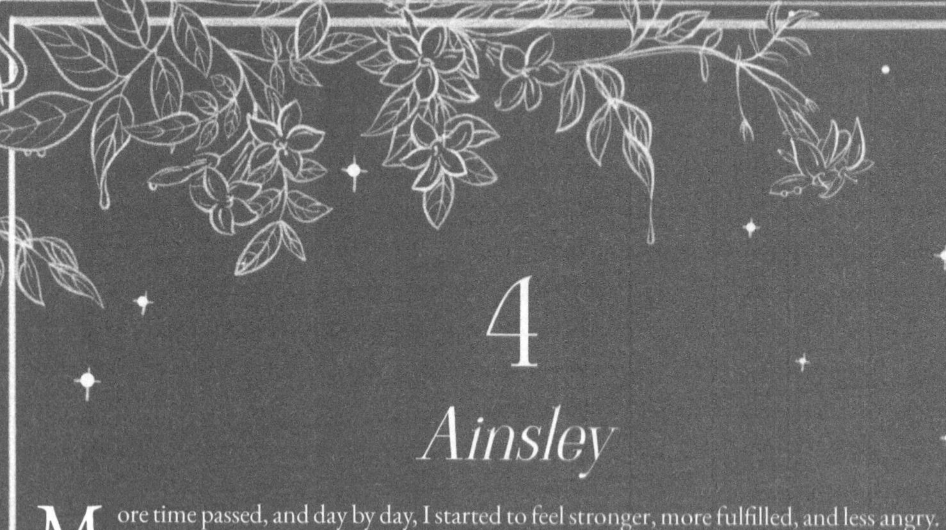

4

Ainsley

More time passed, and day by day, I started to feel stronger, more fulfilled, and less angry. Evander had decided to conduct one of our weekly meetings at the nearest camp and had allowed me to come along and inspect everything. Slowly, I was starting to earn back his trust in my role as a leader of our kingdom. I was starting to become more like my old self, eager to fulfill what was demanded of me and be the person my people deserved. The person *he* deserved.

One night, while the world was quiet and a settled calm fell upon our house, I found myself standing in the center of my room. Not the bedroom I had taken up residence in these past daunting weeks, but the one I shared with Evander.

It smelled the same, like parchment and cedar. Nothing seemed out of place except...there was an emptiness that blanketed the room. The bed looked untouched, neatly made without the imprint of a wolf. The fireplace held fresh wood but no ash, despite us still being in the winter months.

"Love?" Evander called gently, and I turned to see him standing in the doorway with furrowed brows.

As soon as our eyes locked, I felt myself suffocating under the pressure of his gaze. All at once, the emotions I had spent so long trying to fight came rushing forth, consuming me completely. I didn't want to run anymore. I didn't want to hide and shove everything away. I wanted to throw out my misplaced anger and instead throw myself into the arms of the man who loved me. I wanted to *feel*. I was finally ready to.

"He's gone," I whispered as the tears began streaming down my face. My hands clutched my chest, and a heartbeat later, Evander had me wrapped in his arms as I let the agony finally tear its way through me. "He's gone," I cried as my legs gave out and we sank to the floor.

Evander didn't say a word. He knew it wasn't what I needed. Instead, he cradled me against him as I broke and shattered into a million pieces over the loss I had experienced. My best friend was gone because of *me*. I wanted so badly to blame Dashiell, and a part of me still did, but I knew I was just as responsible for that night as he was—if not more. Had I been honest with my plans and not so blinded by my rage and need for vengeance, perhaps he'd still be alive.

When I couldn't control my sobs and my body shook violently, Van quickly lifted me and took me to the shower. As the hot water caressed my skin, I tried my best to regulate my breathing and find solace in its soothing embrace, but my efforts were futile. The intense combination of anger, sadness, frustration, and despair became unbearable as they all surged out of me at once.

"I've got you, love," Evander whispered as he wiped away my tears through the stream of water. "Let it all out. I'm here."

And so I did.

✽ ✽

Life was getting easier as time went on. Throughout the day, I'd find myself smiling, laughing, and even joking with my family, but there was still a hole in my heart I was certain would never fully heal.

"Do you mind if I join you?" Lia asked as I sat by the lake behind our house the way I did every evening when the sky turned a soft hue of amber—the same shade as Felix's eyes.

I nodded and offered an awkward smile as I gestured to the spot at my right. As my eyes darted over the water ahead, my anxious hands slid along the blades of grass and then wrapped around my chest, only for me to settle them in my lap a second later. The deafening silence only made my anxiety grow.

"I don't hate you, Ainsley," Lia whispered, stealing the air from my lungs as my shoulders sagged with relief. My eyes misted over as they met hers, and she placed a comforting hand on my cheek. "I miss him every day, but I don't blame you for what happened. Not for one second."

"No one does," another voice added, and I twisted to find Marceline coming to sit on my other side. The two women sandwiched me between them as we sat shoulder to shoulder, looking out at the dimming horizon.

"I do," I quietly admitted, wiping away the single tear that spilled over. "I'm trying not to, but I do. I hate myself every day for his death."

Lia wrapped her arms around me, pulling me into her side as my head rested on her shoulder. "I can't tell you that your guilt will fade," Lia began as Marce took one of my hands in hers. "But I can tell you that you'll never have to go through it alone."

"We're family. We'll always be here for you whenever you need us—whether you realize you do or not," Marce added, echoing Felix's declaration from months ago.

I didn't respond—I didn't have to. I simply clung to them tighter as the three of us sat in peaceful silence, their love and support meaning the world.

I moved back into the room I shared with Evander and slept in his arms each night, no longer able to pretend I could get through my loss without him by my side. He was my home, my sanctuary. There was still a pang of guilt I felt over how I treated him these past several weeks, and I had no idea if he was still hurt by my attempts to push him away.

Evander was wrapped around my body, caging me in like I was a prisoner he refused to let free, but I didn't mind. His scent of cedar and fresh snow was enough to make me never want to leave; that and the sound of his steady heartbeat against my ear.

"Van?" I whispered, unsure if he was awake even though the sun had risen an hour ago.

"Yes, my love?" he said into my hair before pressing his lips against my head.

"I'm sorry. For everything I did—"

"No."

"But I—"

"No," he interrupted again and pulled back, forcing me to look at him. You don't apologize for grieving, Ainsley."

"I was horrible to you."

I didn't think I'd ever get over the shame that flooded me every time I pictured the door shutting in his face as he begged me not to push him away. It was something I wasn't sure I could ever make up for, but I'd still try. Evander brushed the loose strands of hair from my face before leaning down to kiss my cheek.

"We tend to be our worst to the people who love us most because deep down, we feel safe. We know that no matter what we throw at them, they can take it and won't ever leave," he said, smiling gently.

There was so much truth to his words. In the depths of my soul, I knew Evander would never abandon me. He'd never give up on me—on trying to make me smile or laugh. He would do whatever it took to bring me back to life.

"Are you happy you have me back now?" I asked. My demeanor toward him had improved vastly compared to how I was. Of course he'd welcome that over the sullen ghost I was weeks ago.

Evander cocked his head and narrowed his eyes. "You never left."

"No, I mean—"

"I know what you mean," he interrupted, "and my statement still stands. You never left."

Van brought his hand up to cup my cheek as he stared deep into my eyes. The grey within his was bright and brilliant, and the morning sun made the tiny golden flecks inside more prominent. They weren't usually noticeable, but today, they shone beautifully, and my heart squeezed at the sight of this man I loved so much.

"When I Claimed you, Ainsley, I Claimed every part of you. Not just you at your best—at your happiest—but *every* aspect of who you are. I want your worst, your angriest, your most broken self. All of it." I swallowed hard, feeling my throat tighten with emotion. "You never left me. It was just a different part of you whose turn it was for me to love. And I love that side just as fiercely as I do this one," Evander said before pressing his forehead to mine.

I was entirely captivated by how much he loved me.

"Now love, what would you like to do today?" he asked.

For the first time, I decided to answer. There was only one thing I wanted. I pulled back slightly to meet his gaze and smiled. "I have an idea."

Van arched a questioning brow. Before anything else could be said, I leaned up and pressed my lips to his, claiming the kiss I had gone far too long without.

I could never fully go back to the person I was before that night, but I didn't want to keep pushing him away every time he tried to get close simply because I couldn't cope with the pain and guilt of my actions. I needed him. I had learned just how precious time was and would claim the life I wanted instead of running away.

Sunlight danced on the lake's surface as the soft breeze created tiny ripples. I tried to rub warmth back into my arms when I felt a fur blanket drape over my shoulders. I smiled to myself as Evander pressed a kiss to my cheek, his shadows from traversing drifting into the wind. He pressed his chest to my back and wrapped his strong arms around me.

"It's almost time," I said. His body tensed, and he gave a subtle nod. "Are you nervous?"

"No," he answered, but I could hear an edge in his voice—one of uncertainty and fear. Today wasn't going to be easy, no matter how much Van wanted to pretend.

Last week, the end had finally come. We received a formal letter demanding retribution for my crimes committed against the Crown. We'd acquired such summons before, but now it wasn't coming from just King Dashiell. Now, it was being demanded by every other king in Disparya. Even Tallis had signed his name to the letter, though that wasn't a surprise.

For weeks now, Tallis had been trying to convince Evander to stop delaying the inevitable and agree to the trial, but he wouldn't. He was more concerned about getting me through my dark patch than the politics of our land, and although I loved him for that, we couldn't delay any longer. I had to answer for what I did.

"I am," I admitted. Today would be the day we found out the date of my trial and the punishment for my crimes if found guilty—which I was.

"I'm not going to let anything happen to you, love. You know that, right?"

I did. Of course, I did. Evander would sooner rip the world apart than let harm come to me, especially at the hands of people who we believed were traitors against Disparya. Van was more than ever convinced that King Harbin of Ministro was still working with Pravus's leader, Oberon, to take over our continent. The now very dead King Perceval was his closest ally, so why wouldn't he want to help take over Disparya by getting rid of the biggest threat to that plan?

Oberon's soldiers had stayed mostly quiet in Disparya since I murdered Perceval, instead focusing on attacking the continent of Vorsutos. From one of the many letters we received over the weeks, Declan was struggling to maintain morale over his soldiers in Vorsutos as they constantly were getting pelted in every direction from attacks. I knew it was killing Evander not to be able to help the Lord of Vorsutos—the man he considered family—but there was nothing we could do. Tenebrae couldn't afford to be without her king right now.

"I think I found a place for him," I said, not bothering to answer his question. "I found it the other day while out with Nox. It's close by and overlooks part of the land. You can even see our house in the distance." Evander nodded along as he tightened his embrace. I leaned further back against him.

It had been two months since Felix died, and he still hadn't been put to rest. As soon as everything that night in Caelum happened, our world had been shut down. There was no crossing in or out of a kingdom you didn't belong to. Dashiell had immediately ordered a ban on portal usage, and all kings quickly agreed, fearing they would be Tenebrae's next target. As part of the agreement, guards from each kingdom were placed at the portal locations throughout Disparya, with the exception of the one located inside the cave on our lands. Though they guarded the portals on the opposite side, no one dared to cross through to Tenebrae.

Tallis had sent word that fateful night that Brandle and Elenora had barely made it into Agnitio with Felix's body before the complete shutdown occurred. Luckily, they were safe, but it also meant they weren't able to bring Felix home to me without Dashiell's soldiers intercepting him. Apparently, he wasn't going to stop until he found his best friend's body and brought him home. But Caelum wasn't Felix's home—Tenebrae was. Olivier was. And he deserved to be laid to rest in the place where he was finally free.

Evander offered to traverse into Agnitio, take Felix, and bring him back, but it was too risky. As a sign of good faith, each of the other three kingdoms agreed to allow soldiers from Caelum to patrol their lands, including the palaces. Van assured me he could get in and out undetected, but I wasn't going to take even the slightest risk with him. Not after I had already lost one of my family members.

Tallis assured me through letters that his body was being kept preserved thanks to magic, and as soon as it was safe, he'd find a way to get him to me. I could be patient for a little while longer.

"I think it sounds perfect," Evander replied. "The weather has warmed enough to travel through the mountain pass. We can visit the northern camps as soon as the trial is over."

I didn't miss his confidence in thinking that everything would go well enough with the trial that I would be with him for the journey through our lands and not rotting in a dungeon or beneath the earth.

Our quest to find Inmuto, the mythical sixth kingdom, could soon begin. With the other kingdoms against us for what I did to Perceval and Declan dealing with his own battles in Vorsutos, we were running out of allies—and chances to save Disparya. We needed Inmuto's numbers and whatever potential magic they possessed to even the playing field.

"Has Tallis been able to translate the book yet?" I asked.

Van shook his head solemnly. "The language is apparently old—*very* old—older than anything the scholars living within Agnitio's palace have seen. They're trying to decipher it, but it's apparently taking far more research to do so than we initially expected."

I sighed in frustration. I was so sure that the book Imogen uncovered in Caelum's library would help us in some way, but maybe I was wrong. Perhaps seeing the word *Solum* in the text meant nothing at all. Maybe it was just an entry regarding the sacred bond between the species of wolf that Onyx and Nova were. Maybe it was nothing at all, but it didn't feel that way.

"What if I was wrong and we're just wasting everyone's time and effort?" I said remorsefully. The thought made me sick.

"You're not," Evander replied with utter confidence. "I trust your intuition. If something about that book caught your attention, then that's all I need. We will—"

"Van," a voice interrupted and we both turned to see Olivier approaching.

After we decided we couldn't put off the trial any longer, Evander summoned him home. He wasn't going to let him continue to stay away during a time like this. My gaze locked onto Oli's for only a second before I twisted my head and stared back out at the water. I couldn't bear to see the pain in his turquoise eyes. I was the reason he lost the man he loved; the reason why he and Felix would never have the time together they deserved.

"The meeting's about to start," Olivier said.

My heart dropped into my stomach and the anxiety began to creep faster now. I closed my eyes and forced myself to focus on my breathing and the way Evander's arms were anchoring me in place.

"We'll be there in just a minute," Van replied, giving me a few moments to gather myself.

Once the sound of Oli's sloshing footsteps through the melting snow quieted, and I could be sure he was no longer with us, I spun around to face Evander. He shook his head slightly as if answering the thought in my mind.

"He doesn't hate you, love."

"He should," I responded. "He has every right to."

Evander sighed as he brushed the hair from my face and cupped my cheeks. "Did you ever think that perhaps he blames himself for Felix's death?" I furrowed my brows. How could Oli possibly have been responsible for something that was caused due to my actions? "If roles were reversed and it was me, I would only be able to focus on how I didn't get to you in time. Nothing else would matter to me except that one detail."

I didn't think of it that way, but I could understand what he meant. If Evander had been the one with an arrow through his heart, I would have hated myself for the rest of my life for not saving him.

"Come on," he whispered. "It's time."

5

Ainsley

The study was quiet as Marceline, Calidore, Lia, and I gathered around a table with a large piece of blank parchment in the center. Evander stood behind his desk on the opposite side of the room with Oli. I tried to clear my mind and remember that today was only a meeting to determine the date of the trial and punishment; I knew Van would never let harm come if I was determined guilty. But despite the reassuring words to myself, I didn't feel at ease.

Lia squeezed my shoulder and Marce nudged me with her hip before giving me a command to relax and breathe. I did as instructed and glanced over to find Evander watching a slip of paper on his desk with a deadly calm. He always effortlessly slipped into his role as king when the occasion called for it, but this felt different. His demeanor now was less similar to the way he conducted himself in royal meetings, and more like when he confronted Mishal after finding the bruises that disgusting man had left on my body. It wasn't just the Heir to Tenebrae being threatened, it was his Soul Bonded. His Claimed. The woman he loved.

Evander's body tensed ever so slightly as he stared at the parchment. The motion caused me to turn back to the piece in the center of the table just as black ink magically spilled across it. The meeting was starting.

'*State your presence,*' the parchment read. One by one, the names of the Kings of Disparya appeared in different handwriting. Soft scribbling was the only sound in the space, and the moment it ceased, Evander's name drifted onto the parchment...written significantly larger than everyone else's. I glared at him with an arched brow but he simply smirked and shrugged. I chuckled softly under my breath and his face softened at the sound. I knew at once that was why he had done it—to get a reaction that wasn't laced with fear out of me. Van knew how scared and nervous I was, so he'd never miss the opportunity to try and lighten my mood. I loved him even more for it.

After a moment, the five names of the kings disappeared, and the paper was blank once more. All were present, and the arraignment could officially begin. I sucked in a breath as Lia grabbed my hand.

"It's going to be fine. You were smart not to marry Van that night," she told me, and I turned back to see him nodding along.

The day Felix and I left for Caelum, I was supposed to marry Evander, but I knew it had to wait. I had a feeling that I would have to use a marriage proposal to appease Perceval's quest for power over Tenebrae. If Van and I had been married, I wouldn't have been able to sign the magical contract binding me to that deal, and my ruse would have been uncovered.

When I told Evander of my plan, we spent hours going over the wording and how important it was to be precise and clever with my choices. I couldn't let Perceval back me into a deal I couldn't get out of, especially if the punishment for breaking it were death. But of course, there was another reason I didn't marry Evander that night—a reason he didn't learn of until I came back home bloody—and once again—on death's door.

"You kept Tenebrae safe, love," Evander reassured me. "And now, we will protect *you*."

No one knew of my plan to murder the King of Caelum for his crimes against my family and me. When Felix questioned me about the dishonesty, I claimed it was because I didn't want to be stopped. That was true, but I also didn't want to implicate anyone in my treason. I knew that if I committed regicide as simply the Heir to Tenebrae, I would be punished accordingly. However, if I committed the act as a queen, then it would be me acting on behalf of the kingdom of Tenebrae. I would be declaring war.

As it stood, Evander could truthfully deny involvement, and Tenebrae could uphold her stance on peace with the other four kingdoms. It was why King Dashiell's only demand to end the dispute between our kingdoms was to turn me over. It would only be me who needed to be punished, and not our people.

Words spilled over the paper again and I leaned closer to read.

The trial for the murder of King Perceval of Caelum shall be held in seven days' time in the kingdom where the crime took place.

I recognized Dashiell's handwriting as Calidore blew out a relieved breath, though I didn't understand why. Going back to Caelum for the trial seemed like the last thing anyone should be comforted by.

"Seven days?" Oli said, sounding just as confused as I felt.

"I don't know," Evander admitted. "Perhaps he needs time for whatever he's planning."

At that point, I glanced around to see my family all nodding as they agreed. Apparently, I was the only one not comprehending the significance.

"It would be his right to demand an immediate trial, leaving us with no time to prepare our defense," Cal answered, reading the confusion on my face. "Seven days is a long time to wait, given the crime that was committed."

"He has to be up to something," Oli offered. "Perhaps he's stalling to give Oberon time to send troops over for an ambush." Evander nodded like it was a possibility, but it didn't feel like it to me. I couldn't pinpoint precisely why I didn't think we had anything to worry about, but my magic didn't stir as it usually did when something felt wrong.

'Agreed' appeared on the paper five times before disappearing——all kings accepting Dashiell's terms.

Several minutes passed as we all stood around in silence, staring at the blank parchment in our possession and waiting for it to magically fill again. Once it did, a list of my crimes was spelled out for all of the kings to see. Treason, regicide, and attempted murder of the newest King of Caelum were written in dark, bold letters—all of which I was guilty of. Below, in a much smaller print, more words bled onto the page in fresh ink.

Ainsley, Her Royal Highness, Heir to Tenebrae, has been formally accused of the crimes above. Her punishment shall be determined by the five Kings of Disparya. If found guilty, we call for:

I sucked in a shuddering breath as my hands gripped the table to stop them from trembling. This was it. King Harbin's name appeared first, followed by the unmistakable letters that formed the word *'Death.'*

King Arden of Venator was next with the same request. I could feel Evander's rage through our Soul Bond, but I couldn't turn to face him. My eyes were too glued to the parchment in front of us as Tallis's name appeared with the exact same punishment. Calidore's throat rumbled in something like a quiet growl as I fought the nausea that was forcing its way into my system.

"He has to, love," Evander explained, knowing exactly the deep-set fear I was feeling. "It's all about keeping up appearances, but Tallis *is* on our side. When the time comes, he will argue your case."

I knew Van was right, but it didn't ease the sickening feeling of seeing three kings calling for my death. I didn't think I could possibly feel any lower until Dashiell's name flooded the page in black ink with the demand for an end to my life. I pressed my hands flat onto the table as I gulped down the air in greedy intakes. My walls were closing in, and the room was spinning out of control. I had no idea why. I expected that word to appear next to his name... at least,

I thought I had. But for some reason, seeing it was a shock to the system. It was pain and heartache and grief—a line cut I didn't realize was still tethered.

My family's voices grew muffled as my ears filled with the roaring panic of my thundering heart. Lips pressed into my temple and then again along my cheeks until hands were cupping my face, and I was being forced to stare into the eyes of the man I loved. My fingers dug into his shirt as I worked to slow my breathing and bring myself down. Evander's eyes grew dark and dangerous as he took in just how scared I was. He called for Lia, who took his place, wrapping her arms around me and pressing me into her body.

Only the sound of Van's thunderous footsteps filled the air as he stormed towards the desk and scribbled his note on the paper. A few seconds later, his name appeared at the bottom, followed by the words *'Go fuck yourselves.'*

There was no way in hell Evander was going to play the role of an unbiased king when the others were demanding for my life to be taken. I knew it was a possibility—we all did—but nothing could have prepared me for seeing the words written in ink.

'The trial has been set,' was added last to the paper before everything magically disappeared, and it was left blank once more. In one week, my life could be forfeit.

Lia rubbed her hand up and down my back in an effort to soothe, but it did nothing. I was too afraid, too numb, too in my own head. I closed my eyes as the scent of cedar and snow enveloped me, and the feel of Van's shadows brushed against my skin.

A moment later, we were traversed into our bed, where he held me close as I shattered. I had expected the call for my death, but to see Dashiell demand it as well... It broke something deep inside me that my fractured heart didn't understand.

6

Ainsley

We didn't bother preparing that week. The reality was, I was guilty. I killed the former King of Caelum and was caught doing it. My only option was to plead my case, justifying my decision to commit regicide and relying on Tallis to sway the other kings into pardoning me.

No one would care about what Evander had to say due to his bias, so hoping they would listen to him would be a wasted effort—particularly since he killed King Arden's advisor in Agnitio months ago. I had absolutely no faith in swaying Dashiell to spare my life, either. I was the reason he had lost his father and his best friend in a single night.

"We should take Nova with us and have Onyx stay with Lia as a precaution," Calidore suggested as we clipped our packs onto our horses.

"I'll be fine, and so will Tenebrae," Lia drawled. Cal wasn't enthusiastic about her remaining behind while the rest of us journeyed to Caelum for the trial, but someone had to, and Lia was the logical choice.

Like all of us, she was trained to fight, but she also had the ability to heal our people if something happened while we were away. If she informed us that the other kingdoms delayed their attack until we left Tenebrae, Van would quickly traverse us all back home. None of the other kings besides Tallis knew what his unique ability—known as an Obscure—granted him. We could be home and fighting within minutes—or seconds if we weren't already too far away.

"Lia is right," Marce affirmed as she mounted her mare. "Not to mention, you know we can't separate the two of them right now."

"Why not?" I inquired. Nova and Onyx had been separated in the past, so what set this time apart?

"Because of their Solum Bond," Evander answered, appearing behind me and lifting me up so I could saddle myself onto Nox. "We're walking into dangerous territory, and if we're attacked, they need to be together in case one of them gets hurt. Their bond allows the magic they possess to flow freely between them and heal any injuries."

"That's why Onyx wouldn't leave Nova when she was wounded," I deduced, thinking back on the time we found her bloody and broken in Agnitio. Onyx had been fierce and vicious, refusing to let anyone approach her, and even killing a man who dared to try. Once we managed to calm him down, he stayed by her side, refusing to leave.

"That, as well as loving her," Van answered. "Had he not been there, Sirona and Lia's work may not have been enough to save her. It's too risky to keep them apart right now."

I nodded in agreement with his assessment. We had no clue what we were about to walk into, and it was best to be as prepared for the worst as possible.

Evander climbed onto my mare and settled in behind me. Typically, he would have chosen his own horse, but I could sense he wanted to stay close. I just didn't know if it was for my benefit or for his. Maybe a combination of both.

Suppressing the overwhelming fear that today might be my final day in this world, I leaned back against Evander and closed my eyes as we embarked on our journey to the portal that led to Caelum.

⚘

"We should leave the horses," Oli suggested once we reached the mouth of the cave that would lead us to Caelum. "If something goes wrong, they'll only slow us down." He was right. Van's ability to traverse would be far quicker than trying to ride away.

"We still have a while until the trial starts, so we'll have plenty of time to get there on foot," Marce added. With that, Evander nodded, and the rest of us dismounted.

I gave Nox her usual apple and said a quick goodbye as I stroked her neck. I felt relieved that she wouldn't be joining us. As she had once belonged to my father, she was the only living piece of him I had left. Losing her wasn't an option.

"It's going to be fine," Evander singsonged as he removed our packs from Nox. After he finished, he put three apples in front of her, and she eagerly took them. He was determined to use food to steal her affection from me.

"How do you know that?"

Evander brushed his hand down her side before tapping her gently in a clear order to head back home. "Because I know everything."

I rolled my eyes. "You might be wrong this time."

"I'm never wrong," he replied with that cocky smirk of his. "Plus, I want everything to go well, and I always get what I want." He lifted my hand and pressed his lips above my knuckle. "Case in point."

"You barely have me." I made a deliberate stride away from him towards the cave entrance where the rest of our group was gathered.

"Are you joking?" Evander scoffed and casually tucked his hands in his pockets. "You're completely obsessed with me, love. It gets a little much sometimes." He kissed my cheek and swiftly ran past me before I could smack him.

"So what's the plan?" Cal asked, securing daggers in different holsters across his body.

We were all dressed in our training suits, choosing to travel prepared. Given the state of our world, we couldn't be too cautious.

"I don't care about the result of Ainsley's trial. Regardless of the verdict, we aren't letting anyone touch her," Evander stated as he crafted daggers and shoved them into the holster at my thigh.

"Obviously," Marce added, annoyed Van had to even say that. "But what's our play regarding Oberon? None of the methods we've used before have been effective in getting the other kings to listen. Even your father couldn't convince them to take the threat seriously."

"That's because the other kings were probably always in Oberon's pocket," Olivier pointed out. "Asking for help won't work; we need to take it by force."

Unease settled in my gut at his demand. Oli's desire to go straight for blood was out of character, especially considering the negative impact it would have on Tenebrae. The outcome could be more detrimental for our people.

"Absolutely not," Evander stated. "Our goal is to achieve peace, not make more enemies." This was a non-negotiable matter for him. He looked towards the rest of us, but Oli interrupted again before he could continue.

"Are we just going to let what happened to Felix slide?"

My heart squeezed at the mention of his name. I understood Oli's strong wish for justice, as I felt the same, but it wasn't the right moment. We had too much at stake.

"Yes, Oli, we are." Van was gentle yet firm in his decision, but I could tell how much it hurt him. Although he would have supported Olivier as a friend, he had to prioritize his duties as a king.

"Oli—" I began, approaching the man who was like a brother to me.

I wanted to reason with him—to show him that I understood the pain he was experiencing. We may not have been able to avenge Felix's death, but we could try to honor him in another way.

Olivier gestured with his hand to halt me, his piercing turquoise eyes freezing me in place. He regarded me for a moment before taking a deliberate step forward. "If you had—"

"—No." Evander placed himself between us, his focus fixed solely on Oli. "Don't you fucking dare," he growled, low and deadly. Van's power thrummed through me as shadows swirled in his palms.

Olivier didn't have to finish for me to know what he meant. *If you had been honest, Felix would still be alive. If you hadn't killed Perceval, Felix would still be alive. If you had just followed orders, Felix would still be alive. If you hadn't been such a selfish asshole, Felix would still be alive.*

I had been telling myself the same things for months. Occasionally, I still did. Those were the times Evander always held me tighter.

Oli immediately fell silent. His gaze shifted to me, and I witnessed a flash of regret in his expression. It seemed like he wanted to apologize, but I didn't let him. I turned and walked into the cave, ready to pass through the portal and begin our trek. He didn't owe me an apology, especially when he was right.

"The three of you travel through and secure the area. I need to have a moment with Olivier first," Evander commanded, his voice bouncing off the walls of the cave.

Marce and Cal swiftly caught up to me, while Onyx and Nova silently followed. Taking a slip of transfer paper from my pocket, I swiftly wrote a note indicating to Sirona that we were prepared for her to open the portal.

Soon after, a shimmering glint appeared on the cave wall. Gripping the dagger on my hip, I took a preparatory breath and stepped through to Caelum.

Just like the last time I entered, the sun was blinding, and I threw up a hand to shield my eyes. Spring was just beginning in Tenebrae, but here in this kingdom, it seemed to have been in full swing for quite awhile.

I slowly lowered my hand, blinking several times as I adjusted to the brightness. Caelum was already adorned with blooming flowers and sunny skies. My forehead glistened with sweat, leaving me uncertain if it was because of the warmer weather or my anxiety.

I caught sight of a black blur, followed by Onyx leaping into the air and creating a cloud of dust upon landing.

I marched over to him. "Drop it." Evander's wolf hesitated as if pretending he hadn't done what I had just witnessed. "Now, Onyx. We aren't here to play."

Without breaking eye contact, he opened his mouth and a large blue butterfly, covered in slobber, dropped out. I gestured my chin towards Nova. With his head hanging low, he walked over and sat down beside my grey wolf, clearly showing his displeasure with me.

"For something that can be so deadly, he acts like a child most of the time," Marceline said.

"He gets that from his owner," I replied, my gaze sweeping across the meadow.

"Which one?" Cal jabbed. The smirk in his voice had me rolling my eyes—mostly because I didn't know the answer.

"Since you want to insult your rulers, you get to clear the thick brush," I told him, pointing to the forest beyond. "Marce, you take the meadow to the east and I'll take the south. Onyx and Nova, guard the portal." With that, we all dispersed.

Clearing the area didn't take much time. Even though everything seemed normal, a sense of unease persisted within me. My magic was restless, which was always an indicator that something wasn't right.

"I'm going to check on them," I announced to the group.

Van and Oli hadn't joined us and it had been nearly an hour since we separated. I pushed my hands against the portal's entrance, but instead of going through, they stayed pressed against solid stone. My fingers searched the rock, sliding over cracks and crevices as I frantically tried to get through.

"What's going on?" Cal demanded.

"It won't open."

I started to panic as that strange foreboding feeling grew stronger. A whimper left Nova's throat, only solidifying my fear. Something was definitely wrong.

Shadows pooled in my hands as I crafted two daggers and turned around. Calidore and Marce were already armed and ready. I didn't know who the fight would be with—only that every instinct in me told me enemies were coming.

Before I could think of what our next move should be, a cool breeze brushed past my face, leaving a stinging slice of pain across my cheek. I twisted to see an arrow embedded in a tree behind me.

A second one whizzed past from another direction, this time bouncing off the shield I had thrown up a fraction too late to protect myself against the first attack. One after the other, arrows flung from all directions, either hitting our protective shields or landing just short of us.

We couldn't determine the number of hidden enemies or how we missed any signs of them during our area search. There seemed to be far too many to have overlooked.

"Cal, shadows!" I yelled. He did as instructed and both of us released our Gifts, wrapping our group in darkness. If our attackers couldn't see us, then we had a chance of getting away and catching them off guard.

"How did we miss this?" Marce whispered, slinging a dagger through the darkness in hopes of hitting the enemy.

"We can discuss that later. For now, we need to get the hell out of here. Ainsley, send Van a note while we have a second."

The moment I pulled out the transfer paper, the arrows that had landed short all burst into flames and white smoke came slithering out. I reached for the mask wrapped around my throat, but it was too late. By the time I pulled the fabric over my mouth and nose, the fumes were already in my lungs.

Marce doubled over first, coughing profusely. Seconds later, Cal and I were doing the same. Onyx and Nova were the only two that didn't seem affected by whatever was emitted into the air. The wolves whimpered helplessly as my vision blurred and my limbs went heavy. I was vaguely aware of my knees hitting the hard dirt as I gasped for clean air, only to take in another lungful of the toxin.

My magic strained as if it were being reeled back into me without permission. I pushed against it, trying like hell to shove my power out, but it was no use. Our shadows stirred before slipping through the air and back into us.

Clutching my daggers, I masked my fear as the darkness receded, exposing a group of at least twenty individuals encircling us. All of them were wearing clothes similar to what we had on, but there was no way to distinguish where they hailed from.

Each person looked at us with malice and hunger, ready to strike the prey they had so expertly ensnared. A copper-haired man stepped forward and angled his head to the side as he looked us over.

"I thought you'd be more difficult to catch. That wasn't much of a fight at all," he tsked.

I stood, stepped forward, and banged my fist against the shield that glinted in the sunlight, now keeping us trapped. "Why don't you let us out? I'm sure we can rectify that," I said.

A sinister smile split his face. With a slow shake of his head, he crept forward until he stood inches from me. He tapped the shield with a long finger as if he were trying to get the attention of some kind of strange pet in a cage.

Nova snarled at our enemy's proximity to me and Onyx lunged, his paws clawing at the forcefield around us. It didn't falter.

"Where is he?" the man mused, ignoring the wolves as if they weren't there. I knew who he meant.

"He's probably already at the palace by now. And when he realizes we haven't followed, he'll be back." I meant the words to be a deadly promise of what would happen should any harm come to us, but they seemed to miss the mark.

"Oh, I'm counting on it."

My fingers itched to warn Van, but one look at Cal had me dismissing the idea. We all knew that the second Evander found out we were in danger, he wouldn't hesitate to come rushing in to save us—putting himself at risk in the process.

If he was stuck on the other side of the portal for whatever reason, it meant he was safe—at least for now.

The man looked back at the crowd of our captors before jerking his head toward us. Arrows flew and landed at our feet before bursting into flames once more. This time, the moment the fumes released, it felt as if the exposed skin on my hands and face caught fire.

Screams of pain shredded my throat on its way out, and I collapsed to the ground. Marce grunted as she crawled to me, in too much pain to stay on her feet. Calidore reached me first, not in much better shape than I was, and used a cloth at his side to wipe my forehead.

Nova came to me next, licking one hand as Onyx took the other. Each member of my family worked diligently to remove as much of the poison from my skin as they could despite the effects I knew they were experiencing, too.

Water spilled over my face, but it might as well have been acid for how badly it burned.

"I'm sorry," Marceline whispered as my scream pierced the air. I could hear our enemies laugh at my pain, and I mentally marked each one of them for death. Marce poured more water over Cal's cloth as he continued to scrub my skin clean.

"You both need to take care of yourselves," I said weakly, meaning every word. Just as I knew it would, my command fell on deaf ears.

"You are our priority," Cal said, a final response on the subject.

Onyx's growls tugged at my concentration. We all looked up just as another wave of arrows littered the field around us. They erupted and I held my breath in preparation for the pain that was promised. But it never came.

Blue smoke filled the air with the scent of peppermint and clove. The fumes blanketed my skin, bringing instant relief from the burning sensation. But with the reprieve from the pain, my magic became more sated within me—now just a distant echo of what it usually was.

I tried not to panic as I looked toward Cal and Marce, knowing they were discovering the further slip of their power. Whatever was given to us was nearly as potent as wolf venom.

Nearly.

I curled myself around the one wisp of power I could still feel. It wasn't possible to fully call to it, but I could hold on to the remnants until the sedative started to wane.

My mind raced as I quickly ran through different scenarios. We didn't have access to our magic, but we could fight our way out. Granted, five on nearly twenty wasn't ideal, but they were odds we'd have to take. Of course, that would require our enemy to let us out of the shield, and it didn't look as though they had any plans to.

We could wait until the poison's effects left our system, but I had no doubt they would just release more, and we'd be back where we started. As much as I hated it, Evander and Oli were our only hope for rescue. But with them trapped on the other side of the portal, they weren't really an option either.

The copper-haired man unsheathed a dagger at his hip as his eyes stayed locked on me.

Cal helped me to my feet, and he and Marce took protective stances in front of me. Onyx and Nova flanked my sides, ready to join the impending fight. I grasped my two daggers fiercely, grateful that Van had fully armed me rather than relying solely on our ability to craft weapons at will. That clearly wasn't an option now.

"When he comes for you," the man said menacingly, "I'll have you watch as I kill him first."

I bared my teeth as a low growl rumbled at the base of my throat. The metal hilt of my daggers dug into my skin as I held them tighter, fighting the rage that filled me over his threat.

"I won't make it quick or clean, either," he said.

I lunged at the shield, stabbing my blades into it repeatedly as I yelled my fury, but we were helplessly trapped. I couldn't lose Van because of that. I wouldn't.

"You're dead," I promised.

He chuckled and his audience joined in. The man laughed and laughed until suddenly, a soft thump sounded behind him. We twisted at the noise, and I looked past him to see one of his men on the ground.

Another fell to his knees. Then another. One by one, those who surrounded us crashed to the dirt, their eyes fluttering shut with no visible signs of injury.

"What the fuck is going on?" Cal murmured. Marce and I shook our heads, the three of us angling our weapons to fight the new threat.

I turned around and glanced at the portal to find it was still solid rock. Had Van and Oli made it here through another portal?

"Perhaps they passed through Agnitio's," Marceline commented as she read the confusion on my face. "Van could have traversed here."

"If it's not them, we need to be ready," Cal added.

The shield around us flickered before reinforcing once more. The new attack was distracting whoever was keeping it in place. Onyx moved to the front and dug his paws into the dirt, ready to pounce the second the opportunity arose.

The copper-haired man drew the sword sheathed at his side and turned his back to us. The members of the enemy who hadn't fallen frantically looked left and right, trying to locate the culprits.

An arrow pierced the silence, slicing through the copper-haired man's neck and sending him to the ground in a bloody heap. The shield trapping us disappeared.

Without a breath of hesitation, Onyx and Nova sprinted into the crowd, dodging blows and shredding our initial attackers apart. Screams and pleas erupted as Marce, Cal, and I joined the fight. Thanks to whoever was taking out this group from afar, we were no longer vastly outnumbered, leaving only a handful of our ambushers remaining for us to deal with.

We made quick work of the stragglers, with Cal and Marce executing all but one of the unconscious men. He needed to stay alive for questioning. Though we took out the immediate threat, it didn't mean that we weren't still in danger.

The five of us went back-to-back, searching the treeline as best we could. The mysterious aid stayed hidden.

"It'd be easier if you came out so we'd know whether to kill you or extend our gratitude," Cal announced.

A breath later, a twig snapped in the distance and Cal stiffened against my back. I felt it before turning—scented it on the soft breeze that blew past. Every muscle in my body trembled as a languid voice filled the space and my heart.

"Hey there, cupcake."

7

Ainsley

I was dreaming; I had to have been. There was no way that if I turned around, I would see Felix standing there, alive and well. His voice, his scent, the feel of his presence—it was all just a side effect of the toxin still in my system. It was a hallucinogen designed to cruelly show me what I had lost. There wasn't any other plausible answer.

I held my best friend in my arms while he died. I felt his heart stop as my Imperium Gift tried to fix what was irreparable. I had said goodbye and mourned him. This wasn't real.

Sucking in a shuddering breath, I turned slowly and prepared to see my best friend bloodied and broken. But as my eyes locked onto the figure across the meadow, he was nothing like I expected.

Felix stood tall, dressed in the attire of the Agnitio court. His silver hair was tied back by three thick braids and his amber eyes were bright. His skin was its usual porcelain shade, though there was a slight color in his cheeks—nothing like the pale grey flesh I had clutched to me that fateful night.

My knees went out as I stumbled forward, Cal and Marce both catching my elbows to keep me upright. I looked at my companions who seemed just as shocked. Somehow, the poison was making us visualize the same thing. Because that's what this was—a vision.

I screwed my eyes shut to gather my thoughts. If Felix had survived, I would have known. Tallis would have sent word. Someone would have—

A body collided with mine.

Leather and spice enveloped me nearly as strongly as Felix's arms did. His fingers twined through my hair as he pressed me into his chest. I refused to open my eyes. I knew this would kill me the moment the hallucination faded, but I didn't care. My best friend was here with me, even if it wasn't real.

Inhaling his scent, I buried my face further into his chest.

"I miss you," I whispered.

"I've missed you, too," he said back. The words sliced my heart deeper, reopening the wounds that would never fully heal in his absence.

I pressed my ear to his heart, listening to it beat steadily beneath his chest. The rhythm was a gentle melody accompanied by his lyrical voice. The two, together, made the most beautiful song I never wanted to end.

"I'm home now," Felix said.

I hummed in contentment as Elenora spoke. I had no idea why she was here in the hallucination, but I didn't care enough to inquire. My focus was solely on soaking up the precious seconds with my best friend before he was ripped from my world again.

"That's bullshit," Calidore replied to whatever it was she had said. "He's our family. Tallis had no fucking right."

Felix squeezed me tighter as Elenora spat her retort. I wanted them to shut up. They were ruining what little time I had.

"You will all answer for this," Marce growled, accompanied by a snarl from Nova.

Felix let out a deep sigh, my cheek rising and falling with the movement. "I know you're all pissed—trust me, so am I—but we don't have time for this now," Felix said.

At that, I pulled back slightly to look at him. Why was my mind so eager to have him leave? If anything, I should have wanted to keep him with me for as long as possible.

"Don't go. I'm not ready yet," I pleaded.

Felix's brow furrowed as he stared at me. Slowly, his palm cupped my cheek in a soft caress. I placed my hand over his, holding him there with me.

"I know this isn't real but..." Tears slid from my eyes as I choked out the words. "But I'm not ready to say goodbye again. Please stay—for just a little while longer."

I gripped his shirt as his thumbs swept over my cheeks, delicately catching each fallen tear.

"We don't have time—"

"—Say one more fucking word, Elenora, and I swear to the Gods, even our alliance will not be enough to save you," Marceline warned.

Her sharp words intrigued me, but I didn't let my eyes stray from my best friend.

Felix cradled my face with both hands as he bent to meet me at eye level. We were frozen in time, yet he looked so much different from what I remembered—older, somehow. Maybe a little wiser, and more experienced, too—the lines in his face seemed to tell a story I had yet to hear.

"I'm not going anywhere, Ainsley. I'm right here," Felix said. He pressed my hand to his heart and I savored the consistent thumping against my palm. His eyes bore into mine, his face becoming more serious than I had ever seen before. "This is real. *I'm* real. And I'm right here."

My stare drifted from Felix to Cal and Marce. They nodded in unison as encouraging smiles lit both of their faces. I twisted back to my friend as the knowledge of what I was being told started to sink in.

No.

This couldn't be real. This had to be some trick that even Cal and Marce couldn't decipher. I stepped back, needing to distance myself. It was one thing to enjoy the hallucination; it was another for it to try and convince me of its validity. Felix closed the gap.

"You died." I shook my head repeatedly. "I held you as you died."

"I know," he whispered, pulling me back against him. I tried to wiggle free, but he only tightened his grip.

"I don't understand."

"Brandle. He—" Felix stopped abruptly. He stiffened against me, his arms going slack at his sides. I glanced up to find his eyes wide as he looked past me. Twisting in his arms, I peeked over my shoulder.

Olivier stood still, his body rigid, and a look of shock crossed his features. I slid from beneath my friend's grasp. The moment I did, Felix and Oli moved toward each other, like two magnets pulled together by an invisible force.

They collided, their hands grasping and mouths searching in a deep embrace.

"How?" Oli questioned as he pulled Felix's face from his.

"Brandle."

Olivier let out a relieved chuckle just as a tear slid down his cheek. He crashed his lips to Felix's once more. I should have looked away, given them their privacy, but I couldn't.

This was real. Felix was alive. He was *here*.

A finger pressed to my cheek, and I sucked in a breath at the stinging sensation.

"What the fuck happened?" Evander questioned, raising his hand to show me the blood now coating it. I had forgotten all about that slice from the arrow. His charcoal eyes were frenzied as he surveyed the ground, now littered with bodies.

"We were attacked," Cal answered.

"Clearly," Van responded, less than thrilled.

"And Felix is alive," I breathed in disbelief. He and Oli were still wrapped in each other's arms, smiling and speaking too low for any of us to hear.

"Clearly," he said again, but this time, Evander's voice was soft and joyous as he enclosed his arms around me. I leaned my head back against his chest, letting him hold me as I repeated the mantra in my head.

This is real. Felix is alive. He is here.

"I hate to break up the happy reunion, but we have to fucking go!" Elenora demanded.

Before another word could be uttered, a blade was poised at the Agnitio general's throat.

"My brother suffered for *months,* believing the man he loved was ripped from this world. All the while, you had him captive. Give me one good reason why I shouldn't spill your blood here and now," Marceline demanded.

Elenora lifted her hands in surrender as she carefully began to retreat. "My uncle commanded his survival be kept secret. I understand Felix is part of your family, but I will not betray an order from my king."

"Not good enough."

"Marce," Evander warned before she could cross a line that would lead us further into war. Marceline gritted her teeth but backed down, sheathing her sword on her back.

Elenora breathed a sigh of relief as she lowered her hands. "Thank you, Evan—"

"Just because I spared your life does not mean we are friends. As far as I'm concerned, the Kingdom of Agnitio betrayed Tenebrae."

"It wasn't like that, Evander," Felix chimed in, rejoining the group hand-in-hand with Olivier. "There's a lot that happened, but Elenora is right; we don't have time right now." He gestured to the bodies on the ground. "There are more of them, and they will be coming for us any minute."

"Then we'll stay and fight," Oli said.

Felix shook his head, dismissing the idea. "Ainsley's trial will be starting soon. If she's not there, the kings will see it as her admitting guilt."

We had put off accepting the trial so many times in the first place that Felix's notion didn't seem far-fetched. Why would the kings have any reason to believe I'd actually show up when Evander had been against the idea in the first place?

"Fine," Evander agreed. "They won't believe any note I send, so take Ainsley and—"

"I'm not leaving you," I interrupted.

He could try and argue all he wanted, but there was no way I was going to be apart from him—not after what we had just gone through. He seemed to recognize he'd be fighting a losing battle because he quickly amended his order.

"You all go and try to stall as best you can. Oli, Ainsley, and I will stay and fight."

No one argued with Van's command. Instead, we hastily said our goodbyes and prepared ourselves for another fight.

"We left one of them alive," I told Van.

I jerked my chin toward the still unconscious man whose blonde curls peeked through his black hood. I pulled on that wisp of power I had felt earlier and was relieved to see a small black tendril of shadow form in my hand. My magic wasn't fully restored, but it was on its way.

"I can't say he'll stay that way for long, though."

Van smirked at my comment before placing a tender kiss on my cheek. "Mask up, love," he commanded just as approaching footsteps filled the space. "It's time to remind the world why they fear us so damn much."

8

Felix

We sprinted through the forest. It would have made much more sense for Evander to just traverse us, but alas, he had a show to put on. I had no clue why he bothered. He had already impressed Ainsley sufficiently enough to charm her, and this was the most ill-timed occasion for him to flaunt his skills as a killer.

Not to mention, I didn't like the idea of Ainsley or Oli remaining in imminent danger.

Alright, and I suppose Evander as well. At some point, while I was in Agnitio, I started to actually miss him.

Correction: I missed pissing him off.

"That delay was inconvenient," Elenora whispered to me while we ran.

"You know what else is inconvenient? Believing for months that one of your own is dead," Marce replied.

Calidore agreed with a grunt. I didn't blame them for being furious about the secrecy—so was I. For months, I tried to sneak the word out to my family that I was okay, but each time, I failed. I hated Tallis's reason for keeping everyone in the dark, but I understood it.

There was so much they didn't know, so much that I only learned after waking up in the Medicus facility within Agnitio's palace.

Surviving that night was surprising, but even more jarring was the way Elenora, Tallis, and Brandle regarded me as if I were something to be examined.

The second I found out that Ainsley and Olivier were alive and back home, I demanded to go to them but was immediately shot down. My fury at that moment paled in comparison to the emotions I felt when Tallis explained why I had been brought there.

"I told you, it wasn't my choice," Elenora ground out, pulling me from the memory.

"We can't fight right now," Cal said. "We have a mission to see through. I'm not going to let Ainsley suffer because of shit that Tallis is responsible for. Van will deal with him."

With that, we continued on our journey in silence, save for the thud of boots upon the earth, panting breaths, and my screaming thoughts as I remembered each new piece of information I had learned.

Who I was and what I was capable of.

⁂

"Let me do the talking," Elenora demanded as we hurried down the stone corridors. "Those present will trust my explanation more than yours."

Agnitio was home to Disparya's peacekeepers, lawmakers, and justice wielders. Anything a member of its court said was considered to be the indisputable truth. The hope of extending my best friend's trial was firmly in Elenora's hands. My family seemed to gather as much because her request went unchallenged.

Within minutes of entering the palace, we received curious stares from the halls lined with residents going about their day. Shock flooded their features as some pointed, while others leaned in close, whispering shared secrets as their eyes tracked our advance through the corridors. I was supposed to be dead, after all.

Finally, the four of us reached the throne room. I smoothed my hair and pulled at my clothes, suddenly nervous for what lay beyond the doors. Dash would be there, but he wouldn't be the only one I would have to see.

My palms began to sweat. I wasn't sure I was ready to set my eyes on—

The massive doors creaked loudly as the guards opened them, and I flinched as I refocused on our task. Ainsley—she's what was important. Everything else could wait.

At least for now.

As we entered the room, several sets of eyes fell upon us, but there was only one pair I gravitated toward.

Dash paled, his deep teal stare going wide in disbelief. His posture stiffened and his muscles twitched like he was fighting the desire to stride for me.

He was. I knew it because I was doing the same.

All of our bullshit was so inconsequential in hindsight. Nothing mattered except that he was my brother through and through. We would get over the hurt we caused each other. Perhaps not today, but one day we would.

I would see to it.

If being *dead* had taught me anything, it was that the most important thing in this world was family, and Dash was mine.

A firm hand pressed to his shoulder, keeping him in place. I tried not to gag at the sight of the late King Perceval's most trusted advisor, Gideon. He was always such a dick to Dash growing up, trying desperately to drain any ounce of pure innocence my best friend possessed.

Gideon had been determined to turn Dash into the same ruthless ruler his father had been. Luckily, growing up, his efforts were futile as Dash was busy wasting his days away with me. The two of us were too rebellious to give a shit about what anyone wanted, least of all some dickhead who kissed King Perceval's ass daily.

But seeing Gideon at Dash's side now sent a pang of guilt through my chest. By choosing Ainsley, I had let the wolves descend upon him. I had left his side after I'd once promised to always be there.

Dash's stare turned cold, and I couldn't help but wonder if he was disappointed at the revelation that I was alive.

I banished the thought from my mind immediately.

My gaze swept across the room, taking inventory of the people and space. In the center, there were five thrones set in a wide semi-circle with a single chair in the middle—Ainsley's. Beyond the thrones were several seats, modest in size but larger than the one I was supposed to take. Behind the seated kings sat the three advisors chosen for the meeting, along with two of the Queens of Disparya—one married to King Arden of Venator and the other to King Harbin of Ministro. A handful of guards representing the present kingdoms lined the walls, alert and ready to defend their ruler.

"Apologies for our tardiness, Your Majesties," Elenora stated as we walked through the grand space. "It seems someone has issued an attack against the King and Heir of Tenebrae."

We stopped outside a semi-circle of thrones. Hushed conversation between those in attendance broke out, adding to the already growing tension.

"Are you insinuating that one of us committed treason?" King Harbin sneered.

I clenched my jaw at the sound of my former king's voice. It brought nothing but unpleasant memories and unrealized truths to the forefront of my mind.

"Never, Your Majesty," Elenora bullshitted. "I only mean that a rogue group has taken the opportunity to attack Tenebrae's leaders while they were at a disadvantage."

"And how do you know this?"

"As my king is aware," Elenora gestured to Tallis, "Felix and I were delayed, as I had an official task to complete prior to my arrival. On our way, we encountered a group moving in the distance. Felix picked up on some aggressive emotions, so we decided to follow them. That's when we discovered they had ambushed the Heir to Tenebrae and her advisors."

I reached out to my Empathi Gift in an attempt to detect any clues as to who could have orchestrated this, but everyone kept up a strong internal defense. I couldn't uncover anything besides subtle nerves, a normal response to a meeting of this gravity.

"And then you…"

"Helped," Elenora finished. "King Evander sent us away to relay the situation as he continued the fight. He didn't feel a simple note from him would suffice."

She gave a sweet smile to the King of Ministro that I read for what it was—a very large *fuck you*.

"So you aided criminals," King Arden pointed out.

"Respectfully, her guilt has yet to be determined."

The corner of my mouth lifted at Elenora's confident response. I had to give it to her; she knew exactly how to handle the situation.

"And how do we know you speak the truth?" King Arden added, looking Cal and Marce up and down with disgust.

"Are you suggesting that a member of the Agnitian court is lying? Think wisely before you accuse not only one of my generals, but also my niece, of treason," King Tallis announced.

The room went quiet. Even the gossiping advisors stationed behind their kings had gone silent as they regarded the King of Agnitio.

"Given the state of the two Tenebraen advisors present," Tallis gestured a hand over Cal and Marce's dirtied and bloodstained clothing, "I'm inclined to believe my niece."

Elenora bowed her head in gratitude.

"Does King Evander need any assistance?" Tallis asked.

Calidore shook his head before walking to the throne meant for the ruler of Tenebrae. The rest of us followed as Elenora took up her spot beside her uncle.

"He has it covered and will be present as soon as he's finished," Cal explained

"Very well."

The room went silent again.

⚜

Minutes ticked by as we waited… and waited… and waited. Chairs creaked and throats cleared as people shifted uncomfortably. I didn't like how long this was taking one bit. I had to believe that everything was alright and Evander was just being his usual self—wanting to make a memorable entrance and irritate me simultaneously.

It would be fine. Everything would be fine.

I heard a barely audible whisper and turned to locate its source. Gideon leaned in towards Dash, speaking in such a low tone that I couldn't make out his words. Sensing my presence, Dash glanced up and locked eyes with me before replying. Gideon gave a nod and left the room.

Cal's tension was palpable as we witnessed the advisor leaving. Marce strode for the window and peered out. She scanned the landscape below, as if on the lookout for potential traps. The fact that Dash's advisor was just sent from the room wasn't making them feel at ease.

"Perhaps we should send someone to retrieve whatever is left of them," King Harbin drawled as he lounged on his throne. My teeth ground against each other at the suggestion. "I'm only pointing out that if they haven't arrived yet, chances are they won't."

Cal stalked forward just as Marce pressed a hand to his chest.

"He wants a fight," she said beneath her breath. "Do not give him one."

Tensions were high, tainting the air with anxiety that tasted sour on my tongue. I couldn't penetrate their defenses with my Gift, but that didn't stop their emotions from slipping out from time to time.

I eyed Dash, trying like hell to get a read on him, but he knew me too well to fall prey to my tactics. He was stoic, passive, and seemingly unaffected by the current state of everything. His mask wouldn't be slipping.

"How much longer are we expected to wait?" The King of Venator demanded angrily.

"Has King Evander arrived yet?" Calidore asked, making a show of surveying the room. "No? Then I guess you have your answer... *Your Majesty.*"

King Arden stood abruptly, his throne scraping loudly across the marble floor behind him. He pointed his finger at the Tenebraen advisor as his lip curled in a sneer. Before he could spew his hatred at Cal, Dash pushed up slowly from his seat.

"Quiet," the King of Caelum demanded, though he sounded more distracted than anything else. When I twisted toward my childhood best friend, I saw that he wasn't paying attention to the confrontation in the room. His eyes were fixed on the glass of water to his left.

I followed his stare and watched as tiny ripples moved within the cup in a steady cadence. Dash studied the vibrating liquid, his brow pinched in concentration.

"Your Majesty, what is that?" Gideon asked, but Dash ignored him. Just then, the room dimmed as if clouds had blocked the sun. Marce peered out the window before giving us a subtle shake of her head. She didn't know what was going on either.

I dropped my gaze to the ground, where a small rattling sound snagged my attention. Kneeling, I examined the fragments of pebbles brought in by boots bouncing violently across the marble. The floor was rumbling.

Marceline drifted back to us, unsheathing the weapon at her back. Calidore crafted me a sword before arming himself, just as each king and advisor in the room did the same. Everyone's focus was glued to the large, closed doors.

The rumbling increased in volume, now a booming thump as whatever was causing it loomed closer. I gripped the hilt of my weapon and planted my feet. The room illuminated as flames flickered in Dash's left hand while his right held a sword. We were all prepared to fight.

Boom. Boom. *Boom.*

The sound resembled a large beast approaching, shaking the palace with each massive step. The two queens present shrieked in terror as they ran to the far end of the room to cower alongside their ladies.

Despite the imminent threat, the palace halls lacked screaming or rushed stampedes. It was relatively quiet everywhere except the throne room. I looked around, but no one else seemed to notice.

"It's getting closer," King Hardin announced.

Boom. Boom. Boom. And then…

Silence.

The rumbling ceased, the water stilled, and the sun reappeared. There was nothing but a quiet calm that coated the air in more fear than I had ever tasted. Everyone looked to each other, but held their weapons at the ready, still too on edge to retreat. It was quiet.

Far too quiet.

The massive doors flew off their hinges, slamming into the wall and splintering into a million pieces as darkness erupted into the room. Shields were solidified in place, but Cal, Marce, and I lowered our defenses, knowing instantly what it was. I wasn't afraid of this darkness—it was my home.

Evander, Ainsley, and Oli walked through the shadows, drenched from head to toe in blood. They looked like death itself, coming to claim the lives it was owed.

"Sorry we're late," Evander announced as he sauntered into the room.

There wasn't an inch of his flesh that wasn't dripping in crimson. It made him look all the more menacing, though knowing him, I was sure that was the point. I quickly scanned Ainsley and Oli for any injuries, but they were just as soaked in blood as he was. It was impossible to distinguish which was theirs or the enemy's.

"It seems a few of your friends were a little disappointed they couldn't attend the trial," Evander said, casually slipping his left hand into his pocket. "But don't worry. We had a little talk and I gave my word they could be here."

The King of Tenebrae flashed a smile and snapped his fingers. Bodies poured from the ceiling and landed in a heap on the marble floor. Screams of terror broke out as the kings rushed from the center of the room, creating as much space as possible between them and the deceased.

I surveyed the bloodied mess. Flesh was shredded, heads were missing, and limbs were bent at unnatural angles. Dozens of our enemies were butchered and broken, given no peace, even in death. Evander didn't simply kill these people—he used them to send a message.

"I've never seen these men in my life," Harbin claimed, meeting Evander's stare.

"Nor have I," King Arden added.

Evander's sinister smile only grew. "My mistake," he said. His tone was light and playful, making it all the more terrifying. "Anyway... It seems the heir and I are slightly underdressed. We'll go clean up a bit, and then we can begin the trial."

The three of them began to retreat when King Harbin spoke again. "The heir stays." Evander stopped and turned around slowly. "She has been accused of regicide. We can't afford to be too careful with her roaming the halls."

Evander shook his head. "She's coming with me."

Harbin caught the attention of a guard stationed near the doors and jerked his chin in Ainsley's direction. He moved for her, nearly grabbing her arm before a shadowed dagger was lodged in his throat. The man fell to the ground, his life lost.

"Evander!" Harbin yelled. "That is a punishable offense!"

The King of Tenebrae twirled his fingers, and his dagger disintegrated into thin air.

"Accused or not, Ainsley is still royalty, and he tried to lay a hand on her. I was well within my rights to defend the Heir to Tenebrae," Evander argued. His grey eyes were chips of granite as he glared at King Harbin. "And if you try to take her from me again, I promise you, the results will be the same."

The two kings glowered at one another, each clutching a weapon at their side, ready to attack if necessary.

"Let it go, Harbin," Tallis announced. "We have a trial to conduct, and whether Ainsley remains in this room or leaves to wash the blood and innards from her hair won't change that."

The King of Ministro didn't move. He was determined to make this as difficult as possible for everyone involved.

"Go," Dash said, finally asserting himself into the conversation. "Let the Tenebraen court tend to their needs. I'll have lunch brought up for the rest of us just as soon as we clean this mess." He looked over the dozens of bodies spread along the ground.

Evander's shadows poured from him and blanketed the dead until nothing was visible but a pool of inky black. When the darkness receded, it took the bodies with it, leaving only puddles and streaks of scarlet across the marble floor.

The King of Tenebrae turned, put a gentle hand on the small of Ainsley's back, and led her from the room with Olivier following behind.

It was about to be a long fucking day.

9

Ainsley

I rolled my neck as we walked through the royal corridor of the palace. The battle in the meadow lasted longer than we'd planned, as Van had something of a creative streak when it came to mutilating bodies. Covering ourselves in more blood than necessary seemed a little over the top, but both Van and Oli agreed that it would make the statement we needed.

Following the fight, I briefed them on the specifics of our initial capture. Apparently, Van and Olivier debated for nearly half an hour in Tenebrae about how we should behave during the trial. That was, of course, then followed by a physical altercation, which I knew Van had provoked in order to help Oli release some of the hurt and anger he had bottled up for months.

By the time tensions calmed, the portal had locked and neither of them could get through. Evander explained that Sirona was struggling to reopen it, and when he didn't hear back after writing me, he knew something was wrong. He and Oli journeyed to Agnitio and utilized their portal to access Caelum, locating us shortly thereafter.

We didn't know for sure why the portal had solidified, but the ambush that ensued right after couldn't have been coincidental.

A snarl filled the empty hallway, and I dropped my gaze to find Nova baring her teeth at Onyx as he tried to get close to her. She decided against bathing in the blood of our enemies, while Onyx gleefully played with the corpses. His black fur was now slick and matted to his body. Nova emitted another growl, advising him to keep a safe distance from her mostly clean coat.

"I'm sorry," Evander announced. "I know the plan was for me to stay calm through this entire fucking ordeal, but I just couldn't."

"Stop," I interrupted, grabbing his arm to pause our journey. "Staying calm and collected was never going to get us anywhere. We needed to show force and that we aren't going down without a fight. We needed to remind them why they've feared the Kingdom of Tenebrae for centuries. You showed them exactly what we are capable of."

"She's right," Olivier offered as he wiped the blood from his brow with the back of his hand. "Diplomacy was never going to work with those assholes."

"Then we change course," Evander agreed.

With a smile on his face, he pressed his bloody hand against my cheek. For the first time today, I had a glimmer of belief that we could make it through this in one piece. I pressed myself onto my toes to claim his lips, but before I could, my name echoed off the stone walls around us. The familiar cadence instantly made me turn.

Imogen was rushing towards me from the far end of the hall. Without hesitation, I abandoned Evander and hurried to the woman I loved as a mother. Her safety had been a constant worry for me these past months.

Despite promising to come to Tenebrae the last time we spoke, she never showed. I was terrified that her involvement in King Perceval's murder had been revealed and that retribution had been enacted. There was no one in the palace I was close with, no one I could write to learn of her fate. It was too risky to send correspondence as it was, and I couldn't afford for my letters to wind up in the wrong hands.

Imogen flung her arms around me, not seeming to care one bit that I was covered in blood and pieces of organs that weren't mine. With tears welling, I breathed in her comforting scent while she held me tightly. I felt a sense of clarity and relief knowing she was alive and safe.

"You never came to Tenebrae," I scolded, pulling back to get a good look at her. She appeared unchanged, though her usual polished and pristine look was now marred with gore.

"There were things I needed to take care of here," she answered. "But soon, I should be able—" she trailed off as she looked over my shoulder at the two men slowly approaching. I adjusted my position while waving my hand over the pair.

"Imogen, this is Olivier," I told her, and she nodded curtly. "And this is Evander." She arched a well-groomed brow before dragging her gaze up and down his body as if inspecting a transaction she was, in no way, pleased with. Van's concerned gaze locked onto mine. I shrugged, oblivious to Imogen's issue with him.

"Hello, Imogen. It's a pleasure to finally meet you. "I'm Ev—" he attempted, but Imogen interrupted him with a raised hand.

"I know exactly who you are," she said coldly. With a small step towards him, his eyes widened in panic. "You're the reason she looks like *this*." Imogen gestured towards my body while maintaining eye contact with him. "Ainsley is royalty and should be dressed as such."

"We were attacked—"

"—And instead," Imogen continued, speaking over the king beside me, "You chose to stroke your own ego and flaunt her like a bloodthirsty creature."

"I..." he started but quickly shut his mouth as he looked between Oli and me, desperate for us to save him from the deep waters he was treading. Both of us glanced away. "We... When... But..." Imogen glowered at him as he stumbled through his thoughts.

"But what?" she asked sweetly. Her words were poison coated in sugar and Evander had taken a bite before I could stop him.

"It was imperative that we show our strength and..."

My head shook vigorously behind Imogen as I silently implored Evander to stop talking. As usual, he didn't listen.

"And I stand by that choice," he finished. Oh, dear Gods.

With her arms crossed over her chest, she cocked her head at the king. I screwed my eyes shut and released an exasperated breath, knowing that her stance meant she was about to tear into him.

"Is that so?" she questioned, and Evander nodded like a fucking idiot. "According to you, it was a good idea for her to appear before the kings and prove her capability of committing the crime she's accused of?" Her hand swept slowly over my body, and Van's eyes tracked the movement. "Having her look like something vicious and feral and *terrifying* was the perfect way to show that she's not a threat to them, right?" Evander resembled a scolded child, swallowing hard while looking apprehensive. "Because why would we want her to appear put together, regal, and under control? Why would we want her to look like the royalty she is—worthy of respect and admiration?"

Evander was silent, and I had to bite my lip to hide my amusement at his speechlessness. He was terrified of my maiden and I was enjoying every second of it.

Imogen examined the men in front of her, huffing out air and curling her lip in disgust as she took in the body tissue and blood coating them. Slowly, she shook her head before pinching the bridge of her nose with one hand while pointing to a set of rooms at the end of the hallway with the other.

"Go and clean up, both of you. Perhaps you'll be able to find some dignity in the bath," Imogen said. Oli and Van quickly passed us, following the direction she pointed, until they stopped at one of the doors. "Not that room; it's Ainsley's."

"But we're—" Evander began, but stopped immediately when she raised an eyebrow, challenging him to go on. He sidestepped to the next door and pushed his way through. Imogen waited until the lock clicked before she turned to face me completely.

"He's *very* cute," she said with a bright smile. I laughed under my breath as I nodded.

"Was that whole display really necessary?"

"Oh, absolutely," Imogen teased, leading us to the room I was assigned.

Imogen worked her magic and quickly had me cleaned and looking my best despite the lack of time. Her talent for making me appear so polished never ceased to amaze me. My hair was styled to flow down my back in soft waves, with a comb pinning one side—her signature look for me.

"Where did you get this from?" I asked as I smoothed out the black gown she instructed me to wear.

The dress was beautifully crafted, appearing as a sheer covering over the corset body suit I had on. The piece, embellished with black diamonds, functioned like impenetrable armor rather than a lavish design. The gown had a hip-high slit, giving my legs freedom to move in a fight if necessary. Every aspect of this design was carefully tailored to fit my needs.

"I've been making it since you returned to Caelum with Felix months ago. I wanted to give you something suitable for your Coronation as Queen of Tenebrae, but I suppose you'll just have to wear it now."

I glanced at myself in the mirror one last time before I smiled and turned to Imogen. "It's perfect," I said, but she brushed off my compliment with a wave of her hand.

"I'd have to agree," came a voice from across the room. I looked up and saw Evander leaning against the open doorframe, arms crossed. He was dressed elegantly in all black with a crown dripping with shadows atop his head.

"Do I look breathtaking?" I teased. My favorite crooked grin appeared on his beautiful face.

As Van neared me, he stopped just shy and spun his hand around, crafting a crown adorned in black diamonds. He fashioned it atop my head before leaning down to reach my mouth.

"Devastatingly," he replied against my lips before kissing me deeply.

I melted into him, fisting my hands in his jacket until Imogen cleared her throat vociferously, interrupting our embrace. I whined at his sudden absence as he pulled away too soon. This could very well be the last time we would be this close and I wasn't ready for it to end.

"Banish those thoughts, love," he said, reading the worry etched in my furrowed brows.

"I'm scared," I quietly confessed. Given all we had gone through, he deserved my honest thoughts.

"Me too," he admitted—an answer I wasn't expecting from him. Throughout the week, he had shown no signs of wavering confidence. "I don't know what the other kings will say or how the trial will go. I don't know what the future holds regarding peace between the five kingdoms. The only thing I *am* certain of," he said carefully, sliding a finger under my chin to direct my drifting stare to him, "Is that your death will not be an outcome today."

Evander leaned forward and flicked the tip of my nose up with his own before kissing my cheek. I could see Imogen's smile in my periphery, and then she quickly let it fall, lest anyone see she actually liked the love of my life.

Van gently squeezed my hand and guided me out of the room, where Olivier was waiting for us in the hallway. He was fidgeting with his fingers and bouncing on the balls of his feet impatiently. I suspected he was anxious to see Felix again.

"Ready to go?" Evander asked. Taking a deep breath, I steeled myself and nodded.

Pushing off the wall, Olivier started leading the way down the hall to the throne room. I stopped abruptly after taking just two steps, then turned around and launched myself at Imogen. I clung to her tightly, desperately hoping this wouldn't be our final farewell.

"You'll be fine," she whispered. "He won't let anything happen to you." Her voice dropped even lower as if that final sentence was meant to be more of a secret than a comforting reassurance.

I released a breath as I stepped away, finding solace in her words.

Marce, Calidore, Olivier, Evander, and I stood outside of the throne room, listening to the muffled voices from the other side. We were making the most of the remaining minutes before my trial, cherishing every moment of calm before the inevitable storm.

"How are we playing this?" Marce inquired. All eyes turned to Evander, anticipating the command of their king. He gave a nonchalant shrug and pointed his chin in my direction.

"We follow Ainsley's lead," he said simply.

Van's hand moved upwards to caress my cheek, his eyes fixed on mine. The touch was both searing and reassuring. It felt as if he passed on the confidence he had been carrying to me.

His eyes were warm and lively, and an air of excitement surrounded him. I knew that it had nothing to do with the trial itself but rather the fact that I would be leading us through it. He appeared thrilled by the idea that our family would follow me, not him, today.

"Are you ready, love?" Evander breathed.

I straightened, lifting my chin and calling to my magic. The jasmine blossom tattoo on my neck tingled as I released the shadows hidden inside. Van's eyes sparkled as he looked at my open back, where the ink curled down my spine and settled into place. Instead of keeping it in one spot, I chose to let it delicately swirl over my skin like Van's tattoo always did.

Following that, my Gift emerged as shadows coiling around my fingers and adhering to my dress, revealing a lengthy, shifting train of darkness.

Assessing me, Evander's face displayed a look of pride. I had come a long way from the person I was when I arrived in Tenebrae months ago. She was filled with fear of the power she had and what she could do with it.

But now, I loved it.

"I'm ready," I announced. With a smirk, Van casually slid his left hand into his pocket and motioned for Oli and Cal to open the doors.

10
Ainsley

Evander's hand pressed to my lower back. His comforting magic brushed against my skin, letting me know he was there. That small touch granted me the strength I needed to move forward. With my shoulders back and chin raised, I walked with confidence to the center of the semi-circle.

My heels clinked against the marble floor as I took each deliberate step to what should have been my chair. It was an effort to maintain control over my nerves and not glance curiously about the room. My family split up and walked the perimeter of the circle until they were poised at the top, next to the throne that was designated for Evander. He didn't sit. Instead, he stood stoically at its side, watching me intently.

My stare drifted to King Harbin who examined me with a mix of intrigue, disgust, and—no doubt—recognition. Everyone had always claimed that I resembled my father, and I fully believed that Harbin was noting the similarities himself. I wondered if he knew Perceval had stolen me after arranging the murder of my parents, or if he was just coming to that realization himself upon seeing me for the first time.

Releasing his gaze, I moved mine next to King Arden of Venator. His lip was pulled back in a snarl as he glared at me with such hatred. He obviously blamed me for Evander snapping his advisor's neck that one afternoon. I smirked before moving my stare across the circle to Tallis.

The King of Agnitio wore a beautiful smile and his hands were neatly interlaced in his lap as he studied me curiously. Tallis was someone both Evander and I considered a friend, but I couldn't deny the anger I felt toward him at that moment. He had kept Felix's survival from us for months knowing full well the emotional turmoil I was under believing I had lost him. I couldn't think of a single reason to be so cruel. I clenched my jaw, tasting the venom of my words before swallowing them. This wasn't the time for that. It would have to wait.

Reluctantly, I turned my head and locked eyes on my next target—Dashiell. My chest ached and my magic thrashed against me at the sight of him. Somehow he looked older, his face harder and his deep teal blue eyes cold and haunted. His hands were set upon the armrest and his fingers stretched ever so slightly as if reaching for me before he pulled them back and balled them into fists.

I searched his stare, looking for any trace of the boy I used to know, the one I was so in love with last summer, but all I found looking back at me were the eyes of the king who demanded my death as retribution. My mouth opened just barely, like my body wanted me to speak before my mind had a moment to catch up. Dashiell straightened, his gaze widening with anticipation.

"Take a seat, girl," someone sneered and I blinked out of my trance, seeing Dashiell do the same. I twisted my attention to locate the culprit and met the stares of several men watching me curiously. "Now," he said again, and this time I saw who the demand came from—King Harbin.

My chest rose and fell heavily at the command, my anger reaching for the surface along with my shadows. I let my Gift fall freely from me and slither to the chair that I had been assigned. My darkness swirled over the seat, encasing it wholly in shadows. Keeping my eyes glued to Harbin's, I gritted my teeth and solidified my Gift into metal, letting the heavy weight crush the chair into dust.

Then, with a flick of my wrist, I let my shadows dissipate into nothing. I smiled sweetly before stepping over the remnants of the chair and strolling over to where Evander waited. He twirled his hand and a second throne appeared next to his.

The King of Tenebrae grinned at me before we both took our seats at the head of the semi-circle. I may have been on trial, but I wasn't going to be on display for them.

"Carry on," I stated as I placed my hands on the armrest and leaned back in the newly formed throne. I could feel Evander's pride radiate through me as both Harbin and Arden glowered from their chairs.

"You do not command *us*, child," King Arden remarked, his teeth bared in a growl.

For a moment, I thought about backing down and not drawing any more negative attention to myself. The five kings present would be the ones choosing my fate, so perhaps riling them up wasn't the best idea. But before I could talk myself out of it, a cool wave of magic brushed over my flesh. It was calm, soothing, and cleared the intrusive thoughts and self-doubt from my mind. This was *my* trial. And as Imogen had said: Evander wouldn't let anything happen to me.

I sat straighter and with a new sense of confidence. "It seems like I just did," I replied.

Our audience tensed, their backs going rigid in their seats at my blatant sign of disrespect, but I didn't care. The rulers of Venator and Ministro may have been regarded as callous and merciless kings, but they had three Gifts, while I had four. I held more power and potential than they ever would.

King Arden stood, his face screwed up as he prepared to spew his retort.

"We will begin the trial," Tallis announced before Arden could get a word in. His voice boomed through the room and captured everyone's attention. "Tempers are obviously high, so before matters get out of hand, let us do what we came here for."

King Arden and I locked eyes for another brief moment. Finally, he nodded to the King of Agnitio, mumbled something crude under his breath, and took his seat. Tallis stood and steepled his hands in front of him as he directed his attention to me.

"Ainsley, Heir to Tenebrae, you are on trial for the murder of King Perceval of Caelum. This is a unique situation. As you were caught in the act of the crime you are accused of, the laws of Disparya state that King Dashiell of Caelum has every right to demand immediate retribution, yet here we are," Tallis said, opening his hands to gesture to the room around us. "We are told there may be more to the events that happened that fateful night, so King Dashiell has requested that in lieu of immediate punishment, this trial be given."

Evander straightened in his throne. I didn't miss the subtle look he gave Oli out of my periphery. I reached out my Empathi Gift toward him and he let down his internal defenses just for me. His heart rate was elevated but not out of control and there was tension thick throughout his body. He was on edge.

A barely perceivable dip of his chin had Cal moving slowly away from us. To anyone else, it would seem that he was simply stretching his legs and trying to intimidate the other people in attendance, but I knew Van. It was an order to observe our surroundings closely.

Dashiell's choice to delay the inevitable and have everyone gathered together in one place only furthered Evander's fear that this was all a trap.

When royalty is gathered in one place like this, there is always a chance it's a trap.

Dashiell had once uttered those words to me months ago when the kings had come to Caelum to conduct a meeting on my attack. I swallowed hard and wrapped myself around Evander's heart, letting him sense my magic against him. He sighed in contentment under his breath and I could feel him relax slightly. With that, I withdrew my Gift and focused all of my attention back on Tallis, who was still addressing the crowd.

"You will be asked a series of questions regarding that night and your motivations," King Tallis continued. "Speak truthfully, for your answers will dictate your fate."

"There is nothing to dictate. She is guilty and should be treated as such. We are wasting our time with this nonsense!" The King of Ministro declared.

"A trial was demanded, King Harbin," Tallis argued, his voice taking a tone of agitation rather than its usual collected cadence. "So a trial she shall get."

Harbin leaned back in his chair and strummed his fingers against the throne with disapproval. He didn't take his eyes off me as the King of Agnitio directed his stare to Dashiell before nodding and taking a seat.

Dashiell stood, his eyes glancing over Felix before darting to me. I couldn't help but wonder what thoughts were pacing his mind. Felix wasn't stationed behind the King of Caelum as he once would have been. Instead, he positioned himself directly between Tallis and Evander. He had chosen our side over his childhood best friend's. There was a flicker of pain in Dashiell's features before it vanished and was replaced by something wholly different.

His face was hard, his jaw strong and his eyes dark. He looked like a king. It was the role he was born to play, but he seemed so different from his father. King Perceval was ruthless with an air of cold authority always surrounding him. That wasn't present in his son now. Even as Dashiell stared directly into the eyes of the woman who killed his father, there was something besides hatred swirling in his mind.

But for the life of me, I couldn't figure out what it was.

Dashiell stepped to the center of the semi-circle, finally breaking my stare as he surveyed the kings around us. He took a deep breath before lifting his chin high and addressing the room.

"Let us begin."

11

Ainsley

Dashiell recounted the events from the moment I entered Caelum until I reached Tenebrae through the portal. He left nothing out, including the multiple times I tried to stab him.

Van was aware of the anger I still harbored towards Dashiell for what he had attempted. I had told Van in detail about the strange way my magic would behave around Dashiell, refusing to obey my desires and instead curling deep inside me to sleep. Evander shared my concern and instructed Sirona to investigate the cause.

After a couple of weeks, she stumbled upon a possible reason. We were aware of the Lapsus stone's ability to make things disappear, the Tectus stone's power to conceal them, and the Indico stone's capability to expose the magical signatures left by the first two. But she had found evidence of another stone resembling the ones we sought, capable of negating magic. Van, Cal, and Oli were convinced that was the cause. We were confident that the stones we were searching for were in Caelum, so it wouldn't be a stretch to assume this new stone was as well.

When Dashiell finally shared the details of the night his father was murdered, the room was hushed and everyone was captivated as he recounted the story. However, he was unaware of all the specifics. All he seemed to know was that I had deceived him into talking with an illusion and got caught in King Perceval's room, drenched in blood, before leaping out of the window. I would have to be the one to fill in the gaps for my judges.

Dashiell reached the part where we fought outside—his fire versus my shadows. Throughout his speech, his focus remained fixed on me filled with a soft and imploring gaze, as if he was trying to communicate solely through his eyes. I held his stare as he went over every aspect of our battle, reminding myself of the anger I had felt.

If I hadn't taken advantage of his exhaustion, would I have even been able to escape? If I hadn't cast out my shadows, would I have been captured and killed on the spot, just as I thought Felix had been? The only thing that saved me was that Dashiell was still unfamiliar with his fire ability and lacked skill in using it.

I wasn't sure that held true anymore.

"And then she fled back to Tenebrae before my soldiers could apprehend her for her crimes," Dashiell finished. Brief murmurs broke out among the audience behind the kings, each spectator discussing my guilt. "I then informed the rest of you of what had happened that night."

King Tallis rose from his throne and joined the King of Caelum in the center. "Is your story truthful?" he asked. Dashiell looked him directly in the eyes and nodded once. "Thank you."

Tallis gestured for Dashiell to reclaim his seat before directing his focus on the rest of the kings. My stomach sank, knowing it would be my turn to speak soon.

"I have detected no lies in his answer," the King of Agnitio declared, his voice loud and commanding. "He speaks the truth."

Rushed whispers erupted within the space, and I looked toward Van who was watching Tallis closely, his grey irises fixed on only his friend.

"Do you deny his claims, Heir to Tenebrae?" he asked me. The room fell silent at once as everyone braced for my answer. That cool brush of magic caressed my skin, giving me the strength to hold my chin high as I answered.

"No."

Fury enveloped the room as harsh demands for death rang in my ears. There was an uproar amongst the crowd over the murder of a king who wasn't theirs. Marce appeared at my side a heartbeat later, her hands clutching the hilt of her sword and her chest rising and falling in steady movements. I could tell she was readying her Tremo Gift to call forth if needed.

"We have our answer then," King Harbin voiced. "There is no need to continue this charade."

Cheers of agreement broke out. Tallis raised his hands to silence the disgruntled guests, though it did little to stop the chatter completely.

"A trial was demanded, so a trial shall be conducted. We will not vote on Ainsley's guilt until she has had her say," Tallis argued forcefully. "If you cannot abide by our laws, then you may leave this trial and return to your kingdom, forfeiting your vote. You know the rules, Harbin. We shall not break them for anyone, king or otherwise."

Harbin grumbled under his breath but settled back in his chair. King Tallis brought his gaze back to me before taking a deep and calming breath. He curled his fingers gingerly in a signal for me to rise. Nervously, I obliged.

"You have corroborated King Dashiell's story and therefore admitted your guilt. You killed a king of this land, and the punishment for that is death, Ainsley," Tallis announced.

Evander's throat rumbled, and I could see shadows slip from his hands and fall to the floor. His emotions slammed into me at full force—fear, frustration, and most of all, anger.

"Relax, King Evander," Tallis warned. "No one is threatening her. I am merely stating the facts of the situation at hand."

"Facts that we should not be debating," the King of Ministro tossed out.

Tallis ignored him and continued. "We are not solely here to discuss whether you committed regicide, though we seem to already have that answer. As I stated before, we have been informed there may be more to that night than we are aware of. We know you are guilty, Ainsley, but now we will discern if your actions were justified."

I fought the desire to turn to Evander for comfort and confirmation. Needing him wasn't weak, but the other kings would see it that way. I had to do this entirely on my own. Giving Tallis a single nod of acceptance, I clasped my hands in front of me as I prepared for his questioning.

He offered a small smile of support before diving in.

"Ainsley, Heir to Tenebrae, why did you murder the former King of Caelum?" Tallis held his hands behind his back, the picture of professionalism.

I pondered my answer—not what to say but how to say it. The goal of this trial was to convince these kings to pardon me for my crimes. I had to be strategic about what I said, how I said it, and who I said it to.

The Kings of Venator and Ministro both hated me, so the chances of swaying their decision were slim. Evander was clearly on my side, and I knew Tallis would support me through this endeavor, which meant...

I inhaled deeply as I directed my stare to Dashiell.

"Because he murdered my parents." The new King of Caelum stiffened infinitesimally, but enough that I noticed. "As well as Evander's."

"Lies," King Harbin declared.

"How do you know this?" Tallis directed at me, ignoring his fellow king's outburst.

Dashiell leaned forward, steepling his hands and resting his forearms on his knees. His stare was hard as he prepared to examine my response.

"He admitted it to me—right before I killed him."

Rumbles of disgruntled conversation broke through the room. Accusations of falsities mixed with vicious insults were thrown my way, but I didn't pay them any mind. My gaze was firmly locked on the one king in the room whom I needed to convince.

Dashiell's chest moved steadily, giving me no indication that he was affected or even believed my statement. His face was unreadable stone with no cracks for me to penetrate. King Perceval had withheld so much information from his son regarding me. My only chance now was to cut the threads and watch the truth spill at his feet. I couldn't force Dashiell to believe it, but I could at least present him with my story.

"How convenient for you he isn't here to defend himself!" The King of Ministro yelled, rising from his throne. "You accuse King Perceval of committing treason against our nation. Where is your proof of these crimes?"

I stumbled for my words as I stared at King Harbin. I had no proof. There was never any evidence of his crimes against my parents or the former King and Queen of Tenebrae. We knew this fact was going to be our biggest hurdle and hadn't quite figured out a way to argue it.

"I have none," I admitted.

"I say again, how *convenient*."

Swallowing the bile in my throat, I turned my attention back to Dashiell. He pushed himself straight and leaned back in his throne. For some reason, I couldn't help but feel that his change in posture meant I had failed. That he had realized my answers didn't matter.

"My fellow kings," Harbin announced, moving to the center of the circle where Tallis stood. "The Heir to Tenebrae is guilty of regicide. She has admitted it and provides no proof to back up her outrageous accusations. We have a duty to our great land to uphold its laws."

"Our laws dictate a trial is to be given," Tallis argued.

"Which we have done! And for what? She has admitted her guilt and provided us with nothing but a story she cannot prove legitimate! I will not grant clemency to someone who murdered one of our own for no reason, Tallis."

All eyes were directed to me again, and I shifted uncomfortably on my feet. My blood was pounding, my thoughts screaming, as I tried to come up with a defense.

"Let us be done with this. I move we execute the traitor immediately," Harbin finished. Cheers of agreement combined with applause and chatter bounced around the room.

Evander stood, shadows coiled in his palms as the rest of our court inched closer. We didn't need to fight our way out. Van could simply traverse us to safety, but I could taste the thirst for vengeance spilling off of him like wine. He didn't enjoy the idea of keeping anyone who threatened my safety alive.

"Guards," Harbin ordered, his back to me as he returned to his throne.

"And why were you in Caelum to begin with?" Tallis questioned, his voice breaching the sounds of chaotic shuffling and rapid whispers. Our audience glanced at me with anticipation.

The guards halted their task, and even the King of Ministro hesitated before reclaiming his throne.

I gave in to the desire to set my eyes on Evander. He slowly lowered to his seat, his brow pinching just barely as if a realization had fluttered through his mind. His stare met mine, and after a slight dip of his chin, I turned back to Tallis.

"Because I grew up here. After King Perceval had my parents killed, he stole me. I was raised in Caelum with Caregivers until I was sent to the palace."

"Another wild accusation," the King of Ministro claimed, but Tallis paid him no mind as he went on.

"You did not grow up within these walls?"

"No," I answered

"And when you moved to the palace, did you possess magic at the time?"

"Not that I was aware of."

King Harbin groaned in agitation. "What does that matter? Where are you going with this, Tallis?" he demanded.

"I'm just trying to gather the facts of the situation. We heard from King Dashiell what happened months ago, but nothing prior to that. I believe it is important that we collect all of the information before we make a decision that could very well end a life," he answered.

The King of Agnitio paced within the circle, his hands placed firmly behind his back as he continued his line of questioning.

"King Dashiell," he started, "Is it accurate to say that once someone has received a Gift, they are relocated to the palace of Caelum?"

Dashiell cleared his throat as he straightened. "That is correct."

"And as far as the accused was aware, she did not possess any magic?"

"Correct. At the time of her arrival, she was still mortal. We assumed she would receive a Gift following her birthday."

Tallis nodded in satisfaction as he began pacing again. He turned his attention to me once more, and I prepared myself for his next inquiry. I wasn't sure where he was going with his line of questioning, but I was eager to find out—especially if it could get me out of the hole I dug myself.

"Did it not seem odd to you that you were required to live in the palace though you were not Gifted?" he asked me.

"No."

"And why not?"

I opened my mouth to answer just as the realization hit me. Suddenly, I was filled with hope and determination. We may have never been able to prove Perceval was behind the murders of our parents, but that wasn't the only crime he had committed.

"Because I had been told years prior that I was betrothed to Dashiell," I answered.

Tallis turned to Dashiell for confirmation, and the King of Caelum nodded shallowly. My lips tugged in the corner, ready to bear Perceval's crimes before the royalty of Disparya.

"Perceval brokering a marriage between his son and some *whore* is not a crime," Harbin argued.

Evander's teeth audibly ground at the derogatory term. I peered over my shoulder to find him tense, his fingers digging into the side of his throne while he sat there. It was taking every ounce of willpower he had not to step in and defend me.

I reached my Empathi Gift out, circling around his heart in a gentle reminder of how much I loved him. He relaxed just a fraction, though his eyes didn't leave Harbin.

"It is not," Tallis agreed. "But arranging a marriage between your son and a woman who is the product of Conjoining is very much one. For someone who seems to be so invested in upholding our laws, I would think you would have known that."

"Again, we are accusing a man who cannot defend himself of treason!" King Arden of Venator added. "Who's to say Perceval even knew of her lineage?"

"He claimed to have been childhood friends with my father," I announced, and everyone's attention returned to me.

Arden laughed, the sound menacing and cruel. "*Claimed*. Of course he did," he said sarcastically. "This trial is a joke. The defendant's only argument always seems to be hearsay that cannot be confirmed—"

"—I can corroborate her story."

My heart sank into the pit of my stomach as everyone whirled to the source of the interruption. Dashiell stood from his throne, keeping his gaze fixed on King Arden. His hands twitched, and in response, he balled them into fists at his side, only to place them behind his back a moment later so they were out of view. He was fidgeting—nervous.

"You're going to defend your father's murderer?!" King Harbin demanded, outraged.

Dash drew his focus toward the allegation, his posture going rigid as a look of insult flashed over his features.

"We are here to enact justice for those wronged. Whether that is to be granted to the Heir of Tenebrae or my father has yet to be determined. Until then, I would suggest you refrain from accusing me of misconduct." Dashiell's tone was a deadly threat, coated in ill-will and promises he would make good on.

The King of Caelum joined Tallis in the center and surveyed those in attendance before setting his sights on me. I held my shoulders back and chin high in defiance. He may have backed my claim, but it didn't change the past between us.

"Shortly before Ainsley's twenty-first birthday, my father and I had a disagreement. It was then that he informed me about her lineage."

"So you knew she was the Heir to Tenebrae," King Arden interjected.

"No. He informed me that she was a product of Conjoining but nothing more than that. I was instructed that during our Entwining Ceremony, I was to take all of her power for myself.
"

"And you didn't inquire for more information, let alone inform the rulers of this land that your father was breaking a law. It sounds to me like you and Perceval should both be charged with treason. Since he is no longer with us, perhaps you should claim both sentences," Arden replied.

Quiet claps of encouragement surfaced from the advisors stationed behind the two kingdoms that seemed to hate me the most. I desperately wanted to remind King Arden that he didn't seem too concerned about breaking that law when he came to Agnitio months ago in hopes of brokering a marriage arrangement between his son and myself. The Prince of Venator, Jahier, had told me that the only reason they chose to attend that ball was because his father knew about my Gifts from Tenebrae and Ministro. He wanted the power I possessed to be aligned with his kingdom.

As much as I wanted to share that information, I wasn't sure it would help my case today. A slight shake of Evander's head in my periphery told me he had already come to the same conclusion. If the kings were hellbent on arguing that Conjoining was illegal, our best bet was to prove Perceval's guilt in that matter.

"If that is what this court wishes," Dashiell announced.

"It is not," Tallis hastily replied before anyone else could. "You may have been aware of your fiancé's origins, but I am going to assume your father commanded you to keep it secret." Dashiell nodded his confirmation. "And correct me if I'm wrong, but in the end, no crime was committed on your part." Another nod. "Then we will, once again, focus on the task at hand."

Swallowing, I peered over my shoulder at Evander, who gave me a slight smirk of encouragement. This trial was taking a different turn than originally planned, but I couldn't deny it seemed to benefit us. A breath of relief left my lungs just as Tallis gestured for the King of Caelum to return to his throne, his part in this now over.

"From where I am standing, it appears that the accused is actually the victim of King Perceval's long-standing plot to covet more power for himself," Tallis announced, and for the first time, there were murmurs of agreement. "The punishment for his crime, should he have been charged, would have been death. It seems the Heir to Tenebrae has already served that justice."

The King of Agnitio turned his back to me and peered at each king, holding their stare one by one as if conveying a message through look alone. I was subtly reminded of the way Dashiell and Felix used to do the same thing. A secret conversation only those with the same thought pattern could understand.

"I vote we absolve the charges brought forth against the Heir to Tenebrae," Tallis demanded, his voice a vice over the audience.

"Never!" Harbin yelled, standing from his throne. He pointed a finger in my direction as he addressed the kings in the room. "And I will not pardon some *whore* who deserves to die—"

One second, the room was silent, save for Harbin's vile words—the next, it was full of shocked screams and frantic gasps.

Shadows swirled in dissipating wisps around the King of Ministro. His eyes were wide and frenzied, panicked and confused as he took in Evander now standing less than an inch away from his face.

With a dagger pressed to his throat.

"Call my wife a whore one more time, and she won't be the only one on trial for killing a king."

12
Ainsley

Evander tilted the blade, causing the light streaming through the windows to reflect off the ring on his left hand. The gazes of everyone in the room were directed at me, undoubtedly noticing the black diamond I wore as I finally unclasped my hands for the first time since the trial began.

Our wedding had been simple, and on a day when I woke up and realized I couldn't wait anymore. I was ready to claim the life I wanted, starting with marrying the man I loved. I didn't know what kind of queen I would be, just that Evander would never let me fail at it.

Guards and advisors reached for their weapons, ready to cut down my husband. Arden gave a subtle nod—an order to his men. Jahier's eyes collided with mine, soft and pleading, imploring me to end this before it could begin.

"Evander," I said, my voice dripping with the cadence of a queen.

This wasn't good. In the blink of an eye, we revealed our marriage, threatened a king, and showed the room what Evander's Obscure was, losing the element of surprise.

Shit.

With reluctance, he distanced himself from Harbin and approached me, letting the dagger dissolve into smoke. When he finally reached me, he placed a soft kiss on my cheek before taking my hand and guiding us to our thrones. We sat down, keeping our fingers interlocked as a sign of strength and our union. At least, that's how it was meant to appear to everyone else. To *us*, it was a way to keep each other grounded when we were struggling.

And Evander was.

He had let his anger get the best of him not once but twice today. His stare met mine briefly, relaying his guilt and an apology I didn't need. Evander's desire to protect and defend me was never something I could be mad at him for, even if it hindered us today. We'd find a way to overcome it.

With a disgusted sneer, Harbin shook his head. "How can you let *her* command *you*?" It was intended as an insult, not a question.

Van tightened his grip on me and casually shrugged with one shoulder. "It's easy when you have a queen worth worshipping. I would gladly give anything her lips demanded of me."

I suppressed the smile that pulled at the corner of my mouth while gently caressing the back of his hand with my thumb.

"Pathetic," Harbin finished.

"Yes, you are," Evander quipped.

I squeezed Van's hand, silently signaling him to stop talking. Continuing to anger the King of Ministro wouldn't lead us anywhere. We were on the brink of overcoming this obstacle and shifting our focus to what was truly important: garnering support from the other monarchs for the impending war against Pravus.

"If she is your wife, then you are just as guilty for her crimes against the Kingdom of Caelum as she is," King Arden proclaimed.

"Van had nothing to do with it," I argued. Under no circumstances was I going to allow him to be held accountable for my actions. "Our marriage is only a couple of weeks old, and I never told him of my plan to kill Perceval," I announced to the room.

"I find that hard to believe," Arden scoffed.

"Your lack of intelligence isn't my problem."

I could see my husband's confident smile from the corner of my eye and could feel love and admiration pouring from him. I embraced it, allowing it to consume me and drive away the intrusive thoughts of fear and self-doubt.

"Evander is innocent."

"Well, not entirely, love." I faced him, my brow pinching with worry at whatever stunt he was about to pull. "While I didn't expect the regicide, I knew you wouldn't leave Caelum without seeking retribution."

"And it never occurred to you to stop her?" Dashiell demanded, speaking for the first time since his statement. His tone conveyed a mix of frustration and anger.

Evander cocked his head to the side in that condescending way he loved. Slowly, he leaned forward and narrowed his eyes at the king. Dashiell didn't back down. His unwavering gaze held Evander's in a clear challenge.

"Once her mind was made up, do you honestly think anyone could have changed it? She wasn't going to let anyone get in her way."

"You could have at least tried," he responded. "If you had, she might not be in this mess."

"If I *had*, she wouldn't have listened. If I *had*, she would have had me flat on my back and begging for mercy." Evander's posture eased, and a slow, wicked grin spread across his face. "And I don't mean in the delicious way she does every night."

Dashiell remained tight-lipped, but now all attention, including his, shifted to me. I couldn't help but notice Jahier's smug grin as my feelings for Van were confirmed. He raised a brow, and I responded with an eye roll, making him laugh softly.

"You find this funny, boy?" King Arden asked through gritted teeth.

"Mildly amusing, yes," Jahier responded casually.

King Arden stood up and angrily confronted his son. "She lied and made a fool out of you. Her intention was never to be your princess."

Jahier nonchalantly shrugged, displaying complete indifference to the turn of events. He grinned at me while addressing his father. "I never said I wasn't up for sharing."

I restrained myself from smiling by biting my lip, just as Brandle discreetly disguised his laughter as a cough. Throughout the trial, he maintained a quiet demeanor, mostly observing and occasionally exchanging whispers with Harbin. Though we were tentative allies, I knew Van still didn't trust him. After finding out he had saved Felix and kept it a secret from me, I wasn't sure I did either.

"Well, I'm not," Van declared, leading Jahier to put on a dramatic show of sighing in defeat.

"We are getting grossly off-topic," Tallis announced as he rubbed his temples.

"I concur. So let's end this and execute the traitor," King Harbin suggested. "Voting serves no purpose anymore. By declaring their union, Evander's ability to remain impartial is compromised, if he even had it to begin with."

I glanced at my husband as his eyes closed in frustration. Even if it was accidental, Evander's disclosure of our marriage caused him to forfeit his right to vote.

"It's up to the four remaining kingdoms to make the decision. I can confidently say that Arden and I are on the same page, but should it result in a tie, our advisors and queens shall break it. No matter how you calculate it, The Heir to Tenebrae is outnumbered."

The room buzzed with discussions of plans. I wanted to vomit. My hands began to shake as I glanced around, noting the confident smiles of everyone against me. The King of Ministro was right. It appeared that we were going to lose this vote.

As Tallis and I locked eyes, his expression conveyed a desperate question. Evander had been against this idea from the beginning, but the panic in the King of Agnitio's gaze made it clear that we had no other choice.

We had given our all, and victory felt within reach for a moment. But now... now it was time to take another chance.

I nodded once.

"An attack on Queen Ainsley would be an attack on King Evander," Tallis announced. The chatter didn't cease. The advisors were too bloodthirsty as they discussed how I would be executed.

"She is simply his wife. He'll find another," Arden said, brushing off the comment.

"She is *far* more than that."

"Tallis!" Evander shouted as he stood up from his throne.

Everyone halted their planning and focused on the furious King of Tenebrae as he stormed for Tallis. I promptly followed, seizing his wrist to halt his progress.

"Don't you fucking dare," Van warned the King of Agnitio.

"It's the only way."

I tugged on Evander's arm to get his attention. He turned, and I gave him a pleading look, indicating my agreement with his friend. He shook his head, but this wasn't his call to make—it was *mine*.

"What is that supposed to mean?" King Harbin asked, intrigued by the implications of Tallis's statement.

"None of your fucking business," Evander growled.

I reached up and cupped his face in my hands. He looked so scared, so *broken*. I detested the fear this decision caused him, but it was unavoidable.

"We can just leave," he begged beneath his breath.

"You know we need them."

He didn't respond. Instead, he broke free from my grasp and returned to his throne, leaving me and Tallis alone in the circle. I nodded my approval, and he turned to face the three kings.

"Ainsley and Evander share a soul. They were designed and created by magic—each one half of the other."

"That's impossible," Arden breathed.

"I assure you, it isn't."

I left Tallis's side as he spoke and walked back to Evander. He deliberately averted his gaze from the conversation, so I knelt in front of him and grasped his hands.

"I love you," I told him.

Reluctantly, he turned his attention to me. "They'll use this against us. They know our weaknesses now."

I understood where he was coming from. Knowing what your enemy coveted above all else was a powerful advantage. It has the potential to win wars or even initiate them. I exhaled a long sigh as I brought his hand to my lips. I pressed a kiss to the black ring on his finger, enjoying the cool touch of the metal.

"We were *always* going to be each other's weakness—Soul Bond or not," I told him. As the kings continued their discussion about the strange magic, I rose to my feet, leaned forward, and grabbed his chin. "Now tell your wife you love her."

A concealed smirk formed on his face. "I love you," he quietly mumbled.

"Good boy." I winked and released his chin before taking my seat next to his, catching the tail-end of the kings' conversation.

"—That's not a sufficient reason to save her life," Harbin stated.

"You would jeopardize your kingdom's well-being and success just to make a statement?" Tallis argued.

Before anyone could respond, the King of Venator interjected, "He's right, Harbin. You saw what they did to those bodies today. Imagine what he would do to our people should we rip away the other half of his soul."

"Together, we are stronger than him."

"Perhaps, but I will not risk my people to prove a point. This is not a fight that Venator can afford to be part of right now."

"Arden—" the King of Ministro tried.

"It's not the right time, Harbin." He turned to the other kings and advisors, who were now watching with bated breath. "The Kingdom of Venator votes to pardon the accused of her crimes."

I leaned forward in my chair, my hand clutching Van's as if it alone could keep me grounded. Tallis grinned and declared the same verdict. Although I had anticipated it, I couldn't help but feel a wave of relief.

As expected, Harbin rose and proclaimed my guilt, demanding my execution. The choice of words elicited a low growl from Evander's throat, but my attention remained on the upcoming king.

Dashiell's gaze was fixed on the floor, his forearms resting on his knees. With a thunderous heartbeat in my chest and a stomach tightly knotted, I anxiously awaited his response. I couldn't read him—couldn't decipher what was going through his mind as he stared silently at the ground.

Finally, after what felt like an eternity, Dashiell raised his head, his stare instantly meeting mine. I locked onto his gaze, his blue eyes pulling me beneath the current the same way they always had. He drew a deep breath and exhaled slowly.

"The Kingdom of Caelum pardons the Queen of Tenebrae for her crimes."

I didn't speak, didn't think, didn't do anything but replay Dashiell's words over and over and over and over again. Skin brushed against mine, my body moved without my permission, and words rustled in my ear—I could grasp none of it. I couldn't look away from the King of Caelum.

The room thrummed with power and distant noises rang in my ears, though I couldn't distinguish what they were. Once again, my body shifted and I slowly realized I was being guided. My gaze was reluctantly pulled away as I was shoved behind Calidore.

The room's sounds gradually returned to me, like awakening from a dream while still half-asleep. I blinked several times as I surveyed my surroundings.

Evander stood before me, his hands filled with darkness. My family surrounded me in a protective circle, weapons at the ready.

All the other kings and advisors stood up as Harbin positioned himself in the center of the room, sword drawn and aimed at Evander. He was furious after being denied and ready to take what he believed was owed to him—my life.

13

Ainsley

"Is this really worth it to you?!" Tallis firmly demanded, moving closer to the enraged king. Gone was the diplomatic leader as he dealt with a madman.

"YES!" Harbin bellowed, his frenzied eyes on Evander. "Step aside and allow me to take care of what needs to be done! Her mere existence is a total violation of our laws!"

Harbin's attention shifted to me as he began to pace back and forth, dragging a hand through his brown hair. I sensed he wasn't stalling, but rather using his growing anger to fuel himself before he attacked. His brow pinched and his face twisted in rage as he examined me with a disgusted expression.

"She should have never been born," he said. The words seemed intended solely for him.

I came to the realization that they were.

Whenever his eyes met mine, he saw someone else—someone that wasn't me.

"It kills you, doesn't it?" I asked, stepping around Cal so Harbin could view me fully.

"What does?" Harbin hissed through gritted teeth. His quick temper could only be rivaled by his even quicker impatience.

"That I look so much like him."

The King of Ministro bared his teeth, and I moved forward. Evander stiffened as I passed. His hand pressed to my back, letting me know he would stay at my side. That gentle touch fed me the confidence I needed to continue.

"That you have to sit in this room and see his face every time you look at me."

"I don't know what you're talking about," he tried, but I cut him off, continuing my persistence.

"That you have to be reminded the Gods chose a different bloodline to rule."

He attacked me with his Imperium Gift, but my shield blocked him—mine and the five others that were in place around me, thanks to my family. As soon as I had passed them, I could feel their magic sticking to me like other layers of skin.

"I hold you just as responsible for my father's death as I did Perceval, dear *cousin*," I sneered.

Harbin swung his blade, but before it could connect with my force field, flames erupted between us, causing us both to jump back. Harbin hissed in pain as he clutched his red, burned hand. I whirled, crafting a short sword and positioning it defensively across my body as I faced the source of the fire.

Dashiell stepped forward, keeping the barrier of flames alive and bright in the center of the circle. "Lower your weapons," he commanded.

No one moved an inch.

"*Now.*"

I stole a glance at Evander and watched his eyes shift as his mind ran through a handful of scenarios at once. Harbin wanted a fight, and I was itching to give him one.

Slowly, Evander recalled his shadows and instructed us with a look to do the same. Without hesitation, I let the sword disappear from my hands as I kept my focus on Harbin.

"If you have something else to insinuate, Ainsley, I suggest you do so to the entire group so we may follow along," the King of Caelum announced.

"My father's name was Julian." The statement caused a few quiet gasps and hushed whispers. His name held power and stories that had only been rumors until now.

During my training in Tenebrae, I learned a lot about my parents. Olivier had used the knowledge I wanted as a reward whenever I did something right. Craft a dagger, get a story. Gain a point in sparring, get a story. Not threaten to kill Van for a day, get a story.

That last task I was rarely ever successful with.

One afternoon, after I crafted a dagger free from imperfections, Oli told me about when my parents first met. My mother had hated my father with a passion and even tried to convince King Uriel to return him to Ministro after they learned of the rumors surrounding him.

The story spreading through Ministro and the rest of Disparya was that my father stole from King Harbin and fled north to work as a spy for the King of Tenebrae. The entire continent believed my father was a traitor, and that Uriel was planning to overthrow Ministro with inside information he had been given.

My mother argued that even though it wasn't true, my father wasn't worth the headache and urged the king to turn him over. But Uriel saw something in my father—something he wanted to keep around. He granted him asylum in exchange for his services as a Medicus. Less than a year later, he and my mother married.

"If that is true, then he deserved to die for his treason," King Arden chimed in.

"He wasn't a traitor!" I argued. "He fled not because he stole, but to survive."

There were skeptical looks from the crowd; all but the court of Agnitio seemed to think I was a liar. My heart ached for my father.

"Explain," Dashiell said.

"After Harbin took the throne, my father was given a second Gift from Ministro."

"LIES!" King Harbin yelled. I stalked forward through the flames. They were hot against my skin but didn't burn—at least, I didn't think they did. I was too focused on the vengeful, pathetic king before me to pay attention.

"HE WAS THE RIGHTFUL HEIR TO THE THRONE!"

"HE POSSESSED NO SUCH TITLE!" Harbin shouted back.

We were inches from each other, our anger rising to the surface as the room shook from the weight of our powers slipping through. I couldn't hold back any longer—I didn't want to.

"He did... and now it belongs to me."

The room went deathly silent.

Harbin stepped back, his eyes going wide and panicked as he looked me over in disbelief. I reveled in his terror-stricken expression and the fear rolling off him like dripping blood, hot and thick.

"That's impossible," he whispered to himself.

I lifted my lips in a slow, menacing grin just to piss him off some more.

"PROVE IT!" Harbin demanded. "I know you're an Empathi from your lackluster attempts to infiltrate my emotions but show us your other Gift."

Cocking my head to the side, I didn't respond.

His face flashed through different shades of red before he whirled on the guard next to him, grabbed his arm, and twisted until the crunching of a snapped bone filled the room. The man screamed in pain, slumping to the ground as he cradled the injury.

"HEAL IT!" Harbin demanded.

"What are you doing!" Tallis exclaimed. From my periphery, I could see everyone exchanging worried glances as Harbin teetered closer to the edge of insanity.

I held the King of Ministro's stare as he pointed to the poor guard on the ground, now whimpering from the agony of his protruding bone. Harbin smirked wickedly as he shook his head, looking more deranged by the second.

"You can't, can you?" he said with a soft laugh. I continued to hold his gaze, not deeming a response. "You have no other Gift! You—"

A gurgling sound interrupted his sentence, and he turned his head in the direction of the noise. I kept my eyes on him, studying the side of his face.

There were wrinkles around his eyes, not from age but from obvious lack of sleep, the skin purpling just beneath. His dark brown eyes were nearly bloodshot, and his deep brown hair disheveled from running a hand through it incessantly. He looked less than put together, which seemed so at odds with the way he tried to present himself.

Harbin was power-hungry and always wanted to prove his strength and superiority. But now, he looked like nothing more than a weak, frightened man.

I didn't turn away from the King of Ministro—I didn't need to. I was completely aware of what his eyes beheld as they stayed fixed on the second guard beside him.

I imagined how blood would be pooling out from the man's eyes, his mouth, his ears. His hands were more than likely wrapped around his own throat as he signified his inability to breathe. He sputtered and coughed the red liquid up as his heart slowly gave out. And then, judging by the soft thump, the guard had fallen to the ground.

I called my magic back, and the man gasped for breath. Tallis yelled for a Medicus to tend to both guards, and Harbin's stare drifted back to me.

"I'm not a Medicus," was all I said.

The king swallowed hard and shook his head, denying the rare Gift I obviously possessed.

"She's truly the Heir to Ministro," someone whispered.

"SHE ISN'T! THIS WAS A TRICK! AN ILLUSION SHE CASTED!" Harbin said desperately. Despite my performance, he was still in denial about my abilities. "I WANT A MAGUSIER TO CONFIRM!"

Tallis stepped forward, but Harbin shook his head. "Call for another," he demanded.

Tallis stared Harbin in the eye as he declared a single name.

"Felix. Come forth."

My stomach bottomed out, and my eyes immediately shifted to Dashiell. He appeared just as shocked as I was, his stare somehow finding mine in the crowd, as if we were both checking to see if the other knew.

Neither of us had.

Felix strolled forward, casting a glance in my direction as if to say, *I'll explain later.*

I returned one that said, *Yes, you most certainly fucking will.*

He stopped at Tallis's side, looking just as uncomfortable as I knew he felt. I reached out my Empathi Gift to him and he brushed it with his own magic. Whatever was about to happen, I'd be there for him.

"Tell me, Felix," Tallis asked, crossing his arms over his chest after gesturing to me, "What do you see?" He hesitated for a moment, seemingly unsure of how to answer the question. "Remember what I taught you. Each Gift has a unique aura," Tallis urged.

A long exhale released between Felix's lips as he faced me fully. I stared into his eyes, watching in amazement as they dilated, the amber nearly completely swallowed by two black pupils. His irises darted back and forth as he examined me, seeing the magic that lay within my soul.

"I see her Gifts," he announced.

"Can you describe what they look like?"

Felix's brow furrowed and he shook his head in frustration. Tallis placed a hand on his shoulder and instructed him to breathe and take his time.

Minutes passed when Felix spoke again. "There's a black wisp for her shadows and a grey one for the illusions." Tallis nodded along as his lips tugged in a smile filled with pride. "Her Empathi Gift is like mine, a light shade of pink."

"We already know this! Just tell us if there is a fourth Gift present!" King Harbin sneered, his impatience paper-thin.

Felix clenched his jaw, and I sensed an anger in him that I hadn't felt before. Rage pushed against his flesh, hot and persistent as if finally bubbling to the surface after being shoved away. He tore his eyes from me and set them upon the king. "There is a dark crimson aura present. She is an Imperium. Is that what you wanted to hear... *father?*"

14

Ainsley

I sucked in a sharp breath as the room erupted in chaos. Harbin lunged for Tallis with his sword. But the King of Agnitio was quick, dodging the attack and releasing the staff that had been strapped to his back. Evander was at my side a breath later, traversing me back to the safety of our group as the two kings battled one another with weapons and words.

"You knew!" Harbin accused, thrashing his sword against Tallis's staff.

"Of course I knew! Kiara was my oldest friend. I recognized her son the moment I laid my eyes on him!" Tallis unsheathed a hidden dagger at his hip, swiping the air and only narrowly missing his target.

"No! You knew he was a Magusier and kept it a secret! As my bastard, he belongs to Ministro!"

My heart shattered for Felix as he stood there, watching and listening to every vile word out of that king's mouth. His posture was taut, his face paler than before. I still had my Gift wrapped around him, and the emotions I could feel were...devastating. Hurt, anger, confusion, shame... *so* much fucking shame cascaded from him. He was breaking, but I wouldn't let him crumble.

I threw a pleading look at Van. He didn't need to hear me say the words to know what I was asking. One second, he was standing at my side; the next, he appeared beside my best friend, wrapping him in shadow and returning to me. Darkness twirled where Felix had once stood, and for the first time, I noticed Dashiell just a foot away from where my friend had been.

"I have you," I heard Olivier say. Pulling myself from my thoughts, I peered over my shoulder to find Felix pressed against Oli as he whispered words of reassurance to him. Harbin's name jumped to the top of my kill list.

Fire erupted in the room again, causing the King of Ministro to swear from yet another burn. "WE ARE DONE WITH THIS!" Dashiell bellowed.

"WE ARE NOWHERE NEAR CLOSE TO FINISHED. THE MAGUSIER BELONGS TO ME!" Harbin announced.

Dashiell stalked for the king, walking through his flames, unmarred. "You sold him to my father as a child. I have inherited his kingdom and, therefore, his property. That mark just below his wrist says that he belongs to *me*."

I thought of the small scar on Felix's flesh, barely bigger than a thumbprint. It was a semicircle with an extended line to symbolize the setting sun—the insignia of Caelum. All advisors had them to show their allegiance to the kingdoms they were in servitude to, regardless of what magic they possessed. As long as he bore that mark, he would never be free.

"That was before I knew of the Gift he possessed!"

"Your inability to keep track of who you fucked and the bastards you've produced is not my problem. Until I say otherwise, Felix is in debt to the Kingdom of Caelum, not Ministro."

Harbin eyed Dashiell with distaste and frustration. He was losing his battles at every turn and it was only fueling his rage.

"Did she take the oath?" Harbin asked, though I wasn't sure to whom. We all remained quiet. "You said she's been Queen of Tenebrae for weeks. So, did she take the oath?"

My heart hammered in my chest as the King of Ministro's eyes grew dark and dangerous. He was onto something, and he knew it. As if sensing the same thing, Evander tugged me to his side, shielding half of my body from view.

"Tallis!" Harbin demanded when he didn't get a response.

With a heavy sigh, the King of Agnitio shook his head. "She doesn't possess the land's bond. She is Queen of Tenebrae in name only."

"She takes the oath now! It is our law that upon marriage, the new queen takes the oath of Disparya. She has yet to do so," Harbin argued. I knew what he was getting at—we all did.

As I learned shortly after arriving in Tenebrae, even though the Gods choose the rulers, the land has to accept them. And that hasn't always been the case. Only twice in our history has the land rejected the chosen, resulting in that ruler's immediate death. But a chance was still a chance, and one that neither of us was too keen on taking, especially when my situation was more cause for concern than normal.

I wasn't a queen who inherited the title from marriage alone; I was different—an heir to a kingdom. Someone the Gods themselves had chosen to rule. We had no idea how the land would respond to me, but it was obvious Harbin was eager to find out.

"It will be conducted once we return home," Evander argued.

"You will do it here and now!" The King of Ministro demanded.

"Harbin—"

"No, Tallis!" he interrupted. "This ordeal has gone on long enough! I demand this be done and will not back down on the matter."

"I agree with King Harbin," the King of Venator added. "We have been gracious enough, and there are rules that must be followed."

My eyes fluttered shut as a shaky breath slid from my lips. I didn't want to do this here. If the land claimed my life, I wanted it to be in the kingdom that was my home—the one I should have grown up in with Evander at my side. Not the place that brought countless painful memories.

Discussions were had in the distance. From what I could tell, Harbin was trying to send word to an Incantis currently in Ministro. They were the only ones who could perform the ceremony.

Hands cupped my cheeks and Evander dipped into my line of sight. "We aren't doing this here. We're going back to Tenebrae right now, and if you want to go through with the oath, we'll get Sirona. We'll do it at home like we talked about."

Before I could respond, he pulled me into his chest and wrapped his arms protectively around me. Inhaling the scent of cedar and fresh snow, I closed my eyes and cherished the steady thump of his heart. A heart that belonged only to me. As much as I wanted to give him what he wanted, I couldn't. We had come to Caelum not only in hopes of winning my trial but also to gain allies for an imminent war. If we left now, we would be dooming every kingdom in Disparya.

The land would either accept me or not. It didn't matter where the sacred words were said, the choice would be the same. I would survive, or I wouldn't. Breathing deeply, I pulled out of his hold, meeting his worried stare. He knew what my decision was before I spoke it aloud.

"I can do this," I whispered to him. His thumb swept back and forth over my cheek as he leaned in close and pressed his lips to mine.

"Yes, you can."

15
Ainsley

An Incantis arrived through the Ministrian portal two hours later. I stood at the back end of the room as the seating was rearranged into neat rows to watch the performance. My court, however, chose to remain at my side.

"I can't believe you got married without me," Felix chastised.

My attention was pulled away from the hushed conversations amongst the crowd as they impatiently waited for the Incantis to finish preparing for the ceremony.

I gave Felix an incredulous look. "You were *dead*."

"That's still not a good enough reason. I deserved to be there."

"Take that up with Tallis," I grumbled as I glared at the King of Agnitio from across the room.

"Oh, I plan on it," Marceline cut in.

She was spinning a dagger between her fingers, no doubt picturing all the ways she wanted to deal with him. Marce had just as much right as Evander to be angry at the king. Both of them had watched the people they loved crumble and break over Felix's supposed death.

"I get the first round of torture," she declared.

"We're not going to *torture* him," Van drawled, leaving Cal and Oli's private conversation to join ours.

"Do you think, if I allowed the wolves to sleep on my bed as much as they wanted, they'd—"

"They're not going to eat him, Marceline."

I laughed softly as she groaned and walked away in defeat. Felix kissed my cheek before joining her and the rest of our family.

"You know, if you wanted the land to claim your life just to get away from this lot, I can't say I'd blame you," Van said.

"This lot—no. *You*—perhaps."

I grinned and Evander pulled me close, pressing a kiss to my forehead. "You're such a smartass."

"You start it ninety percent of the time." He gave me a flat look, calling out my lie, and I shrugged. "The land may very well be about to kill me; I'm allowed to over-exaggerate today."

Evander stiffened infinitesimally, but I caught it. We could joke and make light of the situation all we wanted, but it wouldn't change how scared we were. Though the chances were slim, there was still a possibility that I wouldn't make it out alive today.

"If the land rejects me—"

"—No," he interrupted.

"—If the land rejects me," I tried again, speaking over his interjection, "I need you to go through with our plan. You convince the other kings to join the fight, however you have to. You beg, plead, threaten—I don't care. Do whatever it takes." He swallowed hard but didn't stop me. "Then you find Inmuto and do the same with them." Van didn't respond. "Promise me, Evander. My death cannot be for nothing."

"You're not going to die—"

"Promise me," I demanded.

Evander closed his eyes as he took a deep breath and let it out slowly. When they fluttered open again, they were misted and pained. "I promise, love. I promise that I will do whatever it takes to ensure that our people are safe and there is peace in this land. I promise that your memory will live on in everything that I do. I promise that your life will not be lost in vain. I promise to love you until the air is snuffed from my lungs...and even after that."

I fought the thick lump in my throat and blinked away the tears that had formed in my eyes. I grasped our Soul Bond as tightly as I could and kissed him softly.

"Now you have to promise me something in return," he said against my mouth before shifting back. "Promise me you will not die today."

"I can't—"

"Promise me, love. Because I *will* follow you. I will fight every God and form of magic that tries to take you. And once I'm finished, I will drag you back to this realm with me... And we *really* don't have time for that detour."

I laughed softly and nodded. I had no doubt he would try to do exactly that. "I promise."

"I'm ready," the Incantis announced, breaking our tender moment and sending my heart into my stomach.

Evander walked me to the center of the room as the kings, queens, and advisors all took their seats. My family stayed standing just a few feet away. This wasn't a spectacle to them the way it was for everyone else.

The Incantis didn't say a word, looking less than thrilled as she pressed my palms together and began wrapping them with a satin cloth.

"Wait!" Van said, pulling me out of her hold. His hands cupped my cheeks and my skin blazed beneath his gentle touch. "Are you sure?"

"Yes," I whispered.

As much as I wanted to just go home, we couldn't. Harbin wasn't going to stop until he exhausted every legal way to see me killed. If we ran now, we risked losing the aid from any of the kingdoms besides Agnitio. I prayed that this act of compliance would at least show Caelum and Venator that we could be team players. Maybe then they'd be more inclined to hear us out.

"Are you sure about being sure?" he questioned, now grasping at straws.

"Van," I groaned.

My mind was made up and there was no use trying to change it. He was just going to have to accept whatever fate the land had in store for me, though I knew acceptance was not his strong suit.

He leaned forward and pressed his forehead to mine, taking a deep breath as if savoring the feel and scent of me. I did the same.

"I have loved you since I was five years old," he began. "I have searched for you for nearly two decades. You do *not* get to leave yet, do you understand?" His voice cracked, and I felt warmth trace a line down my cheek from a tear that had fallen. One that didn't belong to me.

I nodded because I couldn't speak. My throat was lodged with the despair I was working so hard to keep trapped.

"It'll just be a quick couple of lines, and then you'll be done. You'll feel a tingle of magic when the land accepts you—which it *will*—and then it'll be over, and we can go home," Evander explained.

Again, I nodded.

He dragged the tip of my nose up with his before kissing me deeply. The kind of kiss meant to convey everything words could not. An expression of love in its most delicate and intimate form.

A throat cleared and I instantly remembered we had an audience. Van twisted his head toward the source of the interruption. The Incantis arched an impatient brow and began tapping her foot against the marble floor.

Evander tightened his grip on me and held her stare as he leaned in to kiss me again. My asshole of a husband was not going to let her dictate when he was done. Harbin groaned, Cal snorted, Felix applauded, and I smiled at his antics.

When he determined he was finished, he pulled back, kissed the tip of my nose, and moved a few paces back to stand with the rest of our family. The Incantis rolled her eyes in agitation and aggressively wrapped my hands with the cloth once more.

Once she finished, she stepped back and collected a large bowl containing various items. Her voice was soft and melodic as she chanted words I couldn't comprehend—like they were from another language or time. The Incantis reached inside and fisted a handful of dirt, which she then proceeded to throw over my covered palms. Next, she sprinkled purple flower petals gingerly over them.

I watched in quiet curiosity as she continued her ritual, each item representing one of the five kingdoms. She pulled out a black feather and stuffed it into my bindings, followed by a prick of a dagger to my finger. Blood welled and soaked into the white cloth. Finally, she tipped a small vile of water above my hands, and the droplets spilled onto me one by one.

Evander's deep intake of air caught my attention, but I didn't turn. He was preparing himself for whatever part of the ritual was next, and I needed to do the same. I swallowed my nerves and focused only on the Incantis in front of me.

Her eyes were so dilated that the honey hue that had been present before was nowhere to be found. She threw her head back, chanting her strange language louder. A gentle tremor filled the room with an invisible magic.

It felt older than time itself, powerful and cryptic... and constantly morphing, changing form. I couldn't grasp it. Anytime I reached for it, the magic slipped through my fingers like shifting sand.

I could sense it all around and taste its potency in the air. I felt it in my blood as if this magic was the very essence of what I was made of. It was familiar but also foreign... and something that terrified me.

The power was overwhelming—strong and unforgiving. Mixed within the threads of magic were traces of supremacy, desire, arrogance, and a deep-seated hunger for life. This power was both a warning and a reminder of the Gods.

The Incantis' lips went silent and the thrumming magic in the room fell still.

"Title," she said with a commanding tone, her voice not as gentle as it used to be, almost as if it didn't belong to her anymore. A chill went through my spine, and my pulse quickened.

"Queen of Tenebrae," I answered, trying desperately to mask the pure terror in my voice.

The Incantis gripped my hands tightly as she snapped her head forward. I flinched at what I saw. Her eyes were like two black pits, void of any color. My breathing went ragged and I could feel the tension coil around me.

Evander's stare was like a brand on my skin, but I couldn't look away. The Incantis's dark eyes kept my focus rooted to only her.

The deep, resounding voice slipped between the delicate woman's lips again. "You will repeat after me." I nodded shallowly. This was it. *"I, Queen of Tenebrae, solemnly vow..."*

I recited the words, pushing as much confidence into my shaky voice as I could.

"To support, protect, cherish, and defend the Kingdom of Tenebrae."

With each claim, I could sense Evander's fear increasing. Whatever was about to happen, he was scared enough that it slipped through our Soul Bond and into me. I fought the urge to comfort him. If he knew his terror was so great that I could feel it, he'd never forgive himself for adding to my anxiety.

The voice continued. *"I willingly accept the obligations of my title and bear unwavering allegiance to the Gods, my kingdom, my land, and her people."*

I took a deep breath, filling my lungs with what could be my final intake of air.

"I willingly accept the obligations of my title and bear unwavering allegiance to the Gods, my kingdom, my land, and her people," I announced.

The Incantis raised her arms above her head and recited something in her strange language. My heart pounded in my ears so loudly that I was sure the rest of the room could hear it over her chanting. Finally, she stopped, and I locked eyes with Evander as I waited for the tingle of magic to take place.

I waited and waited... and waited. But nothing. All was too quiet, too calm, too... *wrong*.

Evander's head cocked to the side slowly, and I followed his dropped gaze to my feet. Black shadows pooled beneath me, but they weren't mine. These were different—darker, more dangerous. They expanded quickly, wrapping around my body and slowly lifting me from the ground.

I finally felt that tingle of magic... Followed by the agony of my body breaking in two.

My world went dark.

16
Felix

Darkness swirled around Ainsley like a storm ready to ensue destruction, creating a wind so great I had to use my arms to block its force. The royalty and advisors in the room ducked behind chairs and pillars—anything that could shield them from the strength of the magic. The unmistakable sound of bones snapping penetrated my ears, closely followed by two desperate screams of Ainsley's name.

I gripped the dais, my fingers digging into the stone hard enough that the marble cracked beneath my touch. Her pain was near cataclysmic, stealing the breath from my lungs and threatening to rip the heart from my chest. Gritting my teeth through the agony and the ear-splitting scream that pierced the air, I pushed everything I had out toward her, desperately trying to dull her pain as I separated myself from my feelings of horror as my best friend was shattered bit by bit.

I expected my magic to go straight through the power surrounding her, but it slammed into a barrier unlike anything I had ever felt. The magic was strong and unpredictable, foreign and unfamiliar, yet I knew its ways like I knew my own. It was ancient and ever-present—an impenetrable force that refused to allow my entrance. It wasn't *her* keeping me out, but the magic of our land.

"Felix!" Evander bellowed, his panic seeping into that one word.

"I can't get through!" I yelled back. The whispers of chaos transformed into a thunderous rage. Declaration of ill-intent and murderous plans were ordered by King Harbin, as he wanted to take full advantage of the situation and my new family's distraction.

"It has rejected her!" he rejoiced, and I swallowed the truth of those words.

When Evander's intention to marry Ainsley was made clear, we all discussed the implications of the union. He was a powerful king, yes, but she had the potential to surpass him. We all knew the only reason she hadn't yet was because of her sheltered upbringing—however, her lack of experience wouldn't last forever. And though Evander would only support her growth, the other rulers wouldn't.

Once they were married, it would likely be perceived as a grab for power. Together, Ainsley and Evander would hold six Gifts as king and queen, not including Evander's Obscure. They would be seen as a threat by nearly everyone who wasn't our allies. Neither of them cared about that risk... So, another was brought up.

Ainsley and Evander were created from the same soul, which we theorized was why she had been chosen as the Heir to Tenebrae rather than the succession following Evander's bloodline as it had for millennia. Perhaps the Gods recognized a selection they had already made. But would the land see it as the same, or would it be viewed as an heir trying to claim the power they were not yet entitled to? Would the land bestow upon her its magic for her royal status, or would it view her as an avaricious ruler and enact retribution?

It was a troubling thought that none of us could confidently answer. At the time, Ainsley was grappling with her own doubts about even assuming the role, concerned about her ability to be a good queen, so we tabled the discussion and never picked it back up.

I was seriously regretting that decision now.

"Try harder!" Evander ordered. I could feel the wrath rolling off him like magma just as billowing shadows surged from his body, aimed at his targets behind me.

Marce ran to Ainsley's other side, her hands outstretched as she called for her Tremo Gift. Both Calidore and Oli crafted weapons faster than I could blink as they took their stance to protect our queen in her most vulnerable state.

I pushed more of my Gift out to her, trying desperately to break through the shield that our land had placed upon her. A fight had ensued between kingdoms as they battled to either claim Ainsley's life or protect it. As much as I wanted to help them, *she* needed me. If these were her final breaths, I would stop at nothing to steal away the pain I knew she was experiencing. If this was it for her, she deserved to go peacefully. Not torn apart by a gluttonous land or selfish men who were terrified of her potential.

In my periphery, shadows spooled from Calidore's hands as he crafted creatures that looked like they belonged in the horrors of a nightmare, each one more terrifying than the last. People screamed and took off running, the sound of wet flesh being torn from bodies chasing their retreat.

The heat from flames brushed along my back and arms, the temperature so hot I nearly faltered my task, but a moment later, it was extinguished as quickly as it came. Sweat dripped down the side of my face, my arms trembling as I fought with everything I had to reach her. But nothing worked. I couldn't locate a single fissure in the land's impenetrable armor.

Reluctantly, I turned my gaze to Evander who was releasing more of his darkness into the room, letting his own horrors sink their teeth into their victims. His eyes found mine as if he could feel the weight of my stare. I opened my mouth, but the words wouldn't come out. He shook his head in disbelief, already denying the claim before it could leave my lips.

"No," he said through gritted teeth.

"Evander, I can't get through."

"You're not trying hard enough—"

"I'm trying everything I can! Do you think I want to lose her?!" I yelled back, unable to stop my voice from breaking because of my failure. Ainsley's bones crunched again, and both of us winced at the sound.

Her back was too arched to be natural, and her arms were bent in ways they shouldn't have been. Her name was a desperate plea, with Evander's voice smothering the others. He fought to get to her just as hard as the other kings, though their motivations were dripping with ill-intent. It wouldn't matter though. There wasn't a single thing anyone could do to save her.

The shadows around her spun faster as she cried out over and over again, which only seemed to fuel the fight. The closer she inched to death, the more violent the crowd became. It was as if they wanted to be the ones credited for dealing the final blow rather than having the land claim victory.

"Felix, please," Evander begged.

We never had a good relationship, but it pained me to witness his voice trembling and the anguish in his eyes when he realized he might lose the woman he loved. His Soul Bonded. He wasn't even keeping his emotions from me as he usually did, so I could feel every ounce of grief and physical pain he was going through. Having her ripped from him was like having his own soul cleaved from his chest... and yet he didn't buckle under the pain. He pushed through it as he fought to save her.

"There's nothing I can do," I told him mournfully. My best friend was going to be taken from this world, and there was nothing *any* of us could do. "The land won't accept her since Tenebrae already has a ruler." The words tasted like bile on their way out, clawing up my throat as I struggled to keep them down. But little good that would do. He needed to hear that truth.

Evander's face momentarily reflected defeat before he shifted his gaze towards Brandle, who was strategically positioned behind a pillar utilizing his Imperium Gift to fight. Startled, Ministro's prince reacted as if someone had suddenly appeared before him, even though no one was present. He whipped his head around to us, nodded, and hurried over.

"Cal, cover us!" Evander shouted. Both Marce and Oli moved into position, taking over for Calidore as he shifted to protect his king.

The King of Tenebrae looked up at his wife before meeting Brandle's stare.

"I need you to kill me."

17

Felix

"**W**hat?!" Brandle and I demanded in unison.

We couldn't have heard him right. The room was too loud, too chaotic, too filled with psychotic magic that was doing something to mess with our heads… because there was no way in hell that he just instructed Brandle to kill him.

"There's no way in hell you just instructed Brandle to kill you," I told him, disbelief caressing every word.

"Cal, conceal us!" Evander demanded.

Shadows spilled from Cal and encased us in darkness, away from prying eyes. Evander turned back toward us, pure determination on his face.

"Like you said, the land won't accept her since Tenebrae already has me. There's only one fucking way to fix that!"

He was frantic, desperate to find some way out of this mess and spare her life, even if it meant losing his. Evander spun to Brandle and pointed to his own chest.

"You stop my heart and let me die," the king instructed. "The land will need a new ruler, and she's the only option."

"And then what?" Brandle asked, but I had a sense he already knew the answer.

"Once it's done, you bring me back." The Prince of Ministro opened his mouth to argue but Van spoke first. "Don't try to deny the extent of your abilities. You gave that one away when you saved Felix."

Brandle tongued his cheek and smirked. "What's to stop me from just leaving you dead?"

It was a valid question, but either way, I knew Evander didn't care. Of course, he'd want to live, but if it meant Ainsley's survival, he'd gladly take the risk of never breathing again.

"You want to earn my trust, Brandle? This is how you do it."

The prince perked up at that. For weeks after Ainsley's Imperium Gift manifested, Tallis had tried to convince Evander to allow Brandle to train her, but he refused. His proximity to his stepfather was cause for concern, and regardless of the vital information the prince had provided to our efforts, Evander still didn't trust him when it came to Ainsley.

"But if my trust is not enough to motivate you, there are four people here who would gladly kill you and feed you to my wolves if you cross me." Brandle's face drained of color. "So the question isn't how much *I* value my life—it's how much do *you* value yours?"

Brandle and Evander stared at one another for what seemed like a lifetime. This wasn't only Ainsley's chance at life—it was Van's, and we all knew it. If he refused, the King of Tenebrae would simply do it himself, taking a dagger to his own heart. Brandle was Evander's only hope of surviving the ordeal.

Ainsley yelled in pain again, prompting Brandle to say, "Fuck it," and place a hand on Evander's chest.

He fell to his back, eyes going wide as the prince leaned over him. Brandle placed another hand on Evander as he pushed his Imperium Gift through his body, manipulating the blood flow to his heart. I reached out my own power and eased Evander's raging fear in hopes it would help get him through it, balancing my Gift between him and Ainsley.

I held my breath as Brandle worked, my own anxiety rising the longer he took. Seconds passed, and Evander's eyes fluttered shut, his chest void of movement.

"It's done," Brandle said. "I can only hold this for a short amount of time. If his heart goes too long without blood, I won't be able to bring him back."

Well, fuck.

"You didn't tell him that!" I pointed out.

"Would it have mattered?"

Nope. Evander more than likely would have asked why Brandle was still talking and not doing what he was commanded to. To him, Ainsley's life would always be worth more than any risk.

The light dimmed from darkened clouds as thunder rumbled outside, the room growing louder with screams and the clang of metal on metal. The battle was still going on as the guards and advisors from Venator and Ministro fought their way to my queen, taking advantage of Ainsley's state and getting closer to her by the minute. King Arden might have sided with us earlier, but with the land rejecting her, he'd see it as a clear sign that she was meant to die.

A dagger was flung through the air at her, only to be swallowed by the darkness of the land and spit back out. I watched as the weapon was expertly flicked into the throat of its owner. Apparently, the land wasn't going to make the task easy for them.

The darkness around Ainsley spun and spun and spun until...

It stopped.

Everything just… stopped.

The billowing shadows stretched apart, revealing a broken body suspended in air, her mouth open in a silent scream.

Everyone halted their swings, their attacks, and their defenses to look up at the spectacle as she rose higher toward the vaulted ceiling. I shifted my gaze to Evander and then Brandle, a quiet question on my lips.

"We're almost out of time," he whispered.

The inky blackness slithered around her in a gentle caress. Bone crunched, and though I wanted to turn away from the brutality of it, I couldn't. Her elbow was no longer bending the opposite way. Her legs were next, then her wrists, her fingers, her feet, her hips, and finally, her back.

The land was mending her, gluing back together the fractured pieces. I released a strangled cry of relief as I felt her pain start to subside. Evander's plan had worked. The land needed a ruler, and she was all that was left.

"Do it, now!" I commanded Brandle.

"I can't yet."

"He's running out of time!"

"And *she's* not out of the clear. Until the land releases its grip on her, it's too risky to bring him back."

He was right—I hated that he was right. Ainsley wasn't out of the woods, and we couldn't stop until she was. So, we continued to wait helplessly while Van's life slipped further away.

She'd hate me for agreeing to this plan. It wouldn't matter if I did it to save her life, she'd never forgive me for letting the man she loved willingly die. I couldn't even blame her for it.

"Come the *fuck* on, you piece of shit magical entity," Brandle grumbled.

Sweat had slicked his forehead and his arms were trembling. He wouldn't be able to last for much longer.

As if the land had heard him, the darkness stretched out through the room. Everyone ducked as it shifted overhead, swelling over the entire ceiling, shrouding us in a deep and endless starless sky.

And then…

It retracted—and slammed into Ainsley.

She screamed, her voice so high pitched it shattered dozens of windows. I dove over Van, covering him from the debris of glass that launched through the room. The land's shield around her was now gone, and I plummeted my Empathi Gift into her just as Cal extended a shield to keep her protected.

There was no pain to be found despite the sound she was still making.

I switched my Gift, calling forth my Magusier ability. It was still new to me, and I barely had a grasp on how to use it, but I had to try. I focused on her, channeling my magic in the way Tallis had shown me.

The auras that represented her Gifts swirled around her—black, grey, pink, crimson, and… something *new*. A deep purple wisp tangled between the other colors, moving and stretching like a cat that had been asleep for too long. I sucked in a sharp breath.

A new Gift.

Her Tremo ability.

"Brandle, now!" I demanded.

He raised his hands high above his head and then slammed them down onto Evander's chest. The prince's arms shook, and his breathing was ragged as he tried desperately to undo the damage he had caused. Brandle grunted, his face taut in both concentration and exertion.

"Come on, asshole," he said to the king.

Evander didn't move, his chest still.

"I swear to the Gods, if you don't get your ass back here, I *will* fuck your wife."

"And I'll help him," I added. "You know she listens to me. I'll convince her to do it—I promise you I will."

It may not have been the best tactic, but only Evander would claw himself back from the dead to prevent a total prick from bedding his wife. Brandle looked at me, failure furrowed in his brows as he solemnly shook his head.

"One more try," I begged, and he nodded.

Brandle raised his hands high above his head, took a deep breath, and let them fall. He yelled, his voice straining and hoarse as he pushed and pushed and pushed his magic into Evander one last time.

The King of Tenebrae sat up with a gasping breath.

18

Felix

The moment Evander's lungs filled with oxygen, I threw myself at him. The embrace was not an expression of my joy at his survival, but rather a deliberate act to anger him with my hug. And honestly, he deserved it for making me believe that I would have to deliver the news to Ainsley about her husband's demise.

As I expected, the King of Tenebrae shoved me away and pointed to Brandle.

"You were going to let *him* fuck my wife?!" So he heard that…Well, that just meant another one of my ingenious ideas succeeded.

I nonchalantly shrugged, displaying no shame in my tactics as it clearly worked. With arms crossed, I steeled myself for a volley of insults. But rather than release them, his attention was suddenly drawn to Ainsley, still hovering above us.

She looked asleep, calm and peaceful. Her hair billowed out around her like delicate ripples in a stream and her hands were placed firmly over her chest. I reached out my Empathi Gift once more and found I could effortlessly slip between her defenses.

She wasn't experiencing pain or fear, or even happiness and comfort. I could perceive the steady rhythm of her heartbeat, yet she appeared devoid of any emotion. I withdrew my Gift and subsequently summoned my second one.

The deep purple aura had grown in size as it manifested her Tremo Gift within her. It had reached the same level of potency as the others, whose colors had all intensified as a result of the land's bestowed power.

"She has all three," I said low enough that only Evander could hear.

"I still have mine," he admitted.

We had cheated the land and death today, but I had a foreboding feeling that it wouldn't go unpunished.

"Do you think—" Ainsley's body plummeted toward the floor before I could finish.

Shadows began swirling next to me, and then Evander materialized beneath her, catching her just before she could hit the ground. A sense of relief washed over me as I and the rest of our family quickly moved towards their side. We kept our backs to them as we faced what was left of the room with weapons raised.

She was still unconscious but breathing, her heart a persistent thump that brought joy to my ears. Evander sank to the ground, tenderly holding her in his arms while placing gentle kisses on her face. He didn't care that over two dozen people were watching him. Concealing the affection and love he felt for his wife was never something he attempted. He was admirable in that way, and it made my heart squeeze for my best friend. She had been through so much heartache in her short life and deserved to have someone who would unconditionally put her first.

Ainsley stirred, letting out a soft whimper from between her lips. I could have crumbled at the sound. She was awake, she was *alive*, and she was now unarguably the Queen of Tenebrae.

"Ouch," she mumbled.

Evander's eyes scanned her body, his fingers feeling for any signs of obvious injury. "Where does it hurt?" he demanded.

"Everywhere, but I'm fine. Just sore."

She groaned as she fought to sit up. Oli and I rushed closer to help Van bring her to her feet and support her wobbling frame. She seemed dizzy and out of it, but slowly coming back to herself.

"How much do you remember?" I asked. Her eyes fixed on me as I watched her mind work until, slowly, she shook her head. Van pressed a kiss to her temple and pulled her into his side, taking over for me completely.

"Can you feel your new Gift?" Tallis inquired, electing shocked gasps from the crowd.

No one knew what we did to ensure Ainsley's survival. Cal had hidden the three of us entirely behind the cover of his shadows. The development of a new Gift for her wasn't known to anyone but us and Tallis.

At least not until now.

She nodded, a slight smile tugging at the corner of her mouth.

"What are you talking about? That isn't possible!" the King of Ministro argued as he stepped over one of the bodies that had been cut down during the fight.

"The Queen of Tenebrae possesses all three Gifts of her land and two as the Heir to Ministro. For whatever reason, the Gods and land both chose to bless her. Do you really want to question their decision, Harbin?" Tallis replied, an air of cockiness coating each word.

I watched as Harbin internally struggled. He wanted nothing more than to rid the world of the woman who threatened his line of succession, but with the Gods and land making their support clear, the possibility of angering them wasn't a risk he could take lightly. But if he ever found out the land had actually rejected her, he would stop at nothing to see her life claimed.

Reluctantly, he shook his head. "We're leaving," he announced and stormed for the exit. His queen, advisors, and what was left of his guard hurried to follow, disregarding the puddles of blood and corpses littering the ground.

"I call for an emergency assembly of the rulers!" Evander declared before Harbin could enter the hall.

"We're already assembled, Evander," King Arden pointed out.

"How lucky for me, then."

Harbin strolled back into the room, pointing a finger at Evander. "I'm not staying. We can conduct an assembly another time!"

"No, it must be now."

Harbin's rage began to climb again. I wasn't sure how acquainted Evander was with him, but I knew the King of Ministro as a cruel and unforgiving man, willing and ready to cut anyone down who dared oppose him. He callously determined whether orphaned children were worthy of life. He was a monster.

And apparently, my *father*.

The word twisted my stomach in knots and caused bile to creep up my throat. I hadn't wanted to believe it when Tallis told me of my parentage, but the more I denied it, the more the horrifying pieces fit.

I never understood what prompted him to save my life as a child—why he didn't just cast me aside and discard me as he had done to so many others. I was barely a toddler who wasn't of any importance and didn't possess anything that made me more deserving than the innocents whose lives were forfeit.

But he spared me, and I had chalked it up to just being lucky. Growing up, he rarely paid me any mind. In fact, we were ordered to stay as far away from the king and queen as possible. We were burdens to the land, just extra mouths to feed and backs to clothe, though mine were always slightly nicer than the other orphans'. I was put in a group with the kindest Maiden in the palace and assigned the biggest bed in a room of ten.

Again, I attributed it to just being *lucky*.

When I was ten years old, my magic began to manifest. It was nearly unheard of in Disparya for power to take form so young, especially in those who weren't royalty, so I didn't know what was happening to me until I saw Dash during one of his casual visits to Ministro. His Gift as an Unda had manifested a few months prior, and after he reassured me I could stop planning my own funeral because I was not actually dying—he explained the same sensations had happened to him.

Sure enough, a week later, my Empathi Gift fully formed. I was taken to the throne room under the cover of night, with no one present besides King Harbin and a single guard. Even my Maiden had been ushered away.

The secrecy didn't seem odd to my young brain, as King Harbin had always been a mystery to me. For all I knew, having a meeting in the middle of the night with no witnesses was completely normal.

He had studied me for a long time, asking various questions about my Gift and when I had first discovered the change. He inquired if I had felt anything else out of the ordinary, such as a sudden interest in blood or the strong desire to stay at the side of someone sick. I had not, which only seemed to frustrate him.

"I do not have the need for another worthless Empathi on my Council," he had declared before sending me back to bed without another word.

I told Dash the next morning about the meeting, but he didn't have any insight into what it was about either. However, hours later, I was brought back into that room, this time completely full, and given to King Perceval and Caelum as a *present.*

I do not have the need for another worthless Empathi on my Council.

Those words have lived in my mind ever since, worming their way into every decision placed before me. Now that I knew the truth of who I was, I understood their meaning. I may have been his son, but I wasn't bestowed the title of Heir to Ministro, and that made me worthless—at least in his eyes.

Olivier placed a hand against my back, his thumb swiping back and forth in a gentle gesture to show he knew I was going through shit and that he'd be there through it all. Gods, I loved that man.

"What is this regarding?" King Arden asked.

"Oberon of Pravus," Evander answered, which prompted a groan from several of the advisors and two of the kings present.

"Not this again." Arden pinched the bridge of his nose as he shook his head.

"As we told your father before you, there is nothing to worry about," Harbin added. "The only attacks on Disparya have been from Tenebrae."

"Bullshit!" Evander yelled. "You know just as well as I do that we were set up!"

"Of course, yet another convenient tale," Harbin replied.

Evander let out a frustrated breath as he straightened and raised his voice for the entire room to hear.

"Regardless of your beliefs, I, as king, am owed the chance to plead my case. As we are already gathered together, you all have one day to answer my call. Should you refuse, you will forfeit your right to vote and officially be declaring war on your own nation." Harbin narrowed his eyes at Evander, his face somehow another shade redder. "Whether you like it or not, this right has been granted to me by law. Make your choices wisely, as you put your own kingdoms at risk if you decide incorrectly."

The room was quiet, save for the whispering advisors, no doubt attempting to reason with their kings. Deciding against taking this meeting wouldn't solely be a *fuck you* to Evander—it would mark those kingdoms as traitors to our nation. Trading would cease, supplies would be cut off, and the kings still a part of Disparya would work together to dissolve the traitorous kingdoms, putting millions of lives at risk.

It would be another Great War, and I didn't think even Harbin wanted that.

"The meeting will be set for tomorrow afternoon. Everyone has until then to decide," Tallis announced, breaking the growing tension rooted in silence. A mumble of acceptance rumbled through the room despite the uneasiness I still felt from those present. "As King Harbin suggested before the trial began, I think it would be a great idea to hold a celebratory feast tonight."

"That was when I thought she was going to die—" Harbin tried, but the King of Agnitio stepped on his words like they were dirt beneath his boots.

"—But I believe it should be in Ainsley's honor. We have added a new ruler to this land, and that deserves to be celebrated."

The pride I felt for my best friend warmed my heart. Tallis was absolutely right—she deserved to be celebrating the feat she accomplished today. Even prior to the oath, Ainsley exuded royalty, commanding the trial and the men a part of it like the queen she rightfully was.

"But as you are the hosting kingdom," Tallis said, turning his stare to Dash, "It is, of course, your decision."

"We don't have to—"

"Caelum would be pleased to host a feast in the Queen of Tenebrae's honor," Dash replied, not giving Ainsley a chance to finish her sentence. I pushed my Empathi Gift out to both of them... and was quickly shielded the second they felt me.

Fine, I would just have to be a commoner like everyone else and use my *eyes* to figure out what the fuck they were feeling. As if they knew this would be my tactic, both of them diverted their gaze—Ainsley to Evander and Dash to Tallis. Assholes.

"Caelum will open the portal to each kingdom so you may all have members of your court attend the festivities should you choose. The pathway between our kingdoms will stay open for only three hours, so please send word quickly."

"I assume we are still welcome to stay despite the earlier altercations," Tallis replied as he wiped blood from his palms onto his soiled shirt.

"Of course. Your rooms have already been prepared. I would request getting cleaned up so as not to frighten my residents," he said as he surveyed the mess of bodies and broken chairs scattered across the ground. "The palace staff will assist in any needs you require," he continued. "Now, if you'll excuse me, I have a few matters to attend to before tonight, including getting this mess cleaned up...once again."

With that, Dash bowed and hurried from the room before I had a chance to stop him. There was tension in his movements, a stiffness coupled with a sense of urgency to flee that had me feeling the urge to go after him. But I didn't know if he would want me to.

The remaining advisors, guards, and rulers trickled out of the room one by one, careful to avoid the gore as they discussed the night's planned celebration. Ainsley and Evander departed shortly after Dash, no doubt eager to have a moment to themselves. Familiar hands pressed firmly onto my shoulders, and I leaned back against Oli, enjoying the feel of him so close.

"Well, that whole shitshow went as well as expected," Calidore commented as he gestured over the dead and earned an eye roll from Marce.

"If they don't agree to Van's assembly request, they're all complete idiots—I mean, they're idiots anyway, but this would just make it more evident," she said.

Cal made a reply I didn't hear, too focused on Oli's lips just above my ear.

"How are you?" he breathed as our two friends continued their conversation, oblivious to the private one we were sharing.

I twisted and gazed at him, giving a subtle shake of my head. I wasn't good—nowhere near it—but I couldn't find the words to voice everything going on in my mind. Oli nodded and tightened his hold on me before leaning close and pressing his lips to mine.

For a moment, I didn't have to be the bastard son of a terrible king or even someone who possessed a rare and sought-after Gift that I could barely master.

For this moment, I could just be *loved*.

19

Ainsley

We didn't speak on the walk to my room. Evander's hand was tightly interlocked with mine, but his stare remained straight ahead. He was keeping something from me and I had a feeling I would have to pry it out of him the moment we were behind closed doors.

He twisted the knob once we reached my chamber and gently pushed it open, gesturing for me to enter first. I stepped inside and immediately stopped as I beheld Onyx and Nova lying on the ground with Imogen sitting before them, circling the air with her finger.

Onyx rolled to his back and then his stomach before wagging his tail impatiently. Was she... teaching them tricks?

Imogen's eyes flicked up, and she cleared her throat as she stood and smoothed out her pristine white apron. "I had them bathed," she announced, gesturing to the two wolves who were now sniffing her pocket for the treats she undoubtedly had hidden.

"Thank you," I replied, a smile in my voice. "You didn't have to do that."

"Of course I did. The black one was traipsing blood and bits everywhere. I found him rolling around on a bed in one of the rooms." She leveled Onyx with a flat look, and his ears drooped as if in shame for his actions. I smothered my smile. "I take it everything went well?"

"I don't know if I'd say *that*."

"Well, you're alive, so that's enough," she stated simply.

Imogen strode forward and wrapped me in her arms as Van gave attention to our wolves. He pulled out a cloth from his pocket and unveiled two oatmeal cookies. Onyx whimpered with excitement and Nova sat stoically as they waited.

"What are you giving them?" Imogen demanded. Evander froze, his hand halfway extended to his black wolf in offering. She gasped softly under her breath and released me before moving closer to the king. "*Cookies* are not meant for wolves."

"But he likes them?" Van replied as if he was no longer sure of the fact.

Onyx backed away from his owner while keeping his eyes on Imogen, clearly understanding who actually held the power in this situation. Slowly, Van pocketed the treat without another word. She nodded, pleased with his decision, and strode for the door.

"I'll give you some time alone for now, but I expect to hear the details of everything later," Imogen said.

Halting on the threshold, she glanced down to the left and then the right, seeming to search for something. With a sigh, she snapped her fingers loudly, and Nova and Onyx hurried to her. As soon as she shut the door, I turned toward Evander, ready to demand he tell me what he was keeping secret.

Before I could say a word, he rushed to me and crashed his lips against mine. The kiss was brutal, desperate, scorching, demanding, everything it needed to be, yet still not enough. I wanted more—*needed* more.

His hands roamed over my body, gripping my face, my neck, my waist, like he couldn't decide where to touch me, so he settled on *everywhere*. I moaned into his mouth as his tongue swept over mine, making me forget all about my earlier concerns. Hell, it made me forget my own name.

"I need you," he whispered against my mouth. I nodded the same sentiment. Gods, I needed him just as badly, but more than that, I needed to know what was going on.

"Van—"

His kiss cut me off and for the life of me, I couldn't find annoyance at the interruption. It had been so long since the two of us were this desperate for each other. Since returning from Caelum, we had only been intimate once—the night of our wedding.

Losing Felix had taken its toll on me, and though I was growing and getting back to my old self, I had felt guilty about indulging in life's pleasures when he couldn't. I felt guilty for being with the love of my life when Oli had lost his because of me. I felt guilty for just breathing.

Evander had been patient, of course. Even after our wedding ceremony, he never pressured me to consummate our union. In fact, he had even made up a pillow barrier as a sign of good faith... and also to remind me of the first night we had spent in our room together. But despite his understanding and chivalry, I wanted to be with him. I wanted to feel that love we shared in all its forms, even if only for one night.

We hadn't been together in that way since.

"Talk to me," I begged, pulling back from his intoxicating embrace.

Evander groaned and dragged a frustrated hand through his hair. "I did something you're going to be pissed at me for." I already didn't like where this was going and crossed my arms over my chest in preparation. "Before I tell you, just remember that everything worked out."

"What did you do?"

"—And we're both alive and well."

"Evander!"

"I may have died earlier."

My mouth hung open as indecipherable noises came out. What the hell did that even mean?

"What the hell does that even mean?!" I yelled, my panic mixing with confusion.

He dropped his gaze to the fingers he was pulling on nervously. "Well, the land rejected you at first, because of me…"

I didn't remember much of the ceremony or what occurred after, but I would always be acutely aware of the searing pain that surged through my body before I blacked out. It was one of the most excruciating things I had ever experienced and was unlikely to leave my memory anytime soon.

"So, I kind of forced its hand…" Evander nervously looked at me through lowered lashes.

"You're going to have to give me more than that."

He sighed deeply before giving me all of his attention despite the unease I could feel rolling off of him. "I told Brandle to stop my heart so the land could choose you to rule since Tenebrae's sovereign died."

My eyes widened as a potent cocktail of anger and fear filled my bloodstream. What the *fuck* was he thinking?!

"WHAT THE FUCK WERE YOU THINKING!" I yelled, fury fully rising to the surface. I knew Evander loved me, but this wasn't just about *my* life—he risked his knowing we were in the middle of a war, knowing he had millions of innocent people we were responsible for.

"That I had one chance to save you. I wasn't not going to take that, Ainsley."

"Van, we have a responsibility to—"

"To *you*," he interrupted. "I have a responsibility to *you*. Don't ask me to idly sit by and watch you be broken into pieces before my eyes, and then expect me not to do anything about it because of my fucking crown."

"Van—"

"Tenebrae is taken care of. I have ensured that should anything ever happen to me—to *us*—that she will be looked after. My people mean the world to me, but you mean *everything*. I won't apologize for that."

He turned away and strode a few paces, running a hand through his black hair. I could see his point, and if I were in the same position, I knew I wouldn't have hesitated to do the same. It was unfair of me to be angry with him, but I still hated that he risked his life.

I moved for him, curling my hand around his wrist until his fingers were between mine. His grey eyes met my own, softening to break the tension. I offered a small smile, a white flag. What's done was done and there was no use arguing about it. Evander returned the gesture, adding a kiss to my temple.

"How did you survive?" I asked quietly.

"I told Brandle he'd be fed to our wolves if he didn't bring me back."

I pulled back to look at him, slightly shocked by that response, though I didn't know why. It was a very *Evander* threat to make.

"But Onyx and Nova don't eat people."

"He doesn't need to know that," he replied nonchalantly before kissing my widening smile. I encircled my arms around his neck as he deepened the embrace, once again getting lost in the feel of him.

Within seconds, I was breathless, taking more and more of what I wanted. I couldn't touch enough, taste enough, *have* enough. Evander groaned as his hands traveled down my waist to grip my ass as he stole the thoughts from my mind with his tongue.

"We can't," I reluctantly announced. "Not here."

"I know," he whispered, still searing me with his kiss, though not as forcefully as before. He was pulling back, respecting my boundaries even though my body was giving him different signals.

As much as I wanted to connect with him, it didn't feel right to do so in the home I had shared with my ex-fiancé.

"Two more days," I told him, finally pulling away and taking a deep and full breath. Evander pressed his forehead to mine as he nodded.

"Two more days... And then we will be doing many, *many* things."

"Like what?" I might not have been comfortable acting on my desire, but I could definitely *hear* about it.

Evander's smile grew wicked with dark and delicious promises. "Well," he started, pushing aside my hair as he leaned in to press his lips to my neck, sending a shiver down my spine. "As you are officially a queen, I think it's only right that I show you the throne room."

"I've seen the throne room."

"But you haven't *sat* on your throne," he argued, dragging his tongue over my flesh. I physically melted into him, gripping the fabric of his jacket for support as my traitorous knees buckled beneath me. "So you will sit, with a crown on your head, as I worship you."

His mouth moved lower, sweeping across my collarbone as his fingers dug into my sides. He pulled closer, allowing me to feel just how much he wanted me, and I whimpered in need.

"Worship me how?" I asked breathlessly as his lips continued to tease and trace their way over my body. I could feel his smile on my flesh as he moved his mouth up to mine and claimed another passionate kiss.

"I'm going to fuck you. First, with my tongue," he flicked it over my lips as if to emphasize his point, "And then with my—"

A loud and impatient knock interrupted us, causing Van to groan irritably. "You've got to be fucking kidding me! He's been alive for five hours, and he's already ruining my life."

"You don't know that it's *him*," I argued.

Van's face twisted in confusion as if I had just spoken in another language. "You're kidding, right?" I rolled my eyes and strode for the door.

The second the latch clicked, the door flung open, nearly hitting me. Felix flung out his arms and pulled me into a tight embrace. I quickly stole a glance at Evander as he gestured a hand over my best friend as if to say *I fucking told you so*.

"Look, if you wanna get away from Van, just say so and we can leave, but don't ever go to such lengths again," Felix joked, though I didn't miss the edge of hurt in his words.

"I'll do that next time," I tightened my hold on him. "But only if you tell me what happened with you."

We hadn't had a second of peace since our reunion and there were a million questions I had racing through my head. Had Felix known all along of his Gift as a Maguiser? Had he known Harbin was his father? Why hadn't Tallis allowed him to come home?

"I will as soon as we get back to Tenebrae," he promised, finally releasing me as Oli walked into the room to join us.

"Where is everyone?" Evander asked. "We have a lot to discuss and very little time to do so."

"Cal is getting acquainted with Imogen in the hall, and Marce is trying to find a new room. Apparently, some jackass wiped blood all over her bed," Oli answered.

I clamped my lips shut to smother my smile.

"Did you find out who sent those men we encountered in the woods?" Felix chimed in.

"Not officially, but my gut says Harbin was behind it. They didn't wield any magic, but that could have been a choice so that their identities weren't revealed," Evander replied.

"What about the man you saved for questioning? He didn't talk?"

I shook my head, frustrated at that fact. "The moment he woke and saw us, he slipped a toxic pill into his mouth before we could stop him."

Felix swore under his breath.

"We need proof that it was Harbin who did it," Van said.

"And that he's working with Oberon," Oli added.

Proof—The one thing that had evaded us. It didn't matter how strong our gut instinct was—without proof, it was useless.

I strolled over to the open window as the four of us quietly tried to come up with a useful idea. Peering below, a small thought flittered through my mind. It most likely wouldn't work, but if it did, it could be our one chance at obtaining evidence or, at the very least, a witness.

"I may have an idea," I told the group, earning interested glances. "It's a long shot, and it may possibly do more harm than good—"

"Do *you* believe it could work?" Van asked. After a moment of contemplation, I nodded. "Then trust your gut."

With that, I hurried from the room.

20
Ainsley

My task didn't take long and went surprisingly better than I had anticipated. I still wasn't sure if I could trust that it would work, but for the first time in a while, I felt a pang of hope. I took the long way back to the room, going over my plan repeatedly. There were too many people counting on me to mess this up.

I was completely lost in my thoughts and didn't notice I had taken a different route until I found myself in front of a familiar door. My hands shook as I reached for the golden knob and gently twisted.

Immediately, I was met with the sweet and musky scent of worn leather and parchment. The natural light from the windows flooded the room, illuminating tiny specks of dust floating through the air. Empty goblets with red-stained rims were scattered across a table next to books flipped open to random pages.

I wrapped my arms across my chest as if holding the glued-back pieces of myself together as I surveyed the Sanctuary. Everything was exactly as I had last seen it, frozen in place, untouched by time.

Releasing a wavering breath, I stepped further into the room. As much as it hurt to be there, I had to remind myself I wasn't doing it for me—I was doing it for my people. I was doing it to find those stones. They were in Caelum, and if Dashiell had them, the Sanctuary would be the one place where he would keep them hidden.

I swallowed hard, and then got to work.

⁂

An hour passed and—nothing. Not a single trace of the damn stones. I placed my hands on my hips as I threw my head toward the ceiling, letting out a frustrated groan. Closing my eyes, I willed myself to calm and think through the problem. There had to be something I was missing, some spot I was overlooking.

Another ten minutes passed, but I didn't move. I continued to let my mind travel to each inch of the room I knew so well, hoping the answer was revealed to me before I grew any more irritated.

"Can I help you with something?" Startled, I whipped around to find Dashiell leaning against the closed door, watching me intently. I hadn't even heard him come in.

"No," I answered as I moved toward the exit—toward him. "I shouldn't have come in here."

He pushed off the door and crossed his arms firmly over his chest, stopping me in my tracks. "You're allowed to," he answered softly, no trace of hostility in his voice. "This place belongs to you just as much as it does me."

"No, it doesn't. At least not anymore." My tone was final, leaving no room for argument. This place—this *sanctuary*—was no longer a part of me. I couldn't afford for it to be. The memories that filled this room were tainted by the lies Dashiell had fed me for weeks.

He glanced away, shaking his head subtly as if this fight wasn't worth it to him. I couldn't blame him for that, nor could I explain the uneasy feeling in the pit of my stomach at the sight of it. There was so much bad blood between us that I wasn't sure it would ever subside. And did I even want it to? He hated me because I had killed his father, and my actions were why we almost lost Felix, but my reasons for holding a grudge held far more weight than his ever could.

I reached down for the hurt that was always swimming just below the surface and dipped into the heinous memories. I bathed in the lies and manipulation, the heartbreak and betrayal, and the loss of the person I used to be—thanks to *him*. He didn't deserve my time or the air from my lungs spent on useless words.

I moved again, but he stepped in front of the door, forcing me to halt once more. "Then why are you in here?" Dashiell asked flatly. It was like he could taste the resentment and anger on my tongue before I had the chance to spew them.

My mouth opened and closed as my mind drew a blank. I could lie—I *should* lie—so why was something pulling so hard for me to be honest with him the way he never was with me?

Dashiell's gaze flickered over the space, seeming to land on every place I had touched. I watched his eyes widen and the emotion play out as if he had just now noticed the chaotic state of the room. As if before this moment, the only thing he had been focused on was me.

His stare darkened and his breathing came quick and heavy as he took inventory of what I had done. I felt a slight pang in my chest at the fury I could both see and feel forming within him. A hard lump traveled down his throat as he swallowed, and his eyes sliced back to mine. Gone was any trace of humanity.

"Are you ever going to be done trying to hurt me?" The words snapped through the air like a whip, delivering a blow I physically reeled back from.

"You're one to talk," I shot back, my teeth bared and my anger palpable. He couldn't have been serious. Any concern or guilt I had felt was immediately replaced with rage and intolerance. Dashiell scoffed, and the sound sent a new wave of anger through me. "I'm sorry your desire to claim my life didn't quite pan out the way you wanted. Maybe next time," I added.

With that, Dashiell uncrossed his arms and stormed for me, planting himself just a foot away—a safe distance apart but close enough for me to see every emotional scar etched into his features.

"If I wanted you dead, you would have been by now."

"Is that a threat?"

My shadows seeped out and curled around my fingers on instinct, though they were nothing more than trails of wisps rather than the violent darkness they usually were. If I didn't gain back control of my magic in his presence, his threats wouldn't stay idle for long. I suspected the dulling of my Gifts had something to do with his Obscure.

"No," Dashiell responded. "I'm not you. *I'm* actually aware that there are other ways to deal with an adversary besides removing them from the playing field or writing them off because you're too stubborn to listen—A fact you haven't seemed to realize yet."

"What the hell is that supposed to mean?" My temper was at an all-time high as I mentally added *'insulting me'* to the growing list of marks against him.

"It means you're selfish. You refuse to hear anyone out when their opinion differs from yours."

My teeth ground together as my jaw clenched. He was so damn arrogant and condescending that it made taking his life here and now seem all that much better. At least it did for a split second. Until my magic roared inside me at the idea. It was as if the gesture was meant to talk sense into me and calm my raging mind. I took a deep breath before responding, settling for the poison of my words rather than my actions.

"I bet it must have been hard then." Dashiell's eyes narrowed as he tried to catch my meaning. "Having to pretend to love someone you clearly think so little of."

He tongued his cheek as he shook his head. He was just as done with this conversation as I was. So why the hell were we still both determined to have it?

"I never lied about my feelings," he argued, causing me to release a breathy laugh as I looked away. Did he truly believe he was just in his actions? Did he honestly think that lying and manipulating me was how he showed his love? "But you aren't *her*."

At that, my eyes flicked back to his. There was a rot in my stomach, growing and infecting everything inside me. I felt sick and weak and confused as I began to crack under the pressure of his stare. He was right—I wasn't the same woman as before. But that fact was doing something to me that I couldn't explain. It was shredding me apart while I tried to hold on to the pieces I already deemed were lost long ago.

"*She* was kind-hearted and fierce. She was stubborn, temperamental, funny, and empathetic. She was guarded, but when you broke through her defenses, you saw such mesmerizing beauty within her," he said.

My eyes stung as I blinked back the tears I felt on the cusp. The words were poetry, but he said them as if they tasted vile on his tongue.

"But you..." he started, taking a deliberate step for me. I balled my hands into fists at my side as he approached and took a deep breath to steady myself. "You are *nothing* like her."

I didn't let the words seep in before I snapped my retort. "Because I'm not easily manipulated?"

"Because you're cruel. You're bitter and scorned—I get it—but so am I." His words were like a dagger to the heart, twisting and slicing as blood continued to pour, only worsening the wound. "Believe it or not, I'm hurt too, Ainsley."

Irrational anger coursed through me, and I lifted my chin in pure defiance over his confession.

"After all that you did to me, you have *no* right to—"

"I have *every* right to feel how I do," he argued forcefully, raising his voice louder than I had ever heard him do. "It may have taken me months to realize that I'm entitled to feel anything other than guilt with you, but I'm here now."

I scoffed, a bitter, incredulous laugh beneath my labored breaths. My mind couldn't comprehend how he felt entitled enough to be angry and hurt with *me*. I didn't understand how he could experience anything other than crushing guilt. But I guessed maybe the guilty don't see themselves as such.

Still, I couldn't stop pressing him—couldn't just walk away and let this die even if the more logical part of my brain wanted me to.

"No," I demanded just as angrily as he had. "You don't get to play the victim because you don't want to deal with the outcome of your own actions."

"You're one to talk."

My teeth ground at his mocking use of my earlier words. He was baiting me, tempting me with a challenge he knew I couldn't refuse—a fight I couldn't walk away from. And even though I knew his motive like I knew my own, I couldn't resist the lure of traps he so delicately laid.

He regarded me closely, and I saw something that looked like hope flicker in his eyes as he realized I would not give up this battle between us.

"You continuously lied about your love for me, and yet you paint *me* as the villain?" I sneered.

Dashiell was always a rational and logical thinker. His mind worked at a speed I could never hope to keep up with, and even now, that continued to be the case. He inclined his head as he studied me like I was an elusive object he had never encountered, mystery in my every movement, my every word. And though I wished that were truly the case, I knew Dashiell could read me as easily as if I were the comforting story he favored every night. It made me uneasy and almost reluctant to stay.

Almost.

"You constantly say how I manipulated you, but I can argue the same," he said, his tone cavalier and confident, a man finally getting what he wanted after so long—the chance to argue his case.

Nails dug into my palms as I tried tirelessly to ground myself. I knew what he was doing, but it was a struggle not to retaliate. He could tell.

So he continued.

"I never lied about my feelings for you and never once manipulated you into falling in love with me. I can't say the same about *your* actions, though." My pulse spiked and the metallic taste of blood swept over my tongue as I bit it back. Still, I didn't respond. He cocked a brow, either impressed or furious by my restraint. "You want to defend it, but we both know you can't," he added. "I was in that room just like everyone else as we learned what you are to him. You never once loved me. Every declaration from you was a lie."

That did it.

"Bullshit," I spat. "You don't get to try and turn this around just because you're bitter I've moved on."

An incredulous laugh escaped his lips as he turned his head, trying to locate his next defense, but I struck again before he could.

"The only thing you ever loved was the thought of my power running through your veins." I held up my hand for emphasis as shadows curled around my fingers. "The only thing you ever wanted was the one thing you knew would destroy me."

He shook his head, his blue eyes dark and blazing. "That isn't true." The words came out in a growl beneath his breath.

I shrugged with a single shoulder and no care in the world. "From where I'm standing, it is."

"So then move."

The corner of my lips twitched in smug satisfaction, but he remained calm and calculated—always assessing the situation before reacting. I was envious of his control, of his ability to keep his emotions in check even when I knew he wanted to falter.

Evander was always cautious of what others saw. With the secrets of his emotions being on display thanks to his shifting tattoo, he had to be. But even *he* didn't possess the same level of restraint Dashiell was displaying. I wanted to find an opening, a tiny piece of him left unguarded that I could crawl into and attack. Felix was right—we were opposites in every way. And though he could cool my temper, fire always melted ice.

"I was going to tell you the truth," Dashiell argued.

"But instead, you decided to fuck me," I stated plainly.

That fact filled the air between us, tainting the oxygen until it felt like I was suffocating under its truth. Dashiell turned his head as if my words had struck him across the face, and I reveled in the small bit of shame he displayed.

"I'm curious, though," I added, ensnaring his attention once more. "When did you decide to go through with your plan?"

"After you were attacked in the orchard." His eyes widened for a fraction of a second and a white panic shot across his features before he quickly schooled them again. An answer he wasn't planning on sharing, yet it came out instinctively.

"Interesting," I mused. "Why?"

He shook his head deliberately. "It doesn't matter. What's done is done."

That wasn't good enough. "Was it because I was so weak and pathetic in that moment, you thought it would be easy?"

No answer.

"So while I was fighting for my life, you were plotting how exactly you were going to do it." Again, I was met with his silent, hard stare. His throat bobbed slightly and I knew it was my one and only opening. "Did you think about it while you sat with me while I was bloodied and bruised?"

"That's not—"

"Did you imagine what it would feel like to wield my Gifts while you looked me in the eyes and promised me *forever?*"

"No, I—"

"So then why, Dashiell?" I demanded, cutting him off again. He turned his cheek as he shook his head, unable to provide an answer.

Still not good enough. He wanted to have this fight, so we'd have it, but it would be on my terms.

"Was it difficult to constantly pretend you cared for me? Did it send a thrill down your spine each time you held me, knowing what you were going to do?"

I sent a barrage of countless questions, drilling so deeply that his usual calm exterior began to fracture like fissures in the earth. I almost had him.

"Were you excited about our wedding night?" I tried again. At that, his eyes sliced to mine and his brow pinched. "Fucking me with my power coursing through you," I explained nonchalantly. He flinched at my vulgarity, but I didn't care. "Tell me something. Was it ever *me* that got you off, or just the thought of what you would steal from me?"

"That's not—" he yelled, but I was quicker.

"THEN TELL ME WHY—"

"—BECAUSE YOU ASKED ME TO!"

I stumbled back and watched as his eyes widened and his mouth clamped shut. My chest tightened, and my stomach sank as his confession slipped between my bones and pierced my heart. It had to be another lie.

Dashiell's breathing came quicker, and I could feel the anxious panic seeping from him. This wasn't something he planned on sharing, but that one slip of his tongue caused the fatal blow he never wanted to deal.

"You're lying," I whispered in denial. "I never would have requested that."

Dashiell was quiet for a moment, looking around the room like it held more lies to spin.

"It doesn't matter," he finally answered.

I scoffed to cover up my screaming panic as I scoured through every memory, every hollow interaction between us, to try and pinpoint the precise moment his decision had been made. The sound only seemed to enrage him.

He dragged a hand through his brown hair and inhaled sharply. "You know what? Fuck it," he said before turning those dark blue eyes on me. "I don't know why I bother trying to protect you when you obviously care so little about anyone else." The words were just a breath of air, so low I believed they were said more to himself than me.

His body turned toward me fully, and I immediately tensed as if readying myself for a battle where the victory was slipping between my fingers like sand. His posture was rigid, and his stare held the same burning intensity as the sun. I fought like hell not to balk beneath it—not to shrivel up and wither away into nothing.

"I never wanted to take your Gifts from you, Ainsley. When my father told me what you were and what I was required to do, I said no. Without a single thought, without a whisper of hesitation, I said *no*."

I didn't move, though my fingers began to tremble slightly at my sides. "That choice didn't seem to last long—"

"—Even during your birthday when my father cornered me and used every reason and tactic he possibly could to get me to waver, I still said *no*," he continued, ignoring my outburst. "When you were bloodied and barely breathing in my arms, hanging on to life by a single thread as I carried you to the palace, I said *no*. When I sat outside the Medicus facility and prayed to the Gods for them to take me in your place, I still said *no*."

The world began to sway beneath my feet as his confession sucked the air from my lungs. Lies. Every word he uttered had to be filled to the brim and overflowing with falsities. My mind untangled the web of his words, twisting and turning and inspecting each thread of woven intricacies. He was always smart and careful with what he shared, so why would this be any different? Was this a tactic he was using to throw me off and make me question everything I thought I knew? Had he been aware I had already been doing so?

"It wasn't until I held you in my arms as you healed that my resolve began to slowly shatter." I blinked, and his silhouette came back into focus. I didn't even notice it had blurred from tears to begin with. "It wasn't until I heard your confession that my mind started to falter for the first time. And it wasn't until your pleas that I finally gave in."

The images of that night with Dashiell inundated my vision, replaying every word that had been spoken—both gentle and angry. I searched desperately, digging deeper and deeper into the pit I had filled long ago, determined to get to the center by any means necessary. My fingers were filthy and my bones ached as I clawed and clawed through the memories until I found it.

There, at the very bottom, was the moment everything had altered.

I remembered being pressed close to Dashiell's chest as he rocked me back and forth while I sobbed. I had momentarily shoved away my anger with him and instead opted for him to comfort me as I shattered in his arms and proclaimed the secrets of my darkest thoughts.

"I can't do this anymore. They're never going to leave me alone. It's never going to stop. I just want it to stop."

The words sounded in my mind like an alarm, waking me up and sending a shiver of panic creeping down my spine. A tear slipped from my eye, and with it, the last request I had made.

"Please, just make it stop."

King Perceval's own words from the night I had killed him jumped to the forefront of my mind. *"I'm not sure what you said to him, but whatever it was, it made him agree to my plan."*

Dashiell wasn't looking at me. His eyes shifted back and forth as he gazed in the distance, reliving the exact moment I was. Slowly, he repeated aloud the words I had said in my head, each declaration short and laden with pain from the past. When he reached the final sentence, his throat was thick with emotion, fraying the edges of his words. He swayed slightly in my vision, but I didn't know if the cause was one of my own doing or his. I gripped the back of the nearby couch for support, regardless.

His own response all those months ago fluttered into my thoughts.

"I'll make it stop, I promise," he had told me. I recalled the way the words were off. His pledge was steady, but filled with a sorrow I didn't understand.

Until now.

"There you were, so broken in my arms—so ready to give up—begging me to make it all stop. And I could," he said shallowly. "I was the one person who could take away the fear and the pain for you. I could make it so you never had to feel that low and helpless again."

"You didn't have to agree to it," I responded, barely louder than a whisper as I processed. There must have been residual animosity in my tone because his attention snapped to me, and his face twisted into something unpleasant.

"Don't you think I know that? Do you think I wasn't aware of what the consequence of my choice would be? I accepted that the moment I made that promise to you, I would lose you forever. You would hate me, but it would be worth it because you'd be alive. You would be free."

My pulse pounded in a heavy rhythm and my magic curled around my heart on instinct, willing it to slow. I was thinking too fast and feeling too much. I grasped my sanity with both hands, but no matter how hard I tried to hold onto it, I couldn't. It slipped through my fingers like a rope with Dashiell on the opposite end, pulling harder and harder to steal it away from me.

"And if I had to go back and do it again, I would," he added.

"Proof you never loved me."

"No—proof I did what I could with the information I had at the time. Proof that I loved you so Gods damn much that I would have fucking broken myself over and over again for you," Dashiell argued, his hands gesturing about to punctuate his point. "All I knew was that you were a product of Conjoining, Ainsley. I didn't even know what kingdoms were involved."

"And you didn't think to ask?!" I shouted, matching his temper.

"Of course I did! I spent that entire week we were apart locked in my room, researching the possibilities after my father refused to give me the answer for fear of it getting out." Of course that was King Perceval's excuse. I let out a bitter laugh beneath my breath, annoyed Dashiell had fallen for his father's tricks. It was unfair, but it didn't matter.

"I dove deep into each Gift of Disparya, trying to pinpoint exactly which ones you possessed," Dashiell continued. "I was so sure one of your parents was from Caelum, because why else would you have been here? I had no reason to suspect you were stolen."

"You should have looked harder, and then maybe you would have seen the signs."

Dashiell opened and closed his mouth like I had left him temporarily mute. I recognized the movement. There was something he wanted to say—an excuse he wanted to give—but thought better of it.

"You're right. I should have," he admitted. I was momentarily stunned by his acceptance. "But as I said before, I did what I could with the information I had at the time." He was quiet for a moment as if waiting to see if I was going to fight back. When he realized I wasn't, he continued. "Based on what you told me of your past, I assumed one of your Gifts was fire magic, but I couldn't figure out what your other one could be. I wanted to find a way to save you from your fate, but what could I have done? Nowhere but Caelum was safe."

I snorted at the word and Dashiell seemed to realize his mistake.

"Not *safe*," he corrected, "but Felix and I could protect you here. Any other kingdom would have killed you on the spot. Ministro is known for despising Conjoining the most, followed closely by Venator. Either king would have demanded your death the instant they found out what you were. Agnitio upholds our laws, and your existence goes against our most important one. And we had all believed Tenebrae was trying to kill you. I tried to find a way to get you out, Ainsley; I really did."

It was a pretty explanation, I'd admit, but it did nothing to soothe the sting of his betrayal. It didn't make the heartbreak I had experienced any easier.

"Felix managed to," I said resentfully. That fact alone made me question Dashiell's motivation in the matter. For someone who had researched so much, how was it that Felix figured it out before him?

"From information he didn't bother to share with me," Dashiell argued. I had forgotten Felix had felt my Empathi Gift before I even knew I possessed it. For some reason, his excuse still wasn't enough and only made me angrier.

"And if he had shared it, then what?" I shot back.

Felix had chosen not to tell Dashiell for a reason. Based on what he told me when we first arrived in Tenebrae, Dashiell's mind had been made up, and he refused to budge. Would his knowing who I truly was even matter when his decision seemed to be set?

"I would have helped you get out. I would have gone with you!" he yelled.

His chest rose and fell at a rapid pace, and the sound of thunder cracked so loudly that it felt like the world had been split in two. The vases rattled and shelves shook as his power reverberated through the Sanctuary, each tremble reaching into my bones.

I wanted to deny his claim, but I could taste the truth in the air, thick and coated with hidden emotions. I could see it in the way his eyes glazed over and the bobbing of his throat. I could feel it in the ripples of guilt and hurt and regret and anger that rolled off him like waves.

"I meant every word I ever said to you. I loved you, but you had never felt the same," he said.

"That's not—"

"You listened to Felix. You gave *him* the opportunity to speak, the chance to make everything up to you. But with me, you refused to hear me out. After everything we had been through together, I became painfully aware that it was nothing but a fucking lie. You never loved me. It was always *him*." He didn't understand my Soul Bond with Evander, and I didn't want to explain it to him.

I reeled back as if I had been slapped. Shock and hurt poured from him and into me, mixing our emotions until I couldn't tell them apart. I didn't know whether to fight or lie down and take it. I didn't know if I should be angry or remorseful.

"I had chosen you, and you betrayed me." My words were a whisper on a shaky breath, barely formed.

"No, you didn't. I gave myself fully to you, but you never did the same. That's evident in the way we are with each other now."

"So because I didn't forgive you—"

"I never once asked for your forgiveness," Dashiell interrupted. "I knew I'd never gain that. But I stupidly thought that you knew me. That you and Felix—my *family*—knew who I truly was." Tears slid down his cheeks, and his voice was strained as he continued. "But instead, the two of you cut me out and cast me as the villain. Everything we had built, the trust, the friendship, the love, all of it—gone. In the blink of an eye, I lost the two people who meant more to me than my own life."

My lips trembled as I shuddered. I didn't like where this was going. I didn't like how my anger was transforming into something else, or the way my magic reached for him. I didn't like that I had to focus on keeping my feet rooted in place instead of stepping forward to close the distance between us.

I wanted to wrap myself in the comfort of my vendetta against him. I wanted to curl up against my fury and bathe in my need for vengeance.

I swayed lightly as his declaration slammed into me on repeat.

"I lost *everything* while you seemed to gain it all. You have your magic, a kingdom, a crown, love, family. And I have nothing but a title I didn't want and sure as hell wasn't ready for."

Dashiell glanced around the room, his eyes settling on every inch of the Sanctuary I had overturned. I followed his stare, noting the scattered stack of books, the tilted-over vases, the drawers pulled out of the dressers with their contents spilling onto the ground.

"And yet that *still* isn't enough for you," he said, choking on the words. "You have to try and hurt me every chance you get." He gestured to the state of the Sanctuary. "Including destroying the one place you knew meant everything to me. The one place that was safe. The one place that felt like home." He said the words angrily through gritted teeth.

Out of everything I had done to him, this had affected him the most. Not me killing his father, running away, or when he found out about Evander and me. No, it was seeing his Sanctuary picked apart and scavenged through.

Guilt and shame dripped down my throat like a bitter medicine I was forced to swallow. This place had once been home to me, too. It housed memories of laughter, friendship, and love found. And here I was, soiling any happiness left.

"And for what? For this?" Dashiell reached into his pocket and pulled out his father's gold ring donning a large ruby in the center.

He pinched it between his thumb and forefinger, inspecting it curiously. I couldn't peel my eyes away, every hair on my arm going erect at the sight of the stone in his hand. It was undoubtedly one of the three we had been searching tirelessly for. I had been so certain the Crown of Caelum held our answers, but perhaps it was the ring all along that was pulling me toward it. I mistakenly grabbed the wrong object.

With a flick of his wrist, the ring flew through the air and landed soundlessly in my open palms. I curled my fist around it like a vice, ready to slaughter anyone who so much as looked at it.

"Do you want to hear something pathetic?" he said. It wasn't a question. "Even after everything, all you had to do was ask, and I would have given it to you."

I opened my mouth to speak, unsure of what the hell I was going to say when a small voice cut through the space.

"Your Majesty?" I quickly turned, wiping my damp eyes free from the steady stream of tears.

Dashiell cleared his throat of the emotion lodged within before addressing the man. "Yes, Robert?"

"I apologize for the intrusion, but there are several questions surrounding tonight's event, primarily from the kitchen staff regarding a strange request on the menu." Robert's voice wobbled, clearly uncomfortable with the tense conversation he walked in on. "I assured them it must be a mistake and tried searching for Imogen, but—"

"She's busy with another task," Dashiell interrupted. "Tell the staff there is no mistake and to carry on as previously instructed. I'll be down in a moment to clear up any confusion."

I listened to Robert retreat and wiped my face once more before twisting back to Dashiell. He hadn't bothered to brush away the tear tracks staining his cheeks or blink away the moisture brimming in his eyes. He sucked in one long breath as he broke our stare and looked over the damage of the room one last time.

His brow furrowed, his nose wrinkled, and his lips twisted to the side as he fought the urge to crumble. I had only seen him like this once before—the day I had sent him away following my attack in the orchard.

After a moment, his features fell slack and he nodded to himself, accepting whatever his mind had spoken to him. His eyes turned to me and I inhaled slowly. My magic writhed inside me and I recognized the warning for what it was. Dashiell was about to land his final strike.

"Take whatever you want from here, Ainsley." His hand waved over the destruction without breaking eye contact. "And when you're finished—when this summit is finished—I want you to get the *fuck* out of my kingdom." My knees wobbled beneath me, but I stayed upright, focusing all my energy on that task. "And my life. For good."

With that final declaration, he turned from me but stopped short. His eyes widened just a fraction, and I followed his stare to find Evander standing precariously in the doorway, his arms crossed firmly over his chest.

Van's gaze slid back and forth between Dashiell and me as he assessed the situation without so much as a word passing between his lips. His jaw ticked and I could feel the anger pool around him when his eyes met mine. I could imagine how upset I had looked, how broken and small. But Evander shoved his fury down, knowing this wasn't his fight. It was mine.

He took a long breath before his watchful eyes shifted back to the King of Caelum. Dashiell held his stare, though not in challenge. His shoulders were slumped, and his chest rose and fell in long, shallow movements. He was aching and hurt—a man utterly defeated.

The two regarded each other quietly until Dashiell seemed to have enough. He broke the silent altercation and pushed past Evander, closing the door behind him.

The second it clicked shut, I fell to my knees, gasping for breath like I was tasting air for the first time. I remembered to throw up a shield just before I made impact with the ground, trapping Evander in only a foot of space between the closed door and the rest of the Sanctuary.

His fist slammed against the barrier once, twice, three times, but it held strong, keeping him out and locking me in my graveyard of memories. I had tried hard to ensure they stayed buried beneath the earth, but one by one, they clawed free from the loose soil like the undead I had only read about in stories. They were determined to drag me back below with them until my lungs filled with dirt and I suffocated from the pressure of my own mind.

My eyes frantically darted over the space. There, only a foot away, Dashiell and I had curled up together, basking in each other's warm company. Across the room, he had kissed me deeply against the bookshelf, neither of us caring about the novels that had fallen off because of it. The couch brushing my shoulder was where I had drifted to sleep in his arms, adoring the flame gemstone bracelet he gifted me the hour prior.

Evander's muffled shouts grew louder, but they were drowned out by my pounding thoughts.

To my left, Felix, Dashiell, and I lounged on the window bench and played truth or dare, divulging our deepest secrets and completing outlandish tasks mostly set forth by Felix. The mantle was where I sat with Felix for hours as we made bets as to who could get under Dashiell's skin the quickest. I had lost.

"Ainsley, I swear to the fucking Gods if you don't let down this shield," Evander warned with a worry-coated tongue.

"You can't come in here," I whispered, though I knew he heard it. How could I tear this place apart yet still feel the need to protect it from outsiders?

"The hell I can't."

I ignored his outburst, my mind once again shifting through memories like a deck of cards. As I pulled them out one by one, each held a greater value than its predecessor.

My fingers pressed into the carpet, my nails digging deep, sharpening into dark talons as I recalled the night we sat in this very spot.

I had crawled onto Dashiell's lap, peppering kisses across his neck, his jaw, his lips. His fingers weaved through my hair until his hands slid around to frame my face, holding me still as he whispered sweet declarations. Innocent promises tangled with undying love as I captured his mouth and vowed to never let it go.

We locked Felix out of the Sanctuary that evening, making use of every inch of space we could before sneaking back to my room and swearing to take that secret to the grave.

A well of power brushed along mine as Van worked to pry open my shield, coming too close to success.

"Stop. You can't come in here."

"I'm not leaving you to fall to pieces on the fucking ground, Ainsley."

He pushed more magic into his hands, making my power buckle and bend. My shield was starting to crumble. I knew he could feel my pain, and having to stand there while watching me break from afar was creating a rift in his chest that mirrored my own. He wasn't going to stop until he shattered my defenses.

"Please, go get Felix," I requested quietly.

"Ainsley—"

"Just go get Felix, Evander!" A low growl slid from between his clenched teeth, but reluctantly, he obeyed.

I sank further into the ground—further into myself. I dug a fresh grave and frantically attempted to bury my memories once more. But it was too late. The skeletons were now uncovered, and the ghosts of my past were now free to walk at my side, haunting me with every breath I took.

The sutures upon my heart split, spilling the contents of every wound once healed beneath my fingers until I was sitting in a pool of my own sorrow. Everything hurt. Every painful, blissful, memory lay before me to witness as I unraveled thread by fraying thread.

I tried to breathe through the phantom touches on my skin, the feel of hot lips against mine, the sounds of gentle laughter and comforting silence. It didn't help; it didn't erase the pounding in my head or the tears pouring from my eyes.

A soothing brush of magic stroked mine, and I looked up through lowered lashes to find Felix patiently standing at the entrance. I lowered my shield, and he stepped through before throwing his hand up behind him in a halting gesture.

"Stop," he told Olivier. "You're not allowed in here."

"I'm not allowed in here?" Oli replied slowly, wrapping each word in a question.

"No."

Felix stepped forward as Olivier gave Evander a skeptical look.

"Some stupid fucking rule they made up," Van told him.

To my husband's credit, he didn't try to argue. He looked furious, but he didn't cross over the threshold. He simply folded his arms over his chest and rested his back against the doorframe, regarding me closely. Oli rolled his eyes and followed suit. I didn't bother telling them to leave.

Felix approached slowly as he looked around the room he had loved as fiercely as Dashiell. He didn't comment on its state, and I thanked the Gods for it. If he was hurt or angry, he didn't let it show. There was nothing in his warm eyes other than concern for my well-being.

He slid to the ground next to me, pulling his legs to his chest and resting his forearms on his knees. I gripped the carpet and took one long breath as I tried to garner strength to push myself up.

"I can't tell if what I'm feeling is my own heartache or Dashiell's," I whispered. My emotions still felt muddled and mixed together with the string of a betrayal that wasn't mine.

"Both," Felix replied. He was staring into the distance, his mind lost in a time that wasn't present.

"Did you speak to him, too?"

He was quiet for a long moment as he rubbed the pads of his thumb over his fingers back and forth like a nervous tic. Finally, he spoke.

"I don't think he wants anything to do with me, either."

21
Felix

I was a master at controlling everyone's emotions. I could ease their pain, calm their heart and mind, steady their breathing. But I was complete shit at dealing with my *own* shit. I couldn't make myself stop caring, stop feeling, stop reliving the pain of Dash's hurt every waking moment.

Nor in my dreams.

Ainsley was quiet as she waited for me to elaborate. I didn't think she could speak if she tried. The pain radiating from her was so great, I knew it was sucking the air from her lungs and clouding her mind—it was a mirror to the same agonizing guilt I experienced after my encounter with him months ago.

"I don't think there's a cure for the hurt I caused him," I admitted, the truth of those words slicing like the sting of a blade. "What I did to him... It's not something I think I can fix, nor do I think he wants me to."

Her fingers slid over mine as I blinked away the uninvited tears and observed her sitting in front of me as she tried to summon the strength to endure the pain. That was the worst thing about being an Empathi—experiencing the gut-wrenching emotions of everyone else. It wasn't something that disappeared like puffs of smoke after a fire had long since gone cold; it stayed with you like embers ready to be tended.

"You're his brother," she said, moving to sit beside me. Her hand squeezed mine as if to emphasize her point.

"And I betrayed him."

My regret was a bitter cloud tainting the air around me, each breath like shards of glass shredding my throat on its way down. Concern that wasn't my own flooded through me, and I looked up to see Oli's mournful gaze. He hated that I was hurting, and I loved him even more for that. Evander didn't look much better off as his eyes stayed fixed on his wife.

"We both did," Ainsley offered, her voice a meek version of the strength she commanded earlier in that throne room.

Her eyes shifted back and forth as she stared into the distance, coming to terms with what we had done to Dash. We were his family and we never gave him a chance—a chance we both knew he would have extended to us even if we were in the wrong. That choice was now eating at her just as thoroughly as it did me.

I could imagine how the conversation went between them today, what Dash had said. I was sure their exchange didn't hold much difference from the one he and I had shared months ago. Hearing my transgressions laid out before me and what it did to him had destroyed me. It caused me to hesitate in my decision to depart from Caelum and go back to Tenebrae alongside Ainsley.

I didn't deserve to be happy.

Regardless, in the end, I had made a promise to her and could not betray her trust—not again. I wouldn't fail her in the same way I had failed my oldest friend, my brother. I was the worst kind of person for what I had done. Not because I helped Ainsley, but because I didn't have faith in him the way he always had in me. I chose to believe the worst, acting out of pure terror and panic over what Perceval had planned for her.

I could have shared what I had come to realize about Ainsley and given Dash the opportunity to do the right thing, but instead, I took that chance away from him. In the end, I believed he was no different from his father when, in actuality, the boy I had grown up with had proven time and time again that he was far better.

When I was first learning how to wield my Empathi Gift, I struggled. No child should have to endure the weight of so many feelings at once and be expected to carry on as if they were fine. I'd cry myself to sleep each night as I waited for the overwhelming sensations to transform into dull aches. Dash never left my side. Each night, he'd creep into my room after curfew and crawl beneath the sheets with me. He wouldn't say a word; he just sat there in the role of a comforting presence should I need one.

Occasionally, when the pain became too much and I'd wretch for hours, he'd rub my back, fetch me water, change the bedding if I didn't make it to the toilet—still without so much as a word. Come morning, neither of us would acknowledge the night before or my shortcomings. And each morning, he'd offer himself up as a test subject for me to practice on, even though I knew he hated the emotional manipulation.

As we got older, our bond only deepened. 'Friends' didn't properly encompass all that we were, and 'family' didn't hold enough weight. One could hate family, could hide their truth and only present a front to them. With Dash, there was no room for secrets, no room for being anything other than ourselves. And for the first and only time in my life, I had been accepted by someone, flaws and all.

As a child, my life was tumultuous. The Queen of Ministro hated my existence, so much so that I wasn't sure why King Harbin hadn't just sent me to be discarded to save himself from her wrath. But he always claimed he saw something powerful in me—a gut instinct that I would be of use. That theory proved true when my powers emerged at a young age. Clearly, I was too stupid to put the pieces together of why that had been.

After I was sent to live with King Perceval, I should have found comfort in being away from the demanding king and his cruel wife, but being cast out into the cold only made me feel smaller—unwanted and unworthy of love.

Dash had taken it upon himself to ensure that I experienced anything but that. He provided me with the love of a brother and the protection of a guardian. He had given me a safe place to unravel and feel at peace—a sanctuary currently in shambles—and still, he had never once asked for anything in return.

I vowed to never let his kindness go unnoticed. I would reciprocate what he meant to me: someone who would support and protect him unconditionally, who would trust and defend him without question. Because I *knew* him. Even without my abilities, I knew his heart as well as I knew my own.

After having broken that oath, I couldn't fault him for his anger or pain. I was so preoccupied with trying to make him understand my point of view that I neglected to consider his perspective and the challenges he was facing.

The love he emitted for Ainsley was more than I had ever felt coming from any one person before. I didn't need to be an Empathi to sense it; the way he looked at her left no doubt about his feelings. Nothing made that more clear than when she was barely holding onto life.

So why was I so quick to believe he would cause her harm? Why hadn't I trusted him with the information I figured out?

He asked as much that day in Caelum after he and Ainsley sparred. Just like back then, I didn't have an answer. I couldn't pinpoint the exact reason I chose not to tell Dash about Ainsley, but I knew in my soul, it was a decision I would regret for the rest of my life.

"I have nothing more to say to you."

Ainsley looked at me questioningly, not understanding the comment I had made.

"Those were the last words he spoke to me," I explained, remembering the hard look in his eyes and the way he turned his back on me after he said it.

I have nothing more to say to you.

It was a sentence I had repeated to myself so often that the words had burrowed beneath my skin, becoming a part of me. I couldn't extract them from my flesh, no matter how hard I tried.

And even my escape from death wasn't enough to make Dash reconsider.

I have nothing more to say to you.

"Come on," I told Ainsley, finally rising from the floor and helping her to her feet. "I'll help you clean up in here before we head to the feast."

She nodded, wiping the tears from her eyes as she surveyed the disaster before shuffling over to a pile of books scattered on the ground. This place, which once provided a sense of safety and belonging, now lay in ruins—a fitting symbolism for the state of our friendship. My gaze drifted toward Oli and Van as they stayed put at the doorway, watching us with pained expressions.

I took a deep breath, then turned to help clean up the mess of my former home.

I have nothing more to say to you.

22
Felix

Imogen had outdone herself with the decor, though I'd expect nothing less when it came to Ainsley. She was always a sort of mother figure to us all, but with the Queen of Tenebrae, it had been different from the start.

I knew how much Ainsley had missed Imogen over the months they had been apart, and it warmed my chest to know they were finally reunited. I suspected Imogen would travel to Tenebrae with us when the summit was over.

My lungs filled with the sweet scent of peonies, which was not surprising as every vase was filled with them. Green vines crawled up the delicate curtains draped across every window and balcony doorway. Glass orbs flickered with soft lights like thousands of fireflies overhead, lighting up the world above. It was beyond magical—a celebration fit for a queen.

Oli whistled low beside me. "I know," I told him as my gaze continued to sweep over the decor. "Imogen always exceeds expectations, but when it comes to Ainsley, the limit of what she will do does not exist."

"Good. She deserves this after the hell she's been through."

I nodded and rested my hand against his lower back. "I missed you."

Olivier stared straight ahead, surveying the crowd for any possible threats against his king and queen. He pretended not to care about my declaration, but I could hear the faint smile in his voice as he brought his wine goblet to his mouth before speaking.

"I'm still pissed that you kept me in the dark." He wasn't. Not pissed at *me,* at least. The emotion radiating from him was very much *not* anger. My blood heated as I recognized it.

I leaned in close, placing my lips against the shell of his ear. His heart rate spiked as feelings of desire coated my tongue. "I'll let you punish me for it later."

Oli choked on his drink before disguising it as a cough. He straightened and twisted around, placing those brilliant turquoise eyes on me. A smirk played on his lips as he slowly dragged his stare up and down my body.

"Is that a promise?"

My own pulse quickened. I had been without him for too long. Fuck the party. Fuck the summit. Fuck our mission. And, *my Gods,* just let me fuck—

My thoughts were interrupted by a horn sounding off. Not exactly the instrument I wanted blown, but I guess that'd have to wait. It was time for the rulers of Disparya to enter.

Hundreds of heads turned toward the massive doors opening on their own. The kings and queens needed no formal introduction. There wasn't a soul in this room who wasn't ensnared in the power they exuded by merely existing. As this was his kingdom, Dash entered first.

His presence was commanding. The flawless marble floor quaked beneath each of his steps as if absorbing his magic and emanating it back to us, granting us a glimpse into the strength of the power he wielded. It was more than I had ever felt radiate from King Perceval, and the late ruler never held back what he was capable of... but Dash currently was.

He wasn't like his father, who thrived on power and made those around him bend to it. Dash was always reserved and humble with what he was granted. Even now, he was holding back when he should have showcased everything the Gods bestowed upon him to cement his place among the seasoned rulers.

And that fragment I felt now was still greater than any power his predecessor had wielded.

Dash walked effortlessly through the parted crowd as everyone dipped their chin in respect. His strides were powerful and deliberate, yet calm and gracious at the same time. His hand was dipped in his pocket in a casual gesture, but the gold crown on his head proved he was no longer the boyish prince who breezed through filled rooms without concern for his title. He was a king now, and there was no mistaking that.

There were no polite nods and gentle smiles from him as he passed; no small waves and friendly pleasantries. His focus stayed locked on the dais as he crossed the room, donned in deep blue. It was a change from the emerald his father always wore and claimed as Caelum's color, a subtle yet impactful statement that Dash's reign would be different.

It was already shaping up to be that way from what I had heard while in Agnitio. Besides refurbishing the palace to look less ostentatious—thank the Gods—and putting that wealth into his kingdom, the new King of Caelum had dismissed nearly his entire inherited council. Rather than let the now previous members pass down to his reign, he conducted interviews with all those interested in the newly opened positions. Most of his current council was now made up of new and fresh faces, much to the dismay of its former members. Only a few established advisors, those closest to King Perceval, kept their coveted roles.

To my allies, I knew this fact would only perpetuate their theory of Dash helping to plot against Disparya with his father. The fact that he was spotted leaving Pravus all those months ago made defending him that much harder. But after breaking the trust we had spent nearly our entire lives building, I swore to never do it again. His choice of council members had to be for a bigger reason. I just had to have faith in my oldest friend.

Once Dash climbed the dais, he took his seat among the thrones set out for each member of the royal houses. The doors opened of their own volition again, this time letting through King Harbin of Ministro with his wife one step behind him. My stomach knotted as I felt the unease in the room gather like thick mist upon their entrance.

The residents of Ministro were easily spotted within the crowd. They were the only ones who dipped at the waist as their rulers passed. One man even dropped to his knees, keeping his head down and eyes lowered to the floor as if he wasn't worthy of sipping the same air as his king and queen. My feelings of pity outweighed his fear.

The late King Perceval wasn't a kind or just ruler, but he never evoked the same level of terror King Harbin ensured his subjects possessed. Perceval didn't want love from his people; he desired fear and admiration. His goals vastly differed from what I observed of Evander and King Tallis during my time with them.

Next to enter was King Arden with his queen and Prince Jahier following close behind. The taste of worry slid over my tongue and filled my veins as I examined how the people of Venator reacted to their king. It wasn't as impactful as King Harbin's arrival, but he still brought forth anxiety in his subjects.

When King Tallis entered, the room was swept up in his charisma as he waved and winked at the people of Disparya. As a neutral kingdom known for its benevolence, the reaction among the crowd wasn't a surprising one. King Tallis was loved and respected throughout our continent.

The doors opened for the last time, and the ambiance changed instantly. Unease, wariness, excitement, admiration, fear, love, and desire crashed into me like a tidal wave. So many feelings at once that it was impossible to pinpoint which emotion belonged to whom.

Evander and Ainsley stepped over the threshold, hand in hand and looking more regal than I had ever seen—two rulers born for the roles they possessed. Their crowns were peaks of obsidian made from shadows never quite taking full form. Evander was donned in a black so dark it looked like he was draped in a starless night, swallowing any light whole. Initially, I believed Ainsley was wearing a dress fashioned from identical fabric. However, when she started to move, the light reflected on it, exposing a hidden hue entwined in the material.

My gaze slid to Olivier to find a sly smirk lighting his face. His eyes met mine, and my smile mirrored his as we shared a common thought.

Our queen wasn't dressed in the same dark shade as her husband, though it appeared that way at first glance. Her gown was red, a shade of wine so deep that it looked as though fresh blood spilled over her skin in the form of silk, cascading gently to the floor in delicate ripples.

Tenebrae's color mixed with Ministro's.

She twisted her wrist and dark rubies appeared next to the onyx diamonds in her crown, causing hushed murmurs to fall as realization settled over the crowd. Her choice was a reminder to King Harbin and a statement to the people of Disparya: when he fell, his throne would rightfully belong to her.

My eyes drifted to the King of Ministro, now baring his teeth in an outright snarl as he clutched the arm of his throne. Clearly, Ainsley's inherited title wasn't something he ever planned on releasing to the world. And *clearly,* my best friend knew that.

Ink would spill over parchment, spreading rumors far and wide about the Heir to Ministro, and making King Harbin's plans to rid the world of her that much harder. Any open attack on Ainsley's life after this display would undoubtedly lead back to him. Did I think it would cease his plans to have her killed? Not at all. But it would force him to go about it another way, buying her time.

I knew her choice of attire wasn't only to rattle Harbin, but also to let the people of Ministro—*her people*—know there was another option. There was a kinder ruler from a bigger and more prosperous kingdom who could lead them if they gave her the chance. With King Harbin working closely with Oberon, the most we could hope for was duress amongst his people.

Evander gleamed down at his queen with admiration, love, and respect, never once stepping in front of her as the other kings had done with their wives. She smiled up at him, and for a moment, it seemed like the rest of the world melted away.

The tender scene was interrupted by a quiet insult slung by an unmistakable source. Ainsley halted the moment the word '*whore*' reached her ears. Her hand released Evander's, her stare leaving him to drift to the dais where Dash was now standing, his muscles tense and chest moving heavily. Everyone in the room ceased breathing as they waited for the queen's response.

Ainsley's eyes held Dash's for one heartbeat, then two—far longer than any of us had expected, given her quick temper. Her mind was working, carefully laying out her next move as she bore into him. Finally, a smirk curved her lips.

"Fuck," Oli whispered before we both pushed our way through the crowd.

We had to get to her and stop her from making a rash mistake. Evander stood there, picking at his nails and looking bored by the entire situation. He wasn't going to help. He loved this vengeful side of his wife far too much.

Slowly, the Queen of Tenebrae stepped backward, never taking her eyes off Dash until she reached the woman who insulted her.

Rosella.

Ainsley studied her for a long moment, and to Rosella's credit, she didn't bend beneath the queen's stare. She was far too proud and hated Ainsley far too much to ever bow to her, despite her title.

Rosella held her shoulders back and her chin high as she waited for Ainsley to speak, but my friend never did. Her head swiveled once more, meeting Dash's bewildered gaze before she arched a single brow in question. He stepped forward as if to answer, but it wasn't quick enough.

Ainsley smiled as she wrapped herself and Rosella in darkness. A second later, a strangled scream pierced the air and all hell broke loose.

Rather than put an end to Ainsley's recklessness, Evander stepped backward to give his wife room to work. Oli and I lurched forward, shoving through the stunned guests as they let out shocked gasps.

Another scream broke through. *Shit.*

By the time we reached the cleared aisle, the other Kings of Disparya were there, studying the tornado of shadows and demanding it stop. King Harbin reached a hand outward as if calling to his Gifts. In response, the darkness spun faster and more violently as the lights flickered overhead. I was engulfed in fear, rage, and pride. The witnesses were scared, the kings angry, and Evander proud.

"Stop this instant!" King Arden demanded, moving quickly around her inky shield as if he could find a weak point to penetrate it.

"If she won't end it, then I will," King Harbin added.

Evander scoffed and rolled his shoulders. "You can try, but we both know how that worked out for you earlier."

Harbin charged for the King of Tenebrae so quickly that he was a faceless blur; however, his speed was short of impressive when pitted against Evander's Obscure. One second, Evander was standing before the King of Ministro; the next, he was behind him, spinning a shadowed dagger between his fingers.

"The only reason you're still breathing right now is because that attack was aimed at me and not my wife," Evander said. "But try that again, and it won't be the case."

Tensions peaked as discourse broke out among the crowd. This was supposed to be a celebration of a new queen, and here she was, terrorizing one of Disparya's citizens. Deserved or not, this wasn't the way she should have responded to Rosella.

Ainsley had always steered clear of her, never taking her bait or giving her more than a passing thought. So what made tonight so different? Why did that simple word cause so much fury?

Dash stepped forward as lightning flashed and thunder cracked outside. People screamed, startled by the deafening and sudden storm.

"Enough!" he demanded, flames licking his skin, poised and ready.

Darkness spilled over Evander, forming two blades in his hands as he squared his shoulders and prepared to take on the King of Caelum. In the blink of an eye, he disappeared into shadow and reappeared beside Dash to attack.

But the King of Caelum had anticipated his move, having already observed the strange Obscure he possessed multiple times now. Evander's blade was met with a shield so strong that the sound of metal clanged through the air at the strike.

The King of Tenebrae was momentarily stunned—we all were. Not only at the speed of Dash's defense but the strength of his shield. Evander stepped back, baring his teeth as he tried to figure out another way to attack, but Dash paid him no mind. His focus had never once shifted from the swirling darkness before him. I knew his confidence in the strength he possessed only pissed Evander off more.

"Tear it down now!" Dash yelled to Ainsley just as a whimper and sob escaped her tornado. "I SAID NOW, AINSLEY!"

At his demand, everything stopped. The darkness stopped swirling. The thunder stopped crashing. The crowd stopped murmuring. Everyone stopped breathing.

Slowly, her shadows came down around her like falling rain. Rosella was doubled over on the ground, clutching her head and sobbing as Ainsley stood over her, a predator protecting its kill.

"Please," Rosella whimpered, barely audible. "Please stop."

Dash's eyes flicked to her and then met Ainsley's with angry determination. I didn't try to reach out my Gift to smooth over the rising tensions. My two friends were too far gone.

"Enough," Dash said through clenched teeth. A demand, a promise, a warning, a plea. There were so many emotions radiating from that one word.

Ainsley arched her brow just as she had earlier but didn't move. Rosella whined once more.

"You made your point," he added cautiously. Ainsley didn't speak. She stayed where she was, her gaze flicking to Evander momentarily before moving back to Dash. The silence that passed between them in the long moments was deafening.

Ultimately, in a gesture of surrender, Ainsley reluctantly shifted slightly to the right. Rosella swiftly placed her hands on the ground and pushed herself up. Dash reached out to assist her, but she shoved passed him, sprinting towards the exit as tears flowed from her eyes.

"*Your Majesty*," Ainsley corrected as I tore my attention away from where Rosella had gone. Dash tilted his head, waiting for her to continue. "I'm a queen," she explained.

Dash scoffed, and Ainsley's hands balled into fists at her sides. "If you want to be a ruler, then act like it." He leaned closer, but the Queen of Tenebrae stood her ground. "*Ainsley*," he added.

She pressed forward, her lip curling in disdain.

"Send them away, Dashiell," King Harbin demanded. "Their court attacked yours. You are well within your right."

I anxiously held my breath as Dash meticulously observed first Ainsley, then Evander, and then every member of our present family, before finally turning his attention to me. Our eyes briefly locked, and in that single glance, I caught a glimpse of the boy whom I had grown up beside.

Suddenly we were climbing trees as children and sparring with wooden swords. We were staying up through the early morning hours and getting into far too much trouble. We were lending helping hands and open ears when the other needed it. We were discussing our hopes and dreams and planning a future we knew neither of us would ever have the freedom to claim.

The moment ended too soon, and I was left staring at the side of his face as he addressed the King of Ministro.

"No."

"No? What do you mean *no*?" King Harbin demanded.

"I wasn't aware there were multiple definitions of the word."

"They insult you and Caelum, and you resort to weakness!"

Dash shrugged, and I watched as different hues of red washed over Harbin's face. I could feast on his anger for a solid two weeks and still be full.

"I disagree," Dash said, nonchalantly glancing around at Tenebrae's court. "Ainsley," he dragged her name out like an insult, "has already proven she is rash, foolish, and inexperienced. I won't let my people fall prey to her destruction if she decides to throw another tantrum at the dismissal."

Ainsley's posture was rigid and her nose wrinkled like she was ready to snarl at him over the remark. Was he baiting her into a fight he claimed he didn't want? Her jaw dropped open and the ghost of a word left her mouth before he cut her off.

"Anyway," he said, turning his back on the queen. The disrespect was devouring her... and I would undoubtedly be the one having to listen to her rant about it later. "We've spent enough time entertaining Ainsley's outburst, and I will not have this feast go to waste."

A low rumble left Ainsley at the sound of her name once again on Dash's lips. Harbin smirked as he picked up on her anger too. The King of Ministro seemed delighted by Dash's determination to refrain from using her new title.

"Everyone," Dash announced, meeting the waiting faces of the residents of Disparya, "Take your seats and enjoy the meal."

At once, everyone did as commanded. Low murmurs of Ainsley's transgression bounced from spectator to spectator. Some thought her in the right for taking action, while others believed she had gone too far.

Dash turned and looked over at Ainsley for a fleeting second before his eyes traveled to me. I held his stare, detecting a question subtly interwoven in it—perhaps even an invitation. As I moved closer towards him, he deliberately turned his back on me and redirected his conversation towards Harbin.

"I know you do not want to participate in this facade of an alliance between our kingdoms and Tenebrae. I will respect your decision if you wish to excuse yourself and your court from tonight's events. However, before you do, I would like to discuss some matters that I have recently come across," whispered the King of Caelum. Harbin's eyes filled with curiosity as he looked at him.

My interest piqued.

"What kind of matters?" he asked.

"Plans my father had before his untimely death." Harbin's brow arched in curiosity before he nodded his acceptance of Dash's proposal. "Good. Let us eat first and then speak in private."

I looked around, but no one else had observed this exchange. Ainsley and Evander had already reached their seats at the front of the room, and Oli had joined Marce and Cal at the advisor's designated table. When my gaze traveled back to Dash and Harbin, they were already making their way to the royal table.

My mind circled around the information like a tireless bird in flight, constantly making loops and swirling but never quite landing. I didn't know if I should have shared what I overheard or kept it to myself and trusted that Dash had a bigger plan at play. But if I was wrong about my oldest friend... if I made an error in judgment, then it could cause countless lives to be lost.

"Are you okay?"

I jerked at the interruption and twisted toward the source of the question. Oli was watching me with a wary look, his mind trying to decipher what was flitting through mine.

"You've barely touched your food," he added. I glanced back down to my full plate. Everyone else's was nearly clean as they waited patiently for the ball portion of the night to begin.

"Yeah," I told him. "Being back in this place is just a lot to deal with."

It was not entirely untrue. For more than thirteen years, Caelum had been my home. And now, as I looked around a ballroom I had been in so many times, I felt like an outsider, a foreign stranger, someone who didn't belong. I had no allegiance to this place, no family present anymore. Dash seemed to want nothing to do with me, and I couldn't blame him for that. This place was no longer home to me.

Concern caressed my skin—a gentle touch I knew belonged to Olivier. Knowing me as well as he did, he could sense I wasn't being entirely truthful. My chest tightened with guilt and I turned in my seat, ready to disclose the conversation I had overheard.

But then Dash's face flashed before my mind.

It wasn't him now, but rather months ago, standing outside while the sun beat down on his inked flesh. His features had contorted with rage, acting as a facade to conceal the anguish he was fervently trying to repress. It was the day I divulged the truth about my initial suspicions of Ainsley's identity and the actions I took to protect her.

The word *betrayed* echoed in my thoughts alongside that image, repeating in the same broken cadence it was spoken. Dash had barely croaked out the word in one piece, his voice shaky and distant. His eyes were glassy, his muscles tense and knuckles white as he kept them balled into fists at his side.

The more confessions I made, the more he suffered, and the conversation only emphasized how avoidable it had all been. Every deep cut the three of us felt, the sleepless nights, the countless tears, the broken hearts—all of it. If only I had been honest with him from the start.

Betrayed.

That single word would haunt me forever, its weight measured in pain and a constant pressure in my chest. Each time it played in my mind, it felt as though shards of glass pierced my heart, shredding the organ more and more. I welcomed the agony. I deserved it.

"I love you," I said instead of another confession.

Oli returned the sentiment, though I could tell he wanted to push for the information he knew I was withholding.

A chair scraped loudly across the marble floor as Dash stood to address the subjects of Disparya. Just as I had seen his father do so many times, he made a speech graciously thanking the guests for their attendance and then clapped his hands loudly twice.

The room transformed.

23

Ainsley

The musicians played their instruments with precise expertise. Residents of Disparya whirled around the dance floor, laughing and soaking in the delicate symphonies as well as the more vibrant and upbeat pieces. Everyone seemed to have forgotten about my earlier altercation in their merriment; either that, or they chose not to let it damper their fun. Regardless, there wasn't a sullen face in the crowd.

Following dinner, nearly all of King Harbin's court dismissed themselves, not that the choice was surprising. I had suspected as much after Evander's constant insults and my little outburst.

My gaze swept across the couples twirling around, their bodies lost in the trance of the melody. It was moments like these, seeing the smiles on my people's faces and feeling the joy in their hearts, that I remembered all that we were fighting for and how much we had to lose.

As if he were a magnet, my focus was pulled toward one man standing at the opposite end of the room. He was deep in conversation with someone, but his dark stare was fixed on me. I smiled, and as if that was the signal he had been waiting for, he disappeared and then formed from shadow at my side. Apparently, now that his Obscure had been revealed to the kings, he didn't find the need to keep it hidden.

"Have I told you just how much I love this dress on you?"

His fingers started at the base of my spine and trailed up. Thanks to the design of the gown, my back was completely exposed, revealing my swirling shadow tattoo. He traced the inked darkness and I shivered beneath his warm touch.

"And how happy I am that *I'm* the one you come home to," he added as his mouth grazed the shell of my ear.

"Well then, you sound like a lucky man."

"I'm trying to be, but my wife keeps turning down my advances."

My smile widened as Evander dipped closer and kissed my cheek. I relished in the feel of his lips on my skin, the brush of his fingers, and his intoxicating scent. Images of naked bodies and tangled limbs surged through my thoughts, setting my body and blood on fire. Gods, I missed him. I missed *us*. Just two more days.

Two more days here and I could claim that piece of us back. I could get lost in our passion and drunk off our desire for one another. Two more days and I could be with the man that I loved in the way that only we could.

"I miss you," he murmured as if reading my thoughts. I pulled back and twisted to look up at him. A slight smile curved his lips, revealing the whisper of a dimple. I reached onto my toes and kissed it before pressing my lips softly to his.

"You both are nauseating," Marceline commented.

"Jealous you can't find someone for the night?" Evander jabbed, finally taking his eyes off me.

"Why settle for one when you can have two?"

"So that's what you scurried off to do the moment the celebration started instead of your job."

"The closets are deceivingly large," she replied back with a wink. "Besides, it's not like I missed anything. This place is overwhelmingly boring." Marce released a dramatic sigh as if the lack of carnage, blood, or drama would be the death of her. After my trial, near-death experience, and public dispute with Rosella, I was relieved to finally have a peaceful evening.

"Not to mention obsessed with fruit," Calidore added, coming up to us with Imogen at his side.

I blinked several times at the unexpected guest. Imogen hated parties and refused to attend any while I was living in Caelum. I narrowed my eyes suspiciously as her gaze met mine. She widened them a fraction as if to say, '*What?*' I lifted a brow and then made a show of looking between her and Cal, silently pointing out the distance between them—or, lack thereof.

Imogen rolled her eyes like I was a petulant child and determinedly looked away. Oh, something was *definitely* going on there. I wrote myself a mental note to hound her about it later, though I'd have better luck cracking Cal first.

"It's a bit much," Marce replied, commenting on Calidore's earlier observation. Something about their conversation tugged at me, and I turned to see Marce pinching a small red berry she had plucked from her drink.

"It seems to be everywhere," Evander agreed. I turned around and fully took in the scene for the first time since the room had been transformed for the ball.

My heart stopped.

I had been so caught up in the music, the sound of laughter, the way the room smelled like fresh peonies, and the twinkling lights overhead, that I didn't notice the thousands upon thousands of raspberries. They were incorporated into every pastry, cake, custard, baked, and frozen dessert. They were scattered upon table tops and arranged delicately in bouquets. They were plopped into every crystal glass of white wine.

And as I took a deep inhale, I saw they were placed in patterns atop the dessert table that lined the back wall away from the other food—a table that held nothing but hundreds of chocolate tartlets piped with an overwhelming amount of whipped cream.

My breathing was ragged and my knees buckled beneath me. I barely had time to grip Evander's arm before he caught my side, keeping me upright. "Give us a minute," he directed to our company.

Marce and Cal drifted back through the crowd, but Imogen hovered. I could feel Evander's distress, and I wanted so badly to ease it, but I couldn't. I didn't have words for what I was being wracked with.

"Love, what's going on?"

I turned to Imogen and addressed her instead. "Not you?" I asked. It wasn't a question but more of a desperate need for clarification.

"Not me," she answered.

Imogen hadn't known about the significance of the harmless fruit, but given my reaction to it, I had no doubt she knew now. The room spun as my chest continued to rise and fall heavily. Warmth spread along my cheek, and I reached up to catch a fallen tear. After all that Dashiell and I had been through, all I had done to him, all he had said and felt; After *everything*... he was still proud of me. And he didn't let our fight get in the way of telling me that—in a way that only I would understand.

My eyes darted left and right, frantically searching the crowd for brown hair and deep teal eyes. "Where is he?" I demanded, setting my focus on Imogen. She was hesitant for a reason I didn't understand, a wary look sliding across her features.

"He left just after the ball started," she finally said. "After your conversation earlier, he didn't want to impose on a night meant to celebrate you." I swallowed hard and felt even more like an asshole.

"I need to find him," I told her as I began to do just that. Before I made it more than a step, Imogen grabbed my elbow to stop me.

"No." The word was clipped and final, leaving no room for argument. I met her hazel eyes with a pinched brow. I didn't understand why she wouldn't let me try to make things right.

"Imogen—"

"Evander, will you give us a minute, please?" Imogen said, cutting me off.

My husband looked cautiously between my maiden and me. If he was hurting by my need to find Dashiell, he wasn't letting it show. Without a word, he turned and strode through the crowded room.

Imogen released my arm once Evander was far enough away. "You need to leave him be," she instructed.

"No, I need to—"

"You've done enough, Ainsley." I didn't miss the sternness in her tone or the way she drew out the words like she was exhausted with me.

She didn't understand how badly I needed to fix what was broken. I wanted to step around her and continue on my quest, but her stance told me she'd sooner try to take me down than let me pass. She was being protective—shielding him from the hurt she thought I'd bring. For the first time, I felt anger toward Imogen. She was keeping me from him.

"You didn't see him after your fight," she offered quietly, taking my hand in hers. I pulled it back out of her grasp. I didn't want to be comforted—I wanted to see Dashiell.

Imogen sighed in frustration but not defeat. Something told me there was no way she was going to give in to my demand. This wasn't her usual bout of trying to prevent me from doing something stupid; this was her choosing a side—and it wasn't the one that belonged to me.

"I know you want to make things right, and I truly hope you are able to do that...but not tonight. He needs time and space, Ainsley. He's owed that much."

I wanted to argue, but she was right. I had done enough to him and it wasn't fair to push before he was ready. Perhaps he'd never be. Maybe this raspberry gesture wasn't an olive branch or a white flag; maybe it was a goodbye. I felt sick at the thought.

"Okay," I conceded, my heart fracturing at the word.

Imogen's fingers brushed my arm in a small effort to comfort me. "Try to enjoy your night."

I didn't respond or acknowledge her. My focus was solely on counting my breaths and rapid heartbeat as I worked to calm myself. If I wasn't careful, I'd be dragged below the surface and drowned in the depths of my own mind.

Dashiell's emotions earlier were still a sad song in my blood, with every wave of hurt and rush of betrayal playing on repeat. Coupled with my own feelings on our argument, I was more susceptible to losing myself. I had to channel my energy on not letting my control slip. Even a gentle sway off the path could lead to my temper exploding or my heart shattering into pieces.

I hated my Empathi Gift. I didn't want to feel everything at once. It was too much of a struggle every day to keep it together. And now that I had the third and final Gift from Tenebrae, I had more power thrumming through me than ever before. Somehow, the magic I received from the land sharpened *all* of my Gifts, not just the ones belonging to the kingdom

I now ruled. Which meant that holding myself together and shoving away everyone else's emotions was that much more of a challenge.

An arm snaked around my stomach and I was pulled until my back pressed into a hard chest. I closed my eyes and tilted my head against Evander. "Breathe, love."

His other arm curled around me until I was caged in completely. My fingers gripped his forearms, my nails digging into his flesh as I tried to anchor myself.

"You're okay. I have you," he repeated continuously as he began gently swaying our bodies to the soft music. To anyone watching, we would look like two lovers enjoying a dance.

I thanked the Gods for my observant and attentive husband. I wasn't sure if the depth of what I was feeling was strong enough to translate through our Soul Bond, but I knew it wouldn't matter. He was always acutely aware of what I needed before I was.

We swayed from one song into the next, even though it was the kind meant for quick movements and changing partners. Evander held me through it all as each melody bled into another. I focused on his breathing, on the rise and fall of his chest where his body met mine as I tried to match my rhythm to his. I wasn't sure how much time had passed when I was finally stable enough to turn around in his arms.

My face buried into his chest as I took long, deep inhales, letting his scent of cedar and fresh snow comfort me in the way it always had. "I'm sorry," I whispered.

A finger slid beneath my chin and tilted it up until I was forced to meet his patient stare. He shook his head, rejecting my apology. He always hated when I did that—try to apologize for how I felt. He wanted me to own it.

"I want to try and make things right," I explained. Evander nodded and ran his hands up and down my back as the crowd erupted in soft applause and the next dance began.

"Then you will." His fingers reached down to interlace with mine. He gently spun me out and back into him, this time positioning us for a proper dance.

"Imogen won't allow me to. She's refusing to let me go to him."

My maiden had always been on my side, especially when it came to anything I experienced with Dashiell, so what had changed? Why was she coming to his aid instead of mine? What could possibly have gone on in the months since I returned to Tenebrae to cause her to take such a stance? I huffed out a frustrated breath.

"Would you have wanted him to do the same?" Evander asked.

I pulled back to look at him questioningly. He spun me again, this time keeping a gap between us as I came back to him. We moved quicker to the beat, now truly blending in with the rest of the crowd.

"When you first came to Tenebrae," he elaborated. "When you were hurt and feeling betrayed, would you have wanted him to come to you?"

The inside of my cheek pinched between my teeth as I pondered. Reluctantly, I allowed myself to slink back to those first few days I had been in my home kingdom. My love for Dashiell then was overwhelming, which made the sting of his betrayal feel like a fatal blow. I could barely stomach food and my eyes had always run dry from the constant array of tears streamed every night. No, I would not have wanted Dashiell to come to me. It would have shattered me so thoroughly that time wouldn't have been enough to piece me back together.

The realization in my eyes was all Evander needed for confirmation.

"What am I supposed to do in the meantime?"

The length of my patience wasn't a secret. Not only was I stubborn and quick-tempered, but it was nearly impossible for me not to just take what I wanted. I hated waiting. It always made me feel anxious and uneasy like a thousand spiders were crawling over my skin.

Without my permission, my body flooded with Dashiell's earlier emotions. Not making things better between us was the equivalent of seeing a wounded animal and not offering it aid, instead walking by and letting it suffer and writhe in agony. This Gift was more like a curse. I breathed his pain in deep, letting it fill every crevice before pushing as much of it as I could back out through a long exhale. It didn't help.

A spark of sadness flickered over Evander's face before it disappeared and was replaced with a smile that didn't reach his eyes. I was hurting him, and he was trying not to let it show. Before I could utter an apology, the music transformed into a slower, haunting melody.

Evander pulled me flush against him, his heart a steady beat against my chest.

"It's up to you," he murmured before placing his cheek against my head. "But I, for one, would very much like to dance with my wife."

Guilt wracked through me again, this time aimed at the man who held me in his arms. I had been so consumed with making things right between Dashiell and me that I didn't take into account what it was doing to Evander. Gods, I was selfish, wanting everything but giving nothing in return.

For the second time, Van had to feel the world try to pull me away from him, had to feel my soul being ripped from his grasp as if it was his own. Instead of comforting him, I was complaining about giving Dashiell his well-deserved space.

And he let me.

He stood there, holding me together while I struggled not to break over someone else. If I needed any more proof that I didn't deserve the man I now called my husband, there it was.

I tilted my head and pushed onto my toes. My lips molded to his, moving against them with fervent need. A simple apology wasn't enough to show how sorry I was or how much I loved him.

But this kiss would have to be.

My fingers combed through his soft, dark hair, grabbing hold of the delicate strands to keep him to me. He responded by deepening our embrace. His tongue swept over mine in the barest of touches, exploring, teasing, claiming. This wasn't a kiss shared between lovers behind closed doors. It wasn't undiluted passion and need. This was pure love—an unmistakable desire to express what words could not.

Evander's hands traveled up my back before gliding under my neck and through my hair. He held my face possessively as he angled my head to allow him better access. I didn't mind. Thoughts of anything but his gentle touch and the way he tasted vacated my mind as if nothing else had ever resided there.

"Like I said, nauseating," Marceline said as she passed. I twisted to see her dragging some poor man across the dance floor, seemingly against his will. Tomas had always been nice enough, but right now, he looked utterly terrified at whatever Marce had in store for him.

My stifled smile was interrupted by a nose pressing to mine in a gesture I went from loathing to never wanting to be without. I returned it before crushing my lips to his again to take more of what I wanted.

24

Ainsley

I stared intently at the tendril of shadow that weaved through the fingers of my left hand before jumping to my right. Back and forth it went like a cat chasing its tail. My head lolled toward the ceiling as I let out an annoyed sigh.

We had been sitting in the throne room for over an hour now, unable to begin our meeting thanks to the tardiness of two of Disparya's kings. My suggestion to start without them was unanimously shot down by those who were actually present. Van was determined to wait in hopes his call didn't go unanswered.

A second shadow tendril slithered over my fingers, entwining with the first. I smiled at the way Evander's magic felt against my skin—warm, protective, playful. I glanced to my right to find him twisted toward me on his throne, his cheek resting upon his propped elbow as he watched me.

"I'm bored," I whispered, sending my shadow moving at a quicker speed to chase Van's. "Not to mention insulted," I added, throwing an annoyed glare at the empty thrones designated for King Arden and King Harbin.

Evander smirked as he said, "Welcome to politics, my love." I rolled my eyes and continued to whine.

"Entertain me."

"I'd love to, but I didn't think you'd want an audience. I'd be more than willing to give it a go if that's what you're interested in now." He gave a devious wink, prompting me to smack his arm as he chuckled.

"You know that's not what I was referring to," I scolded.

Evander grinned like he had no shame, and I let out an exhausted sigh. "Why don't you practice your Tremo Gift on Felix?" he suggested. I shrugged, choosing to ignore that he offered my best friend up as a test subject to be terrorized.

"I'd rather practice my Obscure."

"You know what it is?" Evander was excited by the idea.

"No. I can feel an extra layer of magic different from my Gifts but can't access it. It's like it's waiting to be called, but I don't know how to."

Van nodded thoughtfully as if he could relate. "It'll come out when you least expect it. Mine manifested months after I became king when Oli was trying to make me take a bath. I didn't want to, so I ran, and right before he caught me, I disappeared into shadows only to reappear in my closet."

I smiled at the image of my husband as a very stubborn five-year-old running through the halls to avoid something as simple as a bath. It was hard not to resent the life that had been stolen from me when I listened to memories about the boy I should have grown up with. Though it was a bitter sting, it made me cherish the time I had with him now all that much more.

Just then, the doors to the throne room opened with a loud creak. I put my magic away and straightened in my chair, ready to finally get this damn meeting started. Only one figure crested the threshold—Prince Jahier of Venator.

He hurried to the center of the room and quickly took his seat next to his father's throne.

"I apologize for my tardiness. It was a difficult morning," he explained. He looked exhausted as he slumped into his chair and dragged a hand down his face.

"Your father...?" Dashiell asked.

My chest ached at the sound of his voice and the pain I could still feel from him. He was careful to keep his emotions in check, but that didn't stop the tiny traces of hurt from slipping into my grasp, adding to the surmounting pile I already possessed.

Last night, I had done as requested—I let him be. And this morning, I didn't try to speak to him, hoping he would come to me or give me some sign that he was ready.

His obvious determination to avoid eye contact with me was a clear indication that he was not.

Felix seemed to be in a similar boat. Oftentimes, I'd find him staring at Dashiell, moving a fraction closer only to retreat. It was like he couldn't make up his mind on what to do. I knew that my desire to make things right between us was nothing compared to what Felix was experiencing.

"Coming," Jahier replied, pulling my focus from the King of Caelum. "At least, that's what he told me after hours of trying to convince him to. Like I said, it was a difficult morning."

"Good," Dashiell stated. "Then we'll begin the meeting momentarily."

"I'd give it more than a moment. My father went to speak to Harbin. Hopefully, it was to encourage him to join as well."

I wasn't surprised that the King of Ministro and his court withdrew from the celebration last night, but I was slightly unsettled when he hadn't shown up this morning. My trial was now over, and this meeting was to discuss the pending war against Disparya. By choosing not to participate, Harbin was all but declaring his allegiance to Oberon and the land of Pravus.

No one had spoken to Brandle; it was far too risky to do so here. We needed him to keep up the pretense that he was on his stepfather's side for as long as possible. He was our inside source, and if he was discovered, we would lose what little advantage we had over the king.

"Then we wait longer," Evander announced just as Dashiell was beginning to speak. It was a tiny power play to insert dominance and show the new king he wouldn't be making all the decisions for the group. Evander was far too cocky and arrogant to let Dashiell, of all people, have the last say.

As if Dashiell recognized the move for what it was, the corner of his lips twitched. "Yup," he said, claiming that final word.

"Good," Van retorted.

"Great," Dashiell threw back.

Gods help us.

I got up and strode for the table across the room to make myself a cup of coffee. Jahier, Tallis, Felix, and Oli appeared at my side a moment later, looking exhausted and annoyed as random synonyms were thrown back and forth between Evander and Dashiell. Something told me the morning was only about to get more difficult.

"I think it's time," I told Van as he stared at the large oak doors across the room, defeat creasing his brow. After Jahier arrived, we agreed to give the two kings an additional hour, but they hadn't shown up.

"I agree with her," the Prince of Venator added from where he and Cal had been leaning against the windows as they peered over the land.

Evander released a breath and hung his head, frustrated over the situation. I placed a comforting hand on his shoulder, knowing full well he was blaming himself for issuing the assembly to begin with. If it had been me, I would have been doing the same thing, convinced that because I made the request, I was responsible for the millions of lives that were now affected.

At face value, that was true, but when you peeled back the layers, Harbin and Arden were the ones who decided to take the risk. They were the ones who held the lives of their people in their hands.

Van sat straighter and twisted to face me. "Five more minutes," he said, his voice containing a small remnant of hope placed just out of reach. I offered a weak smile and nodded. Five more minutes.

The room was silent as the minutes ticked by, everyone growing increasingly more anxious as time stretched on. I shifted uncomfortably on my throne as my own foreboding feelings began to take root. Evander sensed my distress and threw me a worried glance, his hand reaching for mine in comfort.

"What is it?" he asked.

I shook my head as my brows pinched, unable to form the words. "I can't explain it, but something doesn't feel right."

As soon as the words left my mouth, Dashiell straightened, his features morphing into a confused look. Evander was next, followed by Tallis, all of us rulers receiving the same odd sensation of warning.

"What is that?" Jahier whispered. I turned my attention to find him leaning over the window ledge as he studied the distance.

"I don't see anything," Cal added.

"You don't possess my Gift as an Oculi."

A flittering sound, like the wings of a bird in flight, filled the space. The entire room, excluding Jahier, turned towards the center of the semi-circle of thrones as a piece of transfer parchment materialized out of thin air and floated to the ground.

Dashiell walked to receive the paper and hesitantly flipped it open. A panicked expression appeared on his face as he breathed heavily. The two kings and I immediately rose from our seats.

"It's from Brandle," Dashiell announced, his voice slightly shaking. I swallowed the terror in my throat as my eyes stayed glued to the letter he held open for us to see.

In a delicate script, a single command was written.

Get out. Right now!

"What in the—" was all Jahier could say before the palace shook from an explosion.

Everyone dove to the ground, and Evander covered me with his body as debris rained from the ceiling and pelted his shield. Dust filled the room alongside the screams of thousands of residents as chaos erupted.

Coughing, both Evander and I pushed to our feet and took off into the crowded hall.

"We need to get out of here," I yelled over the commotion as people fled left and right, determined to escape as another explosion rocked the palace.

Evander took my hand, and a heartbeat later, we were standing under the blazing sun in the garden. Fissures crawled up the stone walls of the palace like roots beneath the earth, growing in size with each passing moment. A portion of the western wing had been reduced to rubble, a giant pile of gravel now sitting where a solid structure had once been.

People screamed and cried as they flooded onto the lawn, desperately trying to get free of the damage. I scanned our surroundings, looking for our enemy but coming up short. There was nothing but woods and sprawling hills in the distance.

Another crack whipped through the open air as the palace continued to split, causing pieces of the roof to shift and topple.

"Van!" I screamed, directing my finger at two innocent people standing just below where the stones were about to fall. A heartbeat later, he appeared beside them, traversing them to safety just as the structure crashed to the earth.

"We need to get everyone away from here!" I yelled.

Staying in the vicinity of the attack was going to result in lives lost unless we could quickly stop the enemy; the only problem was that we had no idea where they were. More people spilled from the entrances, including almost everyone who had been in the room with us.

Dashiell and Tallis immediately jumped into the fray, helping to direct everyone to safety as my family ran to our side.

"What do you need?" Felix demanded, looking over the chaotic scene.

"Help get the residents to safety. There are too many people, and I'm not sure how much longer the building is going to hold." As I said the words, a flying arrow caught the corner of my eye.

I watched as it landed in the center of a slightly discolored patch of grass at the far end of the palace, opposite to where we had gathered. A few seconds later, the arrow exploded, causing the foundation to shake again.

"Go and do it now!" I ordered before sprinting off in the direction of where the arrow had landed.

I felt Marce's presence at my side before I saw her. There was no chance my court was going to allow me to go anywhere this dangerous without someone with me.

"What is all of that?" she asked, gesturing to the tiny, dark patches of grass scattered across the lawn.

"Targets."

She swore beneath her breath just as a voice yelled from above. We whipped our heads up to see Jahier pointing from the throne room window.

"Just beyond those oaks on the western side!" he shouted, pointing to the woods across the lawn. "Two on the ground and one in the trees!"

"Shield the palace! Put multiple in place!" I ordered.

Jahier did as I instructed, creating a shimmering force field the length of the building, and yelled at the others with him to do the same. Marce and I didn't waste another second and sprinted to where our attackers were hidden.

We stayed out of sight as we weaved between the trees, watching helplessly as two more arrows were let loose only to slam into Jahier's shield. They exploded on impact, shaking the ground and causing his magic to bend, but not break. I wasn't sure how much longer they would be able to hold the protective barrier in place.

"Can you sense any of them?" I asked Marceline as we stopped momentarily to catch our breath.

She was quiet for a moment as she concentrated on her Gift. "Yes, but I can only take out one person at a time. As soon as I do, they'll know we're here, and we'll lose the element of surprise. They could get away before we claim them all."

It was risky, but we had no other choice.

"Do it," I commanded.

Marce closed her turquoise eyes and raised her hands to the side, calling to her Gift. I watched in amazement as she silently worked, appearing as if she was sleeping rather than slipping into someone's mind to create living nightmares.

Her blond curls swayed in the gentle breeze, and the light filtering through the trees cast dancing shadows across her ebony skin—a beautiful goddess of death. A smirk curved her full lips just as a thump sounded from the distance; someone falling out of a tree.

"We need to hurry," she said, her eyes fluttering open before we took off again to hunt our prey. As long as we kept them on the run, they wouldn't have time to fire off exploding arrows at innocent people. That alone was worth the risk we took by exposing ourselves.

My magic tingled below the surface, that extra power I couldn't yet access making itself more apparent. We ran quicker, closing the distance with each stride we took. Soon, I could make out the two figures rushing through the brush of Caelum's forest.

"I see them!" I told Marce as I crafted a dagger and tossed it through the air, narrowly missing one of the men.

My magic surged again, fueling me with more power than I knew what to do with. I pushed my legs farther and extended my hand, calling for my shadows so I could craft another weapon.

My darkness slipped from between my fingers the way it always had, but this time, it felt different. It shot forward, slithering through the woods until it passed the men and formed a tall barrier of inky black.

Our attackers skidded to a halt, allowing us to catch up. I wasn't sure why they didn't just push through my shadows, as they were only meant as a way to slow them down as they ran in the dark. The men spun around and one of them lurched forward, colliding with Marce in a dance of swords.

I kept my eyes on the second one, something vaguely familiar about him, though I couldn't place what it was.

Until I saw his scarred hands.

"You," I sneered, my mind flashing through my encounter with him in the orchard and again in Agnitio. His face had always been shrouded by shadow, whether from his own making or the bend of the light, but now I could see him clearly.

Scars marred his face from his forehead down to the lips set in a snarl. His dark eyes were made prominent by the blue veining and purple hue beneath his pale flesh. His teeth were yellow, rot and decay encasing nearly every visible patch of bone. Shadows curled in his palms as he readied himself for our fight.

"You should have died long ago, but today will have to do," he vowed, setting his stance as he crafted his Gift into a longsword.

My magic pulsated beneath the surface, a steady thump, thump, thump that reverberated in my bones and roared in my head. The power within me grew intense and heavy like lead, weighing me down as I tried to force it free from my flesh.

But my shadows wouldn't come.

At least, not in a form I had ever seen before.

Pain crackled along my spine, sharp and blazing hot. I squirmed at the agony of trying to stay upright and not lose focus on my target. If my concentration slipped, even for a second, it would cost me my life.

An unavoidable scream tore from my clenched teeth as something strong and unyielding ripped from my back and plunged into the air. The man's eyes sliced upward, widening in horror at whatever he saw. I followed his stare and watched as a long black tendril of shadow attached to my spine lengthened into a spear aimed directly at him.

He turned and sprinted, but a heartbeat later, that tendril shot forward, piercing him in the back like a scorpion's tail, fast and precise. He yelled out in agony, but I wanted to see the look on his face as he suffered. As if the magic knew that, it lifted the man from the ground and turned him towards me.

I walked forward, my back no longer in pain now that I was filled with rage. He had beaten me until I was on the brink of death, enjoying every second of the misery he inflicted. His dark stare grew frantic as I came closer, allowing me to taste his fear in the air. His limbs hung limp at his side, the darkness severing the nerve in his spine that granted him mobility, leaving him paralyzed and utterly at my mercy.

Good.

"You've lived far longer than you deserve to," I told him as I stopped inches away from his broken body. He tried to speak, yet nothing but gargling noises and scarlet blood escaped his lips. What a shame.

I called for my magic again—for my Obscure; that new and vicious part of me that thirsted for this man's death as much as I did. My skin prickled, and I held up my hand curiously as the magic was directed there. The tip of my fingers darkened as if dipped in ink, and my nails lengthened into deadly sharp claws.

A strangled noise came from the man who desired my death, but I paid him no mind as I pressed my new weapon to his chest.

"Ainsley." Evander's voice was a gentle command drowned out by my pounding blood and the strength of this power. I wanted this man to suffer and so did my magic. We were starving—gluttonous—and it was time to feast.

My claws punctured his flesh, slicing through muscle and tissue as easily as if they were soft butter. He choked on a scream, or perhaps a sob, causing his blood to spray across my face. I enclosed my hand, letting the claws shred through his heart piece by piece.

My name was said again, but I was too focused, too angry, too *hungry* for his demise to stop my task. I pulled the flayed heart from his chest, watching the blood pool on the grass as I squeezed the muscle until it burst.

My shadowed scorpion's tail retracted, and the man slumped to the ground, void of life. I dropped the shredded chunk of organ beside him and turned away.

My gaze quickly landed on my audience, my eyes darting between Jahier, Tallis, Dashiell, Marceline, Olivier, Felix, Calidore, and Evander. They were... *afraid.*

I tried to call back my Obscure, but it wasn't finished. There was too much destruction caused by evil people in this world, and my magic didn't want to rest until I made those who were responsible pay for their crimes. It was too angry—*I* was too angry.

I couldn't stop.

My claws lengthened more, and Evander's hands cupped my cheeks as he sank to my eye level.

"Love," he whispered in a soft plea.

"I can't." My voice trembled into a broken whisper as the fear of my magic consumed me. It was too strong and too powerful for me to control. "I don't know how to make it stop."

My fingers shook as I latched onto him, gripping the fabric of his jacket to keep me grounded.

"Just like your Gifts, this magic is a part of you. *You* control *it*, not the other way around. Just breathe and concentrate. Will it to obey," he instructed.

Swallowing my fear, I nodded and closed my eyes to focus. I caressed the strange power, coaxing it like a scared animal, back into its cage. It didn't want to listen, but it also wasn't actively fighting against me. I realized then that this magic was the manifestation of my anger. It was cruel and dangerous and enacted the brutal retribution I longed to claim.

"Breathe," Evander instructed.

I took a long and deep breath as I drank him in, savoring the feel of his heart beneath my touch and his calming scent. Cool and soothing magic brushed along me, further dousing the raging flames of my fire.

Slowly, the tips of my fingers returned to normal and the darkness around me faded into nothing.

"There you go, love," Evander encouraged, kissing my forehead as I continued to lock away each ounce of my Obscure.

Once I was sure nothing remained, my eyes fluttered open. Van let out a relieved sigh as his thumbs swept back and forth over my cheeks tenderly.

"It isn't enough to manifest objects from shadows—you have to control them too?" he joked in an attempt to make light of the fear I knew he felt within me.

"The Obscure is too much power."

"It's not," Evander argued.

"It is," Tallis cut in, causing us both to glance in his direction. "I adore Ainsley, but I won't pretend her Obscure isn't dangerous. If she can't control her anger, then she can't control this magic, and we all just witnessed what it's capable of."

Evander's hands slid to my waist, pulling me closer against him as if readying to battle anyone who tried to harm me because of my power. I sent my Empathi Gift into him, wrapping around his heart and slowing the racing pace. He released a calm breath as the tension eased from his body.

"What can I do to help?" Evander asked.

"She needs balance. Be that for her," Tallis instructed. "Be the peace to her rage, the calm to her chaos. She won't survive without it."

25

Dashiell

My fingers pressed into the wood of the desk as I pored over the names of the people who perished today. It had taken hours to account for everyone and even longer to search amid the rubble. Tallis was gracious enough to use his Gift to scan the area for any signs of magic buried in the debris.

We only pulled out one survivor.

Sixty-three men and women were lost to the attack. Thankfully, Imogen assured me that all the children were safe, only abstaining minor cuts and bruises that would be tended to immediately. Still, those sixty-three souls would be mourned by mothers, fathers, sisters, brothers, husbands, wives, and children. They were my people, *my* responsibility.

And I failed them.

I should have known Harbin and Arden were up to something the moment they chose not to take part in the assembly this morning. For months, I had believed they allied themselves with Lord Oberon of Pravus in the same way I recently discovered my father had. Last night, when I received verification from Harbin himself, I should have suspected this was a possibility.

As soon as the feast was finished, he was eager to learn of the bullshit discovery I had fabricated for the sole purpose of making him believe Caelum was still in his pocket. Ever since Perceval's death, Harbin had been trying to get closer to me so he could manipulate and form me into a king who would do his bidding.

That shit wasn't going to happen.

Judging by the events that transpired this morning, I take it he knew that, too. Disparya was officially at war with itself, and my people were the first of what would be a long list of causalities.

"Have their families been notified?" I asked Dickhead—sorry, Gideon—as I read through the list of names for the third time.

He cleared his throat in that annoying ass way he always did. Gods, I hated him.

"Yes." I looked up from the paper and raised a brow. "Your Majesty," he quickly corrected. He knew my title; he just liked to insult me any chance he could.

Gideon was always a kiss-ass to my father. He respected and feared Perceval, but with me... Well, I would always be that sixteen-year-old boy who pissed on his bed when he ordered Felix to be lashed because I was late to a meeting. Gideon loved his position of power, so he'd put up with me as long as necessary if it meant he got to keep it.

I pointed to a name in the center of the page. "What about her?" I asked. Gideon peered over the paper, his face twisting in confusion. "She and your daughter were close. You may want to inform her—"

"She'll find out when she finds out, Your Majesty," he dismissed.

Nice. What a piece of shit.

I slid the paper away and instead focused on another—the list of damage to the palace. Gideon cleared his throat, once, twice, three times.

"Would you like to see a Medicus, Gideon? It sounds like you may be ill." I didn't look up from the parchment.

"I would like to discuss the agreement you made, Your Majesty."

Of course he wanted to. I had purposely left him out of the arrangement when I made it this afternoon following the attack. Caelum had to choose a side, and I wasn't going to stand with the wrong one.

"My decision is final."

"We cannot trust Tenebrae, but Ministro and Venator have long been allies to the Crown. We should stand with *them* and Lord Oberon like your father wanted."

"My father is no longer here," I pointed out, mentally noting his determination to undermine me.

"I just think—"

"Then don't," I interrupted, finally looking up from my task to glare at him. "Caelum is aligned with Agnitio and Tenebrae, the only other two kingdoms still a part of Disparya. Do not question my decision again. Is that understood?" Dickhead swallowed hard and nodded. "Great. You may leave."

He bowed at my dismissal and rushed angrily from the room. The moment the latch clicked in place and I was alone, I reached for the book Evander had provided me on the mysterious stones. Part of the terms of the three remaining kingdoms working together was complete and total honesty—the deal we were brokering wasn't going to work without it.

Hesitantly, we all agreed and began sharing the secrets we still kept. Tallis didn't have much; only that he had been working with Evander for years and was a loyal ally to Tenebrae. Evander shared information about their quest for a kingdom that had only ever been a myth to me. I wasn't sure it existed, but the King of Tenebrae was certain, so who was I to argue?

Ainsley explained the importance of three rare stones, one of which was in my father's ring. I knew about the ruby's magic, but I had no clue about the others.

When Perceval started requiring his generals to wear rings, I became increasingly suspicious of what they actually were. Enforcing jewelry to be part of a soldier's uniform made little sense to me at the time.

One afternoon, after watching a general disappear into thin air after placing the ring on his finger, I confronted Perceval about where they came from. He told me they were a present from Lord Oberon, our ally from Pravus. My first thought was *Ainsley*.

She had vanished months prior with no sign of her or Felix's whereabouts. Any letter I sent to friends in other kingdoms always yielded in a dead end. So when Perceval wanted to send Caelumian soldiers to Pravus in exchange for more stones, I volunteered to go in hopes of finding my fiancé and best friend.

Instead, I discovered a brewing war.

When it was my turn to share information with the group, I told them all I had seen in Pravus. I divulged the thousands of soldiers from Caelum and Ministro who were mixed into the ranks of Oberon's own army. I explained that nearly every soldier hailing from Pravus had a patch to indicate which two Gifts they possessed. Oberon had created an army fully made up of soldiers who were products of Conjoining.

It wasn't news any of us wanted to hear.

We agreed to join forces in all aspects of our endeavors. We would find the stones, find Inmuto, and fight for what was left of Disparya and our people. Our numbers together were still significantly less than what Pravus now had with Venator and Ministro at its side, but both Jahier and Evander were working on that.

The King of Tenebrae had connections on the continent to our east, Vorsutos, who he ensured we could count on. And Jahier swore that the soldiers he led for over two decades would follow him and not his father, crippling Venator's aid to Pravus by nearly half. The numbers weren't ideal, but they were silver-lined with hope.

I released a heavy breath as I flipped the page to another stone I had never seen before, written in a language that wasn't my tongue. A throat cleared, and I whipped my head up to yell at Gideon once more when a different figure entered my periphery.

"I thought you were leaving," I told Evander as I directed my attention back to the book. He was the last person I expected or wanted to see, especially right now.

Slow and rhythmic footsteps echoed in the room, but I kept my eyes on the paper, refusing to look up. He stopped, just a foot away. "She wants to talk to you first." His voice was soft and calm, not at all how I expected those words to leave his mouth.

My eyes flicked from the book to him as he stood there, patiently waiting for my response. "I'm busy."

I couldn't see her. Not after everything we had said to each other in the Sanctuary. That fight had destroyed me.

As soon as I reached my office, I slumped to the floor and shattered into fragments I never fully pieced back together. There wasn't enough glue in this realm that could mend just how broken I was. Imogen discovered me shortly after and rushed to my side, comforting me just as she had done for months now—like I was still that small child she sat with night after night when my mother died.

Seeing Ainsley this week was hard enough; anything more, and I'd be asking for the pain.

"You owe her this," he said, and my mouth dropped open to argue.

But nothing came out. He was right. I had wronged her in more ways than I could ever count and owed more than I could ever give.

His face softened, and his voice was little more than a gentle request. "Please," he whispered. There was more love for her in that one word than any kiss could hold. He was breaking, and not because she wanted to see her ex-fiance, but because she was in pain. She was hurting, so he was, too.

"Where is she?"

"I don't know," he answered. "She said *you* would." My mind flashed to the one place I knew she would go.

With a deep and steadying exhale, I got up and headed to find her.

26

Felix

I was covered in sweat and filth, but far too exhausted to bathe. By the looks of Oli, Marce, Cal, and Imogen, the same could be said for them. Even Onyx and my newest best friend, Nova, had collapsed onto the bedroom floor in a heap of fur and fangs as they snored the afternoon away.

Despite the exhaustion reverberating through every bone in my body, the effort had been worth it. Thankfully, the only main damage to the palace had been the western wing, which tended to remain empty and unused. Had our enemy attacked the eastern side, the effects would have been catastrophic, resulting in many more lives lost. We were lucky today.

"So she can control shadows now?" Imogen asked for the hundredth time as she tried to make sense of Ainsley's new power.

"Seems like it," I replied through a yawn.

"But why *that* power?"

Oli emitted a soft groan beside me while burying his face deeper into his pillow, equally frustrated by Imogen's incessant stream of questions for which we lacked answers. I knew she was only asking because she was worried and hated not understanding a situation, especially when it came to Ainsley.

I wanted to tell her just to ask the Queen of Tenebrae, but as soon as our little truth circle meeting ended, she and Van disappeared. That had been at least an hour ago and we hadn't seen or heard from them since. If she was having sex, it clearly wasn't good enough to the point of the entire palace hearing her. And if that wasn't the case, there obviously was no point in doing it.

Tonight, *everyone* would know exactly what Oli and I were up to.

"Because that's what she has," Marce added, throwing herself on the other side of Oli as she placed a pillow over her face.

"I don't like your tone," Imogen replied.

"Hey," Cal said gently, coming over to the end of the bed where Imogen was seated. He slid a hand over hers as he looked her in the eyes. "She's okay. We're not going to let anything happen to her."

My mouth dropped open as I watched the exchange. Did no one else see what was going on here? Cal and Imogen were practically fucking in front of us, the sexual tension so thick I could cut it with a knife, and no one else besides me even cared! Gods, where the hell was Ainsley when I needed her?

"This magic..." Imogen began.

"Is called her Obscure," Evander finished, appearing in the bedroom doorway with Tallis at his side.

"I don't know what that means."

Evander disappeared into shadows, reforming a foot away from Imogen. She gasped in shock and nearly fell off the damn bed before Cal caught her and kept her upright.

"Can Ainsley do that too?" she asked, placing her hand over the heart I could feel racing.

"She wishes," he replied through a snort. "But her Obscure differs from mine."

"So, it's not just Dashiell," Imogen said to herself, barely audible beneath her breath. My interest was piqued as I wondered about my childhood best friend's extra power. Would it manifest physically like what Evander and Ainsley possessed, or would it be something that couldn't be seen, like Tallis's Obscure?

My focus drifted to the tall king with white hair braided back like mine. He stood, leaning against the door frame as he watched me intently, just as he had when I had woken in Agnitio months ago. He was trying to gauge whether I had divulged the nature of his Obscure to anyone since that day he had reluctantly shown me.

I hadn't. At least not yet.

"All of the rulers have one, each unique in their own way," Evander continued. "It's something we tend to keep hidden, but since we're on the subject... It's clear that you know what additional ability Dashiell possesses, and I would *very* much like to as well. Care to tell the group?"

Imogen tilted her head to the side as she scrutinized the King of Tenebrae. Slowly, her lips lifted into a terrifying smirk. "You're a bold and cocky little shit, aren't you?" Evander grinned, giving her a shrug of a single shoulder. "Good," she added. "She needs someone who can keep up with her."

Holy shit. Did Imogen just give Evander her blessing in some weird and twisted way? *And where the hell was Ainsley?* My best friend's absence was really starting to piss me off.

"But," the maiden continued, leveling Evander a flat look, "We both know I'm not going to tell you anything regarding Dashiell."

"It was worth a try."

The King of Tenebrae conceded and sat in one of the armchairs across from the bed that was currently full of people. Imogen turned back toward Cal and smiled as he gave her a look that could only be described as *sex*. Just a sex-filled stare in a sexual tension-filled room.

My eyes locked on Evander, who was looking at the couple just as curiously as I was. As if feeling my gaze, he turned his attention to me. I raised my brows and offered a look that said, *You see that too, right? What the hell is going on there? Oh my Gods, we need to talk about this. Maybe shove them in a room somewhere and just press our ear to the door and listen. Do you think Lia knows? Do you think she'd be into it too? She probably would, right? Imogen is about to be the center of the most delicious sandwich.*

Evander stared at me blankly, then deadpanned his own look that conveyed a message that went a little something more like, *Do I look like my wife? No? So then, why are you speaking to me?*

He directed his attention toward Tallis instead. I missed Ainsley.

"Since we're on the subject of *secrets*, I'm still waiting to hear all about why you kept one from me, Tallis," Evander said, and no one in the room missed the hostility in his tone. Marce and Oli both sat up, suddenly no longer tired as they waited for the King of Agnitio's answer.

"I did what I had to."

"Bullshit!" Oli growled. Tallis was going to have to give far more than that response for my family to accept his decision. And even then, I didn't think they would.

"Felix may be part of your court, but he is a member of *my* kingdom and possesses a Gift very few people alive do. I did what I thought was necessary to protect him."

"By keeping him from his family?" Evander bit out. "I watched my wife and best friend grieve for months. There was no Gods damn reason you couldn't have sent word that he was alive."

"His safety—"

"Has never been a concern to you until now! Had it been, you would have removed him from Caelum long ago!" Evander yelled before pointing his next question at me. "How long have you been aware of your Magusier Gift?"

I thought back to when I started realizing there was something not quite right with the magic I carried. "I began noticing signs shortly after my immortal birthday, but it wasn't until Ainsley arrived at the palace that they became more apparent."

"But *you* knew, didn't you, Tallis? You claimed to have been aware of who Felix was the second you laid eyes on him, and I find it hard to believe you didn't once lock into your Gift and check to see what his were. Even if they hadn't manifested yet, you were well aware of what he would be given. For someone you considered to be your childhood best friend, you didn't seem to care about her son's well-being until he could be of use to you," Evander pointed out.

The King of Agnitio didn't respond. With his jaw clenched tightly and his eyes hard, he maintained a piercing gaze on Evander. Tallis's body was tense, the muscles beneath his olive skin straining as he kept his arms firmly locked across his chest as if holding in the anger I could feel rolling off him. He hadn't given me nearly as much information on my mother as I would have liked. Based on what I *did* know, he cared for her deeply—a kind of devotion she hadn't reciprocated.

He stepped further into the room and moved closer to Evander as he spoke with a deadly calm that was far more intimidating than any raised voice could offer. "I did not question your decision to keep Ainsley in Caelum after learning of her whereabouts. I suggest you do not question mine."

The two kings regarded each other intensely, the tension in the room so taut it could be plucked like a stringed instrument. Tallis had his reasons for secrecy, just as Evander had his—a fact the King of Tenebrae seemed to understand.

"Noted," Evander replied, and leaned further back in his chair. Tallis dipped his head in a bow of acceptance, and the two men decided to let sleeping dogs lie. I moved from my spot beside Oli to the edge of the bed next to Imogen and brushed my shoulder against hers lightly as the room broke out in quiet conversations.

"His Obscure," I began, briefly fumbling for the words I wanted to ask. "Is he in any danger when he wields it?" It was a quiet plea for information I wasn't owed, nor did I think I would be granted.

Imogen's smile was sad as she looked at me and shook my head. "He's learning how to use it, but it causes him no harm." I sagged next to her, relief caressing every muscle that sank into place at the news.

"If you tell me what it is, perhaps I could help him use it," Evander offered.

Imogen's eyes sliced in an annoyed movement. "Nice try, but no." The King of Tenebrae dramatically sighed as he steepled his hands together. "However, I'll tell you what I know of Perceval's Obscure."

Chatter completely ceased as we all directed our stares at the maiden and her unexpected offer.

"And how did you stumble across that?" Tallis inquired. "We all know how closely Perceval kept information to his chest."

Imogen cleared her throat and straightened, readying herself to divulge the story of what she learned and how. The twins shifted off the bed and came around to stand near Evander so all eyes could be on the maiden as she spoke.

"I was close with Queen Calida," Imogen said, her tone coated in fondness for Dash's mother. "I was more than just her maiden; I was her best friend. We shared dreams, aspirations, fears, secrets, and just about everything in between with one another. I knew her better than I knew myself most days."

Imogen's stare was fixed on the wall beyond Evander, her mind seeming lost to a time long ago. Sadness flashed across her features, but her gaze stayed locked ahead as if she saw the past playing out before her eyes here and now.

"Perceval was always a cruel man, wanting more than he deserved—his choice to be with Calida was no exception. His love for her was borderline obsession, and I could never understand what she saw in him or why she chose to give up a life she loved so much to move to the palace and become his queen."

Dash had expressed a similar sentiment over the years. The way he described his mother to me left me wondering how she could have ever found Perceval worthy of her love. But for a reason that neither of us could figure out, she had.

"We'd often spent evenings talking about how we could change Caelum for the better. Her ideas spanned from providing fresh produce to the neighboring villages that were experiencing difficulties, to establishing schools throughout the kingdom for underprivileged children. Each thought her mind created was more generous and selfless than the last. But when she would return after proposing these ideas to Perceval, her mind had always changed, deciding against every one. No matter how hard I tried, I could never talk sense back into her. She never loved him, but Perceval was too charismatic, too charming, too *manipulative*," Imogen explained.

She blew out a heavy sigh. With a shake of her head, her eyes focused back on the present, scanning over the group of us who were listening intently to her recollections. My gaze dropped to the hand Calidore was now squeezing gently as if to comfort her.

I thought back to the meetings I had attended as one of Perceval's advisors. As an Empathi, my job was to read the emotions in the room and de-escalate tensions should they ever rise.

But they rarely had.

Thinking back on the situations now, that was odd knowing how intense Perceval had been. However, conflicts rarely ensued because he was always able to control the situation by words alone. Whatever he wanted, he got.

I attributed it to his exceptional negotiating skills, but was there actually some form of magic at work that enabled him to consistently manipulate the situation in his favor? To manipulate *people* to do his bidding?

"It wasn't until Queen Calida gave birth to Dashiell that things began to change. Less and less was Perceval able to coax her into seeing things his way or doing what he wanted. It was as if the love she held for her son allowed her to sift past his lies and manipulation. She finally had something in her life that meant more to her than her own. Someone to love and protect at all costs. Someone who fortified her will and gave her the strength to stand her ground on her beliefs. All Calida wanted was a better life for her son."

Throughout our years together, Dash had shared how much he admired the woman he called his mother. I hoped he knew that her strength and compassion were all because of him.

"So that's why his father always hated him? Because Dash was the reason Calida stopped going along with his ideas?" I inquired, wanting to fully understand the situation.

Imogen was quiet for a moment as she angled her gaze toward me. The feelings I could sense from her were complex and overwhelming as if she were jumping from emotion to emotion, never quite settling on just one. Her eyes narrowed, and there was a thought behind them that I couldn't decipher.

"Among other reasons, yes," she finally answered.

"Does he know?"

"I told him shortly after Perceval died."

My heart sank for my best friend and the storm of emotions I knew the news would have caused him. Not only had his mother been manipulated for years, but so had he. Knowing Dash, he had been dissecting every conversation with his father and every decision that he had ever made because of it.

Every choice he had once made regarding Ainsley.

In the beginning, Dash and I were often in meetings with his father, discussing the new guest to the palace. Ainsley had hated us but Perceval made it clear that we needed to continue trying with her. That had always been our plan, regardless of the king's order, but how much of it was truly *our* idea? How much of it was Perceval using his Obscure to manipulate our own ideas until we agreed with his?

The only solace I could gather for Dash was that his mother was able to find the strength to resist Perceval's manipulation once he was born. Perhaps when Dash had fallen in love with

Ainsley, the same could have been said for him. The truth of that possibility was becoming more apparent the longer I pondered it.

"Where is Ainsley now?" I asked Evander as the room once again began to quietly discuss amongst themselves. She wasn't here, and this seemed like information she should be privy to.

Evander chewed the inside of his cheek as he looked at the open window to his right. "She had something to take care of before we leave."

I swallowed hard before getting up from the bed and strolling for the door.

"Where are you going?" Olivier asked.

"I also have something to take care of before we go."

27
Ainsley

I felt his presence before I saw it. The scent of lemongrass and sea salt drifted toward me, coupled with emotions of hurt and wariness. I swallowed the last of my fear and turned away from the sunlit lake, leaving the small feeling of peace I had found trapped upon the surface of the water.

Dashiell regarded me carefully from halfway across the meadow. He wasn't going to come any closer than that; I would have to be the one to close the distance between us. Taking a deep breath, I moved toward him, stopping a few feet away to give him the space I knew we both still needed.

I opened my mouth to speak but Dashiell did first. "May I say something before you start?" he asked warily. My heart thumped with worry about what else he could throw at me, but my nerves eased at the thought of holding off from having to speak for a little while longer.

It was *my* idea to approach him, but that didn't stop my cowardice from taking root.

I nodded.

Dashiell's gaze flicked to his hands, which he was wringing in front of him nervously. "I want to apologize—"

"You don't have to. In the Sanctuary—"

"Not for that," he interrupted. "I meant what I said in there."

That was fair, but my stomach still dropped as I remembered every detail of our fight.

"I want to apologize for that night... Here," he said, gesturing to the space. I looked around and was instantly transported back to the evening of my Primum Celebration.

I smelled the scent of roses from the petals that had been sprinkled on the grass. Felt the delicate brush of fingers exploring my body, skin on skin. Tasted wine and mint as we exchanged passionate kisses under the stars. Remembered how much I had loved him.

"And for every moment after that," he added, jolting me back to the present.

Dashiell was still playing with his fingers, a sign I knew meant he was searching for the confidence to face me. Finally, he found it.

"Knowing the information I did, I should have never let it get that far. I'm sorry, Ainsley." He looked up as he said the words. I felt the apology in my bones, tasted the truth in the air. "I was always selfish when it came to you. In the beginning, I wanted something I couldn't have, but by some miracle, you granted it. And then I wanted something I knew I couldn't hold on to. Still, I tried, and I deeply regret that."

I shifted uncomfortably, not expecting an apology from him, and certainly not the one I was given.

"Had I stayed away and not taken our relationship to the next level, not proposed, not made promises I knew in the back of my mind I could never truly keep... Had I not told you I loved you, then perhaps it wouldn't have hurt as bad when you learned the truth. Maybe then you wouldn't have been as broken as Felix said you were."

I shut my eyes against the painful memories. My mind was flooded with flashes of cool tile flooring pressed against my cheek, the taste of salt coating my lips as the tears continued to flow, and worst of all, the ache in my chest where my heart had been.

He was right; I had been broken. But would erasing the events between us have changed anything? Sure, the tender moments we shared were beautiful, but I was so far gone in my love for him by that point that I didn't think it would have lessened the pain of my loss if they had never occurred. If anything, those moments only proved how much I loved him.

"I'm sorry, Ainsley," he said again. "Truly, I am. If I could take back every kiss, every touch, every declaration, I would."

His misted-over deep teal eyes met mine, the honesty shining in them overwhelming my thoughts and heart. He was hurting, and by the way he carried himself, I wondered if that pain would ever stop for him.

It was only at that moment that I realized it still hadn't for me.

I let a shaky breath slip between my lips as I nodded to myself, accepting it was my turn to address him. The pressure building in my chest only increased as I forgot everything I wanted to say now that he was standing before me. I had written it out in my head and rehearsed it repeatedly for the past hour as I stared out at the bright blue water of the lake. But now, looking at Dashiell patiently waiting for me to begin, the eloquent words drifted from my mind as if they had never been there to begin with.

Fumbling, I decided to start with the one apology I knew was owed. "I'm so sorry for what I did to the Sanctuary," I told him, my voice already thick with emotion. "I know what that place meant to you, to me, to Felix. It was home, and I destroyed it. I hate myself for what I did in there, and I tried so hard to put everything back—"

"I know," Dashiell interrupted quietly. "I returned that night to clean the mess but saw you already had."

A tear slid down my cheek as I nodded. "I'm sorry, Dashiell."

He was quiet and as still as stone. After a minute, I realized he wasn't going to respond—either he couldn't, or he didn't deem me worthy of a reply. I swallowed the bitter sting of the latter as a possibility.

My gaze scanned our surroundings, searching for the next place to start as I pondered each part of our conversation in the Sanctuary. I didn't want to argue or excuse my actions, but I needed to explain them so he could understand.

"Do you remember when I encountered someone in my room during the kings' meeting?"

"Brandle," he said, and my heart fluttered with hope that he was engaging in the conversation, even if it was only a single word.

"It wasn't Brandle," I admitted, shaking my head. "It was Evander."

Shock and confusion fleeted across Dashiell's features at the confession. His brow pinched and his mouth hung slightly open as if trying to form a question before quickly deciding against it. He narrowed his eyes, and I watched a familiar scene play out as I had so many times before—his mind searching for a logical solution to a puzzle he didn't understand.

"He used an illusion on us," Dashiell announced, solving the mystery before I had the chance to explain.

"Yes."

"So he knew who you were the entire time?"

"He knew who I was to *him*, but not who I was to you."

Dashiell's brow furrowed as he tried to put the pieces together of how one thing led to another, but there was no way he could figure it out without help.

"Tallis saw me that day and knew instantly who I was because of his Gift," I shared, putting Dashiell out of his misery. "He told Evander, and that's how he ended up in my room."

"So, if he knew who you were, why didn't he take you with him?"

It was the question I had both wanted to answer and had hoped was never voiced. Dashiell deserved to know the truth of everything, but that meant I'd have to dive into the feelings and emotions I had worked so hard to keep locked away.

Biting my lip, I turned, unable to look into his blue eyes as I spoke. "Evander and I were created by magic, our soul split from the same one. It has granted us the ability to feel each other. Any strong or intense emotion one of us experiences, the other will as well."

I blew out a shaky breath as my hands trembled nervously at my sides, half expecting Dashiell to question me about the Soul Bond. But he didn't; he stayed quiet as he waited for me to go on.

"For over twenty years, Evander has had to experience my loneliness, fear, anger, sadness—all of it. I remained hidden from him as he had to endure the extent of my misery, unable to help the other half of his soul. He had plans to find and save me," I admitted, finding the courage to meet his stare again.

I inhaled deeply, remembering the pain on Evander's face as he told me the story of why he had changed his mind. Dashiell wasn't owed this part of my relationship with Evander, but I felt it was important he heard it as it involved him.

"Everything changed when I moved to the palace," I continued, prompting a questioning glance from Dashiell. My voice was unsteady, small, and weak as I prepared myself to go back to the summer my world altered. "For the first time in my life, he felt happiness from me."

My lips quivered as tears streamed down my cheeks. The sutures stitched across my broken heart had been snipped, causing the pain and fear and heartache and love to pour out and pool beneath my feet in deep crimson.

"He felt…" I struggled to produce a coherent sentence. "He felt how much I loved you." I choked out the words, sobbing as they came up all at once. "I know you said that you regret us, but I don't. I wouldn't take back a single moment together because I *did* love you, Dashiell. I loved you with all that I had to give and more."

The truth of my confession stung like a blade on its way out, further severing the progress I had made toward moving forward.

"It wasn't always *him*," I admitted, addressing what he said in the Sanctuary.

Tear tracks stained Dashiell's cheeks as he listened, appearing just as pained as I felt. We had both loved each other and ruined what we had in our own way—something we were just now coming to terms with.

"I shouldn't have shut you out the way I did. I felt angry and betrayed, yes, but you deserved better than the way I treated you," I said through sniffles. "I fell in love with your heart and your mind. I fell in love with the boy who gave me patience, grace, and twenty birthdays because I hadn't ever celebrated a single one. I fell in love with my best friend and in the end, *I* was the one who betrayed all of that."

"Ainsley—" he tried, his voice cracking on my name.

"—Please," I interrupted. "Please, let me finish. I need to say this." He nodded and wiped the tears from his face.

I sipped on the air like wine, willing it to calm my nerves just as the drink would have. Straightening and blowing out a long exhale, I pulled my shattering pieces back together.

"I held onto the anger because it hurt less. It was easier to blame you, to curse you, to *hate* you, than it was to admit to myself that I missed you," I choked out, the pain in my chest increasing with each confession. "Because I *do* miss you, Dash. I miss my best friend, and I know you may never forgive me, but I forgive you, and—"

His body collided with mine a breath later as he wrapped his arms around me. I buried my face into his chest and wept.

We both did.

Muffled apologies had mixed with tears and confessions neither of us could fully understand. We were too emotional, too distraught, too hurt, and too hopeful to care.

My magic surged forward and reached for him the way it always had, but this time, instead of keeping it back, I let it go. I knew it wouldn't hurt him. At last, a final piece of myself clicked into place, and I closed my eyes against the sensation, feeling wholly complete for the first time. Dash was part of my family and not having him in my life had left a hole that would never be filled by anyone but him.

I smiled faintly as he released his own magic, sending a cool and soothing brush over me. I sighed in contentment, knowing we were finally going to be okay.

28

Dashiell

I didn't want to let her go; I couldn't. I clung to her tightly, afraid that if I released her, this embrace would be nothing more than a fucked-up hallucination, revealing that I was still battling against the woman who meant everything to me.

I rested my cheek on her hair as my tears continued to fall, willing myself to believe this encounter was real. Ainsley's magic was a gentle caress against me, an odd yet somehow familiar extension of her. She didn't possess the Gift of fire, but her magic was warm and inviting, so different from the way mine felt.

She continued to apologize, though I could barely understand her through the broken sobs. My focus was solely on how different our circumstances were from the last time we were here. But I didn't care. I would gladly take her this way over not having her in my life at all. The only thing that mattered was that I had a piece of my family back. And I wasn't going to do anything to ever risk losing it again.

"I didn't think you'd come," she admitted, and it made me tighten my hold on her.

"I knew it was a chance to make amends. Perhaps my one and only."

We were plunged into strangling silence. A breath later, Ainsley stiffened in my arms before pulling back to look at me. Her brow creased and her eyes scanned my face, her mind seeming to work just as fast as her heart beating against me. I could feel her magic slowly retract back into her as she began taking slow and deliberate breaths, her slightly widened gaze never straying from mine. Did I make a mistake? Had I made her uncomfortable?

This line between us had only been freshly drawn and I feared I may have shattered the fractured friendship we were trying to rebuild. I opened my mouth to breathe back in the tainted words, though I didn't understand why they were wrong. Had we not made amends? Perhaps I had spoken too soon and this was simply the closure we both needed to move on. I wanted to vomit at the thought.

"I'm sorry, I—" I fumbled for the words, my tongue tying.

Ainsley shook her head to deny my apology, only confusing me more. Before either of us could comment further, the snapping of a twig broke the climbing tension. We directed our attention to the far end of the meadow where a familiar figure was making his way through the tree line.

Felix hesitantly stepped forward into the clearing, the sun making his silver hair stand out. His saddened stare bounced from Ainsley to me, no doubt noting our reddened eyes, tear-stained cheeks, and the lack of distance between us. His gaze dropped to the fingers he was nervously pulling on.

"You made up without me?" he whispered—a teasing comment meant to detect where we stood with one another.

As heartbroken as my breakup with Ainsley had left me, my falling out with Felix had been even worse. Our friendship had spanned over fifteen years and countless memories together. When I thought he died, it destroyed me—a grief so great I was sure I'd never recover.

And when he walked into that throne room yesterday, alive and well, I fought every instinct to rush to him, to pull him close and never let him go. But his betrayal had destroyed us both and after the words we exchanged months ago, I didn't know if a relationship with me was something he wanted.

So I stayed seated and observed him from afar. I noticed his smile towards Ainsley and his comfort with the Tenebraen court. I saw the pain and anger flash across his face when it was revealed to the room who his father was. I watched him be whisked away right before I could reach him—the issues between us be damned—and fall into the embrace of a man I didn't know.

My best friend had found the love and acceptance he had always dreamed of and I hadn't been there to witness it. Above all else, that fact hurt the most. With a deep breath, I released one of the arms encircling Ainsley and held it out wide in invitation. Felix sprinted, colliding with us a moment later. Our trio was nothing more than gripping arms, wet eyes, and sobs of indiscernible dialogue.

We cried and apologized and cried some more, all while never letting go of each other. Even as we slumped to the lush grass below, our grasp stayed firm. As usual, Ainsley was crushed in the center of our huddle, struggling for breath, but this time she didn't complain.

"Can we talk about how Felix is a fucking *Magusier*," she croaked, her voice muffled against us.

"And how Harbin is his *father*," I added.

"Please? And also about Imogen and Cal because I'm pretty sure they've fucked and no one seems to care," Felix said through a barely audible sob.

Ainsley wiggled her head until she found a small hole she could push through. Her hair was disheveled, sticking up in random places as she gazed at Felix with wide eyes. I tried not to smile at how ridiculous she looked, but it was a lost cause.

"What?!" she demanded, and Felix shook his head.

"Me first. Then we can discuss them." His words were a string of sniffles we somehow managed to understand.

We both agreed and together, the three of us laid back, looking up at the blue sky as Felix told us the story of what happened the night of Perceval's death and everything after.

"So Elenora and Brandle knew who you were," I stated, trying to follow along.

"Yes, but they were only told recently."

"And they took advantage of the situation by having Brandle stop your heart to make you appear dead so they could smuggle you to Agnitio?" Ainsley clarified.

"Yes. Tallis wanted to make sure I was somewhere safe and alone when he told me what and who I was. He didn't want the truth getting out unless I was the one to spill it."

It made sense to an extent. Harbin was a dangerous and greedy man, so if he found out that his son possessed a rare and coveted Gift, he would have stopped at nothing to retrieve him. In a small way, I was grateful that Tallis provided Felix with safety as he worked through what these revelations meant to him.

"And the whole time you were *dead...*"

"I was learning how to wield my Magusier Gift," Felix told Ainsley.

"And Harbin had no idea?"

"None. He knew of my mother's pregnancy, and after she died while in childbirth, he had me taken to Ministro just so he could learn if I would be heir when I came of age. When that didn't pan out how he wanted, he cast me out to Caelum."

My jaw clenched as I thought back to the hard life I knew Felix had in that shit kingdom. I was so relieved he had been given to my father because it not only meant I would get to grow up beside my best friend, but that he would finally be free of that miserable place. Perceval wasn't a good person, but he was far less cruel than Harbin had always proven to be.

"It's his loss, and I don't just mean because of your second Gift," Ainsley said.

She was right about that. The Kingdom of Ministro never deserved the kindness and grace Felix always bestowed upon the world.

"We're here if you want to talk about your father," I added, prompting Felix to sit up and direct his stare from the clouds to me. He was quiet, his eyes searching mine as he lifted a single brow in confident question. Shit.

"I'll talk about mine if you talk about yours," he singsonged, rolling to his back and looking up at the sky once more. His knowing tune sent Ainsley into a sitting position.

"Why did you say it like that?" she asked him before turning her attention to me. "Why did he say it like that?" Fucking Felix.

"We don't keep secrets from each other," Felix added, none of us missing the irony in that statement. The entire reason we had fallen apart was *because* of the secrets we kept from each other. That choice had nearly destroyed us all.

I exhaled a frustrated breath as I mentally cursed Felix's new Gift. "Perceval wasn't my father," I admitted.

"What?!" Ainsley yelled as she looked down at me. I pushed to my knees and faced them.

Felix may have known the truth about me thanks to his ability to see that fourth Gift I kept hidden, but he didn't know the details of how I found out. He rolled to his side, just as eager to learn as Ainsley.

"After Perceval died and you both left, I was a wreck—barely functioning. Two days later, I took the oath and received the land's magic which only intensified what I already possessed. I had always felt this strange part of magic within me that I couldn't explain. I just assumed it had something to do with me being the Heir to Caelum, that perhaps the land and Gods were just readying me to take over for my father one day."

Ainsley and Felix were quiet as they listened, both of their stares curious yet wary; they knew this conversation wasn't an easy one for me to have. Gods, how I'd missed them and how attuned we all were to each other.

"One evening, I accidentally sliced my palm while opening a letter," I continued, closing my eyes as I recounted the events. "It was just a small cut, but as I swept my thumb across my flesh, the wound began to close. At first, I thought it was because as king, my magic was stronger, allowing me to heal quicker than most. So I tried again, this time a deeper cut, and again, I healed. Over and over and over again, I healed with one swipe of my finger."

I swallowed the lump in my throat as I replayed the events. I knew my mother wasn't from Ministro as I had seen her use fire magic throughout my young life. Which meant there was only one explanation.

"Imogen found me sitting in a pool of my own blood as I sliced a sword across my leg, only to use the magic to stitch it back together. I was an utter mess, covered in crimson with tears pouring down my face. She sat by me that night and told me of the man from Ministro my mother had fallen in love with."

A small smile tugged at my lips as I thought back to hearing all of Imogen's stories of when they met and how happy she was. I knew my mother never loved Perceval and it had always pained me to think she was miserable before she died. But there was solace in knowing that she had found her happiness and that I was a product of it, even if it had to be kept a secret.

"Once Perceval found out about her affair, he had the man killed. My mother learned she was pregnant shortly after and was terrified because she knew who my real father was. Though Perceval had his suspicions, they were never confirmed as he didn't have a Magusier on his council. And when my Unda and Aerian Gifts emerged, he took that as a sign that I was his true son."

"And you had no idea about your Medicus ability?" Ainsley asked, her voice trembling from the emotion I could tell she was trying to keep at bay for me.

I shook my head. "The signs were all there, but I never put them together. Not until that night."

Felix sighed in disbelief as a gentle laugh formed. "So you're telling me that our whole lives, we were raised and groomed for roles of authority meant to eradicate Conjoining... Only for it to turn out we're two bastards who are products of it?"

Felix's hysterics deepened, and I couldn't help joining in at the insane irony of it all. "It seems that way."

Ainsley tipped her head back as she spoke through her own laughter. "And you tried to take my Gifts because my parents were from different kingdoms, only for it to turn out, so were yours?"

We laughed even harder, unable to catch our breaths as the conversation continued.

"You've spent your whole life feeling abandoned and unwanted because Harbin rejected you," I wheezed, directing my strained words to Felix. "Only to discover that he did it by mistake a decade too early?"

"And that he's your *father?*" Ainsley added.

We couldn't stop our laughter, letting our hurt and misfortune transform into the most beautiful sound I had ever heard. The melody was rich and hopeful, drifting through the sky on a breeze composed of love and forgiveness; a song I would play on repeat for the rest of my existence.

We pushed through the final thicket of trees that opened to the sprawling green lawn of the gardens several hours later. I looked over the cracked palace from the distance. So much had been damaged today, yet even more had been repaired.

"We need to figure out who was behind this," I muttered, mentally calculating the work that would need to go into the rebuild.

"I already know who did it," Ainsley admitted nonchalantly as she shrugged. Felix and I both looked at her expectantly. "It was Oberon, with Harbin's help."

"Are we assuming this or…"

"I've received confirmation," she answered Felix.

"From…"

"A source."

I couldn't tell if she was purposely being evasive to annoy our best friend or if she was trying to protect the person who had fed her the information. Seeing as it had only taken me about three seconds to figure out who it was, I assumed I could speak freely on the subject.

"What did you have to give her?" I asked, earning a mischievous smirk from the Queen of Tenebrae.

"Who?" Felix asked, but Ainsley ignored him, answering me instead.

"Besides getting to choose what insult to throw at me?"

"Wait… Rosella? Your source was *Rosella*?" Felix asked incredulously, but Ainsley kept her eyes firmly on me.

When she looked at me that night before the feast, it was as if she was the same woman I had known for months. In that gaze, gone was the animosity and anger—just an unspoken need for help.

Rosella's public insult wasn't entirely out of character, but the way Ainsley reacted to it was. That was the moment I knew it was a ploy. I couldn't tell why she was setting a scene but I trusted it was for a bigger reason, especially when I picked up on the fact she was stalling. So I played my part of the scorned ex-fiancé while she carried out whatever plan she cooked up.

"I promised to introduce her to Jahier," Ainsley said, answering my earlier question. There was more she wasn't saying, and I gave her a knowing look. "And I offered her asylum in Tenebrae. I know she's your citizen, but it was a term she requested and I would like to honor it. I can't believe I'm saying this, but she proved useful."

"I'm not understanding the point of the performance," Felix cut in, still two steps behind.

"She needed an excuse to leave the room and also a public display that showed her hatred toward the queen. Whoever Rosella was instructed to seduce would be more inclined to divulge information if they believed the two women were enemies."

Ainsley's wide smile proved my deduction correct.

"So does that mean the two of you are friends now?" Felix teased.

She snorted and rolled her eyes. "Gods no. We only made a deal because it was mutually beneficial. I may hate Rosella, but she's good at what she does," Ainsley reluctantly confessed. "She was able to find out the next time Harbin plans to travel to Pravus, and even how many people he sent to assist Oberon's men with ambushing us yesterday."

Rosella was notorious in the palace for her ability to know everyone's business at all times. It looked like she finally used it to serve a purpose other than useless gossip and collateral. I couldn't help but think over the deal she and Ainsley had made. If she wanted freedom from Caelum, I would grant it, but not before finding out why.

"There's something else," Ainsley added, ensnaring my attention again. "Rosella told me the man she seduced hinted that there may be a traitor in the palace. I'm more inclined to believe her after seeing the targets all over the grass and the proximity they were to the building. It's something to think about."

I nodded just as Evander, Olivier, Imogen, and Jahier spilled from the palace entrance, deep in lighthearted conversation. Felix jogged ahead of us, determined to get to the man he loved as quickly as possible.

"He treats him well?" I asked, jerking my head toward Evander's advisor. She smiled as if deep in thought and I couldn't help but return the gesture.

"Felix annoyed the shit out of Oli at first."

"Naturally."

"But now, they're very much in love, and happy."

"Good. He deserves that."

I glanced away from him and focused on Evander, who stood alone, leaning against the palace wall, his eyes fixed on Ainsley and me with intense interest. I could feel her follow my stare and settle on the man she now called her husband.

"Is this going to be okay?" she asked, spinning around to face me as she walked backward to the palace. I slowed my pace and looked between her and Evander curiously.

There was still so much I didn't understand about what they were and what it meant. But the one thing I did know was that her love for him was undeniable.

"Are you happy?" I asked, swallowing the pain I had no right to feel. She peered over her shoulder, a smile curving her lips.

"Yes," she whispered.

"Then that's all that matters."

Her eyes found mine again, and that beautiful smile widened more than I had seen in a long, *long* time. My heart thumped heavily in my chest, healing itself just from that one sight alone.

She spun again to face the palace, walking slowly at my side. I bumped her with my shoulder. "But did you have to move on with *him*?" I let the mocking disgust coat my words and ease the tension. "He's such a prick."

She laughed at that and nodded. "You get used to it," she said before hurrying off to her husband. I kept my eyes on her a moment longer before I changed my path to meet with everyone else.

"And we're meeting in Tenebrae?" Jahier asked.

"Yes, in three weeks. The leader of Vorsutos will join us there," Olivier replied.

Something wet pressed against my fingers and I glanced down to find Ainsley's giant fucking grey wolf with its nose against my hand. I jumped back on instinct, which only prompted the black one at my other side to bare its teeth in a vicious snarl.

"I wouldn't do that," Olivier suggested.

I looked at him with wide eyes. "Then what *would* you do?"

Felix's boyfriend grinned and only offered a shrug, clearly enjoying the prospect of me being eaten alive by overgrown dogs. I threw Felix a desperate look that said, '*a little help would be nice,*' but he was too busy flopping the grey one's ears back and forth as she sniffed me to care.

"Can you call your killer dogs back, please?" I asked as Ainsley and Evander watched the scene play out.

"Sorry, I can't hear you," Evander shouted back, definitely able to hear every word I said; partly because of his immortal hearing, and partly because he was only twenty fucking feet away.

A Gods damn prick, indeed.

29

Ainsley

"It's good they get acquainted with him, especially if he'll be around now," Evander explained as we watched Nova and Onyx relentlessly inspect Dash. I didn't miss the hint of amusement in my husband's tone as he observed the King of Caelum's terrified face during every moment of the encounter.

Onyx had listened to Imogen's command to back off for only two seconds before he jumped back in, snarling whenever Dash made a sudden movement. The wolves were extremely interested in him, and Evander was right; it was better they became accustomed to his presence now rather than later.

"You seem happier," Van whispered, snaking an arm around my waist. I smiled as I twisted around to face him, pressing myself into his hold.

"I am."

"Good." His grin widened and I reached onto my toes to kiss each dimple.

Our goodbyes were quick, and after five minutes of making Imogen swear she would come to Tenebrae once she finished helping rebuild the palace, I was ready to leave Caelum for what would no longer be the last time.

Things between Dash, Felix, and I were on the mend. I could picture summers spent swimming in the lake and late nights drinking and laughing in the Sanctuary as we caught up with one another. We would win this war and get to experience those days together.

Tallis left several hours ago, followed shortly by Marce and Cal, eager to return home and make arrangements for the upcoming gathering in Tenebrae to discuss our war strategy and search for Inmuto. Plans were finally coming together, and I was hopeful we would all come out okay in the end.

Felix ran his thumb back and forth over the smooth patch of skin that once held his brand of Caelum. Without permission, Dash burned it off and quickly healed the wound, declaring Felix a free man. The level of his involvement with Caelum would solely be at his discretion.

I could feel a mix of emotions radiating from my best friend, so I drifted closer and bumped him with my hip. "Are you okay?" I asked. He looked up from the task he was lost in, his brows pinching as he nodded.

"Yeah, I just…" he trailed off as his stare wandered to Dash, who was still trying to get the wolves to leave him alone as he spoke to Jahier. When Felix glanced back at me, I offered him a comforting smile.

"Stay."

"Ainsley, I can't—"

"Stay," I said again, interlocking our fingers and squeezing tight for emphasis. "Stay here and repair what was broken. And I don't just mean the palace."

Felix's eyes welled as he smiled weakly and pulled me in for an embrace. Oli and Van appeared as we parted, understanding washing over their features. Before Oli could speak, Evander's voice flooded the space.

"Just be back before training begins in three weeks," he commanded his advisor. "Marce can take over preparations while you're away."

Oli released a relieved breath before saying his goodbyes and walking hand-in-hand with Felix to the palace entrance. I couldn't help but grin as I watched Dash's face light up at the news Felix would be staying in Caelum for a little while longer.

"You can stay, too," Evander offered, his voice a low whisper above my ear as he hugged me from behind.

I shook my head as I observed the happiness pouring off of the two boys who meant the world to me. "No," I said gently. "They need this time together."

Felix and Dash had so much hurt to work through, and I wanted to give them the chance to do so. There would be plenty of time for our trio to be together and heal the past pain we all had caused.

I spun, wrapping my arms around Evander's neck as I pulled him close, his lips brushing along mine. "And *I* want to go home and be with my husband."

Van smiled against my mouth as he kissed me, letting his shadows encircle our bodies and bring us home.

30
Felix

I hurried through the corridors, pulling Oli along as I pointed to another random room.

"And in there—"

"Let me guess. You woke up naked and with the worst hangover of your life," he deadpanned.

"How did you know?"

"Given that it was the plot of the last four rooms we passed, it was a safe bet."

I smiled and shrugged, prompting Oli to form a grin. He could act annoyed all he wanted, but I knew deep down he was enjoying this quiet moment together. I had never experienced the loss of a loved one to death and couldn't fathom the unimaginable anguish he must have endured, believing that I had perished and our time together had abruptly ended.

As if remembering the pain of the past few months, Oli leaned in and pressed his lips to mine. Never in my wildest dreams did I think I would get to walk hand-in-hand through these halls with someone I loved without fear of repercussions, let alone kiss him in the open. Of course, I had lovers before, but this was different. Oli was far more than just someone to casually sleep with when I wanted to cure the sting of loneliness.

I pulled him closer, deepening our embrace and letting the love I felt for him drift between us. He sighed and swept his tongue over mine as my Gift wrapped around him, displaying the depth of my devotion.

"You can't do that to me here in the middle of a damn hallway," he murmured. His complaint didn't seem to deter his actions as his hands wound through my hair, gripping me tighter against him as our mouths moved in perfect harmony.

My hand slid over the smooth wood of the door, frantically searching for the damn knob as Oli tried to kill me with his kiss. Finally, my fingers felt cool metal, and I smiled at the victory. "Well, it's a good thing we're right outside my room," I told him, twisting the handle and pushing open the door.

Olivier broke our kiss the second we crossed over the threshold, doing the very opposite of what I had intended. His attention was suddenly drawn to the wide space we were now occupying instead of me...which was annoying.

He pulled away completely despite my objections and began studying the room that had once been the only thing that belonged solely to me. I bit my lip as I watched him, unexpectedly feeling nervous about what he thought.

Everything I had owned, all of myself, was laid bare before him in the most vulnerable way. I pressed my back against the wall and pulled on my fingers as he slowly scanned the room. He walked forward, stopping at a desk littered with parchment, and I inhaled as he read my heart spilled before him in ink.

His lips twitched as his eyes darted across a piece of paper, and then another... and another, until he had gone through them all. Once he was finished, he strolled to the worn books stacked haphazardly in the corner of the room. He crouched, looking over each of the titles before selecting one and flipping it open to a random page.

Oli's brow rose and his eyes flicked to me as he held the book up. "You wrote in this?"

I nodded, once again self-conscious as I tried to remember what I had scribbled in that particular novel.

"*If only it were that simple,*" he recited, showing the text I had underlined with my note written sloppily beside it. "I annotate my thoughts when I read, too." He smiled warmly, and the tension instantly eased from my body at the sight of it. Gods, that smile alone could cure any illness.

He placed the book back on top of the pile and then peered out the open window. The change was subtle, but enough for me to sense it.

"What's wrong?"

He shook his head, directing his attention back to me as he walked away from whatever he had seen below. A few strides later, his lips were on mine again, though I could tell his mood had soured from the earlier passion.

"Oli," I warned, reluctantly withdrawing. He sighed as he dragged his hands down his face, a gesture I had come to learn meant he was struggling to gather his thoughts. As I had always done with him, I waited patiently.

"It's just this place," he confessed, bringing his bright blue eyes to me. "Every time I look around, I'm reminded that I'm in the home of the man who killed my family. And his son—"

"Had nothing to do with that," I interrupted.

"I know, but it doesn't change how hard this is for me. Julian and Viviette were the only parents I'd ever known, and his father had them killed in front of my eyes. And he didn't stop there. He had to go after Evander's parents and take Uriel and Dahlia from me too. That's not just something I can overlook." His voice broke with each painful word slicing deeper than the last. We had never discussed his relationship with Ainsley's parents in great detail, but I could tell by the love he displayed for her that they meant the world to him.

Oli took a deep breath as I stayed quiet, allowing him to work through the haunting memories and strangling emotions. I could empathize with his hurt and anger, but what I couldn't do was let him blame an innocent. Dash was my family, and as much as I didn't want to lose the love of my life, there wasn't anyone I would choose over him and Ainsley.

"He's my brother, Oli."

"I know—"

"—And had *nothing* to do with the death of your family."

"I know that, Felix," he argued, his voice rising just barely to showcase his frustration. "But he *did* hurt Ainsley."

I opened and closed my mouth, failing to defend my best friend because Oli was right. There was no denying how shattered our queen had been upon her arrival in Tenebrae. And we all knew Dash was the cause.

"Just as Dashiell is your brother, *she* is my sister. I made a promise to her parents to protect her, and you're asking me to play nice with the man who broke her heart and destroyed so much of who she was for so long." I took a deep breath, willing the instinct to defend Dash to dissolve. I was at a loss, and there wasn't anything I was going to be able to say or do to change Oli's mind on the matter.

The silence was heavy between us, thick with unspoken grievances and justifications neither of us wanted to throw at the other. Our time spent together was supposed to be fueled by passion and desire, making up for the precious months we had lost, but instead, we landed on the one topic that would forever cause a disagreement.

"Even feeling this way," Oli said through a sigh as a soft, ebony hand curved my cheek. "I'm still trying because I love you. I'd never ask you to choose between us." A faint smile ghosted his lips—a sign of truce. "I just need you to be patient with me." He pressed his forehead to mine, and I slid my hands over the hard ridges of his back, savoring the feel of strong muscle beneath.

I nodded as I pressed my lips gently to his in a peace offering. I could give him the grace he requested as long as he could do the same with me.

"When you say *patient*," I said, moving my mouth against his, "Do you mean in every aspect or just pertaining to Dash?"

My fingers dragged down the side of his ribs until I reached his belt buckle. Oli grinned as understanding and desire flooded his emotions and drifted into me. His hands worked their way into my hair as he forced my mouth open wider, stroking his tongue over mine.

I yanked on the belt harder, pulling him flush against me as I made quick work of the clasp that was in my damn way. The second the leather was free, my hand dove beneath the waistband of his pants, gripping his hard length. We both groaned into each other as I slid my thumb over his sensitive tip, wishing it was my tongue instead. I needed him. Needed to taste, suck, stroke, lick, *feel* every inch of him.

"Felix," he whispered, the desperation in his plea making my cock swell and pants strain even more than they already had.

I moved my hand quicker along his shaft, stroking him hard and deliberately. A growl rumbled at the base of Oli's throat, and he wrapped his hand around my wrist before pulling it free from his pants and pinning it above my head.

"I want my way with you first," he said, sucking on my tongue before nipping at my lip.

Fucking Gods. If this was my 'Welcome Back to Life Party,' I'd gladly 'die' ten times over.

"You'll have to fight me for that honor." As much as I loved when Oli took over, I needed to feel that control just as badly. His lips spread in a sinister smile at the challenge.

"Gladly."

He reached for my pants buckle.

"I'm sorry," a voice who shouldn't have fucking been there, said.

Oli hastily turned away from the intruder as he fastened his belt and readjusted himself, though that would do little to hide the very obvious, very *large* evidence of what we were up to.

"Am I interrupting?"

"Yes—" I said.

"—No," Oli declared at the same time.

I glowered at Dash as he worked extremely hard to hide his cocky as fuck smirk. "Well then. I just came by to make sure you both had everything you needed."

Not even close, thanks to him.

"We're fine," I said through clenched teeth as Oli stayed focused on the wall across the room, refusing to glance Dash's way.

"That's good," my brother replied as he held my stare.

"Yup."

He didn't leave, didn't so much as make an effort to retreat.

"Great."

"I'm going to go… check… do… Fuck it. I'm just going to go," Oli said, rushing for the exit while keeping his hand held strategically over the center of his pants.

"Oh, you don't have to do that," Dash replied as if he were the most accommodating host in the realm.

He wasn't. I knew what the fuck he was doing.

"It's fine," Oli called over his shoulder as he pushed through the door, slamming it loudly behind him.

My glower was deadly as Dash sighed in false apology and brought a cup of wine to his lips, slurping loudly as he gripped my gaze.

"Really? Are you actually serious right now?"

"What do you mean?"

"Don't play stupid. You know damn well what you're doing."

His lips twitched before he quickly schooled his features and cleared his throat.

"I'm not sure what you're referring to," he said innocently.

"You're out to ruin my sex life."

"Stop being so dramatic. It was by complete coincidence—"

"Bullshit!"

"Oh, come on, Felix. Do you honestly think I followed the two of you, waited until you slipped into your room, counted to three minutes in my head, then came barging in here to purposely disrupt your alone time, knowing full well what it was going to lead to?"

We blinked at each other through the silence as Dash took another loud sip of his wine.

"Holy shit. That's exactly what you fucking did!"

"I did not," Dash argued as he directed his gaze toward the open window, his finger swirling around the rim of the cup absentmindedly. "I counted to four minutes. Just to be sure."

I tried to grasp for a thread of anger but came up empty. As much as I wanted to be with Oli—and I *really* wanted to be with Oli—I wouldn't have exchanged this moment with Dash for anything. It was the first time in too damn long that things felt *normal* between us. There was no outside pressure, no world crashing down around us; we were just two carefree brothers playing immature pranks on each other for fun.

"I hate you," I murmured, meaning nothing of the sort.

"No, you don't."

I felt the corner of my lips lift at the familiar bit we always did. "No, I don't," I agreed. Dash grinned wide before taking another sip of his drink. "But I wouldn't have ever done that to you." He choked on his wine, and for the life of me, I didn't understand why.

"You're joking," he coughed.

I wasn't. I was a great friend. The *best* friend, actually.

"When have I ever—"

"Sasha, Talia, Gerard, Rosella, Amy," he rattled off, ticking off his fingers in a tally. "Aiden, Elsie, Ainsley—"

"Okay, okay. I get it."

"And let's not forget what you did with Lola."

"Hey! I am not responsible—"

"You set me up!" Dash argued dramatically. "You arranged the whole thing knowing damn well what was going to happen."

"That isn't true! I had only heard rumors. That's not the same as actually *knowing*."

"Close enough!"

"—and what she did wasn't even that bad!" I tried. Honestly, he was being a bit overdramatic about an ordeal that happened over eight years ago.

"Wasn't *that bad*?! It took the Medicus three hours to fix my damn dick, you asshole!"

I burst out in laughter.

"And much like you are now, you were amused the entire time I was being mended!" he yelled, though his voice was a broken cadence between feigning anger and fighting humor.

I threw my head back, unable to stop the deep laughter from surfacing as I remembered when we were sixteen and specialized in getting into as much trouble as possible. Dash followed me into hysterics, and I basked in the familiar sound of home.

As much as I wanted Oli, I needed *this* more.

Forks scraped across full plates of food no one seemed to be touching. The tension was uncomfortably palpable and no amount of clearing my throat dramatically was going to ease it. I glanced over to find Oli prodding his chicken as if it was still alive, a look of contempt souring his face.

"Is something wrong with the meal?" Dash asked—the first sentence spoken by anyone in what had to have been twenty minutes.

"Just trying to determine if it's poison," he jabbed.

Oh Gods.

I set my utensils down and reached for my wine, taking a generous gulp while wishing it was liquor instead. As uncomfortable as the silence was, I'd much prefer it to the pissing contest that was about to take place.

Dash scoffed as he ran his tongue along the inside of his cheek, indicating his internal struggle between delivering a retort and maintaining composure. A sparkle in his blue eyes caught the light and he straightened in his chair, letting me know the former had won the battle. Great.

"That's only in the tea," Dash quipped. "But I can have some brought to you if you'd like." He raised a finger to gesture to the waitstaff.

"I'm fine," Oli ground out with a pleasant smile.

"You sure? It's really no trouble."

"I said, I'm fine."

My eyes closed and I pressed my fingers to my temple to massage away the headache beginning to form. I didn't expect them to be best friends, but I had hoped we could have gotten through just one meal without the personal attacks.

I could feel their stares branding my skin, but I wasn't ready to give them my attention and let them see the disappointment I couldn't hide. I knew how selfish I was being for trying to push Oli to get past his hurt and anger over what happened to Ainsley's parents, but I couldn't help wanting the man I loved to have a cordial relationship with my brother.

"Let's air this shit out, Olivier. What's your problem with me?" My eyes fluttered open to find Dash leaning back in his chair, his arms crossed firmly over his chest. Oli mirrored his movements, whether by coincidence or spite, I didn't know.

My boyfriend's hard glower was his only response. My instincts were screaming at me to ease the obvious tension, but if I did, nothing would come of it. The two most important men in my life would stay on the path of hating each other.

Dash's fingers drummed lightly on the tabletop in a steady rhythm, his head cocking to the side as he examined Olivier. "This isn't about Ainsley's parents," Dash announced as he continued to tap against the iron. "Or Evander's. You may hate my father for that heinous act, but you're much too intelligent to hold someone who was a toddler at the time responsible."

Oli arched a brow but offered no other indication that Dash was on the right path. Only the slight unease I felt drifting from him and into me gave him away.

"Evander and you are close, but again, you seem too level-headed to let any animosity he feels toward me sway your judgment, even if you *were* the one who raised him," Dash continued, leaning forward to rest his elbows on the table.

I turned to Oli to find the corded muscles in his arms tense. His mouth was set in a hard line, and a muscle in his jaw feathered as he clenched his teeth. How did Dash know Oli wasn't only an advisor, but also the man who had raised the King of Tenebrae since he was five years old? That wasn't information even King Perceval had been privy to. My entire time as his advisor, we assumed Evander was brought up by maidens just as every other orphan in Disparya had been.

Dash steepled his hands and placed his chin onto his interlaced fingers as he continued to study Olivier. I threw a sidelong glance at my boyfriend just as he shifted in his seat—his first tell.

"I could say your issues stem from what transpired between Felix and me, but I know him too well. He'd never allow you to take your frustrations out on me when our problems don't concern you. Which means this is about Ainsley."

Oli remained quiet.

"Seeing your reaction to her rejection by the land, the pride you exhibit whenever she asserts herself, and your evident wish for retribution regarding her parents' demise, it's clear she's your family—a sibling, perhaps? Not by blood, but in the same way Felix is mine," Dash deduced, a sly smile creeping up his face.

I had known Dash was a logical thinker, his mind constantly working to solve puzzles only he could see, but he had always moved through his steps silently until he reached a point in which he was ready to share. This was the first time he had ever recited his thought process aloud.

"You hurt her," Oli said, offering his first response since the assessment began.

"I did. But that's not your concern."

"Like hell it isn't."

I swallowed hard, feeling the tension turn to anger and settle in my gut like a sinking rock in a pond, coarse and heavy. I shoved away their emotions and instead focused on my own, though they weren't much better.

"With all due respect, I don't owe you an explanation, an apology, or a damn thing. What happened between Ainsley and me is something *we* are working through—not you."

"I have every right to look out for her. She's my sister," Oli said, angrily rising from the table.

"And her own person," Dash countered but remained seated. "While I commend your protectiveness and love for Ainsley, the matter between us does not involve you. You don't have to like me, Olivier, but you have to respect that I'm in her life for as long as she'll allow me to be, and in whatever capacity she'll have me."

"You don't deserve her forgiveness."

"I never said I did."

Oli opened his mouth on instinct to argue, but promptly shut it at Dash's unexpected response. He reeled back slightly, looking at a loss for words as he regarded the seated king in front of him. Oli's anger spiked for the briefest of moments before a shallow wave of acceptance blanketed him.

Thank the Gods.

Dash released a long exhale as if realizing the argument would soon be over. "Listen, Olivier. Felix loves you, and that holds weight with me. I don't expect us to be friends, but I want to at least try to be civil for his sake," Dash explained, gesturing his chin in my direction.

I smiled weakly at my friend for the restraint he was still displaying for my benefit. Twisting my attention to Oli, I was met with softened eyes and a sad lift of his lips. Guilt was flooding my senses, radiating from both men at the table as they watched me silently.

"But in order for this to work, Olivier, you have to understand that the relationship I have with Felix and Ainsley is between us. You don't have to like that they chose to forgive me for past discretions, but you have to accept that it's their choice."

In a move that stunned even me, Dash extended his hand across the table. I knew that Dash was nothing like Perceval, who would have simply ordered Oli to get over himself and shut up. But to offer his hand... A king performing the gesture of a truce with someone below the status of royalty just wasn't done, at least not that I had ever witnessed except while in Tenebrae.

By the widening of Oli's eyes, he had only ever seen it with Evander.

Hesitantly, the Tenebraen advisor reached out his hand and clasped it with the King of Caelum's, shaking once and releasing it.

Peace and understanding had finally been brokered between the two men. And their love for me was the reason—as if there would have ever been a better one.

Dash smiled as he stood, tossing the cloth napkin that had been in his lap onto the table.

"On that note, I'm going to head to bed and leave you to it."

"What? No!" I exclaimed. The two most important men in my life just agreed to become friends for my benefit, and I wasn't going to let either of them leave the table until that happened.

"I know what you're trying to do, and as glad as I am that your boyfriend and I reached an agreement, I think it's best not to push your luck with this," Dash responded.

"Agreed," Oli added, taking a long drink of his previously untouched wine.

"But—"

"Goodnight," Dash interrupted as he backed away from the table and disappeared into the palace, leaving Oli and me alone with the servants. Fine. My plans to mold their relationship now that Olivier was willing to stop being a dick would just have to wait.

I leaned back in my chair and began poking at my chicken just as Oli had done earlier.

"Are you going to continue pouting, or are you going to come to bed?" he asked, and I turned in the chair to see him already halfway across the terrace. A wicked smile curved my lips as I jumped up and ran after him.

31
Ainsley

Inviting warmth and the scent of home enveloped me as we crested the threshold, shortly followed by Lia's excited squeals and body slamming into me as she wrapped her arms around my neck and squeezed me tight while sobbing.

She gripped my hand and tugged me through the house as she explained that Calidore and Marce had filled her in on everything that had transpired since crossing into Caelum when they arrived home shortly before us. Lia was just as pissed as the rest of us regarding the secrecy and stashing of our closest friend in a kingdom he didn't belong to. It was going to take a lot to regain that trust with Tallis after his stunt, regardless of his reasoning.

"So you're officially queen now?" she asked, handing me a cup of coffee as we settled onto the hearth next to the roaring fire in the library, just the two of us.

Evander had traveled to the palace to begin preparations for our future guests. Jahier, Tallis, and Dash would soon be traveling to our kingdom to strategize for the pending war. Declan had sent word while we were away that he would also be joining us to offer as much help as he could.

"It seems that way," I answered, blowing against the steam wafting from my drink.

I glanced inwardly at the new door that kept my Tremo Gift in place, running my magic along the deep purple doorframe curiously. It felt different from my shadows and illusions like it harbored something darker, deeper, and more complex.

"Where's Marce and Cal?" I asked, wanting to direct my focus away from the strange new magic I didn't yet understand.

"Marce went to get ingredients to make dinner, but she should be back any second."

"And Cal?"

"Running an errand."

"Because that's not a cryptic answer at all," I deadpanned.

Lia smiled, but it didn't reach her eyes. I could tell it was a topic she didn't want to elaborate on.

"Are you okay?" I asked instead.

She sighed and placed her mug down on the brick hearth. "Not really, no." I followed suit, straightening as I fully faced her. "Do you remember what I told you about why I left Ministro?"

"You said you wanted a change of scenery. I knew there was more to the story, but I didn't want to pry. You never made me talk before I was ready."

She smiled gently and squeezed my hand. "Thank you for that." I returned the gesture and waited for her to continue. "When I lived in Ministro, Harbin wasn't yet king, and as bad as he is, his father was worse. There wasn't a day that went by where people didn't fear for their lives."

Felix had recounted tales of the harsh and inhumane practices in his homeland, but it was difficult to imagine a worse situation than the current one.

"What do you mean?"

"Felix explained to you what happens to orphans, right?"

I nodded, thinking back to the sick act of discarding children on a whim as if their lives didn't matter, all because their rulers couldn't be bothered with caring for them.

"When Harbin's father, King Casimir, reigned, it wasn't just the children."

Bile crept into my throat as I read the history of pain written plainly on Lia's beautiful face. She didn't need to say any more for me to know she had lost so much during that time.

"Ministro doesn't possess physical Gifts like Caelum, or even ones that could defend and kill like Tenebrae, save for the Imperiums, though very few people are Gifted that magic. King Casimir was constantly paranoid that the other kingdoms were plotting to overthrow him and take the land for their own, despite Disparya being in a period of peace. He became obsessed with filling Ministro with only the strongest magic wielders," Lia continued, her eyes glazing over as she stared into the distance, remembering a time centuries ago.

She picked her cup back up and took a small sip of her tea. With a deep breath, she prepared to dive deeper into a story she seemed unsure she wanted to tell.

"At first, he rounded up every person who didn't possess a Gift, uprooting them from their homes and forcing them to move to the eastern coast. We assumed he would have stopped there... But then the assessments began." Her voice was distant, holding a sorrow so deep it could rival the depths of an ocean.

My heart splintered at the haunting agony that rolled off her, wrapping around me and filling every crevice of my being. I didn't raise a shield, didn't protect myself from the heartache that deserved to be felt.

Lia closed her eyes and spoke through the emotion already thick in her throat. "Casimir claimed the process was part of a new hierarchy system he had in place, though I suppose that wasn't a lie—it just wasn't what we thought it was," she recounted bitterly. "Each Gift wielder was examined to determine their magic level and then assigned a rank based on it."

"But how—"

"Casimir had a Magusier on his council," Lia answered before I could finish.

Harbin didn't have one in his rank of advisors, which was why he was so furious the truth of Felix's abilities had been kept a secret from him. That meant that something had to have happened to the Magusier Lia was speaking of.

"For two weeks, we were called to the throne room to line up and be given a status based on our baseline. Those who held the most magic were assigned the rank of gold and moved into the palace. Everyone just below them was given a silver rank, and they were directed to move into the surrounding villages."

Lia went eerily quiet, the room seeming to still with her silence. I grabbed her cup and placed it back down with mine before grasping both of her hands, holding on tight as she worked for the courage to continue.

"Everyone else was given a red status and removed from their homes. Casimir claimed they weren't worth the resources needed to keep them alive and had them escorted to the coast to live out their days with the nonmagic wielders. Even their children weren't permitted to stay. The Magusier attempted to inform Casimir that certain individuals would have a higher baseline once their Gift manifested, but the king considered their bloodline impure and undeserving, regardless."

When Lia's green eyes fluttered open, they were misted, a single tear languidly slipping down her porcelain cheek. My chest constricted as I brushed my thumbs over the back of her hands, and a revolting thought entered my mind. As much as I wanted to push it away, I couldn't.

"They weren't sent to the coast, were they? None of them were," I whispered, already knowing the answer.

Her lip wobbled as more tears streamed down her face. "It took us a week to realize what was truly happening. Even the Magusier didn't know at first." Her voice broke on each word like shattered glass, sending jagged-edged shards directly into my heart.

I swallowed down the nausea as my eyes welled and Lia's silhouette blurred in my vision. Her misery and regret surged into me as if it were my own, and I welcomed it with open arms, refusing to allow Lia to have to feel it all on her own.

"I remember my assessment as if it were yesterday." She took deep and steady breaths as she held my stare like it could keep her grounded to the world. "There was a woman a few people ahead of me with a young daughter, only six years old. The closer the line shifted to the Magusier, the more nervous the mother became. I couldn't blame her. It wasn't just *her* life at stake, but her child's too."

My stomach knotted, realizing this was the world my father had grown up in—the world *I* might have grown up in. How many people had he watched being dragged away to their deaths during Casimir's reign of terror? Did he try to stop it?

"Right before the mother's turn for assessment, she moved out of line and walked to me as she clung tightly to her child," Lia continued. "I'll never forget her soft mahogany eyes or the way they silently pleaded for her daughter's safety." I grasped her hands tighter as she sobbed through her story, her body shaking as she recounted each horrendous moment. "She kissed her daughter on the cheek and handed her to me before stepping back in line. I didn't hesitate—just took her and held her against me as if she were my own. Her eyes never left her child as the Magusier called the color she had known would be her fate from the start."

I pulled Lia to me, wrapping my arms around her neck as she cried into my shoulder, letting the memories of that fateful day flow from her. My cheeks were wet as I wept for my friend, for the mother, for the six-year-old child whose entire world was ripped away from her because of one selfish man. They all deserved so much better.

"When it was my turn, the Magusier knew," she whispered, her voice barely audible as we clung to each other. "He knew she wasn't mine, but he didn't say anything. We just stared at each other as the silence carried the guilt and grief and hopelessness between us. He announced my rank as gold without ever calling to his Gift."

A shaky breath escaped my lips as I listened, unable to fully comprehend what she, the mother, and the child had gone through that day. I wasn't sure I would ever be able to, and I thanked the Gods for that. My people would never have to know that fear as long as Evander and I ruled.

"The next day, the Magusier took his own life." I shifted back from her, feeling my eyes widen in shock. "He didn't want to be complicit, and there was no other way out for him."

Judging by Lia's story, I didn't think simply refusing to aid the king would have worked out for the Magusier. Casimir didn't seem above torturing the man or those he cared about to get his way. In this case, death was the kinder escape.

"Did it stop after that?" I asked tentatively.

Lia wiped her eyes with the back of her hand as she nodded. "Yes and no. The assessments shifted to having to showcase the strength and ability of your Gift. Those who couldn't perform well enough were given the red status."

"And their children?"

"They were either handed off for safekeeping before the assessments or stashed in orphanages where no proof of the child's parentage could be found. Without a Magusier, Casimir had no choice but to wait until their Gift manifested as an adult to test them."

I breathed a shallow sigh of relief. It was still a horrible situation for those children to be in, but at least their parents found a way to keep them alive.

"I'm so sorry, Lia." The words stumbled off my tongue, small and insignificant. I struggled to come up with anything that would carry weight after hearing her story.

She pulled back and tucked a red strand of hair behind her ear as she nodded, her sad eyes finding mine.

"Did the girl know what happened to her mother?"

"Not for a long while. That first night, she—Tessa—told me that her mother had gone to build them a house on the coast, and she was to stay with me until it was completed. She had told Tessa that it might not be done for quite some time, but eventually, they would be together again."

My heart squeezed at Lia's story and how deeply this mother had loved her daughter. She couldn't give Tessa the life she knew her child deserved, so instead, she gave her the one thing that she could hold onto—hope.

"Every night, when I would tuck Tessa into bed, I'd tell her a story of a mother and daughter who lived by the sea. They spent their days bathing in the warm sun and swimming in the waves. They would collect the colorful shells and sea glass scattered across the sandy shore. They would laugh and play and love. They were happy," she said, her voice so distant despite being so close. "Eventually, it became more than just a story; it became the life I wanted for Tessa, for every child in Ministro, and for *me*. And I wasn't going to give up until I made it happen."

"Is that when you came to Tenebrae?"

A faint smile ghosted her lips as she lost herself in her memories. "After learning that both Agnitio and Tenebrae were safe havens for anyone needing refuge, I spent the next several years slowly smuggling children out of Ministro. I was good at it, too, never once getting caught by anyone... Until—"

"Me," Cal interrupted. Lia's grin grew as he stepped through the room and took a seat by her side on the hearth.

"Only because I let you."

"I'd gladly fall into any trap you set." Calidore kissed her cheek, causing it to flush the moment his lips parted from her skin. "But we both know that was the last thing you wanted."

"Perhaps," she teased playfully as Cal wiped away the few tears that had fallen down her cheeks. The love they shared drifted around them, filling the room with warmth and comfort that rivaled the flames beside us.

"Why the secrecy if Tenebrae and Agnitio were safe?" I asked.

"I didn't know who I could trust or the extent of the two kingdoms' generosity. For all I knew, there were protocols to follow, and I could have been turned away and forced to return to Ministro with the children in tow. It was safer for me to drop them off at an orphanage and wait in the shadows until they were taken inside."

"And then..." Cal pushed, letting me know this was his favorite part of the story. His excitement over the otherwise somber memory made it clear that this was where he came into her life. Lia's answering smile at the man she loved confirmed as much.

"And then, this one here," she enclosed her arms around his middle to emphasize her point, "Was visiting a friend in Agnitio where he saw me drop two children off and not-so-stealthily scramble behind a nearby tree as I waited for them to be let in."

"And she looked adorable doing it."

Cal kissed the tip of her nose before running a hand through her long, red hair and staring into her eyes with nothing but admiration. She melted into his touch, scooting even closer to him as a smile split her full lips.

"For five years, he met me at the border of Ministro and took each child I brought to a new home so I wouldn't have to risk my own life more than necessary. With his help, we managed to save over two hundred children throughout all of Ministro."

Arms slid around my stomach from behind, and I sank back against the familiar presence. I hadn't even noticed him enter the room or sit by my side, too engrossed in Lia's story. Van pulled me onto his lap, twisting my body until I was sitting the way he wanted. I squirmed to get more comfortable, which only caused him to tighten his hold, not allowing me to gain an inch.

"Van," I pleaded as I continued to struggle.

He didn't let up. "Shhh, you're missing the story."

Knowing my attempts were a lost cause, I sighed in defeat and relaxed into him. I could practically feel his victorious smirk as he rested his cheek on my head. I didn't have it in me to be annoyed with him, even when he was acting like a child.

"We were doing so well with our mission until one night, everything went wrong," Lia continued. "Somehow, I had been found out, and soldiers were placed along my path to the border. I had to divert our route, and when I didn't show up at our meeting time—"

"I went looking for her," Cal finished. "She was surrounded, a sword held to her throat as the soldiers began dragging the children away."

"Cal used his shadows and managed to kill every last one of them, saving us all."

"As soon as the children were brought somewhere safe, I took her home with me. And we've been together ever since."

I smiled fondly at the pair and the strength they exuded, my chest filling with pride. I was lucky to call them my family.

"What happened to Tessa?" I asked curiously.

My friend smiled brightly as she directed her attention away from the man at her side. "She lives on the northern coast. In a house by the sea."

I smiled just as wide. "Do you see her often?"

Lia's face fell just a fraction, but it was enough for me to notice. "Not as much as I'd like," she admitted solemnly.

"But one day you will," Cal said. The way he spoke the words was as if they were more than a promise—they were a vow.

I watched the exchange between the two, an integral part of the story clicking into place. Tessa's life was what Lia wanted for herself, and instead of living it, she was here with us. She read the realization on my face, and her hands reached out and clasped mine again.

"It's not that I don't love you all, because I do," she began quickly. "You, Van, Marce, Oli, and Felix mean *everything* to me. You're my family, and I wouldn't have it any other way."

Her green eyes darted across mine as she frantically searched for signs that I believed her.

"But you want a quiet life in a house by the sea," I said through a small smile.

She nodded slowly, seeming to understand I wasn't angry with her for the choice. How could I be? Lia had seen and been through more than anyone should in a lifetime. She deserved to finally experience the peace she fought so hard to grant others.

"When will you leave?" I asked.

"Tomorrow," Cal answered for her without hesitation. My eyes widened in surprise, and my heart dropped into my stomach at the thought of being separated from one of my closest friends so soon.

Lia threw him a sidelong glance that had me breathing a sigh of relief. "Not anytime soon," she corrected, not taking her gaze from him.

"I just returned from finalizing the plans. You could leave first thing in the morning and meet her when she arrives in—"

"No."

"You'd be safer with her in Vorsutos."

"I'm not leaving you, Cal." Lia's tone was final, inviting no room for arguments. Her mind was made up.

The two stared at each other for a long moment, the silent tension carrying unexchanged words between them. I couldn't argue with her logic. There would never be a situation in which I would voluntarily leave Evander, especially when our time in this world could be over so soon.

"We are in this life together," she told him, raising a hand to cup his cheek as she spoke. I will not abandon you or our family. And when this war is over, you and I will move to our house by the sea, just as you've been promising me for centuries."

Cal nodded against her palm as he released a deep exhale, accepting her choice.

"I only ask that you not choose something astronomical in price," Evander quipped, and my brows furrowed in question.

"Van is paying for the house," Lia clarified, a grin stretching across her face as she looked at my husband. "He owes us."

"You act as if I was *that* bad growing up."

"Oh, you absolutely were."

A tiny laugh bubbled up through my throat as I listened to them squabble, Lia giving Van countless instances in which he was miserable to deal with as an adolescent. Knowing him as well as I did, she wasn't exaggerating in the least.

"Lia, you have the Queen of Tenebrae's blessing to choose whatever house you see fit. Raising the asshole behind me couldn't have been easy," I told her. Van poked the sensitive side of my stomach, and I squirmed against his touch.

"You're supposed to be loyal to *me*," he pointed out. "I'm pretty sure it was in our vows."

"Really? I don't remember that." I twisted to look at him, then shrugged casually. "But I *do* try to block out any time I'm forced to spend with you, so that makes sense." His lips quirked into a smirk he was trying to hide.

"Smartass."

I turned back toward Lia, ready to give her my full attention when soft lips grazed the shell of my ear. "I'll be sure to punish you for that later," he whispered low enough for only me to hear.

My throat tightened and my thighs clenched with immediate need that only he could sate. I shifted in his lap, trying to readjust and put his filthy promise out of my mind, but the fingers that stroked my arm slowly weren't helping. I knew him, and his gentle touch was just a heated reminder of where those fingers would be later. He wasn't playing fair.

"I will gladly take your offer, Your Majesty," Lia said happily, pulling me from Evander's distraction. "But the credit for raising him goes entirely to Oli and Marce. I didn't even meet Van until he was eight. And for years, we only visited to celebrate birthdays and holidays."

I looked to Van for confirmation, and he nodded. This whole time, I had been under the assumption that the four of them had raised Evander together from the moment his parents were killed.

"It wasn't until Van was about fourteen that I received a letter from Oli, begging for help. Apparently, your husband was so much of a handful that even Marce couldn't deal with him," Cal added.

A heavy thump sounded at the other side of the room and we all turned to find Marceline standing in the doorway, a full bag of groceries dropped at her feet.

"That's total bullshit," she argued, striding into the library. "Olivier was the pushover, not me. He's the one who refused to dish out any tough love to *that* little asshole," she said, pointing a finger at her king, "So he got away with *everything*." She drew out the last word for emphasis.

A guilty grin formed on Evander's face as if he were proud of his younger self. Of course he was.

"Anyway," Cal cut in, drawing out the word in mock annoyance. "I obviously said yes, and a week later, I received my new orders to move into the palace to help train the king."

"And naturally, I joined," Lia chirped.

Evander had been through so much with losing his parents at such a young age and inheriting an entire kingdom on top of it. But through that heartache and loss, he earned four people who dropped everything to help him become the man he is today. Four people who raised him, who loved him, and who would gladly lay down their lives for him.

I tilted my head back, causing his eyes to drop to mine, and lifted my chin in a clear demand. Evander leaned forward and his lips brushed mine in the barest of kisses before he straightened again and sought Marce.

"For the record," he said arrogantly, "I got away with so much shit with you, too—*more* than with Olivier, actually."

"Liar," Marce growled.

"It's true. You were far easier to manipulate than he was. All I had to do was start talking shit about someone you were mad at, and anything I wanted would be mine."

Cal and Lia both laughed as Marceline's face transformed two shades redder. I bit my lip to stop my own smile, knowing it would only fuel her obvious irritation. She said a string of indecipherable words, like she couldn't quite figure out what she wanted to throw at Evander.

With an agitated grunt, she turned and headed for the door, calling over her shoulder, "Dinner will be ready in an hour for everyone except Evander."

He chuckled low in my ear, her anger only amusing him more. "Actually, we have to head to the palace shortly," he countered.

"Meeting not go well?" Cal asked.

Van shook his head. My stomach bottomed out. If there was pushback from our council about the peace deal we made with Agnitio, Caelum, and Prince Jahier, it could lead to an uprising in our own kingdom. The last thing any of us needed was for our people to revolt.

"They don't think it's a good idea?" I questioned, the worry thick in my throat.

"It doesn't matter what they think. The rulers of what's left of Disparya made a decision, and we're not going to back out of it simply because of their misplaced fear. It's going to take trust on all of our parts for this plan to work. Our council is just going to have to learn to deal with that."

Evander's statement exuded confidence and determination, but there was an underlying note of worry woven within. His charcoal eyes met mine, and a wrinkle creased his forehead as he read the nervous thoughts written on my face.

"We're staying there tonight because I don't want to let unease fester before I can fully present the arrangement to our generals tomorrow," he explained. "If I'm not present, it gives time for doubt to spread before that. With the stakes being this high, it's better to be safe than sorry, and I want them to be able to come to me immediately should they need to express their apprehension."

My jaw flexed as I pondered the possibility of our council turning against us at a time like this. Regardless of their skepticism about the other kings, this was Tenebrae's only chance at survival. Without working together, none of the kingdoms would survive this war.

"Have fun with that," Marce said as she reached down to pick up her bag of forgotten groceries.

"You're coming too."

"I'll show up to the meeting tomorrow, but it's already late, and I don't feel like going tonight."

"Even if Kenji is there?" Van asked, his question low and nonchalant as he picked at his nails.

"He's at the palace?!"

"Saw him when I first got there."

"AND YOU'RE ONLY JUST NOW TELLING ME! Dammit, Van, that was hours ago!"

The bag she had picked up dropped to the floor once again as she sprinted out of the room. "WE'RE LEAVING IN FIVE MINUTES!" she yelled from the hall as thunderous stomps echoed in her wake.

My family let out a giggle, and I suddenly felt like I was missing out on something important.

"Who's Kenji?" I whispered only to Evander, in case I was supposed to know who that was.

"Marceline's husband."

32

Ainsley

Steam from the shower I had just stepped out of filled our bathing room, leading condensation to cling to the mirror above the sink. With one hand, I wiped away the moisture while the other grasped a soft white towel around me.

"If Tessa lives in northern Tenebrae, why did Cal want Lia to meet her in Vorsutos?" I called into the bedroom as I worked a brush through my wet hair.

Evander hadn't joined me to bathe, claiming he wanted to stop by the dining room to make an appearance so the council would know he was staying in the building tonight. He only arrived back in the room a few minutes before I had finished, explaining that the council members were more than a little uncomfortable to see him again so unexpectedly. Before I could voice any concern and suggest going back downstairs to ensure tensions remained calm, Van informed me that Marce and Kenji were already on it. Kenji. Marce's damn *husband*.

"During times of war, it's common to move your loved ones as far from harm as you can. Though Vorsutos is involved in this conflict, Disparya is far more dangerous of a place to be," Evander explained. "Lia and Cal have arranged for Tessa and her family to travel there, and Declan has already agreed to provide them with land in the south of Vorsutos, far from where any battles have taken place. Cal's mother was sent there during the Second Great War and loved it so much that she chose not to come back. Tessa and her family will be staying near her."

I nodded, though Evander couldn't see from where I was in the bathing room. It was good they both were able to get the people who meant the most to them out of the continent before harm had a chance to come to them.

"Is there anyone you'd like to send?" he asked. My mind rummaged through the list of people I knew, coming up with only Imogen as a viable answer.

"Did you make arrangements for anyone?" Evander didn't answer. At first, I thought he hadn't heard me, but then an idea wrenched itself into my mind, filling me with only defiance. "I'm not going," I said immediately.

"I know." The words were soft and sad.

"You can't make me, Evander. I'm not leaving you. We stay together."

"I know."

"So if you knew, then why would you bother arranging for me to leave?"

"Because, I wanted to give you the option, and selfishly, I wish you would take it. Lives will be lost to this war; that's just a fact. Don't blame me for wanting to ensure yours won't be one of them."

I blew out a heavy breath, unable to fault him for his attempt to keep me safe. If I had known about the option, I probably would have arranged it for him as well.

"So tell me, why the hell didn't I know Marce was married?" I asked, changing the subject. I could hear the smile in his voice when he spoke again, knowing I wasn't going to fight him on the issue.

"Because it's not a big deal. They were close friends while both stationed in one of the western camps alongside the border of Venator. One night, they drank entirely too much and got married just for fun," he answered from the other room.

"Just for fun? They weren't in love?"

"Nope. At least not back then," Van said.

"And now?"

"Marce will still deny it if you call her out. But we all saw how quickly she ran to get ready."

"What about Kenji?"

"He'll deny it too... And then act as if he didn't barge into my meeting earlier all out of breath and frantic because he thought she'd be in there."

I laughed, picturing the shocked, then amused look on Evander's face at the interruption. Tomorrow, I would finally get to meet Marce's mysterious husband and force him to tell me stories about her when they were younger. I couldn't wait.

My stomach rumbled and I was suddenly aware I hadn't eaten a single thing today. "Are you hungry?" I asked, placing the brush down and turning to head into the next room. My steps froze the moment my gaze locked onto Van's. His eyes dragged up my body, darkening as his jaw ticked and fingers clenched at his side.

"Starving."

My heart pounded at the blatant need on his face as he stormed for me, tugging the towel away and dropping it at our feet. His lips crashed to mine a second later, his hand fisting in my hair as he held me against him.

My fingers pressed into his arm to steady myself as his tongue dove between my lips, sweeping across mine and coaxing a moan from me. I melted into him, savoring the feel of him hardening against my stomach.

"You know what that little sound does to me, love." His voice was a deep and desperate rasp as his free hand trailed down the length of my body and dipped between my legs. Silken fingers parted my thighs as his mouth continued to move against mine with fervent need, stealing the breath from my lungs and fogging my mind.

A gasp escaped me as his hand drew higher along the sensitive inside of my thighs. Higher and higher and higher he climbed, until...

"Fuck," he growled the second he felt the warm wetness waiting for him.

I arched into the touch, urging him to continue his ascent so he would finally reach the spot I was so desperate for. Evander didn't hesitate, thank the Gods. He dragged a single long finger from my entrance to my clit, causing my knees to buckle beneath me as I cried out.

His hand moved from my hair to wrap around my waist, keeping me upright as he swirled his thumb around me while kissing me harder. My nails bit into his skin as I gasped for breath and rolled my hips over him to meet each passing of his thumb. I was coiled tight, that delicious tension building at the friction of his hand pressing against me and moving in time to my thrusts.

"Van," I begged, as I sank my teeth into his shoulder, trying desperately to anchor myself to the edge before I tumbled off of it. He groaned at the sharp pain but didn't pull away, seeming to get off on my feral need for him. I wanted that promised relief, but I wasn't ready for this to be over already.

It had been far too long since we were together, but now I couldn't wait any longer. I needed him to kiss me, touch me, taste me, *everywhere*. I needed to get lost in him forever without coming to an end because no amount of time would ever be enough with him. My thighs clenched around his hand, desperate to hold on for a little while longer.

"I don't think so, wife." Evander slid a long finger inside me, his tongue lapping over mine and keeping pace with his rhythm. My eyes screwed shut, stars exploding behind my lids as he brought me closer and closer to my release. Holy fucking *Gods*.

"Your Majesty?" a voice called, accompanied by a knock on our bedroom door. No, no no no no. This was not happening right now.

Van's eyes met mine, and just as I thought he was going to pull away, a crooked and devious smile curved his lips. He released my waist and plunged a second finger inside me. I cried out in pleasure half a second before Evander's hand clasped around my mouth to quiet the sound.

"What is it, Clyde?" he asked as he continued to fuck me with his hand. I held my breath, trying like hell not to make a sound as my body coiled and clenched around him.

"I just wanted to see if you and Her Majesty would like dinner brought to your room," the servant replied.

Van quirked an eyebrow at me in question. I shook my head violently against his palm. How could he ask me that right now? Van shrugged, and pressed his thumb to my clit, causing me to buck forward against him and let out a strangled sound.

"What's on the menu?" My husband asked before giving me a mischievous wink. What the hell was he *doing*? Why wasn't he sending Clyde away?!

Evander's fingers curled inside me, drawing a deep pleasure to the pit of my stomach. I bit down on his palm as tears pricked my eyes from trying to stave off my release until we were alone again. He moved even faster, determined to drive me to the brink of madness, and a soft whimper pressed into his hand.

"Quiet, love. He'll hear you," Evander warned. All at once, a thought entered my mind.

My eyes narrowed a fraction, and I studied him while Clyde rattled off meal options that Van wasn't listening to. He grinned, confirming my idea.

This asshole was *trying* to get me to lose control—trying to make it known to the man outside the door exactly what he was in the middle of doing. He wanted me shattered so entirely that I could be heard even with his hand blocking the sound. My jaw clenched as I lifted my chin in challenge. It wasn't going to happen without a fight, that's for damn sure.

Evander's smirk grew, a shine in his eyes coming forth at the sight of my defiance. "You're not going to win this battle. But Gods, do I love it when you try." His mouth was on mine again, his tongue scorching hot and searching for every inch it hadn't yet touched.

"Does any of that meet your desire, Your Majesty?"

I tried to pull away, but the hand that had once clasped my mouth was now at my waist, holding me still as his fingers pumped in and out of me. He wasn't playing fair, so neither would I.

"What is there for dessert—" His voice dropped on the last word as I cupped his hard cock through his pants, catching him off guard. I moved my hand up and down, stroking every ready inch of him as he struggled to catch his breath.

Clyde listed the options, though neither of us was paying attention as we worked each other. Our hands and tongue roamed over teeth and flesh as we both tried to keep quiet and not give in to our desperate need for release.

My fingers speared through his black hair, grabbing it hard as he hit a marvelous spot that had my entire body quaking and shadows spilling from my skin. Evander groaned at the sensation. I wasn't going to last much longer and he knew it. Sheer will and determination weren't going to be enough to stop me from cascading over that glorious edge and tumbling into oblivion.

"I already told you; you won't be winning this match," he whispered. I could hear the truth in that promise. He needed this and wouldn't stop his torment until I was clenching around him and screaming his name.

Fuck it.

I shoved my face into his chest, releasing him to fist his shirt as I barreled into my release. His hand curled around the back of my head, keeping me pressed against him as I came hard around his fingers with his muffled name on my lips.

Spots danced in my vision, my breathing went ragged, and my legs shook from the aftermath of my orgasm. Evander's chest rose and fell beneath me heavily, his own restraint slipping.

"We're fine, Clyde, thank you," Evander called breathlessly. He pressed a soft kiss to my forehead, his hand stroking down my hair as I worked to catch my breath.

Van's fingers pulled out of me, leaving me empty and aching for him all over again. I wanted more—*needed* more. As if he knew exactly that, he dropped to his knees before me, hands gripping my waist to keep me upright as he trailed wet kisses up the inside of my trembling thigh.

"You're not going to eat?"

Van smiled against my hot flesh. "Oh, I plan on doing exactly that, Clyde. Now go away."

His mouth was on me a breath later, sucking and licking along my entrance. The moan that came out of me was just loud enough for the whole damn palace to hear. I didn't care anymore. Let them know exactly what we were doing. I closed my eyes and focused on nothing but the way his tongue felt against me, letting myself fall back into the endless void of desire.

33

Ainsley

The cold stone bit into my flesh, sending prickles of goosebumps over my body. I shifted to get more comfortable and ran my fingers across the hard marble beneath my hands. Ten minutes had passed since I slid from the comfort of my bed beside Evander and journeyed down the dark halls. Any minute now, he would notice my absence and find the note I left for him on my pillow.

Come and find me.

My eyes scanned the massive room. Dozens of floor-to-ceiling windows lined the walls, bathing the space in moonlight and causing the white veining in the black marble floors to appear as an illuminated path along the ground. A smirk lifted my lips as I thought back to the first time I had been in here and how different things were then. Before, I was frightened and unaware of who I was, not only in the sense of my familial ties but as a person. And now...

Tendrils of darkness licked my bare flesh, cascading down my body in gentle ripples like a sheer robe made entirely of my shifting magic. I crossed my legs and straightened my posture as I waited...wearing nothing but my shadows and a crown atop my head.

Less than a minute later, shadows swirled in the center of the room. Evander stepped through them, his gaze on the slip of paper held between his index and middle finger. I knew it wouldn't take him long to find me. We could sense each other's presence whenever in the same place, the sensation growing stronger the closer we were.

My eyes roamed down his bare chest, tracing the lines of the chiseled muscle that dipped below the waistband of his soft pants. I wet my lips, practically salivating at the sight of him making his way toward me with one casual hand tucked into his pocket.

"Very cryptic note, my—" The words died on his lips, and his feet fumbled to a stop the second he turned his gaze straight ahead.

Evander's mouth dropped, his eyes shifting back and forth, up and down, like he didn't know where to let them settle. His pupils dilated, swallowing the deep grey and leaving me with dark pits of hunger.

My note slid from between his fingers and floated to the ground like a feather in the breeze. Evander didn't seem to notice—didn't seem to see anything but me.

His jaw clenched, the muscles in his body visibly straining as he tried to control that flow of animalistic desire I could feel radiate from him. I uncrossed my legs, spreading them just barely as my shadows drifted down over me, blocking the view he so desperately wanted to see.

"I seem to recall you promising to show me the throne room," I said, waving a hand to gesture over the space we were in. "You haven't done so."

Evander stepped forward as if my words were pulling him on a string. In five long strides, he reached the dais and climbed the few steps separating us. His silhouette towered over me as he rested his palms on the arms of my throne and leaned forward, peering down from only a few inches away.

"How unforgivable of me," he whispered, his stare dipping to my full lips. "Let me make it up to you." My thighs clenched together at the hunger in his words, but as much as I wanted his mouth on mine, that wasn't why I came here. It wasn't the promise I was given.

Before Evander could close the gap between our lips, my Obscure rushed from me, a single black strand slamming into his chest to halt him. It had anticipated my desire before my mind could fully form the thought. It was like the instinct of my intentions, knowing what I wanted before even I did. Our eyes left each other, both of us now focusing on the strange magic that emerged.

My head tilted to the side as I examined it. I wasn't physically touching Evander, but it *felt* as if I was. I could feel the warmth of his flesh and beating heart as if it were my hand there rather than my Obscure.

The magic slid up his bare chest, over his neck, and paused at his cheek a breath before I could tell my mind to do it. Evander hummed against the touch of darkness, closing his eyes and leaning into it. His hand pressed to the Obscure, slipping right through the wisps of black.

"What does it feel like?" I asked.

He smiled and stroked his fingers over the tendrils that broke apart and reformed to accommodate his touch—letting him in because that's what *I* would want.

"You," he answered. My lips twitched as my Obscure moved to his hair, running through it and tugging gently on the roots. His throat rumbled in a groan of desire as his eyes fluttered open and sought mine again. "Now, where were we?"

My shadows dissipated in winding wisps over me as I called them back until he could see every inch of my bare flesh. I spread my legs wider.

"You said something about wanting to worship your queen."

A gluttonous grin split his face as he raked his gaze over my bare body as if marking each spot he wanted to touch, nip, and taste. "That I do." The words were barely more than a strangled breath.

I lifted my chin and raised a brow. "So then kneel." As the last word left my lips, my Obscure slammed into his shoulders hard, forcing him to his knees with a cracking sound to the marble floor.

Evander's hands were immediately at my thighs, parting my legs to give himself better access. "I really fucking like this Obscure—"

My magic cut him off by fisting his black hair and shoving his face right where I wanted. I didn't want his remarks—I wanted his tongue. I wanted to get lost in the way he worshipped me. But more than that, I wanted to be the one in control of how he did it.

Evander groaned as his mouth moved against me like a man starved and not one who already had me several times tonight. And if he kept rolling his tongue that way, it would be several more times as well.

A moan tore from my throat as he alternated between fervent strokes and slow languid licks, savoring the taste of me. He was always so attuned to my body's desires that he knew when to slow down or go faster, harder, bringing me to the brink of ecstasy. However, when *he* was in control, he loved to push me to the verge of bliss just to pull me back and delay my pleasure. But not tonight.

I leaned back on my throne, tilting my pelvis up to take more of what he was giving.

"Love," he growled in warning as my walls fluttered around his tongue. My gods, I was so damn close. There was no way in hell I was going to stop until I got what I wanted.

"Shut up." I rocked my hips, grinding myself against his face harder as I chased that promise of release.

"Not yet," he begged, his fingers pressing into my waist to slow my movements. That wouldn't do.

My Obscure raked through his hair, grabbing the strands and yanking hard until he was forced to look up at me. Evander hissed at the pain, but I knew he loved it. His wild, frenzied eyes met mine, and my blood heated as he licked my wetness from his lips.

Another black tendril broke apart from his hair and traveled down his face, caressing gently until it wrapped around his chin and squeezed forcefully so he had no choice but to hold my stare. I was in control here, not him.

"I am your queen. You do as *I* command," I told him. Evander swallowed hard, his chest heaving with each word that left my lips. I leaned forward and pressed a soft kiss to his forehead as my Obscure released him completely. "Now finish."

Van dove forward, shoving me hard until my back slammed against the marble, causing a crack to split the stone. I didn't care. The pain was a welcomed bliss when paired with his mouth moving between my thighs.

Evander gripped my legs, spreading them wide and setting them on the arms of the throne, leaving me open and bare for him to continue his work. A scream of pleasure ripped through me as his tongue plunged in and out at a pace that had my entire body trembling with need.

"Right there," I said through a shaky breath. "Don't you fucking dare stop."

He flicked and lapped and sucked and nipped until I couldn't take it anymore. The tips of my fingers darkened, my nails sharpening into deadly points as they scraped and scratched and clawed at the black marble of my throne.

I couldn't hold on any longer—didn't want to. The windows rattled violently and the room shook from our combined power, neither of us able to contain it within our bodies.

I moaned as my eyes screwed shut and a large chunk of marble crumbled beneath the pressure of my hand. "Fucking Gods."

"It should be *my* name on your lips."

"Make me come, and it will be."

He growled at the challenge and the room rumbled even louder. A deafening crash echoed and my eyes flew open to see pieces of the stone ceiling cascading to the ground. Too much power was being released, but something about the danger—the *chaos*—of it all was so beautifully *us*. I didn't want it to stop.

"More," I demanded, throwing my head back and getting lost in him all over again, the damage falling around us only adding to my pleasure.

Evander obliged, giving me even more of what I craved. My legs began to shake uncontrollably and my hands reached for him, needing to feel his skin and not the cold stone now slick from sweat.

"Yes!" I cried as my inky claws scraped down his flesh, marking him as mine. He moaned against me in pleasure, and the sound alone sent me falling down, down, down, over that edge and straight into oblivion as I screamed his name for all of Tenebrae to hear.

Evander's mouth continued to move against me slowly, drawing out each wave of pleasure until I whimpered from the sensitivity. He retreated from between my thighs and moved up my body, licking along my rib cage, my breast, my neck, until his lips were on mine, stealing the moans of pleasure from my lungs.

"Turn around," he whispered, sucking on my tongue before biting my bottom lip hard enough that I could taste the metallic tang of blood. I shook my head, too tired to think, let alone attempt to move. "I made you a promise," he said, brushing my sweat-slicked hair from my face. "I fucked you first with my tongue, and now my cock."

"Actually, you never said the last word," I pointed out, remembering how Felix interrupted us right before he could.

"It was implied."

"*Implied* doesn't count."

Evander stood at once, grabbing hold of my arm to bring me to my feet. My legs wobbled, threatening to give out at any second. Before I could say as much, he spun me around so my back pressed to his chest, one hand sliding around my waist to keep me upright while the other curved around my throat.

I swallowed against his palm, my thighs instantly becoming slick with need again as his breath tickled the shell of my ear. Van's hand traveled an inch higher, tilting my head back as his grip tightened with the barest of pressure against my throat, letting me know this time *he* was the one in control.

"You gave me an order and I obeyed. Now it's *my* turn to take what I want from my queen," he whispered seductively, sending my heart galloping in my chest. "Do you have any objections to that?"

Fucking Gods, absolutely not. The only problem with it was that I wasn't sure if I could handle any more.

I shook my head. "But I don't think I can take it," I admitted honestly. We had already gone several rounds in our bedroom, and after this last time, I was completely weak and struggling to even stand.

"You can, and you will."

He slid the hand that held my waist to my thighs, parting them with a gentle push and finding me already wet and ready despite my fatigue. He groaned at the feel of me and then withdrew, the sound of clothes hitting the floor echoing a heartbeat later. His knee moved in between my legs, knocking them wider and keeping them separated.

"Gods, you're perfect," he said, dragging the tip of his length through my wetness. I gasped and trembled, my legs giving out beneath me a split second before Van caught me with both hands on my waist. "You can," he reminded, wrapping an arm around me and lifting me higher as he positioned himself at my entrance. "And you will."

He slid inside with one powerful thrust, and I threw my head against his shoulder, moaning loudly as he pushed and stretched and filled me completely. My body instinctively moved back against him, wanting to feel him harder, deeper.

"I told you," he whispered arrogantly. The prick loved being right.

"Just shut up and fuck me."

"There's my girl."

Evander grasped the back of my thigh, lifting it slightly to hit a spot so deep I saw stars. Faster and faster he moved, sliding out to the tip and plunging to the base repeatedly, creating that delicious friction I loved.

"Lean forward and grab the arms of your throne," he demanded. I swallowed hard before setting my eyes on the chair.

"How about we move over to yours?" I suggested, noticing that there was nothing but fractured chunks of rock where the arms of my throne should have been. Evander pressed his mouth to my neck and flicked his tongue over my flesh as he continued to move inside me.

"I said *your* throne. Figure it out."

Normally, I would have thrown back a snide remark and challenged him, but there was something in the command his voice held that made me actually *want* to give in to his demands. I wanted him to take charge and seize control of my body as if it were meant to cater to his every whim and desire. We were fire on fire, and that passion was never hotter than when we were fighting or fucking. I was kindling in his hands, ready to burn alongside him.

My eyes scanned the fragments of the black marble chair, locating the spots that would give me the best grip to hold. I leaned forward, grabbing the jagged pieces of stone and arching my ass higher for him. Evander's fingers moved from my hips and curved around me as he fell forward and dragged his tongue up my spine until he reached my neck.

My head tipped back to see him grabbing the top of the broken throne so hard that more cracks formed beneath his touch. His mouth found my ear and he bit down, tugging gently as our bodies moved as one.

"Do you know why I wanted you on *your* throne?" he asked, the hand that was curved around my stomach now trailing down to circle my clit. I gasped at the sensation and shook my head. "Because tomorrow, when you walk toward me, I want you to look at this throne and remember how it felt to have my tongue buried beneath your thighs until you couldn't take it anymore."

He pulled out of me to give way to his fingers, plunging them in deep only to withdraw and rub them around my swollen clit. A moan spilled from my lips, my body on the brink of reaching pure euphoria. Evander moved his hand away, and I whimpered at the loss of touch and promise of bliss.

"And when I place that crown on your head..." Before I had a chance to fully miss the absence, he slammed his cock back into me, sending white-hot pleasure trickling down my spine. "When you look out at your people..."

His hand slid from the top of the throne and fell to my hair, twisting around the strands until he had a fistful. Evander straightened, his chest no longer pressed to my back as he moved inside me.

"When you're sitting on your throne…" My scalp stung as he yanked my hair back, thrusting harder, deeper, faster. Oh Gods, I was so damn close. "I want you to think about how I had you bent over it, fucking you until you couldn't speak."

He gripped my hip as he angled his, allowing himself to go deeper and hit a spot that stole the air from my lungs. My Obscure ripped from my back, spilling all around us in tendrils. I couldn't see where it went, but I could feel what it was doing as if it were my own two hands. The magic twisted around the pillars and slammed into the walls. It shattered the glass windows and clawed at the rust-colored curtains until they were nothing but tattered shreds of fabric. It went *wild*.

"Until you couldn't think of anything but the way I feel inside you," Evander said, refusing to relinquish his pace.

My mind fogged, zeroing in on every sensation firing off in my body at once. The feel of his fingers digging into my skin, the way the cool hard stone felt against my breasts as I slid against it, the prickling of my scalp from Evander's tight hold on my hair. Every delicious morsel further stoked the fire, letting me burn hotter and hotter and hotter. My walls clenched tight around him, indicating I was ready to fall. All he had to do was push me. And he did.

With one final slamming of his hips, he shoved me over the cliff and into my release. And there was nothing in my mind but the euphoric way he felt as he spilled inside me, groaning my name as he followed me into ecstasy.

34
Felix

The stone walls of the hall were illuminated by the brilliant light that streamed in from the rays of the late-morning sun. For the past week, Oli and I worked diligently alongside Dash and the residents to rebuild the damaged palace, often laboring through the late hours of the night and into the next day. We were still far from finished, but I had high hopes the restoration would be fully complete within the next few months.

I wandered aimlessly through the corridors in search of Dash, checking all of our usual haunts but coming up empty. He wasn't at our best friend breakfast this morning, nor did he leave a note letting me know he was skipping the meal, and to be honest, that was a little selfish of him. Naturally, if I were to mention that, he would simply highlight the fact that I neglected to attend the one two days ago in favor of remaining entwined in bed with Oli throughout the morning. However, that wasn't the same thing.

Rounding a corner, I practically slammed into Imogen as she rushed through the palace with her arms full of clean bedding. "Watch where you're going!" she demanded as a sheet fell to the ground.

"Or you could just slow down," I said as I knelt down to pick it up.

"I don't have time. There's still so much to do before we leave."

"And there are plenty of people here who can contribute. Just try to relax a bit," I told her, placing the sheet back on top of her pile. "And if you can't, then I'm sure Cal will help you when you get to Tenebrae." I dodged her attack before she could even think to swing her fist at me.

"Don't you have anything better to do than be a constant nuisance?!" Imogen called over her shoulder angrily as she made her way back down the hall in a hurry.

"Not until I find Dash."

"He's in the Royal Corridor."

What? As far as I knew, Dash never went to that side of the palace. Even after he became the King of Caelum, he kept his room in the Royal Wing rather than move to the suite now meant for him.

I rushed towards the direction Imogen mentioned with fear sinking in my stomach. Dash hated that area of the palace, never wanting to step foot near where his mother had died. Throughout the time that I knew him, he would only enter her room when he was in a state of darkness. It would take me hours of trying to coax him out of both her bedroom and his mind.

Skidding to a halt in front of the door, I reached for the handle and twisted. Locked. It was never locked. "Dash," I said, rattling on the metal knob. There was no answer but a distinct shuffling coming from inside. "Dash, open the door!"

My closed fist met the wood, banging as hard as I could as my Empathi Gift surged out of me on instinct and flooded out as far as I could reach. His shields were up, refusing to let me in, but I could detect him close.

"Dash, I swear to the fucking Gods, if you don't open this damn door!" I yelled, and all at once, a baby's wail sounded from the other side of the door. My hand halted mid-air, my eyes going wide. What the fuck? Did Dash have a child I didn't know about?!

The door to his mother's bedroom yanked open, and a woman with long blonde hair and light blue eyes stood there holding a crying infant in her arms. "You asshole! I just got him to sleep!" she growled, bouncing the child against her. "What do you want—"

"Shhh," I interrupted, holding out my fingers as I counted off the months beneath my breath. The math was slightly off and the child looked nothing like him, but what did I know about genetics?

"Felix?" Dash's voice broke over my panic and I turned to see him half-dressed, standing in the doorway of the next bedroom over with a different woman at his side. "What are you—Oh shit, breakfast," he said as if realizing he had missed it.

My eyes darted between my best friend and the small infant, my mind moving at breakneck speed as I tried to figure out what the hell was going on.

"I had just gotten him down when..." the blonde woman announced, glaring in my direction like it was somehow *my* fault that Dash's love child was now awake.

"It's alright, Judith. I'll feed him, and he'll go right back to sleep," the woman at Dash's side said, moving forward and taking the child.

"I'm so sorry about this. I know how hard it's been—"

"It's perfectly okay, Your Majesty," she replied, cutting Dash off. "But if you wouldn't mind..." she shot me an accusatory glance before setting her stare back on my friend.

He nodded at once in understanding. "We'll leave right now."

She offered an appreciative smile before both women dipped their heads in a bow and entered the former queen's chambers, latching the lock behind them. I turned my attention to Dash, arching a skeptical brow and giving him a look that demanded an explanation.

"What?" he asked, reaching for the bottom button near the hem of his shirt.

"Were you just never going to tell me?"

"Tell you what?" The dickhead was playing dumb.

I scoffed and rolled my eyes, irritated at his choice to hide this monumental life event from me. I knew we were on shaky ground still, both of us trying to navigate through the hurt as we repaired our friendship, but for him to keep something like this from me...

"You're really going to pretend like I didn't just come face to face with your child?!"

Dash's fingers halted on the button, his gaze flying to mine as pure shock flooded his features. "Collin is *not* my son," he said, stammering through the sentence. Likely story.

"I'm not an idiot, Dash. Why else would he be in the royal section of the palace? And in your mother's old room of all places."

He dropped his shirt, the buttons left undone so his bare chest was on display as something black peeked through the fabric. Dash's shoulders sagged as he exhaled a long, annoyed breath.

"Because the family in the room next to Melody's has kept Collin up for a week straight. She came to me asking if there was somewhere she could move, so I assigned her my mother's old room. No one uses this part of the palace, so I figured it would be quiet enough for a child."

I narrowed my eyes. It was a believable story except for the part about the two women staying in his mother's room. As if he read my mind, Dash let out an annoyed sigh.

"I didn't want to be haunted by my past anymore. If something good could come from the places that brought me pain, then so be it."

"So he's not yours..."

"No, Felix. I did not father a secret child behind your and Ainsley's back," he said flatly, like he was reciting a grievance rather than an explanation as he went back to re-dressing.

Well, that was a relief. As much as I would have been happy for my best friend if that were the case, we were far too young to be thinking about bringing children into this world—especially one on the cusp of war.

"So you're just fucking his mom, then?"

His fingers halted again and he shook his head vehemently. "What? No!"

"It's completely fine if you are. I think it's good that you've moved on—"

"Felix, I'm not having sex with Melody."

"Right, and I'm not having sex with Olivier either," I said with a wink and then gave a pointed look at his open shirt. I didn't know why he was trying to deny it so forcefully after practically being caught in the act.

Dash would have to move on from Ainsley eventually, and it couldn't have been easy for him to find out she was married the way he had. He deserved to find the same happiness, and if that were with Melody, that'd be okay. He shouldn't feel shame for spending his time with someone else—someone who could offer him what Ainsley no longer could.

"Dear Gods, Felix, she's *married*."

"Hey, I'm not judging."

"Because there's no reason to. Nothing like that happened between us."

"Then why are you half dressed, *Your Majesty*?" I asked, dragging out his title like an insult. Why did he constantly insist on lying to me? Was this some kind of punishment for everything that happened between us all those months ago?

"Oh, for fuck's sake," he growled, rolling up the sleeve of his shirt. "She was doing my tattoo."

"Right. Because the King's Suite is the optimal place for—"

Dash shoved his arm in my face, showcasing the fresh black ink that adorned his flesh. The tattoo was a curved line that resembled the letter *S* stretching the inside of his forearm from his wrist to his elbow. I traced my fingers over the straight black line that cut the wave in half. The symbol of a Medicus.

"Melody learned about my Gift one night when Collin had gotten a small cut on his foot. I was in the Medicus facility alone, practicing my magic, when she rushed inside in a panic. I took Collin and healed him without so much as thinking," Dash explained, twisting his arm as he peered at the black ink. "She promised to never reveal my secret before I was ready, so I thought it was only fitting that she be the one to etch my tattoo."

Nodding to myself, I lifted his arm closer, noticing the discoloration and scarred flesh beneath the design. Burn marks, perhaps?

"Having trouble controlling yourself?" I asked, realizing it had to have been from him trying to wield his new fire magic. The Medicus always shared stories of new Ignisian wielders practically burning their faces off as they learned to manipulate flames.

"Something like that."

His tone of voice told me not to press the subject, so instead, I marveled at the delicate design, a smile tugging at my lips as I realized what it meant. Dash would be putting an end to the law against Conjoining in Caelum.

"When?" I asked as my eyes flicked up to his.

"The decree was signed an hour ago. I'll make an official announcement this afternoon and reveal my Medicus Gift. I know you're not technically a part of this kingdom anymore, but it would mean a lot if you were there."

Letting go of his arm, I embraced him tightly, never having felt prouder of him than I did at that moment. We had dreamed of making Caelum a better place, and here he was, actually doing it, little by little.

"Of course I'll be there." I pulled back to see a wide grin split his face in answer. "But only if we can eat first. I'm fucking starving." Dash laughed and shoved me before working to re-button his shirt.

"Yes, but I have something I need to take care of first. And before you try to suggest the 'something' I'm referring to is sleeping with Melody's sister, Judith, the answer is no."

I closed my mouth and swallowed that very suggestion. "Fine, then is it having Melody finish whatever that tattoo on your chest is?"

His stare dropped as he pulled open his shirt to reveal a different inked design just above his heart. A small tracing of flames, twisting and climbing as if reaching for life. Dash shook his head as he observed the tattoo barely bigger than a child's palm.

"This one is finished. I had it done a few days after I became king."

I squinted, taking in the tiny fire meant to signify his ability as an Ignisian. "But it's so tiny compared to the Unda and Aerian symbols on your back. Plus, you're king now, so the tattoo needs to be fitting of one," I argued.

He rolled his eyes as he finished dressing and trekked down the hall, completely dismissing my qualms about the minuscule marking meant to showcase his Gift. I had no idea why he was being so stubborn about it. For years, we had discussed and designed his tattoos, even being so bold as to decide the flames would lick up the side of Dash's face. Though now that I thought about it, I could understand why he wanted to forgo that idea.

"Fine, I'll drop it," I conceded reluctantly. "But at least tell me what mysterious task you have to do before we're allowed to eat."

We stopped outside the throne room doors as a mischievous smirk curved Dash's lips. "I have to punish a traitor."

35

Felix

I stood at the side of Dash's throne as he sat looking more regal than I had ever seen him. After entering the room, he gave me a quick explanation of what exactly was going on and who he had learned was responsible for the attack on Caelum. Upon being informed, I found myself not surprised by the revelation, but rather curious about how Dash was going to handle the situation.

It was his right as king to dole out whatever punishment he saw fit, but every choice he made as ruler came with its own set of risks and repercussions. Dash would have to meticulously analyze every possible option, understanding that there would be individuals who would dispute his decision regardless of the path he decided to follow.

The King of Caelum straightened in his throne and sucked in a deep inhale before letting it out slowly. "Let's get this over with," he said before nodding to the guards to let his first awaiting guest in.

The doors creaked ominously, opening wide enough to allow just one person through before shutting again. Rosella strolled through the grand space as if she owned it, her light blue dress hissing as it dragged along the white marble floors. Though her shoulders were held back and her chin high, her eyes darted quickly over the room, betraying her false confidence.

"I assume by your summons that you've realized the error in your ways and want to beg for me back," she claimed, holding her voice strong. Dash didn't respond, and that sent a wave of worry rushing toward me.

As a prince, Dash was trained to shield against intrusive Gifts like mine. Even some of the noblest families and those belonging to the king's advisory had received instruction on how to best protect themselves. But as a woman in Caelum, Rosella would have never been offered the opportunity to learn.

"It took you long enough," she tried again, stopping twenty feet away. Dash remained quiet.

Rosella glanced at the two guards flanking the sides of the platform Dash's throne was on, and then to me briefly before settling back on the king. She crossed her arms over her chest to show defiance or perhaps boredom, but I sensed the gesture for what it truly was—a way to hide her rapidly moving chest. Panic seeped from every pore of her flesh, spreading over her like wildfire.

"To be honest, I thought you would never get over that whiny woman you were obsessed with. I always thought you deserved far better than—"

"Enough," Dash demanded, stealing the words from her lungs.

Rosella flinched at the forcefulness of his tone but quickly covered the movement with an exaggerated roll of her eyes. I smothered my smile at her constant defiance. Even now, when she was absolutely terrified, she'd never let it show.

She grew quiet, clinging even tighter to herself as she continued to scan the room as if notating all possible exits to freedom.

"Why am I here, Your Majesty?" she asked, breaking the uncomfortable silence.

Dash shot a look in my direction with a question furrowed between his brows. I nodded once, indicating that she was terrified enough to be less combative than usual.

"The Queen of Tenebrae informed me of the deal the two of you made," he finally said, turning his attention back to his former lover.

Rosella stiffened, her face going pale as a sheet as the blood drained from it. Her head swiveled to the closed door and then to the windows as if contemplating the best way to escape. Working with another kingdom behind your ruler's back was treason—and she knew it.

"Of course she did," she whispered on a shaky breath. "She got what she wanted from me, and instead of fulfilling her end of our bargain, she exposed my crimes to you." Betrayal and anger muddled with her fear, diluting it to the point where all I could feel was her wrath. She was tipping too far to one side and needed to be reigned back in.

I placed a gentle hand on Dash's shoulder and he nodded in understanding without ever taking his gaze from her. "Ainsley intends to honor her word," he announced.

Rosella's eyes widened in shock, her anger turning to confusion and hope and skepticism all at once. She shook her head as if silently denying his claim. I sent my Gift forward and seeped into her icy interior, wrapping around her racing heart and willing it to calm.

"And I will not stop you from leaving," Dash added.

A sharp intake of air slid between Rosella's teeth as her eyes shifted quickly over Dash's features, searching for any trace of a lie. Her brow creased, her mind working endlessly to solve the puzzle she couldn't understand—why Dash wasn't claiming her life.

"But before you decide to accept, know that I'm prepared to counter Ainsley's offer."

Her head angled to the side as she studied her king, skepticism making its way into the space surrounding her. She wasn't off base for that emotion. She and Dash weren't exactly friendly toward each other ever since Ainsley's arrival last summer. Even before that, the two barely tolerated each other, only desiring a physical connection, so of course she would be cautious of Dash's generosity.

Rosella narrowed her eyes as her arms relaxed at her sides, her worry transforming into curiosity. She took a tentative step forward, holding Dash's stare as she lifted her chin to speak.

"I want your crown and a seat at your side as Queen."

I disguised my laughter as a cough to portray as much professionalism as I could. Although she was irritating, I had to commend her for never backing down from her desires, even when they were ludicrous.

Dash chuckled under his breath as he shook his head. "We both know you want me as little as I want you."

"It has nothing to do with wanting *you*. You said you were prepared to counter," Rosella said. "Well, this is what I desire."

"We both can't stand each other," Dash pointed out, gesturing a hand between them. "So, why would you want this?"

Rosella swallowed hard as she collected her thoughts, prepared to argue. Determination swelled inside her, boiling her blood and pumping her heart faster. I threw Dash a sidelong glance that said, '*Good luck.*'

"As much as I hate her, Ainsley is offering me a chance to better my life. She's introducing me to Prince Jahier, who has no romantic attachments. If that meeting goes well, I could rule and finally be someone," she explained.

For the very first time, I found myself feeling sorry for Rosella. Her father was a dickhead, and it was no secret to the palace residents that he treated his wife like shit. I had long held the belief that Rosella had inherited his qualities, but the sadness underlying her words implied she might be as much a victim as her mother. Perhaps her father was the primary force behind her inclination towards Dash, rather than it being her own volition.

"If I don't have that crown, then I don't have a future here in Caelum. My status will have climbed as high as it can, and there will be nothing left for me to gain," she finished, the words coming out in a somber whisper.

The King of Caelum leaned back on his throne, propping an elbow on the arm as he rested his cheek against his fist and exhaled deeply. "I can't give you that title," he answered.

Rosella's shoulders sagged as the breath she had been holding in preparation for his response left her lungs. Her face deflated. She nodded once and then gracefully stood straighter. Her chin lifted and her mouth dropped open to officially accept Ainsley's offer when Dash spoke again.

"My counter will not hold as much value compared to what the Queen of Tenebrae has promised, and any normal person would think you were insane to accept it over hers," Dash began. Rosella closed her mouth and her brow arched in intrigue. "But I think it holds something far greater to you than a royal crown does."

"And what's that?"

"Your freedom. The chance to be your own person without the pressure of someone dictating what you can and cannot do, who you should and should not be with. The opportunity to accomplish something entirely on your own."

Desire enveloped Rosella wholly, and she reached forward as if wanting to pluck the truth of Dash's words from the air. I glanced down at the king to find his lips lifted in a small smile.

"I don't think you truly want to leave Caelum or your family." Rosella's lips peeled back in the barest hint of a sneer. "Leave your *little brother*," Dash quickly amended. "I know how much young Gideon means to you." She nodded absentmindedly as if it were nothing more than a reflex.

I released my hold on her emotions as I observed her successfully regulating herself. Despite her distaste for Ainsley, she resembled her in one aspect—a perpetual struggle to maintain control. If they were ever able to overcome their differences and work together, their anger alone could reduce kingdoms to rubble.

Rosella fidgeted with her fingers and then the fabric of her dress, her nerves seeping through with every uncertain action. "What exactly are you offering me?" she finally asked.

Dash stood and sauntered down the steps of the dais, his hands slipping into his pockets casually as he made his way toward Rosella. "A position on my royal council recently opened up, and I'd like you to fill it."

She laughed. Loudly. "Women cannot be advisors."

"That was during my father's reign. Mine *will* be different." Dash said the words like a vow.

In a short period of time, Dash had emerged as the ruler his father failed to become. The majority of his people already held him in high regard, and his progressive initiatives only served to drive Caelum towards a future marked by prosperity and equality. He was finally becoming the man he swore to his mother he would one day be.

"Why me, Dash? I have no experience or formal training in politics. I'm completely unqualified." It was Dash's turn to laugh.

"You're kidding me, right?" he questioned. She looked at him quizzically, and then over to me as if I could provide her an answer. "Rosella, there isn't a single thing that happens in this palace that you don't know about. You're in everyone's ear, you have minions who do your bidding, and you keep a journal full of incriminating information to use as leverage should you ever need it." Her lips lifted in a proud smirk as if Dash were rattling off her greatest accomplishments. "The information you provided Ainsley was crucial, and you potentially saved thousands of lives. I need someone on my council who I can trust has the best interest of this kingdom in mind. Someone who I can trust will fight to make it better."

He approached her, narrowing the distance between them to just a few inches, while casting his gaze downwards. The atmosphere within the room shifted, taking on a more serious and solemn tone.

"You, Rosella, are capable of far more than simply stroking a man's ego and being a beautiful piece of art by his side, viewed as nothing more than a silent decoration for others to admire."

She drew in a shuddering breath, her chest visibly rising and falling as she wrestled with her emotions. It proved to be a futile struggle for both of us as Rosella's eyes welled up with tears, and I averted my gaze to wipe my own. Dash's compassionate words and his capacity to perceive the inherent goodness in others deeply resonated with me, serving as a reminder of why I chose him as my best friend and brother.

Rosella blinked back her tears before they could fall, placing her hands on her hips defensively as she shook away the last of the vulnerability she never meant to show.

"What position? And I swear, if you say something that has to do with charity or children, then respectfully, you can go fuck yourself, Your Majesty," Rosella stated.

"Gods no. You'd be terrible at that," Dash answered with a laugh. "If you accept my offer, you will be my personal Ambassador. The position will require traveling to other kingdoms as my representative. You will sit in on meetings I cannot attend and be the voice of Caelum, as well as perform various other tasks."

My lips quirked as Rosella stumbled backward, and Dash had to grab her elbow to keep her upright.

"But that..." she stammered as her eyes darted between mine and Dash's, "Is my father's position."

"It was."

She visibly trembled as the king took her other arm to steady her, pure disbelief morphing her features. I gestured across the room for the guard to bring her a glass of water as I pushed my Empathi Gift back into her. Rosella's heart was pumping too fast, her breaths coming too wildly from the shock of Dash's offer and news of her father's displacement.

"Does he know?" she asked weakly, taking the water from the guard the moment he presented it and chugging it in one gulp.

"Not yet."

"Can I be the one to tell him?" There was a wicked pleasure in her eyes that had me rethinking my aversion to her.

Dash took a long, deep breath as he prepared himself to divulge the other reason he had summoned her to this room. "Rosella," he said gently as he held her stare. "I'm about to bring your father in to inform him of his removal, and I need you to be here when that happens so you can fully decide if this position is one you'd like to accept."

"I do—"

Dash held up a hand, cutting her off from fully being able to agree to his offer. "I need you to observe the meeting, and only after it's finished do I want you to decide, though you can take as much time as you want to do so."

A small wrinkle appeared between her brows as she tried to understand the dire need for her to wait. I wrapped myself around her worry, easing it and sending a jolt of calm through her. Rosella nodded and walked over to the chair on the side of the room Dash directed her toward.

With a final wary look at one another, we returned to the dais. The King of Caelum sat upon his throne as I stationed myself at his right side, ready for our next task.

"And Rosella?" he called, claiming her attention again. "I will ensure your brother is looked after, regardless of what you decide about the queen's offer." She dipped her head in a grateful bow and then shifted her focus to the large oak doors creaking to life once more.

"How can I be of service, Your Majesty?" that dickhead, Gideon, said as he strutted through the room.

His gaze snagged on his only daughter, prompting a fleeting furrow of his brow before he swiftly composed himself. My Empathi Gift's strength was unparalleled in Caelum; however, Gideon possessed centuries of experience in protecting himself from magic like mine. Although it did not prevent me from breaching his defenses, it required a significantly greater amount of focus than my usual approach.

With intense concentration, I slipped through the cracks in his barrier undetected and rooted myself in his emotions should I need to manipulate them at any point.

"I don't suppose this summons is for you to inform me you have finally agreed to marry my daughter?" Gideon said smoothly.

From my periphery, I could see Dash shift in his throne from annoyance. The former advisor seemed to recognize it as a flood of uncertainty wrapped around my magic.

"Apologies, Your Majesty. You can't blame a father for trying."

"Your daughter has been plenty tenacious in that matter," Dash replied, the playful jab meant more for Rosella than anyone else. I stole a quick glance to find her rearranging the smirk that had come and gone from her lips.

"But clearly not persistent enough," Gideon joked, but there was no trace of humor in the way he spoke the words or the disappointed look he shot his daughter. There was a promise of malice in his gaze. A sudden rush of terror slammed into me.

I whipped my head toward Rosella to see her pulling the sleeves of her dress over her wrist. Perhaps a nervous habit...or to hide something she didn't want to be seen. She was frightened of her father, that much was certain.

I sent a sliver of my Gift toward her, twisting around her fear and calming her emotions. Rosella's eyes flickered up to mine, her brow puckered in a brief moment of confusion before smoothing into recognition. *Thank you*, she mouthed, and I could have fallen over at the two words I didn't think she was capable of forming. Rather than express my shock, I simply nodded.

"How many lives were lost during the attack last week?" Dash asked Gideon, bringing my focus back to the conversation at hand.

"I'm sorry?"

"Do we need to have a Medicus examine your hearing, Gideon? I thought my question was rather clear."

The former advisor ground his teeth in irritation before plastering a fake smile on his face. "I heard the question, Your Majesty. I just don't understand *why* you are asking it."

"It is not your job to *understand*; it is your job to answer."

The room became dim as storm clouds swiftly approached, accompanied by the sound of thunder rumbling overhead. The floor quaked under the force of Dash's power, leaving no question who reigned over this kingdom and its people.

Gideon swallowed hard and sipped quickly on the air as his heart pounded beneath his chest. I didn't allow him to calm himself, instead keeping his emotions heightened. He deserved to feel fear.

"Not off the top of my head, Your Majesty, but I'm sure I can retrieve the list if you'd—"

"Sixty-three." Dash's words sliced through the air like a knife, clean and precise. Gideon stayed quiet, letting the patter of rain against the glass windows fill the silence. "Given that you didn't know the count, I'll assume you can't provide me with the names of the dead."

Gideon's eyes dropped to the floor. "No, Your Majesty. But as I said before, I can retrieve the list—"

Dash shifted and the movement halted the former advisor's words. Slowly, the king pulled a piece of folded parchment from his pocket and held it up between his index and middle finger. The crease was so prominent and the paper so tattered and worn that it looked as if the owner had unfolded and read through it dozens, if not hundreds, of times.

I stepped forward, following Dash's unspoken request, and slid the parchment from between his fingers. Without opening it, I walked down to Gideon and shoved the rumpled paper into his chest before turning and ascending back up the dais.

He dropped his gaze to the parchment and then to his king, a question etched into the hard lines of his face.

"Read it," Dash commanded, leaving no room for arguments. Lightning flashed, illuminating the room ominously as the rain outside intensified.

Gideon's fear was potent on my tongue as he carefully unfolded the paper and scanned over its contents.

"Out loud," the King of Caelum added.

One by one, the names of the fallen were spoken into existence until all sixty-three had been accounted for. Gideon's hands moved to the corners, prepared to close the parchment and be finished with his task.

"Again."

His stare darted to Dash. "Your Majesty—"

The room violently shook as if lightning had split the building in two. Gideon flinched and crouched, his hands flying over his head as if to protect himself from a collision that wouldn't come. Terrified, he straightened after the last of the thunder's boom echoed, his hands trembling so badly I wasn't sure how he could make the words out on the paper. He read the names aloud.

Once finished, Dash demanded, "Again."

Over and over, for more than an hour straight, Gideon listed the names of the dead. He didn't dare stop to request a break or offer some bullshit thought I knew was swirling in his mind.

Occasionally, he would glance over at his daughter who only watched him with intent interest, no doubt trying to figure out the point of Dash's display of power over her father. Other times he would glare at me. It had taken him all of twenty minutes to realize why he couldn't calm himself and that I wouldn't be relinquishing my hold.

Dash turned his attention to me and nodded once in a clear order. I jogged down the steps, casually strolled to Gideon, and ripped the parchment from his hands before returning it to the king's waiting palm.

"Recite them," Dash commanded.

"Your Maj—"

"Recite. Them." The venom in Dash's tone was just as deadly as the power he wielded.

"I—I..." Gideon stammered and stuttered, unable to fulfill his king's demand. For over an hour he had been listing those names, and now he couldn't recall any of them.

Dash's teeth audibly ground as he clenched his jaw and fist, sheer fury rolling off him in molten waves. He stood, the marble floor vibrating with each step of his foot as he made his way down the dais.

"You sent sixty-three of my people to their deaths and can't remember a single one?"

Gideon's eyes widened in shock and panic, his fear churning around my magic like a storm of distress. He shook his head, instantly denying the claim.

"I wouldn't—"

"Do not lie to me," Dash growled, inching closer and closer to the frightened man.

"I..." The singular word left Gideon's lips in a whisper as the king stopped a foot away, towering over the man.

"Are you really going to try and deny that you weren't conspiring with Lord Oberon and King Harbin? That you didn't mark targets for their archers to sink into the earth and destroy the palace, taking sixty-three innocents before their time?"

Gideon's chest moved rapidly as he looked up at his sovereign, unable to articulate another lie to convey. "I never meant for anyone to die."

"I SAID DO NOT LIE TO ME!"

The throne room shook and fragments of stone rained down from the ceiling as Dash's power surged, causing the storm outside to transform into a ferocious force of nature. The rain forcefully pounded against the windows with such intensity that I feared it would fracture and splinter the glass, unleashing the tumultuous roar of the wind as it ravaged the landscape.

Gideon dropped to his knees, his hands cupping in front of him as if his king was a God and he was nothing but a worthless servant, praying to his deity.

"I did what was necessary," he argued on borrowed breath. "You needed to see the strength of the alliance you should have chosen—what *they* can provide."

Lightning cracked and I threw a hand up to shield against the sudden brightness.

"I DECIDED—"

"Wrong," Gideon bravely interrupted. "You decided *wrong*. Your father helped build this unbeatable alliance. By not joining it, *you* are condemning all of Caelum to fall!" Demonstrating his defiance, he rose to his feet with a lifted chin and stiff stance. The King of Caelum leaned in, baring his teeth as he sneered at the traitorous piece of shit.

"You're a coward. And you will pay for what you did with your life."

Fear flashed momentarily through Gideon before it was replaced with rage and disgust. "And the people of this kingdom will pay with theirs for your foolish choices." His gaze shifted, and he abruptly jerked his chin towards the guards who were now tightly gripping their swords. "Be done with it then," he demanded.

Dash followed his gaze before a cruel smile split his lips and he turned back to the former advisor. "You do not deserve the privilege of a swift death," Dash told him. "No. I will ensure you pay thoroughly for each life you stole." He closed the gap and whispered his final promise. "I will make you suffer. I will make it slow. And I will enjoy every second of your screams."

Gideon rushed backward as if he could escape his fate, but ran straight into a shield Dash had surrounded him with. He banged on the forcefield, causing shimmering ripples to vibrate with each pound of his fist. Dash turned and strolled casually back to his throne with his hands dipped in his pockets.

"You don't have to stay here for this," he said to Rosella once he was seated.

She turned her ice-blue eyes on him and pulled her shoulders back. "I'm fine," she said. I checked the small piece of magic I had wrapped around her, feeling emotions of anger, hurt, confusion, and betrayal as she glowered at her father.

Dash's focus shifted to me as he ran his thumb over the pads of his fingertips, preparing to call his magic forth. "Pull out," he directed, and I withdrew my hold on Gideon at once.

With a deep breath, Dash straightened and set his sights on his traitor. "Joseph," he announced as Gideon fell to the ground with an ear-splitting scream. "Carolynne. Bryson. Hektor." Each name was punctuated with a painful wail from the criminal.

Gideon held up his hands, now red and blistered, as if he...

Rosella's lips parted in a soft gasp as she realized the same. Dash was using his Ignisian Gift to burn him from the inside out. My jaw dropped and my eyes widened at the sight. It was not the torture that caught me off guard, but rather the fact that Dash possessed the ability to carry out such actions from a distance. Never before had I witnessed a fire wielder with the ability to ignite an object without physical contact or projecting flames toward it. Dash was doing neither.

"Walter. Yara. Felicity."

Gideon writhed in pain and raised his hands, his bloodshot eyes going wide as he took in the damaged skin. Dash showed no mercy, persisting in his onslaught of names as the criminal's insides blackened.

It was at that point the begging began.

Empty promises and regretful confessions polluted the air, mingling with the stench of charred flesh. I breathed through my mouth, but it did nothing to cure my sour stomach from the rancid fragrance and taste of Gideon's anguish.

"Vincent. Annabeth. Timothy."

Dash's relentless torment endured until all sixty-three names were uttered, reducing Gideon to a pile of liquefying flesh on the ground, red and covered in sores and blisters. The stench was awful, causing a churning in my stomach and one of the guards to vomit onto the ground. Gideon's breathing was strained, yet Dash persisted. He was unwilling to end his suffering until the task was finished.

Finally, the King of Caelum stood and swiftly snapped his fingers, engulfing what remained of Gideon in flames. I placed a comforting hand on my brother's shoulder as we watched the fire reduce the traitor to nothing but ashes.

Rosella's presence loomed nearer as the last of the flames died out. Both Dash and I turned to find her standing a foot away, arms crossed over her chest.

"I accept your offer, Dash," was all she said as she looked at the pile of dust as if it didn't hold the remnants of her father's body, but the fragments of her chains.

She was finally free.

36
Dashiell

With a steady motion, I slid my hands along the velvety fabric of my bedding and flattened my palms against it. I shut my eyes and counted to fifty, practicing the slow breathing technique that Imogen had taught me. A feeling of unease settled in my stomach as I battled leaving my kingdom in its current state.

I was aware that killing Gideon would not be well received, even though I had made it clear to my people that he was responsible for the palace attack. Many of them held the belief that it was a lie, asserting that I was too young, too inexperienced, too impulsive to be king. However, those reactions paled in comparison to those regarding the announcement of my repeal of the law against Conjoining.

Foolishly, I thought my people would be happy and proud of the progressive movement forward, but I was wrong. In the two weeks following the announcement, more than half of the residents in the palace tried to revolt, with failed assassination attempts on my life.

Prejudice against individuals who were the result of Conjoining was widespread within the palace, with people too afraid to come forward due to potential consequences. Entire parties were formed with the sole purpose of hunting down anyone in the palace they suspected of possessing a Gift from another kingdom.

"And the people of this kingdom will pay with theirs for your foolish choices."

Gideon's final words of warning echoed in my mind endlessly, his promise already coming to fruition. Although he may have been referring to the war, the chaos had already commenced.

I counted to fifty again.

A few days ago, I commanded the residents to assemble, occupying every ballroom and dining room within the premises. One by one, I visited the spaces and asked the same question: who present wants to reimplement the law against Conjoining? Hands were raised and people stepped forward, unwavering in their stance.

The groups were sorted by the guards and myself, with the individuals who did not object to the new law being taken to the throne room to wait until all residents had cast their votes. Following the completion of the tally, I made my way into the throne room for the final time accompanied by the last group. It was then that I relayed the news to everyone that those who had voted against Conjoining had been expelled from the palace.

As king, I understood that not everyone would agree with the choices I made, and I welcomed grievances to be brought to my attention. However, I would not stand for my people being subjected to threats and harm due to prejudice and ignorance. Over half of the palace residents had been removed, including some of those in the throne room who chose not to be split from family members who were forced to vacate.

I counted to fifty for the third time.

I felt like shit for leaving my people while tensions were still high and our future uncertain, but this new alliance between the three remaining kingdoms and part of Venator was just as fragile. I couldn't abandon it either.

"How many sets?"

My lips twitched and I exhaled deeply as my eyes fluttered open. "Three," I told Imogen.

She whistled low as her approaching steps sounded in my ears. "That bad?"

I twisted and held up my unsteady hand to show her just how much it was shaking. Imogen slid a palm over and above it as she gazed upward at me.

"I'm not going with you today," she said. "I already wrote to her to let her know."

I immediately shook my head. She had been counting down the days until she would finally be reunited with Ainsley and I wasn't going to let my issues keep her from that.

"Imogen, no. You promised her you'd go to Tenebrae."

"And I promised your mother I would look after you," she argued.

"I'm fine."

She dropped a pointed stare to the trembling hand she still clutched. "Clearly." I opened my mouth to argue, but she cut me off. "Can you honestly say you'll be completely present in Tenebrae if you're concerned about what's happening here?"

"No, which is why I should stay."

"No, it's why *I* should stay." Imogen squeezed my hand as her hazel stare held mine. "You have to be there, Dashiell. Let me look after Caelum for you while you're gone."

I swallowed hard, wanting to fight her on it, but unable to deny the comfort I felt knowing my kingdom would be in the hands of someone I trusted. Someone who would ensure peace was maintained, seeing as the residents were more terrified of enduring *her* wrath than mine.

I blew out a long breath in surrender and dragged a hand through my hair. "Are you sure you can handle it?"

Imogen dropped my hand at once and rolled her eyes as if that was the most ridiculous question I could have ever uttered. "I'm going to pretend you didn't just ask me that. We both know I have far more control over these residents than you do." I stifled a smile knowing just how right she was. "Nevertheless, I suggest that you find a method to help you cope with needing to leave again, as I will not give up the opportunity to see Ainsley in Tenebrae next month."

"Of course," I said at once and pulled her into a tight hug.

I wouldn't have made it through half the shit thrown my way if it wasn't for Imogen at my side these past months. She was there to talk me through my heartache, my depression, my grief, and my fear, never once balking or shying from my darkness.

She pushed away from me when she deemed the embrace had gone on long enough. After all, she had a persona of pretending not to care nearly as much as she did to uphold.

"Now, hurry and be on your way. Felix won't stop checking the time every thirty seconds and Rosella is ruining the marble floor from all of her pacing," Imogen declared. I huffed a laughed as I nodded. "Why are you bringing that girl with you, anyway?"

"She needs to learn how to perform in her new position," I explained simply. "Plus, would you rather I have left her here with you?"

"Dear Gods, no. But keep her away from Ainsley, please. We both know how they feel about each other. I don't see Rosella playing nicely despite being in the queen's kingdom as a guest."

"I'll do my best to ensure she behaves," I promised, suddenly painfully aware that bringing Rosella along might not have been the best decision. Moments after accepting the position of advisor, she went on and on about how happy she was she wouldn't have to live in the same kingdom as Ainsley. Great. Just add it to the growing list of my royal fuck ups.

A tingle of magic and then a chill brushed over my skin as we left Caelum and entered Tenebrae, the portal depositing us in some sort of dark cavern. Olivier immediately led the way out of the long and twisting tunnels of the cave until we were standing beneath the early afternoon sun.

I blinked several times against the blaring light, waiting for my eyes to adjust to the sudden brightness. Once they finally did, my jaw dropped at the sight.

Tenebrae was breathtaking.

Mammoth grey mountains kissed with snow bordered the horizon as far as the eye could see. Sprawling deep green hills were peppered with wildflowers only just now coming into bloom. Though spring had long since made her presence known in Caelum, it seemed she had only recently graced Tenebrae. There was still a nip of cold and the taste of fresh snow in the air as it blew around us, ruffling our coats in the gentle breeze.

My lips tilted in a smile as I thought about how miserable Ainsley must have been in the winter months if *this* was a normal spring day. She absolutely hated the cold. In my periphery, I spied Felix staring at me with a sly grin of his own as if he could read my thoughts.

"She complained about it daily," he said knowing exactly where my mind had gone. "Still does, actually. And I'd be willing to bet that when we arrive at the palace, we'll find her in wool socks."

I narrowed my eyes as I tried to picture the image. The air was brisk but nowhere near as cold as it would have to be to warrant clothing of that degree. "Nah. She's dramatic, but not *that* dramatic."

Felix stuck out his hand. "Care to make a wager?" I arched a brow in intrigue. "Three gold coins says she's dressed as if it's still dead of winter."

"Deal," I said and clasped my hand with his to solidify the bet. I swear to the Gods if he was right...

Something wet pressed into my other palm, and I looked down to find Nova sniffing me again. Onyx stood close by, baring his teeth as my eyes met his. For some reason, the two wolves had stayed behind in Caelum, most likely as a form of protection for Olivier since they usually followed him wherever he wandered.

Sometimes, though, the grey wolf would scratch at the door of the study or Sanctuary until I let her in, the black one always a step behind her. He never seemed thrilled at her choice to be in the same vicinity as me, and to be honest, I never understood it either. I just chalked it up to curiosity or the desire to keep an eye on me and ensure I wasn't out to hurt Felix or Olivier.

I flexed my fingers, subtly petting the soft fur of her snout. Whenever I tried to do anything else, Onyx would growl and snarl until I released her, so my affection toward the grey wolf had to be minimal.

"Are you excited to see her?" I whispered to Nova as her tongue swept across my open palm, taking the treat I slid to her from the sleeve of my jacket where I kept them hidden. If Onyx wanted to continue being a dick, he didn't deserve any. A soft grunt rumbled at the base of her throat and the corner of my mouth lifted in response. "Me too," I replied.

Onyx let loose a warning growl, letting me know I had spent enough time with Nova. I slipped her one more treat before strolling over to where Rosella and Felix had joined Olivier at the front of our group.

"The portal is now closed," Olivier said, tucking a piece of transfer parchment away before removing another from his jacket. "We have two options. Either we take the horses," he gestured his chin toward four mares stationed near the cave's entrance, "Or Evander can come and retrieve us."

Back in Caelum, Felix had told me that Evander's Obscure enables him to effortlessly travel to different locations in mere seconds. As much as I didn't want to spend hours on horseback and further delay seeing my best friend, I was still apprehensive about trusting the King of Tenebrae.

Everything I had ever been told about the Dark Kingdom and its ruler had led me to believe that nothing good could come of this place or its people. Even though I now knew that my father had fabricated many of the stories to seek vengeance against Tenebrae, I still harbored uncertainty. It was going to require some time to train myself out of the unease I felt but now was as opportune a time as any to extend a modicum of trust.

"Evander can take us," I announced and received a surprised look from Olivier. "What?"

"Nothing. I just figured you'd be too proud to take the easy route." He scribbled a message on the parchment.

"We have a meeting to conduct. Why risk being late?"

Olivier shrugged and stashed away the note as soon as the ink disappeared.

"Yeah, because the *meeting* is the reason you want to get to the palace as soon as possible," Felix whispered as he jabbed me with his elbow. I rolled my eyes and shoved him back.

"As if you're not just as anxious to see her."

"Of course I am. The only difference is, I'm not pretending that I'm not."

He had a point.

I had been practically crawling out of my skin with excitement from the second we departed the palace in Caelum, much to Rosella's annoyance. I couldn't contain myself no matter how hard I tried not to fidget or walk faster than the rest of the group, my feelings too overwhelming to remain calm and collected.

"Stop bouncing in place. You look like an idiot," Rosella chastised. I turned to my right and offered her a glare as I planted my heels firmly on the ground. She supplied a saccharine sweet smile and before I could come up with a retort, black smoke swirled before us.

"You two first," Evander commanded, stepping through the shadows without so much as a greeting as he pointed to Felix and me.

Off to a great start.

"No!" Rosella objected, the fear of being left behind evident in her voice. "I should go with His Majesty first."

Evander arched a brow but didn't offer her a response. "Let's go." He held out his arm for Felix and me to take.

"But—" she tried again.

"My wife wants *them*," Evander interrupted as Felix and I grabbed just below his elbow. "Consider the delay in your arrival a kindness. Something tells me it won't be pleasant when she finds out you're here."

With that, we disappeared into shadow.

37

Dashiell

The sensation of pins and needles spread throughout my entire body as Evander's magic flowed around us. In an instant, our surroundings shifted from the foothills of Tenebrae to an environment of black marble and a soothing warmth.

I stumbled back, my head whipping around at the sudden change in scenery. We were now standing in a long corridor, one side of which was bordered by open windows, revealing a sweeping view of the snowcapped mountains in the distance, while the other side presented a solid wall of dark stone.

"I'll be back in a minute with your *friend*," Evander stated, uncertain of the precise term to call Rosella. He gestured towards a set of wide double doors. "She's in there."

The King of Tenebrae stepped away from us and strolled to a man I recognized as Calidore, most likely delaying his trip just to get under Rosella's skin. It seemed like a dick thing to do, so I could only assume that was his plan.

Felix rushed toward the room with me following closely behind on his heels, the anticipation of seeing Ainsley again growing with each thunderous pound of my heart. He forcefully swung the door open, and numerous sets of eyes zeroed in on us, but I only scanned the area for one—light brown with dark red flecks.

Ainsley shoved away from her chair at the large round table big enough for twenty and hurried around it. While Felix ran towards her, I remained firmly rooted on the threshold. With everything so different now, I felt lost and uncertain about how to behave or what was considered appropriate. Was it okay to sprint to her? To hug her? Or was I simply to wave and greet her as if we were new acquaintances? A sense of panic consumed me as my thoughts became jumbled, leaving me clueless about what to do.

Felix wrapped his arms around her, showering her face and the top of her head with tender kisses. I envied him. I yearned for that certainty of friendship—that closeness—back. He spoke softly to her, too quietly for me to understand, but my chest tightened as she laughed and nodded in reply.

Felix had been with me for weeks, but it was only now that I realized this was the first time she could really be with him after learning he was alive. Things in Caelum had been so tense, hectic, and focused solely on the tasks at hand that the two of them never got to enjoy each other before it was time for her to leave. It suddenly hit me that I had been selfish to keep him with me for so long, knowing Ainsley must have been longing for him, too. Another item to add to my list of things to make up for.

With another giggle, she withdrew from him and moved backward. I anxiously waited for her to look at me, pulling on my fingers and bouncing my knee. Every instinct in my body was screaming at me to go to her, but I fought against the urge, choosing to let her dictate how things between us were going to go.

Her gaze drifted to mine, and somehow, her grin grew even wider, sending my heart into a full gallop. She rushed for me, my arms going wide before enclosing tightly around her. Gods, it was like I could finally take a full breath. All the pieces fell into place within me, like a puzzle that could only be solved with her by my side. Felix and I were brothers; however, Ainsley held an equal place within our family. Nothing felt whole unless we were all together.

A set of fingers snapped, and I reached into my pocket, pulling out three gold coins and placing them into Felix's awaiting palm without ever picking my head up or releasing Ainsley. I didn't even care that I lost the bet the second she rounded the table, dressed in a thick sweater that extended to her thighs, soft pants and chunky knit socks that reached above her knees. She wasn't even wearing shoes, appearing more like she was about to lounge by a fire and read all day rather than take part in a meeting of rulers.

She pulled back, a bright smile still stretched across her face, mirroring my own.

"Hi," she told me breathlessly.

"Hi," I said back, just as winded.

We were both nervously trying to navigate our relationship, and I was immediately sent back to when Ainsley had first let me in last summer. This strange sense of uncertainty, coupled with the strongest desire not to fuck things up, felt so familiar. I had maneuvered my way through those awkward times once before; I could do it again.

"I want to show you around," she replied, still holding me close as she peered up.

My gaze went beyond her and landed on the guards from Caelum, who had taken their positions against the back wall of the room alongside Agnitio, Tenebrae, and Jahier's selected soldiers. As part of our agreement, rulers were required to send soldiers ahead to survey the area to ensure there were no traps set. We did this for protection and to satisfy our council members and generals, who were not entirely supportive of our collaboration. "Won't we be starting soon?" I asked, noting that nearly everyone was present.

"Jahier is slightly delayed, so we have some time."

"Any word on Brandle?" Felix had filled me in on him being Tenebrae and Agnitio's inside source into the inner workings of Ministro. The more I learned, the less I realized I knew about alliances and motivations in this world. People who I thought were enemies turned into allies, and those I thought I could trust turned out to be nothing more than traitors conspiring to overthrow kingdoms.

"He sent correspondence last week stating that he'd be here, but he's running late too, I guess," she answered. "So, how about that tour?"

"I'd love one," a deadly, sweet voice called from behind me.

Ainsley's hold on me dropped at once, her eyes going wide and the blood draining from her face.

Shit.

"Why is *she* here?" Ainsley demanded just as Rosella came into view at my side.

"She's...one of my advisors?" I answered, though it sounded more like a damn question. Gods, why the hell did I think bringing her was a good idea?

"Why?" Ainsley dragged out the word like a question that had no logical answer.

I opened my mouth, but before I could respond, Rosella did. "You weren't capable of fulfilling something he was after," she said before leaning in to whisper her final words to the queen. "And I offered something he really, *really*, wanted."

She winked before straightening again, a vicious smile plastered on her face. Ainsley's stare went flat as shadows seeped from beneath her sleeves and swirled around her fingers. Great.

"Rosella," I warned in a growl.

"What? I only meant that as queen, Ainsley cannot fulfill a position on your council." The explanation was spoken as innocently as if a child had uttered it.

I rolled my eyes, already over her games. "That's not what you were insinuating and we both know it." She shrugged guiltlessly, and Ainsley huffed a bitter laugh as she pushed past us and stormed for the door. Felix chased after her and I dragged a hand through my hair in frustration. "Go mingle with the other advisors," I commanded, backing toward the exit.

"Can't you bring me with you?" she argued, and it was my turn to laugh.

"Not after that shit you just pulled, Rosella."

"But—"

"Go. I'll be back later."

Reaching the door, I cast a final glance around the room. The guards from different kingdoms stood stoically as Tallis addressed the two advisors next to him. At the far end of the round table, Olivier's sister was engrossed in conversation with a man I had never seen.

Observing their close proximity and the intimate way he leaned in to speak, I surmised that he was her lover.

My gaze snagged on Rosella standing alone and looking as if she didn't belong. Even when she was out of her depth, she was an expert at exuding false confidence, but now she seemed too terrified to even try. I released a long sigh and sauntered back over to her.

"Please let me come with you," she whispered, refusing to glance in my direction. "I'll be nice to her. I just...I don't have anyone." Her ice-blue eyes met mine and her face filled with a vulnerability I had never seen before. She was scared.

I felt a pang of guilt as I looked at her, remembering that she had lost her best friend in the attack on the palace only weeks ago. Ever since that day, Rosella had kept mostly to herself. I'd spy her sitting alone in the gardens, in the library, or on the terrace. It didn't matter where she was—she was always alone.

"I don't know what to do, Dash," she admitted under her breath.

Despite my anger toward her deliberate action of provoking Ainsley, I acknowledged it as an attempt to cling to something familiar amidst the uncertainty of the situation. I had received political training throughout my entire life, but this world was new to Rosella. Even though she was well-versed about the people of Caelum and the way the court operated, this was a completely different scenario that she clearly felt unprepared for.

I gently placed my hand on her shoulder. Pissed at her or not, she was one of my people...and she was struggling. "Do what I hired you for," I told her. She looked up at me with imploring eyes, needing more than just that. "Do what you're good at." Her brows scrunched, and she turned away, scanning the room of people before finally nodding. "You're going to do fine. I'll be back soon."

Feeling like I had gotten through to her, I hurried through the door and into the long corridor. I had to jog to catch up with my friends, who were already halfway down the hallway and going at a brisk pace. The moment I approached, Felix shot me a *'Now you've fucking done it'* glare.

"That's a bedroom, that's a hallway; over there is a ballroom," Ainsley announced angrily, pointing at random places around us in a fury.

I threw a pleading look at Felix.

"Yeah, she's fucking pissed," he murmured.

"I can see that," I whisper-yelled back. "How do we make it better?"

"Don't you think that if I knew, I would have done it?"

"Well, we have to try something!"

"Oh, I have an idea! How about you go back in time *and not bring Rosella!*" Felix demanded, his voice still barely louder than an angry hush. I narrowed my eyes in a *'Really helpful suggestion, dickhead'* kind of way.

"That's a stairwell, that's another hallway, that's a window you can go jump out of," Ainsley continued.

Fuck, she was furious.

"You ruined trio bonding time," Felix declared in an angry huff of air. "We're supposed to be getting back to normal and now you've pissed her off!"

"Well then help me make it better!"

"There's no making it better! It's *Ainsley* we're talking about. She's going to hold a grudge for the next ten years!"

She whirled around, her hands flying to her hips and her brow arching in irritation. Felix and I froze in place, shooting each other a wary glance before setting our stares on the very angry queen in front of us.

"I'm sorry. Am I boring you with this tour?" she demanded, obviously catching wind of my and Felix's hushed conversation.

"No," I stated.

"Yes," Felix offered at the same time. Fucking Gods. Her attention shifted to him as she waited for an elaboration. "I only mean that this is the boring part of the palace. Why don't we show Dash the library?"

Her eyes drifted to me, and I nodded enthusiastically. Ainsley loved books and places that housed them. The library could be the one place that could help turn her sour mood.

"It's a big room with books like all the other big rooms with books," she replied and my tentative and hopeful smile wilted. She wasn't going to let go of this any time soon.

"Ains," I tried. She cocked her head and arched a single brow. "*Ley. Ains-ley,*" I corrected, emphasizing the syllables. She clearly was not in the headspace to accept nicknames. "I know you're mad..."

She threw her head back and laughed incredulously. Oh no.

"You think I'm *mad?*" she questioned through a bitter scoff.

"Don't answer that," Felix whispered as if I would be stupid enough to.

"I mean, what reason would I possibly have to be *mad?*" Ainsley demanded, taking a deliberate step forward. Felix and I both stepped back on instinct, our shoulders brushing as we moved as one. "It's not like you brought a woman whose list of hobbies involves insulting me at every turn..." She took another step and so did we. "Or trying as hard as she can to get under my skin."

"Ainsley, I—"

"Because that would be crazy, right?" she said, cutting me off. I didn't dare respond. I may have been stupid, but I wasn't an idiot.

"Completely crazy," Felix answered. Ainsley whirled on him, her finger pointing to his chest as she raged on.

"And you," she seethed. Felix's eyes widened in shock as if he hadn't expected to be the subject of her wrath. "You *knew* he was bringing her. We had been writing to each other all damn morning, and you couldn't once tell me she was with you? Sure, you found the time to ask me what I planned on wearing today, but couldn't locate a split second to let me know my nemesis was traveling with you?!"

I shot Felix a sidelong glance and his shoulders sagged in irritation at being caught. Carefully, without drawing attention to myself, I slid my hand behind Felix's back. He shifted slightly, and three gold coins fell into my waiting palm. I pocketed his false win before Ainsley could notice what had just transpired.

"What are you two doing?!" she demanded.

Shit.

"Nothing," Felix and I said in unison, the same way we had every time we had been caught doing something we shouldn't have been. She narrowed her eyes, clearly not buying a word I was selling. I drew in a deep breath as I took a tentative step closer.

"I'm sorry, Ainsley. We both are," I said before the flames of her wrath could burn any brighter. "I should have let you know that Rosella was on my council and that I'd be bringing her today, especially knowing the history between the two of you." She perked up and her brows scrunched as if internally fighting between holding onto her anger and letting it dissipate. "Please don't be angry."

She stared up at me as she contemplated her choices. I had barely just gotten her back and the last thing I wanted was to unsettle the already shaky ground beneath us. My thumbs ran nervously over the tips of my fingers as I held my breath in anticipation of her response.

Felix's snickering broke the tense silence, and both Ainsley and I directed our attention to him.

"Is something funny?" she demanded tersely.

"Kind of," he replied, covering his mouth with his hand.

Irritation flooded my system, hot and thick. On the list of things Ainsley hated, just beneath *lying* and right above *geese*, was *being laughed at*. We were supposed to be diffusing the situation, not setting her off again.

"I wanted so badly for things to go back to normal between us," Felix explained.

"But yet, here we are—arguing," Ainsley added.

"Yeah, but about Rosella. I mean, how much more normal does it get?"

A shallow laugh escaped me as I acknowledged the validity of Felix's point. It was reminiscent of our time in Caelum before our world was flipped upside down, bickering about insignificant things. I directed my gaze towards Ainsley, who was struggling to contain a faint smile that was eager to be revealed as she arrived at the same realization.

Taking a chance, I stepped forward and pulled her into a hug. "I'm really sorry for catching you off guard." She nodded against me, her body relaxing as I held her. "And I promise to have a talk with Rosella about her attitude. She may not like you, but you're a queen and you deserve that respect. Especially in your own kingdom."

"Thank you, Dash."

I squeezed her once and then stepped away, needing a bit of space. I was still learning my own boundaries regarding our relationship and what I could handle.

"How about a real tour now?" I suggested, and she nodded before leading Felix and me down the long corridor.

38
Dashiell

We rounded a corner an hour later, now in a different part of the palace than we had started. This place felt like a maze to me, but Ainsley navigated its halls effortlessly. I couldn't help but smile to see her in her element and so at ease in the kingdom that belonged to her.

She had taken me to every room that flittered through her mind, her excitement rising with her growing list as we hurried through corridors and pushed past doors that led to unknown places. Felix didn't seem to mind exploring the rooms he was already familiar with, completely content just for the three of us to be reunited once again.

Eventually, we spotted Olivier as we departed the massive library with elongated bookcases lined with thousands of tomes. I could picture Ainsley there, sprawled out on one of the dark velvet couches next to a roaring fire with Felix at her side—both of them utterly consumed by the stories at their fingertips. A pang of unwarranted loneliness overtook me at the image.

Upon seeing Olivier, Felix had excused himself from the tour, opting to steal a quiet moment with the man he loved before we were all called to partake in a game of politics none of us wanted to play.

"And then we assign them a punishment that fits their crime," Ainsley said as we walked closely together to our next destination.

"And after?" I asked.

She shrugged nonchalantly. "We release them. The goal is not to have them in the holding quarters forever."

Holding quarters—a place I had only ever referred to as 'the dungeons.' However, the long hallway lined with cells was nothing like what was held beneath the palace in Caelum. There was no other way to describe Tenebrae's prison other than humane.

At first, I had wondered why Ainsley had brought me down there; exploring the kingdom's dungeon wasn't a usual location to include when showing visitors around. But as I observed the spacious cells stocked with food, clean bedding, and items to pass the time, I understood why.

When Ainsley and I were first getting to know one another, I shared with her my reluctance and fear of ruling one day. I had dreams and aspirations that didn't align with my father's, and anytime I would make a suggestion or comment, it was quickly shot down with my ignorance and naivety thrown back in my face.

'You know nothing of ruling a kingdom, Dashiell,' my father would say. Every time I walked out of a meeting with him, I felt that much lesser of a person, beat down and heavy. I felt like a failure—like I wasn't fit to ever rule.

The former King of Caelum had this unexplainable way of always transforming my hopeful ideals into streams of nightmares. He'd force me to stand there while he dissected every thought, every suggestion, every possibility, twisting and bending them until they morphed into unimaginable chaos. The path of my aspirations always led to destruction, starvation, revolt, and death.

Each lashing of my father's tongue was like a brand on my flesh, burning and searing until my mind was scarred and I was too afraid to ever utter another dream aloud. I would walk away from my father feeling like if I had ever ruled Caelum, I would bring about the end for my people unless I stayed the course—*his* course.

I wish that I could say when I learned of his Obscure from Imogen, I was relieved. I should have been, but I wasn't. For years, I had been played and manipulated into believing he knew best, feeling that falsity in my bones as if it were a blinding truth. Finding out it was just my father's power making my beliefs flex and waver wasn't reassuring. If anything, I felt even more inferior at the revelation.

I hadn't been smart enough to see the signs or strong enough to fight through his magic. I was weak and naive, and even now, I battled with the haunting words that rang true in my mind. Even now, with the changes I was trying to implement in my home, I was still failing.

'You know nothing of ruling a kingdom, Dashiell.'

"Felix wrote to me about you dissolving the law against Conjoining," Ainsley said, spearing through my clouded thoughts. I blinked to clear my mind and then turned to her, nodding once. A soft smile curved her full lips. I wanted so badly to return the gesture but found myself instead picturing the disarray my kingdom was now in for that choice. I'd never regret that decision, but it didn't make the consequences of my actions any easier to digest.

She looked up at me, her caramel eyes imploring a belief I couldn't force myself to seize. Ainsley had always known how much my kingdom and people meant to me, and never once had she ever questioned or doubted my capability to be a fair and just leader.

"I know it isn't going how you hoped," she whispered, the crimson streaks in her irises ensnaring my focus as usual.

"Felix told you about that too, did he?" I replied, willing some lightness into my tone to mask my embarrassment. I broke her stare, unable to look at her as my cheeks flushed.

"To be honest, I'm a little upset that *you* didn't."

Ainsley moved in front of me, coming into my line of sight as if refusing to allow me to retreat into myself as we stopped in the middle of the hallway. My throat bobbed as I swallowed every ounce of disappointment etched into her soft face.

"I didn't know if I could...If I was allowed to," I admitted. Understanding washed over her features.

She took a deep breath and stepped forward, closing the gap between us to a distance it would have been this summer when all that mattered was our little family. "You can always come to me, Dash." I wasn't sure if those words truly held weight or if she only wished they had.

Despite the pushback and my stumbles, I wanted to believe that I could honestly change the ways of my kingdom and lead my people into more progressive times. But having to undo centuries of ignorance and prejudice was proving harder than I could have ever imagined. It wasn't difficult to wonder if my father had been right all along and that I would bring about the end of Caelum.

'You know nothing of ruling a kingdom, Dashiell.'

"If anyone can alter Caelum for the better, it's you," Ainsley said, seeming to sense where my thoughts had gone. My heart nearly fractured at her faith in me. "And I'll be here to support you in any way that I can."

That's exactly what she was doing with the tour of the holding quarters—showing me a part of her kingdom that she believed could benefit mine.

"Thank you," was all I could manage to say.

She nodded in a self asserting way and looped her arm through mine as she steered us back on the path of our next destination.

"You've made a great king so far and will continue to do so," she added with an air of nonchalance as if it were a simple fact and not an opinion.

"You don't know that."

"I do. Because I'm always right."

She was rarely right. But I didn't point that out as I conceded the unwinnable debate with a long exhale and polite smile. When Ainsley had her mind made up, there was never any use trying to change it. She always had to come to conclusions or realizations on her own time and not a moment before.

"Oh, Your Majesty!" a frantic woman called, capturing both mine and Ainsley's attention.

She hurried through a door on our right and rushed to her queen. Her curly blonde hair wildly framed her freckled face as a small child sat on her hip while another clung to her leg. The woman seemed both frantic and exhausted as she approached and unfurled a closed fist revealing broken pieces of a candle.

"I'm so sorry to disturb you, but Tommy broke them all…again," the woman gritted the last word while peering over her shoulder as if she could scold Tommy through the now-closed door.

"How many this time?" Ainsley asked.

"All of them. He's quite interested in their magic but hasn't grasped the concept of gentleness."

Ainsley chuckled softly under her breath before nodding to herself. All at once her hands began to move, fingers twirling delicately as shadows encompassed them. I watched in amazement as her magic spun and whirled, transforming from gentle wisps of darkness into something that held shape.

She twisted her hands, and suddenly, the object morphed into a basket, its handle resting on her forearm. Ainsley's fingers moved again, this time creating long, slender cylinders that turned into candles. One by one, she placed them into the basket before extending the handle for the woman to take.

"I crafted a few extra, just in case," Ainsley said with a comforting smile in her voice.

The woman released a relieved breath before taking the candles from her queen and attempting to adjust the child at her hip. "Thank you so much, Your Majesty."

"Of course, Miriam." Ainsley waved off her gratitude and reached for the child Miriam was struggling to hold on to. "I'm going to take Alec and Penelope," she explained, removing the small boy from his mother's arms as the little girl shifted from her leg to the queen's side, "as well as Tommy, to the children's quarters for the night."

"You don't have to do that," Miriam argued as Ainsley moved past her and opened the door that little Tommy clearly had his ear pressed against as a small boy no older than four tumbled to the ground.

"You need to rest, Miriam," she said, giving a pointed look at the woman's stomach. Now that her son wasn't impending my view, I could see that she was pregnant. "You know the maidens will take good care of them."

"I know; I just don't want to burden anyone."

"You won't be, I promise."

Miriam seemed reluctant as she looked over the three small children, but eventually gave her queen a shallow nod.

Ainsley's grin grew as she cast her gaze in my direction. "Dash, will you grab Tommy for me?"

I did as she asked, kneeling and picking up the small boy who was sliding his limbs over the ground as if pretending to make imprints in invisible snow. He fought me at first, wiggling in my hold, until I opened my palm and offered a small heatless flame for him to take. Tommy grabbed it at once, his blue eyes widening in amazement as the magic fire twisted around his tiny fingers.

"Do you wield?" Ainsley asked. I directed my focus back to her, prepared to answer her very obvious question, but it wasn't me whom she was speaking to.

A few feet away stood a man nodding enthusiastically at his queen. "Perfect. I need you to follow Miriam and illuminate these candles," Ainsley said, gesturing to the full basket in the woman's arms. "Make sure you place them high enough so they can't be reached."

The man bowed, and with a quick thank you from Miriam, the two disappeared into the room. Ainsley wasted no time as she led the way through another hallway I assumed would take us to the children's quarters she mentioned.

"Miriam doesn't possess magic?" I whispered close to Ainsley's ear, not wanting to offend the children. In Caelum, non-wielders were always thought to be lesser, unworthy, and never would have been invited to the palace. I didn't exactly agree with the prejudice, but it was present in my kingdom, nonetheless.

"No," Ainsley answered at a normal volume. "Most people visiting the palace don't."

Visiting—not living. I noted the distinct choice of wording before crooking a brow as her stare met my eyes. Everything about her world was so different from mine that I couldn't help but want to understand it all.

In Caelum, the palace was the designated home to anyone who possessed magic. There were no *visitors* unless invited by the king, and even then, those invitations were only given to magic wielders from other kingdoms. Ainsley made it seem as if Tenebrae operated differently, prompting my curiosity.

We stopped outside a set of double doors before she could answer my unspoken request for elaboration, and Penelope began banging loudly on the wood. The doors creaked open immediately, and a pissed-off-looking maiden popped her head through the crack, clearly prepared to berate whoever had caused the sudden disturbance. It was only when she saw the Queen of Tenebrae that her furious mask faltered and transformed into something that resembled respect and admiration.

"I know it's short notice, but is it alright if the children stay the night?" Ainsley asked.

"Of course, Your Majesty. I've been telling Miriam to bring them by for days now," the maiden said, taking the boy from her arms just as Penelope pushed past us and ran into the room where several other children were playing with wooden blocks.

"Thank you, Claudia."

I shifted to set Tommy on the ground but he fisted his tiny hand in my shirt, refusing to allow me to do so. "I don't want to go," he whispered. I turned to Ainsley for help, but she and the maiden were engrossed in a quiet conversation, paying us no mind. When I looked back at Tommy, his too-large eyes were aimed at the magical flame in his palm and I finally understood his reluctance.

My lips tugged at the corners and my chest tightened as I remembered feeling just as captivated by the small display of magic when my mother had done the same for me. There was something so beautiful and innocent about seeing the wonder on a child's face at the power we took for granted every day. I bent down, keeping myself at Tommy's height as I placed his feet on the floor.

"Do you think you can help me with something?" I asked conspiratorially. The boy's interest piqued as he looked at me with a curious stare. The magical flame disappeared from Tommy's grasp, but before he could object, I held my palm open and called for my Unda Gift.

Water appeared in my hand, spinning around itself faster and faster as it formed a ball of swirling liquid. Tommy's jaw dropped and my smile grew as I watched joy, curiosity, and amazement flood his features. Placing a finger on the sphere with my free hand, I channeled my magic into it, allowing it to glow just as the candles he was so interested in did.

"This is a very important item, and I can't bring it with me into my meetings today," I told Tommy, extending the magical orb of water to him. "Do you think you can keep it safe for me while I'm busy?" He nodded enthusiastically and reached for the ball. "You'll have to be extremely gentle with it so it doesn't break. Can you do that?"

"I think so," Tommy answered, and ever so carefully, he wrapped his small fingers around the illuminated sphere.

"I think so too."

His face lit up and a shallow gasp escaped him as he held the glowing ball of water between his hands. I drew in a shaky breath as my mind flashed to another place and time—a balcony in Caelum beneath the warm summer sun. Ainsley's back was pressed to my chest; her floral scent mixed with winter air was intoxicating and addictive as I breathed her in. I slid my arms around her, my hands cradling the back of hers as I called for my magic.

That spark I always felt when close to her only grew, as if my magic had craved her just as strongly as I had. There had never been an instance where I shared that magic with someone, and to be honest, I hadn't known it was possible until I did it. I should have known that she was different from that moment.

As my magic surged through her, I felt fire, strength, and mystery, like a part of her hid in the shadows. Rather than cluing me in to who she truly was, I just wrote it off as her being my opposite. Where I was ice, she was fire; my calm was her rage, and my desperation her resilience. My magic was soothing and bright, so why wouldn't hers have been fury and darkness?

A ripple of my power gathered into her palms and she spun, her brown eyes wide and the biggest smile I had ever seen stretching across her face. She whispered my name but the word held so much more than just an acknowledgment. There was gratitude and wonder and admiration and hunger, and *my Gods,* she was everything I had never known I wanted.

I blew out a breath and blinked away the memory I didn't ask for. It wasn't that I didn't cherish the time Ainsley and I had spent together, but it was far too painful to reflect on those moments without preparation. I was still working through my shit, and each happy recollection was accompanied by a darker one.

With every image of Felix laughing or Ainsley's head resting on my chest, I was plagued with memories of heartache, of loss, of loneliness, of pain, of..." My fingers grazed the curved lines of scarred flesh on my forearm absentmindedly.

I took in a long inhale and counted to fifty.

"Thank you," Tommy whispered just as I finished.

I smiled briefly and motioned for him to enter the room where the other children were. As I rose to my feet, Ainsley said goodbye to the maiden and then faced me. Our gazes collided and my heart stuttered as the smile she wore wilted away like rose petals. She knew something was wrong.

"Where to next?" I asked, stealing the words from the air before she could claim them first.

Her mouth closed and her eyes roamed fervently over my face, searching for a way in. A crease formed between her brows as she studied me, and I fought the urge to smooth it away with reassurance. She had always been adept at picking up when I was being tormented by thoughts, but I couldn't allow her to read me now.

More than anything, I desired to get back to the level of trust and friendship we had fought so hard to build, but even I knew I wasn't capable of that yet. I needed a moment—a minute to count, a second to breathe. Just *something* to help me not feel the weight of her angered words or how quickly she had cast me out without so much as a glance back. I needed to shove away the intrusive ideas that she had never once truly loved me.

'What if it was all a lie?' the darker, insecure part of my mind suggested. It wasn't. She *had* loved me as fiercely as I had her. The trust, the foundation, the friendship; that was all real. And we'd get there again someday.

"Your room," Ainsley finally answered, her brows still furrowed as she inspected me. I counted to fifty as she led the way.

By the time we arrived at the room designated for me, Ainsley had shared all about the inner workings of the palace and the people. Miriam was a widow and had recently lost her husband when Oberon attacked the camp he was stationed at several months ago. She had no family and with three small children and one on the way, she needed all the help she could get. So she came here.

In Caelum, the place I called home was a residence solely for magic wielders—people my father and the kings before him believed were deserving of a life of luxury and freedom. But in this kingdom, the palace was a shelter that anyone could come to if they were in need of a warm meal or safe place to sleep. It was meant to be a refuge for the people of Tenebrae for as long as they needed one. I was most surprised to learn that even Ainsley didn't live within its stone walls, instead choosing to dwell with her new family in a house not too far from the premises.

"Here we are," she said, pushing the door wide to allow me to enter first.

The room was spacious and flooded with sunlight from the wide windows that lined the eastern wall. I walked closer and peered out at the view, catching a glimpse of the sparkling light reflecting off the surface of a large crystal blue lake. My lips tilted into a smile, knowing this was why she had assigned me this space. It wasn't *my* lake, but it was a small reminder of home in a foreign and unknown land.

"It's perfect," I told her, twisting around to meet her gaze.

Her grin matched mine as she nervously pulled at her fingers as if waiting with bated breath for my reaction. "Good, because—" The word barely escaped her lips when the door slammed into the wall with a crack and a smear of grey and white bolted through the room. Fire danced at my fingertips a heartbeat before I watched the large wolf collide with her owner.

"Nova!" Ainsley squealed, her body half covered by the massive animal as she sank to the ground. The queen lovingly offered her pet attention by scratching its ears while the wolf affectionately nuzzled and licked her face.

"They didn't cause any problems, did they? I didn't know they weren't planning on coming home with us when we left."

My head cocked to the side at that response. I had assumed the wolves were given an order to stay behind as a precaution and protection for Olivier, but apparently, that wasn't the case.

"They were no trouble at all," I answered and moved to her side.

Nova perked up at the sound of my voice and pushed off Ainsley to come to me. She sniffed at my hand as she always did and I tentatively ran my fingers over her snout.

"She wants you to pet her," Ainsley said. On instinct, my eyes flicked up and I scanned the room for any signs of Onyx. "What are you doing?"

"The black one won't let me touch her."

Ainsley let out a breathy laugh, and I watched as she rose to her feet, strolled for the door, and shut it. She spun and gave me an expectant look. I still didn't move. With an annoyed sigh and roll of her eyes, she latched the lock on the door. My knees hit the floor a second later.

I ran my fingers through Nova's soft grey fur as I gave her the affection I hadn't been allowed to for weeks now, thanks to her dickhead protector. Ainsley's presence loomed close before she slid to the floor next to me and petted her wolf as well.

"She likes you," she said. For some reason, the statement sent a bolt of pride through me.

"At least one of them does."

She nodded along thoughtfully like she had expected me to say as much. "It can be difficult to break down Onyx's walls, but once he trusts you and lets you in, he's the sweetest, most attention-seeking creature in the world."

My face scrunched as I tried to picture the mammoth black wolf as anything but angry and vicious. These past weeks in Caelum, I couldn't so much as look at him without garnering a snarl and display of his razor-sharp fangs.

"Nova is the more logical thinker out of the two of them. She knew you wouldn't hurt me or the people I care about, so she had no reason to be anything other than friendly," Ainsley continued. "She doesn't hold grudges against anyone except her Solum." Her voice dropped an octave and her words were smushed together as if she were talking to a baby and not a fully grown wolf.

"Am I supposed to know what that is?" I asked, twisting the foreign word in my mind as I inspected it. I couldn't help but feel I should have known what that meant. Ainsley's gaze held mine for a moment before narrowing, a question sparking in her eyes. "Felix didn't tell you about them?"

I ran through every conversation I had with my best friend about the canine visitors, but there was nothing of substance besides *'Don't touch the black one or you'll die.'* I shook my head.

"Solum means one and only. It's said that the Gods created two souls to mold and match each other in every way—a perfect pair written in the stars. When they find their other half, an undeniable bond forms. A love deep and pure." She spoke of the connection with an unmatched admiration.

"And that's what you and Evander share…" I deduced. Ainsley's silence lingered for a moment, causing the tension in the air to intensify. She didn't want to answer. "Was that not okay to ask?"

The question seemed to break her from her trance. "Why wouldn't it be?"

"I don't know…" I said, shrugging awkwardly. "It just seems like you don't want to tell me about your bond. Like it's too personal—too intimate."

"It is." It was barely a whisper yet deafening at the same time.

I continued to pet Nova to cover up the fact that I felt like a complete dick for prying into her life when this topic was obviously something she didn't feel comfortable discussing. The longer this day went on, the more I fucked it up. First with Rosella, then with my inability to regulate my emotions, and now with inserting myself where I didn't belong. I released a shaky breath and turned toward her with an apology poised on my tongue.

"But it's okay that you asked," Ainsley suddenly added. "The Solum Bond has only ever been proven to occur in a specific wolf species. What Evander and I share is different." She shifted her position to face me more fully as her fingers continued to stroke Nova's coat. "We were created by magic—two souls split from one. Though it's not the same, the connection Van and I have mirrors Onyx and Nova's in many ways. The more I examine it, the more I believe that our parents were trying to replicate the Solum bond through us."

"They wanted you two to be together?"

Ainsley shook her head as she replied, "Not in that way. Magic can't create love." I had once said the same words to her.

I tongued my cheek as a million questions ran through my mind. What does it feel like? What can you do? When did you find out? Do you *want* this? There was once a time when she would have been bound to me without any say in the matter, and the prospect of her choice being stripped away again sent a shudder down my spine.

But I didn't have a right to the answers I longed to know. So instead, I let the questions stick in the back of my throat until I swallowed them down like a bitter tonic.

"So Nova knows my intentions are pure, but Onyx doesn't?" I asked, changing the subject. Ainsley's shoulders visibly sagged in relief as a breath escaped her disguised as a careless chuckle.

"No, he's well aware you're harmless to me. He's just choosing to be an asshole."

"Joy." I slipped a hidden treat from my sleeve and offered it to Nova, which she gladly took. I could see Ainsley's head cock to the side in my periphery and I shrugged. "Onyx tried to attack me the one time I openly handed her food, so now I do it in secret."

She laughed hard, the sound pulling on the strings of my heart as joyous memories of ice slides, children's games, and sharing embarrassing stories flooded my mind. I held onto them with both hands, wanting to sink into the depths and drown in the happiness that filled me—needing to cherish this moment of peace before the darkness came and swallowed me whole the way it always did.

"He won't attack you, you know?" Ainsley said, breaking through my paralyzing fear. I looked at her questioningly, not remembering what we had just been discussing. "Onyx might snarl and growl and lunge, but he won't ever hurt you." That seemed like a load of shit.

"That seems like a load of shit." She rolled her eyes and shook off my claim.

"He won't. Trust me."

I narrowed my eyes and she repeated the gesture, mocking me in that asshole way of hers.

"Or…" I said conspiratorially. "You're lying and just want to watch me get my ass handed to me by an overgrown ball of fluff."

Her smile grew just as big as it had the day she held my water sphere in her hands. "Or that."

Before I could offer a single quip in return, inky shadows swirled around us, followed by the appearance of Evander. I quickly scooted away from Ainsley as if I had been caught doing something I shouldn't have. We were friends, but I didn't know what extent of friendship Ainsley's husband was going to tolerate.

The King of Tenebrae looked us over but barely seemed to register my presence as he extended a hand to his wife in haste. "We need to go. Right now." A second later, Ainsley's hand was in his, and they disappeared before my eyes. What the fuck just happened?

I looked left and right, utterly confused as to what had transpired before me. Did I do something wrong? Was I sitting too close to her and that's why he decided to whisk her away on a whim? Was he pissed we were alone together? Should we not have been?

My panic mind raced for all of three seconds before dark wisps found me again. Evander had barely stepped through his shadows as he snapped his fingers and shoved his hand in my face in a clear sign for me to take it. Apparently *speaking* was too much of an inconvenience for him. With gritted teeth, I grabbed hold of his palm and drifted into the darkness.

In a single blink, there was nothing but bright light and fresh air enveloping me. I shielded my eyes from the sun as I tried to get my bearings straight, focusing on the soft ground beneath my feet to anchor me in the moment.

"What the hell happened?!" Ainsley demanded, panic slicing each word.

I brought my hand down and fully observed my surroundings. We found ourselves in a grassy field filled with an abundance of wildflowers. To our left, there lay a narrow creek that gently curved through the terrain, while to our right, a dense forest loomed. The scenery stretched endlessly, devoid of any structures, villages, or people.

"We don't know, Your Majesty," someone replied.

I turned my attention to the conversation, my gaze dropping to where Ainsley was kneeling, her fingers covered in crimson. On pure instinct, I sank to the ground, my hands flying over the body before us as I called to my Gift.

"Did you find anyone else?" Evander implored, an edge of worry slipping between his mask of calm.

"No, My King."

My eyes roamed frantically over each bruise, each cut, each broken bone protruding from the skin. I wasn't skilled in my Medicus Gift yet, only mastering the repair of small wounds, and with the amount of damage done here, I didn't know where to begin. His busted lip and the blood dripping from his mouth? The purple flesh beneath his eyes? The foot that was bent in the wrong direction? The injury to his abdomen that he was clutching?

Someone had tortured Brandle to the brink of death.

39
Ainsley

My hands trembled as I pressed them to Brandle's stomach and tried not to focus on the feel of his hot blood slipping through my fingers. I kept my head turned away and sipped on the air, not daring to breathe through my nose. The stench of infected flesh due to obvious weeks of torture was nearly too much to bear. But that wasn't why I directed my stare elsewhere.

"Keep applying pressure," Dash commanded, and I nodded but kept my eyes on the distant horizon. Without having full control of my Imperium Gift, it was too risky to attempt to regulate his blood flow, and I could end up doing more harm than good.

Drawing in a full breath through my mouth, I pressed harder onto his wound. Brandle released a strangled whimper and my instincts had me turning toward the sound before my mind could stop me. My breathing quickened, the panic rising so high I could do nothing but let the force of the current drag me under. I froze as my eyes landed on his face; it wasn't a Prince of Ministro dying in the grass—it was Felix.

I blinked, and suddenly, I was cradling my best friend as he bled out. My throat was thick with emotion as I stared down at him, knowing there was nothing I could do to save him from his fate. I was going to lose the person who meant everything to me all because of my need for revenge.

I could hear my name in the distance, urging me back to reality, but I was too far gone. Felix's amber eyes were losing their brightness, the honey hue fading away. His voice was barely more than a whisper as he pleaded for me not to leave him—not to let him die alone. I clutched him closer. A tear streaked down my cheek as my arms became heavy with his weight. My chest was warm from the blood seeping through his shirt and soaking into mine.

"Ainsley!" the voice said again, and my shoulder shook forcefully. I snapped back to the present, my hands still firmly pressed to Brandle's stomach as my tears dropped to the ground. Lia was now sitting at my side with a tender look of concern on her face.

"I've got him," she whispered, but I didn't back away. "It's okay, Ainsley. You can let go now; I've got him." When I was still too paralyzed to move, Evander gently pried my hands from Brandle's body so Lia could take over.

"Breathe, love," he whispered as he helped me to my feet. "Just breathe." I buried my face in his chest as I tried to anchor myself back in the present.

It's not Felix. It's not Felix. It's not Felix.

Over and over again, I repeated the mantra. Despite being aware that my best friend was alive and well, the traumatic events of that night still lingered in my mind. Even now, there were times when I would wake up with a scream lodged in my throat, the result of reliving the image of that arrow piercing his heart in my nightmares.

"What have you done so far?" Lia asked as I continued to regulate my breathing.

"I healed a few minor lacerations, and now I'm trying to mend his shattered ankle. The rest of his damage is far too extensive for my knowledge base," Dash answered.

"Will he survive?" Evander said, voicing the question I had been too terrified to ask.

Lia's response was not immediate, and as the third minute of silence approached, I turned to face her. She must have torn away his shirt because her hands roamed slowly over his bare skin. I swallowed back bile as I took in the deep purple splotches across his chest and the ribs pressing against his side as if trying to break free from his flesh.

"Yes," she said definitively. "I'm confident that Sirona and I will be able to repair the internal injuries. It won't be an easy recovery, but he'll live."

Evander and I released a relieved breath at the same time. "I still don't understand what happened," I admitted.

"Harbin," Brandle croaked, his voice so low I barely caught it. The eye that was not swollen shut opened slightly, revealing a shade of blood red that consumed the circulating white around the pupil. "He knows about me." The words were broken and raspy, possibly from fluid filling his lungs. Before any of us could question him further, his eye closed and his head lulled to the side.

"We need to get him somewhere safe right now," Lia commanded. With a kiss on my forehead, Evander released me to grab ahold of her and Brandle before traversing away.

I swayed gently on my feet from the lack of support, my knees slightly wobbly from my earlier panic. We didn't have time for me to have a mental breakdown and get lost in the labyrinth of my fear. There were far too many important questions we needed to focus on.

"I can't believe Harbin found out. Brandle had been so careful to cover his tracks for years," I said.

Twisting at the sound of dirt beneath boots, I found Dash now at my side, his hand curling around my elbow to offer me some stability. "I may have an idea about that." My brows scrunched in curiosity as I looked into his deep navy and teal eyes. "That traitor in my court you told me to look out for... It was Gideon."

I gritted my teeth in disgust. "That isn't surprising. From what you and Felix have shared with me, he's always been a dick." He refrained from responding to my assessment, his demeanor instead displaying the lingering impact of the betrayal. "Did he suffer?"

Dash's eyes narrowed a fraction, as if reluctant to answer. Finally, he dipped his head in a single nod.

"Good," I declared. "He didn't deserve to draw breath after what he did."

The King of Caelum studied me for a moment, and it occurred to me that he was still becoming familiar with this side of me. When I lived in his kingdom, I had been so naive and afraid of the evil in the world. I heavily depended on his and Felix's protection, allowing fear to prevent me from asking questions and seeking answers. But now, after everything I had gone through, I found solace in the darkness.

"When we get back to the palace, we need to change," I announced to get back on track and gestured to our blood-drenched clothes. "No one can see us like this."

"Probably smart not to cause a panic."

"It's not just that," I said, wiping the blood from my hands onto my sweater. "Gideon might very well have been the one to inform Harbin about Brandle, but it's also possible that he wasn't. Right now, we're in the dark about too many things." I scanned the area, trying to pick up on clues overlooked by the soldiers who made the discovery. "Brandle showed up on my kingdom's doorstep, tortured and barely breathing. We don't know if he was dropped here as some sort of a message or if he managed to escape and fled. Until we have those answers, I'm not taking any risks with vital information falling into the wrong hands." My stare dropped to the flattened grass now streaked with crimson.

I traced the red outline of Brandle's lost blood with my mind, noticing how comparable it was to the one Felix left behind when I thought he had died. Even the blood pooled in a similar manner, gradually soaking into the soil as if the earth had longed for it.

"I refuse to lose anyone because I was careless and didn't think every scenario through before acting," I added.

When I moved my attention back to Dash, his firm stare was on me. I noted the subtleties he wore like clothing, layering them over himself like complex fashions. The way the pad of his thumb ran across the tip of his fingers. The way his weight shifted to one side as he readjusted his stance. The way his gaze gradually roved over my face, trying to seep into me as thoroughly as the blood now coating the land. His mind was at work, putting together a puzzle he didn't possess all the pieces for.

But the most profound thing I noticed was the way his pupil dilated slightly—a clear tell an Obscure was at play.

Evander appeared in a billow of shadows, and I broke Dash's stare. We had more important matters to attend to at the moment, and I couldn't let an ounce of my current focus wander to what extra power he possessed.

"Brandle?"

"Alive," Van replied. "Sirona and Lia are tending to him at the house."

"Good. Gideon was the traitor in Caelum." We exchanged sentences in quick bursts, needing to relay as much information as we could in the shortest amount of time.

Van's grey eyes drifted to Dash and he arched a brow in silent question. "He's taken care of," Dash answered. My husband only nodded and turned back to me.

"We can't be sure that was the only leak," he said.

"I agree. For now, we need to carry on as if nothing out of the ordinary has happened."

Van concurred and slid his fingers between mine. His voice dropped low and the sharp edge of a worried king drifted away on the wind around us. "Are you okay?" he asked, tightening his hold.

I didn't have time not to be. Tensions were already high with our advisors not being particularly happy about our new alliance with Caelum, and I could imagine Dash was getting just as much pushback on the subject as we were. My main concern had to be getting through these meetings.

"Take us to my room so I can get cleaned up, then to Dash's," I told him. He held out his hand without hesitation, understanding that I didn't want to talk further about his inquiry.

Once I had finished wiping the blood from my hands and changing clothes, Evander brought us to Dash's room, where the King of Caelum quickly did the same. My husband didn't stick around and wait for him to finish, citing his desire to discreetly let Tallis know what had occurred with Brandle before we started the meeting from hell.

As I waited for Dash to emerge from the bathing room, I absentmindedly ran my fingers over the velvet blanket adorning his bed and tried to focus on how best not to lose my temper this afternoon. Today's assembly was not going to be a pleasant one, as our selected participants were bound to air out grievances about our partnership.

Given the vast number of rumors and general unfriendliness between the kingdoms, I couldn't exactly blame them for their apprehension, but it didn't mean I would be okay with hearing slander and accusations thrown about. Gods knew I had a difficult time reining in my quick tongue on a good day, so this afternoon was *definitely* going to be a challenge.

"What happened back there?" Dash asked as he emerged from the bathing room while fastening a gold button on his tailored jacket.

I admired the way the new title of king suited him despite his reservations, and how he seemed to tackle the role in such a different manner than his father. Even the way he dressed was a drastic change from the former king. Where Perceval's attire was always an ostentatious show of wealth and power, Dash's look was much more austere.

He wore a deep shade of navy blue, and the only gold that adorned his jacket were the buttons fastened at his cuffs and down the middle. Perceval would have sported a gaudy embellishment sprawling across the breast, but that wasn't the case here. At first, I had thought that Dash had chosen a plain fabric, but upon further inspection, I noticed the nearly invisible detail. There *was* a design, but the threads were the same dark shade as the rest of his jacket, making the pattern that resembled cresting waves virtually unnoticeable.

It embodied him in every way; simple yet elegant, and containing complex layers that were hidden unless you got close enough to uncover the truth.

"I don't know, but hopefully, when Brandle wakes up, we'll find out."

"I meant with *you*," he said, and I shifted my gaze from his attire to discover his intense eyes on me. "You didn't respond when I called your name, and it took Lia a few times to get through to you."

My stare dropped to the hands folded in my lap. "Felix died in my arms. Well, at least I thought he had." Dash didn't answer, but I heard the slight breath he sucked in. "And seeing Brandle like that..."

"You were reliving that night."

I nodded and finally looked up to meet his gaze. His features were soft—thoughtful—yet there was an ounce of pain behind his eyes. I couldn't tell if it was directed at what I had experienced or if he was remembering his own agony from that night.

"We should go," I said, not wanting to know the answer. Dash didn't argue, and together, we left the room and walked silently through the palace.

40
Ainsley

I spied Evander and Tallis speaking quietly next to one of the open windows that lined the long corridor leading to our council room. The air grew thick with tension and my stomach curled into a knot as I studied the scene before me. The King of Agnitio's lips were moving quickly, only pausing when Van interrupted with a sentence uttered too low for my ears to pick up. With a subtle shake of Tallis's head, my husband's face shifted into a grim display of despair.

I picked up the pace, cautious of the eyes on me from the palace goers passing through the hallway. Dash seemed to tune into my distress and quickened his steps beside me. Tallis spoke again, and this time Evander's shoulders visibly sagged and he stumbled backward a single step before righting himself. Something was wrong.

Evander must have felt my panic because his eyes snapped to mine. He only offered me a brief moment of seeing the terror on his face before morphing his features into that neutral mask he always donned in the presence of company. A slight shake of his head indicated this wasn't the time nor place for him to disclose the contents of the conversation, and it took everything inside me not to fight him on it.

My heart was racing alongside my magic, and my intuition was like a warning bell going off in my mind, setting my entire body on edge. I didn't like being kept in the dark for any amount of time. Especially when I could tell that something was very, *very* wrong.

With his stare still locked on mine, Van tilted his head toward the door that led to the council room. We were only feet away from it now, but my steps slowed as I fought to obey his order for me to enter. I trusted that Evander would fill me in on his conversation with Tallis eventually, but that stubborn and fearful part of me I couldn't always beat into submission was roaring with impatience.

"Ugh, finally..." Rosella whined, dragging out the words. My attention automatically shifted toward the shrill voice that constantly made my hair stand on edge.

She widened the opening of the door as she pushed through, allowing me to see everyone assembled inside. Some sat at the large round table, while others stood and chatted while they waited. The common factor from just that glance was that everyone kept the conversations reserved for only those who belonged to the same kingdom, refusing to mingle amongst the other magic wielders. I wasn't surprised, but it confirmed how difficult this meeting was going to be.

"You took forever," Rosella continued.

My attention drifted back to Evander, but he was no longer looking at me. His focus was firmly on Tallis and the hushed exchange that passed between them, but I couldn't look away.

"I'm sure you managed to entertain yourself just fine," Dash said.

"Obviously, but I'll need a new notebook before we start the meeting."

Evander crossed his arms firmly over his chest, and I narrowed my gaze as I observed the tension in the movement. Tallis seemed relatively calm, but as that was always his demeanor, I couldn't tell if Van was overreacting or if the King of Agnitio was just masking his emotions better than my husband.

"Already? I just gave you that one," Dash replied.

Evander sighed before dragging a hand through his black hair in frustration and directed his stare out the window to their right.

"What information have you gathered?" Dash asked.

Tallis moved closer to Van's side and placed a comforting hand on his shoulder as he peered out at the landscape as well. Their backs were now to me, so I couldn't tell if they were speaking, but the subtle nod of Van's head told me Tallis must have said something.

"Elenora is going through a breakup. She won't stop looking all sad and like she doesn't want to be here," Rosella answered.

"Maybe she doesn't. That's not telling of her personal life," Dash countered.

"Please. I watched you mope around the palace for months. I know what a breakup looks like, and that's exactly what's happening there."

I could practically hear Dash's eyes roll when he said, "What else?"

"The woman sitting next to her seems like a bitch," Rosella answered. "She's quietly reprimanded Elenora at least ten times about the way she's acting. Given her general annoyance and the fact that they look alike, I'm going to guess that it's her older sister."

"Delyth is her mother. What else?"

Evander nodded again and his back moved as if he had taken a deep breath. I could pick up on trace amounts of fear from him through our Soul Bond, but it was as dull and quiet as a whisper—as if he had thrown up that barricade between us that Sirona had taught him all those years ago.

"Evander and Ainsley are fighting."

At Rosella's accusation, I turned away from my husband and set my sights on her.

"No, we aren't," I claimed.

She looked toward Evander and then back at me, a sly smile creeping across her face. "Well, it seems like it."

"Well, you're wrong."

Her grin grew, and my blood heated to a molten degree. "My mistake." I pushed past her and into the council room, driven by the pure joy in her voice. I couldn't stand her condescending tone or Evander's suffering any longer.

"Dashiell," a familiar voice called from outside the room, and I twisted back around in time to see Dash look at the source. "A moment."

Dash nodded at Evander's request and moved in his direction, disappearing from my sight completely as Rosella shut the council room door before finding her seat. What the hell? My worry shifted into anger. He could include Dash in his conversation, but he couldn't include me?

I stormed around the table, ignoring the stares that flickered away from their discussions to watch me. My temper was getting the best of me and I knew that, but the will to rein it in was fleeting.

My chair moved loudly across the marble floor as I took my seat and crossed my arms over my chest. Marce caught my eye as she and Kenji watched my silent outburst with amused expressions. I had known Marceline's secret husband for all of three weeks and yet couldn't picture a future where he wasn't a part of our family. Kenji was not only kind, but also intelligent, funny, and rivaled Evander as the most sarcastic member of our group. But perhaps my favorite thing about him was how much he loved his wife.

The two denied they were anything but two friends who engaged in a drunken activity of randomly marrying, but to me and everyone else, their connection was undeniable. The tender way I'd catch him staring at her whenever she smiled or trained or laughed or was deep in conversation with someone always melted my heart. And when Evander asked if Kenji would consider being reassigned to join our royal council, I had never seen someone accept a proposal so quickly. Once he agreed, his gaze immediately landed on Marce, leaving no room for doubt that he accepted in order to be closer to her.

Kenji and Marceline were a perfect pair, complementing and strengthening each other in every way that mattered. Normally, it was a fact that I loved, but right now, when their sarcastic sights were set on me, it only pissed me off. Just as I was about to offer a snarky response to their ogling, Prince Jahier slid into the chair next to mine.

"I apologize for being late," he said, not seeming to pick up on my attitude—or if he did, he was simply too polite to point it out.

"That's alright," I replied, peeling my glare from a smirking Marce and Kenji.

"Evander told me about..." Jahier looked around the room before deciding to place a silencing shield around us. "Any idea what happened?"

I shook my head as I noted Rosella leaning back in her chair with a pen and notebook in her hand while she examined us. "I haven't had a chance to speak to Van since he took Brandle away to be tended to." Jahier hummed in thoughtful acknowledgment, and I leaned in closer while keeping my stare on Rosella. She held my gaze, narrowing her eyes as she scribbled something in her stupid notebook. "There was a traitor among Dash's council the day we were attacked in Caelum."

"So I've been told." I arched a brow and met his gaze. His green eyes sparkled and the corner of his mouth lifted in a way that said *I have my sources*. Of course he did.

The people of Venator were Disparya's fighters. With their unique Gifts of stealth magic, they made up the spies and assassins of our land, protecting her against potential threats. Given that fact, I would have found it surprising if Jahier *didn't* know the inner workings of the other kingdoms.

"We can't be sure Gideon was the reason Brandle was caught until he tells us what happened himself," I continued.

"Agreed. For now, everyone is a suspect." Jahier pushed back from his chair and stood. "They're coming," he said, pointing to his ear. He dropped the shield around us before returning to where he was previously sitting.

The door opened a heartbeat later and Tallis, Evander, and Dash strolled in. At the sight of the kings, every advisor took up their assigned seat, with the generals standing at their backs and several guards stationed along the walls. All in all, there were nearly fifty people in the council room, ready to get the meeting started.

I locked eyes with Evander as he sat in the chair to my right. There wasn't a hint of worry or doubt etched into his features but I could still feel those emotions lingering faintly through our Soul Bond. His hand slid over mine beneath the table and squeezed my fingers lightly as if to say *we'll talk later*, and *I love you*. I squeezed his hand back.

Evander offered me a crooked grin before turning to address the now silent room. "Let's begin, shall we?"

41

Felix

I pressed my fingers to the side of my temples and massaged vigorously as casual insults were thrown about the room. Two hours had transpired in this seemingly endless meeting, and yet we found ourselves no closer to reaching a peaceful understanding among kingdoms.

My eyes drifted around the space, needing to focus on anything but the current slew of obscenities being hurled about things that happened before half of the people here were even born. The kings and Ainsley were positioned around the table like a compass, each ruler representing where their kingdom was on the map of Disparya. Ainsley and Evander sat at the north of the table, Tallis to the east, Dash to the south, and Jahier to the west, with their advisors placed on either side of them. I had learned in the first thirty minutes that Disparya's rulers would not be partaking in the discourse around the table, instead leaning back in their chairs to watch the show unfold as they casually scribbled down thoughts in their notebooks.

It didn't matter that the advisors in the room didn't think it wise to work with each other; the sovereigns of our land had already made up their minds. The main purpose of this assembly was to extend a courtesy to the members of the councils by allowing them to voice their concerns. Even if the rulers had no intention of acting on those worries, it was still vital that they heard their advisors out.

Despite the kings' ultimate authority over their kingdoms, their advisors played a crucial role in ensuring the implementation of those decisions and the satisfaction of the people. Advisors were always chosen from among the nobility, their expertise in court matters and ability to socialize with individuals of all social standings making them invaluable to the royal family as trusted confidants.

While the kings may have been bestowed with three Gifts, it could be argued that their council members held more power in various ways. They possessed the trust of the kingdom's people, enabling them to effortlessly incite a revolution if desired. Naturally, a king has the option to completely eliminate the threat, although doing so would potentially elevate the traitor to the status of a martyr. Dash had been concerned about that very thing when he made the decision to bring an end to Gideon's life.

Regardless of whether or not the rulers in the room agreed with their council members, it was still wise to make them believe their opinion on this subject was being taken into consideration—something I had done many times during my years as an advisor to King Perceval. The last thing any of us needed was a pissed-off advisor spreading discontent among their people and causing an uproar while we were in the midst of a war.

"That's laughable," Ezra, an advisor from Venator, scoffed. "This council room is no place for the daughter of a traitor."

Dash tensed and shifted as if getting ready to defend Rosella, but she spoke before he could. "Funny," she said in that sickly sweet voice of hers. "I said the same thing about men with small dicks, yet here you still are."

I struggled immensely to stifle my laughter, and as I cast my gaze around the room, I observed the same struggle mirrored on the faces of everyone else, including Ainsley. Despite it being her first time taking part in kingdom affairs, Rosella seemed to hold her own just fine.

Ezra leaned forward, pressing his palms flat against the top of the table as he glared at Rosella. "That's enough," Jahier said before his advisor could sling another insult at his target. "You both got a shot in; move on."

"She has no right being here," Ezra argued. "If we are to work together, then we should be able to trust one another. How can we possibly do that when he chooses the daughter of a traitor to not only join his council but sit on his right side, no less?"

That specific position next to the king was reserved exclusively for their right hand—the person they had complete confidence in. Sitting to the right of Ainsley and Evander was Oli, to the right of Tallis was his sister, Delyth, and to the right of Jahier was Ezra. It was not so much a matter of trust, but rather a strategic move on Dash's part to place Rosella on his right side so he could help her navigate through her first royal meeting. However, it would not appear that way to most.

"The last time I checked, Ezra, it was the Kingdom of Venator that broke the Treaty of Disparya. It was *our* king who betrayed our land and joined forces with the enemy," Jahier pointed out calmly. "If anyone should have to prove their trust, it should be us, don't you think?"

Venator's advisor didn't move right away, but after a minute, he slowly slid his hands from the table and placed them back into his lap. "Yes, Your Highness," he replied.

Jahier nodded in satisfaction and waved a hand over the room. "Carry on."

After the passing of another hour, we had finally begun to make progress. Although there was still a lack of enthusiasm over our union, the amount of yelling and accusations decreased substantially, so that had to count for something.

At the conclusion of the fourth hour, a unanimous agreement was reached that our primary objective should be achieving victory in the war and preserving as many lives as possible. Funny enough, our sovereigns had cited that as their reason for uniting at the start of our meeting... nearly five hours ago.

As no one appeared to have any additional points to contribute to the conversation, I breathed a heavy sigh of relief, knowing the meeting from hell was now over. Tomorrow, we would figure out the schedule of our next assembly and the logistics of getting our soldiers ready for war.

"Before we disperse, there was an incident this morning that I believe you all should be made aware of," Evander declared just as everyone started to stand up.

The ominous tone in his voice caused a chilling sensation to run down my back, prompting me to immediately shift my gaze towards Ainsley, who was engaged in a wordless exchange with Dash. They knew what was going on and didn't bother to clue me in. I directed my focus towards Oli, only to discover him observing his king with a passive demeanor. Evidently, he was also aware of the situation but neglected to inform his boyfriend.

The advisors slowly sat back down, each throwing concerned glances at one another as Evander leaned back and drummed his fingers over the tabletop, the very picture of casual confidence. His eyes flicked to mine before he cast his stare across the crowd. The look was only a split second long but held a quiet command I caught immediately.

I called for my Empathi Gift and let it roll over the unsuspecting group, prepared to catch the first hint of anything that felt odd or out of place. I had been trained my entire adolescence to perform this exact job, though it was in service of a different king. Under intense circumstances, my ability to pick up an elevated heart rate or a heightened emotion such as fear, nervousness, or guilt was invaluable.

"This morning, a Prince of Ministro was found tortured and barely breathing on Tenebrean soil," Evander elaborated.

A wave of unease sparked throughout the room.

"Which one?" Elenora asked. Her tone was steady, but I recognized the quiver of fear in her voice.

During my unscheduled time in Agnitio, I became aware of the close bond between Brandle and Tallis's niece. It had developed as a result of her years of serving as his point of contact for information exchange. Their relationship bore a striking resemblance to Ainsley's and mine, intensifying the difficulty of being apart from her during those months when I was supposedly deceased.

"Brandle," he answered.

Elenora slumped into her chair, her body sagging as the air left her lungs. The room erupted into a chaotic chatter, but I still wasn't picking up on any traces that things were amiss.

"But he's fine," Evander continued.

A tiny pang of uncertainty seeped out from the left side of the room—the area that held most of Caelum, all of Venator, Marce, and Kenji. Trying to monitor nearly fifty people's emotions was difficult, but luckily, I was now able to narrow it down to just half of the room.

"I don't understand. Why was he in Tenebrae?" Ezra asked quietly to Jahier, though we all heard the question.

Evander repositioned himself in his seat and leaned towards Ainsley, murmuring in her ear. With an arched brow of intrigue, she responded with a single nod. Instead of dwelling on my frustration at being kept out of the loop, I made a conscious decision to concentrate on my immediate task and cast more of my power out over the room.

"Brandle has been working with Tenebrae and Agnitio for years, providing us inside information about Ministro and Harbin's dealings. All of this time, he's gone undetected," Ainsley announced, pulling away from Evander. There was a noticeable shift in her expression as her calm demeanor gave way to one of fury. The strength of her anger was palpable as it radiated in forceful waves.

At that revelation, the gossip among the advisors from Venator and Caelum commenced as they fired off rapid questions about the collaboration, but the rulers didn't bother to answer.

"Someone sold him out," Evander said, commanding attention and quieting the room once more. "And I'd *very* much like to know who it was."

There it was again—that hint of uncertainty now muddled with fear. With intense concentration, I meticulously eliminated additional individuals from my list until I was left with two advisors and one general from Venator, two advisors from Caelum, and a small group of guards positioned along the walls. I unleashed my full power on those ten people, infiltrating their beings and gripping their emotions tightly.

"What about my father?" Rosella whispered to Dash.

"She makes a good point, Your Majesty," one of the King of Caelum's advisors, Johan, said. "We already know Gideon betrayed us. Perhaps he was the one who informed Harbin of his stepson's betrayal."

The sense of relief my Gift picked up on prompted me to eliminate five additional individuals from my list, all of whom were from Venator. I captured Evander's gaze for a heartbeat, hoping the look was enough to convey that I was close to uncovering what he was after.

Dash reclined in his chair, extending his arms above his head and rotating his neck from left to right. "Ah, you see, I too had the same thought initially," he replied.

The calm yet callous tone he employed echoed the manner in which he had addressed Gideon prior to his demise. I had a strong sense that something of the same nature would be carried out here today.

"Then I recalled that Gideon had left the room to check on the progress between the King of Ministro and King of Venator. He wasn't there when Brandle's note appeared," Dash explained as he sat forward once again, a fire now blazing in his eyes.

"But conveniently, everyone who was present in that room is now present in this one," Evander added, his tone just as icy as the King of Caelum's had been.

I was suddenly overwhelmed by an unprecedented sense of fear and panic. Suppressing the flood of emotions, I clenched my teeth and locked eyes with Evander once more. With a quick flick of my gaze, I pointed out who the culprit was and pulled my magic back into myself.

I dug my fingers into the table and concentrated on silently catching my breath as I felt the depleting consequences of using an excessive amount of magic at once. Oli softly nudged a glass of water in my direction accompanied by a subdued plea to drink as he placed a reassuring hand on my knee. I was too close to my baseline and would need to refrain from using any more of my magic today.

"Would anyone like to confess?" Tallis asked.

"I can't promise it'll help you in this case, but it would save us time. There's no point in delaying the inevitable," Ainsley added cooly as shadows spilled from her body and billowed on the floor.

Although I wasn't actively using my Gift, it didn't prevent me from being able to feel the emotions others shoved onto me. I took a deep breath and tried to dismiss the terror radiating from everyone like a sickness.

"No one?" Ainsley asked after a minute of silence. "Well, that's unfortunate." She clicked her tongue in irritation and sighed.

Rapidly beating hearts echoed throughout the room as glances were exchanged, each person searching for the perpetrator of betrayal. Finally, Dash stood and slid his hands into his pockets as he cast his gaze over his court.

"Anything you want to confess to, William?" he asked his advisor.

The room fell deathly silent. Not even the sound of breathing could be heard as all eyes fell on the man to Dash's left. "I'm not sure what you mean—"

"Let's not play coy," Dash interrupted. "At least go out with some dignity for a change."

With a sneer forming on his face, William's features contorted into a display of disgust. In a rapid movement, he forcefully pushed himself away from his chair and quickly stood up, causing all guards to instinctively reach for their weapons. Dash didn't so much as flinch.

"Caelum has been loyal to Ministro for centuries," William growled. "Brandle deserved to be killed after betraying that alliance—and so do *you*." Caelum's guards stepped closer, but Dash raised a hand to halt their advance before dipping it back into his pocket. "You're dooming our kingdom all because of *her*," William spat and pointed a finger across the table at Ainsley.

Oli stiffened at my side while the rest of our family adjusted themselves in their seats, clearly displeased with his disrespect for our queen. But as protective as we all were, we knew Ainsley could handle herself. And sure enough, like the asshole she was, she offered a small, enthusiastic wave to Dash, the gesture serving as a means to highlight the utter ridiculousness of that insult.

In a display of anger, William's hand moved swiftly towards the sword at his side. Yet just as he was about to grab the hilt, his hand froze and instead rushed towards his throat. He coughed and sputtered, his attempts to gasp for air proving fruitless.

"William, William, William," Dash reproached, tilting his head to the side. "I once told you what would happen if you tested me."

The advisor stumbled away from the table, his eyes going wide with panic as he clutched his throat. His attempt to escape was abruptly stopped when his back collided with the stone wall, and water trickled out from between his lips, now displaying a violet hue.

"Did you think I was lying?" Dash inquired. With a head shake, William descended to the ground, his irises transforming from white to red.

Every pore of his body seemed to exude moisture, causing him to be drenched in sweat as blood started to trickle from his mouth and nose, intensifying the grotesque scene. Dash walked over to him and knelt just a foot away, attentively studying the man who was slowly drowning on his own bodily fluids.

"I made you a promise, William," he said, the calm tone he used utterly terrifying. "And I always keep my word."

William fell over, his head hitting the marble floor with a smack. His flesh became heavily wrinkled, resembling leather that had been exposed to the sun for an extended period of time, as Dash used his Gift to suck the moisture from his body. His mouth widened further, yet only a strangled gurgle combined with blood flowed out while his body convulsed in a slow and agonizing demise.

After William ceased all movement, Dash gently touched his body and covered his flesh in a layer of frost. I watched in horror as he shoved down onto the corpse, and it shattered into a million shards of ice. The King of Caelum stood again and set his attention back on the terror-stricken eyes of the room.

Dash's choice to end William's life so brutally was deliberate, aimed at reminding all those present of the grave consequences awaiting those who dare to betray a king or queen of this realm. It might have been a gruesome choice, but it was a necessary one.

"Seeing as my kingdom continuously seems to be the issue, does anyone else have anything they want to confess?" Dash asked with a strained smile on his face. He encountered vehement denials. "Fantastic."

Evander stood up from his seat and signaled for everyone to rise. "In that case, it seems our work for the day has come to an end."

"Not quite," Dash interrupted and I audibly groaned as I sank back into my seat. Today was never going to end. "At least not for the rulers. There is still one more matter of business I think we should discuss before we can fully move forward." A mixture of confusion and intrigue filled the exchanged glances between Tallis, Jahier, Evander, and Ainsley.

"And what's that?" Evander asked.

"Our Obscures."

42

Felix

The current number of people sitting around the council room table made its size appear absurd. Both Dash and Tallis chose to dismiss all members from their respective kingdoms, while Jahier retained only Ezra by his side. Evander and Ainsley kept our family present but dismissed the generals and guards just as everyone else had. Marce and Kenji were the sole exceptions, volunteering to leave and monitor the sent-away advisors.

The majority of the nine individuals present were silent as servants placed plates brimming with food on the table, yet no one made any attempt to eat. The day had been both draining and daunting, and its conclusion seemed distant. I lifted my fork and gently prodded the chicken, feeling too exhausted to consume it.

"You need to eat," Oli scolded in that protective way of his.

He was right, of course. Sustenance would help restore my depleted magic faster, but I couldn't muster the will. A peculiar sensation lingered in the room, yet I couldn't discern its origin. The emotion was all-encompassing, bright, overwhelming, and heavy, and the more I concentrated on it, the more it drifted between my fingers like sand. I was incapable of retaining my hold.

"Please," he said, interrupting my focus. I ripped off a small piece of bread and popped it into my mouth to give him a sense of peace I couldn't attain. "Thank you," he responded, and I nodded.

Ainsley and Evander were conversing softly, neglecting their meals as well. Just as he moved closer for a kiss, she abruptly turned her face, presenting her cheek instead.

"As it was you who desired this meeting, Dashiell, feel free to commence it," Evander stated as he distanced himself from his wife. Everyone's attention was drawn to the King of Caelum as he reclined in his chair and shrugged.

"I just can't see how we can trust each other completely if we're all still keeping our magic a secret," he answered.

A smirk curved Evander's lips. "It seems to me like *you* are the one keeping secrets. Everyone in this room knows what my Obscure is."

Dash's finger gracefully followed the intricate patterns of the wood grain on the table as his unwavering gaze remained fixed on the King of Tenebrae. "Your capabilities, yes. But not your limitations."

Evander's smile widened further.

"Who said I have limitations?"

Dash's lips displayed a subtle lift at the corner as he interlocked his fingers and adjusted his posture to sit in a more upright manner. The room was filled with a tense silence as the two men engaged in a silent power struggle, their gazes locked on each other.

"How far can you travel?" he asked.

"Far," Evander replied.

"How often can you use it?"

"Often."

"Is there anywhere you can't go?"

"That would imply I have limitations."

I internally groaned at the continuous back and forth, though it was not unexpected. Not only was Evander a prick 99% of the time, but why would he willingly divulge his weaknesses to a room of people he didn't fully trust?

"Van," Ainsley gently coaxed.

Reluctantly, he averted his gaze from Dash and turned it towards his wife, a silent communication occurring between them. If there was one individual who could ensure his cooperation, it would be Ainsley.

After a hushed moment, Evander sighed dramatically and lulled his head back as he interlaced his and Ainsley's fingers. With a triumphant smirk, the queen shifted her attention to Dash, prompting Evander to do the same.

"I can travel anywhere," the King of Tenebrae said. Dash scoffed and made to point out the vague explanation, but Evander continued before he could. "As long as I'm familiar with the territory."

"And if you aren't?" Dash asked.

"I'll get lost."

The answer was simple but accurate. Evander was extremely careful about when he chose to traverse, unwilling to jeopardize the safety of himself or his companions.

"How often can you use your Obscure?" Dash requested next.

"As often as I'd like. However, the more I use it in quick succession, the faster it drains my magic."

Dash nodded to himself and turned his focus on Ainsley, the next target for questioning. Instead of waiting to be asked about her Obscure, she immediately delved into the information.

"I'm still learning what mine is," she explained, and called forth a tendril of darkness. Emerging from her fingers, it glided across the table and wound itself around a wine goblet, effortlessly lifting it into the air. "But I can control my shadows as if they are a physical extension of myself."

"And that's different from your Gift?" Tallis inquired, gazing at the Obscure with profound fascination.

Shadows danced across Evander's hand as he extended it toward his own goblet. The darkness encircled the glass in scattered wisps, passing through the object, never able to grasp it the way Ainsley's magic had.

"Our shadows are just that—shadows. They cannot harden themselves in their current form. If we want to solidify them, we must do so in the form of an object," Evander explained. As his fist tightened, the shadows encircling his glass underwent a captivating change, assuming the form of an elaborate handle. He inclined his body and retrieved the goblet, which now had an ornate metal protrusion on the side. Meanwhile, Ainsley's glass rose higher, lifted by the inky darkness.

"Have you encountered any limitations?" Dash asked her.

Ainsley carefully returned her drink to the table and summoned her Obscure back into herself. "Not yet, but like Evander, if I use it often, I find it drains my magic at a faster rate than my Gifts do."

"How is your control?" Tallis inquired with a touch of worry present in his voice.

We had all seen what she was capable of in Caelum when she used her Obscure to rip a man's heart from his body. Her actions were driven solely by anger and a desire for vengeance, and given Ainsley's quick temper, that was cause for concern.

"Better. As I become more familiar with it, it becomes easier to handle."

"And does it only manifest when you're angry?" I inquired casually, determining that now was the ideal moment to participate in the conversation. Ainsley's attention drifted to me, her eyes narrowing as she scrutinized my intentions. I presented an innocent smile as she shifted uncomfortably in her seat.

The day after she went back to Tenebrae, I received a slip of transfer paper, detailing her and Evander's night in the throne room. Ainsley had been very descriptive about how her Obscure came out to play and what exactly she used it for. She explained how utterly mortified she felt upon witnessing the space in the daylight the morning after and learning the extensive amount of time it would take to repair all the damage she had caused. It was the reason behind today's meeting being held here rather than in the throne room.

Evander skillfully provided an explanation to the people repairing the space, stating that the destruction occurred because the new queen was in the process of honing her abilities. Although not a direct falsehood, he intentionally withheld the specifics of their activities at the time the damage occurred.

"I don't see how that's relevant," she replied.

"Arguably, it's very relevant. If we are to trust each other, we should know as much as we can about the magic each of us wields," I answered with a knowing smirk.

Ainsley audibly clenched her teeth. "No. It's not solely limited to anger. It can slip out when other emotions are heightened." The words were clipped and held a dark promise that she would get me back for this.

"Like what?" Evander asked innocently. She turned to him, her eyes widening in horror as a sly smile played on his lips. "As Felix said, we need to be able to trust each other."

"You're an asshole," she whispered.

"And yet you love me for it."

"I'm debating that fact at the moment."

I concealed my amusement by disguising it as a cough and immediately reached for my glass of water. She was certainly going to ensure that we suffered for this small act of betrayal, but the horrified expression on her face made it all worthwhile.

Evander's grin grew, and Ainsley had trouble hiding the small curve of her lips, displaying her own amusement.

"Happiness," she growled as she held her husband's stare.

"Care to elaborate—"

"No." She cut him off before he could get the last word fully out. "Tallis, it's your turn."

Ainsley swatted at Evander as he attempted to kiss her cheek and redirected her focus towards the King of Agnitio. I jabbed a piece of chicken with my fork and promptly placed it into my mouth, sensing my appetite resurface as I began to relax. Although the odd sensation persisted in the room, I deliberately chose to ignore it and instead paid attention to Tallis who leaned forward in his chair.

"I can show people things," he answered and held his hand out for Ainsley to take. She did so hesitantly, a crease forming between her brows.

The atmosphere in the room grew still as all in attendance observed the subtle conversation unfolding between the two rulers. Ainsley drew in a breath of astonishment, swiftly scanning the room with her eyes, as though witnessing a spectacle unbeknownst to the rest of us.

"I have the ability to share any experience I have had, whether it be a dream, a memory, or a vision," Tallis announced to the rest of the room as they watched Ainsley with intense curiosity.

I proceeded to take another bite of food, unaffected by the surprise in everyone's reaction, as I had already encountered Tallis's Obscure firsthand.

During my involuntary stay in Agnitio, Tallis had disclosed his ability to me. I didn't believe him when he informed me that Harbin was my father or that he and my mother were childhood friends, so showing me was the only way to gain my trust.

My entire world collapsed the moment I took his hand.

The sight of my mother for the first time had been quite unsettling, to say the least, yet it also mended a part of me that I was unaware had been damaged. I bore a striking resemblance to her, with matching silver hair and amber eyes. Her skin tone appeared slightly darker, yet our facial structures were remarkably similar—a slender nose, full lips, and prominent cheekbones. I was grateful that I took after her rather than the dickhead who attributed to my genetics.

Through Tallis's eyes, I watched her rush to him and confess she had spent a night with Harbin and was now pregnant. Agnitio had extended a warm welcome to those who were the result of Conjoining. Thus, I understood that the tremor in my mother's voice had no relation to my potential abilities but rather to the matter of my lineage.

She detailed her decision to keep their time spent together a secret, learning Harbin's identity only after their intimate encounter. Upon his arrival at the local pub, she had presumed him to be yet another visitor from Ministro, present for the Solstice celebration. Unbeknownst to my mother, the individual who sat at her table and engaged in a quiet conversation was none other than the king himself.

Tallis and she agreed to hide the truth of her pregnancy for as long as possible, but somehow, he found out.

"Holy Gods," Ainsley whispered, pulling her hand from Tallis's and blinking rapidly as the vision cleared.

A smile graced his face as he reached for his water. "Similar to both of you, the utilization of my Obscure requires a substantial amount of energy, thus I seldom employ it."

I wanted desperately to call for my Magusier Gift to check the status of his magic level and how close he was to his baseline, but doing so would potentially make me dip below mine. It was a lesson ingrained in us from the start: never to let our magic reach such a low level, as there was a risk it would not replenish.

"Regarding limitations, I am only able to display my abilities to a small group of individuals at a time. I can do so without establishing physical contact if I choose, however, it requires more energy that way. In addition, the greater the number of individuals participating in my Obscure, the quicker my magic depletes."

I finished my plate and twisted to find Oli casting a thankful glance my way. I could already feel my power starting to recover, slowly rising from the depths and bringing me to a more secure level. Still, I didn't feel comfortable using any of my Gifts until I was completely back to normal.

"Your turn, Dashiell," Evander said. He rested his elbow on the arm of his chair while tilting his head, gently pressing his cheek against his fingers.

"Like Ainsley, I'm still learning what mine is," Dash explained as he leaned forward and placed his forearms on the table. "But...I pick up on things—notice details that others don't, and can draw conclusions based on what I gather."

"So you're just... observant?" Oli said, seeming less than impressed.

"I guess you could say that. It's how I knew you raised him," Dash said as he angled his chin toward the King of Tenebrae. Evander lifted a skeptical brow at the king before twisting to look at Oli. Evidently, he hadn't been informed of Dash's assumption.

"Lucky guess," Evander claimed.

"Perhaps. But I haven't been wrong yet." Dash peered down at the fingers he was currently fiddling with—a nervous tic that mirrored my own. "I knew Olivier raised you, that Gideon was a traitor, and that William was behind exposing Brandle before you cast an illusion to tell me. It's just a feeling I get based on what I see."

"Can you try to elaborate?" Ainsley asked gently, capturing Dash's attention. "What was the reason behind your belief that Oli raised Van?"

Dash's brows furrowed as he observed her, his eyes shifting rapidly as his mind scrambled to devise a rationale. At last, he nodded to himself and expelled a breath.

"Take right now, for example," Dash stated, his voice exuding the confidence of a man who knew far more than anyone expected. "Olivier is stationed at his king's right side; that alone tells me they're close and there's a deep trust between them. Moreover, they frequently exchange glances."

"You're basing this assumption off a look?" Evander asked flatly.

Dash rolled his eyes and shook his head. He was never good at explaining the way his mind worked and Evander sure as hell wasn't going to make it easy for him.

"Whenever a decision is made, or a statement is expressed that does not align with your personal views, you exchange glances. You did the same thing during the trial in Caelum. Olivier's opinion seems to be the one that matters to you the most," Dash told the king. "One might argue that you simply rely on the judgment of your advisor, yet the subtle raise of your eyebrow and Olivier's discreet nod tells me that you seek more than just his opinion. You want his approval. This fact indicates that Olivier possesses expertise beyond that of a typical advisor. He knows how to rule a kingdom."

Oli and Evander maintained their silence, refusing to provide Dash with any form of affirmation.

"Were you the one who assumed the duties of the king until Evander was old enough?" he asked the advisor. Still, Oli stayed silent. "You did," Dash concluded, a smile playing on his lips.

No one spoke as we all waited for the King of Caelum to finish his assessment. Dash's mind consistently intrigued me, and it appeared that his Obscure had only served to heighten his preexisting ability to read people.

"The validation you're after extends beyond a king seeking reassurance in their ability to guide their subjects," Dash elaborated, as he firmly placed his fingers on the tabletop and leaned in closer. "No, it seems to be more in the realm of a son seeking his father's approval. I would know; I often gave Perceval the same look after making a suggestion."

Dash pushed back from his chair and stood. He extended his arms above his head before pacing back and forth, his mind still engaged in conveying his thought process.

"The way your bodies are positioned was another indicator," he added.

I felt my lips curve into a smile at watching my best friend grow more secure with himself by the minute. For years, he had always questioned if he was capable of handling the role he was born into. I never doubted his ability and hoped others wouldn't either after seeing him now.

"Olivier is slightly angled towards Evander, ready to act as a shield for the king if needed. Calidore is also an advisor, but the way he's positioned next to Ainsley is entirely different. However, I know he'd still protect her, given the subtle flex in his shoulder muscle that tells me he's fiddling with a weapon of some sort beneath the table."

Cal let out a breathy laugh as he withdrew his hand from its concealed position and forcefully plunged a dagger into the wooden surface. Ainsley and I locked eyes as we both grinned at Dash's correct assumption.

"Olivier's fondness for Evander extends well beyond mere loyalty to a king. No, he loves him in a way that resembles the love a person has for their child," Dash concluded before exhaling deeply.

The chair emitted a creaking sound as Ainsley reclined in it, crossing her arms over her chest and gazing at her husband with a broad smile.

"That is truly impressive, Dashiell," commented Tallis, while Jahier enthusiastically concurred.

"It is," the King of Tenebrae agreed. "But I don't see how your Obscure will be useful in this war."

"I never implied that it would be," Dash responded, resuming his seat. "But it's not all that I can do." Ainsley and I locked eyes again, her brow arching in question. I shook my head, letting her know I had no idea what else Dash was capable of. "My Obscure isn't limited to just observing *people*. I can study and replicate tasks. Things I've never done before I can somehow master after a minute or two of examining how it works."

"Show us," Evander commanded, motioning for Cal to retrieve the dagger that remained lodged in the table. The advisor did as silently instructed and walked the dagger over to Dash before crafting another one to wield.

Cal skillfully twirled the weapon, deftly weaving it between his fingers. He intensified his speed, rotating the dagger so swiftly that his hands appeared as a blur, before forcefully launching the weapon across the room. All of us directed our attention toward the dagger, which was now firmly lodged in the center of the intricate design on the patterned wallpaper.

"Your turn," Cal said arrogantly.

Dash had always excelled in sparring, yet I had never observed him successfully strike the center of a target during our rare dagger-throwing practices.

"Show me one more time," he requested. Cal nodded and skillfully fashioned another weapon shrouded in darkness, artfully manipulating it between his fingers once again. I observed Dash's pupils dilate as he fixated on the trick, his own fingers starting to imitate the motions.

Dash mirrored Cal's actions, executing them meticulously before forcefully hurling the dagger, which found its mark in the center of another pattern. Enthusiastic clapping was demonstrated by both Jahier and Tallis, with Ainsley and I eventually joining in.

Dash's chest heaved with effort as he surveyed the room, a subtle smile of pride adorning his face.

"Impressive *and* useful," Tallis claimed, giving Evander a knowing look. Ainsley's Soul Bonded shrugged it off and instead focused back on the King of Caelum.

"Limitations?" he asked.

"Besides it using a lot of my magic, I'm not sure," Dash confessed through labored breathing.

I poured him a fresh glass of water and walked it over as everyone chatted about Dash's potential and what it could do for the war. With gratitude, he accepted it from my hands and proceeded to drink it all in one gulp.

"What happened to not keeping secrets from each other?" I pointed out, refilling his glass.

"I don't trust speaking freely in my palace. At least not yet."

He made a valid point. Caelum was on shaky ground, and if secrets made their way into the wrong hands, it could be detrimental to our cause.

"Perhaps Brandle knows what Harbin's is," I heard Ainsley say and directed my focus back to that end of the table as Dash continued to drink.

"He would have told us," Evander pointed out, to which Tallis agreed.

"While our knowledge about the King of Ministro's Obscure may be limited, I am well-informed about my father's," Jahier interjected.

A wave of surprise from everyone rushed into me, mirroring my own. The kings maintained a high level of secrecy regarding their additional power, making it all the more shocking that Jahier happened to possess knowledge of it. Even Perceval decided not to reveal the knowledge to his son, leaving Dash to be informed about it by Imogen.

"It's an extension of his Sonor Gift," Jahier explained. "Typically, individuals possessing the Gift have the ability to perceive almost any conversation provided we are in close enough proximity. However, my father possesses the remarkable ability to detect sounds from significant distances."

"How far?" Evander asked.

The Prince of Venator directed his attention towards Ezra, engaging in a debate over the question at hand. "I've seen him relay an entire conversation between two people who were located in Ministro," Ezra replied.

I let out a profound sigh while observing the expressions of panic throughout the room. If King Arden were able to covertly intercept our plans regardless of his location, our chances of success would be minuscule.

"Can he penetrate a shield?" Evander inquired.

"No," stated the Prince of Venator firmly. "While his Obscure is powerful, it is not without limitations, with a shield being one of them."

"And another?"

"His ability to concentrate is restricted to one conversation at a time, and the more distant the conversation, the quicker it depletes his magic."

The visible relief on Evander's face was apparent as his shoulders drooped, with Ainsley matching his sentiment by exhaling a long breath.

"Regardless, important conversations shouldn't be held outside of a silencing shield," Jahier continued.

"Agreed."

"Furthermore, I would strongly recommend that they no longer be held in this building." I raised an eyebrow and cast a downward gaze at Dash, who seemed just as apprehensive as I did. "Venator has spies everywhere, Evander. Tenebrae's court is no exception. Consider this warning my extension of trust as I do not have an Obscure to display like the rest of you."

"Noted," Evander muttered through gritted teeth, visibly displeased by the presence of Venator spies who had covertly infiltrated his kingdom for an unknown length of time.

"You are welcome to stay at our house," Ainsley said, rising from her chair. "We have shields in place and can speak freely without fear of being overheard." The kings who were visiting exchanged glances, displaying uncertainty regarding whether they should accept.

"My wife is right," Evander said. "We have plenty of room, and it'll be far safer to discuss our strategies."

"But please bring only one advisor, should you choose. The others should stay with the generals and guards here in the palace. We don't want to be entirely too conspicuous and my home cannot fit fifty people."

Oli emitted a subdued groan beside me as I suppressed a smile. He had been looking forward to returning to a sense of normalcy, but now our home would be full of visitors. I moved away from Dash's side and went back to my boyfriend's, giving him a kiss on the cheek before taking my seat beside him.

"I'll accept your invitation, but Ezra will stay behind," Jahier announced. "Tensions are still high so I want him to keep an eye on the other members of my court."

"Elenora will join me," Tallis added.

"I'll come alone," Dash said. "I don't trust anyone from my kingdom right now."

Evander stood up and gently placed his hand on the small of Ainsley's back before tenderly kissing her temple. "Then it's settled. You'll come home with us."

43
Ainsley

Absentmindedly, I ran my fingers across a page of the book I had no intention of reading. My mind was so tangled with thoughts of Brandle's health and the meeting today that I couldn't focus on anything else. Despite the assembly going better than expected, the presence of another traitor in Dash's court and Venator's spies in ours made it impossible for me to relax.

As soon as the conversation regarding our Obscures ended, Evander traversed all of us home. We offered a quick tour of the house and assigned rooms, but after that, no one seemed up for much of anything else.

Onyx's loud snoring filled the room as I stretched my feet over his body at the foot of our bed. As soon as Van left to check on Brandle's progress, Onyx tried to take his spot, but I didn't allow it. On any other typical evening, I would have enjoyed observing Van and his wolf engage in their usual bedtime dispute over who slept where. However, tonight all I wanted was to nestle beside my husband and forget about the burdens of the day.

The room was filled with swirling shadows and the comforting scent of home, causing me to toss my book aside and sit forward.

"How is he?" I demanded before Van could fully step through his Obscure.

He moved closer, pausing suddenly as his gaze traveled across my body. "How the hell did you find it?!" Van asked, his eyes locked onto the shirt I was wearing.

"You act like it was difficult," I replied, dismissing his question.

Despite Evander's attempts to hide his favorite shirt from me for months, I always managed to locate it. Though to be honest, I almost hadn't tonight. It was merely by chance that I noticed the rug was slightly askew. As I walked over to fix it, I suddenly heard a subtle creak in the floor. Not until I dropped to my hands and knees did I realize the wooden board under the dresser was off-level. I pushed aside the furniture and pulled up the floor, revealing my favorite shirt hidden beneath. I didn't want to admit how much better he was getting at the game or that my losing was now a very real possibility.

He let out an annoyed groan and climbed onto the bed, only to be surprised by the sight of a sleeping wolf at the foot.

"I saved your spot."

"I appreciate it," he responded, kissing my temple and then positioning himself on his stomach with a pillow supporting his chest. "And Brandle is doing well. Tallis and Dashiell are currently overseeing his progress to give Sirona and Lia a break. They've been at it all day and need to replenish."

"Has he said anything?"

He gave a shake of his head. "No. He's been asleep the entire time, but Lia says that's a good thing. His body is keeping him unconscious as it repairs itself."

"That's good," I murmured, running my hand through his dark hair. He tilted his head into my touch.

"Today was... interesting."

I chuckled and nodded in agreement. "That's putting it mildly. I can't believe the extent of everyone's Obscures."

"I can't believe it only took five hours for the advisors to agree to work together."

Evander's hand found mine, and he lovingly traced his fingers over my wedding ring. I surrendered to the gentle caress, enjoying the way his skin felt against mine. It was quiet moments like these that always made my heart beat faster—that made me want to cherish each second with him as if it could be our last.

"You were right to tell Declan to wait until next month to come," I said, watching the way he brought my hand to his lips.

Yesterday, Van told me that he asked the man he considered an uncle to stay behind instead of attending this initial meeting. He understood that convincing the advisors of Disparya to trust each other was already a challenge, and adding Vorsutos into the mix could have jeopardized the peace we sought. It was more effective to first illustrate how easily the advisors could cooperate before pressuring them to include a foreign continent in the alliance.

Van nodded but didn't offer an opinion.

"When will the book get here?" I inquired.

As the advisors conducted their meeting, we rulers held our own. Once the conversation was far enough along, the King of Tenebrae cast an illusion over the room, making himself appear to be observing the meeting, when in actuality, he was informing the sovereigns about his conversation with Tallis.

He explained that a vision had come to Tallis this morning, thanks to his Seer Gift, which showed sickness and devastation plaguing Disparya. Tallis couldn't tell how far into the future it was, but from what he saw, the land appeared devastated by war, with entire villages destroyed and bodies of all ages scattered amidst the ruins. The only hint about the timeline we received was the king spotting late summer dahlias growing all over the ground. If Tallis's vision was for this year, we only had a few months until it became reality.

During our secret meeting, only Evander and I could speak due to our shared Gift of illusions. Others wrote down their questions and concerns for Van to read aloud as he walked around the room. Although it wasn't the easiest way to communicate, it was the safest.

Tallis scribbled a note stating his intention to request the book I took from Caelum to be sent here. Although his scholars hadn't finished transcribing it, we couldn't wait any longer and had to make do with what he had due to the development of his vision.

We debated back and forth on whether it was wise to inform everyone in the room about Brandle, but ultimately we concluded that the risk was worth it in order to potentially uncover another traitor. Luckily, once Dash exposed and killed William, Tallis had the same vision, but with one noticeable difference—the ground was blanketed in snow. Removing him from existence altered the future, potentially granting us additional time.

"Tomorrow, if not the day after," Evander replied, cocking his head and giving my hand a squeeze. "You seem worried about something more than just the events of today."

I smiled weakly, torn between hating and loving how well he understood me. Looking down at him, I shrugged my shoulder in a dismissive manner. "I miss Imogen," I admitted. "It's starting to become more evident that we don't have much time left and I hate that I'm not spending it with her."

With a thoughtful nod, Evander kissed my hand again to offer solace. "Why didn't she come today? I remember you mentioned she couldn't, but we didn't get a chance to talk about why."

"Things aren't going well in Caelum," I answered, suddenly feeling a stab of guilt for being disappointed in Imogen's absence. She was helping Dash to ensure his kingdom didn't collapse while he was away, and here I was, upset she wasn't with me.

"What do you mean?"

I let out a long sigh while pondering where to start. "Dash has made changes that aren't going over well."

"Like?" He elongated the word like he was unhappy with my vague responses.

"Killing Gideon."

Van scoffed and then intertwined his hand with mine, finally done fidgeting with my wedding ring. "That was never going to go over well, but it doesn't mean it wasn't the right decision." I tilted my head, surprised at Van's opinion.

"Really?"

Nodding, he redirected his gaze from our hands to my eyes. "Not only did Gideon betray his kingdom, but he was also responsible for several deaths. It was a situation that didn't require any mercy whatsoever. Dashiell needed to show his strength and establish authority as Caelum's king, and he did just that."

I knew Evander was right in his assessment and would have imposed the same punishment. Even though I agreed with Dash's choice, it was comforting to hear that Evander felt the same way. It demonstrated that my instincts were correct and I was on the right path for ruling.

"He also disbanded the law against Conjoining," I added.

"So I've heard," Van replied flatly. I furrowed my brow in confusion as I struggled to understand my husband's response to the news and why he seemed unhappy.

"You don't agree with that decision?"

"No," he breathed.

I retracted my hand from his grasp, feeling an immediate surge of anger at his response. I, the woman he loved, his Soul Bonded, his Claimed, his *wife*, was a product of Conjoining and yet he didn't agree that others like me in Caelum should be allowed to live?

My mouth hung open, and I desperately searched my thoughts for words to express, but I found myself at a loss.

"Before you give into your temper, at least let me explain," Van said, rolling his eyes as he sat up. "And I'll try not to take offense at your assumption that I would ever approve of a law that takes the lives of innocent people simply because of the magical abilities they were born with."

I closed my lips tightly, overwhelmed by guilt after making a hasty assumption. I was still so quick to dive into anger, despite knowing his heart.

"I realize that trust is still something you're getting used to," Evander said tenderly. "Given the life you've had, I understand if you can't let go of your anger—it's been your sole source of comfort over the years. I promise to always be patient with you, but I also ask that you try your best to resist your natural instinct to reach for that rage." As he leaned closer, his hand brushed against my cheek, gently holding it as he pressed his lips against mine. "With what your Obscure is capable of, it's even more important for you to learn how to control your emotions."

A lump formed in my throat as I recalled killing that man in Caelum—how effortlessly my nails dug into his chest, how desperate my thirst for his death was, and the immense gratification I felt while tearing his heart apart and extracting it from his body.

I won't pretend her Obscure isn't dangerous. If she can't control her anger, then she can't control this magic. Tallis's words drifted into my mind and I released a shaky breath.

"I'm sorry," I whispered, but Van brushed off the apology and kissed me again.

Releasing my lips, he pulled us down onto the bed and spun me around so that his chest was pressed against my back. He embraced me, intertwining his limbs with mine, and nuzzled against the back of my neck, placing a delicate kiss on my tattoo. It instantly brought back memories of the first time we laid like this in Agnitio. It was at that moment I knew there was something between us—something more than just friendship or attraction. Something deeper—something real.

"When a kingdom has adhered to its established traditions for hundreds, if not thousands of years, you can't expect immediate reform," he explained, his lips caressing my skin as he spoke. "I'm not saying you can't enact ideas, but you have to do so gradually or else—"

"It can cause an uproar."

"Exactly," Van agreed. "Change to that extent should be introduced slowly and over a period of time."

I sank further into him, grabbing his hand and running my thumb over the black metal of his wedding ring. "What do you think he should have done instead?"

There was a brief silence as he considered his response. "Both of his closest friends have multiple Gifts. If I were in his position, I would utilize that fact to demonstrate that you pose no threat. I would slowly incorporate individuals from mixed kingdoms into daily life, making their existence less unfamiliar. It would take time—decades, perhaps centuries—but eventually, those with magic from one kingdom and those with multiple Gifts would blend together."

"Would it really take that long?" I asked, twisting my body around to face him. The thought that it might take hundreds of years for individuals like myself to experience peaceful lives without constant threats made bile creep up my throat.

"Potentially."

I exhaled with frustration and concentrated on Evander's steady heartbeat while my mind contemplated numerous strategies to expedite Caelum's acceptance of individuals with multiple Gifts. But no matter how long I pondered the predicament, I couldn't seem to come up with a solution. My knowledge of politics was too limited, especially compared to Evander's.

"You did well in the meeting today," he said, changing the subject.

"I was nervous."

"I could tell, but you found your stride toward the end."

When I didn't respond, the tip of his nose brushed against mine, forcing my head to tilt back and meet his stare.

"Talk to me," he said gently.

I shook my head as I dug through my jumbled thoughts, embarrassed at what I knew I had to voice. "Sometimes I feel like I don't belong; like I'm lacking," I admitted. Van's brows knitted together in a combination of confusion and subtle encouragement, silently requesting for me to elaborate. "I don't possess as much knowledge, and I definitely feel like I don't command a room like you do."

His features wilted, and his eyes grew sad as he nodded. "That's because you don't," he replied. My stomach bottomed out. "But that's not to say you can't, or that you haven't before."

I averted my gaze as I quickly blinked to dispel the moisture that was gathering. Evander firmly grasped my chin and gently raised it, forcing me to meet his piercing grey gaze once more.

"In nearly a year, you have grown and blossomed into something extraordinary, but you often seem to forget that fact," he said. "You are a queen, love. You've already gained the loyalty of our people, but you must also command their respect. It won't be granted to you solely based on your title. You'll have to earn it."

"That's easier said than done."

"Because you have a tendency to question yourself," he replied quickly, like the words had been ready and waiting on his tongue. "It's okay not to have all of the answers. You're still learning how to navigate this world, and experience will come with time. But when you *do* know what you want, you need to have confidence in yourself to speak it aloud. Don't request that the kings stay at our home, *demand* it. If you believe something is the best and safest course of action, then don't give anyone a chance to argue."

I clutched onto his words like a lifeline. He had always believed in me, but from his observations, I could sense that I was reverting to old habits of being too fearful to express my thoughts because of my inexperience.

"You are a new ruler—a *young* ruler. You'll have to fight for the respect you desire, just like all the kings before you have. You'll have to prove that you are capable and worthy of the position you were given. It's what Dashiell and Jahier are doing now, and it's what *you* must also do."

Evander's gaze pierced into me, his grasp on my chin becoming tighter.

"Do you want everyone to treat you the same as they do me?" he asked. Clinging to his intense stare, I nodded. "Then make them."

44

Ainsley

I yawned and stretched my arms above my head as I padded to the kitchen, bleary-eyed and exhausted. Evander slid from our bed this morning before dawn, stating he wanted to check on how things were going at the palace before we started our day. When I proposed going along with him, he insisted that I go back to sleep. I would have thought it a sweet gesture if not for him mumbling something under his breath about how cranky and difficult I am to deal with that early in the morning.

It felt strange in our house with so many people occupying its rooms. The space reverberated with a constant flow of power, ensuring that the kings' presence was always felt, intentional or not. Based on my conversation with Van last night, I assumed it was deliberate. I released my magic, joining the rest to put on a show of strength and firmly establish my place among the other rulers.

Once I got to the kitchen, I glanced around, noticing that I was the final person to arrive. Dash and Elenora sat side-by-side, quietly laughing while they ignored their half-eaten plates of food. Lia, Cal, and Felix stood against the countertop, grinning from ear to ear as they finally got to catch up since Felix's return to Tenebrae. Jahier occupied the seat next to Oli, both of them too focused on the books in their hands to notice my arrival.

"It's about time," Van said as I strolled over to him and took the cup of coffee he held between his hands. He leaned forward and I offered him my cheek, which he kissed lightly, and then stole his drink back before I could take a sip.

"How did this morning go?" I asked, trying to retrieve the mug he now held behind his back.

"Surprisingly, everyone is still alive. Marce and Kenji said the night was relatively peaceful." He spun and drained the contents of his mug before handing me the now-empty cup. "Better luck next time, love." I groaned as I stared into the clean mug and then at the empty kettle of coffee on the stove.

"I no longer want you to be my Claimed."

"Too bad."

He tried to plant a kiss on my forehead but I deflected his attempt and narrowed my eyes.

"There's a fresh cup on the counter behind him," Oli muttered, his stare fixed on the pages of his book. This type of interaction between the two of us every morning had become routine for him.

In a display of frustration, Evander rolled his eyes and audibly sighed. "You weren't supposed to tell her," he complained.

"It's too early to listen to her whine," Oli replied.

I paid no attention to the playful jab and soft snickering of the people in the room as I reached around Van and grabbed my hidden coffee cup. I couldn't defend myself because they were right, but more than that, I relished the laughter of my family and our everyday routine, even though this morning was unlike any other. It had been months since we were last all together like this, and I wanted to make the most of it.

"Are you ready for training?" Van asked as I blew on my hot coffee and served myself breakfast.

"Of course," I replied, and quickly made my way to the table, taking a seat next to Dash while Felix joined me on the other side.

"What's the plan for today?" Dash asked, finally peeling his attention from Elenora to his two best friends.

"Our advisors and generals will collaborate to devise a training schedule and battle strategy to present to us," Evander answered before I could finish chewing my food. "After that, we will be going to the tavern for our own training session."

"Before that, actually," I corrected around a mouthful of eggs. I could sense the gazes of both him and the others fixed upon me as I chewed, yet I disregarded them, focusing instead on loading my fork for my next bite.

"Afterwards," Van amended. "It's already been arranged."

With a smile adorning my face, I reached for my cup and took a sip. "And I rearranged it after you left this morning," I replied innocently. "Giselle is expecting us in the next hour, so we'll leave right after I finish eating."

The room fell into silence as Evander gracefully walked around the table and settled in a seat across from me, his eyes fixed on me with curiosity. He had shared his plans for our training today before we went to sleep, so it wasn't difficult for me to alter them.

In the wake of our discussion last night, his words lingered persistently in my thoughts. If I wanted everyone to treat me like they did him—If I wanted to earn their respect and be considered just as important and worthy as the king sitting across from me, I would need to assert my dominance. I had to make them see that I could lead as effectively as he could. And that started with hijacking his training today.

"I've already instructed Tallis that he's to return to the palace and observe the generals' meeting with Cal, Marce, and Kenji," I announced to no one in particular, and set aside my drink in favor of a slice of toast. "Jahier, you'll bring Ezra." In my periphery, I could see him nod in response. "And Dash, as much as I hate to admit this, Rosella would benefit from the lesson."

Though I couldn't stand the newly appointed advisor, I couldn't deny she had a flare for extracting information. Given the instability of his court, the skill could be beneficial for Dash.

"I'll send for her," the King of Caelum replied without hesitation.

"No need," I told him, taking a large bite of my bread. "Van will go retrieve her and Ezra and then meet us at the tavern."

"Oh, will he now?" Evander questioned with a smirk in his voice. My eyes flicked up to meet his and found an unmistakable flair of pride shining within.

"Yup."

I pushed my chair away from the table, stood up, and dropped my partially consumed toast onto the plate before brushing the crumbs off my hands.

"Let's go," I ordered and sauntered out of the room without giving anyone a chance to argue.

Van was right; I was a queen, and this kingdom belonged to me just as much as it did to him. While I may not have possessed the necessary expertise or training to conduct an assembly on battle tactics, I knew the inner workings of the tavern. This was *my* chance to prove my worth.

45

Felix

We gathered on the main floor of the tavern and sat at the various tables in groups chatting as we waited for Ainsley and Evander to finish prepping the workers. His spies were masterful at extracting and relaying information covertly, and something told me we were about to get a firsthand lesson on how to do just that.

"Everyone line up," the Queen of Tenebrae commanded, gesturing toward the back of the empty establishment.

They had closed the tavern to the public so we could conduct our meeting in secret. To any of the patrons who were forced to leave the premises, it would simply look as though the rulers and their guests wanted to enjoy the tavern's offerings in private.

We did as instructed and Evander walked the line, tapping Oli on the shoulder and instructing him to have a seat. Apparently, he wouldn't be participating in today's training. That left just Dash, Rosella, Elenora, Jahier, Ezra, and myself.

I watched with anticipation as Evander handed one of his spies a yellow slip of paper and then strode away from the group. "Your task is simple," he stated, his hands firmly grasped behind his back as if he were instructing a line of soldiers. "Each worker has information that you need to retrieve. First, you must receive an invitation to go upstairs," he pointed to the rooms above us and we all glanced up, "Then, you'll need to extract said information by whatever means necessary. Provide us with what you've gathered and you pass. Oh, and no using any form of magic," Evander finished, giving a pointed glare to Dash.

The rules were simple enough, and as nervous murmurs broke out amongst the participants, I rubbed my hands together, excited that the first task was one that I would flourish at. Roaming my eyes over the selection, I mentally chose who I would want.

"When you say, '*by whatever means necessary*'..." Elenora said, a hint of trepidation in her voice.

"We mean exactly that," Ainsley answered, strolling away from the spies to stand at Evander's side. "Anything goes, aside from harming our employees."

Jahier swore quietly under his breath, and I stifled my laughter knowing the Prince of Venator was probably used to applying torture as a tactic to extract information, given that his kingdom was full of Disparya's assassins.

"When conducting this type of training, we normally start with learning how to interact when being approached for information exchange," Ainsley began, holding her chin high as she instructed. "But given our lack of time, I think it would be more beneficial for us to teach you how to interact like our spies."

Elenora asked another question, and I faintly heard Oli call for Evander, but I was too focused on the lineup of workers. Giselle would be unbeatable as she was the most experienced of them all. Flynn and Jasmine would both be a challenge but not impossible. Carl was newer, but—

I turned suddenly as I felt a looming presence before me. When my gaze met Evander's, he angled his head toward the table where Oli was seated, silently instructing me to join him.

"No," I begged, looking between the king and my boyfriend. "I want to participate!"

"It's not my call," Evander claimed, gesturing an impatient hand toward the table. I instantly turned to look at Ainsley since she was the one leading this damn meeting.

"It's not mine either," she replied, holding her hands up in innocence.

A groan rumbled in the base of my throat as I whirled around, setting my sights on the man sitting across the space. His lips lifted in a grin as he placatingly patted the seat next to him. Slowly, I shook my head, and he raised a brow in response before tapping the open chair again.

I crossed my arms firmly over my chest and narrowed my eyes.

Oli huffed a dramatic sigh and rose from his seat before striding across the room to stand before me. I lifted my chin in defiance as we held each other's stare, though his possessed none of the hard edges mine did. His blue eyes were soft and thoughtful, holding a quiet request I was fighting to accept.

"Please?" he whispered, and my body tingled at the touch of his fingers weaving between mine. My jaw clenched as I fought how much I wanted to give in to him. Even when I desired to be angry with him, I couldn't find the means to—not truly.

I was only the second person Oli had ever fallen in love with during his seventy-eight years in this world. The first had been a woman who lost her life during a careless act of violence while Oli was away on a mission for the late King Uriel. In the aftermath of losing her, Ainsley's parents, and then Evander's, he firmly resolved to never open his heart to anyone else other than the few individuals he had remaining.

Until he met me.

Although I was furious at Tallis for keeping my recovery hidden from my family, I'd never forgive him for what that secret did to Oli. The man I loved had spent months alone and broken, thinking that he was somehow at fault for my demise and blaming himself just like he did for every other death he had experienced.

Olivier had always been overprotective and overbearing at times, but lately, it had reached a new degree. Whenever I felt the urge to resist, I recalled that his unwavering determination to protect those dearest to him was one of the qualities that made me fall in love with him, to begin with. Given everything he had gone through before—and especially recently—I couldn't find it in me to fault him for acting on his fears.

Without a word, I nodded and allowed him to lead us to our small table. "Thank you," he said quietly and kissed my cheek once we sat down.

"You know no one was going to attempt to kill me, right?"

Oli pursed his lips and rolled his eyes just as Ainsley began her instruction once more. "Yes, but I also don't like the idea of anyone touching you, act or not."

I inclined my head as a self-satisfying smirk played on my lips. "So you're saying you're jealous?"

"No," he stated at once, barely allowing me to breathe the last word.

My grin widened as I leaned back against the table, propping my elbows on the top. "You were," I replied happily. Jealousy was never something Oli admitted to feeling, even when the emotion was evident in his every movement. He was stubborn in that way.

"Whatever," he grumbled as he shifted forward to watch the show.

I reached out and encircled my fingers around his chin, gripping tightly as I directed his face back to me. His eyes dipped to my mouth and I nearly said to hell with the meeting and opted to drag him to one of the upstairs rooms.

"You better make it up to me later," I said, unable to stop from biting my lip as Oli's gaze grew dark with a hunger that rivaled my own.

"I already have several ways I plan to do just that."

Someone clapped their hands together loudly, sending a force as strong as thunder reverberating through the room. Oli and I whirled forward, locking eyes with a very pissed-off queen.

"Pay. Attention," she demanded, clipping each word as her icy stare held ours. We both vehemently nodded and straightened in our seats. When she was satisfied that we weren't going to interrupt again, she faced her participants once more.

"Ainsley and I will demonstrate—"

"Actually," she replied, interrupting Evander. "Flynn will be the one assisting me today."

She gestured for Flynn to join her, and he eagerly complied, happy to assist his queen in the lesson.

"Sure," Evander said, unfazed, and crossed his arms over his chest as he surveyed the man standing next to his wife. "If Flynn wants to die today."

Oli redirected his attention to me, and I turned to see a smug look on his face as if Evander's reaction justified his. I shook my head, letting him know it absolutely did not, and then turned back to the show at hand.

"He doesn't!" Flynn said at once, his voice flying up an octave as his eyes widened in fear.

"You won't," Ainsley replied as she glowered at the king.

Flynn didn't seem too convinced, but as he attempted to retreat back into the lineup, she grabbed his arm and forced him to her side. She narrowed her glare at Evander, a silent command passing from her to him.

With a roll of his eyes, he dropped his arms to his side. "I'm not going to kill you, Flynn," he said. Ainsley turned back to the worker whose fear was slamming into me like a tidal wave, persistent and heavy. She offered a warm smile as if to say, '*See, you'll be fine,*' but then Evander spoke again. "As long as you keep your hands to yourself."

The poor man shook his head back and forth and tried to pull out of Ainsley's hold, but her grip held strong. "You're not going to die, Flynn," she told him. "And if my husband doesn't sit down and shut up, then *he'll* be the one keeping his hands to himself for a very, *very*, long time."

With a shallow growl blooming in his throat, Evander turned and marched for the empty table next to ours. I bit back my smile as his stomps echoed off the walls, his boots pounding against the floor with each forceful step. Once he was finally seated, he offered a tight-lipped smile to his queen, which she gracefully mirrored before facing the other rulers with Flynn's arm still clutched tightly in hers.

"The first thing you'll need to do is pick your target," Ainsley announced, gesturing a hand over Flynn. He offered a weak wave to the crowd and diligently kept his stare averted from his king as he strode for the small round table she had set up for the two of them in the center of the room. "Next, capture their attention." Flynn and Ainsley locked eyes for only a heartbeat before she grinned and turned away. "You don't want to be too willing or forceful, or it will come off as suspicious. Try to be as natural as possible. It may take hours before you've established enough of a quiet curiosity and can finally interact with your target, so be patient."

She sauntered over to Flynn and offered a questioning glance as she pointed at the open seat. He smiled and nodded, happily accepting her offer of company. Once seated, Ainsley struck up a conversation and got to work.

In between flirting and politely laughing at Flynn's less-than-amusing jokes, she'd address the onlookers and give various instructions about maintaining eye contact, body language, and how to pick up on clues of whether the target was interested or becoming discouraged.

Everyone watched her intently, occasionally chatting amongst themselves as they quietly pointed out helpful observations about her performance. The only one who seemed to be less than interested over the entire ordeal was Rosella, who could often be seen eyeing the group of tavern workers rather than watching Ainsley's lesson.

Finally, after about thirty minutes of the performance, Flynn extended his invitation for the queen to join him upstairs.

"So all we have to do is have a friendly conversation with them?" Elenora said, sounding skeptical. "That doesn't seem hard." The unimpressed tone she used regarding Ainsley's instruction had Rosella giggling under her breath.

"Perhaps," Ainsley answered tightly. "But it might not be the most useful tactic. It's all about reading what your target is after and choosing whichever path will lead you to success the quickest."

She stood and approached Flynn with an extended hand. He grabbed it and smiled, pushing his chair back from the table to give the queen ample room as she climbed onto his lap. Evander shifted in his seat, the irritation pouring from him in thick waves as Flynn's hands slid up Ainsley's thighs to rest on her waist.

She started her performance up again, running her hands through his hair as she softly chuckled and flirted, her lips sometimes running over the length of his jaw or neck. Flynn was less hands-on than I'd usually seen him be while he worked, never moving his grip anywhere other than Ainsley's waist, though I was sure that had something to do with the tense king at my side.

The entire exchange lasted only five minutes before Flynn extended his invitation and the queen removed herself from his lap. The crowd applauded the performance, and the worker hurriedly walked back to the line-up just as Evander stood and made his way to his wife's side.

"Evander will decide which spy to assign to you, as he's the most familiar with their strengths," Ainsley announced. "Remember, you must receive an invitation to join them upstairs and then present us with the information you've gathered. Do both, and you pass." She crossed her arms and scanned the waiting group of participants. "Since you seem so confident in your abilities and ease of my task, you can go first, Elenora," she added.

Evander called for Flynn to return to the center of the room, and both Tenebrean rulers strode for the sidelines. With a smug grin, the advisor of Agnitio traipsed forward, her eyes roaming over the crowd before they landed on her target.

"Fail," Ainsley said. Elenora's mouth dropped, her eyes widening in question. "You looked around and brought suspicion upon yourself."

"I didn't know we started!" she argued.

The Queen of Tenebrae shrugged as if that fact wasn't her problem, and I didn't bother hiding my smile at her sass. *This* side of Ainsley was always my favorite. The side that refused to be questioned or proven wrong. The side that would put you in your place simply because she felt like it.

"Try again," she demanded.

With a clenched jaw and harsh stare, Elenora rolled her neck and directed her attention to Flynn. She moved forward and extended a hand for him to take in greeting.

"Hi, I'm..."

"Fail," Ainsley interjected before the advisor had time to finish that sentence. "You are the niece of a king, one of his generals, *and* a close advisor. There is a slim chance he won't know who you are. But for argument's sake, let's say that he didn't. Given that it took you entirely too long to say your name, it leads me to believe you were attempting to create a fake one. He would know you were lying, so you fail. Sometimes we need to embrace exactly who we are and use that to our advantage. Try again."

Elenora never made it more than ten seconds before Ainsley called her out for fidgeting, looking around, stuttering, or being too forward.

"Would you like to go back in line now or continue thinking that this task is too easy for you?" the queen asked with a passive tone as she picked at her nails.

Elenora didn't respond, but with a huff of irritation, she left the center of the room and stood at Dash's side once more. He leaned down to whisper something I couldn't hear, and when she shook her head, he slung a comforting arm across her shoulders. I would be questioning him about *that* later.

"A hefty bonus will be applied to your paychecks should they fail in their attempt to gather the information," the King of Tenebrae announced to his spies.

"That's not fair!" Elenora complained. "They're just going to make sure we don't pass on purpose."

Evander stepped forward, his glare steadily piercing the advisor's. "Given our friendship over the years and my fondness for your uncle, I'm going to let your questioning of the integrity of my employees slide. We may be friendly, Elenora, but I am a king. I suggest you remember that the next time you want to have an outburst."

Ainsley moved next to her husband, her gaze sweeping over those standing before her. "This may seem like a fruitless task, but it isn't," she said. "The information Rosella provided us potentially saved thousands of lives. If she hadn't uncovered the knowledge that a traitor was among Caelum's court, Gideon would have had the opportunity to betray his kingdom again. This training is meant to help you ensure something like that doesn't happen, so take it seriously."

The crowd nodded, and Elenora dipped her head in a bow. "Apologies, Your Majesties," she replied.

I could feel the mood in the atmosphere shift after Ainsley's speech. What was once a steady flow of challenging excitement had morphed into tense feelings of apprehension and pressure. Even *I* began to view the task through a new lens as I realized just how important this lesson was and how it could help.

Ainsley and I had both undergone training in the ways of the tavern spies during our months in Tenebrae, but until now, until Gideon was exposed, I hadn't realized just how important their work was.

"Do we have any volunteers who'd like to go next?" Ainsley asked as she paced in front of everyone.

"I'll go," Rosella stated, stepping forward and marching over to the group of spies with confident determination. Before Evander could assign her someone, she grabbed Carl's hand and pulled him to her. "I want this one."

Ainsley looked toward the king and he shrugged, finding no issue in Rosella's selection.

"Fine," Ainsley agreed. "Take a seat, and the two of you—"

"Yeah, I won't be doing any of that," Rosella answered as she strolled right past the king and queen while tugging Carl along behind her. I could see the fury brewing in Ainsley's eyes as she looked at Dash for some assistance in dealing with his advisor.

"Rose," Dash tried, but Rosella waved a hand over her shoulder as she reached the base of the stairs leading to the rooms, dismissing him. "You already said yourselves that the information I provided helped, so clearly, I know what I'm doing and this lesson is useless."

Dash shook his head, and I could feel anger and frustration billow around him like a smothering fog. "That doesn't mean you can just take him," he tried again.

"Actually," Rosella pulled several gold coins out of her pocket and held them above her head as she ascended the stairs. "Given that I'm a paying customer, that's exactly what I can do."

"Rose—"

"Just let her go, Dash," Ainsley interjected gently, her voice soft and compassionate as she and the King of Caelum stared after the woman now entering a vacant room.

My heart shattered for the pang of defeat I felt surge into me before Dash had the chance to regain control of his emotions. He turned his back to me as if realizing his mistake and interlaced his hands over his head.

"I'm sorry, Ains," he whispered, keeping his broken gaze on the back of the room.

I couldn't stand Rosella, but I had never hated her more than at that moment. Dash had given her a chance. He had believed that she was capable and worthy of more than she had been dealt in this life. And for what? For her to throw away the opportunity Dash had given her and instead prove just how selfish she was.

My best friend dropped his hands to his side and took a long, deep breath before turning around and rejoining the others. I released my Empathi Gift, weaving my way toward him in the hope that he'd let me in and offer just the smallest amount of comfort. As I suspected, a cold barrier was in place to keep me out.

"Go ahead," Dash commanded, breaking the silence, though everyone's stares remained awkwardly on him.

Ainsley looked toward me, but I shook my head, completely at a loss for what to say or do. I knew Dash better than anyone, but even I didn't know how to help with the situation. Between his kingdom revolting, him having no one he could trust there, and now Rosella neglecting her duties as his advisor, I wasn't sure there was anything I could offer to ease his struggles.

"Dash..."

"I'm fine, Ainsley. Continue with the lesson," he replied.

She opened her mouth and then shut it, swallowing whatever words of comfort she wanted to offer as Evander cut in. "Jahier, you're next," he ordered, pressing a hand to his queen's lower back and ushering her away from the center. "Jasmine will be your target."

The tall woman with raven hair stepped away from the other spies and took her seat at the performance table, ready to be seduced by the Prince of Venator.

Each participant was granted several attempts to successfully receive an invitation. If their spy failed them three times in a row, they were dismissed, and it was the next participant's turn to try. Jahier came the closest, lasting over an hour before receiving his third fail for glancing at the audience. Ezra didn't make it more than ten minutes, and Elenora, who demanded to go again, made it twenty before ultimately succumbing to her nervous fidgeting. Dash was the final ruler to step forward and take his place in the center of the room.

The workers straightened, their eyes roving over the King of Caelum hungrily, each seeming hopeful they would be chosen as the target. I snorted and Dash smirked as we locked eyes, both of us far too familiar with this sight.

While in our teenage years and just prior to Ainsley wandering into our lives, we'd often have a competition during the monthly celebrations in Caelum to see who could secure the most invitations to bed. It was never about actually accepting the offers but rather a way to entertain ourselves during mundane events and see which of us could outdo the other. I usually won, but the last time we played, Dash had claimed the victory by a single invitation extended by none other than Rosella. Before I could reclaim my title, Ainsley decided to enter into our world, and Dash was done for.

Knowing him as well as I did, he was viewing this task in the same way as our friendly games back in Caelum. And if I had been allowed to participate, we would have been competing to see who could complete this challenge in the fastest time. But unluckily for me, my boyfriend wanted to deprive me of fun.

Evander leaned back in his chair as he scanned the list of hopefuls across the room, all vying for a chance to ask the newest King of Disparya to join them upstairs. To be honest, I didn't think any of them would have been disappointed to lose their potential bonus if he passed.

"I think either Jasmine or Elise," Ainsley murmured to her husband, but he shook his head.

Evander sat forward and rested his forearms on his thighs as a mischievous grin crested his lips. "Giselle," he announced.

My eyes immediately shifted to Ainsley as she slowly turned to glower at the side of Evander's face, though he kept his stare straight ahead. He was being a dick, and she and I both knew it. This task was difficult enough, with not a single person able to pass it today, and still, Evander decided to select the one spy Dash had no hopes of breaking.

With an audible grind of her teeth, Ainsley faced forward again. Disappointed grumbles echoed in the space, and I turned in time to see the gorgeous blonde make her way toward Dash.

Rather than stop at the table set for the two of them, Giselle continued past it until she reached the far wall where she twisted around to face him, her back pressing against the stone. He took a deep breath in preparation and strolled to the spy, his posture and attitude relaxing and shifting into something I had seen so many times during our competitions.

He strolled toward Giselle, his gaze dipping to trail slowly up her body, as if assessing his prey and the best way to capture it.

"See something you like?" she asked, mirroring his movements. Tilting her head to the side, she marked each inch of his body until she reached his eyes.

"Several things," he replied as he reached her. I snickered and elbowed Oli, but he didn't seem to find Dash's response as entertaining as I did. But someday soon—when they were best friends—he would.

Quiet introductions were exchanged, but given that they were practically undressing each other with their eyes, the pleasantries were far less formal than those with the previous participants.

Dash leaned in, whispering something I couldn't hear and pulling forth a laugh from Giselle that sounded anything but faked. Noting the soft blush that donned her cheeks as she replied with a sly smile, I shifted forward, completely entranced by Dash's performance but also fighting the urge to sabotage him like we used to do when we were younger.

He twisted and rested his left shoulder against the wall in a casual lean as he continued to whisper to her. Unfortunately, that meant his back was now to me, blocking my view of the show. I quickly got up and rushed to the other side of the room where the spies, advisors, and Jahier were all gawking.

Thanks to my somewhat loud interruption, Giselle and Dash's attention darted to me, and I apologetically whispered, "Sorry."

"Fail," she quietly told the King of Caelum.

Dash released my gaze and redirected his focus back to the beautiful woman before him. "Sorry," he replied cooly. "I just had to size up the competition for your attention."

Smooth, Dash.

"Nice recovery," Giselle replied, her brow arching in amused appreciation.

"I thought so too." Dash's eyes lowered to the spy's lips, and he positioned himself fully in front of her, his hands finding her waist as he pressed his body closer. His mouth dipped to her ear, and though I couldn't hear what he whispered, I was met with an immeasurable amount of lust, desire, and infatuation pouring from the spy in his hold.

A gasp, barely more than a shallow breath, slid from between her lips as she nodded. In a swift motion, Dash lifted her, keeping her back pressed firmly to the wall as his hands traveled to her backside. Giselle's legs wrapped around his middle, her arms encircling his neck as her fingers dug into his brown hair. There wasn't a single person in the group I was standing with who didn't move closer to the couple to get a better view.

Giselle turned her head at the sudden motion, clocking our advance. A hand slid around her throat, traveling up until fingers pressed against her jaw, and her face was redirected to the man holding her.

"Eyes on me," Dash quietly commanded, his lips just a breath above hers.

Oh, he was good.

She swallowed hard, her throat bobbing with the movement as her eyes fluttered and she arched further into his hold.

"Sorry. Something distracted me," she murmured.

Smirking, Dash's thumb brushed lightly over her full bottom lip as he pushed closer, nearly erasing the gap between their bodies completely. "That seems to happen a lot."

Giselle tilted her chin, desperately trying to close the slight distance between their lips, but Dash held firm, keeping himself just out of reach. "I know how we can remedy that," she said breathlessly. Dash arched a brow in question but didn't reply. "How about you take me upstairs where it can be just the two of us?"

Dash smiled at his victory and moved his hands down Giselle's body, slowly lowering her to the floor as a round of applause echoed through the room. To my surprise, he replied, "Not today."

I looked around to try and locate Dash's lost sense of logic, but landed on Elenora's somber gaze instead. She watched him mournfully, a thought seeming to plague her mind that I didn't understand. Okay, I was *definitely* going to be questioning him about that later.

"Are you sure?" Giselle asked as Dash took a step back. She laced her fingers through his and pulled gently to bring him closer. "I won't even charge you," she said.

He offered a polite smile as he brought her hand to his mouth and placed a soft kiss. "Perhaps another time," he replied and released his hold before backing away to his spot among the group.

Jahier and I offered enthusiastic pats on the back and not-so-subtly pointed out how he was an absolute idiot to turn down an offer from Giselle. Not only was she incredibly gorgeous and experienced, but she was the most expensive and sought-after worker in the establishment.

Dash was single as far as I knew—though that could be changing given the interesting exchanges between him and Elenora—and had been through hell these past few months. He deserved to unwind and release the obvious tension he was carrying around, and a night with Giselle would do exactly that. I was about to tell him as much when a sly voice cut above my thoughts.

"Fail," Evander said, and everyone's excitement and chatter ceased. He sauntered to the center of the room, stopping a few feet away as Ainsley joined him. "Fail," Evander repeated.

"He received an invitation," Jahier argued. "After less than ten minutes."

Evander ground his teeth and inclined his attention towards Giselle. "I'm well aware," he growled, but Giselle didn't seem fazed by his anger, only offering an innocent shrug. "But the task was not only to receive an invitation but to join your target upstairs," Evander continued, turning back to the crowd, his eyes locked on Dash. "And then provide us with the information you extracted. You didn't do that, so you failed. Perhaps if you were capable of following directions then—"

His words were cut off as Dash stepped forward and held up his middle and index finger with a slip of yellow paper wedged between them. The same paper the King of Tenebrae had given Giselle prior to the start of the lesson. Evander took it from Dash and directed his attention back to the spy who was frantically checking her pockets, now realizing it had been lifted from her.

"You only said that we had to receive an invitation to go upstairs, not that we had to accept it," Dash claimed, sliding his hands into his pockets. "And then provide you with retrieved information from your spies. I did just that."

My mind quickly ran through the given rules, searching for any flaws but coming up empty. Even Oli seemed amused, though he dropped the surprised smirk the second our gazes collided and instead fixed his features into something that resembled unimpressed boredom.

I loved him.

Ainsley cleared her throat as she clasped her hands behind her back. "Giselle," she announced, turning to the spy now striding for her. "There is no conceivable reason why the King of Caelum should have broken you in that short amount of time. Clearly, you don't take your position seriously if—"

"I do, Your Majesty!" she interrupted.

Ainsley held up a hand, silencing the woman. "I don't care how long you've been in service to the Crown. Perform poorly like that again, allow someone to remove valuable information from you like that again, and I will find someone else to lead our establishment. Is that understood?"

"Yes, Your Majesty."

"Every one of your shifts will be closing duty for the next two months. Flynn will take over your usual responsibilities during that time, and we will reevaluate your status after," she continued, earning an eager nod of acceptance from Giselle. "We've finished here, so prepare the tavern to reopen to the public this evening."

With a bow, the spy hurried away behind the bar and began reorganizing glasses and various containers of liquor. The rest of the workers followed suit, unstacking chairs and getting tables ready for the many patrons that would fill the room in a matter of hours.

Ainsley took a single step forward as she held Dash's gaze, the corner of her lip lifting in a proud smile before she spoke.

"Pass."

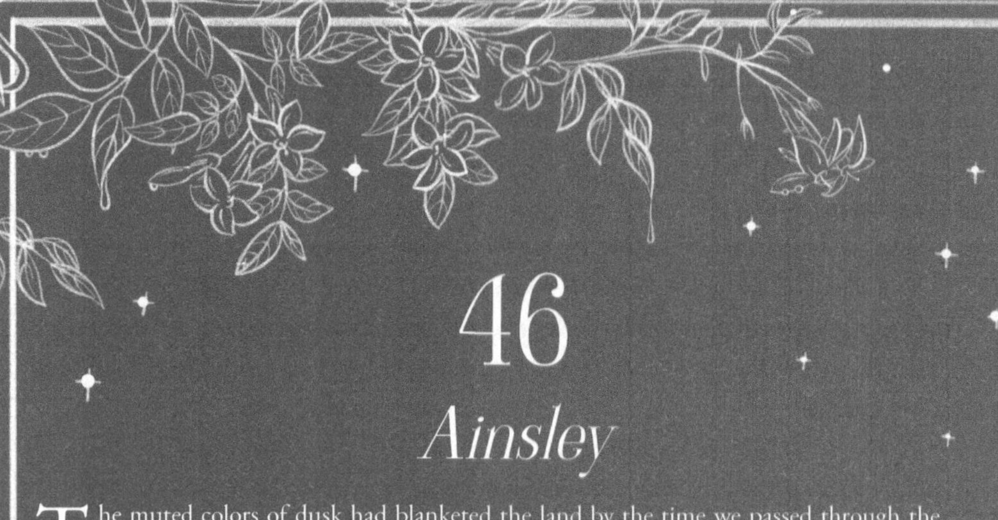

46
Ainsley

The muted colors of dusk had blanketed the land by the time we passed through the doors of our home and into the kitchen where Marce, Cal, and Kenji had just finished preparing dinner. The meeting this afternoon to hear the plans that our generals and advisors had devised went surprisingly well. Each kingdom worked together to develop a battle strategy and designate safe locations for people to seek refuge in times of attack.

"I'm just saying! If I was allowed to play, I would have easily beaten your time by two minutes," Felix said for the thousandth time since we left the tavern this morning.

"Bullshit," Dash argued yet again. "Olivier, tomorrow let him—"

"No," Oli replied before Dash could complete the sentence.

I rolled my eyes and pressed my fingers to my temples, massaging away the headache from their constant back and forth about who was better than who at seducing. As much as I loved those two boys, I finally understood Imogen's constant gripes over their behavior. She deserved a raise and all the luxury in the world for having to deal with them since childhood—even though it seemed they hadn't ever left that stage of their lives.

Turning away from their squabble, I spied Evander taking a seat at the table with a helping of food in front of him as he placed a second plate at his side. We locked eyes as he pulled the chair next to him out in offering, and though I was still pissed at him for purposely trying to sabotage Dash during my lesson, he had my food, so...

Before I could take a step in that direction, the front door slammed loudly, followed by the telltale high-pitched voice of Rosella. My focus immediately darted to Dash as he noticed her entrance too, his carefree expression wilting away like fallen petals. Everyone in the kitchen tensed as he stormed out of the room for his advisor, with me following closely behind. Dash had no allies and constantly encountered betrayal and rebellion. I wasn't going to let him face this alone after Rosella disappointed him.

"This place is far smaller than I would have imagined," Rosella drawled, looking over the space with a hint of boredom and disdain as my spy, Carl, stood at her side.

"Enough," Dash commanded. The room trembled with his power, the curtains shifting in an invisible breeze as vases and various objects rattled on the tabletop and mantle.

Rosella snapped her mouth shut, her eyes widening in slight fear as she took in Dash's furious demeanor. Her throat bobbed as she swallowed hard, nervously looking between her king and me as if I would be the one to grant her protection from his wrath. I wouldn't be, not this time.

"Is there a problem?" she asked, somehow finding the strength to stand straighter, her chin tilting upward as she held her head high.

Dash scoffed, and the mocking sound sent a shudder down my spine. I never envied Rosella, and especially not at that moment.

"Are you fucking serious right now?" he demanded. His tone was as cold and sharp as the edge of a blade poised to pierce its target. "You have the audacity to stroll in after that shit you pulled today and act like nothing happened?"

"I'm not—"

"I agreed to have you at that lesson today because I thought it would be a good opportunity for you to prove yourself and learn a useful skill. All you had to do was stand there and follow instructions," he said, interrupting her.

"Dash, I—"

"But instead, you did what you always do, Rosella. You proved just how selfish and unwilling to change you are. I don't know what I was thinking, offering you a council position." He muttered the last sentence under his breath as if it were intended solely for his own ears. Carl looked at me, a question written on his pinched brow, but I shook my head, denying his request to leave.

The advisor kept her chin high, but I could see the hurt swimming in her icy blue eyes, though I couldn't discern if the emotion was founded on guilt or embarrassment. Her stare finally released Dash and she turned, blinking quickly as she visibly tried to fight back tears.

"Carl is twenty-eight," she whispered, still not looking in our direction.

"What does that—"

"He's only been working for the tavern for three months," Rosella continued, stepping onto Dash's words. "He has seven siblings: two sisters and five brothers. None of them have children of their own, much to his mother, Lucinda's, dismay. His oldest sister is the only one in his family to possess magic, the Gift of shadows, and she's currently on the northern coast in one of Tenebrae's camps."

Dash opened his mouth to interrupt again, but I placed a gentle hand on his arm, halting that decision as she spoke again.

"Carl is an artist, and when he's not at the tavern, he spends most of his time at the local markets where he has a booth showcasing all of his work. That's partly why he was accepted when he applied to work as a spy: the fact that he's around people constantly, picking up tidbits of gossip and information others may find futile."

Rosella twisted her head toward her king, her cold stare now full of resolve and determination.

"His real name is Alyx, but since he was named after his father, he goes by his middle name to spare any confusion. He enjoys being employed at the tavern but admits that he's still finding his footing and that half of the patrons and Giselle terrify him."

My attention drifted to Carl where he awkwardly shifted from foot to foot, a blush now donning his cheeks.

"Thank you for walking me here," Rosella whispered to the spy. He offered a polite smile before returning his stare to me. I nodded once, giving him permission at last to retreat.

"Carl," I called before he reached the front door. "Tell Giselle that you'll be joining her for closing duties for the next week."

"Yes, Your Majesty," he replied and then gently closed the door behind him as he left.

Carl was the newest employee of the tavern, and even though he lacked experience, he had spilled far too much to Rosella than what was acceptable. Either he needed to attend more training, or she was just *that* good at what she did.

"I did listen to the instructions," she said, her voice coming out more timid than I had ever heard from her.

Rosella clasped her hands in front of her as she pushed her shoulders back in a fight to regain some of her confidence. Even *I* had to admire her tenacity as I studied her, sending out my Empathi Gift and picking up the traces of courage now diluting the fear.

"Ainsley said sometimes we need to embrace exactly who we are and use that to our advantage," she continued. "Well, I did that. This is who I am, and in what world would I ever wait for an invitation to be extended to me?"

I arched a brow, fighting the curve of my lips as my eyes shifted to the man on my left. Dash crossed his arms as he examined her, likely attempting to decipher whether this was an explanation or an excuse.

"Then you should have told me that," he argued.

Rosella laughed and shook her head. "And let Ainsley fail me for giving away my strategy? Please, I'd rather die than let her hold that over my head for eternity."

"She wouldn't..." Dash stopped mid-sentence, thinking better of it as he realized that was, indeed, exactly what I would have done. He sucked in a long inhale and released it slowly as his head tipped back and he stared at the ceiling. He was at a loss for words, conflicted, and I hated seeing him like that.

Rosella took a tentative step forward, her gaze locked on the King of Caelum. "I know things have been really difficult for you," she said, and the soft tenor of her voice captured his attention again. "You've struggled with your new role, and your council is full of people you can't rely on, but..." she looked away as her voice cracked on the last word. "But I thought I was the exception to that."

My gaze shot to Dash to see his brows pinch and his eyes dart back and forth as he tried to comprehend what Rosella was saying. He looked just as surprised as I felt.

"I thought you asked me to be a part of your council because you trusted me," she continued. "I was under the impression that you believed in me, believed that I was worthy of this role." When she directed her stare back to the king, her eyes were glassed over, but she didn't let a single tear spill. "I meant every vow I spoke when I was sworn in to serve. I am loyal to you and our kingdom, but if you can't trust in that—trust in *me*—then please accept this as my resignation. I love my position as your advisor, but I will not fight every day to prove myself just for you to doubt me the moment you don't understand or agree. I have been treated and looked down on my entire life, and like you said: I am capable of far more. I will not move backward."

For the first time, I felt an immense understanding of the woman before me. I didn't believe there would ever be a time when I would call her a friend, but I could say that I respected her. Like me, Rosella was now coming into her own—her own life, her own voice, her own autonomy, her own power. I couldn't help but root for the woman I hated.

"You're right," Dash said, dropping his hands to his side. "I offered you my trust and then immediately withdrew it without giving you the benefit of the doubt. You deserve better than how I treated you, and for that, I am deeply sorry, Rosella."

She lifted her shoulders, shrugging off the apology as if it meant nothing, but I could tell it did. Her focus dropped to her still clasped hands as she spoke in barely more than a whisper. "I'm sorry that I haven't always given you a reason to believe in me, to begin with."

"Wait a minute..." Dash said, a crooked grin forming. "Did you actually just apologize for something?"

Rosella rolled her eyes but didn't look at us.

"I think she did," I added, unable to stop a smile from forming. At my input, Rosella's head snapped up, any tentativeness in her features was now replaced with fury and annoyance.

"Oh, whatever," she barked. "Can I go back now? I missed an entire day of work all because you wanted me to sit in on some boring lesson I could have done in my sleep." She reached into her pocket and pulled out another notebook, different from the one I saw her with yesterday. "And I need a new one." She threw it, slamming Dash in the chest.

"Again?" he demanded. "Fine, but I don't need you to write every frivolous detail."

"You told me to observe. That's what I'm doing."

"The color of everyone's clothes isn't a detail that needs a three-page description with your thoughts about how hideous it looks with their skin tone," he argued.

"If you want my job done *your* way, then do it yourself."

"That's not what I'm saying…"

"I'm going to go get Van so he can take you back to the palace," I announced, backing away from the squabble. Before I made it to the door that led to the kitchen, I called out, "Oh, and Rosella…" She looked up, locking eyes with me. "You passed today."

Her brows pinched, and her nose wrinkled in disgust. "Like I care," she replied and then went back to arguing with Dash about what was considered an important observation. I grinned as I pushed my way into the kitchen, feeling the bright sense of happiness and pride radiating from the advisor at my declaration.

47

Ainsley

By my third bite of potatoes, Evander reappeared at my side, taking his seat next to me at the table while the rest of our family and guests enjoyed their meals. He was reluctant to traverse Rosella back to the palace, stating that the crisp fresh air and several-hour walk could do her some good. I was more than half-tempted to agree with him, but I didn't want to cause a bigger headache for Dash, who would undoubtedly escort her back himself.

"Does this mean I have your forgiveness now?" Van asked, leaning in to kiss me. I turned my face, offering my cheek as I took another bite of food.

"Let me have your dinner roll and I'll consider it."

His eyes narrowed in contemplation before he picked up his bread and slowly took a bite while holding my stare. "I'll take my chances. You'll forgive me eventually," he replied with a full mouth before he moved the dinner roll to the far left side of his plate.

I ground my teeth and then leaned across him to grab the piece of food, but he lifted it above his head, just out of my reach. Hurrying out of my seat, I crawled onto his lap and continued to scramble my way toward the bread, but Evander wouldn't have it. He pushed back from the table and stood, causing me to tumble to the ground before I righted myself with a new determination.

"Ainsley, there's plenty more. Including the two you still have on your plate," Oli groaned, and I noted the subtle exchange of wagers passing between Felix and Kenji as they observed the show.

My fire within burned brighter as I called for my Obscure, sending it sprawling for my husband.

"I don't care. I want *that* one," I answered, twisting my magic around his arm until it climbed up to his wrist.

"That's cheating," Evander said and dropped the dinner roll before my Obscure could pry it from his fingers. I watched it plummet to the ground only for him to catch it with his opposite hand a heartbeat later before he spun his back to me. Normally, I would have applauded the move, but I was already annoyed he had managed to evade my attack.

I leapt for him, landing on his back as I continued my attempt to take what I wanted. Evander chuckled as he reached up to lock his hands around my neck and flipped me forward. My body tumbled over his shoulder and my spine slammed into the floor hard as he freed himself from me.

"I taught you better than that," Evander said. "You're far too obvious."

He barely finished the sentence before I spun on the ground, sweeping my leg out and hooking his ankle, taking him to the ground with me. I climbed over his torso, my focus firmly on the now-crumpled bread in the locked fist above his head. With me just a breath away from my target, Van wrapped his legs around my middle, squeezing so hard I let out a gasp as the air was stolen from my lungs.

I doubled over from the sharp stab of pain around my ribs, and he took that as his opportunity to roll us over. Before I had the chance to worm out from beneath him, he flipped me, grabbing my wrists and pressing them to the small of my back. He shifted his body weight so it was entirely on my legs, pinning them beneath him and giving me no hope of escape.

"Is that the best you've got, love?" he taunted, and a frustrated growl rumbled in my throat as I struggled beneath him. I shifted from side to side, but any time I thought I could gain leverage, he pressed my stomach harder against the floor and tightened his hold on my wrists. "Now take it," he commanded.

"You *do* know that's the last time you'll ever mutter those words to me," I gritted out, still trying to get free.

Evander laughed, and I felt his presence looming closer. "Again, I think I'll take my chances. You like it far too much." His lips pressed to my cheek as he whispered, his breath softly tickling my skin, "Your growl is very adorable, by the way." I thrashed again, which only seemed to make him laugh harder as he pulled away from my face.

My eyes drifted upward, noticing the watchful glances and quiet conversations of our audience, and the passing of money between Kenji and Felix. I swore to the Gods, if I found out Felix had bet against me...

"Now take the *bread*," Evander demanded, putting emphasis on the subject.

"What the hell do you think I'm trying to do?!"

Both of my legs and wrists were pinned down, and in this position I couldn't gain the leverage or momentum I needed to get him off of me. Physically, I was useless, but I still had another option. I took a deep breath and called for the magic swimming in my veins.

"Not your Obscure," Evander said before I could pull a single tendril from myself. "Your Imperium Gift."

I stopped fighting and instead twisted my neck as far as I could to try and catch a glimpse of the man behind me. "You're not serious," I told him incredulously.

"On the contrary, my love. I'm very eager to see what you can do."

The room quieted as I shook my head vehemently, everyone seeming to grasp the danger of what he was asking. He was insane if he thought I was going to use *that* Gift on him. It was the one source of power that seemed to thrive on my anger and fear more than any other. The more I focused on accessing that magic, the harder it was for me to control, and risking his life to appease him during this game was certainly not going to happen.

"Van, no. I could kill you."

"Perhaps," he drawled. "But you need to learn how to wield the Gift so— "

"—I swear to the Gods if you say *'I'll take my chances'...*" I said, mocking the cadence of his voice, and earning a quiet chuckle from the crowd and him.

"I, for one, think it's worth the risk," a barely familiar voice called from across the room. Everyone present directed their attention to the door where Brandle was slowly making his way into the kitchen with both Tallis and Lia at his side.

His appearance was truly horrific, his flesh marred by purple and yellow marks. Brandle's left eye was still swollen shut while his right was bloodshot, and his leg was wrapped in a bandage that extended from his thigh down to his ankle.

"With him out of the way, I could have a shot with you," he added.

Pressure was released from my back as Evander made his way off of me, extending a hand for me to grab, which I slapped away and instead lunged for the dinner roll. He once again anticipated my attack and pulled it out of reach before I could even get close.

"Lia and Sirona worked so hard to heal you. It'd be a shame for me to add a few more cracked ribs for them to mend," Evander replied to the prince.

Brandle let out of a wheeze of amusement, and then promptly pressed his hand to his side while wincing, the laughter obviously causing him pain.

"Your husband may be an idiot for attempting to provoke an untrained Imperium," Brandle directed to me. "But he isn't wrong. You need to learn how to properly wield it."

I pushed myself to my feet, eyeing the damaged bread Evander was now happily chomping on. "That may be true, but I'm not going to let Van be the test subject of what I can do," I answered.

Brandle limped forward, grunting with the daunting movement, and Lia grabbed his arm as she helped him take another step. "Fair enough. I have a different training tactic in mind for you anyway, and as soon as I've recovered, we'll begin. Given how well I've been taken care of, I have no doubt that I'll be fully restored in no time." He turned his attention to Lia and winked, earning a blush from her and a snort from Cal.

"What kind of tactic?" Van asked skeptically, as we both took our seats at the dining table once again.

He had never been thrilled at the idea of Brandle training me, shooting down Tallis nearly anytime he suggested it. The Prince of Ministro's proximity to his stepfather had always worried him, despite the aid and information Brandle had supplied for our cause. And though I was more than willing to take the risk for an opportunity to learn how to hone my magic, I couldn't blame Van for his trepidation in regards to my safety.

"And give away my secrets this early?" Brandle replied with a *tsk* and took another painful step until he reached one of the empty chairs at the table.

My eyes narrowed in question as I realized there were three vacancies rather than only the one meant for Tallis. I did a quick inventory of those present, and then shifted my attention to Felix at my left.

Our gazes collided, and he leaned in close as he whispered, "He and Elenora snuck off to eat on the roof." I lifted an intrigued brow, and he nodded in response. "Trust me; I already planned on ambushing him about it later."

"Do you really think he'll willingly tell you?"

Dash and Felix had usually shared every aspect of their lives, never keeping a single detail from the other. But once Dash and I began to bloom into something greater, he had chosen to keep the specifics surrounding our relationship from his best friend. I couldn't help but wonder if the same would be said with Elenora.

"It's Dash, so no. But that doesn't mean I'm not going to annoy the shit out of him until he does. I'm not buying his *'we're just friends'* bullshit he tried to feed me earlier on the way home from the tavern." Felix replied.

I snorted and rolled my eyes. "Because it worked so well when you tried that tactic last time."

Felix had been relentless with Dash, trying like hell to get any information from him regarding our relationship and failing every time. It didn't matter that I had already shared the details with him—he wanted the satisfaction of prying it from Dash.

"Yeah, but that was different because it was you."

Dash's reason for keeping our relationship private was because of how much he valued and cherished it. I was the first person he had ever loved, and there was a simplistic beauty in keeping what we shared just between us. If Elenora meant even a fraction of what I did to him, he may have decided to go that route again.

"Perhaps it'll be the same with her," I said before leaning away.

I focused back on my plate, ignoring the gentle conversations in the background as I spied a third dinner roll next to my two uneaten pieces. My lips curved as I turned to Evander to find him watching me intently with a grin. I arched closer, moving my lips as close as I could to his face, and waited for him to close the distance.

"Thank you," I said once his mouth was on mine. He nodded against me and I deepened the kiss, sweeping my tongue softly over his as I reached over and pried the half-eaten portion of bread from his fingers. "But I want this one too."

"Rude," he replied, but didn't let up in our embrace.

"Since you're giving away food, I'll take an extra helping of chicken. I've got to regain my strength," Brandle declared.

Van reluctantly pulled back and directed his attention to the injured Prince of Ministro now seated across from us. "Get your own plate."

"I'm injured."

"I don't care."

"You owe me."

"For what?" Van asked incredulously. "Showing up half dead on my land and delaying the meeting you were supposed to be at?"

"I saved your wife's life," he replied, and Evander snorted.

"And I saved yours. Looks to me like we're even."

I popped a piece of bread into my mouth, thoroughly enjoying the back and forth between the two men. Brandle leaned back in his chair and crossed his arms over his chest as he and Van stared each other down, both locked in a power struggle.

There were far too many egos in my house.

"I saved Felix's life, too," the Prince announced with a satisfied grin.

"Great," Van replied. "Then *he* can fix your plate for you."

"Just think about how sad she would have been if he hadn't survived," Brandle continued, ignoring the King of Tenebrae's counter.

"Perhaps. But she would have gotten over it quickly enough."

"Okay, I don't think it would have been *that* quickly," Felix interrupted. The outrage he held for Van's assumption was clear in the gravel of his voice and the way he adjusted in his chair. "Her best friend *died*. I'm sure she would have mourned for quite a while."

Van bobbed his head from side to side noncommittally as he grunted. I clamped my lips together to keep from smiling at his love for getting under Felix's skin and turned to face my friend. His eyes widened, imploring me to confirm that he would have been missed for an appropriate amount of time.

"My grief would have known no bounds," I said. It wasn't even an explanation meant to placate him—it was the truth. His loss was something I'd never be able to fully recover from.

"That's all I'm asking for," Felix replied.

I released a soft chuckle, then turned to Evander. "Just go fix Brandle a plate." With wide eyes, he whirled his head to me, completely appalled by my request. "He's our guest," I added.

"He's a prick," Van answered.

"That may be true, but he's the only one who can teach me how to wield the Gift you stated I need to learn. The least we can do is give him dinner."

Evander audibly ground his teeth but didn't argue. With a tight smile toward me and then to Brandle, he pushed away from the table and strode for the display of food.

"Hold off on the potatoes," Brandle called. "I'm watching my figure."

The King of Tenebrae's back went stiff and his hands clenched at his sides, but by some miracle, he didn't offer a snide retort. I reached out with my Empathi Gift and wrapped it around his rage, willing his heart to steady and his nerves to calm. His magic enveloped mine, squeezing gently in a sign of gratitude.

"Continue to antagonize my husband, and I won't stop him from adding to your injury count," I promised Brandle, and the arrogant smirk he possessed faltered. "Understand?" He reluctantly nodded and shifted in his seat.

"I think it's time you tell us what exactly happened to you."

48

Ainsley

It was relatively quiet around the table as we waited for Elenora and Brandle to finish their reunion. Felix had retrieved both her and Dash from the roof so they could be present for the prince's story as Evander used his shadows to craft two new chairs. If our guest list continued to grow, we would soon need a larger dining table as well.

"Is the food alright?" I asked, leaning across Felix to speak to the King of Caelum. He pinched his brow in confusion and I gestured to his mostly untouched plate, which made me start to question what exactly they were doing up there.

"Yeah," he replied. "I'm just not very hungry."

I nodded before sliding back to my seat, throwing Felix a knowing glance that he mirrored.

"You better tell me as soon as you find out what's going on between them," I whispered beneath my breath, only loud enough for my best friend's ears.

"Obviously," he replied just as Elenora sank into the chair next to the right of Dash. I offered her a warm smile before facing forward once again. I wasn't sure how I felt about the prospect of her and Dash, or if I even had the right to care, but until Felix retrieved more information, I wouldn't let the thought fester.

"I want to start by saying that I didn't know about the plan to attack the Palace of Caelum that day," Brandle began, capturing the attention of the room, though his focus was solely on Dash.

The Prince of Ministro waited for a response, but none came. Dash stayed quiet and reserved, his head tilting to the side as if studying Brandle and what his motives could be. He seemed to trust him as little as Evander did.

"You had no idea, yet somehow made it out before the attack occurred. How convenient," Evander mused as he drummed his fingers over the table.

Brandle turned slowly to look at Evander, his blue eyes sparking with frustration. "If I wanted you dead, why bother warning you at all?

"To keep up the facade," Van answered without hesitation. "You escape harm, make us believe you're on our side by warning us just in time, and then show up here in desperate need of help and in the prime position to leak information back to your stepfather." He leaned back in his chair as he cast a skeptical glance over Brandle. "Seems like the perfect plan to me."

"That's such bullshit and you know it!" the Prince of Ministro exclaimed.

"Do I?"

"I've proven myself for years, risking my life to help this cause. What more do you want from me, Evander?"

The King of Tenebrae was silent as he regarded Brandle. To anyone else, they'd think it was because he didn't think the prince was worthy of a response, but to me, it was obvious he didn't have one. Evander was running out of reasons not to trust Brandle, especially after he saved my life when he could have so easily taken it.

"When did you find out what was going to happen?" I asked, wanting to diffuse the pending fight I could see brewing.

Brandle reluctantly pulled his focus from Van and settled his eyes on me as he answered. "I didn't know anything about it until we were already outside the palace grounds. It wasn't until his father showed up," he said with a gesturing hand toward Jahier, "That I started to become suspicious. Refusing Evander's demand for an emergency assembly—a right that is granted to our kings by law—is essentially declaring war against the kingdoms. Harbin is just stubborn and arrogant enough to do it, but Arden..."

Brandle shifted his focus to the Prince of Venator sitting quietly to his left. Jahier lifted his chin, those light green eyes alert as he held the injured prince's gaze.

"Your father is a dick," Brandle began, "But it doesn't change the fact that he's been loyal to Disparya despite Harbin's attempts to sway him over the years. Seeing him arrive outside the gates with us was an immediate cause for concern."

"And that's when you sent the note," I deduced, but Brandle shook his head.

"No. I planned to just gather information to feed to you as I always have, but once Arden made a comment about Jahier, I knew something bigger was going on."

Jahier spoke before I could. "What comment?" he asked, his tone a mix of ice and betrayal.

Brandle glanced at the prince with pity—a look I could tell Jahier despised by the audible clenching of his jaw.

"When Harbin inquired about your whereabouts, your father stated that you weren't coming and..." he trailed off as if fighting the desire to continue. "And that you deserved what was coming to you.".

Jahier snorted and leaned back in his chair, averting his stare as his eyes flashed with unspoken fury. I'd never gotten the sense that he and the King of Venator were close, but it couldn't have been easy to hear that his father wanted him dead.

"His loss is our gain," Evander directed at Jahier.

I smiled at his kind words, my hand finding his beneath the table and squeezing gently. He returned the gesture before sliding his fingers between mine and bringing them to his mouth for a tender kiss.

"Agreed," Tallis said just as Dash nodded. None seemed to lessen Jahier's heartache though as his stare stayed firmly glued to paintings decorating the far wall.

Brandle noted the quiet tension before clearing his throat and continuing. "I knew it was dangerous to send that note, but it was worth risking my cover if it bought you any time at all."

We were all quiet as we sat there, no one seeming to have the heart to tell him that it hadn't. His letter had come too late—only seconds before the attack began.

"If it wasn't for your note, I'd still have a traitor on my council," Dash said into the silence. "So thank you."

Brandle loosed a heavy sigh of relief, his shoulders and the crease between his brows easing as visible tension left his body. My chest tightened as I realized he had been holding onto that burden for weeks now, never knowing if what he had done was enough.

"What happened next?" I asked.

He shrugged and shook his head as he said, "Everything went back to normal. Or so I thought."

Brandle leaned forward and rested his forearms on the table, his fingers fidgeting nervously with each other as if he truly couldn't figure out what went wrong.

"Harbin and Arden were to return to the Palace of Ministro to sort out their next steps. I, on the other hand, was sent back to the northern camps with the task of ensuring our forces were strong enough to fight off any potential attacks from Agnitio now that the Kingdom of Ministro was an enemy of Disparya. Over the next two weeks, I did just that. Occasionally, I'd receive updates and new orders from my stepfather, but any questions I had regarding his motives or next move went unanswered," he finished.

"And that wasn't a red flag to you?" Evander asked skeptically.

"Not particularly, no," he replied. "Harbin's always been secretive. Most of the time I don't get let in on his plans until the last possible second, so I didn't take his silence as cause for concern. It wasn't until I was fighting off a group of men who ambushed me in the middle of the night that I realized I was fucked."

My eyes darted over the watchful crowd as I tried to discern their thoughts on Brandle's story, but no one was giving anything away. All had been trained in the art of maintaining passive expressions as the wheels of their mind spun. It was unbelievably annoying.

"They broke in when I was in the dead of sleep and filled the room with some type of gas that prevented me from reaching for my magic," Brandle added. My gaze immediately locked with Evander's.

We had assumed the attack on me before the trial had been orchestrated by King Harbin, and though it was an educated guess, we had no hard evidence until now. Harbin had a deadly weapon in his possession—one that would be catastrophic for our side in this war.

"They said Harbin ordered to have me sent back to him in pieces, but they wanted to have their fun first. So they did," Brandle continued, reaching for his wine and taking a long sip like he could drink away the memories.

He didn't elaborate on the torture he went through. By the pain and fear I could feel radiating from him, I didn't think he could. So I tightened my grip on Evander's hand, giving a silent command not to press the prince on the matter.

"How did you escape?" Evander asked instead.

An incredulous, breathy laugh escaped from Brandle's lips. "One morning I woke and the restraints attached to the post I had been tied to had loosened. I don't know if someone did it or if it occurred naturally. The fuckers kept me unfed for the entire week."

"Whatever the cause, thank the Gods for it," Tallis remarked.

"The Gods can get fucked," Brandle replied. My lips twitched and I didn't miss seeing Van's do the same from the corner of my eye.

"Anyway," he continued, picking up his fork and stabbing a potato he'd instructed Evander not to give him. "I waited until the middle of the night before I freed myself. I wasn't too far from the portal that led to my and Ele's rendezvous point in Agnitio, so I headed there."

"Why didn't you write to me and tell me that?" Elenora demanded, worry dripping over every word. "I could have come and gotten you."

"I wasn't going to risk your safety, Ele," he answered. "If Harbin had somehow known about me, he might have found out that you were the one I'd been meeting with. There wasn't a chance in hell I was going to lead him right to you."

Elenora watched her friend with sympathetic eyes. Regardless of is she agreed with his choice or not, Brandle had made the smartest call. If I had been in his shoes, there wouldn't have been the slightest possibility that I would've reached out to my best friend.

"Our meeting spot was only a few hours away from the border of Tenebrae. It was a struggle to get there, but I knew I had to if I wanted to survive," Brandle added.

"Why not just ask my men for help?" Tallis inquired. "We have camps all along that border. Surely you would encounter at least *some* of my people before crossing over."

The Prince of Ministro chuckled before plopping the potato into his mouth and spearing another. "No offense, Your Majesty," he replied around a mouthful, "But your people are known for upholding the law. I couldn't trust they wouldn't return me to my stepfather, especially after seeing my condition. Anyone with half a brain cell would have been able to tell that I was on the run."

Tallis looked as if he was ready to defend his people, but Elenora cut in. "He's right, uncle. Only a select few knew about our alliance with Brandle. It isn't off base to assume they would do what they felt was right and return the deserter to his home kingdom."

"Exactly my thought," Brandle agreed. "Evander's people on the other hand…" he tossed a pointed glance at my husband and took another bite of food. "They'd bring me right to him. Probably in hopes of getting to watch him flay me alive."

A slow smile curved Van's lips as he said, "Probably."

I turned Brandle's story over in my mind, inspecting it for clues that proved to the contrary but came up empty. A quick glance at Dash showed that he was doing the same, his pupils going back to their normal size—his Obscure being put aside.

"So what now?" I asked Brandle, tentatively reaching out with my Empathi Gift and being met with the prince's solid internal shield.

He gave a knowing grin before saying, "You tell me. I'm entirely at your mercy, Your Majesty." Brandle winked and I squeezed Van's hand harder as I felt him tense.

"Flirting with me will only hinder my desire to help you."

"Because of your husband?"

"Because I don't like you," I answered, earning a flash of surprise from Brandle and a wave of relief from Van.

"You barely know me."

"You're right, but what I *do* know, I don't like." He snorted and cocked his head to the side, ready to spew more of his bullshit. "You're insufferable and arrogant—"

"So is your husband," he argued.

"I never said he wasn't. But even so, you're sitting here—in our personal home—displaying anything but gratitude." I leaned forward ready to drive each point into this thick skull. "Evander could have left you for dead, but instead he brought you here," I said, gesturing over the inviting space. "He spared our best healers to mend you. He's clothed you, fed you, given you a bed and place to stay. And yet here you sit, flirting with his wife and insulting him at every turn."

"I think your memory might be a little fuzzy, Ainsley. He's the one who questions my loyalty every chance he gets, regardless of what I've done for this alliance for years now. *He's* the one who needs to get over himself."

Rage, white-hot and blinding sliced through me, and it was all I could do to keep myself from diving across the table and strangling the condescending prick. Evander's hold on me tightened, his magic brushing over me in a delicate caress as it tried to deescalate my growing anger. It almost worked... Until Brandle spoke again.

"He doesn't get to—"

I shot to my feet, my fists slamming down onto the table so hard it split the wood. Plates and silverware rattled as wine goblets tipped over, spilling across the surface in a sea of red.

"He *does*," I growled.

The room thrummed with my power, my Gifts banging against their doors, begging me to choose one to free. One door in particular, the color of dark crimson, boomed the loudest.

"He can do whatever the hell he wants to, Brandle," I continued as my blood pounded in my ears. "You forget his title. And given your familiarity with me, you seem to have forgotten mine as well. You are in the presence of the people who rule this land. People who have more power than you could possibly imagine. People who could end you with barely a thought. And two of those people, in particular, have graciously welcomed you into their home despite their judgment of you."

More power than I knew what to do with poured from me. The floor and walls and furniture trembled as I leaned forward and braced my hands on the splintered wood. The strength of my magic continued to climb as my anger did, reaching, reaching, reaching. I couldn't hold it back any longer—didn't *want* to.

"Love," Evander whispered, but it was too late. There would be no calm to my chaos right now.

I closed my eyes and with a faint click, the door to my Imperium Gift creaked open.

Red smoke, as dark and warm as blood, infected my veins, sprawling out inside me in every direction like a spider's web. It grew more potent, more deadly, more ravenous as it tasted the tension in the air, feeding on the fear. The Imperium Gift's magic was addicting, making me crave revenge and destruction, the bloodlust sending me into a near frenzy.

Evander's hand pressed to my back and I felt him instantly at my side. But I ignored that touch that always grounded me and led me to reason as my eyes sprung open and I settled them on Brandle.

"He has every right not to trust you," I gritted through clenched teeth.

Brandle's eyes went wide, his hands moving to his throat as he felt my magic pierce his internal shield. I tightened my hold, severely reducing the flow of blood to his brain. Brandle's magic pushed and clawed and fought against mine, but it was useless. He may have been more experienced, but I was stronger.

"He has every right to be skeptical and question your motives when he is putting the people he is responsible for—the people he *cares* about—around someone who can do exactly what I can, right now."

His face and eyes reddened as my Imperium Gift continued to manipulate his blood. I sent it through his body, wrapping around his lungs and heart, not to cause him harm, but just to remind him that I could. One small slip and Brandle would cease to exist. My Gift urged me to do it—to hold his life in my hands while I took it. To savor the way his organs would feel as they shriveled beneath my power.

At the sight of the small drip of blood from his nostril, I took a deep breath and released my hold. Brandle fell forward, his head hitting the table as he gasped for air.

"Evander may not like you, Brandle," I told the prince, and he weakly picked his head up to meet my stare. "But he's offered you shelter, safety, and is entrusting you with the care and training of his Soul Bonded. I'd call that a fucking win."

Brandle's heavy breathing matched my own as he pushed his head off the table and settled back into his chair. I hurriedly shoved my Gift back through its door, making sure to call my shadows forth the second the Imperium was locked away. I had never been more grateful that we could only access one Gift at a time.

Evander's shadows slipped beneath my shirt, skirting up and down my spine in comfort as his hand splayed along my lower back. Another deep and steadying breath in and out, and I focused on Brandle again.

"You either stay or go," I said, keeping my voice low and my eyes locked on his. "But if you choose to remain, then I suggest you learn your place." Brandle didn't respond, but I could see the fear and contemplation in his eyes. "I'll require an answer by tomorrow. For now, you're dismissed."

He didn't argue or offer a single thought as the room stayed wholly silent.

Brandle stood slowly, wincing as he hobbled around his chair. Lia's subtly raised hand caught my eye, and I offered her a single nod without looking. She quickly pushed away from the table and hurried to the prince, slinging his arm over her shoulder as she helped him to the exit.

They stopped just before passing through as Brandle bent and whispered something into Lia's ear. She nodded, ducked beneath his arm, and strolled back to the table to retrieve his half-eaten plate. I raised a brow and she apologetically mouthed *he's hungry*, before rushing back to his side.

I closed my eyes against the bubbling irritation with the Prince of Ministro and focused on Evander's shadows trailing along my flesh, letting it clear my raging mind the way it always did.

"Thank you," I breathed, only loud enough for him to hear, and let my lids flutter open...

To find Lia once again at the table, this time scraping the potatoes from Jahier's plate onto Brandle's.

"Lia..." I growled in warning.

"I know, I know. We're leaving—right now," she said quickly and ran back to him as she struggled to keep all of the potatoes on the plate. He said something to her again, but she shook her head vehemently.

"Why?" I heard Brandle say.

"Because you don't deserve dessert. Now let's go!" she whisper yelled back, pulling him over the threshold and out of the kitchen.

Gods fucking help me.

I heard Felix snicker, but I paid him no mind as Evander pulled my hands from the table and spun me to face him. He interlaced our fingers out of both love and the desire to help conceal the fact that mine were trembling. I didn't put my shadows away, keeping them twisting over our conjoined hands as my Imperium Gift continued to bang at its door.

He pressed his lips to my forehead, and I closed my eyes against the touch as he said, "I'm proud of you."

"Because I hurt Brandle or because I defended you?"

I moved my fingers out of his hold now that the shaking had eased and held onto his wrists instead, running my thumb back and forth over his silver bracelet with encrusted black stones that matched my necklace. I traced the delicate etching of the bird that was the symbol for Tenebrae—A species said to always be able to lead you home no matter how lost you are. I wondered if that applied to more than just a physical location. If those birds could lead your mind away from the darkness and back to the light.

He smiled against my skin. "I was going to say because you called your Gift back on your own, but I'll add those to the continuously growing list, too." He kissed my forehead again before pulling back to look at me with a wide grin, his dimples making my stomach flip at the sight.

I held onto his piercing stare, letting it keep me anchored as I added another lock to my Imperium's door.

49
Felix

I tried like hell to remain the professional advisor that I was. Even when Kenji's stare was burning a brand into the side of my head. I knew what he wanted—knew that the moment I made eye contact with him, I'd have to acknowledge what transpired between us.

He cleared his throat softly, but I stayed focused on the tender moment passing between Ainsley and Evander. Stayed focused on the way his thumbs gently swept over the backs of her hands, and how his lips pressed into her forehead again and again as he helped her reign in the anger I could feel still whirling around her. Stayed focused on—

He cleared his throat again, this time loudly. My eyes fluttered as I drew in a deep breath and reluctantly shifted my attention to the smug soldier sitting across from me with an arm draped over the back of Marce's chair.

Kenji wore a crooked grin as he raised a brow in expectation. I offered a tight smile before reaching into my pocket and pulling out two gold coins. Without drawing too much attention to myself, I slid them across the dining room table through the spilled wine no one had bothered to tend to yet. He tipped an invisible hat to me and pocketed his bullshit win.

The moment Brandle had opened his mouth earlier, my pocket tingled from magic—an indicator I had an unread message. I pulled out the transfer paper and read the note Kenji had scribbled from across the table, propositioning me with a wager.

He assumed Ainsley and Brandle would go toe to toe, and bet one gold coin that the Prince of Ministro would come out the victor. I knew better than to bet against my best friend; not only because she would kill me if she ever found out, but because I knew *her*. Knew her temper and her lack of control over it.

Gladly, I took that wager.

Where it all went wrong for me was when Kenji offered to raise the stakes by two additional coins. Ainsley's tongue was brutal, but she rarely ever won with her sharp words alone, always calling forth the assistance of her Gift to finish the job. The question was, which form of magic would she use?

Her shadows were always her first choice, but unless she crafted a dagger and threw it at him, they wouldn't do much damage. Her Obscure on the other hand...

I practically snorted when Kenji chose her Imperium given her blatant refusal to call it forth not five minutes prior. It was going to be the easiest three coins I'd ever won without cheating, until Ainsley had to go and ruin it all.

"So you're just going to kick him out?!" Elenora demanded, shooting to her feet and breaking the relative quiet we all had just reached.

Dash attempted to touch her arm, but she shook him off, her eyes firmly on the king and queen across the table.

"Ainsley gave him a choice. What he decides is up to him," Evander said with deadly calm as he held onto his wife.

"He's injured! He needs Lia and Sirona to continue looking after him. You can't just send him away!"

Evander shrugged, the lack of concern clear in his casual demeanor. "I'm sure he'll factor that into his consideration."

Elenora's hands balled into fists at her side as her eyes shifted back and forth between Ainsley and Evander as if she couldn't decide who to settle her furious stare upon. Finally, she shook her head and stormed around the table and out of the kitchen. Dash quickly followed after her without a word.

Tallis sighed heavily before offering the king and queen a sympathetic smile. "He's her best friend," he explained.

It was Ainsley who answered this time. "I'd be disappointed if she didn't try to defend him."

Tallis nodded in appreciation before twisting his hand in front of him and pulling the large tome Ainsley had stolen from Caelum from thin air. "Since dinner seems to be over, I guess it's time to give you this."

We huddled around the massive map of Disparya displayed across a table in the study as Ainsley flipped through the book, comparing it to the detailed pages of notes the scholars of Agnitio had written about the translation.

"You were correct in your assumption about Solum," Tallis announced. Ainsley gave a questioning grunt but didn't pick her gaze up from the book. "But from what we can tell it's describing a location, not a bond."

"Where our wolves descend from," she answered, her finger moving back and forth along the text. "There's an old map with it somewhere in this study. I remember seeing it during one of Van's boring history lessons." She finally picked her head up and her gaze immediately found her husband's. "Find it for us?" Ainsley didn't wait for a reply, dipping her head back down to read.

Oli and I hurried over to help Evander sift through the ancient maps, each of us delicately unrolling the parchment in search of the one Ainsley was after. It took nearly twenty minutes before I came across a map so tattered and worn that the barest pressure would tear the paper.

With Oli's help, we carefully laid it across the table and spread it out. There, nestled within a mountain range, marked the words *Solum Pass*.

"Is this it, cupcake?" I asked as I looked over the map.

It looked like Disparya, yet didn't. There were landforms, towns, rivers, and boundaries that no longer existed or were changed entirely. My finger traced a prominent mountain range in Caelum that I knew to be on the western coast, yet this map showed it ran along the northern border that touched Ministro. No such landforms there currently existed.

Ainsley appeared at my side a heartbeat later, the book and papers clutched to her chest.

"Yes!" she said, pointing to the *Solum Pass*.

Everyone hurried over to the table and peered at the chart that seemed to be older than time itself, displaying locations that predated anything I'd ever learned about.

"How old is this?" Kenji asked, pointing to a large body of water in eastern Tenebrae. "There isn't anything like this here."

Evander shrugged as he exchanged a look with Tallis. "My ancestors were given this map from his," he said, gesturing to the King of Agnitio who appeared to have no clue as to the map's origins either.

"The titles are all related to lore," Marce commented as she traced her fingers along the ink. "Many of these locations are named for the Gods and Goddesses that are said to have created our world—not just Disparya."

I looked over the chart but was familiar only with the ones who were said to have created our continent. As Perceval's advisor, I was trained in the history of the Gods and our land, but rarely the world itself. Other continents existed, but I wasn't educated about them or the magic their people possessed besides what was described in the fairytales I've read—much like the stories about Inmuto.

"This predates even *my* knowledge," Tallis said, leaning close as he scanned the chart. "You may want to call on Sirona, Evander. With her experience as an Incantis, she'll know more about this than any of us."

Evander nodded and pulled a slip of transfer paper from his pocket to quickly write the note. I continued looking over the map, barely recognizing any of the landmarks in Caelum. Even the shape of the coast was drastically different than what I knew.

Ainsley squeezed herself in between Oli and me and laid a different map next to the ancient one we had found. We looked over them both, comparing the strange land to the current one and pointing out the vast differences between them—including the exclusion of the *Solum Pass*.

Where that landmark had once been in northern Tenebrae, there was nothing but an ocean now, and the only mountain range in that area was currently to the west. It was as if the peaks had simply gotten up and moved.

"This is where it was at some point—where it *should* still be," Ainsley said, placing her finger on the map where the water was. "And this," she continued, pointing to another location where Tenebrae met Venator and the Northern Sea, "Is where Van and I always feel a tugging." She ran her fingers over the drawing, exhaling deeply. "I can feel it even now."

"I feel it even more where the Solum Pass is on the older map," Evander said.

Ainsley nodded in agreement before adding, "I think the Solum Pass is still there and this mountain range connects to it. And I think we should go there instead of the camps to the north like we were planning." She directed the last statement to her husband.

"Nothing is there, Ainsley," Calidore said as he looked over the map. "Kenji and I have both been assigned to numerous camps that stretch that coastline."

"It's nothing but cliffs that drop directly into the ocean. There's no evidence that there was once a mountain range there at all—no rock formations or anything jutting up from the water," Kenji contributed.

"Exactly," Cal said. "Maybe this is just inaccurate. Something drawn up before the continent was fully discovered."

They had a point. If there had truly been a landform of that stature, there would be evidence of it even today. And given all of the errors on the map, their argument was the most logical one. But Ainsley shook her head.

"No," she said, looking over the crowd. "There's something here. I can't explain it, but I can *feel* it. I wouldn't be risking time we don't have if I didn't believe in this fully."

Evander came to her side and placed a comforting hand on her shoulder. Ainsley swallowed hard as she looked up at him, her eyes so big and pleading that it broke my heart.

"You believe me, right?" she asked, her voice breaking slightly.

He cupped her face and pressed his forehead against hers. "I trust your instincts, love. If that's where you want to go, then we will." She nodded and claimed his lips, kissing him softly as she smiled.

My heart lodged in my throat as I watched them so happy and in love. There was a time I didn't think Ainsley would ever recover from her heartbreak—ever *want* to love again. As much as I couldn't stand the man she chose, I would be forever grateful to him for holding the pieces as she picked them up. For standing at her side, handing them to her one by one as she learned how to fit them back together. And for loving her unconditionally through every mishap and mistake, every angry outburst and attempt to run.

Even now, when tensions and unease leaked through every crack and crevice in this room, I sensed nothing but the utmost faith from him. He trusted her entirely, with everything he was, and it was exactly what she deserved.

"Can you look ahead and *see* what we find?" Ainsley asked, pulling back from Evander and settling her attention on Tallis who was still studying the map.

"I'm afraid my Seer Gift doesn't quite work that way," he answered and righted himself. "Once a decision is made, I can see how an event will unfold to a certain point."

Tallis braced his hands on the edge of the table for support and took several deep breaths as he readied himself. His pupils dilated and I gripped Oli's hand to keep steady, knowing exactly what was about to happen.

"What are you doing?" Evander demanded as the room began to tremble beneath our feet.

Tallis'ss deep olive skin stretched over his knuckles, his muscles shaking as his copper irises were swallowed completely by black. The table shook and furniture rattled as paintings plummeted from the walls and crashed to the floors.

"Showing you my Obscure," he said through clenched teeth.

And then everything around us changed.

50

Felix

The view continuously flickered, alternating between the current room and the envisioned scene that Tallis was attempting to present to us. Utilizing his Obscure ability with a single individual alone was an immense display of power and strength, not to mention the challenge of doing so with every individual gathered around the table.

I called for my Magusier Gift and focused it on his magic level. It was currently lower than I had ever seen from him during our training sessions as I learned to access my Gift's abilities, hovering above his baseline, but not dangerously close.

Finally, the view became stable and we found ourselves no longer situated within the study of our residence, but rather amidst a landscape of debris. I instinctively brought my hand to my mouth and nose, trying to shield myself from the putrid and smoky smell of decomposing flesh that pervaded the air. Everywhere we looked, there was death and destruction.

A village was left in ruins, with houses reduced to rubble and small fires scattered throughout, extinguishing any remaining signs of life. The acrid flavor of ash lingered on my tongue as I averted my gaze from the smoke and the large stack of charred remains at my back.

Ainsley knelt and gently brushed her hand over the small children's toy buried in the debris as she said, "Is this the future you *saw* for us?"

I carefully observed my surroundings, attempting to determine our exact whereabouts, but there were no distinctive indications at first. The smoke rendered the sky completely dark, blotting out the sun, and the horizon appeared as a dense, hazy grey, obstructing my view of anything in the distance.

"Yes," Tallis answered mournfully, "And this is what I *saw* after William was killed."

Only a single flicker and our surroundings displayed the same scene, but an unmistakable coldness filled the air that wasn't there previously. As I moved closer for a clearer view, I heard a crunch under my boot. Glancing down, I observed a delicate layer of snow enveloping the earth. Everything was unchanged, except this particular scene now unfolded at a different moment in time.

I swallowed thickly, my heart pounding in my ears as I noticed the remains poking through the snow, demanding to be seen despite my reluctance. All around me, decaying flesh was stretched over exposed bones, some bodies more gruesome than others. Belongings were also scattered amongst the dead, ranging from basic household tools to clothing and weapons that proved useless in this fight.

My eyes watered and my chest tightened to the point of pain as I turned away from the artifacts.

"Where are we?" Ainsley asked.

"I'm not entirely sure," Tallis remarked, none of them hearing me as I whispered the answer beneath a strained breath.

A brilliant burst of light flooded my sight, prompting me to shield my eyes from the glaring brightness. When I looked around again, I noticed that our surroundings had altered once more, returning us to the study.

"Are you okay?" Ainsley asked as she rushed to Tallis.

He raised his hand to halt her, his chest heaving and body trembling while clutching the table's edge. "I just need a minute," he said through labored breaths.

Evander emerged from his shadows at Tallis's side, promptly placing a glass of water beside his fellow king. Tallis dipped his head in gratitude and drained the contents at once.

"If you wouldn't mind, could you please provide me with a chair?" Tallis politely requested. Evander immediately obliged, assisting the King of Agnitio in seating himself before replenishing his water and presenting it to him again.

He took another sip and then set his gaze on the quiet room. "The future only alters after a decision has been made," Tallis explained, holding the glass firm between his hands. "I cannot *see* if you find the Solum Pass or Inmuto, only that you will search for it. A choice to go left at a fork instead of right would change the path of your future. Until those decisions are made, I'm blind to the outcome."

Ainsley's posture deflated, her hopeful eyes dimming to bitter acceptance. There would be no way to know if this mission of hers would be for nothing. I moved behind my friend, wrapping my arms around her shoulders and pulling her against me.

"I trust your instincts, too," I reassured and gingerly kissed her cheek.

Ainsley didn't respond, instead twisting her head to peer back over the map as if the answers would appear simply because she willed it hard enough. Though she kept a firm grip on her emotions and a shield up to prevent me from accessing them, I knew she wasn't entirely okay. Her body was tense in my arms and her heart hammered loud enough for my immortal ears to pick up. I looked to Evander, hoping he would sense her distress too.

"It's been a long day. Why don't we all get some rest?" Evander said, extending a hand to his wife.

"But what about the map and Sirona? We still haven't figured out—"

"She wrote back to let me know she'll be here first thing in the morning," he cut in. "Let's give ourselves a break so we can come back refreshed. Maybe we'll see something we hadn't before."

Ainsley looked at the map once more before hesitantly nodding and stepping out of my hold to take his hand. Everyone slowly cleared out of the room, until Oli and I were the only two left. I rested my hands on the table, glancing over the worn charts and shaking my head.

"Do you think she'll find it? The stones, Inmuto—whatever the hell it is she's searching for?" I asked.

Olivier was quiet for a moment before prying my hands away from the table and spinning me to face him. His fingers skated softly down my arms, tracing my muscles until he found my wrists. He guided them to rest over his shoulders and his grip went to my waist, pulling our bodies flush.

"I think Ainsley is a lot like her parents," Oli replied, pressing a tender kiss to one cheek and then the other. "Julien was intelligent, tenacious, and clever. And Viviette was loving, stubborn, and never knew when to give up. My sister is a perfect mix of the two." I smiled as he kissed my forehead and then the tip of my nose. "If anyone can find a kingdom said to have never existed, it's her."

With a grunt of agreement, I nodded.

"And if she doesn't," he continued, "After we win this war, she'll just designate a portion of Tenebrae to be called Inmuto out of spite."

His lips crashed to mine, swallowing the sound of my laugh at his perfect observation of our queen. Oli was right, of course. If anyone could find what we needed, it was Ainsley and the man who would be at her side every step of the way. Not just to support her, but to find it first so he could hold that fact over her head for the rest of her life.

"You seem off," Oli observed, pulling his face from mine. It was ironic that as a trained Empathi I could manipulate anyone's emotions, yet never seemed to master my own around him.

"What Tallis showed us..." I trailed off as flashes of the decimated town sprang to life in my mind.

"I know." He placed another quick kiss on my cheek. "But I don't want to think about that tonight. Besides, I'm pretty sure I still have a lot of making up to do for this afternoon." A devilish grin curved the edge of his mouth and my chest twisted at the sight.

Belongings scattered in snow surged to the forefront of my thoughts and I blinked rapidly to clear them.

"Are you okay?"

"Yeah," I lied. "I'm just tired. Any chance I can take you up on the offer another time?"

"Are you sure you're—"

"I'm as fine as I can be, Oli. I promise." He examined me skeptically, but as always, didn't push the subject. I tightened my hold, bringing him closer again until our faces were barely an inch apart. "I just want to hold each other tonight."

"I think I can arrange that," he said, before bringing his lips to mine.

I let the kiss consume me—let it wash away the images of crumbled homes and destroyed land. Of charred remains so mutilated, the victim had to have suffered an unimaginable death. And as Oli kissed me harder, I begged for it to take away the image of the dagger that body had been clutching.

The very one currently fastened to the thigh of the man I loved.

As promised, Sirona arrived but was unable to provide any further insight apart from confirming Marce's accuracy regarding the titles on the map being named after deities of the world. During her time as an Incantis, she received training in such matters. However, the society emphasized their devotion and communication solely with the Gods responsible for Disparya. It was regarded as an act of blasphemy to mention any others.

She promised to conduct research on the ancient map after the meeting and inform us of any new findings.

That was three days ago.

I stood over Ainsley's sleeping form, regretting my brilliant idea.

"Pssst," I whispered into the early morning, but she didn't wake. "Ainsley..." Still, nothing.

I grabbed a dagger from the top of her dresser, then immediately put it down as I thought better of it. Perhaps it would have been wiser to refrain from prodding the famously cranky queen with a blade. A deep sigh escaped from me. I'd risk my hand then.

With bated breath, I gently nudged her. "Ainsley..." I whispered. Nothing. I groaned softly and then poked harder. "Ainsley..."

A shroud of darkness erupted from her, enveloping my wrist and forcibly twisting it backward, causing me to collapse to the floor in excruciating pain as a sob escaped me, merging with the resonant chuckles emitted by Evander.

"Felix?!" Ainsley demanded, calling for her Obscure to release me. "What the hell are you doing here? Is everything okay? Did something happen?" The magic that enveloped me dissipated and returned to her as she attempted to rise, only to be forcefully pushed back down by Evander.

He buried his face against the back of her neck again as he spoke. "Nothing's wrong. He's been standing there for the past five minutes trying to wake you," he mumbled.

"You knew I was here and didn't say anything?"

"You weren't calling for *me*," he argued sleepily, tightening his hold around his wife.

Before I could mutter a derogatory remark, Ainsley inquired, "Once again, what are you doing here? I could have hurt you."

I gently massaged my aching wrist. "You already did," I argued, glaring at the visible part of Evander's head. He was such an asshole. "We were wondering if you wanted to have an early breakfast with us."

"Us?"

I angled my chin toward the other side of the room where Dash stood leaning against the doorframe, utterly quiet and no help at all. Upon revealing my plan to him this morning, he responded with laughter and informed me that his only intention for accompanying me was to witness my attempts to rouse Ainsley. It was evident to both of us that the consequences could range from injury to loss of life. She was *not* a morning person, but Trio Time was worth the risk.

"She can't," Evander said.

"She can," Ainsley corrected as she fought against his hold, her face brightening with a smile.

"I'm comfortable."

"I don't care. Go cuddle with Nova." Ainsley wiggled free, sitting up and smoothing her hair before slipping from the bed. "Wait, where is she?"

I traced the queen's gaze to locate the vacant corner of the room where Nova usually slept. The black wolf, who had been pretending to be asleep this entire time, perked up from his spot at the end of the bed.

"In my room," Dash admitted sheepishly. "I tried to get her to leave but she wouldn't."

Onyx propelled himself off the bed, accompanied by a guttural growl emanating from his throat. With bared teeth, he rushed across the room, forcefully passing Dash, and proceeded into the hall. Like his owner, he was also an asshole.

"Give me two minutes," Ainsley said as she sprinted into the bathing room, slamming the door behind her and leaving Evander, Dash, and me alone.

Because for some reason, she thought that was a good idea...

Time passed in an uncomfortable silence as Evander elegantly emerged from the sheets and made his way to the dresser. He rummaged through it, eventually retrieving a dark shirt, and tugged it over his head before coming over to sit on the edge of the bed and glare at the two of us.

"Ainsley," I exclaimed as the silence grew unbearable.

"Two minutes!" she yelled.

"You said that five minutes ago."

She didn't respond and all was quiet again.

Another minute ticked by and Onyx stomped into the room, his ears and tail low as he jumped onto the bed and sat stoically next to his master. Nova padded in next, stopping at Dash to affectionately lick his hand before sauntering over to the bed. In a swift motion, she jumped onto it, joining Evander on his other side as she locked eyes with him. He arched an inquisitive brow and she licked his cheek in answer.

"Traitor," he murmured, yet still proceeded to scratch behind her ears.

She reclined and nestled beside him, disregarding Onyx's persistent snarls aimed at her. Clearly, there was a dispute happening that she had no interest in being a part of. I suppressed my smile upon realizing the striking similarity in demeanor and attitude between her and her owner.

"Love..." Evander called.

"I said *two minutes*!" she snapped. He drooped his head and firmly pinched the bridge of his nose as a collective sigh of frustration escaped the three of us.

After several additional minutes elapsed, I reached my breaking point. Waiting patiently—*silently*—was never my forte. I cast a questioning look at Dash, subtly conveying my intentions. He shook his head, imploring me to reconsider.

I would not.

"You could have told her I was here," I said to Van.

He stopped petting his wolf and deliberately turned his head to me. "And miss out on seeing her hurt you?" His eyes dropped to the hand I still clutched.

Gods, I was so over his shit. "Do you remember that one time I saved your wife's life, nearly losing my own?" I drew nearer, locking gazes with him as I crossed my arms over my chest and tilted my head. "Or how about when I brought her to you in the first place?"

Evander mirrored my movements, his brow furrowing in puzzlement. "Was that before or after the two of you poisoned her and plotted to steal her magic?" he quipped. "I apologize, I'm always hazy on the timeline."

I marched towards him as he promptly got up, his shadowed tattoo slithering down his bare arms.

"Nope," Ainsley interjected, finally emerging from the bathing room. "We are *not* doing this."

She quickly placed herself between the two of us, her hand going flat against Evander's chest as he bared his teeth to me.

"He started it," he argued, pointing in my direction. I covertly extended my middle finger behind Ainsley's back and promptly retracted it before she directed her attention towards me.

"I doubt that," she said, and gave Evander a flat look.

The King of Tenebrae regarded his wife with disbelief, his mouth agape as if to object, but she shook her head, putting a stop to his attempt. He tightly sealed his lips, giving me a final menacing look before running his hand through his hair and relinquishing the argument.

"Training starts at noon," he grumbled.

"We won't be late," she replied and turned her cheek just as Evander leaned down to kiss her.

The moment we stepped into the hallway, I wore a beaming smile and casually draped my arm around Ainsley, filled with excitement for the morning ahead with my two best friends.

And that display of affection was reciprocated by a sucker punch to the stomach.

I doubled over, my arms going around my middle from the unexpected blow. "Don't be a dick to him," she ordered before stepping past me and continuing in the direction of the kitchen.

I gulped down the air while working to right myself. She had put a significant amount of her power behind that punch, evident by the bruise I could feel already forming on my flesh. Dash firmly placed his hand on my back, delivering a forceful slap as he moved past me to follow Ainsley's trail.

"I told you not to talk to him," he called over his shoulder. Whatever.

51

Ainsley

"That's not what happened!" I argued while Felix's fingers moved through my hair, meticulously weaving the strands together. "I already told you both—I fell." My eyes squeezed shut against the bright sun as he yanked down on the braid, forcing me to tilt my chin to the sky.

"Right..." he replied, stretching out the vowel.

"How?" Dash cut in. I glanced at him with one eye slightly open, silently asking for clarification. "What made you fall?"

"I must have tripped on a rock or something."

"By the lake," he verified.

"Hence why I was wet and covered in filth."

He pressed his lips together and gave a nod filled with skepticism. The two had been on my case since I returned home the other morning drenched and coated in a thick layer of muck. When I told them why, they refused to accept my explanation as truth.

"And the feathers?" Felix added.

Shit. I really didn't like where this questioning was headed. I cleared my throat and straightened my posture just as Felix uttered a curse for forgetting a band to secure my hair.

"They must have been stuck in the mud and transferred to me when—"

"You fell," Dash finished.

I lowered my chin and opened my eyes as Felix moved from behind me. As soon as he released his grip, my hair flowed gracefully down my shoulder, undoing the hard work he had put in. I tucked the copper strands behind my ears and reclined, propping myself up on my elbows.

"Exactly," I replied.

"Mmmm," Dash said, not buying a single word. "And the reason you had a whole loaf of bread with you was in case you got hungry on the walk?"

"Obviously."

"But you didn't get hungry," Felix pointed out.

I cast a gaze over my right shoulder and observed him reclining on the blanket, hands situated behind his head, and eyes peacefully closed—a mirror image of Dash's current position.

"So?" I said.

"So we find it interesting that in all the time we've known you, there hasn't been a single instance you've been around bread and not taken at least one bite," Dash contributed. He opened an eye to peer up at me and grinned.

My mouth dropped open, and I stuttered through a response that was nothing but sounds that I couldn't formulate into words. He grinned even wider, knowing I didn't have a defense.

Conceding, I dragged a frustrated hand down my face. "I just don't understand why they won't let me feed them! Every time I get close, they attack."

An arm draped around me, and I twisted to find Felix now sitting up. He patted the top of my head with his free hand as he said, "Then take that as your sign to leave the geese alone."

Groaning, I shoved away from him and laid back down on the blanket next to Dash. I turned over to face the King of Caelum, making my eyes as big and sad as possible in hopes he would take my side or offer assistance. However, he shook his head.

"Let the dream go, Ains," he whispered.

I rolled my eyes and sighed, fixing my attention back on the expansive blue overhead. Felix's shoulder brushed mine as he settled next to me, the three of us now lying side by side like we always used to. Breathing in their comforting scents, I sighed in contentment and happiness. It had been too long since we'd done this.

Picnics were an almost daily event during our time in Caelum, and we rarely spent any more time apart than required. We used to have a simpler, calmer life in the past, spending our days under the summer sun, laughing, playing games, and simply enjoying each other's presence. However, our schedule now primarily revolved around training, strategy meetings, and discussions about war.

"I can't believe this is the last day we have together," Felix said through the comforting silence. Our week of training had come and gone entirely too fast.

"Don't be so dramatic. It's only for a month," Dash argued.

It still felt like too long of a separation, especially since Felix would be remaining in Tenebrae this time. Once again, Dash would be by himself.

"I could always come for a couple of weeks," Felix suggested, his mind seeming to be in the same place mine was. "We could hang out and catch up some more. Plus we still have to celebrate your birthday since I missed it being *dead* and all."

"Maybe another time. Elenora and I will be busy the next few weeks getting everything under control at the palace."

Felix and I exchanged curious glances at the news. "She's going with you?" I asked.

"Yeah. She offered to help in whatever way she could."

"I bet she did," Felix whispered.

"*Just friends* my ass," I replied and then rolled to face Felix. I let a silencing shield expand over just the two of us as I raised a skeptical brow. "She's going back with him."

Felix shrugged as he said, "It seems that way."

"Why?"

He gave a look that said I should know *exactly* why. I rolled my eyes. "He's known her for like a week." For some reason, my tone came out harsher than I intended.

"First of all, like that would ever stop Dash. And second, they've known each other since they were children, Creampuff. The three of us used to spend a lot of time together whenever she and Tallis would visit Caelum."

That didn't make me feel any better.

Dropping the shield, I reached into my pocket, pulled out a slip of transfer paper, and scribbled a quick note. Felix craned his neck as he peered at my request just as the ink disappeared. '*Imogen?*' he mouthed, and I nodded. We waited in silence as the seconds passed until black swirls formed the response.

I'm not your spy.

Groaning, I tucked the paper away. I'd have to learn about Dash and Elenora's blooming relationship another way since no one seemed to want to tell me. With a heavy sigh, I got to my feet, placing my hands on my hips as I surveyed our surroundings.

Felix had chosen a cozy spot in a meadow enclosed by trees a short walk from the house—the place where I had met Onyx and Nova. It was also the first time I had ever willingly called my magic forward.

So much had changed since then. I was no longer the brokenhearted girl who had nothing and was too afraid to embrace what she was. And now I had magic, friends, family, a kingdom, and love. I had everything I could ever want, and it made me that much more terrified to lose it.

A flash of moving white between the trees caught my eye, and my head snapped in its direction. Squinting, I peered into the distance but found nothing out of the ordinary.

"You okay?" Dash asked, rising to his feet, his line of sight following mine.

"Yeah," I replied as I continued watching the forest. "I thought I saw something." The temperature around us plummeted as Dash called his Unda Gift forward in preparation. "It was probably just an animal," I reasoned and directed my focus to him and Felix. "We should get going anyway. It's almost noon and Van will kill us if we're late."

Quickly, we packed our belongings and made our way toward the house. But no matter how hard I tried, I couldn't stop my eyes from slipping to the trees.

Evander stood in the center of the sparring ring with Tallis at his side while the rest of us gathered around the perimeter. Over the past week, we had engaged in other training activities besides the tavern. Elenora and Tallis taught us useful tips on how to read people; how to pick up subtle clues in body movements and breathing habits that indicate when a lie is being told.

But Jahier's orchestrated training session a few days ago was by far the worst.

His Gifts as an Oculi and Sonor allowed him to see and hear things from distances no one else could. And though he didn't possess the Gift of the Venari, his father ensured he was trained in all areas of stealth.

Jahier's planned lesson had seemed simple enough: retrieve the flag that was hanging at the opposite end of the field. We had to do so without being caught and could not use any magic during our turn.

One by one we crept up to the meadow's edge, and one by one, we received a ball of ice to the face, stomach, or back, not two steps into the grass. Dash was far too enthusiastic about contributing the weapon that left a blooming bruise on my cheek, my spine, and my ass. We had all failed miserably, including Evander, which kept him pissed off that entire day.

After an hour of the onslaught, Jahier ended the session, proclaiming we were all worthless and needed to think outside of the box. That we needed to learn how to adapt to our situation and solve the problem. I was determined to be the first to complete his challenge when we tried it again next month.

"When your name is called, step into the ring to fight," Evander announced, his voice booming over the expectant crowd. "You'll be matched based on skill and experience."

"However, you may be paired with someone who exceeds your level in both areas," Tallis added. "Use this as a learning opportunity to gauge where improvements are needed. You won't progress unless challenged."

Van turned and pointed to the weapons that were neatly set up in the equipment area. "You may select anything you'd like, but you're encouraged to use your magic in conjunction. If you possess multiple Gifts, you'll want to alter them as well. It'll use up more of your energy, but the more you train yourself, the faster your stamina will grow."

The King of Tenebrae scanned the crowd, slowly sizing up everyone in attendance. While Felix, Dash, and I were enjoying our morning, he traversed to the palace to pick up Delyth and Ezra so they could partake in today's training. Of course, when Rosella caught wind of that, she wrote Dash and demanded to be brought to the house as well. She didn't want to participate in the fighting but claimed it would be beneficial for her to observe it. I didn't see how, but nonetheless, Dash gave in to her request.

After a moment, he leaned to his right and whispered low to his fellow king. Tallis nodded in agreement and cleared his throat before declaring, "Olivier and Calidore will go first."

The two kings strolled out of the ring as Cal and Oli headed for the weapons table. Each carefully selected a longsword and then made their way to the center.

"How are we declaring a winner?" Oli questioned as he twisted his wrist, spinning the sword skillfully.

"The fight won't end until someone either crosses over the boundary, falls unconscious, or concedes," Evander declared.

Oli and Cal grinned wickedly as they said, "Unconscious it is," in unison, and ran at each other.

Metal clashed, mixing with the sound of their laughter as they tried to best one another. The two advisors had been friends and fought together for decades, their tactics and strategies completely known to the other. They were perfectly equal in nearly every way.

Cal lunged and Oli jumped back, narrowly evading the blade as he crafted a dagger and flung it at his opponent. Calidore leapt to the ground and rolled, quickly jumping back to his feet with a smile on his face. Felix's boyfriend used his shadows to craft another sword before thinking better of it and calling back the magic.

"How often can you do that?" Dash asked. I turned to him with pinched brows. "Make the shadows come and go," he clarified while attempting to mime the action.

Smiling, I held up my palm. Darkness swirled there, collecting until a dagger appeared. I passed it to him, and as he examined it, I summoned the magic back, causing the weapon to dissipate into shadows within his hand.

"Most Shadow Shifters can have their creations returned to their original state within the first few hours. After that, they stay permanently in their crafted form. Of course, the length of time always depends on the strength of the wielder."

"How long can you do it for?" he asked.

"The dagger that rests on my dresser is the first one I ever crafted. It's several months old and I can still feel the pull to return it to the shadows. Oli and Marce are up to a week on their creations, and Van has a sword he made at fifteen that can still be called back."

He bobbed his head thoughtfully as I spoke, his eyes still on the shadows in his palm. My mind traveled back to a time when I stood on a balcony beneath the summer sun. Smiling, I directed my magic to gather and form into a twirling ball of darkness. Dash smirked and threw me a sidelong glance.

"Now we're even," I explained.

Before Dash could reply, the moment was interrupted by Olivier swearing loudly. I turned my attention back to the fight at hand to find Cal smiling victoriously as Oli stood just a step outside the painted edge of the circle.

"We agreed to a knockout!" Olivier argued.

Cal shrugged and walked his sword back to the weapons table. "It was taking too long," he said. "Plus, you're just pissed you didn't think of it first."

Oli snorted but didn't offer a retort as he tossed his sword amongst the others and strolled back to the crowd.

"Good job, baby!" Lia yelled, applauding wildly as she escorted Brandle across the lawn.

After the Prince of Ministro had decided to stay, he kept relatively quiet and to himself. I didn't much care for the man, but I couldn't deny that he was a valuable asset for our side, or that I was in desperate need of a tutor when it came to controlling my Gift.

"Elenora and Dashiell," Tallis announced next.

The two came forward and headed for the weapons. They stood at the table exchanging smiles, soft chuckles, and a whispered conversation that was far too low for me to hear. After a minute, Dash extended his hand and they shook—a wager made.

He stepped back from the table and held his hands behind his back as Elenora scanned her options. "Are you sure you want to do this?" she teased.

"Just pick," he replied.

Elenora shrugged and selected two long wooden staffs, one for each of them. She tossed Dash his and together they made their way into the center of the ring. "Last chance to change your mind," she offered with a glint in her eye.

Dash grinned and inspected his weapon. "I'll take my chances."

"Very well, then."

Elenora twisted her wrist, the staff picking up speed as she spun it around and around, moving it behind her back and above her head with expert precision. Her gaze stayed locked on Dash as she threw the rotating weapon high in the air and then caught it with one hand.

Everyone applauded at her display of skill and she gracefully bowed before tilting her head expectantly at the King of Caelum.

Dash cleared his throat and stepped forward to showcase his own skill with the staff. He inhaled and exhaled deeply, focusing all his concentration on the pending task. Slowly, he raised the wooden staff in his left hand and with one last deep breath, he tossed it to his right and then smirked.

Felix roared and applauded as Dash gracefully bowed and waved to his audience. "You're an idiot," Elenora remarked playfully.

"Never said I wasn't. You ready?" Dash took up a fighting stance, holding the staff across his body as he stared at the advisor.

"Are you?"

With that, Elenora lunged.

52
Ainsley

The Agnitian advisor was skilled in her craft, offering blow after blow that Dash narrowly evaded. She didn't let up, offering him no reprieve to collect his breath or thoughts before she struck again. In all the times I watched Dash and Felix spar, I had never seen them choose to do so with a wooden staff—a decision I'm sure the King of Caelum was thoroughly regretting as Elenora swept his feet with the stick, knocking him to his back.

Dash rolled as she slammed the tip of the weapon against the spot where he had just been, causing dirt particles to drift into the air. He jumped to his feet and thrust his hand forward, throwing a ball of water at her. She dove out of the way, allowing Dash the time and space he required to catch his breath and plan out his next move.

They circled, giving each other a wide birth as Elenora spun her stick tauntingly. "I warned you," she said through a smile. "You had a chance to back out."

Dash rolled his neck as his knuckles whitened over the staff. "And miss out on all this fun?"

She rushed him again, but he aimed another wave of water at her feet, causing her to call off the attack as he created more space between them.

"Are you just going to run from me the whole time?"

"Perhaps," he said and offered her a dazzling smile. She laughed, and Dash took that momentary distraction to attack.

He ran at her, putting her on the defense for the first time since the match began. Elenora skillfully blocked each strike until Dash finally let up and jumped back. She charged again, wanting to claim the offense, but he wouldn't let her, using his fire this time to create a line of flames between them.

"Scared?" she asked.

"Terrified," Dash replied cooly, remaining hidden from sight on the opposite side of his Gift.

The intense heat emanating from his flames gently brushed against the audience, making my brow bead with sweat. In an instant, the fire was extinguished as Dash swiftly lunged towards Elenora, their staffs colliding with a resounding clash as they resumed their battle.

He switched his magic yet again, this time opting for water and using it to force her back a few feet as he focused on catching his breath. He was using up his energy, but so was she.

"Felix?" I whispered.

"On it," he answered, and I waited as he accessed his Magusier Gift. "He's nowhere close to his baseline, but he's still exerting a lot of magic."

I acknowledged with a nod and stayed focused on the developing fight. Dash attempted to deceive Elenora by lunging left and then attacking right, but she wasn't fooled. Easily avoiding the blow, she swiftly struck his spine, resulting in him falling face-first onto the ground. Not only did she excel in speed, but she also outperformed him in skill with this specific weapon.

He got to his feet before she could land another strike. "Ready to concede?" Elenora questioned as she watched the King of Caelum wipe away the dirt from his face with his water magic.

"And why would I do that?"

She shrugged nonchalantly as she replied, "To save face. It's obvious you're going to lose."

A crooked grin appeared on the king's face. "Is it now?" Elenora didn't respond but offered a wink. "Well, in that case..."

Dash launched himself at her once again, performing the same failed move he had just executed. Just as Elenora was about to strike, he swiftly dropped to the ground, twisting and using his staff to sweep her legs out from under her. The Agnitian advisor's back hit the dirt, and Dash righted himself before backing away.

As she stood up, he raised the stick and began spinning it rapidly, mirroring what Elenora had done at the start. He skillfully maneuvered it behind his back, above his head, launched it into the air, and finally caught it with a single hand. The corners of my mouth curled upwards.

Elenora's display had been her downfall. Dash had accessed his Obscure at the start of their match, luring her into a false sense of security as he studied her moves, mastering them in his mind. And then he waited until she was already worn out to put them into play.

"Shall we begin?" Dash taunted.

He didn't wait for her to answer before he attacked.

Elenora tried her best, but Dash was relentless, refusing to let up an inch. There was no more calling his magic forth to give himself space—that had only been a trick designed for Elenora to believe she had the upper hand in this match.

She spun and evaded, but eventually, Dash's newly mastered skill was too much for her to overcome. With one last blow to her legs, she fell backward into the dirt. Before Elenora could even think about getting up, Dash was on her. He pinned her body down with his, moving his staff over her throat to keep her in place.

"If that's what losing looks like, sign me up," Marce mumbled, and Lia enthusiastically agreed.

I cleared my throat loudly, promptly shutting both of them up just as everyone else applauded. Dash pulled Elenora back to her feet and the two of them put their weapons away before joining the large group once again.

"Good job, Dashiell. Excellent use of all forms of your magic," Tallis announced. "Once your levels replenish, you'll be called back to the center. I'm eager to see more of your Obscure, as I think it could be extremely useful for our side."

"Not a problem," Dash replied as he took up his spot between Felix and me.

I scooted closer, my arm brushing his as I nudged him. "Couldn't win without cheating?" I teased.

"I won fair and square. It's not my fault you're just worried your Obscure will lose to mine."

"Please," I snorted. "If I recall correctly, the last time we sparred I had a sword to your chest without its help."

"Because you played me."

"And you underestimated me."

His lip quirked in the corner as he gave me a sidelong glance. "Touché," he said and we both faced forward as two more names were called into the ring.

53

Felix

As the hours passed, each participant had the opportunity to enter the ring and engage in combat on at least two separate occasions. Dash, on the other hand, had the unfortunate responsibility of being paired with nearly every individual. Without fail, he replicated his opponent's fighting style and emerged victorious. Regrettably, I was not as lucky.

My initial encounter, in which I was pitted against Marce, went exceedingly poorly. It started out fine, both of us engaged in a battle of swords, but then she managed to ensnare me with her Tremo Gift. Because of that, I found myself in the burned village from Tallis's vision, spending what felt like an hour mourning over the charred remnants and clutching the dagger I had discovered. As the images eventually dissipated, giving way to my actual surroundings, Marce appeared in front of me, brandishing her blade at my throat.

My match with Delyth had gone significantly better. However, her mastery of the wooden staff proved an insurmountable feat for me and my longsword, and she had me conceding within the first fifteen minutes.

"How much longer of this?" I whined as Ainsley and Evander met in the center of the ring sans weapons.

Oli glared at me from the corner of his eye. "Until we get an order that we're done. Now stop complaining and pay attention. Maybe you'll learn something so you don't lose so quickly next time."

With my mouth open in disbelief, I fixated my gaze upon him and his audacity. "You're not my boyfriend anymore."

A slight smile flickered across his lips. "I'm finally free?"

"Actually, no," I retorted, crossing my arms over my chest and shifting my attention towards Ainsley and Evander, who seemed to be engaged in a battle of words rather than weaponry. "You're stuck with me forever. That's your punishment."

"Dammit," he deadpanned. Our hands met, and together we observed our rulers engaging in a battle of insults instead of fists.

Ainsley continued to find creative ways to insinuate that everything her husband said and did was in order to compensate for his dick size. Furthermore, Evander seized every opportunity to highlight his wife's educational deficiencies and her inability to wield her magic effectively.

"Are they always this vicious?" Dash murmured softly.

A snort escaped me as I vigorously shook my head. "This is basically just foreplay for them." Dash stilled at my side and I immediately cursed myself for my callousness. "Dash, I—"

"It's fine," he replied, adjusting his stance as he continued watching the king and queen.

"Dash—"

"Really, Felix, it's okay."

Since our argument in Caelum, there had been no further discussion regarding Ainsley. That day in the sparring ring I had told Dash the truth of everything—of how I had come to know where she was truly from, and how I chose to keep that truth from him.

I knew that decision—that *betrayal*—had devastated him and put a damper on our relationship that I wasn't sure we'd ever fully recover from. He had been in love with Ainsley, more deeply than I had thought possible, and part of me had chosen not to bring her up in fear it would cause the pain of losing her to rush back into him.

The other part of me felt like an absolute asshole for not ensuring he was doing right by her.

"Is that so?" Evander teased, pulling my attention away from my thoughts.

"I guess we'll find out," Ainsley replied, and in a move as swift as changing tides, she crafted a dagger and thrust her hand forward.

Evander caught her by the wrist, the pointed tip of the steel blade a mere breath away from his shoulder. "You'll want to aim lower," he purred.

"My mistake." She uncurled her fingers, and the dagger plummeted between them. Ainsley quickly caught it with her free hand and lunged.

"NOT THAT LOW!" Evander exclaimed, leaping backward as his wife aimed for a spot I was confident she'd miss despite her earlier insults. She flashed a mischievous grin as two short swords appeared in her hands. In response, he mirrored the gesture by fashioning his own weapons and assuming a crouched stance. "Let's play, love."

⁕⁕⁕

The King and Queen of Tenebrae's battle waged on for longer than any of ours. Although Ainsley was lacking in skill and experience, she more than made up for it with her sheer determination and stubbornness. She knew Evander would hold a win over her head, and *he* knew that dragging the fight on for as long as possible would piss her off. He'd dangle that hope of victory in front of her just to take it away the second she got too close. Like I said—foreplay.

Eventually, he decided enough was enough and lured her into a false sense of security. When he traversed away, Ainsley moved to the spot she had expected he'd appear, just as he had done several times before. Once Evander did as predicted and stepped through the shadows with his back to her, she placed a knife against his throat.

"You almost had me," she said breathlessly, her chest heaving from exertion. Her husband smirked and then disappeared—not through his shadows, but just *vanished*. One second he was present and the next, Ainsley was holding her dagger against nothing but the thin spring air.

I surveyed the area, diligently scanning for any indications of Evander as a muted murmuring of worry engulfed the onlookers. But there was nothing I could discern. Just as I was about to address Ainsley, she became rigid. Her chin lifted and her throat flexed with a heavy swallow.

A steel blade, glistening under the sunlight, materialized along with an arm and the complete form of a towering, muscular body. "I still plan to, tonight," Evander whispered, leaning close to his wife's ear.

I was taken aback, my mouth agape and my eyes wide in astonishment, while the rest of the audience erupted into resounding applause.

"An illusion," Dash murmured. I turned to him, my brow furrowing in curiosity. "It's what Ainsley did to me and how she killed my father."

I had never seen the strength or skill of Evander's Illusio Gift. He would only utilize his illusions during Ainsley's training and very rarely ensnared me in them unless I pissed him off. Or made *her* angry enough that she allowed him to make me believe bees were chasing me through the house.

"You stole my move," Ainsley accused through clenched teeth.

"You stole mine first," he replied. "And then aimed for my dick."

The corners of her mouth turned upwards. "Whoops."

Evander summoned the dagger back into the shadows while Ainsley pivoted to face him. He skillfully glided his hands to her waist and then leaned down to kiss her. She immediately stepped out of his hold and turned, presenting her cheek to him instead, before rushing back over to our group.

The King of Tenebrae stood alone in the center of the ring as he stared after her, his features briefly betraying a mix of hurt, confusion, and frustration. With a clench of his jaw, he turned and retreated to the other side of the circle to stand with Tallis once again.

As the matches persisted, the sky overhead gradually transformed into a delicate orange and pink hue. My stomach rumbled as I rolled my neck, stretching out my sore muscles. The extensive sparring sessions had left me feeling hungry, weak, and severely lacking in both energy and magic. It became evident that Tallis and Evander had intended this from the beginning, with the goal of testing the limits of our bodies and magic.

Following a victorious match for the Prince of Venator, Jahier and Delyth departed the ring, clearing the way for Tallis to step forward. I held my breath, fervently wishing that his decision to enter the circle indicated he was going to offer his observations on the day's event and then order a dismissal. To my great disappointment, I was mistaken.

"Next up," the King of Agnitio announced, his voice reverberating across the open area. "Evander versus..." His gaze skimmed across every face before fixing upon the one he wanted. "Dashiell."

Ainsley tensed as the crowd grew quiet, everyone refraining from even the slightest breath. He had to have been joking. The air was thick with tension, accompanied by the pounding of Ainsley's heartbeat in my ears. A combination of anticipation and uneasiness permeated the spectators. The rival kings stepped into the ring and directed themselves towards the table containing the weapons.

"Do you really think that's a good idea?" Ainsley hissed, as Tallis settled to her right, ready to watch the performance.

A broad smile appeared on his face as he observed the men each choose a longsword and assume their positions at the center of the circle. "Oh, not at all," he replied with confidence, shifting his gaze towards her. "But I'm dying to see what happens." Before Ainsley could continue debating the matter, Tallis swiftly turned his attention to the figures across the space. "Begin!"

The fight didn't start quickly like the others had. The kings didn't engage in a clash of metal and brutality, running towards each other with weapons drawn. Nor did they immediately reach for their magic. They simply circled one another, watching, assessing, strategizing. Their battle unfolded gradually, with both fighters engaging in a series of strikes and defenses, meticulously observing each other for weaknesses and opportunities.

Eventually, Evander came to a stop and elegantly twirled his wrist, gracefully spinning his sword. Dash waited patiently, but when the King of Tenebrae didn't resume their careful battle, he asked, "Is something wrong?"

Evander let out an exasperated sigh of boredom. "This is usually when you use your Obscure on your opponent. I'm merely waiting for you to be finished."

"I appreciate the courtesy, but there's no need. I won't be calling it forth," he replied and assumed his fighting stance once more.

With a disapproving click of his tongue, the King of Tenebrae languidly aimed his sword at Dash. "You sure? You don't seem capable of winning anything without it."

I held my breath as Ainsley stiffened beside me. Deliberately, she rotated her head to direct a piercing glare at the amused King of Agnitio, who watched the exchange with just as much interest as everyone else. The spectators conversed softly among themselves, exchanging thoughts about the match and placing bets on a range of topics, including who the victor would be and how long the fight would last.

Glancing downward, I observed the dark tendril gracefully entwining Ainsley's fingers in a perpetual loop. Thank the Gods she was unable to call her Imperium Gift as long as her shadows were out to play. It wouldn't have come as a shock to discover that was her intention from the start.

Dash averted his gaze from Evander and the surrounding audience, his chest heaving with each deep breath. He was never quick to anger, always carefully considering situations and maintaining composure even during conflicts. But given Evander's obvious hatred for him since their first encounter, I wasn't sure how much longer he could keep himself composed.

"I'm sure," Dash eventually replied, dismissing Evander's insult as he refocused his gaze on him.

The King of Tenebrae casually dismissed the matter with a shrug. "Suit yourself," he declared, and the conflict resumed.

The kings began to engage more, focusing less on circling and more on clashing weapons. Their pace quickened with each successive attack, deftly avoiding the razor-sharp blades as they spun and deflected. Nearly a half hour passed, and neither successfully landed a blow.

Evander halted and took several steps back as he studied his opponent, likely trying to discern the best course to take. The King of Caelum was different from the other matches he faced today. Thanks to his Obscure, he had mastered various combat techniques, leaving Evander unable to figure out his next move.

Dash paced, focusing on the hilt spinning between his fingers as he patiently waited for the King of Tenebrae to join the fight again.

"Well, he seems... skilled," Lia murmured, and Marce concurred with a soft chuckle.

"If you think he's good with his hands, you should see what his tongue can do," Rosella added, just loud enough for everyone in the vicinity to hear. The sound of her voice caused Ainsley's teeth to audibly grind together. "Something Ainsley is well acquainted with," Rosella continued... because apparently, she wanted to die today.

In a calm manner, I firmly took hold of my best friend's hand, swiftly confiscated the dagger I knew she would craft, and strategically positioned her on my opposite side, ensuring she was now positioned between Oli and myself. Hopefully, he would add an extra line of defense in case her Obscure decided to make an appearance and shred Rosella into pieces. While I didn't necessarily have any objections to that, I was aware that finding a replacement for her would be a troublesome task for Dash, who was already burdened with stress.

"You *do* remember that, don't you, Ainsley?" Rosella inquired. With a firmer grasp on the queen's wrist, I shifted my body to speak to the advisor.

"If you enjoy breathing, I'd suggest you quit while you're ahead," I told her. Rosella's smile widened even more.

As I refocused on the ring, I noticed Evander's intense gaze fixed upon Ainsley, his eyes filled with darkness, his features tense, and a muscle twitching in his jaw. With a deliberate and gradual motion, he redirected his attention back to Dash. The ruler of Tenebrae inhaled deeply, releasing his grasp on the sword and allowing it to fall to the ground.

A moment before it clattered to the dirt, he disappeared into shadow.

Only one heartbeat passed before Evander emerged silently, poised to strike Dash with a shadowy wooden staff. In one swift motion, he swung his arms, knocking the King of Caelum to the ground before any of us could take a breath.

Employing the same technique he had used earlier with Elenora, Dash skillfully maneuvered to the left, evading the stick's forceful contact with the ground. He quickly rose to his feet and hastily retreated, diligently surveying the surroundings for the two abandoned blades resting on the ground. Evander disappeared once more.

This time, Dash spun, ready for the surprise attack, but Evander was clever and had anticipated his opponent's move. He reemerged behind him and firmly struck his foot into his spine, sending him flying forward.

Again, Evander traversed.

He had no intention of granting Dash a second to recover, breathe, or formulate a plan. He knew if he did, it would be his downfall, just as it was for everyone else who faced the King of Caelum today.

Evander suddenly appeared, raising his knee to strike Dash's ribs, but my oldest friend successfully defended and retaliated with a powerful right hook, connecting with Evander's jaw instead. The King of Tenebrae stumbled back a step, his hand pressing to his face as his tongue swept over his split lip. Both men locked eyes, emanating intense anger, as Dash positioned himself ready for combat. Evander bared his teeth and did the same. It was decided that there was no longer a need for weapons.

The kings ran for each other.

Ainsley bounced on the balls of her feet, her shadows swirling faster around our now locked hands as our surroundings filled with pained grunts and bones cracking. The men didn't let up, each now equally matched in terms of a physical fight. In response to each kick Dash executed, Evander delivered a punch of equal force.

The King of Tenebrae traversed again, and Dash swiftly extended his arms above his right shoulder, firmly clasping them around Evander's neck upon his reappearance. Dash forcefully threw him over his body, and Evander's back collided with the ground, emitting a loud crack. Evander then disappeared into the shadows, only to reappear a few feet away, visibly exhausted and wearing a sneer.

Oli snorted a chuckle, prompting me to twist towards him, my brows creased with curiosity. "Van's pissed," he explained.

"Because Dash is besting him?"

Oli gestured with a head shake, but it was Ainsley who took the initiative to answer. "Because Dash stole Van's technique."

I observed once more the two kings locked in physical combat, exchanging blows with their fists and legs. "But Dash said he didn't need his Obscure," I argued.

"No, he said he wasn't going to call it forth," Olivier pointed out, stealing my attention. "And that's because he already had. He must have anticipated he would have to face Evander so he used his Obscure to study him prior to their match." A smile appeared on Oli's face as he remained fixated on the brawl. "He learned everything he needed to beforehand so he didn't have to waste his energy during the actual fight. It's actually a brilliant strategy on his part," Olivier added with a touch of admiration underlying his words.

They were *definitely* going to be best friends soon.

The battle continued while the sky gradually darkened with the onset of dusk. Thunder reverberated overhead. "Having trouble controlling your magic?" Evander asked with ragged breath as he wiped a thumb over his swollen lip.

Glancing upwards, Dash smirked, his teeth tinged with a red hue of blood. "You *are* aware that the weather can change on its own, correct?"

Evander shrugged lazily, the movement looking like it was taking far more energy than it should have. "I am," he answered. "But considering your expertise in manipulation, I naturally assumed it was you." Another dig. Another test.

Dash averted his gaze and spit the blood from his mouth, his composure visibly waning.

"Relax, Your Majesty," Rosella called. "Unless you hear it throughout the night and your wife is missing from your bed, you have nothing to worry about."

My heart plummeted to the depths of my being. Ainsley's hand trembled in my grasp, her shadows slowly creeping up my arm and enveloping my entire form, as she battled to keep her Obscure from emerging. Oli firmly clasped her other hand and whispered into her ear. She acknowledged with a nod and directed her attention towards the sky, taking several deep breaths.

Evander charged at Dash, baring his teeth, and the ensuing fight escalated in speed. The men were blurs of motion as they blocked and struck, drawing blood and blooming bruises. Evander was faster than Dash, but his anger was making him sloppy and the King of Caelum was able to offer more blows than he took.

Evander skillfully traversed into the depths of his shadows, and upon resurfacing, he effortlessly sliced through the air with a crafted dagger. Dash barely managed to get away, using his water to knock his opponent several feet back and create a momentary barrier between him. Everyone's attention, including Evander's, shifted to Dash's shirt, where a large slash across his stomach had left the thin grey fabric stained with crimson.

"Need a Medicus?" Evander asked, spinning his dagger tauntingly.

Dash huffed a breathy laugh. "For a scratch?" He pulled the cloth over his head, exposing a gash that extended several inches across his abdomen. "I'm fine," he said, and then tossed the shirt into the dirt.

"Yeah he is," Marce muttered and Lia agreed as they cast their gazes over the King of Caelum appraisingly. Even Cal and Kenji expressed their admiration for the man, appreciating the muscles visible beneath the dark ink of his back tattoo, which symbolized his Unda Gift.

"How far down do you think that goes?" Elenora whispered, pointing to the deep cut of muscle that dipped below the waistband of Dash's pants.

"I'm more concerned about how far down *he* goes," Lia replied.

"As far as you want," Rosella answered, and they all snickered.

I smothered my smile as I listened to their conversation, fully intending to disclose everything to Dash afterward. So much had changed, yet so much remained exactly the same. The display was nearly identical to our sparring sessions in Caelum, where we extensively utilized our code word.

"Good. I'd hate to end the fun early," Evander replied as he removed his now-drenched shirt. He maintained a furious stare at his rival as he vigorously squeezed it, splashing water onto the dirt beneath him.

"My bad," Dash offered, appearing far from remorseful.

With tensions already heightened, Evander's anger intensified as he flung the shirt to the ground with a resounding, wet smack. He rotated his neck and loosened his arms, bracing himself to resume the battle.

"It's fine. I don't mind getting wet..." Evander said accompanied by a newfound glimmer in his eyes. "Much like my wife every night."

Dash's stare narrowed slightly at the response, but not out of anger. No, he was carefully devising his next move against the king. His gaze drifted to Ainsley for a longing moment before he spoke.

"Ah, yes. I seem to recall that about her," he stated as if lost in the memories. Dash turned his focus back to Evander as a smirk curved his lips. "But with *me*, it wasn't only at night."

Fucking Gods.

They sprinted for each other, colliding in fists and magic as flames licked over shadow, their rage a bitter taste on my tongue. Evander unleashed a forceful strike, propelling Dash backward. But he recovered quickly, returning a kick to Evander's stomach that had the snapping of his ribs echoing over the ring.

Black, as thick and ominous as night, shot between them, forcing them apart as Ainsley entered the ring. Her Obscure snaked through the air with a promise of evisceration should anyone challenge it.

"*ENOUGH!*" she yelled, calling back her magic as she stopped before the two kings covered in blood and bruises. "Are you two done, or would you like to whip your dicks out and measure them while you're at it?!"

"Please" and "Dear Gods, yes," erupted from the observing crowd as they found immense pleasure in Ainsley's rhetorical proposal.

"Love," Evander uttered, but she held up her hand.

"No," she ordered. "Don't you dare speak to me."

"Ains," Dash attempted, and she redirected her anger towards him.

"The same goes for you."

The queen clasped her arms around herself, her eyes flashing between the two kings, shaking her head and rendered speechless. I reached out with my Empathi Gift, softly gliding it over her shield to indicate I was here if she needed me.

"I expected more from both of you," Ainsley croaked, the emotion lodging thick in her throat. She promptly exited the ring and made her way into the house.

The space was quiet for some time; no one knew if the fight was over and we were free to leave, or if it would resume again. "Well then," Tallis finally said, stepping forward into the sparring circle. "I think we can call it a day. As everyone is to return home tomorrow, ensure you're making improvements where you need to and are ready for the matches next time we meet."

Everyone agreed and then resumed their discussion over the latest fight. Evander walked purposefully towards Tallis, while the King of Caelum grabbed his shirt and headed towards the house with Elenora following behind.

"Dashiell," Evander called, halting my friend in his tracks and ceasing all chatter as everyone waited to hear what he had to say. "You fought well today. Next time, you'll skip the matches and train with knives alongside the Lord of Vorsutos."

"I already know how to use them," Dash said.

Van's mouth curved into a lopsided smirk. "Not like him, you don't."

Dash accepted by nodding and then entered the house, taking the last remnants of the setting sun with him.

54

Ainsley

I paced my bedroom for hours, curling my hands into fists as I wrapped my shadows around them. My anger was past the point of no return after two of the men I cared about the most humiliated me in front of everyone for their own personal gain. I was a piece to play—something to use to outwit the other. A pawn, not a fucking queen.

A tear slid down my cheek as I took several deep breaths and I quickly wiped it away, hating that I cried when I was angry. They didn't deserve my tears. They deserved my damn wrath. But I knew if I had stayed in that sparring ring for another second, I would have done or said something I couldn't take back. I was trying not to always give in to my anger—to grow as a person—and yet they seemed to want to make it as difficult as possible for me to do just that.

"Much like my wife every night," I mocked, interlacing my fingers and placing them on top of my head. *"With me, it wasn't only at night."* My impression of Evander and Dashiell was spot on, encapsulating their giant egos and general dickheadedness.

I counted my steps, my heartbeat, my breaths, as I continued to pace the room. No matter what I did to try and reduce my rage, nothing helped. The cool breeze of an open door bringing in the scent of cedar and crisp, fresh snow, only fueled that fire.

"I thought this might help," Evander said from the doorway.

I halted my walking and turned to find him holding up a container of salve. My shoulders ached and muscles screamed, the sight of the balm instantly reminding my body of its earlier pain. Gritting my teeth, I held out my palm.

"I could help apply it," he offered.

I moved my hand further out, extending my reach as far as my sore arm would allow. He released a sigh, entered the room, and placed the metal container into my hand. I turned my back on him and stepped closer to the bed to put some much-needed distance between us.

The lid fell to the floor a moment later as I dug my fingers into the salve and pressed them to the harsh bruise along my ribs. I moaned in satisfaction as the balm seeped into my skin, offering me immediate relief from the injury.

"Would you like me to tend to your back?"

I ignored him again, focusing my attention on spreading the cooling balm over various patches of discolored flesh and massaging it vigorously into my aching shoulders. The hardest part of the application was trying to get the injuries that brushed along my spine.

"Are you sure you don't need my help?" Evander asked.

I spun in circles, my arms at odd angles as I tried my damndest to reach. But little good that did. With a grunt of frustration, I threw the container at his chest. He caught it, of course, and I turned my back to him, lifting my shirt over my head and covering my chest.

Evander's fingers dug into my back a moment later, and I bit back my cry of pain as he worked to alleviate the tension.

"You did well today," he said as his thumb moved in a circular motion. I snorted and shook my head. "You don't think so?"

He couldn't be serious.

I clenched my jaw and pulled my shirt back on, ignoring the sudden jolt of pain as I stepped away from him.

"Love?"

"No!" I yelled, whirling around and pointing a finger to his chest. "You don't get to pretend like you didn't just pull that shit down there." My arms crossed over my chest as I glared at him with the intensity of a burning star.

He turned his head and directed his stare to the open window where the curtain blew in the night breeze. His grey eyes darkened and the muscle in his jaw flexed as he growled his response.

"Are you going to tear into Dashiell too, or am I the only one lucky enough to experience this?"

I startled at the unexpected question. "What is that supposed to mean?"

Evander's stare met mine, fury and hurt embedded so deeply in his features that it threw me off. He looked me over before shaking his head. "Forget it," he mumbled and headed for the door.

"No!" I demanded and he stopped before reaching the exit. "We agreed—we don't run." I took a few steps closer and halted in the center of the room. "When we chose each other, we agreed."

Evander's head tilted toward the ceiling and his shoulders lifted and sagged as he took a deep, long breath before reluctantly turning back around and coming to stand a foot away.

We regarded each other for another moment before I tried again. "What did you mean by that?"

"I thought it was pretty obvious."

My eyes narrowed as I studied him, trying to decipher what exactly he was implying. The moment it clicked I breathed an incredulous laugh, bracing my hands on my head again as I stepped further back.

"We cannot seriously be having this discussion again," I said as I closed my eyes to the frustration. We had been over this—over my feelings toward Dashiell and him—and yet for some reason, here we were again. "This is ridiculous," I added, opening my eyes and dragging my hands down my face.

"Is it?" he replied, crossing his arms tightly over his chest.

"Yes!"

A bitter laugh escaped him, and I cringed at the sound. "Then tell me something, Ainsley," he said, bending down to meet me at eye level. "Why can't I kiss you when he's around?"

My mouth dropped open and my brows furrowed at the lie. "What are you talking about? You do!"

"Please. If I try to hold you, you evade. If I try to kiss you, you turn and offer me your cheek. Why is that?"

I started and stopped, stuttering through a response that was just repeating sounds. I tore my gaze from him as I looked around our bedroom in an attempt to find an answer as to how this was happening. Besides today, Van had given no indication that anything was wrong, so why now?

"I don't have the need to flaunt our relationship in his face," I answered cooly. "Just because your jealousy—"

"I am *not* jealous."

"Clearly," I snarked, waving a hand over his rigid posture and this insane argument we were having. "You're being absurd, Van. I love *you*. I chose *you*. I married *you*."

He snorted, the sound vile and so much unlike him. "Please. You were more concerned with the title you'd earn than the man you were marrying."

The room was plunged into a strangling silence.

Too far. He had gone too far, and he knew it.

Realization of what he'd done leached the color from his face, his eyes wide with panic as he reached for me. "Ainsley, I didn't mean—"

I pulled my hand away before he could touch me, my heart shredded and bleeding out as I looked at him. I couldn't speak, couldn't move, couldn't *breathe*, as his words played in my addled mind. He knew my concern for my title was only from fear of not being good enough, and yet he twisted that worry to suit his needs.

My heart slammed chaotically against my chest as I sipped on the tainted air around us, willing my eyes not to shed the tears that had welled. He didn't deserve them.

A war between logic and emotion raged on in my very being. I knew, without a shadow of a doubt, that Evander had said what he did out of anger. I knew he loved me—knew he wanted to take back the words the second they slipped from his lips. But I didn't want to give in to reason. I didn't want to forgive—not yet.

With a shaky exhale, I stepped around him and headed for the door, ignoring my name once again on his lips.

"We don't run!" he called. "You said it yourself. We don't run. We agreed." The panicked desperation in his voice was nearly too much to bear. He was hurting and hating himself for what he did—for the pain cutting me so deep, I knew he could feel it through our Soul Bond.

As my hand hovered over the knob, I mustered up the last of my will and said, "And you promised to never hurt me again. So I guess we're both liars."

And then I left.

55

Ainsley

A warm spring breeze brushed over my skin, doing nothing to douse the heat burning inside me. Trying and failing miserably to reign in my rage, my knuckles whitened as I gripped the balcony railing that overlooked the grounds from the roof. I had hoped the fresh air would help clear my roaring thoughts, but they were too loud, too persistent, too furious.

My mind was racing with anger and accusations. Each time I closed my eyes and deepened my breathing, all I could hear was Evander's insinuation that I only married him for his title. A rumble rattled my throat as I bit back my growl.

"How fucking dare he," I said beneath my breath, my cheeks growing wet with my inability to stop the angry tears from spilling over. Out of all the words that were exchanged between us, the notion that I would use him for a crown hurt the worst. It didn't matter that he tried to take back the claim the moment it left his mouth, or how I felt his guilt immediately slam into me. Nothing mattered except for how low he stooped.

My Obscure slid from my shoulders and glided down my arms, coiling around my flesh like a serpent. I opened my palms, letting it gather between my fingers until it formed into a shape I could easily squeeze while I pictured Evander's stupid face. Gods, I was angry.

The door leading to the roof's balcony opened, accompanied by quick footfalls and soft laughter. On instinct, I twisted toward the interruption to find Dash and Elenora making their way outside. We locked eyes for all of one second before I turned away and swiftly wiped my traitorous tears.

"I'm sorry, we didn't know anyone was up here," Elenora explained, sounding slightly embarrassed like *she* was the one caught crying alone on the roof.

I shook my head to diffuse the situation. "It's okay. I was just leaving," I told her, my voice catching in my throat.

I kept my back facing the pair, hoping it was enough of a signal that I wouldn't be leaving until they were far away from the only exit... unless I wanted to jump over the side of the house.

Given how mortified I was at the moment, it wasn't looking like such a bad idea. My shadows would break my fall and I could walk away with one, maybe two, minor injuries.

"Can you give us a minute?" I heard Dash whisper as I peered over the edge, contemplating my choice of escape.

I felt his approach rather than hearing it. That cool and soothing magic I was becoming accustomed to reached tentatively for mine, but I didn't reciprocate. I didn't want to be comforted; I wanted to stew in my anger.

"You okay?" he asked, resting his arm leisurely on the railing so he could face me fully.

I shook my head as another tear broke free before I could stop it.

Dash didn't press the issue, taking my silence for what it was—a desire not to elaborate.

"I'm sorry for earlier," he said instead. "I should have found another way to rattle him without using you as collateral." I chose not to reply, and a minute went by before Dash spoke once more. "I also apologize about Rosella. She was trying to help and—"

"By getting under my skin?" I said sarcastically, refusing to hide the bite in my tone.

"By getting under Evander's," Dash corrected. "She figured out quickly that his weakness was you and tried to rile him up to help me."

I released a frustrated breath. "I understand why it was done, but going forward, I don't want to be used as a pawn again."

"You won't be; at least not by me."

"Then you're forgiven," I stole a glance in his direction, no longer relying on what I saw in my periphery. He looked exactly how I felt—frustrated, confused, hurt.

My brow pinched as I tried to decipher his emotions without using my Empathi Gift. I didn't want to encroach on his hidden feelings the same way I didn't want to divulge mine. He twisted slightly, his attention now directed at Elenora who was at the opposite end of the house, sitting patiently on the shingles of the roof rather than on the solid ground of the balcony.

Dammit. I was clearly keeping him from his plans with her.

When he looked back at me, I could tell his mind was working. Though his posture seemed relaxed with an air of nonchalance, his muscles were taut and his jaw tight—a sign of distress. I was about to put him out of his misery and excuse myself but he spoke before I could.

"Is that what your fight was about?"

Apparently prying was back on the table. This wasn't a subject I wanted to dive into, especially with Dash. So why did I find myself nodding as I looked back out over the grounds?

"It started that way, but then turned into more," I said.

"Do you want to talk about it?" The words were soft, hesitant. Like we were standing on a thin sheet of ice that could crack and fracture beneath us with one wrong step.

Did I want to talk about it? Absolutely not.

And yet— "He said that I... And then he just... But that was *completely* unfair and—"

"Ains, I'm going to need full sentences."

I placed my face in my hands and groaned loudly in frustration. "I know. I'm sorry, I'm just so damn angry at him. I thought everything was fine, but it's obviously not."

Tipping my head back, I sighed as I took in the expansive night sky sprinkled with twinkling stars overhead. I should have been with Evander, enjoying the view somewhere quiet, just the two of us. But instead, I stood on the roof of our house, interrupting my ex-fiancé's date.

"I didn't mean for what I said to cause this," Dash offered, but I shook my head.

"It's not your fault. This had evidently been stewing for a while." I directed my attention to him and gave a shrug of my shoulder in a gesture of emotional defeat.

"And this is only the first time he got upset about me?" Dash's brows furrowed as if the idea confused him.

"Yeah."

"Wow," he said, his features flooding with surprise as he turned his focus to the sprawling grass undulating in the gentle wind.

"What do you mean, *wow*?"

"Just that I'm stunned it didn't happen sooner." Was that supposed to be a dig at my husband's ill-restraint?

"It shouldn't have happened at all," I mumbled, looking down at my wedding band.

Dash scoffed, tugging on my attention like a string.

"Is something funny?" I accused, my tone reflecting my irritation. I wasn't in the damn mood to be laughed at. Dash shook his head, either to deny or brush me off—I didn't know which. "I wouldn't have done this to *him*," I claimed, feeling the irrational need to defend myself.

Dash whipped his stare to me, his eyes wide and jaw dropped. "You're kidding, right?"

"Excuse me?"

"Ainsley, the two of you act exactly the same."

A bitter laugh escaped my lips. I turned my body fully toward him and crossed my arms over my chest, preparing for the verbal fight that was about to ensue.

"So not only do I get to fight with my husband, I get to be insulted by my friend as well. Yay for me."

"Oh, come on." Dash pinched the bridge of his nose and rolled his eyes. "You're being a bit dramatic, don't you think?"

"Fuck you—I am not! What else are you going to say? That I'm overreacting? I'm being irrational?"

Dash sighed and mimicked my stance, adding in a raised eyebrow like he was impatiently waiting for me to shut up. What an asshole.

"How about that *I'm* the one in the wrong, or that I have no reason to be angry?" I continued, each sentence coming out a sharper bite than the last.

He continued to stare at me quietly with an annoyed look, as if he were dealing with a petulant child.

"Well?!" I demanded when he didn't speak.

"I'm just waiting for you to tire yourself out." I clenched my jaw, causing my teeth to audibly grind. He smirked and my Obscure went right back to my palms, forming a squeezable sphere that I could picture as Dash's head as I closed my fists tightly around it. "By my calculations, it'll be about another two minutes before your temper subsides and you're ready to have a civil conversation."

"Glad I'm so predictable."

"You're not," he argued. "I just *know* you. I know your heart and mind—the way you think. Yes, you're very stubborn, defensive, quick to anger—"

"—For your sake, I really hope there's a *'but'* coming."

"But you're also compassionate and you hate being at odds with the people you care about, regardless of how angry you are at them. That empathic side is what I'm waiting for. Sometimes it takes you a little while to get there, but you always find your way, eventually."

My shoulders eased without my consent, causing my hands to fall to my sides, effectively confirming Dash's assertion. He had a point and I hated it.

I turned away, letting my Obscure glide away from my hands so I could grasp the metal railing once more. Dash was quiet at my side, still waiting for my temper to fully dissipate before we continued the conversation.

Inhaling deeply, I focused on the subtle sweet scent of the blooming jasmine throughout our property. My tattoo tingled and I could feel the delicate shadowed petals transforming into wisps as if they could dissolve and join the other flowers in the land. A subtle smile graced my lips as I reminisced about the night Van delicately etched the jasmine blossom onto my skin and the way his fingers felt as they caressed my bare flesh.

I missed him.

I hated fighting with him, hated being mad. More than anything, I hated that he questioned how I felt about him, as if what we had built together was so easily breakable. As if I would change my mind so callously like he didn't matter—like *we* didn't matter. He was mine and I was his, and it crushed me that anything would ever make him doubt that.

My grip on the railing loosened and I began tracing tiny patterns along the cool metal. "What were you going to say?" I asked, barely more than a whisper. I could picture the victorious grin Dash was no doubt displaying as he scooted closer, his shoulder lightly brushing mine.

"That I think you could be a little more patient with him." Our gazes collided and mine softened as I took his in. There was so much compassion and understanding swirling in his deep blue eyes, which most of the time, I didn't feel I deserved. "How many times did I tell you that Rosella and I were nothing?"

"That was different," I argued.

"It took you months to finally accept my word for truth. And you're right, Ainsley, it *is* different. Rosella and I weren't serious. We casually spent time together with no feelings involved, and when it was over, it was over. But you and I were so much more than that; we still are."

"It's not the same thing."

"Exactly," Dash countered as if I had made his point for him. "Think about how much harder this has to be for him. I'm not just someone who briefly flittered in and out of your life on rare occasions, Ains. We built something real and fell in love doing it. Given what you told me back in Caelum about Evander being able to feel your emotions, he knows that too."

There was a dull pang in my chest at the mention of Van being all too familiar with the love I had felt for someone else. I hated that he had to experience it, but those feelings were no longer there. He felt only my love for *him*.

"Listen," Dash said as he leaned his forearms over the railing.

The moonlight caught on a patch of damaged flesh starting a few inches below his wrist and crawling beneath the fabric of his rolled sleeve. It looked strangely like an unhealed burn; perhaps from when he was learning to wield his fire magic. Why wouldn't he have had a Medicus tend to it and repair the skin fully?

"I'm not an ex he has to see on rare occasions when our royal titles require it," he continued, jolting me from my staring. "I'm currently in the house the two of you share, which I'm pretty sure he isn't exactly thrilled about. He has to walk downstairs and see me every single day because you made the decision to have me in your life. Think about how hard that choice must be for him. And he hasn't complained until now because he loves you; anyone can see that. Try to cut him some slack."

I dragged a hand through my hair as I let out a deep breath. Dash was right, of course. Evander had been far more gracious about the entire ordeal than I gave him credit for. Instead, I was furious at him for something he had every right to feel, even if I didn't fully understand why.

"I'm struggling too," I said, not in defense but in explanation. "I'm still trying to figure out this thing between us, which hasn't been easy, and factoring in Evander's emotions too... I don't know how to handle this."

Dash nodded before directing his attention straight ahead. "I'm not sure either. But I can tell you, tiptoeing around me isn't the answer."

"I'm not—"

"You are."

I didn't argue because—surprise, surprise!—once again, Dash was right. My Obscure twisted over my palm as if sensing my need for a distraction and I rubbed my thumb over the dark tendrils absentmindedly.

"I don't want to hurt anyone," I admitted, not taking my eyes off my task. "And the way you and I ended... Well, we never really..." I stammered, trying to figure out how to word my racing thoughts.

"Officially ended? Had closure?"

"Exactly. One morning we were together and then—"

"You were trying to stab me." There was a slight smile in his voice and I could tell he was now watching me.

"Yes, and then it was made public that I was married to someone else."

"I know; I was there for that reveal," he said, that grin still present in his tone.

My lips lifted as I continued to play with my magic and not make eye contact. We had broken up, even if it didn't happen face to face, so why was talking about this now so awkward?

"I suppose you were," I whispered before taking a deep breath and finally deciding to meet his stare. "We never discussed *us*, and I guess I just don't know where you stand on the subject."

"Where I stand," he mused to himself.

Dash's eyes narrowed as he studied my face, like he was trying to fit the pieces into a puzzle he was solving. Watching his mind work was always fascinating to me. If I stared close enough, I could detect the subtle shift in his thoughts; the tick of a muscle, the dart of his eyes, the way his thumbs would run across the tips of his fingers. And when he reached a solution, he always,

always, performed a barely perceivable dip of his head, as if accepting whatever his mind had conjured.

He blew out a breath and straightened after giving his subtle nod. "Where I stand is: I want you in my life, in whatever capacity you desire. I'm trying to navigate this thing," he said, gesturing a hand between us, "Just like you are. Sometimes it's strange and awkward, but what I want is for our friendship to be what it once was. I want to be someone you can come to when you need to vent or talk things through. And I want *you* to be that for me, too. We had it once, and I hope to again."

I felt the same. Although it hurt to go through, it wasn't only the loss of my fiancé that had broken my heart—it was losing one of my best friends. Felix and I were close, but Dash was an integral part of our trio. Without him, I was incomplete.

"The fact of the matter is, we aren't together anymore, and I chose to be in your life knowing you were married to another. It's on me to figure out what that looks like, not you. As much as I appreciate you trying to consider my feelings, it isn't necessary. I've accepted you've moved on, so don't sacrifice his feelings for mine, Ainsley."

As much as I wanted to excuse my actions, I couldn't. Dash was right; I had been so concerned with trying to make things as comfortable and seamless between us that I was blind to how that was making Evander feel. He was struggling right in front of me, and I had been so selfishly wrapped up in trying to do right by everyone else that he got lost in the shuffle.

I let Dash's words sink into me and settle, filling the fear and doubt and unknown until there was nothing left to be afraid of. It was as if the last piece of uncertainty had vanished, and I could fully move on, knowing Dash and I had received the closure we both needed. Our time together as lovers was over, but there was peace in that. It gave way for us to establish something even stronger and more beautiful.

"He insinuated I only married him for his crown," I admitted, testing out the waters of our newly formed friendship and wondering if I truly could come to him with my problems. Even if they pertained to Evander. Dash's lips quirked as if he understood what I was offering.

"He didn't mean it."

"Maybe there's a part of him that does."

Dash gave a sympathetic smile as he shook his head. "Nah, I don't think that's the case. Sometimes people just say really stupid shit they don't mean when they're angry. Trust me; I once compared the woman I was falling in love with to a snake because I was pissed off."

An involuntary laugh bubbled to the surface and slipped softly from my lips as I remembered that night.

"Was she mad?"

"Oh, furious. She threw a necklace at me the next day."

"You probably deserved it."

"Meh," he said with a shrug, and I rolled my eyes. "Maybe I wasn't so far off with the comparison, after all."

His eyes dipped, and I followed his stare to the black strand of my Obscure slithering over my flesh. I raised my arm and admired the way it moved delicately. Perhaps Dash had a point.

"I still think it's weird," he commented.

My eyes shot to his. "It is not!"

"It really is."

"*You're* weird," I said like a defensive five-year-old.

"Great insult."

"Whatever." I pulled my Obscure back into myself, taking it out of view of Dash's scrutiny. "I'm not going to listen to the opinion of someone named after a form of movement."

His jaw dropped and he chuckled. Hard.

"Okay, first of all, it's a nickname," he said through the laughter. "And second of all, at least I know my name."

It was my turn to let my mouth hang open. "Oh, so we're stooping so low as to bring up dead parents and a lost childhood?"

He raised his hands in defense, palms up. "You're the one who picked the game without establishing the rules." My Obscure came back out and shot forward to smack him in the chest like a whip before disappearing faster than he could blink. He winced from the quick pain but didn't let up on his laughter, causing my own to come forth.

I had missed how easy things always were with Dash. He was one of the one people in the world, including Felix, who could always get me out of my rut and make me forget about whatever ill thoughts plagued my mind. It was nice to be like this with him again.

Movement in our periphery caught both of our attention as Elenora shifted her position to get more comfortable. She had been waiting patiently for him and the realization of that now felt like a sword hanging overhead.

"Would you like to join us?" Dash asked, gesturing to the woman across the way.

I breathed a nervous laugh as we were about to get into another topic I wasn't sure we were ready for. "And impose on your date?"

"It's not a date," Dash said flatly, like he had denied the claim several times already. Something told me that Felix was behind his frustration on the subject.

"Right." I drew out the vowel in exaggeration.

"It's not!"

"The two of you came up here to sit on the roof, in the dark, under the stars, completely alone." I widened my eyes in a very obvious call-out. "But sure. It's not a date."

"We're just friends." A response he had recited all week.

"I'm pretty sure I said that to myself regarding *you* once."

"Whatever. Do you want to join us or not?" Dash said. He wasn't angry, but he clearly wanted to change the subject of his love life.

I looked past him to the dark-haired woman waiting patiently for the King of Caelum to return and shook my head. I had absolutely no desire to impose on whatever was going on there.

"Thanks, but maybe another time. I should really go and find Evander, anyway. We have a lot to talk through."

He nodded and took a few steps back.

"Dash," I called before he could turn and continue his way to Elenora. He stopped his retreat and waited for me to continue, curiosity bright in his eyes. "Thanks for checking on me... and calming me down."

"Always, Ains," he said softly before turning around and strolling over to his not-date.

I stood there for another minute, watching as he reached the other side of the balcony, climbed over the railing, and slid next to Elenora. She looked up at him as her lips moved, but I couldn't hear what she was saying, or if he responded. His back stayed to me, his stare directed at the dark horizon in front of him and not at the woman whose eyes were glued to his profile.

She spoke again, and this time, Dash nodded once. Her arms curled around his as she leaned into his side and rested her head against his shoulder. At the sight, I headed for the door that led inside, not wanting to invade what was obviously a private and intimate moment. Dash deserved to be happy, and perhaps Elenora was the answer to that. And if not... If she hurt him...

I would rip her to shreds.

Literally.

56

Ainsley

I scanned the space as moonlight splashed across the floor, illuminating the vacant bedroom. Creeping forward, the cool wooden floorboards squeaked beneath my weight as I settled myself onto the middle of the mattress. I wrapped the small blanket that was draped across the end around my shoulders as my skin pebbled from the cool breeze the open window brought in. Though I shivered, I didn't bother to shut it.

Twisting, I reached for the small stuffed Onyx that Evander had given to me this past Solstice. I brought it to my chest as I laid back, curling into a ball as I kept my eyes on the door. My fingers absentmindedly combed over the soft fur of the wolf that looked more like a bear. Van had been a child when he crafted it, which made the present that much more meaningful.

I didn't bother to wipe away the gentle tears that fell onto the bed as I lay there waiting. It was stupid of me to hold onto hope that I would have found him here. I could always sense his presence, even if we weren't in the same room, and this house was currently void of it. He wasn't here and my heart cracked knowing I didn't know when or even *if* he'd be back.

I shut my eyes, breathing deeply as I replayed the words we exchanged, and wished I could take them all back.

Soft fingers brushed across my flesh as a blanket was placed higher over my shoulders, bringing instant warmth to my body. My eyes fluttered open to find Evander sitting on the bed next to me, continuously readjusting the fur that was now draped over my body. Our gazes locked in a quiet embrace, both of us trying to assess the other.

I hated seeing him in such a state of distress—his hair overly unkempt from his hands rummaging through it, his eyes hollow and dull and rimmed with red, his shoulders sagging in defeat.

"Hi," he said, his voice breaking on the small word.

"Hi," I replied, in no better shape.

"Can we talk?"

I nodded and sat up, the blanket falling to my lap as I continued to observe his disheveled appearance. I wanted so much to embrace him, to kiss him, to take away the pain we were both feeling, but I knew I couldn't. There would need to be a discussion before any forgiveness could take place.

"If you don't mind, I'd like to take you somewhere," he added, extending his hand to me. Without thought, I placed my palm in his, noting the heavy sigh of relief that slipped between his lips as he pulled us through the shadows.

My hair immediately tangled in the spring breeze as we appeared under the dark sky lit with millions of twinkling stars. Before us stood a line of trees washed in a faint glow of a flickering light to my back. I deeply inhaled the familiar scents of pine, cedar, snow, and crisp air, recognizing at once where that combination meant we were.

"Come on," Evander said, sliding his fingers between mine and tugging my hand in the opposite direction.

I turned to face the expansive meadow and the cliff's edge we had once danced over—the place where I had chosen him to be mine more than once. My steps immediately faltered as I cast my gaze upon the scene. I sucked in a gasp and my hand flew to my heart as Evander squeezed the other one tighter.

Hundreds of magical candles littered the ground while others floated aimlessly through the air, drifting along the breeze but remaining trapped over the meadow. At the edge of the cliff sat a pile of blankets, pillows, books, a basket that I presumed contained food, and a... Was that a copper tub?

"Van, what is all of this?"

He didn't answer, instead pulling me along across the meadow that was dusted with a thin layer of frost. The ground crunched under my shoes as I playfully tapped the floating candles we passed, sending them spinning through the air until they slowed and settled in place once more. Peering up at Evander, I caught him watching me with a smile of admiration.

We stopped a few feet short of the blanket setup as Van took my hands in his and turned me to face him. His gaze was cast downward between us as his chest rose and fell, the air still and quiet while he worked through the words in his mind.

"I want to start by saying how sorry I am for how I acted, what I said, and for hurting you the way I did," Evander stated, his eyes locking onto mine as he spoke. "I need you to know that I don't—nor have I ever once thought—that you married me for my title."

I held his stare for what felt like an eternity, turning over the declaration in my mind as I watched candlelight reflect in his grey eyes. There wasn't a need for me to question him further about it. I could feel the truth in his words in the way his hand curved around my cheek, the way he pressed his forehead into mine as we stood in the silence, the way he breathed me in as if I was the only air he needed.

"I've been struggling this week," Van continued, almost like he had been ashamed of the fact. "And I didn't tell you because I thought I could push past the insecurities and get through this, but…"

He adverted his gaze, sweeping it over our surroundings as a muscle ticked in his jaw. His head shook with frustration, hating that he failed himself.

"I'm not jealous of Dashiell," he said.

A sigh escaped me before I could help it. Everything he had said and done today seemed to prove otherwise. "It's okay if you are—"

"I'm not. At least not in the way you're referring to." He turned his attention back to me as his hand slid from mine to rest on the small of my back, pulling me closer to him. "I'm not worried about the feelings you once had for him, nor am I concerned that you'll replace me." His fingers traced the delicate line of my jaw as he whispered, "I know that you love *me*, you claimed *me*, you chose *me*. Nothing could ever make me doubt the love we share."

My heart softened at the reassurance he felt, but it didn't stop my brows from furrowing. "Then what exactly are you struggling with?" He was quiet as he watched me and I didn't know if it was because he couldn't answer or didn't want to. "Is it how close we are? How much time we spend together? The things we talk and joke about?"

"Yes—I mean, no… It's—*ugh*." He growled his frustration, dropping my face to run a hand down his.

His eyes darted around the vicinity as he shook his head, battling himself and the thoughts he was having so much trouble conveying. Evander tilted his chin toward the sky, the flickering light from the candles dancing across his beautiful face, somehow making him more captivating than he already was.

"Take your time," I whispered reassuringly. "I'm not going anywhere." I pressed my body flush against his and skated my fingers up and down his back as comfortingly as I could.

Several minutes passed when Evander blew out a long breath and turned those brilliant eyes back on me. "Now that you have Dashiell back in your life, I see a happiness in you I haven't before," he explained. His hands moved to cup my cheeks as he brought his face closer. "I see how *complete* you are. That's not something I wish to ever take away from you, but…"

I swallowed hard, fearful of whatever hung at the end of that sentence. His thumbs caressed my cheeks as his stare continued to bore into mine. I admired the subtle flecks in his eyes that could only be seen from this close—a marker of our Soul Bond, I had learned. Where mine shone a deep red, his were a muted gold.

"The logical part of me knows that you've distanced yourself from me because you don't want to hurt him," Evander continued, his hold on my face slipping as he nervously gripped his fingers between us. "But the other part of me—the part that's insecure and terrified—keeps trying to convince me it's for another reason. That maybe it's because you prefer the life you had with the two of them more than the one you now share with me. That perhaps what we've built doesn't compare to what the three of you already have."

Heavy and solid, my heart felt like a stone in my chest, dragging me down. My throat closed up and my lungs constricted, making it impossible to breathe as the panic rooted itself. Evander blurred in my vision, his silhouette gently swaying side to side as my head swam from the dizziness. I was so wracked with shame I couldn't even form the words to tell him he was wrong.

He nodded to himself and looked away. "I know I messed up this week," he continued when I didn't respond. "But I'll do better next time, I promise. I was just struggling to figure out where I fit now, but—"

"That's because you don't," I blurted out, my hands flying to his face to force him to look at me. I inhaled a long, shaky breath, greedily gulping down the air and willing it to calm my racing mind. "*You* are my world. It is everyone else who has to figure out how *they* fit into it, but not you. *Never* you, Evander."

His brow pinched as his eyes softened, glassing over and making the gold in them reflect brighter from the candlelight overhead. Seeing this side of him was always my favorite. Not his sadness, but his vulnerability. The part of him he reserved solely for me.

"I'm sorry that I ever made you feel like you had to fight for a place that already belonged to you," I continued, speaking every word with purpose. "*I'm* the one who will do better next time."

He shook his head, his cheeks plumping from my hold on them. "You were just trying not to hurt him."

My heart tightened as I wondered how many times he had recited that to himself over the past week. Every time I stepped out of his hold? Moved away from his touch? Every time I turned to offer him my cheek instead of my lips?

The earlier conversation I had with Dash drifted into my thoughts. "Dash chose to be in my life knowing I married another," I said slowly, remembering each word between us. "I won't sacrifice your feelings for his." A shy, thankful smile graced Evander's lips. He moved his hands to my waist, his fingers pressing into my sides as he held me firm against him. "Now, kiss your wife, please."

He didn't let me get out the last word before his mouth claimed mine in an embrace that had my knees trembling. His tongue swept over mine, hot and demanding, as a moan escaped me from his taste alone. He was sweet and addicting and all *mine*. My fingers raked through his hair, my body moving against his as I tried to get closer.

Too soon, Evander pulled back and even though I was gasping for air, I still wasn't ready for our embrace to be over. His lips spread against mine in a cocky smirk as I tried and failed to take more of what I wanted, but he held me just out of reach.

I groaned in frustration and crossed my arms over my chest as I turned my head, spying the bed of blankets a few feet away. "Fine. If you're not going to let me kiss you, at least tell me what all of this is for," I demanded, waving my hand over the inviting display.

His lips pressed into my temple and I instantly forgot any irritation I possessed toward him. "If you wanted to run, then I wanted you to have a place to run *to*," he explained. "I didn't think you'd feel comfortable staying at the house or palace, but I also knew you wanted to be close enough that you could return home tomorrow morning to see your friend off."

My bewildered gaze sought his as my heart thumped wildly beneath my ribs. He was offering me respite in a place he knew I would feel safe. Somewhere quiet and peaceful, where I could bathe in my thoughts and emotions until I was ready to come home.

Evander pointed to various spots, directing my attention to them as he spoke. "The basket has all your favorite foods, and the books over there—" he said, gesturing a finger toward the large stack next to the pillows, "Are the ones you had on your list of what you wanted to read next. I wasn't sure if there was a specific order to it, so I stacked them chronologically of what you had written down." My hand rested against my heart, and tears formed in my eyes as he continued rattling off what he had done. "The water in the tub won't lose its heat, and I made sure it was practically boiling—just how you like it. There's a stack of nightclothes for you, too. I didn't know if you wanted my shirt tonight, but I included it, just in case. It's not your favorite, though. That's currently hidden somewhere where you'll never find it."

I laughed through a sob as the tears spilled down my cheeks. This entire week I had made him feel less than he was, yet he was still here, taking care of me as if none of that mattered. It was moments like these when I knew I'd never understand what I did to deserve him.

"The candles on the ground were for light, but the ones in the air were because I knew you'd like them," he explained, wiping the tears from my cheeks. "Oh, and there's this too..."

Van grabbed hold of my hand and pulled me a few steps closer to the blanket. I felt his magic wash over my skin before I caught sight of the shimmering shield around us. Comforting, inviting heat enveloped me.

"It's warm," I breathed, looking up at him curiously.

"The candles beneath the dome are heated. I know how much even a slight breeze sends you into a fit of rage."

I wanted to argue and deny the overdramatic accusation, but instead, I reached onto my toes and kissed him deeply. "Thank you," I whispered.

"I'll be here tomorrow morning to take you home. If you want to return after we say goodbye to our company, I'll replenish your food and clothes and bring you back. If you'd rather not see me at all, Nox is at the forest's edge should you need her instead." He dragged the tip of my nose up with his.

"And if I want you to stay with me?"

"Then there's nothing in this world that would keep me away."

With a satisfied smile, I led him to our makeshift bed and waited as he crafted more pillows to sit against. Once he was situated, he guided me between his legs, spinning me so my back rested against his chest. I covered us with a blanket and then scanned the books for which title I wanted to select.

His arms tightly wrapped around me as I snuggled into him, cherishing this much-needed moment with the man I loved. "Can you do something for me?" I asked. He nodded, placing a kiss against my hair. "I want you to access your magic—the strands of it that rest around your heart." Van did as instructed without question, breathing deeply as he reached into himself. "Whenever that fear tries to win again, I want you to grab onto that piece of me you took. I want you to hold on to it as tightly as you can, and remember that I gave it to you willingly. That I chose *you* and our life together. That there will never be a world where I would choose any differently."

Again, he nodded as his body constricted around mine. It was his turn to ask, "Can you do something for me?"

"Anything."

His fingers found my jaw, then glided down my neck, between my breasts, and settled on the pendant that always hung there—the sister to his bracelet. As he traced the stones and bird etched onto the metal, I wondered if his mind was where mine had been as I did the same thing nights prior.

"I want ten minutes of uninterrupted time with you each day," he stated. I smiled at the memory of when he first made such a request on his birthday. "It can be before bed, in the bath, at breakfast, or on a walk. I don't care when it happens, but I just want time with you alone. No talks of war or strategy or the state of our world. Ten minutes where we aren't the King and Queen of Tenebrae, and can be—"

"Just Van and Love," I answered.

"Yes," he whispered, squeezing me in emphasis.

I nodded enthusiastically, wanting nothing more than that. With war on the horizon, we didn't know how much time we had left together and I would steal any free moments I had with him.

"We can start now," I said, plucking two books from the pile and handing one to Evander.

"Perfect," he mumbled against my hair. "But before we begin, I have one more thing to apologize for." I twisted, peering up at him as my brows scrunched. "For what I said during my match with Dashiell. I may not have been *jealous*, but I got a bit territorial, and for that, I'm sorry."

I puckered my lips in demand for a kiss and he quickly obliged. Given that I could barely control my own anger on a daily basis, I couldn't fault him for slipping up after being continuously provoked.

"You are forgiven," I announced, turning back to my book. "Try not to let Rosella bait you next time."

Evander growled, the sound reverberating against my back. "I hate her."

"That makes two of us."

57

Ainsley

I was dying. There would be no future with Evander, no days spent laughing in bed or stealing kisses or finding ways to antagonize the other just for fun. There would be no more picnics with Felix and Dash, no more dinners with my family where I listened to tales of their past amongst their playful bickering of its accuracy. I was dying, and no one seemed to care.

I wheezed through a painful sip of air as I tried to force my muscles to move forward, the motion pure agony. I couldn't do it—couldn't continue any longer. Everything I had left to give was simply gone. This was it—the end for me. I inhaled again, savoring the way the oxygen felt as it burned its way down to my lungs for what could have been the last time.

"Will you stop being so dramatic and move your ass?!" Marceline yelled from above.

My eyes met hers to find her already nearing the top of Mammoth Hill, dozens of yards away. With a hand as unsteady as an earthquake, I raised my middle finger as high as I could manage. Which happened to be barely past my hips.

"It's not my fault you're so damn out of shape. You're the one who chose to do nothing but mope around for months," she called over her shoulder as she turned around to continue her journey.

"I was mourning my dead best friend!"

"Actually," Kenji interjected from a few feet away as he tied his black hair into a knot at the top of his head, "He wasn't really dead." I glared at the man casually walking backward up the steep incline as if this were a simple nature walk and not the hike of death. One look at my sneer had him promptly wiping the smug smirk off his face.

"Hurry up!" Marce exclaimed.

"I'm going to kill her," I muttered, forcing my legs to take another agonizing step.

"Please don't," Kenji said. "She has several attributes I'm rather fond of." His hand appeared before me and I gladly took it, letting him help support my weight as I struggled up the stupid fucking hill.

"And by *attributes*, you mean her personality, right? Or are you both done pretending you're not sleeping together?"

"We aren't!" Marce yelled from the top of the hill. Apparently, her immortal hearing was far better than I gave her credit for.

"Yeah. We're just two friends who are absolutely *not* sleeping together," Kenji replied, his loud voice stretching over the open space. He gave Marce a playful thumbs up, which she accepted before walking out of view. "And we *definitely* aren't doing it multiple times a night." He winked, and I chuckled, shaking my head as I took another weak step.

Kenji's hands slid around my back and then a beat later, I was in his arms. My stare immediately shot to the summit for any trace of Marce. "She'll be pissed if she finds out," I whispered, clinging to his neck as he carried me up the hill.

"I won't tell if you don't," he replied. "Plus, at this rate, we wouldn't reach the top for hours... and I'm starving. So this is entirely for selfish reasons."

"Good enough for me."

When we were still several yards away, he placed me back on my feet so Marce wouldn't catch us. But given how quick we were to crest the top, I was sure she knew exactly what had happened.

"Van will be here in five minutes to traverse us home," she announced, stuffing the transfer paper back into her pocket.

I collapsed onto the ground, not caring one bit about the grass that stuck to my sweat-slicked skin, as I thanked the Gods I wouldn't have to walk another step. Marce was persistent in her efforts to get me back into the same physical condition I had been in before the night I mistakenly thought Felix had perished. In the weeks leading up to now, I had only afforded myself minimal training and instead threw my focus into planning a war. But not five minutes after I said goodbye to Dash and the rest of our company yesterday, Marce forced me to go on a run with her.

"I finally figured out what that old map reminded me of," she said, running her fingers through the short strands of hair on the side of Kenji's head, "That story your grandmother always likes to tell about your ancestor." Kenji groaned in agreement and I narrowed my eyes in curiosity.

"She has a map too?" I asked.

"Not exactly," he replied, taking a seat next to me. Marce silently knelt behind him, freeing his hair from the band and combing her fingers through it. "*Supposedly*—and I would very much like to stress that word—one of my ancestors came to Disparya from another part of the world."

"Where?"

"It was said to have happened eons ago, and conveniently enough, no one seems to remember the land it was that they came from. Another reason why it's most likely untrue." He directed the last sentence to the woman twisting his hair into the perfect knot.

"Just because there's no proof doesn't mean it didn't happen," she singsonged as she fastened the band in place on the top of his head. Something told me this was a point they had discussed multiple times in the past.

I smiled as she shoved his head forward before moving to sit at his side. "And that's the reason my grandmother likes Marce so much; she believes all of her tall tales." Marceline rolled her eyes and snorted, tipping her head back and closing her eyes against the bright sun as Kenji continued. "Anyway, long ago, the Gods supposedly walked amongst us, ruling over the land."

"Like the kings do now?" I inquired.

"Similarly, yes. And much like the kings, some Gods were benevolent, while others were cruel, seeing the immortals they ruled over as mere forms of entertainment. They believed themselves superior in every way without a care for the lives of their subjects. Centuries passed before the people decided to fight back against the vile Gods, but they were no match for the power the deities held."

Captivated by his story, I pushed myself to a sitting position, giving him my full attention. The more I learned about the world, the more fascinated I became with it. The Gods, the land, the magic—each part drawing me in and holding me hostage.

"The Gods made quick work of their dissenters, but they knew it was only a matter of time before it happened again," he continued.

"So, what did they do?"

Kenji's fingers twisted absentmindedly over a long blade of grass, his gaze distant as if trying to remember every detail of the story. He blew out a long breath as he turned to face me. "They cleansed the land."

I angled my head as I played the response in my mind, trying to understand his meaning.

"They killed everyone," Marce explained, seeming to read the confusion on my face. "And then they started over."

My chest tightened, and the taste of bile filled my mouth as I thought about all of those lives needlessly taken. And for no reason other than simply because the Gods could.

"They reconstructed the land, forming new terrain. Where there were once flat plains and valleys, now stood expansive rivers and towering mountains to make it more difficult for the people of the land to unite," Kenji said, pushing himself to his feet. He braced his hands over his head, stretching side to side, before shaking out his arms. "But it didn't work. Again and again and again, the people revolted."

"And they kept losing," I deduced.

Kenji widened his legs, reaching down to touch one set of toes and then the next. "Eventually, a group of them caught word the Gods were planning on cleansing the land once more. In the middle of the night, they crept onto a ship and fled, hoping to get as far away from the cruel Gods as possible. But before long, they encountered a storm that swallowed their ship and killed all of the passengers, except for—"

"Your ancestor," I finished. Kenji nodded and straightened, grabbing his ankle to bring up to his side. "But if the Gods continuously wiped all immortals of the land from existence, how did the people know to flee?"

He snapped his fingers and pointed to me as he said, "Exactly."

"Because..." Marce said, elongating the word as she directed a sharp glare at her husband, "There were deities who didn't agree with the ones who sought to purge the land time and again. Eventually, they told the immortals of what happened and joined them in their fight. Together, they overthrew the vengeful Gods, but Kenji likes to forget that part of the story."

She angled her head and smugly grinned up at Kenji, her blond curls shifting over her shoulder as she did. His eyes thinned and face scrunched as he offered her a tight smile back. I didn't know why the two kept denying there was far more between them than just friendship when it was as clear as day for the rest of us.

"So there are Gods that still walk this world now?" I asked, excitement at the prospect pumping through my veins. If they helped immortals before, then perhaps they would do it again.

"No," Kenji answered. "After that, the people were apprehensive of the Gods and began to see them all as enemies, even the ones who had assisted in their war. Ultimately, the Gods decided to banish themselves to another realm where they sit now, watching over the land and biding their time until they can return."

Marce checked her slip of transfer paper before tucking it away and rising to her feet. My heart thumped a beat faster, knowing it meant Evander would be here any minute. He was gone before I was forced to get up this morning, and I had been aching for him ever since.

"What about the magic?" I asked as Kenji pulled me to my feet. He gave a puzzled look, prompting me to elaborate. "Wouldn't your family have different Gifts if they originated from another land?"

"Ahh," he replied, nodding. "Immortals didn't possess magic when the Gods walked the land. They didn't want anyone to compete with their power."

"Though not as violent as Kenji's story, our history of the Gods is similar," Marce added, rolling her neck. "*We* were taught that the Gods and Goddesses of Disparya lived amongst us peacefully as they created our world. Once they deemed the people ready to prosper without them, they left the land, granting select individuals from each kingdom magic as a gift—which is why we call it as such."

"So your ancestor, or their descendants, were given the magic of Tenebrae instead," I said to Kenji.

"Supposedly," he drawled, not seeming to believe his grandmother's story one bit.

"And *you*," I said to Marce, "Believe that Disparya was altered just like wherever Kenji's ancestor came from. And that's why the map looks so different."

"I think it's possible," she agreed just as familiar tendrils of shadow appeared in the space.

Evander stepped through, his black hair a mess and his shirtless body glistening in sweat. My stare followed the beads of moisture that dripped down his chest, falling into the cuts of his abdominal muscles and along the line that dipped below his waistband—the one I very much wanted to run my tongue over this very minute.

"Think what's possible?" the King of Tenebrae asked as he came before me, his lips pressing into my forehead as my gaze stayed glued to the way his muscles rippled beneath his skin.

"The Gods are assholes," I answered absentmindedly as I traced the ridges of his stomach.

He laughed, and I hooked two fingers into his waistband as I pulled him closer. One tug and his pants would be off, and I could drop to my knees and have my way with him. Our present company didn't matter—Marce and Kenji would leave the second they realized what was going on.

"Your trembling hands and the note from Marce indicate you're too tired to carry out whatever you're thinking right now," he whispered as his hands rested on my waist, his thumbs stroking the exposed skin there.

I shook my head, shivering beneath his touch. "I can manage."

"You can't," he argued. "But lucky for *me*, I exerted barely any energy during my match with Cal, so you can just lie there while I work."

"You could at least wait for us to leave before you two start with that nonsense," Marce quipped.

I paid her no mind, instead imagining dragging my tongue along his length before taking him as deep as I could. I pictured his fingers digging into my hair, the sounds he'd make, and the way he'd taste as he hit the back of my throat.

"And you could throw up a silencing shield before the two of you start with yours each night, but you don't hear me complaining," he snarked back.

"You said you had one up!" Marceline whisper yelled at Kenji.

I was too distracted to hear his response as the heat deep in my stomach burned hotter with each second that passed. My mouth went dry as I continued to watch the droplets of sweat roll down his body, jealous of every place they touched him. On instinct, my nails sharpened into claws and Evander sucked in a sharp breath.

"You're making it *very* hard to say no to you right now," he breathed.

"I'm trying to make something else *very* hard as well."

He groaned in desire before wrapping his hands around my wrists and prying my fingers from his pants. "Tonight, I swear."

"Why not now?" I begged, my eyes finally lifting and locking onto his. His pupils were completely blown, making me want to further test his restraint. I wouldn't have to push much harder for him to cave—he was already teetering on that edge.

"Because I have a surprise for you."

58

Ainsley

Evander's hand pressed to my lower back as he steered me away from the stairs that led to our bedroom. My throat rumbled in protest, but thanks to Marce's hike of torture, I didn't have any physical strength left to fight him as he navigated us through the house. "It'll be worth it," he promised.

I rolled my eyes, ready to argue when a familiar voice filled my ears, making my heart stop. My body moved on pure instinct and adrenaline as I sprinted through the house, ignoring my aching muscles and pushing myself as fast as I could to the kitchen. The moment I stepped over the threshold, my gaze landed on warm hazel eyes and a bright, loving smile. My breath caught as Imogen shoved away from the dining room table and ran for me. We clumsily collided, wrapping our arms tight around each other as we struggled to get our questions out, each of us continuously interrupting the other.

"What are you doing here?" I demanded through a laugh. "You weren't supposed to arrive for another four weeks!"

Imogen pulled back, tucking her long obsidian hair behind her ears. It dawned on me that I had never seen it styled in any way other than a neatly piled bun. My eyes dropped to her outfit, noting the difference there, too. Gone was the deep emerald Maiden's uniform with a pristine white apron, and in its place was an airy dress in the softest shade of blue that complimented her olive skin. She had always been beautiful to me, but something about the happiness that exuded from her now made her even more exquisite.

"After Dashiell came home yesterday, he told me to make sure my things were packed because your husband was coming to pick me up in the morning," she answered, tossing a glance over her shoulder to Evander, who was now entering the kitchen.

"Are you sure Dash doesn't still need help?"

"When I imposed that question, he wouldn't hear of it. He said he refused to keep us apart for any longer."

I weakly smiled, happy she was standing before me but sad that I had taken away the last person Dash had. "So you're here *for good*?"

Imogen's grin broadened, her warm eyes brightening as she reached up to cup my cheeks. "I'm here with you *for good*."

A lump of emotion rose as I stood there, looking at the only mother figure I had ever known. I had missed her, but I didn't realize the extent until I was in her arms again. Imogen had been through so much—*lost* so much—because of me; and now here she was, willing to do it all again.

She cleared her throat, averting her eyes as she blinked rapidly. "Now, enough of this nonsense," she said, backing away and straightening her posture, "Lia and I prepared lunch for everyone, so let's eat."

I followed her to the table where a massive spread had already been set out. Chicken, fish, pork, fruits, vegetables, bread, and an array of desserts were scattered elegantly across the table. It was without a doubt Imogen's doing as we rarely had feasts of this magnitude unless at the palace. I took a seat between Felix and Imogen and cast my gaze across the table, taking in everyone's smiling faces as they chatted, laughed, and passed around platters of food. With Imogen here, my home was now complete, finally taking in the last member of my family.

When my stare found Evander's, he was quietly watching me, the corner of his lips turned upwards. *Thank you*, I mouthed as I gazed lovingly at him. *I love you*, he mouthed back in response. Before I could say it back, Felix violently kneed me beneath the table.

I pivoted, a sneer on my face as I rubbed my already aching muscles. "What the hell was that for?!" I demanded under my breath.

"I need you to stop making eyes at your husband so you can pay attention to me."

"And you couldn't have just *said* that?"

"Ainsley, there is a time and place for dramatics, and this is it." I rolled my eyes and leaned in, copying his movements. "They are a hundred percent sleeping together," Felix whispered.

"Who?"

He gave me a flat look and then very inconspicuously pointed to Cal, Imogen, and Lia. I directed my focus to his targets... all sitting spaced out from one another and not so much as making eye contact. Cal was engaged in conversation with Marce, Lia was chatting away with Kenji, and Imogen was entirely focused on her discussion with Oli.

"Did something happen?" I asked.

"Yeah, they've been avoiding each other."

"Felix, that doesn't mean they're sleeping together."

"Bullshit." He had been completely fixated on the idea of Cal and Imogen ever since my trial in Caelum, but I never saw anything that led me to believe his accusations. And the way the three of them were now certainly didn't help his theory.

"I think you need to let this idea of yours go," I said, turning to my plate and piling food onto it. My stomach rumbled and I wasn't going to deny it any longer in favor of hearing Felix's baseless theories.

"Whatever. I'll prove it eventually."

Lunch passed slowly as we lost ourselves in conversation, everyone desperate to know more about the woman who meant the world to their queen. They had welcomed her into our family with open arms and I couldn't wipe the smile off my face at how well she fit in. Marce's questions were always answered with eloquent replies, and Evander's quips were returned with equal ferocity. She seemed intrigued about Kenji and Calidore's time as soldiers and they were just as happy to have someone to share tales of their adventures with. Imogen finally had a home with people who would love and protect her just like she deserved.

"I should probably go and unpack," she said to me when the conversations died down and branched into groups.

"We can show her to her room," Calidore announced at a volume and intensity that was far too high for what the situation warranted. Everyone in the room ceased their discussions and directed their attention to the built man with russet brown hair and golden eyes currently rising to his feet, his chair collapsing to the ground behind him from the speed at which he stood.

"What I think he means..." Lia said through a forced smile as she pushed away from the table, "Is that we have no issue taking Imogen there since her room is right next to ours."

I looked between the three of them, noting how Imogen's stare stayed on her plate. Lia and Cal, however, threw glances at one another as if having a silent argument. "Plus, you should go shower, Ainsley. You smell horrible," Cal added.

My mouth dropped open as Lia groaned and pinched the bridge of her nose. I was just about to sling an insult his way when Imogen placed a gentle hand on my arm. "It's really not an issue," she said and gestured toward Lia and Cal. "They can show me to my room while you bathe and change. And once you're finished, come find me." Cal cleared his throat not-so-subtly. "I mean *I* will come and find *you*," Imogen amended.

I felt the color leech from my face. Felix grabbed hold of my leg under the table, his fingers digging into my flesh as he tried to contain himself. My heart was thunderous as I plastered a polite, tight smile onto my face and nodded. Imogen stood and allowed Cal to escort both her and Lia out of the kitchen and through the house.

The room was utterly silent as I waited and waited and waited. Finally, the sounds of boots hitting the stairs reached my ears, and I loudly let out the breath I had been holding as I turned to Felix with wide, panicked eyes.

"I fucking told you!" he said, pointing a finger at me.

"Oh my Gods," I breathed, my hands shaking as I tried to fan myself off. "All three of them?!"

"Good for Imogen," Evander said as he leaned back comfortably in his chair. "She's about to have the time of her life." Oli, Marce, and Kenji all laughed at his response, but I flung a dagger across the table.

Everyone went silent as the blade embedded itself into the wood an inch from the table's edge and Evander's lap. I stood, pressing my palms onto the surface as I glared at my target. "Do *not* talk about my mother that way. She's yours now too for all intents and purposes." I pointed a finger to the door that led to the rest of the house and leaned further across the table. "*Your* mother is upstairs getting railed right now and you want to joke about that?" Like a wise man, Evander shook his head.

"Do you want to talk about it? About how right I was?" Felix asked.

"No. I want to go shower and perhaps vomit. I'm not sure in which order," I replied and left the kitchen.

I slammed my dresser drawer shut as I worked to banish images of Lia, Cal, and Imogen together in a way that was anything but innocent. Maybe Felix's theory was wrong and I was misreading the situation. I sat on the edge of my bed, sliding thick socks onto my feet as I replayed the exchange at lunch. The way Cal abruptly demanded that they be the ones to show Imogen to her room. The way Lia chimed in to back him up. The way Imogen agreed so quickly. Nope—Felix was definitely right.

"Has *anyone* been doing your hair properly?" a gentle voice called. I jerked out of my thoughts to find Imogen standing in my doorframe, curiously looking over the space.

"What's wrong with the way it is now?" I asked, running my fingers through the wet, tangled mess and almost immediately getting stuck. She arched a brow—her point proven.

"Come along," she ordered and walked into the hallway without waiting to see if I'd follow. It was as if I were still in Caelum and she was the Maiden assigned to ensure I looked and acted appropriately. With a wide grin, I leapt from the bed and hurried after her.

Imogen combed through the knots, quietly mumbling to herself about how, as the queen, I should be presentable at all times. Though I continuously agreed, she knew I was full of shit, only saying what she wanted to hear just as I used to when she was in charge of my wellbeing. I'd missed this.

"Where's Cal and Lia?" I asked once her fingers began sectioning off pieces of my damp hair.

"How should I know?" Clearly, she wanted to play coy. "I met Elenora," Imogen added, knowing damn well that I would drop my original line of questioning for that one.

I huffed an annoyed sigh at her deflection and straightened. "And?"

Imogen's fingers began deftly weaving the sectioned strands into a delicate braid as she said, "And... She seems lovely." I remained quiet, impatiently waiting for her to stop dragging out this conversation on purpose. "And very kind, beautiful, intelligent—"

"You got all of that from meeting her *once.*"

"No, I *got all that,*" she said, mocking my tone, "When the three of us had dinner together." I didn't care for the amused smile in her voice. "Does that bother you?"

I snorted. "No. Why would it?"

Imogen fastened one braid and began working on the next. "You tell me." The implication in her statement reminded me so much of when she thought there was something going on between Felix and me. I rolled my eyes, shaking off the unspoken suggestion.

"If you want to have dinner with Dash and your new daughter, I have no issues with it."

Imogen chuckled loudly as I kept my hard stare straight ahead. I didn't see what was so damn funny. "Sometimes I miss you, and then I remember how dramatic you are," she said through her laughter.

"Whatever." I crossed my arms over my chest like the child I knew I was acting like would have. After a moment of quiet, save for her gentle snickering, I continued. "He said he wants to get back to the friendship we once had but then refuses to admit what's going on between them."

"Perhaps it's a topic he's not ready to discuss with you."

"But we talked about Evander," I said, throwing up my hands in frustration. "And *he's* the one who brought it up!" Imogen groaned and released my head, the hair she had been almost done braiding falling undone in loose waves. I mumbled a quick apology, placed my hands firmly in my lap, and tried to remain perfectly still so I wouldn't mess her up again.

"Then maybe there really *isn't* anything more than friendship blooming between them," she offered as she weaved my long strands back together. "Perhaps he—" A gentle knock on the door interrupted her sentence and we both lifted our eyes to find Evander standing there.

"I was checking to see if you wanted dinner brought up here tonight, so you two could continue catching up," he said slowly as his gaze drifted over us, skeptically assessing the situation. "Is everything okay?"

"Yes!" Imogen and I said in unison. Evander's eyes narrowed into slits.

"We're just gossiping about how you and Dashiell tried to kill each other this past week," she lied. Van stiffened as he swallowed hard, still ashamed for how he had acted. "But dinner up here later sounds great, thank you."

Evander nodded, taking the dismissal for what it was, and departed the room. Imogen quickly tied the other band around my hair and crept off the bed and over to the doorway. She peered into the hall, checking left and right before shutting the door quietly and turning to face me with an expectant look.

"I don't entirely believe that they're just friends," I explained, commenting on her earlier suggestion. She raised a brow and I breathed a long exhale before my eyes dipped to my fidgeting fingers. "And though I want Dash to be honest with me about it, I guess I can understand that he may not be ready to. I just want to make sure she's good enough for him," I said truthfully.

Imogen was at my side a breath later, sliding her warm hands over mine and squeezing gently. I lifted my eyes to hers as she offered a reassuring smile. "That's something he's going to have to figure out on his own," she whispered.

"I know." The words were barely audible.

Imogen reached for a pillow and set it on her lap, tapping it twice in request. My lips pulled into an excited grin as I obliged, laying my head down. Her fingers trailed over my braid as she leaned close and said, "Now tell me all about what happened with Dashiell and Evander this week."

I twisted, a crease between my brows forming as I peered up at her. "I thought you already knew."

"Oh, I just assumed," she said, waving a dismissive hand. "And clearly, I was correct."

I couldn't help but laugh at her accurate assumption and immediately dove into the entire ordeal. Imogen was here. She was *finally* with me. But that only meant it was one more person I had to protect—one more person I stood to lose should everything go wrong.

59
Dashiell

I set down my pen and rolled my neck. It had been hours since I last stepped foot out of my office and I was sure I would get an earful from Elenora about it once I finally emerged. But there was still so much work that needed to be done. My kingdom was slowly falling apart, and with war looming closely, I wasn't sure it would survive it.

A knock rasped against the aging wood door and without picking my head up from the parchment in my hands, I called out, "Yes?"

The door groaned as it opened, followed by the steady sound of booted footsteps. I redirected my attention toward the visitor, recognizing the cadence of a general's approach.

"Your Majesty," Silas said as he reached the desk, bowing deeply at the waist before righting himself and straightening his otherwise pristine uniform. "There's been movement on the front." He extended a piece of paper in offering.

"Anything we should be worried about?" I asked.

I unrolled and scanned the report quickly, but there was nothing out of the ordinary. Mostly just families moving about after catching wind of the war and Ministro's forces repositioning themselves on the neighboring border. The latter had been a common occurrence these past three weeks since returning from Tenebrae, and though Ministro hadn't attacked, it was something we were keeping a close eye on.

"Just the usual, Your Majesty, but…" Silas trailed off and I glanced up in curiosity.

"But something feels *off*," I finished for him. He nodded, and looked toward the open window, his eyes narrowing as if he could find the words in the distance. "I sense it too."

"I'd like to bring more soldiers to the front," Silas said, moving his focus back to me.

"Is that necessary?"

About a third of our forces fled once my father was slain and the soldiers learned where my allegiances lie. With a number of my men helping to find homes for the residents who were exiled from the palace, and others lining our borders, we were already stretched thin.

"I'm not sure, but I'd rather be safe than sorry," he answered.

I took a deep breath and nodded, replying, "Then take what you need." The general bowed again and retreated for the door. "Silas," I called before he could reach the exit, a thought popping into my mind. I pulled a golden key from my pocket and unlocked the drawer to my left. "What do you know about this?" I held out my open palm, revealing my father's ruby ring.

After Ainsley told us about the stones they had been searching for and what she believed they could do, she gave the ring back to me. I wasn't sure if it was done as more of a gesture of trust, or if she thought I'd had better luck figuring out exactly what it was.

The rings I had seen adorning the knuckles of a few of Perceval's generals were more modest renditions of the oversized and gaudy original I held in my palm. A bit too coincidental for it to be taken as chance. As soon as Ainsley shared what she learned about the stones, I sought the men who were given the rings. Unfortunately, they were loyalists of my father, and the moment I made my intentions clear to stand with Disparya, they fled.

Silas stalked closer and peered at the ring I held. "Not much, Your Majesty," he answered. His brow furrowed in question and I extended my hand. He picked up the ring and brought it to his eyes, examining every facet as he turned it over. "However, it resembles the pieces he gave some of his generals."

"And what do you know of those?"

He loosed a breath and shook his head, handing the ring back to me. "Again, not much. Your father only provided them to those he trusted most. Those in his—" Silas cut himself off, his frantic eyes darting to mine as if suddenly realizing who his remarks were about.

"You may speak freely." I leaned back in my chair, trying to seem as casual as possible to ease his worry. "Perceval was a dick and a traitor. We don't have to pretend he wasn't."

Silas worked extremely hard to stop the corner of his lips from tilting upward. "Those in his pocket," he finished. "Your father was very good at getting whatever he wanted from whoever he wanted."

I drummed my fingers along the surface of the desk as I studied the general before me. "But not from you," I observed.

Silas opened and closed his mouth as he tried to come up with a response, his eyes flicking around the space as the room filled with tension. He was wondering if he had said too much, gone too far. Like he had walked into a delicate trap I had laid. I tilted my head, deciding to forgo any reassurances of the contrary as I waited to see how Silas would choose to play this.

He was quiet for another moment, an obvious battle waging behind his ocher eyes. Finally, he shook his head—a decision made. "King Perceval had a talent for convincing people to do his bidding. He made promises of greatness and prosperity. Promises of rewards and riches," Silas said, settling his steady gaze upon mine. "But I never bought into any of it."

I sat forward and rested my forearms on the desk, interlacing my fingers together. "Do you have a family, Silas?" I asked. He nodded slowly, his skepticism seeping into the movement.

"A wife, children, and several grandchildren."

"And they mean more to you than anything my father offered." Again he nodded, this time surer of himself. It seemed Imogen's theory of how to get around my father's Obscure had proven correct. My mother's love for me had freed her from his hold, just as my love for Ainsley had done the same for me. "Do they reside here in the palace?" I questioned.

There was no reason for me to assume otherwise given his current position as a general in my army, but the way he slightly stiffened at the inquiry gave me pause to trust him fully. If my father wasn't able to entice him with his Obscure, there wasn't anything this man wouldn't say or do for his family.

"Most of them do, Your Majesty," he replied hesitantly, but an arch of my brow had him expanding on his answer. "My youngest son is assigned to our northernmost camp boarding Venator. And my oldest is..." Silas's throat flexed as he swallowed and crossed his hands behind his back. It wasn't a formal gesture—a soldier's stance in front of his king—but as a way to remove his trembling fingers from view. "He's in Pravus."

My muscles tensed as my Obscure came out on instinct, picking apart each subtle movement of the man before me to try and detect what, if anything, he had shared with his oldest son.

"A traitor?" I mused, cocking my head to the side.

"No." The word was a deep growl with Silas's features hardening at the accusation. I straightened, lifting my brows at his tone, but to his credit, he didn't back down—didn't show any sign of fear. In that moment he wasn't a general of Caelum, but a father defending his son. I couldn't help but admire the loyalty. "He would never."

We held each other's stares as I called back my Obscure, putting away the unique magic for now. "Explain," I ordered.

I didn't miss the faint flash of surprise in Silas's gaze. The late king would have never offered anyone the opportunity to elaborate on a situation if there was even the slightest hint of a conspiracy. And even though I was apprehensive about whatever Silas would say...

I wasn't my father.

"My son, Xavier," the general began with a cautious step forward, "Is—*was*—a good man." I noted the correction but didn't comment as he continued to move closer. "He was part of one of the units sent to oversee whatever plan King Perceval and Lord Oberon had orchestrated."

"A plan you're pretending to have no knowledge of," I said, cutting in before he could say another word. Silas's boot squeaked across the marble floor as he skidded to a halt, the fear in his eyes evident either for his son's sake or his own.

"I'm not privy to the information that Xavier is. I may technically outrank him, but his missions were far more covert than mine ever were. Your father was a secretive man, only granting those he believed he could trust with sensitive information. My son was one of those people." My lips lifted at the deflection and careful wording.

It was obvious Silas had far more information than he had ever led me to believe, but it remained to be seen if he would ever willingly share it with me. Torture wasn't a route I wanted to take, nor did I think it would do any good in this case.

Elenora had been relentless in her task of trying to get me to trust my instincts and not overthink every little decision. And right now those very instincts were telling me to trust Silas. To win him over and keep him close. I internally groaned at having to tell her about this conversation later and hearing her brag about how right she always was.

"You said he *was* a good man," I said, trusting my intuition. "How did he die?"

Silas opened and closed his mouth before shaking his head. "I don't know that he has, Your Majesty." I angled my head in question and the general released a long breath before pressing on. "Like I said, he was close to your father... but he was also a good man. In my experience, you couldn't have been both."

I offered a grunt of acknowledgment, knowing exactly what he meant. There hadn't been a single person who was close to my father who hadn't either fled or attempted to usurp my reign. It was part of the reason Elenora had come back with me to Caelum to begin with. Her Gift as a Verus allowed her the innate ability to detect untruths. Even if they weren't outright lies, she could pick up on underlying notes of falsities. She had been crucial in snuffing out the remnants of traitors in my court.

"There have been rumblings about what King Perceval and Lord Oberon were doing. Stories of soldiers with multiple Gifts and unmatched power. Tales of fortunes, misdeeds, and vile plans. All rumors, of course." He added the last sentence like an innocent afterthought.

"Of course," I replied with a smirk and leaned back in my chair once again. If we were going to dance around each other, I might as well get comfortable while doing so.

Silas regarded me for another moment before continuing. "After your father died, there were many questions about the operations in Pravus, and what would happen once you were sworn in as king." He paused as if waiting for me to offer my thoughts on that matter. Once he realized that I wouldn't, he carried on. "Many soldiers didn't like what was happening in Pravus, and once you made it clear that Caelum's dealings with them would cease, it caused an uproar amongst those who disagreed with the order. And those who were loyal to Disparya—to *you*—never made it back to Caelum.”

I traced a circular pattern along the wooden desk with my finger as I pondered his statement. “So you don’t know for certain if your son is truly dead,” I pointed out.

Silas’s stare dropped to the floor, his shoulders sagging as he let out a defeated breath. His voice came out little more than a whisper as he said, “I’ve been a soldier for a long time, Your Majesty. Over my centuries of service, I’ve seen things I wish I could forget, and am no stranger to the brutality of war or the costs. Once you made your stance clear, those men who were faithful to Disparya were surrounded by the enemy. I’m not naive enough to believe that my son is alive—that any of them are.”

His words sent a pang of guilt through me, and for the first time, I wished I had gone about things differently. Regardless of my intentions, it seemed I had been doing far more harm than good ever since stepping into my reign. Whether it was from my lack of council, inexperience, or a deadly combination of the two, every choice I made had dire consequences that only seemed to get worse as time went on. No matter what I did, I couldn’t seem to find my footing as king.

I reached for my pen and directed my gaze back to the paper on my desk, unable to look into the eyes of a father who would never see his son again because of my choices. “Gather the names of the soldiers unaccounted for and see to it that their families are taken care of,” I ordered as I scribbled on the parchment just to give my trembling hand something to do.

“Of course, Your Majesty, but...” he trailed off. My eyes flicked up just long enough to silently request he continue before darting back to my mindless task. “But there’s no way to tell for certain which soldiers were loyal to you versus who chose to stand with Lord Oberon.”

I contemplated his response for only a moment before doing what Elenora had been advising. I trusted my instincts. “That doesn’t matter,” I told Silas, as I met his curious stare. “The families are not at fault for the crimes of their brother, father, son, or whoever it was they lost. I will not have the memory of their loved ones tainted by declaring them a traitor, nor will I let those who were honorable die in vain. *All* of my people deserve to grieve in peace.”

I didn’t wait for the general to respond before I lowered my eyes back to my desk and wrote down another note. Silas took the dismissal for what it was and retreated to the exit, granting me the false peace of solitude once again.

“Your Majesty?” he called before he left. I grunted in question but kept my eyes on the paper as shame continued to plague me. “They hide things.” The confession snagged my attention and I glanced up through lowered lashes. “The rings,” he continued, pointing to the one still clutched in my left hand. “They can conceal any object or person from view.”

Unfurling my fist, I directed my attention to the oversized ruby that left an imprint in my palm from how tightly I had been holding it. "I thought you didn't know anything," I accused.

A muscle in Silas's lip twitched as he replied. "I said that I didn't know *much*, not that I knew *nothing*." I couldn't stop my own smile from forming at the sly wording.

"How does it work?"

"I'm not sure." I offered a skeptical glare. "Truly, Your Majesty," he said, his hands raised in innocence. "All I know is that your father had very few to offer but was in search of more. The rings can keep the bearer hidden, but I don't know for how long or what other limitations it may have."

I closed my fingers around the ring and pocketed the Tectus stone Ainsley had been right about. One down, two to go. We just had to figure out how to use it. I hoped it could give us an edge in this war.

"Some of Pravus's soldiers have rings of their own, but they're different than the rubies," Silas continued. My heart plummeted with the news I definitely did not want to hear. "They're sapphires, and before you ask, I don't know what they can do. Only that Xavier was terrified and didn't think we could survive." He reached into the pocket on the breast of his uniform and pulled out a piece of paper that looked like it had been opened and refolded a thousand times.

"Another rumor?" I asked as he walked the note over to me and placed it on my desk.

"The last one I received."

Delicately, I opened the slip of paper, careful not to tear its already worn edges, and read.

It's worse than we suspected. If Pravus marches on Disparya, our world as we know it will end. Call in every favor you have and get our family out of there. Sail as far as Memini if you have to. Just get out.

Memini was a land on the other side of the world, and if he wanted his family to travel *that* far, Xavier didn't believe we could win this war.

I fought the sinking pit in my stomach as I picked up the small ring that had fallen from the parchment. The item looked so much like the one my father had possessed in nearly every way except for one—the stone wasn't a ruby, but a deep blue sapphire.

"Thank you," I told him as I handed him back the note from his son and tucked the new ring into my pocket. He bowed and turned on his heel. "Silas..." I said before he could leave. "Why did you tell me all of this? Why not keep it to yourself, as you have been?"

His questioning eyes were bright and thoughtful as they met mine. "Do I still have permission to speak freely, Your Majesty?" I nodded and tried to shove down the anxiety still pumping hard through my blood. Silas's lip quirked up in the corner as he said, "Because you're turning out to be a far better man and king than that piece of shit ever was."

Before I could take a single breath—say a single thing—he bowed deeply and departed the room.

60
Dashiell

"He's not wrong, you know," Elenora said as she leaned across the space and shoved a nibbled-on piece of toast into my mouth. "Now eat, dammit. I'm not going to be held responsible if another King of Caelum keels over dead."

I rolled my eyes and playfully shoved her back into her seat on the makeshift bed of pillows and blankets she set up on the floor of my office. I had refused to leave until I figured out how to use the Tectus stone in my father's ring.

That was two days ago.

"You don't have to stay here if you don't want to," I replied, taking an exaggerated bite of food just to shut her up.

She smiled as she threw her back against the pillows and plucked a book from the stack to flip through. "It's true that your bed is far more comfortable, but contrary to popular belief, I actually enjoy your company from time to time." Elenora tossed a wink my way just as the voice of a guard reached a level of panic outside the office door.

"It's fine!" an all-too-familiar woman demanded as she shoved her way into the room, despite the guard trying to pull her back. Ice shot over the hands that grabbed Rosella as she continued to fight her way out of his hold.

"Let her pass," I drawled and plopped back into the cushions next to Elenora. The Agnitian advisor shoved another piece of bread into my mouth and snickered as I struggled to chew.

"Aww, how cute," Rosella cooed sarcastically. I didn't miss the way Elenora tensed at my side or how she moved an inch away, creating a small gap where our shoulders had been pressed together. "I'm bored," Rosella whined and came over to sit where we were, the sunlight shining through the windows giving her golden hair a soft glow.

"I don't really care," I replied. Rose rolled her eyes as she stole my plate of breakfast and threw a blanket over herself to cover the upper thigh that was exposed from the long slit in her dress. Elenora cleared her throat and directed her gaze toward anywhere but the blonde across from us as she brought a cup of tea to her lips.

"So are we having a threesome or…"

Elenora choked on her drink before dissolving into a coughing fit. A warning growl rumbled at the base of my throat as I patted the Agnitian advisor on the back until she calmed down.

"What? It was just a suggestion," Rosella replied before digging into my food. "And don't pretend like you wouldn't enjoy it." At the insinuation, Elenora coughed again but quickly recovered and drained the rest of her cup.

"I'm fine, thank you," I said. My thumb and forefinger pinched the bridge of my nose as I worked to reign in the flood of irritation I always felt in Rosella's presence.

"Your loss," she shrugged and then continued around another mouthful of the food she stole from me. "I'm sure Ele wouldn't object seeing how cozy you two seem to be."

Elenora's face turned four different shades of red in the span of three seconds as her eyes dropped nervously to the hands in her lap. If making a situation uncomfortable was a sport, Rosella would excel at it.

"Rose—"

"Oh don't even bother trying to deny it. She slips into your room every night."

Elenora's head twisted, her eyes going wide as she frantically looked between me and my advisor.

"I…We…" she sputtered, gesturing a hand between us as I tried and failed miserably not to smile at her floundering. "I mean, we… Dash and I—" Elenora's focus landed on me as she whispered low, gritting the words through a clenched jaw, "A little help here, please?"

"Nah, you seem to be doing just fine," I told her with a satisfied smirk.

"Relax," Rose cut in before Elenora could chastise me further. "No one is blaming you for enjoying yourself. I, for one, know exactly how good his—"

"Rosella," I growled.

"Oh, lighten up," she snapped, dropping her fork to the plate with a clatter. "All I'm stating is that there's no harm in whatever is going on there. And I'm not going to say anything to anyone, so Ele can calm down. She looks like she's about to have a heart attack."

I glanced at Elenora to find her face in the palms of her hands, her ears now matching the hue of her cheeks. Nudging her with my elbow, I offered a wink as she peeked at me through her fingers. There wasn't a chance I was going to let her live down her embarrassment any time soon, and the death glare she gave me told me she knew it, too.

"Besides, it's not like there's anyone interesting enough to share those details with," Rosella was quiet for only a heartbeat before she continued, mischievous intent coating every whispered word. "Except for…"

"Don't," I bit out in a clear order. She attempted to wave me off, but I wouldn't let her. "I mean it, Rosella. Leave Ainsley alone."

She held my stare for a quiet moment before finally saying through a forced smile, "Fine. But I don't get why you're still protecting her."

"It's a good thing you don't need to." I felt Elenora's curious and thoughtful eyes on me but I didn't relinquish Rosella's stare to give her my attention. "Now, don't you have something you should be doing rather than devising a plan to rile up the Queen of Tenebrae?"

"Perhaps," she mused, setting the now empty plate onto the ground. "But it's an ungodly hour so most of my proteges are still asleep."

"How's that going, by the way?" Elenora asked.

Rosella and I both turned toward the advisor, surprised she had chosen to speak up at all. For the past three weeks, my visitor had been relatively quiet and kept to herself whenever Rosella was in my company, though I couldn't blame her for that. Rose was far too intimidating for her own good most days.

"Surprisingly well," she answered. "But they're not as good as me, obviously."

"Obviously."

Elenora clamped her mouth shut as if the word had tumbled from her lips of its own volition. Rose's perfectly groomed brow lifted as I watched her attempt to discern whether the simple acknowledgment was a compliment or an insult.

"So they're progressing in their training?" I asked before Rosella could think on it any longer.

"They are," she said, finally directing her focus back to me. I could practically feel the wave of relief roll off of Elenora now that she was free from scrutiny. "But they need several more lessons before I'll consider them ready."

After I realized how valuable the tavern in Tenebrae was, I knew it would be crucial to my success as king to implement my own system of spies. People I could trust and count on to keep me informed about the palace's people and happenings. And who better to train them than the woman who had been mastering the art of gathering information for years?

Before leaving The Dark Kingdom, I requested Ainsley tell me everything she knew about how to accomplish my task. I recognized that Evander was the one I should have gone to for the advice, but given his clear hatred for me, I figured it'd be best to keep my interactions with him as brief and nonexistent as possible.

"We don't have—"

"Time. I know," Rosella interrupted. "That's why my main focus has been on Bradly and Kodie. The others show promise, but those two are naturals. They master every lesson within a few tries."

I crossed my arms over my chest as I regarded her. "You're sure about them?" Without hesitation, she nodded, so I did the same, trusting her instincts. "Give them a mission as a final test. Assign them someone on our list of those suspected of still being loyal to my father's cause. Someone like Lord—"

"Nathaniel," she finished, a sly smile spreading across her full lips. "Where do you think Bradly and Kodie are right now? Better yet, where do you think they've been all night? I know what I'm doing, Dash." Rosella stood and dusted off invisible crumbs from her hands. "Have fun you two," she said as she headed toward the exit. "And don't forget to take your contraceptive tonics." With a roguish wink at the woman to my right, she departed from the room.

As soon as the door clicked shut, Elenora and I turned to one another.

"Well, that was..." I began, the corner of my lips lifting in a small grin.

"Horrible." She leaned forward and buried her face in my chest.

My smile grew as I wrapped my arms around her, stroking her soft black hair to offer comfort. "It wasn't *that* bad. You did just fine."

"Please. I was a mumbling idiot." The words were muffled as she spoke them into my shirt.

"Maybe. But when are you not?" She slammed her fist into my stomach and I winced from the surprisingly strong punch.

"You're an asshole," Elenora declared, and I laughed before bringing her with me as I laid back on our makeshift bed.

"Still doesn't change the fact that you can barely get out a coherent sentence whenever Rosella is around."

"She makes me nervous!"

"Clearly."

"I hate you," she mumbled with a yawn and I tucked her closer to me.

We'd barely gotten any sleep the past couple of weeks let alone the last two nights as we tried to learn more about my father's ring. A quick nap before diving back into our research wouldn't be completely detrimental to our timeline, especially with Ainsley trying to uncover answers on her end too.

"I know," I said with a yawn just as big, and let my eyes flutter closed. "Five minutes to rest and we'll get back to work."

Elenora's steady breathing was her only response as we both drifted off.

"YOUR MAJESTY!"

Silas's frantic plea yanked me from sleep. My Gift stretched over my arms, coating my flesh in ice crystals up to my elbows as I shot to my feet, my stare darting across the space as I searched for any sign of disaster.

"There's been more attacks!" the general confirmed.

My immortal ears strained as I tried to hone in on where to go and what exactly was going on. Elenora was on her feet a heartbeat behind me, reaching for the transfer paper she always kept on her, probably checking to see if this was an isolated incident in Caelum or if her own kingdom was also under siege.

"Where?!" I demanded as I stepped away from the blankets.

"Nearly all of our bordering camps. Ministro is fighting their way through our land to get to the western coast." I swore beneath my breath as I dragged a hand through my hair, my mind quickly assessing the situation and what we needed to do. "There's more, though," Silas continued and my heart plummeted in my chest. "We aren't only fighting off Ministrian soldiers. Many of our own have turned on us."

"What?" Elenora breathed.

"This was an organized attack. Something in the making for who the hell knows how long," the general said.

I shook my head, my blood pumping hard as I struggled for breath. My soldiers were outnumbered as it was, but with their own turning on them... They didn't stand a chance of survival.

I stormed for my desk, ripping open drawers until I found the stack of untouched transfer paper shoved in the very back. Something I never planned on using.

"What are you doing?" Elenora asked as I grabbed a pen and quickly scribbled on the paper. It felt like a lifetime had passed before the ink finally disappeared and delivered my message.

"The last thing I ever wanted to."

61

Dashiell

Less than a minute later, darkness as black as night spilled into the room.

"*I need your help*," Evander recited as he stepped through his shadows, reading from the slip of paper he casually held between his fingers.

Once we formed our new alliance of Disparya, the King of Tenebrae provided each of us rulers with transfer paper enchanted with his magic. Should we ever need him, the paper would allow him to traverse to us without the requirement of him being familiar with the location. He had warned Tallis, Jahier, and me that he wasn't a dog to be summoned, and given the amount of magic it required from him, it was only to be used for emergencies.

"To be honest, I never thought you'd actually use it," he continued as his Obscure dissipated around him. "And now it seems I owe Oli twenty—" Evander's relaxed demeanor and arrogant smirk faltered the second his eyes locked on mine. "What happened?" he demanded, all trace of arrogance gone.

Silas quickly ran through everything the reports disclosed, including the updates he was constantly receiving as the minutes ticked by.

"Do you have a map I can see?" Evander asked.

I pointed across the room to the large table with a detailed chart of Caelum spread across it. We hurried over, and Silas indicated each camp that had been targeted and how many soldiers were assigned there.

Evander released a heavy breath as he turned to face me, his features grim as he said, "Which one?" My brows furrowed in question as I looked between him and the map. "I take it you called me here because my Obscure is useful to you. Without it, it would take hours at the very least to get to even one of them."

"Exactly," I answered. "But with your help, we can make it to multiple—"

"No, Dashiell, we can't." He leaned over the table and pointed at various camps across the land. "From what you and your general have told me, you don't have a substantial amount of soldiers at these locations. It would be pointless to waste our time—"

"The lives of my people are not a *waste*," I growled, my tone giving way to the fury I felt coursing through me. "If that's how you feel, then you can leave. I'll figure something else out."

"Relax, Dashiell, I'm not saying they are."

"You're saying I should abandon them."

"I'm saying you have a decision to make," he argued, once again placing a finger over the map. "You can't save everyone, and these are the weak spots of your army. Even if we go there, there's no guarantee we can successfully hold our line and survive. We don't have the manpower, Dashiell. It makes more sense to focus our attention over here, or here." His index finger landed on two camps with the biggest population.

He stepped away from the table, crossing his arms over his chest as he waited for my answer. I shook my head, fighting against his logic. He was asking me to condemn my people to a fate they didn't deserve, and there was no way to stomach that.

"You expect me to just go along with this? To be okay with sentencing my soldiers to death?" I said through gritted teeth as I fought between what I felt was right and what I needed to do.

"No, Dashiell," Evander replied. A tinge of sadness slicing through the answer had my eyes drifting to his. "I don't expect you to ever be okay with it. No king worthy of the title ever would be." His arms relaxed, his hands dipping into his pockets as he cleared his throat. "But with this role comes decisions we have to make, regardless of if we want to. And some of those choices will cut so deep they will leave permanent scars on your soul."

I swallowed hard as my eyes closed tight against his logic. Elenora's hand found mine, warm and comforting as she squeezed my fingers.

"Sometimes you have to sacrifice the few to save the many, Your Majesty," Silas offered, but it didn't help. I knew what I had to do, but it didn't make the bitter pill any easier to swallow. I was leaving my soldiers to suffer and die at the hands of traitors without lifting a finger to help. What kind of king was I?

"It's your call, Dashiell," Evander said. "I'll take you wherever you want to go, but you should decide quickly. Every minute spent discussing is another life lost."

A shaky breath slipped from between my lips as I came to terms with the only choice I truly had. "Okay," I said, my eyes fluttering open and landing on the king across the room. "How close can you get us to where we need to go?"

We were only about a twenty-minute sprint outside the boundary of Caelum's largest camp. Evander had done his best, and given how unfamiliar he was with the land, it was far closer than I expected.

The taste of smoke coated my tongue the moment we stepped through the king's shadows, and the screams in the distance made it easy to tell which direction we needed to head.

I led the way, running as fast as my legs could take me, with Evander following a step behind. I had half expected him just to drop me off and leave, but for whatever reason, he stayed.

"How much farther?" he yelled over the booming sound of explosions up ahead.

"A few minutes!" I replied and picked up the pace, letting fire bloom in my palms as I readied myself for the fight.

The frantic pleas and sounds of destruction grew louder with each thunderous footfall as I pushed myself to my limit. I had to get there. I had to save as many as I could so those I had chosen to forsake would not die in vain.

At last, we pushed through a thicket of trees, revealing a meadow littered with fallen bodies beneath a smoke-darkened sky. Fire spread through the land in patches, weaving its way between tents and structures. Some of the flames engulfed soldiers as they ran for safety, naively giving the fire food to thrive and burn even brighter.

"Holy shit," Evander breathed as we scanned the battlefield that lay before us.

Soldiers donned in crimson were scattered throughout the camp, cutting their way through my men clad in emerald. The soldiers of Ministro were known for their ruthlessness, their brutality—their sheer thirst for blood. Unlike in Caelum, the Gods didn't bestow their kingdom with Gifts that could be physically seen, so those from Ministro made up for it with their relentless cruelty on the battlefield.

"There's no way to tell who's on our side," Evander said, pointing to two men dressed in green whose swords clashed with one another. The scene was chaotic with people fleeing and fighting, which made discerning which soldiers were loyal to me nearly impossible.

I reached for my Obscure, hoping it would allow me to see what we were clearly missing. If my men had joined Harbin's side and now fought for Oberon's cause, there had to have been a marker of some sort so Ministro's soldiers could tell friend from foe.

Under normal circumstances, I would have assumed Harbin would take the risk and kill anyone not donned in his colors, but he needed the numbers on his side in this war.

I felt the heaviness from my pupils dilating as my magic surged to the surface like it so often did these days. Time seemed to slow in my mind as my eyes focused on the details before me, picking them apart and inspecting them for clues.

At first, nothing seemed to distinguish the men apart from one another. They fought the same, both holding a sword in one hand while shards of ice coated the other. Their movements matched as they struck and parried in the same style we taught in Caelum, neither of them seeming to develop a new tactic from another kingdom.

I looked harder, observing their uniform next as Evander urged me to hurry up. Just as I was about to tell him to fuck off, I spotted it. I set my eyes on the next set of Caelumian soldiers locked in a battle, finding the same small red ribbon tied to one of their wrists.

The fabric was small enough to stay concealed beneath the sleeve of their jacket—making sneaking up on their victim easy—but accessible enough to reveal should one of the allied Ministro soldiers attempt to attack.

"There!" I yelled and held up my wrist. "Take out the ones with the ribbons."

"Took you long enough," Evander replied back as we both sprinted into the fray.

As grateful as I was to have him there, it was a fight not to give into the urge to burn every slip of his transfer paper just to not have to deal with his smugness. At least not without Ainsley present, seeing as she always knew how to deal with him. But that was a concern for another day.

Sprawling shadows shot past me, enveloping the entirety of the camp in a darkness that smothered any light from the rouge flames. More panicked screams rang out at the sudden loss of sight and I glanced over to find Evander smirking to himself, thoroughly enjoying the chaos he caused.

"Pretty sure we need the ability to see, asshole," I hissed as we skidded to a halt outside a barrier of inky black.

"No shit," he replied. "My Gift will conceal everything but their hands, so why don't you make yourself useful, go in, and kill as many of them as you can while they can't see you?"

Dammit. That was actually a decent plan.

"You've got five minutes," Evander continued, and I raised a brow as I made a sharp spear of ice with my magic.

"Not strong enough to hold it any longer than that?"

Evander snorted and tucked one hand into his pocket while the other kept the shadow barrier in place. "Please. I just don't want you having all the fun without me."

A chuckle I certainly didn't want to produce emerged from the base of my throat as I ran into the darkness.

As much as I hated the man, I couldn't help but marvel at the power he held. Just as he said, the shadows kissed every inch of the space, only leaving each soldier's hands exposed. They fought each other in the darkness the best they could, but with no light entering the area, it made the battle that much more dangerous.

I put a shield in place, feeling metal and magic bouncing off it from the second I entered the camp. Yells of pain and thumps onto the ground sounded around me as soldiers frantically sliced their weapons through the air in hopes of landing a fatal blow, but more often than not, hurting themselves or their allies.

"MY SOLDIERS, HALT!" I bellowed, my voice magically thundering over the bloodied battlefield.

They needed to know I was there—that I came for them. That I would stand beside my men and fight for my kingdom... And that I would tear down anyone who stood in my way.

"SHIELDS *UP!*" I commanded, knowing the second they stood still, the enemy would try and cut them down.

I ran then, not waiting to watch and see if my soldiers obeyed. Time wasn't on our side, so rather than making sure to kill each member of the enemy I encountered, I simply sliced off the ribboned hand and continued working my way through the crowd until the shadows began to drift away on the wind.

Light again filled the space as Ministrian soldiers and traitors alike knelt on the ground, clutching their severed limbs. "I gave you five whole minutes, and this is all you did?" Evander said as he walked forward, scanning the casualties. "I expected at least double the amount." He tossed a dagger over his shoulder without looking, stabbing an attacker straight through his eye as he shook his head at me in disappointment.

Asshole.

"Fuck off," I said breathlessly as I pulled a sword from a dead man's chest and joined the current battle. I was thrown into a sea of red, not just from bloodshed but from fallen Ministrian soldiers. It gave me hope that we might have had only a small portion of traitors in this group.

I could only relish in that prospect for a moment before my mind traveled to all the other camps throughout Caelum that might not have been able to say the same. I shoved the guilt away and forced myself to focus on the task before me. There would be time to grieve, to mourn, and to rage later. Right now, my people needed me.

While I aimed to dismember each Caelumian soldier who possessed a red ribbon and make it easier for my men to make quick work of them, Evander opted for the straight kill. When I told him to save the extra energy, the prick stated he didn't want other people to have credit for his hard work. I still didn't understand what Ainsley saw in him.

Coated in blood and grime, I ran through the battlefield, cutting through flesh and bone as quickly as I could while occasionally alternating between my water and fire magic.

"You need to use your Gifts more!" Evander ordered as he slid across the muddied earth, slicing through an enemy soldier's ankles as he passed him and jumped back to his feet, instantly ready to take on the next wave.

"It'll wear me out too quickly!" I argued back, spinning and plunging my sword into the gut of a man in a crimson uniform.

"I'm sure your two girlfriends would be more than happy to help you with your stamina issues," he replied, narrowly avoiding an attack but quickly recovering as he cast a dagger and flung it at his target. "But right now, your mediocre abilities are more useful than your subpar fighting technique."

I ignored both the insult and girlfriend insinuation as I called for my magic again, keeping a burning flame permanently in my palm.

Evander applauded loudly like the asshole he was before taking down another two charging soldiers.

"If I get near my baseline, that's on you," I called, slamming my fire into the face of an approaching attacker. He screamed in pain before crashing to the ground, my flames engulfing him fully until he was nothing but a crisp pile of flesh.

"If we survive this, your magic depletion will be the least of your concerns," he replied. "Duck!"

I did as he commanded and watched two daggers fly over my head and embed themselves in the hearts of the men rushing toward us. I stood and spun, feeling Evander's back collide with mine as we fought together in perfect unison.

"Unfortunately, you're right, and I have no idea how we're going to recover," I told him. With the severe losses we were taking with my people, there wasn't much I could continue offering to our alliances.

"I wasn't referring to your kingdom," Evander said through a humorless laugh. "We'll figure that shit out. Move!"

We twirled around each other, expertly wielding our weapons as we took out more Ministrian soldiers. I had completely given up my quest of severing limbs and instead went for the proven method of claiming the kill.

"I meant with Ainsley," he continued the moment we finished with the current onslaught. I peeked over my shoulder to find his stare on mine. "She's going to be pissed when she finds out you called for my help and not hers."

I faced forward again just in time to kick away a soldier in emerald green with a red ribbon tied around his wrist. My hands didn't touch him as I used my Gift to burn him from the inside out just like I had with Gideon. The traitor didn't deserve a swift or painless death.

"She can't traverse. I needed to get here!" I explained through a heaving breath. The exhaustion from the battle and my magic usage was kicking in, but I pushed past the pain. There would be time for rest later.

"I'm not arguing with your logic. I'm merely pointing out that the woman in our lives does not possess the capability to see said logic. Especially when she's angry."

Shit. If Evander had ever been right about anything, it was that.

"Can't you just explain—"

"—Nope. You're on your own," he said, pushing off my back as he lunged forward again. Fucking great.

We developed our own technique over the passing minutes, using each of our strengths to our advantage. We'd fight with steel and blades until we pushed our enemy back far enough. Only then would Evander call for his shadows and shove them forward, enveloping our enemy in darkness to steal away their sight. At that point, I'd fling sharp spheres of ice or fire into the black, hitting our targets and eliminating the immediate threat.

Again and again, we worked in tandem until fewer soldiers came, allowing us to finally split up and cover more ground.

⁕

An hour later, with the fight still raging on, Evander swore loud enough that I heard him from a fair distance away. I turned suddenly toward him just as four men fell at his feet, their bodies now withered grey husks void of life from his Tremo Gift.

"What's wrong?" I demanded as I ran over to him, his stare firmly on his forearm. I watched in amazement as his tattoo whirled over his flesh, forming letters in a delicate script. A message.

"Jahier needs me," he answered, his grey eyes flicking up to meet mine. "Are you good here?"

"Go," I said, "I've got it." More and more Ministrian soldiers and traitors had been fleeing the scene, realizing they wouldn't be able to defeat us. It was only a matter of time until the fight was over.

He nodded once before letting his Obscure pull him away.

62

Dashiell

Not long following Evander's departure, the battle was won. My soldiers laughed and cheered as they celebrated, but with over half of my men either dead or deserters, could I really call it a victory?

I spent the rest of the morning helping tend to the injured as we prepared everyone to head back to the palace. With only a few thousand remaining, there was no point in keeping the camp filled. For now, it was best to get those who survived back home and regroup as I assessed the damages from the other battles that had taken place today.

Dusk swept over the land by the time we strode through the palace gates, utterly exhausted. While I was away, Elenora took over things here, making sure the Medicus facility was fully stocked and beds were empty for the incoming soldiers who would need them. She even arranged for hundreds of cots to be set up in each of the three ballrooms as makeshift housing until we could find a more permanent solution.

Many of the palace residents had even offered to share their rooms with the displaced soldiers, going so far as to give up their beds as they took the added cots or the floor.

"I owe you," I told her as she slung one of my arms over her shoulders and helped me to my office after I refused to be seen by a Medicus. My injuries were minor cuts and bruises, all of which I could tend to myself, so there was no point in taking a bed from someone who needed it more.

"You can pay me back by resting," she replied, depositing me on the couch before hurrying off to retrieve food and water.

As much as I wanted to argue, I could barely move. I was closer to my baseline than I wanted to admit after tending to the soldiers during the hours-long trip back to the palace. Unfortunately for us, most of the Medicus stationed at the camp either fled or were killed once the attack occurred, leaving us with only ten remaining.

I ran from cart to cart, healing as many as I could with whatever energy I could muster. A few hours into the journey, I was only able to scrounge up enough magic to mend minor cuts.

Any more than that, I would dip below my baseline, putting myself at risk of my magic not replenishing at all.

Closing my eyes, I tilted my head toward the ceiling and focused on my breathing, my body feeling heavier than it had ever been.

"You used too much," Elenora scolded as she reentered the room. I cracked open an eye to see her striding for me with a tray full of bread, meat, and fruits.

"I didn't have a choice," I replied through a groan of pain as I tried to reposition myself on the couch. Her hands were on me at once, gently adjusting my limbs as I assisted her the best I could.

"Whatever. Just eat."

She furiously set the tray on my lap and walked across the room to pour a glass of water. I didn't dare defend myself further as I dug into the food, sighing in relief as I felt it hit my stomach. I could already sense my magic beginning to refill and said a silent prayer of thanks to the Gods for it.

"Any word from Silas or the other camps?" I asked. She whirled on me, eyes bright and scrutinizing as she gave me a pointed glare. I quickly shoveled more food into my mouth.

"Silas arrived at one a few hours after you left. Thankfully, they pulled out the victory as well. It seemed that very few of your soldiers were willing to turn on you there."

I blew out a grateful breath. We had claimed victory at our two largest camps, keeping a significant amount of our forces intact. It wasn't much, but given what we had been through the past few weeks, it was a small win.

"The locations that bordered Venator along the western coast..." she continued, her voice going grim as she walked over and took a seat at my right. "Dash, I'm so sorry."

I closed my eyes against the news, the pain and guilt far too overwhelming. I knew this would be the case—we all did—but it didn't make the words given life any easier to digest.

"You did what you had to."

"Is that supposed to make me feel better?" I bit out.

She didn't deserve my anger, but I couldn't help it from coming forward. Regardless of if I made the right decision today, thousands of innocent people died. And I would have to live with the consequences of my choice for the rest of my life.

"I'm sorry," I whispered.

Elenora placed a delicate hand on my shoulder, her brown eyes soft and pleading as she said, "Is there anything I can do?"

I shook my head but offered a grateful smile. She had already done more than enough—more than I could have ever asked for. "I just need to be alone for a bit."

Her lips pressed into my cheek before she stood, granting my request of solitude. "Promise me you'll finish that," she said, pointing to the still-full tray on my lap.

"I promise."

Once the latch from the closed door clicked into place, I let the guilt finally drag me under.

⁂

I had no idea what time it was—just that darkness had claimed the sky hours ago—when a swooshing sound I was becoming far too familiar with echoed in the space. My fingers stayed pressed firmly to my temples, my eyes glued to the reports scattered across the desk I was now seated at, as the swaggering cadence of his footfalls approached.

"Your friend is beyond annoying," Evander said as he plopped himself into the chair opposite me. "I told him to let you be, but he won't give it a rest."

I didn't respond, but my gaze shifted to the parchment on my left and the paragraphs of text written upon it. I read through every sentence Felix wrote, but couldn't bring myself to reply. Even Ainsley's concerned notes went unanswered as I sat in this room, too ashamed to do anything but go over the countless casualties each report detailed.

Maybe I was selfish for making them worry, but I couldn't concern myself with that—couldn't force myself to care. They had their own lives now, their own people and kingdoms to look after. And though they were my best friends and Felix had once been my second in command, things were different now.

As much as they loved me, I was alone and needed to face that reality. I needed to learn how to overcome the insurmountable hard times on my own, because we weren't a trio anymore. It was a fact I had been struggling with accepting for a long time, but it was the truth. Felix and Ainsley both had partners—people they loved... a *home*. This place had stopped being that for me the moment they left.

Our lives were going in different directions and as much as it hurt, I had to be okay with that.

"You'll get used to him," I replied as I cleared my throat, ignoring the way the words felt as I pushed them through my harbored emotions.

"I really don't want to."

I exhaled a shallow breath that was a mix of a laugh and sigh as I picked my head up to meet his gaze. To his credit, Evander didn't comment on how terrible and pathetic I looked, though we both knew it was the case. I could feel the redness in my cheeks and the way my lids were slightly swollen from hours of shedding tears.

Evander's stare dropped to a slip of paper he held between his hands as he said, "I heard about the other camps." He inhaled and exhaled deeply, his shoulders sagging with the movement as he continued. "I'm sorry, Dashiell." Evander leaned forward and placed the paper on my desk. "A list of the generals I now have occupying those camps," he explained as I flipped open the parchment.

"What are you talking about?"

My eyes scanned over the paper, noting the names of Tenebrean generals, the Gift they possessed, and where they were now stationed, along with a few additions of Venator soldiers loyal to Jahier.

"As there's no point in false pretenses any longer, I moved every soldier I had along the boundary of Agnitio to your land. They'll keep the camps up and running and defend Caelum's border until your soldiers are ready to occupy them again."

"But—"

"Jahier's men were also targeted today," he continued. I thought back to the message I saw appear on his arm and realized it must have been the prince's plea for help. "Somehow King Arden knew which villages were loyal to his son, and sent in soldiers to burn them all to the ground."

I sat straighter, my eyes widening in panic at the news and what it might mean for the Prince of Venator.

"Is he..."

"He's fine," Evander answered and leaned forward to rest his forearms on his thighs. "Thankfully he has spies within his father's court and caught wind of the planned ambushes. He was able to get most of the villages evacuated before dawn, but some of his people got caught in a battle as they were trying to flee. Luckily though, there were minimal casualties."

"Thank the Gods," I breathed as my posture relaxed with relief. "Is there anything I can do?"

He pointed to the list still clutched in my hands. "My kingdom is currently housing thousands of Venator's refugees, so all I ask is that you let Jahier's soldiers stay at the camps even after yours are ready to return. I know we talked about easing our people into this alliance, but we don't have time for that now."

"Agreed."

"Good."

"Fantastic."

"Wonderful," he replied with a smirk and pushed himself out of the chair. "Oh," he paused before taking a step toward the door, "And for the love of the Gods, write them back."

I smiled and peered at the transfer papers with Felix and Ainsley's handwriting. "I will eventually. I just..." I didn't know how to explain the depth of loneliness I possessed or how sometimes I felt like I didn't fit into their lives anymore.

Turning back toward Evander, I shrugged. He was smart enough to fill in the unspoken words the silence held hostage. I glanced again at the notes, my fingers suddenly inching to go against my better judgment and respond to my friends.

"Being king can be lonely," Evander said, snagging my attention. "You can be surrounded by people who love and support you, but they'll never truly understand what it's like to rule. To make decisions that affect hundreds, thousands, or even millions of lives. They'll never understand what those choices do to a person—what they cost us."

Before I could question it, I found myself asking, "How do you cope?"

A soft smile lit his face as he angled his chin toward the letters. "By allowing them to try," he answered. "Those in your life may never fully grasp what you're dealing with, but they won't want you to go through it alone."

I shifted awkwardly in the chair as Evander tucked both hands into his pockets. We weren't friends; hell, we were barely acquaintances. And this definitely wasn't the type of conversation I ever thought we'd be sharing. His focus drifted toward the door and then back to me as if he was unnerved by this tentative peace between us just as much as I was.

"Is she pissed?" I asked, sliding Ainsley's note in front of me.

"That you haven't responded, or that you came to *me* for help instead of her? Because either way, the answer is the same."

Groaning, I picked up the pen on my desk. "And I don't suppose you explained to her my reason for calling on you?"

His lips twisted in a wicked grin. "And give up the opportunity of having her anger directed at someone other than me for once? Not a chance."

"Of course."

Evander winked before striding across the office and stopping at the door. My head tilted in curiosity, wondering why he was choosing to use the exit rather than traverse out of my office as he had already done before.

"It isn't just being around the important people in my life that helps me cope," he called, half turning to look at me. "You have to let yourself feel the losses. You have to go through the pain and the guilt and the heartbreak because it makes you that much stronger—that much more determined to never feel it again."

His gaze held mine and there was an untold sadness imbued in his dark eyes—a history I was sure he'd only ever share with Ainsley. I regarded him for another quiet passing of time before finally nodding and accepting the advice.

"Let yourself go through the motions tonight so that you may move on and move forward," he added and turned back to the door. "I'll see you next week."

"Evander," I called and he halted, angling his head in my direction. "Thank you... For everything."

He dipped his chin in a delicate bow before facing the exit again. "I'll be back tomorrow afternoon to retrieve them."

My eyes narrowed and brows pinched with confusion. "Who?"

He didn't look back as he answered, "They may be a part of my court, but they're still your family, Dashiell." He twisted the knob and pulled open my office door, revealing two people pacing impatiently in the hallway.

A shimmering shield placed over the entryway disappeared and Felix rushed for me as Ainsley's angry scolding reached my ears.

"You said two minutes," she snapped. Her arms were crossed over her chest as if it was helping her contain her rage as she stared up at her husband. "That was ten."

"Your sense of time is extremely flawed, my love," he replied, tapping her on the tip of her nose with his finger. A gesture I knew was not going to help de-escalate the situation at hand.

Felix collided with me, his arms embracing me with all the love of a brother. I held him back but kept my eyes on the missing piece of my family still entirely too far from my reach.

Ainsley batted Evander away before reaching onto her toes, kissing his lips, and running for us. A heartbeat later, her face was buried in my chest as I constricted my hold on the two people who meant everything to me.

"You're an ass for not writing us back," Felix said.

"And for not asking *me* for help," Ainsley added.

I smiled as I nodded, knowing that if I tried to utter a word, it would come out strained from the tightness in my throat. Picking my head up, I locked eyes with Evander one final time, a moment of understanding passing between us before he disappeared into his shadows once more.

63

Ainsley

I inhaled deeply, savoring the scent of lemongrass and sea salt before my turn to say goodbye was over. With the attacks yesterday and the residents of my kingdom working tirelessly to find housing for the displaced people of Venator, we could only afford one night away from Tenebrae.

Even that amount of time wasn't ideal, but after learning of what happened in Caelum's camps and with Dash refusing to answer any of my or Felix's notes, not going to him wasn't an option.

Shockingly enough, it was Evander who held out his hand for me, knowing exactly what I needed before I even had to voice it. And now he stood yards away, waiting to whisk us back to our kingdom where so much work still needed to be done.

"Promise me you'll write if you need me," I whispered against Dash's shirt as his chin rested on the top of my head.

We talked through most of the night, diving into more dark and traumatic topics once Felix had fallen asleep. I shared with him the details of the night I thought Felix had died, when I fought at one of the camps Pravus had attacked months ago, and even the evening my Imperium Gift had emerged and what I had done to the man who attacked me.

I told him how scared I was on each occasion. How those scenes were forever seared into my memories. How I still wake from the nightmares even now.

And then I listened as Dash told me his horrors.

"I mean it," I added, his shirt muffling my voice. "You're not in this alone and never will be." I tightened my grip on him as my heart twisted, remembering all that he told me during our conversation and how broken he had been.

"I'll be fine," he whispered, his chin shifting my hair as he spoke.

With that, he pulled back and offered a soft smile that didn't reach his eyes. I fought every instinct to bring him back to me, knowing in my very bones that he still wasn't okay. But before

I could close the gap once more, Felix slid between us, taking my spot as he wrapped his arms around his brother.

"Don't freeze me out again, prick," Felix said, bringing forth a laugh from Dash that sounded forced and unnatural.

"Sorry," Dash replied, slapping him on the back before taking a step away just as Elenora emerged from the terrace entrance as if she had been waiting in the shadows the whole time.

I blinked in surprise, unaware that she had still been in Caelum. Last night, the three of us locked ourselves in the Sanctuary, never speaking to anyone but the guards who came by this morning to deliver breakfast, but Dash hadn't so much as mentioned that Elenora was present in the palace.

"I'll see you in a week," Dash said and backed away toward the Agnitian advisor, leaving Felix and I standing alone.

I watched him reach Elenora's side and her arms go around his waist as she stood on her toes to whisper something in his ear. He nodded shallowly while his eyes stayed firmly on Felix and I. Nothing about it felt right.

Dash was still pushing me out—still keeping me at bay when I could feel so clearly that there was more going on. My magic sensed it too, clawing against my skin in a demand to be let free. But I kept it chained as I observed Elenora ask another question, this time yanking Dash's attention away from us.

"We have to go, Ainsley," Evander called.

But I didn't move.

We had to leave, but I couldn't force my feet to take a step. It was beyond evident that Dash was filled with pain and despair, and now I was being expected to just walk away as if everything was fine.

But it wasn't.

We were a family. We were supposed to always be there for one another. I had no qualms or ill will toward Elenora, but she wasn't his—

"Ainsley," Van called again and I closed my mind to the thoughts.

I turned to Felix, frantic and desperate. "Stay with him," I said.

He looked at me with sad eyes as his hand found mine, interlocking our fingers together. "He doesn't want me to."

"I don't care. Just stay with him."

"Ainsley."

"Felix, he's not okay. We can both see that," I argued, my voice a broken plea of panic.

He looked between Dash and me, shaking his head against the idea. It became clear he wasn't going to give in to my request no matter how much I begged. Felix was going to side with Dash on this one. I released a long exhale, knowing exactly what I had to do.

"You're staying," I stated, my tone adjusting to where I needed it to be.

Felix's stare left Dash and landed on me, his eyes wide and features hardening. His jaw clenched, an anger I rarely ever saw within him bubbling forward. "Is that a command?" he asked, though it sounded like an accusation.

"Yes."

Felix didn't wait for me to finish the small word before he backed away and reluctantly headed to our friend. Elenora patted Dash's stomach, pointing out our change of plans as she caught sight of them.

"Felix is staying with you," I announced, turning my back to the King of Caelum just as I saw his mouth open to argue.

"He's not," Dash yelled.

"He is." I reached Evander a moment later, taking the arm he extended for me.

"Ainsley, I'm fine. I don't need a damn babysitter." The words were clipped and coated in ice.

"Good, because I don't have one to spare."

He waved a hand over the man with silver hair coming to a stop beside him. "Then what the fuck is this?"

"Ouch," Felix mumbled under his breath, his arms crossing over his chest as he toed a small rock angrily with his boot.

"You know what I mean," Dash told him in a gentle but still pissed-off way. "*Her Majesty* is the one playing coy." Those deep teal eyes settled back on me, threatening to sweep me away in the ocean's storm brewing behind them.

"We don't have time for this, love," Van whispered only to me. I acknowledged him and then directed my focus to Dash as I slipped into the role of a queen who had made up her mind and wouldn't bend.

"Felix isn't staying for you."

"Bullshit—"

"—He's staying for the alliance," I continued, stepping over Dash's outburst.

"You're lying and we both know it."

"I don't give a damn what you think you know," I snapped, letting venom seep into every word.

Dash's features hardened, his eyes going dark as his glower stripped me bare. It crushed me nearly as much as leaving him did, but I couldn't back down now. I couldn't force myself to go without knowing someone would be looking out for him.

"Evander, Jahier, and I have enough to concern ourselves with right now without worrying about what disaster will strike in your kingdom next." Dash reeled back as if I had hit him, and I supposed I had, but it was too late to change course now.

"That's a low fucking blow, Ainsley, even for you," he growled, straightening his posture to match mine as we went head to head.

"Your people are suffering and scared right now. You've taken a detrimental hit not only to Caelum but to our already struggling cause. Put your damn pride aside and realize not everything is about you!" The lie tasted bitter on my tongue.

Dash was anything but prideful, especially when it came to his rule, and losing so many of his people yesterday had been heartbreaking for him. It felt cruel to throw that defeat in his face given that my choice had nothing to do with the situation and everything to do with my inability to see him hurting.

"Use Felix exactly as you would have if he was still your second in command. Have him ease tensions and ensure no defectors made it back within your palace walls because we don't have the time or resources to come and save you again," I added.

I directed my gaze toward Evander's, meeting his calm but watchful stare. He offered nothing besides a gentle and supportive hand at the base of my spine.

"We'll see you in a week," I announced as Van's shadows licked over my skin.

"We are not done here!" Dash yelled, moving forward as if he planned to pull me from the darkness.

"Yes, Dash, we are."

And then the view disappeared beneath a plume of shadows.

Evander's hands moved to my waist as I blinked against the brightness of Tenebrae's afternoon sun. Gripping his arms for support, I inhaled several lungfuls of the spring air as I fought against my thrashing magic and its clear disapproval for how much I had hurt Dash.

"Are you okay?" Van asked, his breath warm against the shell of my ear.

"I'm fine," I replied. "If I wasn't a complete ass about the situation, Felix would already be headed toward the portal."

"You don't think that'll be the case anyway?"

I released a heavy breath and shook my head as I stepped out of his hold.

"Dash may be furious, but he isn't stupid. He knows it makes sense to utilize Felix's Gift and allow him to do what he's been trained to do his whole life. Keeping him there was the right call for the alliance."

My gaze wandered from my husband, and for the first time, I noticed the landscape surrounding us. Giant snowcapped mountains and sprawling hills of lush forests and wildflowers filled the space. I quirked a brow, wondering why he had brought us to a random field.

"I figured you'd need time to work through all your bullshit political responses before telling me what's really going on," he said, answering my unasked question. A delicate, strong finger slipped under my chin, directing my stare back to him. "Once you do that, I'll take us home."

"We don't have time for this."

"Then I suggest you start talking."

"Van—"

"Ainsley, you are the most important thing in my life," he interrupted, keeping his grip on my chin firm. "We are not leaving here until I know for certain that my wife is okay." He leaned down holding his lips just above mine. An echo of a promised embrace. "Now, love, tell me what's going on." His mouth molded to mine and I savored the gentle kiss and all of the love, support, and honesty that came with it.

"I feel guilty every day for taking Felix from him," I admitted once his lips receded from mine. "Seeing him last night and hearing about everything he was going through—it made me realize just how alone he was. And it…" I looked away from Evander's stare as my eyes burned with tears. "It hurt. I can *feel* how broken he is, and I hate it."

Van cupped my cheeks and his thumbs swept back and forth, catching the trails of moisture that welled over as I blinked.

"Do you feel better now that Felix is there?"

I nodded in his hold, my answer coming out on instinct. Even though I would have preferred to be there myself, an enormous pressure had been lifted from my chest to know Dash would have his brother there—a man who would willingly sacrifice his life, his happiness, and his freedom for him.

"We have important matters that need our attention, and I won't be able to give myself fully to them if I don't know that he's okay," I replied truthfully. "With Felix in Caelum, I know he'll make looking after Dash his priority."

"You don't think Dashiell is capable of looking after himself?"

I chewed the inside of my cheek as I worked out the best way to reply. Dash was strong, clever, skilled, and plenty capable, but that wasn't the point.

"I think..." I began slowly as I peered into the captivating eyes of the man I loved, "That I wouldn't have made it this past year if it weren't for the unconditional love and support of you and our family." I reached onto my toes and stole one more kiss, loving the way his smile tasted as his lips lifted in the corners. "And I want him to have that too."

Evander deepened the embrace as his hands slid down my sides to encircle around my waist. "Okay," he murmured against me and I felt his Obscure brush over my skin. "Let's go get to work."

64

Ainsley

I stumbled through our dimly lit house exhausted and weak. The entire day had been spent taking care of the refugees from Venator—finding them housing, food, and supplies. Thankfully, between the palace, schools, tavern, and numerous Tenebraen volunteers, we were able to secure temporary lodging for them all.

The house was quieter than usual as Van untied my boots and slipped them from my feet, seeing that I was too tired to do so. Imogen, Lia, and Brandle were all at the palace, helping to situate the new residents, while Cal, Oli, Kenji, and Marce would be heading home with dinner as soon as they were finished distributing provisions to the refugees in the village.

The only reason Van and I had left our work early was that I had taken a two-minute break and accidentally tipped out of my chair after falling asleep. The small gash on my temple from when my head hit the ground was enough for Van to dismiss my protests and traverse us away.

"Did you sleep at all last night?" he asked, rising to his feet and winding his hands around my waist.

Yawning, I shook my head. Dash and I had been lost in conversation until the sun began to crest the lush hills in the distance. Once we decided to finally shut our eyes, only an hour or so passed before Felix woke us up for more Trio Time.

"That's unfortunate," Van said, pressing his lips to my right cheek, then my left, then my neck. "I don't plan on letting you have any tonight either."

I smiled as my eyes fluttered close against the feel of his mouth on me, my skin burning hotter with each pass. "And why should I extend the pleasure of my company?"

"Because I was nice to your friend."

A soft laugh escaped me as he continued to kiss his way over my flesh. "Is that so?"

"*Extremely* nice. Like, really, really, *really* nice. I didn't even threaten to kill him once."

"Did you *think* about doing it, though?"

He went quiet, his lips halting their journey. My smile widened.

"That's not the point," he argued and pressed his mouth back to my neck as he worked his way to my collarbone. "The point is: I didn't act on those thoughts. And I came when summoned... *and* I saved his kingdom." His lips moved to my mouth, demanding small kisses from me between each word. "Some would even say I saved the *world* with my selflessness, yesterday. I think that's worthy of a prize."

"Do you, now?"

Evander nodded enthusiastically as a bright smile graced his face. I slid my hands up his stomach and over his chest until they reached his jaw. My fingers gently trailed over the light stubble on his face and the curve of his full lips.

"Some would say that saving your fellow king—saving the *world* itself—should be fulfilling enough," I whispered. "Don't you agree?"

Van looked at me blankly for a solid minute before he shook his head. "No, I want my reward, please."

A laugh escaped me as Evander claimed the sound, molding his mouth to mine as he stole what he wanted. "Fine, but I'm taking this out of your ten minutes," I said against him.

"Absolutely not. We agreed sex does *not* count for that."

His hands moved to my cheeks as he gripped my face to keep me still, and his tongue swept over mine in the barest of touches that had me melting in his hold. Evander kissed me harder, the soft moans I was making gently feeding his fire like they always did. He pushed his body flush against mine as his fingers pressed into my face before stilling for the briefest of seconds. It was subtle—barely there—but enough to tell me everything I needed to know. Wrong—something was wrong.

Evander kissed me once, twice, before hovering his lips just above mine as he whispered, "Craft a dagger and be ready." He didn't wait for any form of acknowledgment before pressing his lips to mine and smiling as if nothing was out of the ordinary.

My shadows gathered discreetly in my palm, forming a small blade as Van continued our ruse of two lovers lost in themselves. I counted my breaths, my heartbeat, the ticks of the clock on the mantle, and the number of kisses Evander took before finally pulling back from me. I offered him a weak smile that felt so forced, I was sure whoever was in our house would see right through the charade. The air was thin, heavy, and charged, and I was unsure how I didn't pick up on the intrusion the moment we stepped through the door.

My heart continued to pound in my chest as I tried to work through how anyone could break into our house. We had protections in place—shields that prevented anyone uninvited from entering, so how could this have happened?

Evander's stare held mine as he gave a barely perceivable dip of his chin. I took one deep, steadying breath, and together we spun, flinging our daggers across the room at the figure lurking in the shadows. Our weapons flew straight, but the sound of the blades embedding into the wall came from the far right of the figure. As if our target had simply swatted away our daggers before they reached them. I crafted two more at the same time Evander traversed and collided with the intruder on the other side of the room.

The intruder crashed into the wall as Van pinned him in place, a strip of candlelight illuminating part of his face. He was the same height as Evander and of a similar build. He possessed dark grey hair streaked with black, and ivory skin that made his deep emerald eyes stand out as they stayed transfixed on my husband.

"You missed," he said, his voice as smooth as silk.

My heart was in my throat as the light glinted off the sharp blade now poised at Evander's throat. I was rooted to the spot as I tried to figure out how best to save him. I couldn't traverse as he could, and any movement the intruder caught from me could mean death for Van. And there was no clear path for me to sling my dagger without risking hitting my husband instead.

"Did I?" Evander questioned and calmly angled his head down. I followed the dropped stare to the blade pressed between the intruder's legs.

The strange man picked up his head, a smirk now gracing his lips. "Is that any way to welcome your uncle?"

"It is when he breaks into my home," Evander replied as the dagger against his throat disappeared.

My grip on my weapons tightened, the pure adrenaline coursing through my veins not allowing me to fully believe the exchange.

"If I recall, we were invited."

"Yes, but I expected you a week from now... And perhaps in the light of day."

The intruder laughed and said, "Fair enough."

Evander turned to me then, those haunting grey eyes soft and calm as they sought me. At the sight, I let the daggers in my hands disappear and hesitantly walked toward the two men. "Love," he said and waved a hand toward our visitor, "This is my uncle, Declan."

Evander twirled his wrists and the candles in our house lit up, illuminating the entire space. Declan's eyes widened and his features fell as he watched me slowly approach.

"And Dec," Van continued, now angling his hand toward me, "This is Ainsley."

Declan nodded as his bewildered gaze tracked my every movement. He didn't respond as I stopped before him and extended my hand in offering. I looked to Evander, my brows pinching with concern.

"Everything okay?" the King of Tenebrae asked.

Declan shook his head as he pulled himself out of whatever trance he had been in. "Yeah, sorry. She just…" he stumbled over his words as his eyes darted across my face. "You look so much like—"

"My father," I finished with a smile. "I get that a lot."

"No," Declan said. "I mean, you *do* resemble him with certain features, but I was going to say your mother." The smile I wore faltered slightly as he continued to study me. "The way you move, the hesitance behind your eyes, the way your mind seems to be calculating every step before you take it… That's all Viv."

"You knew her well?" I said, a mix of a question and request for more.

Declan laughed and nodded. "Like nearly the entire population of Tenebrae, I was crazy about her." He ran a hand through his windblown hair, the overgrown ends flopping to the side and landing just above his brow bone. "But also like nearly the entire population, she shot me down. For some reason, she only had eyes for that bastard of a man you call your father." There was no malice in his voice, just playful jealousy of past events I desperately wanted to know more of.

"Not a big fan of his?" I commented and Evander came to stand behind me. I leaned back into him as his arms snaked around my waist, gingerly swaying us as Dec snorted dramatically.

"Not even slightly," he replied, crossing his arms over his chest. "He not only stole the woman I wanted, but he tried to steal my best friend, too." My smile grew as I remembered how Evander had once told me that Declan and his father were childhood friends, and what it would have been like for my father to squeeze in-between them. "Everyone thought Julian to be valiant, selfless, and kind, but I knew him for what he truly was. A mischievous little snake with a personal vendetta against me," he said, through a lighthearted smile. Evander and I both chuckled in response and Declan threw his hands up as he pushed off the wall and strode for the kitchen. "Fine, don't believe me! No one ever did."

Once he passed into the next room, I peered up at Evander, taking in his brilliant smile.

"So that's Declan," I said. He nodded with pride before tugging me along through the house. "I find it interesting though…" Evander glanced down at me with curious brows. "That you hate Felix so much when he and Declan are basically the same person," I explained.

"They couldn't be more different," he argued.

My smile broadened and I rolled my eyes as we stepped into the kitchen to find a woman lounging lazily in one of the dining room chairs. She stared at a page from a small worn book she held in one hand, while the fingers on her other absentmindedly twirled the ends of her long obsidian braid.

"I told him to write you ahead of time," she said, her voice light and airy like a songbird's. The woman placed the book on the table's surface while tossing Declan a flat stare just as he plopped into the seat to her left.

"And where would the fun have been in that?" the Lord of Vorsutos inquired. Without a word, he lunged for her book and immediately halted just as a knife was slammed down in between his fingers.

"Touch it, and I won't hesitate to remove your hand," she said sweetly, sliding the book to her opposite side.

Oh, I *very* much liked her.

"Ainsley, this is Isla. Declan's better, more level-headed, and sensible other half," Evander introduced. Isla wiggled the fingers of her light brown hand in a small wave.

"I don't know about *sensible*," I heard Declan mutter under his breath as he pulled away from the sharp blade stuck in the table.

"Says the one who thought it a good idea to sneak up on a king," she replied.

Declan rolled his eyes and settled his hands behind his head as he leaned back comfortably in his chair. "Ainsley, tell my fiancé not to be so dramatic."

"Why would I do that when she's right?" I quipped as Evander led us to the table to sit across from our company.

Declan scoffed as his head lulled back to the ceiling. "I withdraw my earlier comment. You're actually more like your father. He was never any fun either."

"I'll take that as a compliment," I replied, earning a playful smirk from Declan.

Evander's arm draped across the back of my chair and I twisted to glance up at him, catching a smile that sent my heart racing. For the first time in a while, he looked truly happy and at peace. I puckered my lips in demand for the small kiss he eagerly granted, his thumb and forefinger pinching my chin as he did.

I heard a group of our family rush into the kitchen and enthusiastically greet Declan and Isla, but I couldn't take my eyes away from the man looking down at me as if I were his entire world. His lips tugged upward as his gaze trailed over my face like he was memorizing every facet, every freckle, every line. I could barely breathe beneath his stare, the pressure of his love pushing into me so hard, that I felt as if my heart would explode under its weight.

I scooted myself higher and dragged the tip of my nose over his.

"Mine," I whispered, and then took the kisses that would always belong to me.

65

Ainsley

"Wait, wait, wait," I said through my laughter. "You tried to change Onyx's name and then got pissed when he refused to answer to it?"

"I WAS SEVEN!" Evander argued and the rest of us dove back into our fit of hysterics.

"It wasn't just Onyx," Oli chimed in near breathless. "When that didn't work, he tried to change *all* of our names and refused to address us by anything else."

I peered up at Van to find him fighting his smile as he shook his head. "But why the name Kaiden?" I asked him.

Before he could answer, Marce cut in as she wiped the amused tears from her eyes. "Because it was the hero in a children's story he was obsessed with. We'd have to read it to him nearly every night."

"IT WAS A GOOD BOOK!" Evander argued, sending everyone into another roar of laughter. Van rolled his eyes as he reached for his wine and took a long sip. "Can we fill the conversation with something other than embarrassing stories from my childhood, please?"

"As someone who missed out on said childhood, absolutely not," I declared and raised my glass to the table. Everyone cheered and the next story about my husband was shared.

Dinner had stretched into the late hours of the night as old friends caught up and stories of the past were exchanged. Once the conversation had quieted substantially, and most of our family excused themselves in favor of sleep, Evander offered to bring me upstairs before heading back down to carry on with Declan. I refused to go, enjoying the happiness Van exuded in the presence of his uncle far too much to want to call it a night despite exhaustion weighing heavily on my body.

Isla pushed Declan back onto the couch and then crawled over him, resting her body over his as she laid her head on his chest. I followed suit, shoving Evander as I draped myself across him to get comfortable. His lips pressed to my hair as I placed my ear over his heart, enjoying the rhythmic *thump, thump, thump* that would beat only for me. A blanket fell over me a second later as I directed my stare to the couple on the couch across from us.

I lay curled against my husband as the two men continued their conversation in our library, sipping on their amber liquor and occasionally kissing the foreheads of the women they loved as our eyes fluttered close to the smooth cadence of their voices.

The soft rumble of Evander's quiet laughter pulled me from the claws of sleep. Though I was too exhausted to open my eyes, I shifted against him, burrowing my face between his chest and the blanket as I attempted to get more comfortable. His hand rested against the back of my head, stroking my hair softly as I sighed in contentment and relaxed.

"I can't believe I found her," Evander said, holding me a little tighter against him.

"I can," Declan replied, his voice echoing as if spoken into a glass. A moment later, ice rattled and a light thud of a drink being placed onto the table sounded. "There was never a doubt in my mind that you wouldn't. To be completely honest, I'm more surprised by the fact you convinced her to marry you."

"To be honest, so am I." My lips tugged upward as Evander offered a small laugh, careful not to jostle me too much. A silent minute passed before he spoke again, the tone in his voice shifting from playful to serious. "I can't lose her again, Dec. I won't."

"Send her to Vorsutos."

"You don't think I've tried? She refuses to go."

It was Declan's turn to laugh this time. "And Isla refuses to stay. Tell me why, out of all the women in the world, did we have to fall in love with the two most stubborn?"

Van's lips pressed to the top of my hair as he replied, "I wouldn't have had it any other way."

"Neither would I," Declan agreed, and I could hear the sound of a soft kiss upon flesh from across the space, followed by Isla's gentle snore. "This war isn't going to be easy, Van."

"I know."

"It's going to be long with a string of battles, each more brutal than the last. Lives *will* be lost."

"I know."

"Do you?" Declan questioned. The words weren't harsh, but rather hesitant, as if he truly wanted to ensure the King of Tenebrae grasped the severity of our situation. "You know I love you, and I will be at your side until the very, bitter end. But I need to ensure that you truly understand what could happen. I need to know that you're aware losing her is a possibility."

"No."

"Evander—"

"No!" His voice rose an octave and I flinched on instinct at the sound. His arms curled around me tighter and his hands trailed up and down my back slowly as if trying to lull me back to sleep. Evander cleared his throat, his tone now softer, more controlled than it was before as he said, "She's mine Declan. Losing her is not an option I will ever accept. And if that somehow happens..." His heart was a thunderous beat against my ear, mirroring my own. "Then I will rip the world apart to get her back."

I wasn't sure how much time had passed when I was pulled from sleep again, this time from a cool mattress replacing the warm chest I had been nestled against. At some point during Declan and Evander's conversation I had fallen back asleep, and mentally cursed myself for doing so. Imogen would have given me an earful for eavesdropping, but I didn't care—I wanted to know more.

Evander climbed onto the bed and repositioned us so our noses touched as he wrapped himself around me. "We never got our ten minutes," I said sleepily.

"What would you like to talk about?" I could hear the smile in his voice which made my own come forth. It didn't matter how tired I was, I wouldn't ever miss out on our ten-minute dates.

"Tell me about that story you were obsessed with as a child."

"You're never going to let that go are you?" Evander groaned.

"Unless you'd rather tell me about the time you pissed your pants when you were seventeen."

"So Kaiden was the main character in the story," he said without missing a beat. "A young prince who was my age at the time. He was completely alone, with no one but his people and his pet dragon. Together they would go on adventures to protect Kaiden's kingdom and save the young princess who had been stolen by an evil sorcerer."

Evander pressed a kiss to my nose and smoothed the hair away from my face. "Did they find her?" I asked.

"Every time," he replied.

I scooted closer, moving my head down to bury my face against his neck as I ran my hand down the hard muscles of his arm. "What was your reasoning for trying to rename Onyx, and everyone else for that matter?"

He let out a long sigh, his breath tickling my forehead as my hair shifted. "I thought that if I had someone like Kaiden in my life, then I could do all of the amazing things he did. I could protect my kingdom and find my princess. I could be just as brave and strong and intelligent. Kaiden became a symbol of what I wanted for my future."

I pressed a kiss into the hollow of his throat as I said, "Then Onyx is a dick for not letting you rename him."

Evander laughed and squeezed me tighter before throwing a blanket over us. I settled into it—into *him*—as I thought about how he had become exactly like the fictional character he admired. He was brave, strong, intelligent, and a million other things. And just like Kaiden, he had found his princess and brought her home.

"Van?"

"Hmmm?" he said, the strings of sleep pulling on the word.

"I'd rip the world apart for you, too."

66
Ainsley

Sweat beaded across my brow, but it wasn't from the sun beating down on me as I stood in the middle of the sparring ring. No, it was from the amount of energy I was exerting as I tried to unlock my Imperium's door without resorting to anger—a feat that was proving to be impossible. My hands smacked into my knees as I doubled over, gasping for air. A grunt of frustration rumbled up from my throat as I shoved away from my Imperium door, still feeling Brandle's hold on my blood.

"Push me out!" he demanded.

"I'm trying!"

The crimson smoke leaked from the cracks, the anger in my blood causing it to become more active. I took a deep and calming breath, but the moment I did, the Gift drifted back beneath the doorframe and out of sight.

"Dammit!" I yelled and braced my hands over my head as I began pacing.

"Incapable of progressing," Rosella mused aloud as she scribbled incessantly in her stupid fucking notebook.

My gaze snapped in her direction as I glared at her. "Why the hell does *she* have to be here?"

Rosella offered a smug grin from where she sat just outside of the training ring. "My king told me to observe in his absence, so that's what I'm doing."

I wanted to strangle Dash for sending her here in his stead. Not long after my visit to Caelum, he informed Evander via transfer paper that he would be a day or two late to our next training session, citing the desire to stop by one of the camps our soldiers were now occupying before he made his way to Tenebrae. I tried not to let the fact that he refused to respond to any of my letters this past week sting, but that was useless. Even Felix hadn't spoken to me since arriving home the other day.

"Go observe someone else," I replied.

"Why would I do that when watching you fail is so much fun?"

My Obscure shot from me, snapping like a whip against the shield Brandle was smart enough to keep around her the moment he brought her out here.

"Obvious... inability... to... contain... anger," she recited, her pen flying across the paper. "Fit...for...queenhood...question mark...question mark...question mark..."

"Make her leave!" I growled.

"I'm liaisoning!"

"THAT'S NOT EVEN A WORD!" Another tendril of darkness smacked against her shield, a shimmer rippling over the protective barrier as it did.

The crimson smoke began to slither through the crevices again as my Imperium's door seemed to pulse in time to my quickened heartbeat. My hand hovered over the knob as Rosella's snide comeback was drowned out by the pounding in my ears.

"Ainsley..." Brandle warned, his magic pushing against me harder to the point of pain. "You need to focus."

"It's a little hard to do that with her here!"

My hand flexed around the metal knob as my Imperium whispered to me softly, luring me to it like a siren in the night. One twist of my wrist and my Gift would be free.

"Ainsley..." he scolded.

I ground my teeth together and yanked my hand away from the magic that urged me to let it out. Turning away from the woman who thrived on baiting me, I faced Brandle, crossing my arms over my chest as I stood defensively.

The Prince of Ministro had finally recovered enough from his injuries and, for the past two weeks, had been training me on how to use my Imperium Gift. At first, we started with the basics: calling forth the magic and then sending it away. Although it was initially a struggle, it became apparent that the fastest way for me to access the Gift was through anger. This method usually consisted of several insults thrown my way, along with sparring matches.

Every day, Brandle would push his Gift into me, restricting the blood supply in my hands, arms, or legs. And every day, I would get angry enough to call forth my Imperium and shove him forcefully out, regaining control of my body. Once the action became like second nature, Brandle declared that the next step in my training would be accessing the Gift without using the help of my anger. That was three days ago. And I was still unsuccessful.

"She's here to make it more challenging for you," Brandle explained as he mimicked my stance. "If you can push past your feelings now, the easier it'll become."

I shook my head, the feelings of frustration and failure crawling over my skin like ants. "Her presence shouldn't matter. I should have gotten it by now."

Brandle's posture relaxed just slightly as he tilted his head and took a single step in my direction. "Ainsley, you've had this Gift for less than a year and have already progressed a tremendous amount in just these two weeks."

"That's not good enough."

He rolled his eyes and shrugged as he watched me. "I hate to break it to you, but you're not the main character in one of your stories who masters every piece of information after a few training sessions."

"I should be," I muttered to myself beneath my breath.

"Well, you're not," he argued. "Plus, that's entirely unrealistic." Brandle lowered himself to the ground, crossing his legs and gesturing for me to do the same. "Now, we already know you're in touch with your Koler side. We just need to figure out how to access your Yuna."

I stared at him blankly, my mind running through the names he said and coming up blank. "Am I supposed to know what that means?"

"Sorry, I forgot you're stupid."

"Watch it..." Evander warned from his spot beneath the shade of an oak tree on the other side of the yard. He may have agreed to let Brandle train me, but he said nothing about not supervising the session. A fact he lovingly pointed out to me after he refused to leave on my first day of lessons with the Prince of Ministro.

"I apologize. I meant *uneducated*," Brandle corrected—though it wasn't much of a correction if you asked me. "Koler and Yuna are the deities who created Ministro. They were split from a single star—twins and opposites in every way. Yuna is the Goddess of health, healing, and fertility." He threw a seductive wink at Rosella who flirtatiously giggled back as I suppressed a gag. "Koler is the God of chaos, bloodshed, and fury. Like I said, they couldn't be more different."

Brandle reclined on his elbows and tilted his head back to catch the sun's rays on his face, the picture of unbothered relaxation.

"Together, they created the Empathi Gift, pouring qualities from each of themselves into the magic. The ability to calm, soothe, and grant empathy to individuals was Yuna's doing. But the ease with which one could manipulate emotions—heighten them to the point of destruction—that was entirely Koler," Brandle explained. "Unhappy with his sister's attributes, Koler decided he would create the next Gift without her knowledge. And thus, the Imperium was born." He gestured a hand between the two of us. "Our Gift thrives on pain, fear, and control. The more intense our emotions get, the more we feed the magic's desire to cause chaos."

I thought back to every instance where my Imperium surged to life, finding the indisputable truth in Brandle's explanation. The more unstable I became in a situation, the more that Gift tried to escape.

"When Yuna found out about her brother's wrongdoing, she brought it to the other Gods and Goddesses. Together, they agreed to ban Koler from this world and ordered him to return to their realm," Brandle said, as he stretched his arms over his head. "After that, Yuna created the Medicus to correct the power imbalance of Ministro. But little good that did, if you ask me."

I snorted my agreement as he jumped to his feet and offered his hand to pull me to mine. "Every day it feels like my anger intensifies, making it harder to ignore," I admitted. If Brandle was going to help me, it was best he knew exactly what my struggles were. "I've always been quick-tempered, but it's becoming even harder not to give in to those emotions."

"It's because of how powerful you are," he answered. "Like I said, that Gift thrives on your chaos. It's going to try to exploit it in any way it can so that you'll feed it what it wants most."

"So, how do *you* do it?"

Brandle may have been an arrogant jerk most of the time, but he was also kind and empathetic. It was hard to believe that someone with those attributes would resort only to anger when calling forth their Gift.

"I hold on to the things that ground me," he explained. I felt his magic once again pierce my flesh and sink into my blood, wrapping around the liquid until he had full control of its flow. "The love I have for my siblings and my friends, as well as my desire to be a better person than those who came before me, are what keep me going. It's *those* thoughts and emotions I reach for instead of the rage that tries to surface."

"And the things that ground you are stronger than that anger?" I asked hopefully.

With a smirk, he nodded. "We just need to find your anchor."

My stare automatically drifted to the man sitting in the shade of the large tree across the space. He shifted forward slightly, his finger frantically turning the page as his mouth hung open, completely engrossed in the story in his grasp. *He* was my anchor and my love for him was what grounded me.

"Let's go again," I demanded and shut my eyes to focus on the way Brandle's magic took mine hostage. I inspected it, looking for cracks and weaknesses that would allow me to shove him out easier. Of course, there were none.

He pushed, and I gritted my teeth against the pain as my blood tried to flow in the wrong direction. My Imperium gently knocked at its door in a peaceful request. It had never been that docile before, and I wondered if it had somehow known my intentions. My hand hovered above the knob while another wave of pain surged through me as Brandle shoved again. The door knocked harder and crimson smoke leaked from the cracks around the frame as a familiar shadow loomed closer.

It was my rage, heartache, and fear all rolled into one—and watching me intently. A darkened red tendril reached out and stroked down my cheek in comfort as it coaxed me to grab onto it and use it to my full might. I knew how easy it would be to say yes and let that wisp wrap around me, granting me the strength I needed to beat this task.

So instead, I reached for my anchor. I dove deep and clung to the cadence of Evander's laugh, the way his eyes light up when he sees me, how his arms embrace me for just a second too long as if he can't bear to let go. I held onto his scent, to his taste, to the way his bare skin felt against mine. And as I plummeted further, I found the love that was so much stronger than my rage.

I dragged it to the surface, letting it burn through me as I twisted the knob and let my Imperium free. It surged out, enveloping me in crimson smoke as it rushed past to take back control of my body. My Imperium slammed into Brandle's, sinking its claws in so deep that I heard Brandle release a hiss of pain. I shoved, shoved, shoved, pushing myself to the limit and ignoring the physical agony and exhaustion of the task.

Finally, with one last thrust, Brandle's magic retracted from my body. I fell to the ground, panting and eagerly gulping down the fresh air. I had done it. A round of applause echoed around the ring, and I picked my head up to find nearly everyone in our company outside. Weakly, I smiled at our guests just as Evander traversed in front of me and swiftly helped me stand.

"I knew you could do it," he said, planting a proud kiss on my temple.

"It took her long enough," Rosella quipped.

With an insult poised on my tongue, I turned to address her but stopped short at the unexpected sight of Dash. He looked just as furious with me as he had when I left him last week.

I waved tentatively, but the King of Caelum merely looked me over before directing his stare at his advisor. "Ready?" he asked her, extending his hand to help Rosella to her feet. She took it and immediately flipped to the beginning of her notebook to recite all she had seen over the past two days as they made their way into the house.

I swallowed the bitter sting of rejection as I watched after him until he disappeared from view. "Let's go again," I said, turning to Brandle.

"A little later, love," Evander objected as his fingers slid between mine. A gentle squeeze was all it took for me to know he could tell how hurt I was. "Sirona just arrived to discuss the rings."

67

Ainsley

We stood scattered throughout the study as Sirona sat at the desk, neatly unfolding a piece of fabric to reveal two golden rings—one with a cut ruby and the other a sapphire. I tried not to let my gaze travel to Dash where he leaned against the wall with Elenora at his side, but it proved impossible. His stare remained blank as he focused his attention straight ahead, actively ignoring my existence, so I turned to my right to find Felix's eyes already on mine.

He bounced impatiently on the balls of his feet and I knew it had nothing to do with his excitement over the pending conversation and everything to do with *us*. He was missing me just as much as I was him.

I'm sorry, I mouthed. Felix smiled gratefully and nodded, allowing me to release my first full breath in days. Being at odds with my two best friends was keeping me on edge and I needed to put an end to it. Today, I'd corner Dash and force him to hear me out.

"The stones are tethered by blood magic," Sirona announced, capturing the attention of the room. "That's why you were not able to use its abilities. But since the bearer is now deceased with no living blood relatives, we can tie it to another line."

"I don't want it," Dash announced to the room before anyone had the chance to suggest he take it. "I'll go with whoever the group decides, but it won't be me. I want nothing to do with that man."

I didn't blame him for his reluctance.

"We'll discuss a new bearer this afternoon," Evander declared.

"Once you all come up with a decision, let me know. This one, however..." Sirona said, pinching the sapphire between her thumb and forefinger as she held it up, "Will be a bit trickier. Whoever it's tied to is still alive."

"So we're screwed," Evander commented, his shoulders slumping with dejection.

"Not necessarily," Sirona argued as she inspected the gemstone. "I may be able to find a workaround to the blood magic like I did with your Soul Bond. Perhaps binding it to something more powerful will overshadow its current ties, just as I theorized would happen if we Entwined you to someone."

"Would that work?"

"I obviously don't know for certain, but it's worth a try," she remarked. "I'll have to break the gem down significantly, and I'll need a drop of each of your blood in there." She pointed to a small vial at the edge of the desk.

Without hesitation, Van crafted a dagger and pricked his finger. I watched the tiny bead of blood rise to the surface of his skin and then fall into the vial before I took the blade and did the same. One by one, everyone stepped forward and deposited their drops.

"How long will it take?" Evander questioned as Sirona pushed a cork into the bottle to keep the contents inside.

"I'm honestly unsure, as this is magic I'm not well versed in," she replied as she pocketed our offering and rose from the desk, "But I promise to be as quick as possible."

"Thank you, Sirona," I said.

She bowed her head and then grabbed Evander's hand to be traversed away. We were one step closer to figuring out how the stones could help us, which meant we were one step closer to winning this war.

Unsurprisingly enough, Dash avoided me at all costs throughout the day. Anytime I entered a room, he found a reason to exit it without so much as a glance in my direction. As much as it hurt to be ignored by him, I wouldn't stop trying.

There was no reason for me to wander the halls other than that I couldn't sleep. No matter what I did, I couldn't shut off my mind to all that today had contained. My Imperium training, the rings, and Dash's purposeful distance plagued every thought until I slipped from the bed I shared with Evander and took a walk, hoping to wear myself out.

As I finished what had to be my hundredth lap through the house, which ended at the door of Onyx and Nova's room down the hall, I turned around and prepared myself to start again. Two steps into my journey, the stairs at the other end creaked and a moment later, Elenora appeared at the top.

Great.

Although we hadn't had any issues with each other besides her disagreement over the way Brandle was treated at dinner, we weren't exactly friends. Furthermore, her spending the majority of her time with Rosella when she wasn't with Dash or Brandle didn't particularly make me want to change that status either.

We each offered a polite, yet awkward, smile as we passed one another on the way to our rooms.

"Elenora," I turned and called before I could think better of it. She stopped and twisted, giving me her full attention.

Panic came crashing into me as I realized I had no logical reason for stopping this woman. I searched my mind for something—*anything*—to say as I stared at her blankly like a Godsdamn idiot.

"Don't hurt him," I blurted, because it was the only thing that came to mind.

Her brown eyes widened a fraction from surprise and I wanted to die right at that moment. Dash had every right to be angry at me. I was a reckless asshole who shoved her way into situations that didn't concern her.

"I've put him through enough," I added, for no sensible reason.

Elenora tilted her head to the side, her longer strands spilling over her shoulder as she studied me. She didn't say a word as a crease between her brows formed, and I suddenly felt naked beneath her stare. Like she could somehow see all of my thoughts and the secrets I kept hidden.

I could see why Dash liked her. Not only was she one of the most gorgeous women I'd ever seen, but she seemed just as perceptive as him—picking apart and closely analyzing every minute detail.

After what felt like a lifetime, Elenora took a deep breath and nodded. She offered nothing more than that before heading back down the long hall to her room. I stood there unable to move a muscle until her door clicked shut. What the hell was I thinking? If Dash wasn't pissed enough at me, he definitely would be once his not-girlfriend told him about this little encounter.

I closed my eyes, cursing myself for my impulsive behavior when I heard the sound of a door opening. Most likely Elenora coming back to tell me to mind my own damn business. I sighed, prepared to receive the tongue-lashing I deserved when I opened my eyes to find Dash emerging from his room not five feet away.

He stumbled the moment his stare met mine, clearly not expecting to see me out here in the middle of the night. "Hey," I whispered.

Dash didn't respond.

His gaze darted left and right like he was plotting an escape route rather than just ducking back into his room like a coward. "Couldn't sleep?" I tried, and once again, there was no response. Dash averted his stare to the ground as the tension in the hall grew by the second.

"So you can't even look at me now?" I snapped, unable to hide my hurt. He brought his blue eyes to mine, but still couldn't find it in himself to speak.

Another door opening had both of us directing our attention to the source of the sound just as Felix slipped out of his room. "Oh thank the Gods," he said and rushed toward us. "We can all agree that giving Brandle the ruby over me is ridiculous, right?"

Felix had been annoyed ever since this afternoon when the vote for who would receive the ruby ring came down to him and Brandle. Ultimately, after a long discussion, the rulers of Disparya unanimously chose the Prince of Ministro.

"Actually, it makes the most sense," Dash replied, much to Felix's dismay. "The Tectus stone conceals its bearer and Brandle is a wanted man. Now he'll be able to help our alliance without the fear of being captured by Harbin."

Felix crossed his arms, prepared to argue that point just as yet another door opened. The three of us shifted our focus to find Imogen entering the hall… from Cal and Lia's room. I watched in disbelief as she quietly closed the door and turned in our direction. She froze the instant she beheld the three of us, the smile on her face falling into something that looked like pure terror.

Imogen swallowed hard and quickly adjusted her features, lifting her chin high as she strode for us wearing a long silk nightgown. Her hair was in a wild state, which meant she was either a restless sleeper or… I didn't even want to think about the other option.

"Why are the three of you consorting in the hall at this hour?" Imogen scolded as she stopped before us and placed her hands on her hips. Dash, Felix, and I exchanged glances, each of us silently communicating a panicked *You saw what room she just came out of, right?!*

"Someone better answer me," Imogen demanded and shifted her stare to Felix first.

"I was hungry," he answered.

"You'll eat in the morning." Next, she looked to Dash.

"I was going to grab a glass of water," he replied nervously. Imogen's features fell flat as she lifted a brow. "But since I have water magic, I can just make it myself." She nodded in satisfaction and finally turned her attention to me.

"It's my house, so—" The harsh look she gave had me instantly changing directions with my response. "So… I have a bedroom that I'm going to head to right now."

"Good," Imogen answered and waved her hands in a shooing motion. "Now disperse."

The three of us hurried back to our rooms like children caught out of bed past curfew. It didn't matter that we were grown adults in our early twenties, Imogen was not someone to be tested. Before fully disappearing inside my room, I threw one last look into the hall. Dash's gaze collided with mine for only a heartbeat before he closed his door without a moment of hesitation.

⚜

The days carried on in the same fashion—little sleep and cold interactions with Dash.

All week, we focused on Jahier's stealth training as no one had yet to pass his test. We were getting closer each day, with Evander making it as far as halfway to the flag before taking a ball of ice to the face. We quickly learned that going straight through the meadow had been our downfall and decided to use the cover of the trees along the perimeter to advance.

It seemed like we were going to finish another week with no winner until Dash's name was called for his turn. As we all had, he disappeared into the treeline at the start of the task.

Five minutes went by, then ten, then twenty. Still, there was no sign of Dash.

We waited and waited and waited, everyone deathly quiet as we tried to pick up any sign of the King of Caelum within the forest. But there was nothing. No rustling of leaves, snapping of branches, or quiet footfalls could be heard. It was as if Dash had simply vanished.

Another thirty minutes later, Dash emerged at the start, covered in mud and holding the flag with a lopsided smirk. We all rushed for him and demanded he tell us how he did it without being caught. He turned and pointed to a large hole in the ground near the base of a tree.

"The rules were we couldn't use our magic during our turn," Dash explained breathlessly. "Jahier never said we couldn't use it when it wasn't." My lips lifted in the corner at his response. Leave it to Dash to find his way around the rules. "So every night I came out here and used my Gift to create a tunnel from here to the flag. Then I crawled through, climbed the tree, grabbed the flag, and came back."

"Way to adapt and solve the problem," Jahier said appreciatively as everyone expressed their congratulations. Even Evander admitted to the King of Caelum that his execution was clever and impressive. I seemed to be the only one Dash didn't speak to.

When I woke up the next morning, Dash had already left without saying goodbye, and for the first time, I started to worry I had crossed a line we wouldn't recover from.

68
Dashiell

"Are you almost done over there?" Felix asked skeptically. I glanced into the soapy water to see that I had been scrubbing the same dish for the last three minutes, the ceramic perfectly spotless. Handing the bowl to him without a word, my eyes flittered back to the window where I continued to observe Evander and Ainsley lounging on the dock in the distance.

Her smile was as captivating as it always was as she sat before him, her legs wrapped around his middle and her arms snaked around his neck. My lips tugged at the corners as I watched her tip her head to the sky, her bright laughter loud enough to reach me inside. Evander's face lit up with a smile filled with so much love and adoration as he gazed at his queen.

"You should go talk to her," Felix said. My stare dropped back down to the sink where I plucked another dish and began scrubbing without a word. "So you're just going to continue to ignore her? Dash, you've been keeping her out for over six weeks —"

"Felix," I warned.

"I just got my parents back. I don't need you both fighting again." I threw a sidelong glance to find him wearing that sly smirk that always got him out of any trouble we found ourselves in growing up. Rolling my eyes, I directed my stare back to my task as I fought my lips from curving.

"She crossed a line."

"I'm not saying she didn't," he replied. "I don't agree with her choice or that she pulled rank on me... but it's Ainsley. We both know she'd never be that extreme unless she were truly afraid." My lungs deflated with a defeated breath as I opened my mouth to argue once more. "And I'd like to think that you, better than anyone, would know the depths of desperation that fear can drive one to."

I clamped my lips shut as the memories of Ainsley and me in Caelum surfaced again—memories I had since tried to bury. My mind quickly flashed through images of standing in the Council Room with my father as he shared with me that the woman I loved was a product of Conjoining, and then dove into details of what I was to do to her.

I pushed through the unwanted thoughts and was taken to another—Ainsley in my arms broken and bloody and dying. My teeth ground together as I shoved that memory away only to land in one that took place mere hours later. She clung to me in tears, begging for me to take away the fear, the pain, the horrors she was so afraid of.

Finally, my mind drew me to another moment in time, standing before my father in the Council Room again, where I agreed to his terms.

My eyes screwed shut as I nodded, a long exhale escaping me. My reluctance to forgive Ainsley didn't stem from unwillingness, but rather from my ignorance of the truth. Did she order Felix to stay with me because she feared for my safety—my *sanity*—or did the words she uttered that day hold the true merit? Did she believe that my kingdom and I were a liability? A burden she and the other rulers would have to look after?

I glanced back up at the window, finding Evander flat on his stomach, his arm outstretched as he reached for something too far away. A piece of cake, perhaps? But thanks to Ainsley's knee in his back, he was pinned in place, unable to get to it.

She crawled over his body to reach the slice of dessert first, but as soon as she cleared his head, Evander's hands wrapped around her ankles. One second they were on the dock and the next there were nothing but shadows swirling over the wood as the king and queen reappeared over the lake... several feet in the air.

Only a heartbeat passed before Evander manifested back onto solid ground next to the discarded piece of cake as his wife plummeted toward the lake, her piercing scream soon swallowed by the water. He bent down and casually picked up the food, inspecting it for dirt before turning around to face the water. He took a bite just as his wife breached the surface, spewing every colorful word in her vocabulary. I hadn't known so many insults existed.

"Sometimes I wonder if he has a death wish," Felix mused as we watched Ainsley flail around like a drowned rat in the center of the lake while Evander finished off the last of the dessert, occasionally waving to her from dry land.

"Maybe," I told him thoughtfully. "But perhaps that's what she needs—someone just as stubborn and fiery as her."

"Not according to him," he replied, gesturing to the King of Agnitio making his way outside. I was taken back to the warning Tallis had given Evander about Ainsley in Caelum after her Obscure had emerged. He had said she needed calm to her chaos or else she wouldn't survive.

Evander headed for the king, trepidation in every heavy footfall that had the hair on the back of my neck rising with worry.

"She and Evander may be the same, but they also know how to be what the other needs," I said, my focus entirely on the slight pinch between the King of Tenebrae's brows as he listened to Tallis speak. "Ainsley will be fine as long as they're together. He's what she needs."

Felix responded, but I couldn't hear a word he said as my attention stayed transfixed on the sight before me. Ainsley hastened her paddling towards the shore, as if she also possessed a sense of unease. Water and soap splashed onto my surroundings as I accidentally dropped the dish I had been attending to into the sink. I then leaned forward to study the scene through the window.

"What do you think that's about?" Felix asked, that calm and calculated cadence of an advisor who spent his life observing individuals slipping into his tone. I shook my head as I summoned my Obscure to the surface.

Time seemed to still as the scene before me flipped through my mind in slow motion. Tallis's posture was rigid with an air of distress in the way his throat flexed gently with each swallow—as if the words he spoke were painful to utter.

Evander's mask had become easier to read the more I watched him these past weeks, studying his motives and reactions until I had a general sense of when he was hiding something—usually bad news. I had seen it in his eyes when he told me I had to choose which of my people to save, and I could see it now as his gaze flittered to the woman emerging from the lake.

Evander's hands moved quickly to his pockets to conceal that he balled them into fists a split-second prior. He pushed his shoulders back just barely, as if to make himself seem more put together and in control as Ainsley made her way closer, but the slight shift of weight from one hip to the next gave away that facade of a calm exterior. One tight bob of his throat and a deep inhale later, she had reached them.

The King of Tenebrae placed a reassuring hand on the small of her back, but I could tell by the skeptical glint in her eye that she wasn't buying his performance, either. Tallis spoke then, most likely relaying what he already had since Evander's gaze stayed glued to Ainsley and her reactions. Whatever news he was delivering, it wasn't good.

Ainsley exchanged several glances with her husband and comments to them both, before she inevitably left and hurried into the house. The front door slammed shut, rattling the windows and paintings that hung on the walls. Her wet boots hit the wooden stairs at a thunderous pace, skipping two steps at a time by the sound of it. Felix and I stared at each other for one heartbeat before we both pushed away from the half-full sink and rushed into the living room where Tallis and Evander had both entered.

"Where's Olivier?" Evander asked.

"What's going on?" Felix replied at the same time. I could hear the worry in his voice and knew it was from whatever intense emotions he was picking up from the room.

"Where is Oli?" Evander demanded again. We both shook our heads and, with a grunt of irritation, Evander pushed past us with Tallis following on his heels.

Felix and I trailed after them until we ended up in the library where the entirety of Ainsley's family had been enjoying their leisurely afternoon.

Olivier shot to his feet from where he had been lounging in a large armchair the moment his eyes met Evander's. "What is it?" he demanded. Everyone else halted their tasks, placing down game pieces and books as they moved to stand.

"A shift in the vision. If we do not leave today, we have no hope of winning this war," Tallis admitted gravely.

"Will they find something that can help us?" I asked, but Tallis shook his head.

"I cannot *see* if they will. Only that our fates are sealed if they don't go now."

In fresh, dry clothes, Ainsley pushed into the library with two full bags in her arms and Declan and Isla at her side. Evander met her in the center of the room, wordlessly relieving her of the packs before she hurried out of the space once more.

"Carry on with the training while we're gone," he instructed Oli as he rummaged through the bag, occasionally reshuffling items and using his shadows to craft weapons to place inside. "But make sure our soldiers are prepared. They need to be ready to mobilize at a moment's notice."

Olivier shook off the command. "I'm going with you," he said.

"Not anymore."

Satisfied, Evander closed the bag and began working on the other just as Ainsley appeared, holding an ancient and worn roll of parchment. Her husband uncurled it, his eyes quickly scanning over the outdated map of Disparya Ainsley and Felix had shown me. He nodded to himself before carefully rolling it up and placing it into the bag he was going through.

"With the change of plans, you're more valuable here," the King of Tenebrae added as he finally closed the pack and directed his attention to the Lord of Vorsutos. "Are you both ready?"

"Obviously," Declan said, effortlessly weaving four daggers between his fingers as Isla shoved her weapons into various holsters strapped to her body.

"I'm coming too," I announced and reached into my pocket for a slip of transfer paper so I could inform Rosella of my change of plans.

"We have enough people going," Ainsley cut in, not looking up from her task of arming herself with daggers still dripping in shadows. "You aren't needed."

"Actually, you are," Evander corrected, turning away from Declan to address me. "With Ainsley staying behind, we could use the additional magic."

"I'm going," she demanded.

"You aren't, and that's final," he replied.

"Van, what's going on?" Marce questioned.

In my short time around them, I had never seen Evander so domineering when it came to Ainsley or her choices. As I glanced around the room and noted the looks of concern gracing every member of their family's faces, I gathered neither had they.

"He's being overprotective because of Tallis's new vision," Ainsley offered as she continued to glare at her husband.

Evander had supported her decision to return to the home of her enemy all those months ago, escorted her to her murder trial, and had been training her for war. Yet for some reason, the risk of her traveling to Inmuto was now too great in his eyes. None of it made any sense.

Marceline jumped in. "Van, if finding the lost kingdom could secure a victory in this war, then—"

"Not that vision," Ainsley said, cutting her off. The room was silent as we all exchanged curious glances. "The one where I die."

69

Felix

The balance of my entire existence was disrupted when those five succinct words penetrated my heart, shredding the organ as I repeatedly recalled them in my mind. Tallis had to be lying. Mistaken. Confused.

Dash confidently moved forward, enunciating each word meticulously while asking, "What do you mean?" Ainsley chose not to respond, reciprocating the silent treatment that he had been subjecting her to for almost two months. "When and where does it happen?" Dash pleaded urgently, his voice filled with more anger than fear.

"I'm greatly interested in knowing that too," Evander uttered with a low, menacing tone, shifting his gaze from his wife to fix it upon the King of Agnitio.

Tallis shook his head with a solemn expression, exuding both frustration and regret in every aspect of his demeanor. "I told you; it doesn't work like that. I can't dictate what is shown to me, Evander. I can't tell you when or where—"

"Then what *can* you tell us?!" Dash's demand reverberated through the room as his power caused it to tremble.

Tallis let out a deep, exasperated sigh and closed his eyes, undoubtedly invoking his Seer Gift to replay the vision once again. "It looks as if Ainsley is in the midst of battle," he answered. "And before you ask, I cannot see her adversary. I see no one in this vision but her." Both Evander and Dash tightly gripped their fists, exuding a palpable sense of irritation that tainted the atmosphere.

Oli appeared beside me with a glass of water. I accepted it with gratitude, appreciating his constant attentiveness to my needs and his understanding of how the uncontrolled emotions of others impacted my well-being.

"Her hands are outstretched toward the sky as she expels her magic," the King of Agnitio continued. "She appears to be using too much, too quickly, and soon falls. The vision then skips ahead to her lying on the ground in someone's arms. She whispers Evander's name and *I love you*, before she passes on. That is the entirety of what was presented to me."

The room was utterly silent as we listened to the fate of our queen. To her credit, her chin remained high and face blank as she met everyone's mournful stares. She was just stubborn enough to tell death to go fuck itself.

"And you don't know when this happens," Dash clarified, more than a little agitated at Tallis's lack of information. "So there's a distinct possibility it may happen during this journey."

"Yes."

"Then she stays," Dash stated with a simple shrug.

"Agreed," Evander added.

Ainsley released a bitter laugh while aiming her index finger at Evander, "This is not a call you get to make," she said before pointing at Dash. "And you don't get to ignore me for over a month and then decide what I can and cannot do."

"Oh, so you're the only one who gets to make decisions for other people?" he angrily quipped. I wasn't sure bringing up his disagreement with Ainsley was the best choice at that precise moment, but I also wasn't stupid enough to interrupt.

"I made that choice for the good of the alliance."

"Great. Now so am I," he countered, nonchalantly slipping his hands into his pockets as if declaring his triumph. That was only going to set her off even more, and he knew it. "You're now a liability to our cause. At least if you stay here, we know you aren't going to die during a potentially pointless mission to find a stupid fucking mythical kingdom we don't even know for certain exists!"

"Fuck you!" Ainsley yelled and defiantly crossed her arms over her chest, prepared to fight him on this.

"Could everyone please give us a moment? I need to talk sense into my wife," Evander added, just as angry as Dash seemed to be. For two men who swore to know her better than anyone, they were clearly idiots when it came to dealing with her now.

Ainsley scoffed and shook her head. "There's no need," she announced to everyone. "It doesn't matter what my husband says. I'm going."

"The answer is *no*," he bit out.

"Evander—"

"Losing you is not an option."

"YES IT IS!" Ainsley exclaimed and extended her arms to encompass the entire space. "Look around, Evander. Look at who is here—at the months we've spent preparing ourselves for *war*. It's always been an option, and we all knew that going in." She made a gentle motion towards him, aiming to cup his face, but he promptly seized her extended wrists, forbidding any form of contact. "We could lose any one of our family members."

"They are not *you*!" Evander cried out and released her wrists abruptly. He forcefully ran his hand down his face in frustration, then gestured with a pointed finger towards the various individuals dispersed throughout the room. "They all know exactly how I feel about them," he continued as he leaned closer, "However, they are also aware of my feelings for you. They know the lengths I have gone to find you and how far I'll go to keep you safe. Do not push me on this, Ainsley."

My heart was filled with profound sympathy for her. Not only because I could see how hard it was for her to not give in to Evander knowing the pain he was experiencing over Tallis's vision, but because I knew how scared she must have been to hear it, too. Ainsley had been through so much heartache and finally found peace, only to be told it was temporary.

"If she stays, will she survive? Does the vision change?" Dash asked, a spark of hope igniting in his voice for the first time today.

"I do not know," Tallis answered and just like that, the flicker died.

"How the hell do you not know?" the King of Caelum gritted out. "You said the future changes based on decisions. If she remains here, the vision either alters or it doesn't. So which is it?"

Amidst the ongoing argument between the men, Ainsley's eyes discreetly turned to meet mine. Immediately, I recognized an unwavering determination in her gaze. "Tallis doesn't know what happens if Ainsley stays, because she won't be," I announced, silencing the kings. "Her mind is made up, and there's no possibility of changing it."

With a raised chin, she looked back at the King of Tenebrae. "I'm going."

"If you try to, I'll just traverse you right back home."

"You wouldn't dare."

"Care to test that theory?"

Crimson rage, frustration, and resolve drifted around her as thick as the air. Ainsley's fists tightened at her side as her chest rose and fell with an overwhelming fury, each breath becoming more labored than the last. Evander remained unfazed by her distress, resolute in his own stance, with no apparent likelihood of altering it.

She shoved past him without a glance and stormed out of the library, slamming the door loudly behind her. "Show me again what you saw," Evander said to Tallis.

"Me too," Dash added.

The two kings approached him and eagerly extended their hands. I averted my gaze from the scene and shifted my attention towards Oli, who was fixated on the closed door leading to the hall.

"She's going to hate us for not speaking up," he said.

"I don't think she will," I reasoned and placed a reassuring kiss on his cheek. "She knows we support her choices, but she's also aware that this conflict between them doesn't involve us," I added, gripping his chin to force his attention on me. "Nothing any of us said would have changed Evander's mind."

It took everything in me not to chase after my best friend. While I strongly supported her autonomy in decision-making, I wasn't able to offer her the reassurance she wanted to hear. Specifically, because I fully understood the reasoning behind Dash and Evander's stance.

From the moment I open my eyes each day, I am plagued by the fear that it might be my final one with Oli. If there was a possibility to lengthen the potential outcome of his fate, I would go to any lengths.

"Felix, I need you with us," Evander declared, abruptly interrupting my train of thought. I knew I should have been concerned that Oli tensed beside me, but I was more perplexed by Evander using the phrase 'I need you' in conjunction with my name.

"Alright?" I uttered the word like a question, mentally working out how I would hold that declaration over his head for the rest of his life.

"If Felix is going, so am I," Olivier claimed.

"No, I need you here."

With determination, my boyfriend approached his king, his head shaking in refusal. "The last time he went on a mission without me, I nearly lost him. I'm not going through that again, Evander."

Prior to the incident, the room was bustling with quiet conversation among those preparing for the trip, but all noise abruptly ceased when Oli confronted the king.

"You don't think I know that, Oli?" Evander argued. "I don't enjoy keeping you apart from the person you love, but this mission and our kingdom are bigger than that. I need Felix's Gifts to potentially ease tensions with a kingdom we know nothing about, and to know which individuals we encounter possess magic."

"And he can't do that if I'm there?"

Evander let out a deep sigh and proceeded to shake his head. "I need you to stay and look after our kingdom. Continue running our training here and organizing with the advisors back at the palace."

"Cal can do that shit," Oli spat.

"I have other plans for Calidore," the King of Tenebrae replied. "I'm sorry, Oli. My decision is final."

Following Ainsley's earlier example, the Tenebraen advisor forcefully pushed past everyone and angrily charged out of the room. I refrained from pursuing him, recognizing that no words of solace or reassurance would be effective.

Especially when I agreed with Evander's order.

I didn't want to be separated from Oli, but the king was right when he said this was bigger than our relationship. As much as it pained me to admit, for us to have the greatest chance of succeeding overall, we had to stay apart.

"Marce and Kenji, you'll also be with us," Evander commanded, and the two nodded their acceptance. "Jahier—"

"I'm not leaving my people right now," the Prince of Venator interjected, "But I believe that Venator should be represented in negotiations should you find Inmuto. So Ezra will go in my stead."

Evander remained silent on his stance regarding Jahier's decision. Nevertheless, he proceeded to accept the terms. Next, he directed his attention towards the King of Agnitio.

"I'll be my kingdom's voice," Tallis said, before turning toward Delyth and Elenora. "Both of you tend to matters here." Elenora seemed inclined to challenge the instruction until her mother interceded by gently touching her arm.

"We will," Tallis's sister replied with a small dip of her head. Elenora reluctantly closed her mouth and imitated the action, shifting her gaze towards Dash, who looked too withdrawn to notice.

"The nine of us will head out in an hour. I need to stop by Sirona's and see if she's made any progress with the sapphires before we do," Evander explained, his hands sliding into his pockets as the shadows of his Obscure began slithering around him. "Make sure you're changed and ready once I return."

After close to an hour, we were outfitted in our new training attire courtesy of Jahier's refugees. The clothing bore resemblance to the black suits we typically wore during our training, but showcased significant improvements due to our collaboration with the artisans responsible for crafting attire for Venator's skilled assassins.

Jahier ensured that our clothing remained lightweight, yet demonstrated a significant improvement in strength. The fabric possessed a soft yet impenetrable quality, exemplified by the dagger's failure to pierce Declan's chest as it rebounded when Isla hurled it. Furthermore, the boots effectively muffled our footfalls, regardless of the nature of the terrain. Additionally, the mask, designed to cover the lower part of our faces, was easily within reach.

"Given additional time, I would have been able to accomplish more," Sirona declared firmly, casting a sidelong glance at the King of Tenebrae.

"You've done more than enough," he responded, examining the small blue gem embedded in the silver ring adorning his finger.

As Oli stood behind me, I briefly looked down at my left hand. Following a solid twenty-minute episode of expressing his frustration in our room regarding Evander's decision, he eventually dropped the matter and proceeded to accompany me downstairs.

"It looks good," Oli quietly remarked, seemingly more engrossed in his own thoughts than in conveying his opinion to me.

"Blue is my color," I replied.

"No," he began hesitantly, his voice fading away. I turned my head to glance behind me, noticing the subtle blush on his cheeks. "I just meant that it suits you. The ring."

I raised one of my eyebrows in curiosity as his gaze moved from my hand to my face. He swallowed with a hint of unease, his demeanor exuding an adorable sense of embarrassment. "Does it?" I asked as a smirk graced my lips.

Oli nodded with a shallow gesture as we ventured into unfamiliar territory. Given my previous position in Caelum and their laws on Conjoining, I had never considered the possibility of marrying someone. I couldn't help but direct my gaze towards the matching ring on his left hand, appreciating its visual appeal.

"I think yours suits you, too," I stated, delicately running my finger over the band.

"Does it?" he asked, the smile clear in his voice.

"Perfectly."

I wanted this with him. I wanted memories filled with love and happiness and no regrets. I wanted the fights, the reconciliations, and every quiet moment in between. I wanted the life we deserved, and I would fight like hell to ensure we got it.

"The magic of the Lapsus stone is simple," Sirona announced, snagging my attention away from my fleeting moment of joy. "Will yourself to a location you've been to and it'll take you there. There are stipulations, of course," she continued, holding one of the rings up as she spoke, "And I will go over those now."

"In order for me to overshadow the stone's blood tie, I had to break it into several pieces, which is why I made rings for all of you. Unfortunately, it also means the stone's magic is weaker," Sirona said. Taking her place at the center of the room, she diligently surveyed each individual present, tucking a strand of her long black hair behind her ear as she carried on with her instructions. "It is important to remember that even at this size, these stones require an exorbitant amount of power to be used. Because of that, your strength will directly affect the ring's capability. The stronger you are, the further you'll journey. Any questions?"

"Can we travel together?" Isla asked, stealing the very inquiry from my tongue.

"Theoretically, yes. But like I said, the stone requires an excessive amount of power, so it would be even more draining to attempt to bring someone else with you on that journey. There is a strong possibility that you will not reach your desired location... And this leads me to a crucial detail. These rings can only be used once—twice, at most. With their size and the fact that they're already tied to a bearer, there's only so much I could do. If I had more time, perhaps I could figure out a way to make it permanent. Maybe if I—"

"Sirona," Evander said as he placed a gentle hand on her shoulder, "You've done more than I could have hoped for. Thank you." Evander drew his gaze over the entire room as he said, "We will be purposeful with calling on its magic." Each person nodded in agreement, and I observed Sirona visibly relax, although a noticeable undercurrent of frustration persisted.

"If there's anything else I can do, please do not hesitate to ask."

Following Sirona's dismissal of Evander's proposal to traverse her back to her shop, the King of Tenebrae directed his attention to the sole remaining member of our family who was still awaiting instructions.

"I need you to go to Vella and arrange to have double the shipments of wheat and grain sent to the palace. Provide Marcas and his family with whatever they need to make it happen, but just ensure that it gets taken care of," Evander commanded before walking around his desk and scribbling on a piece of parchment. "After that's handled, go to the nearby outer towns and advise their evacuation to the palace or one of the closer villages."

"They won't like that," Calidore replied.

"I know. We won't force them to leave, but I need you to convince them it's in their best interest to do so. If that doesn't work, then offer to take the children." Evander handed the now-rolled parchment to Cal. "Everything I've asked of you, just in my hand with my signature. If anyone argues the validity of your request, give them that." Cal dipped his head before retreating to the far wall where Lia and Imogen stood, quietly watching the meetings play out.

Lia swiftly embraced him, enveloping her arms around his neck as she passionately pressed her lips against his, urging him to hurry with his mission and return home promptly. After nodding in acknowledgment, he gently placed her on the ground and shifted his attention to Imogen, whose expression displayed a stern pout.

As his gentle finger slipped beneath her chin and lifted it upwards, my heart quickened and I struggled to maintain composure. Oh my Gods, it was really happening. And my best friend wasn't here to see it.

"I'll be quick, I promise," he said with a crooked grin. "And then much, *much* longer with other things." He softly pressed his lips against her pleased smile.

"You better, or else Lia and I will start without you."

Holy Gods...

"You wouldn't dare," Cal replied, but apprehensively glanced back and forth between the two women.

"Do you really want to risk it?" Lia added, coming over to wrap her arms around Imogen's waist and placing a kiss on her cheek.

"Give me three days!"

"Very well," Imogen stated in a composed manner, "However, if you exceed that timeframe, the proposed activity we all discussed will just have to proceed without your presence."

With a loud curse, Calidore rushed from the room and sprinted down the hall.

A wide smile adorned my face and I raised an eyebrow suggestively upon meeting Imogen's intense gaze. While everyone else doubted my sanity, I was overjoyed to discover that my assumption about Imogen's destination was correct—the center of the most beautiful sandwich ever crafted. I couldn't wait to tell Ainsley.

"Oh, stop. Like you didn't already know what was going on," she scolded and then turned her back to me to face her girlfriend.

I definitely did, but it was still extremely satisfying to see it confirmed.

"Let's head out," Evander directed before traversing away, presumably to find his wife before we had to leave.

I swiftly turned, placing my hands on Oli's waist while he protruded his lower lip in a pout. "I hate this," he grumbled.

"I know," I told him placatingly, and pulled him in for a kiss. "But there's something incredibly important I need you to do for me while I'm gone." Olivier pulled back to cast his curious turquoise eyes my way. "Find out what Imogen, Lia, and Cal discussed doing." He expressed his dissatisfaction by groaning and rolling his eyes, clearly failing to recognize the gravity of this task.

"Felix—"

"Fine, don't love me. Whatever."

Oli kissed me once more and remarked, "Stop being so dramatic. I'm obviously going to do it. I'm just not going to be happy about it."

"I can live with that."

Five minutes later, we were huddled in the living room ready to go. With an air of hurt and confusion, Evander descended the stairs, his gaze appearing to pierce through us.

"Everything okay?" Declan asked as he shrugged his pack on.

"I can't find her," Evander confessed quietly. "Ainsley isn't in our room or the rest of the house. Maybe if I go check—"

"You can't, Evander," Tallis interrupted. "I'm truly sorry, but we have to leave right now."

My heart fractured for the King of Tenebrae. This could have potentially been his final opportunity to say goodbye to his wife, but he wouldn't have the chance. Did Ainsley genuinely harbor so much hurt that she would withhold that from both of them?

With a gesture of acceptance tinged with sadness, Evander took charge and guided us all towards the exit located at the front of the house.

And there was Ainsley. Sitting patiently on a large rock at the edge of the lawn, fully dressed with a travel bag slung over her shoulder, a sapphire ring on her finger, and a *fuck you* expression on her face.

70
Dashiell

"A bsolutely not!" Evander growled as he angrily charged across the lawn toward the Queen of Tenebrae.

Ainsley gracefully jumped down from where she was perched with Nova and Onyx snoozing soundly in the grass. "Everyone ready?" she asked cheerfully, completely ignoring Evander's command.

"You are not going!"

"Watch me." With a swift motion, Evander thrust his hand forward, only to encounter an almost undetectable shield instead of her arm. Without physical contact, he wouldn't be able to use his Obscure on her. "Like I said," she replied with a self-serving smirk, "I'm coming with you."

"You agreed to stay behind," I blurted and rushed forward. Her brown eyes shifted to me, the red streaks within so much darker than usual.

"No, *you* agreed. I simply decided to walk away from that pointless conversation because we weren't going to get anywhere thanks to your bullshit," she quipped, dragging a finger through the air to gesture between Evander and me. "It was more productive for me to get dressed and ready than it would have been to stand there and argue."

I had always admired her tenacity and stubbornness. Even in moments of irrationality, complexity, and unreasonableness, I found her behavior to possess a certain charm. She was my opposite in every way, and I loved how her demeanor always challenged me. However, at this particular moment... it was only pissing me off.

Ainsley was too set in her ways to see the sense in her staying behind. How could she expect any of us to focus on anything other than her fate? Every sudden movement or breeze of the wind would set us on edge.

"I'll traverse everyone right now and leave you behind," Evander stated casually, and crossed his arms over his chest. Ainsley removed a map she had strapped to the side of her bag and carefully unrolled it.

"You can't," she said confidently. "The furthest place you're familiar enough to take us is too far away." Ainsley pointed to the section of the map with a tiny X scribbled on it. "We're at least a few hours' walk from where you can safely do it."

"I'll take the risk."

She grinned and shook her head. "Perhaps if it were just you, but with this many in our traveling party, you'd be too drained to make the jump that many times and our group would be separated."

My gaze shifted to Evander. The audible clench of his jaw had me swearing beneath my breath. Ainsley had him, and now we all knew it.

"Fine," he replied with a tight smile. "I'll just leave you behind once it's time to traverse everyone to the designated spot."

"That's well within your right," she said and offered a casual shrug. "Just as it is well within mine to follow along on my own."

"Ainsley—"

"You either take me with you, or I continue this journey by myself. It's your call, but either way, Evander, I'm going to search for Inmuto."

The tension stayed suspended in the air for one minute, then two. Finally, with a growl of irritation, Evander pushed past his wife and headed for the dirt path that led away from the house. Her annoyed stare met mine next, holding it as my breathing came in heavy inhales. As much as I wanted to fight her, I knew it would be pointless. Once Ainsley's mind had been made up, there was virtually no way to change it.

Regardless of how wrong she was.

With a frustrated sneer, I pushed past her next and followed after the King of Tenebrae.

The journey was anything but pleasant with Ainsley picking small fights with me about how I had no right to try and make her stay back. No matter how many times I argued my extremely valid point, she didn't care. Half the time she angrily stormed away before I could finish my sentence only to come back thirty minutes later and have it out once more, further delaying our journey.

Anytime I'd try to walk away when she started the argument, Nova would snarl at me until I stopped and let Ainsley insult me. Apparently, being in the wolf's good graces didn't matter if her owner was pissed at me.

"Here should be close enough," Evander announced, rolling a map and placing it into the bag strapped to his back. "I can traverse us the rest of the way."

Marceline and Kenji stepped forward first. The three of them would ensure the location was safe and clear before Evander risked bringing any more of us along.

"Us next," Ainsley said once he reappeared five minutes later. Her hand rested between Nova's ears as the wolf sat obediently at her side.

"How do you know I won't just take you home?" he questioned as he stepped toward her.

"Because Nova is my traveling partner and you know she can't be separate from Onyx on a mission like this. Nor do I think Onyx would let you try." She subtly inclined her chin towards the black wolf, who attentively observed his master while baring his teeth, showcasing his sharp canines.

Evander clenched his hands at his sides. "We aren't done discussing this," he said, extending his hand for her to take.

Once we had all been traversed to the location, everyone slumped to the ground, stretching out their limbs or laying down as they relaxed. The trek had been brutal and took far longer than necessary thanks to Ainsley's persistent attitude. The only one who didn't seem exhausted enough to take a breather was Evander as he strode for his wife while holding out his hand.

"I already told you, I'm not going back," she said, tugging off her boot and massaging her ankle.

"Yes, you are." He reached for her hand, but she pulled it away before he could make contact.

"You don't want to do that."

"Trust me, I really do." He lunged again, but she evaded, scrambling to her feet. "I vowed to keep you safe."

"You also vowed to love me, and this isn't how you do that, Evander."

The hurt that flashed across her face nearly wrecked me. It only took me a few seconds to understand why she didn't just put her shield back up—she was testing him. And he was failing.

"If you take me back, I'll never forgive you," she whispered, her sad stare imploring him to reconsider.

She wasn't bluffing. I could see it in her eyes that if Evander crossed this line, they'd never recover. He'd lose her.

He'd lose her just like I had.

"Evander, take a walk," I ordered, coming to stand between them. "You aren't going to solve anything right now and we have more important issues we need to worry about."

It was a lie. Ainsley was the most important thing. She always was. Even when I was pissed at her, her life meant more to me than my own. And if I was barely holding it together after learning of Tallis's vision, I knew Evander wasn't any better off.

Right now, he wasn't thinking logically, only operating off of pure terror and escalated emotions. It wasn't doing anyone any good, most of all Ainsley.

"Take a walk," I said again, letting my voice dip into the command of a king. Evander's eyes reluctantly shifted from his wife's to mine, a clear challenge within.

"Go, Evander," Tallis added before the King of Tenebrae could tear into me like I knew he wanted to. We had been on the same side regarding Ainsley staying behind, so I had no doubt he was feeling betrayed by my interference. I didn't care.

With one final glare in my direction, he turned and charged across the meadow, disappearing behind a thin line of trees that partially concealed a pond. Ainsley didn't say a word as she sat back down and tended to her sore muscles. I guessed that was my cue to leave.

I headed back to my pack and riffled through it, pulling out my container of water and taking a long sip.

"Hey, Dash?" Felix whispered. I gave him a curious sidelong glance as I continued drinking. "Oli pretty much told me he wanted to marry me."

Water spilled from my mouth as I coughed in surprise. "Are you serious?" He nodded, and I grinned from ear to ear. If anyone in this world deserved love and happiness, it was Felix. "He'd be stupid not to," I told him as I shoved the container of water away.

"I'd believe that more if you weren't so withdrawn," he replied, always so attuned to my every emotion. "What's going on? And don't say the vision of Ainsley, because I can tell there's something else too."

My stare automatically dropped to the sapphire ring. "Silas's son was terrified of this," I said, holding up my right hand, "But all they can do is something similar to Evander's Obscure. An annoying inconvenience for us to deal with in battle, sure. But something terrifying enough to instruct your family to flee halfway across the world?" I shook my head, dropping my arm to my side. "I don't think so."

Felix nodded along as he listened intently. "Perhaps there's more they can do when they're whole," he offered. "Sirona said the stone's power is weaker because it's been broken down so many times."

"Maybe. But I still feel like we're missing something." My gaze traveled to the man pacing frantically beyond the trees, his hand dragging through his hair every few seconds as he appeared to be having a furious conversation with himself. "I'll be back," I told Felix and headed for the King of Tenebrae.

The short walk seemed to stretch for hours as I tried and failed to plan the conversation in my head. There were no lessons on how to give your ex-fiancé's husband advice regarding their relationship and I understood why—it was awkward as fuck. But for Ainsley, I would endure the torture.

"We have to stop meeting like this," I quipped once I reached the other side of the trees. Humor seemed like a good place to start.

"What do you want, traitor?" he growled, halting his pacing to face the water.

Okay, so maybe humor wasn't the right choice.

"Just here to repay the kindness of your advice with some of my own," I told him and slipped my hands into my pockets just to have something to do.

He snorted and I could sense his dramatic eye roll without needing to see it. "I'm fine. If anyone needs advice—" he said and angled his head to call over his shoulder, "IT'S MY *WIFE*, WHO'S TOO STUBBORN FOR HER OWN *GOOD*!" I had zero doubts his intended target heard him.

This conversation was going to be far more difficult than I had anticipated, but for Ainsley's sake, I had to press on. "I once had what you have now," I began slowly, resenting that I had to bring this matter up again. "And I lost it all because I thought I knew best. I was selfish and scared and I took away her choice."

"This is different," he argued as he twisted to face me and vehemently shook his head. "You were terrified of a possibility—something that *may* or *may not* have come to fruition. This isn't the case, Dashiell. We both *saw* her fate, her death!"

"I know, but—"

"But nothing!" He turned his back on me and stared at the small pond as the sunlight bounced off the ripples. "She'll be pissed at me for a while, but she'll get over it."

I didn't know how to reach him on the matter. He was too far gone, just as I had been when Felix tried to talk sense into me. His fear was going to win, and it was going to cost them both. I couldn't let it happen.

"I thought the same thing. I thought I could take her hate. That it would be worth it because at least she'd be alive," I admitted, grappling with any reasonable explanation I could find. "But it wasn't. Trust me on that, Evander."

"You may not have been able to deal with it, but it doesn't mean I can't. It's a choice I can live with."

"But can *she*?" I questioned. Evander's mouth opened, only to hesitate, seemingly unable to find the right words. "I made the mistake of only thinking of my own losses when I hurt her. Sure, I knew she'd more than likely want nothing to do with me, but I never took the time to truly imagine what it would be like for *her* to lose *me.*"

I ground my teeth against the images that rushed forward from the snippets Felix had shared with me, each picture worse than the last.

"I was told only details of what it was like for her, but you were there. You saw and felt and experienced all of her heartbreak. You watched her fracture and break over that pain." My stomach rolled with nausea as I pictured Ainsley lying on the ground in a puddle of her own tears. "It'll be worse this time," I added, fighting against the images that still rushed. Ainsley refusing to eat, refusing to speak, blaming herself for what happened, each onslaught intensifying my regret. "She won't only be losing the man she loves, but also the piece of herself she only just found. Putting your fear aside, can you honestly take that from her?"

Evander's eyes wandered away from mine, coming to rest upon a patch of dirt that lay between us. I could see his resolve begin to buckle. He discreetly shook his head, barely perceptible, yet I managed to observe it and sighed with relief. He wouldn't force her on this, at least not today.

"So what now?" Evander muttered, the question more to himself than to me.

I shrugged, knowing there was only one right answer.

"Now we continue as planned and fight like hell to prove Tallis wrong."

71

Ainsley

I held the large map up as I attempted to discern the best path to continue forward once we started again. That is, unless Evander decided to traverse me away, making me have to start my journey from the beginning. My stomach knotted as I pushed away the thought of him crossing that line. I didn't want to believe he was capable of it. Even while scared, I had to trust that he would support me.

The sapphire gem on my finger sparkled beneath the late afternoon sun, and I was reminded of my conversation with Sirona earlier when she gave it to me. The vision of my death had plagued my thoughts for the hour I spent getting ready and settling outside in the fresh air. I didn't want to die, but I found myself more concerned over what that loss would do to Evander—to his soul.

"It would be an impossible loss to deal with," Sirona had said. *"To have one's soul split from this world... Well, I can't imagine the turmoil the survivor would face."*

I emptied my stomach the moment she disappeared from view down the path that would lead her to the closest village.

Yet even after the revelation of the pain Evander would experience should I die, I still decided to come because this mission was bigger than that. It was more important than the life I had planned for us. It was a way to save countless lives and if I had to sacrifice my own to do it, I would. Because that's what a queen would do.

I held the map higher as my eyes darted across the chart I barely knew how to read. A hand pressed into the small of my back and I inhaled a shaky breath in preparation for Evander to traverse me away now that I'd dropped my shield. I fought off the pain of knowing this could be the last time he ever touched me.

"We'll go this way," Evander said, removing the right corner of the map from my hand as he replaced it with his own and pointed with his left to a location we were close to.

I looked up at him, trying not to let the relief I felt show, but the softness of his eyes and the way his lips quirked up just slightly had me smiling through a long exhale. He leaned down, whispering his love for me before planting a small kiss on my lips and focusing again on the map.

I followed his lead and redirected my attention to the chart we both held up. "Why not this way?" I asked, drawing a direct trail with my finger from where we were currently to where we needed to be.

"The forest is too dense," he argued and used his finger to do the same with his path. "That way may be the more direct path, but it could take us twice as long because of the terrain."

"Then we'll go your way." I rolled the map again and shoved it back into my bag before facing Evander.

My arms snaked around his neck, and his wrapped around my waist, pulling me flush to him. I reached up on my toes and flicked his nose with mine, earning that dimpled grin I'd first fallen in love with.

"I can't apologize for my stance on you staying behind," he whispered, rubbing the length of my spine. "But I'm sorry for how I went about it. I don't like or agree with your choice, but it's still yours to make."

I nodded, appreciating the apology. "That understanding is all I wanted."

My hands ran through the hair at his nape as I gently pulled his face down to meet mine. He kissed me softly and with more devotion than I knew what to do with. I arched into him, grateful that this wouldn't be our last embrace. But before I could fully enjoy that knowledge, there was an issue that needed to be taken care of.

"There's something I need you to do for me," I whispered against his mouth and opened wider for his tongue to slip over mine.

"Hmmm?"

I pulled back and brushed my lips lightly over his as I said, "Craft a dagger and be ready."

Evander kissed me hard, pressing his fingers into my back as he slid them down to my waist. "Where?"

I moved my mouth to the hollow of his throat, working my way to the side just below his ear. "Directly to your right, just beyond the tree line," I replied, pressing small kisses to his flesh between each word.

He glided his left hand around my side and I instantly felt his shadows followed by the press of a sharp blade concealed from view between our bodies. I pulled my face from his neck, offering a loving smile as I crafted my dagger and took a deep breath. With a gentle dip of my chin, we both spun and flung our weapons at the target hidden under the cover of the forest.

A roar of pain, loud and *definitely* not human—to my surprise—echoed through the space, causing birds to take to the skies from the branches they had been perched on. Evander and

I took off, ignoring the shouts of confusion from our traveling party. We didn't have time to explain.

"There!" I yelled, pointing ahead to the flash of white moving to our left beyond the dense forest.

"Call for it!" Evander commanded. I knew what he meant and reached deep for my Obscure, sending it out for the white thing that had been watching us for months. "Now hold it down!"

I pushed harder, feeling my dark tendrils collide with the creature. It ducked away, trying its best to evade capture, but I wouldn't let up. My Obscure wrapped around its limbs and I pulled my arms back, taking the creature to the ground.

"Good!" Evander yelled and disappeared into his shadows.

I ran faster, finally entering the clearing where the creature had been caught just as Evander appeared before it with a sword poised in his hand. The animal bellowed as it got up, its teeth snapping at the tendrils that restrained it.

Evander's shoulders slumped as he lowered his weapon. "It's just a bear," he said, relieved. "It was probably just hunting us, thinking we'd be an easy meal."

I didn't call back my magic as an uneasy feeling swam in the pit of my stomach.

"What the hell is going on?" Declan demanded as he and the rest of our group entered the clearing.

"Ainsley saved us from being dinner," Van said, letting his sword dissipate into swirling mist. "You can let it go. I think we scared it enough that it got the message to stay away."

Again, I kept my magic in place.

The white bear stood on its haunches, opening its mouth to let out a thunderous roar at the King of Tenebrae. Gods, it had to be at least eight feet tall, with sharp canines primed to tear through flesh and bone. As his jaw finally shut, something familiar caught my attention, and I rushed forward to get a better look at the animal.

"I know you," I whispered in realization, finding a long scar over the bear's eye. I elongated my dagger into a short sword and pointed it at the animal. "Talk, you asshole."

The creature didn't move as it stood there, its deadly claws ready to strike us down should we attempt to attack it.

"Love," Evander said, his tone dripping with amusement, "You were very, very, *very* high that day."

My bear's eyes drifted from me to my husband, and it released a sound I swore resembled a snicker.

"Where's your little friend, huh? The fucking fish with the hat!" I demanded, pointing my blade over the expanse of the clearing as my eyes scanned the space.

The bear grumbled a sound of confusion—something that didn't sound animalistic, though it reminded me of how Onyx and Nova behaved. They felt like more than just wolves, but I could never put my finger on why exactly that was.

"Umm, cupcake?" Felix said as I fervently continued my search, pushing aside long blades of grass as if I'd find the fish that way. "That one I think really *was* a hallucination from the berries."

I righted myself, finding everyone watching me with either a confused expression or a delighted smile. Kenji wasn't even trying to hide his enjoyment as he laughed at my antics.

"Whatever!" I yelled, aiming my sword back at the white bear. "The fish may not have been real, but *he* is."

The animal narrowed its eyes at me in challenge, only solidifying my belief that it was more than it was leading on.

"I don't know what it is, but it's *something*... Something different," Dash added. I turned to find him halfway between me and the rest of the group, his blue eyes blown out with black from his Obscure. "It's too cognizant. More than a typical animal should be. Its focus drifts to whoever is speaking and there are subtle movements in his facial expressions, as if he understands the conversation."

"It's been watching us train for months now," I announced, redirecting my attention to the crowd. "He stays mostly hidden beyond the trees, but he's there. He leaves whenever you all do, but comes back for the next training session."

At first, I thought I was seeing things—my paranoia getting to me—but after the third time, I told Evander what was going on. We always kept our eyes peeled for it each week, but by the time we caught sight of that flash of white, it was already gone. So we reinforced our shields, ensuring that nothing could penetrate it and no sounds could escape.

That is, until this afternoon.

After I climbed onto the rock at the edge of our yard, I spotted our watcher lurking closer than usual. Onyx and Nova seemed to sense him too, but I ordered them to stand down and keep their focus on me. If we were going to catch whatever it was, it was going to be today.

I dropped the shield and unrolled the map I had packed. Carefully, and louder than necessary, I relayed the plan of our trip to the wolves. I told them where we would be going, how long the journey would take, and even pointed to the spot Van would traverse us to where we would make camp for the night. I made sure to hold the map high as I indicated each area so the watcher to my back could see. Five minutes later, he was gone.

I had a feeling he would show up at the location Van traversed us to, so I delayed the journey as much as I could, walking slower than usual and picking fights with Dash because I knew it would hold us up. I needed to give our onlooker as much time as possible to get to the spot since we'd arrive in seconds once Van took us. My assumption was that I would find an enemy soldier hidden in the trees, not a bear that talked to me when I was high.

"What should we do with it?" Marce asked

"My vote is to kill it," Dec chimed in. "I'm starving and who's to say it's the same bear Ainsley talked to?"

"It is," Felix confirmed. "I'd never forget the first bear I ever rode."

"You did what?" Marce replied.

"I'm sorry, but why are we discounting this whole 'fish with a hat' thing so quickly?" Kenji cut in.

I looked over to find Van pinching the bridge of his nose over the ridiculous discussion everyone was having. Even Dash, who was normally focused when it came to things like this, said, "I'm more interested in hearing about Ainsley being high." To which Kenji agreed by enthusiastically high-fiving the King of Caelum.

"Okay, enough of this," Evander declared, crafting a new sword, "We're running out of daylight and if he doesn't want to talk willingly, then I'm sure we could torture his voice out of him."

Van took a step and the space flooded with a bright flash of light that had us all shielding our eyes. When I lowered my arm, there was nothing but my black tendrils drifting along the air. The bear was gone.

"What the hell?" Van demanded.

I scanned the clearing, frantically searching for any signs of the missing bear. How could something that big simply disappear without a trace?

"There!" Dash yelled, pointing across the clearing to a small white animal sprinting—a weasel, by the looks of it.

"Onyx, Nova!" Evander commanded.

Our wolves took off at full speed in pursuit of the creature as we followed behind as fast as we could. My lungs were burning and muscles aching, but I didn't stop. Van was right—the forest was dense and difficult to navigate. Too many times I tripped over fallen branches or got stuck in hanging leaves. But thankfully, I kept up the pace enough to keep Onyx and Nova in my sights, even if they were just tiny figures in the distance.

Their snarls were loud enough to reach me as they took a sharp left turn into a tunnel. It wasn't ideal to run into a dark space that we weren't sure had an exit, but we didn't have much of a choice. Van was the first one to sprint through, followed by Declan, Marce, and Kenji, while the rest of us brought up the rear. Luckily, the tunnel was short, but when we came out of it, the forest appeared to have changed.

The tree trunks were thinner here and the species of leaves were entirely different from the ones that had constantly smacked me in the face. The grass beneath my boots was a lighter shade of green and felt bouncier under each step. Even the air tasted odd—tinged with salt.

Just when I was about to fall for the tenth time, Van's shadows shifted around me and he materialized a foot away. I immediately reached for his hand and let him traverse me the final distance. We appeared under the sun with the forest to our back and the sound of crashing waves straight ahead.

I blinked against the brightness as the rest of our family pushed through the trees behind us. We were several yards away from a massive cave entrance with a cliff on either side. Onyx and Nova were stopped before it, but there was no sign of the white weasel.

"You don't think it jumped, do you?" Kenji questioned.

"Why would it kill itself?" Marce asked.

"Maybe it didn't want to tell us about the fish."

I swiveled my head and gave our group a curious look. "It probably just went inside," I reasoned and faced forward once more.

"What are you talking about?" Felix asked, coming up to my side. "Inside where? The ocean?"

I glanced to my left, furrowing my brows as I slowly replied, "The cave." The answer seemed more than obvious to me. Felix looked straight ahead and then I followed his stare to the group behind us, noticing that everyone appeared confused.

"Ainsley," Dash said, taking a tentative step forward as his gaze swept over the view before us. "What cave?"

My heart dropped, and I immediately turned to Evander with a question ready on my tongue. He nodded without hesitation and I felt a sense of relief that I wasn't crazy. "I see it too," he announced.

"To us, there's only flat grass followed by a cliff, with a steep drop by the looks of it," Declan added.

I turned to Felix again. "You seriously don't see it?" He shook his head. "Maybe if you got closer," I suggested after seeing I was one step ahead of him. I grabbed his hand to pull him forward and his eyes grew wide as he stiffened in my hold.

"What the fuck?" Felix yelled, as his stare darted across the space in front of us. "Where the hell did that come from?"

"You see it now?" He nodded and stepped closer, still clutching my hand tight.

Together, we looked over the massive natural structure with dark brown stone and cracks spidering out in all directions. There was one tall entrance framed by two large boulders and a tunnel too dark to see inside.

"Dec," Van called, not taking his eyes from the cave we both saw. "Give me your hand." The Lord of Vorsutos swore loudly the second he did.

I shook my head and studied the rock again, unable to understand why we were able to see it when no one else could. It couldn't be because we were rulers or else it would have appeared to Tallis and Dash as well. Perhaps it was because of our connection to Tenebrae; this was our land.

"You've got to be fucking kidding me," Evander said through an incredulous laugh. I curiously turned toward my husband to find him staring down at his wrist.

At the silver band with black encrusted stones.

I reached for the chain around my neck, pulling my pendant out of my training suit and placing it in my palm. My fingers ran over the matching black gems as a smile tugged at my lips. The Indico stone—the one with the power to reveal hidden secrets.

"We've had it this entire time," I commented.

Evander nodded as he laughed even harder, bordering on hysterics. We had spent all that time poring over ancient texts and maps when all along our stones had been telling us the answer. I joined in his fit, unable to control myself as I laughed about how blind we had been.

"If someone could clue us in, that would be really helpful," Kenji said, a hint of agitation in his voice that only made the situation funnier.

"Their items contain the Indico stone," Dash said, answering the question. "That's why they can see it. Everyone needs to touch them in order to as well."

With several deep breaths, I managed to calm down just as Evander did, a bright smile on his face as he looked at me. This was what we had been searching for. This was it.

"Ready?" he asked.

"Ready," I replied.

"Then let's go see Inmuto."

72

Ainsley

The ten of us stayed huddled together as we entered the cave with Nova and Onyx leading the way. The air was still with a cold mist looming through a tunnel so dark that even our immortal eyes couldn't penetrate it. Dash snapped his fingers and a spark of flame ignited, illuminating our small vicinity just enough to see our nearby surroundings.

"Holy shit," Felix whispered as Dash's fire flickered in the facets of thousands of rubies embedded in the walls of the cave. "Are these..."

"Tectus stones," I answered on a soft breath and trailed my hands over the gems. "I can feel their magic." My shadows slipped out and I crafted a dagger before carefully prying one of the stones free.

How did I not realize that all this time I had the power to find Inmuto? I should have known when I felt that pull while studying the maps with Van. Hell, I should have known after I killed Perceval and felt that same pull in his room. Only then I had been mistaken about the crown, when all along it was his ring that was calling to me.

"We should take enough for everyone, including those at home," I said as I continued to pop more stones from the wall, taking a few extra to ensure Sirona had some.

"They *really* didn't want anyone to find this place, huh?" Ezra said, whistling over the sheer number of concealing gems contained within the walls.

"Whoops," I replied innocently as I backed away from my task, ready to continue our journey through the cave. Inmuto may have gone to extensive lengths not to be found, but that didn't matter. My kingdom was under attack and I'd stop at nothing to win this war for them.

We walked down the long passage for what felt like hours, nothing but the sounds of our steps, Felix and Kenji's shit jokes, Kenji's constant attempts to get me to allow him to see me high, and Felix shoving in Kenji's face that *he* got to see me high echoing against the stone walls.

At that moment, I would gladly take Dash's silent treatment over spending another minute in their company.

Finally, the long stretch of the cave opened up, revealing a circular chamber that appeared too perfectly cylindrical in shape to be created by nature alone. The ground was a mix of sand and dirt and the walls were smooth as they stretched up so high we couldn't see where they ended. There was an exit on the opposite side from where we entered with another narrow passage beyond it.

"There's art on the walls," Isla announced, hurrying over to the left side of the space.

"Over here, too," Ezra chimed in.

I jogged over and wiped my hand across the wall, freeing it from dust, but the chamber was so dim I could barely see.

"A little light would be nice," Evander called, as I spied him struggling to make out the image he was standing before. Small balls of flame settled into the ground, subtly illuminating the walls. "That's it?" Van scoffed.

"Since you're so concerned with size," Dash quipped, and the firelight grew brighter though the flame remained small. "Size means shit when you don't know how to use it, though I don't have a problem with either."

I rolled my eyes and focused on my wall. Depicted on the stone was a figure, her hands outstretched toward the sky with a bolt of lightning nestled between them. I moved to the right to find a similar figure, this time with a skull where the lightning had been. Beneath the figure were smaller ones, seeming to bow at the larger illustrations.

I moved over to another portion of the chamber at the opposite end, finding the same depictions with only the objects that the beings held differing. A droplet, a tree, fire, a heart, a scale, a book, a sword, a feather... On and on and on, they changed.

"These are the Gods of this world," I said as the realization hit me. "This chamber is a representation of all of them."

Evander came over to my side as I pointed out the similarities and variations in each illustration. "I think you may be right, love."

I opened my mouth to offer a snide remark, but his face fell, sensing the same feeling of unease I had just been hit with as well. We both turned toward the exit to find Onyx and Nova heading into the passage before we were ready to leave.

We called for the wolves, but they continued forward as if they didn't hear us. Van yelled louder and whistled, but they still kept going until they rounded a corner and disappeared entirely from view. I shoved away from the cave's wall and hurried toward where Onyx and Nova had gone, looking just as worried as Evander as his eyes met mine.

But not three steps in that direction later, the cavern shook violently, knocking us all to the ground as a massive slate of stone slammed into the dirt, blocking the entrance we had come from. I took several gulps of air as my instincts took over, warning me something was wrong, wrong, *wrong*.

I dove into myself, frantically searching, although I already knew the answer. "Evander!" I yelled as I yanked on each door to my Gifts.

But they lay dormant.

"I know," he said back weakly. "I feel it, too."

"My wind, it's... gone," Declan announced.

I threw myself against my doors, clawing, banging, and pulling against the handles, but it was no use. What frustrated me the most was that I could feel my magic present within me, but I couldn't access it.

"I can still call for my Obscure," Dash said, looking toward Evander, Tallis, and myself. I reached for it, letting out a long sigh of relief when the black tendrils wrapped around my hands."

"Why take only our Gifts?" I asked.

"Why take our magic at all?" he countered.

Good point. Although I knew nothing about the mythical kingdom, my dislike for it was already strong.

"Let's just get out of here," I suggested.

Everyone eagerly agreed, and together we took a step toward the exit—

Only to fall to the ground as an arrow whizzed through the air, slicing Isla across her cheek. She screamed from the sudden sting, and Declan rushed for her just as another arrow shot in his direction. He dove out of the way, taking his fiancé to the ground with him as he covered her body with his.

"Nobody else moves!" Evander bellowed with outstretched hands.

My chest rose and fell at a rapid pace as I tried not to panic. It was my fault we were here—my choice to come to Inmuto—and now we were stuck in a chamber while magical arrows tried to kill us.

"There are triggers hidden everywhere," Dash explained. I turned my attention toward the King of Caelum to find him lying close to the ground as he pointed to various spots. "There are slight shifts in the way the sand moves, and some spots are more raised than others until it reaches the passage where Onyx and Nova went. That threshold where the cavern meets the tunnel is where the traps end."

"Can you see a path to safely get us there?" I asked.

Dash carefully pushed himself to his feet as he continued to study the ground. He tilted his head from side to side while he considered before turning to me and saying, "Even with all the firelight, it'll be difficult. Some spots are so subtle that it's possible I could mistake them for a safe area."

"I'm just going to traverse us out," Evander said impatiently as he called for his Obscure.

"Van, no!" I demanded, stopping him at once. "You can't guarantee you'll land in a safe area. Don't risk it."

"Whether we do it Dashiell's way or mine, there's a risk. At least with my Obscure, we can get out of here faster. I'll test it on myself first."

"Van—"

"You made your choice, love. This one's mine."

Evander didn't wait for me to argue as his shadows enveloped him and took him away. A breath later, he appeared safely on the threshold... as dozens of arrows rained down over the rest of the cavern.

73

Ainsley

Screams tore through the chamber as we all took cover the best we could without being able to leave our spots. My name on Evander's lips flooded my ears as I felt small slices across my hands and back as the weapons rushed past me, landing in the dirt and setting off even more traps. I shouldn't have been able to feel the stings across my spine, which meant our attire wasn't holding up. Not only did this place render our Gifts useless, but it also affected the magic sewn into our suits to keep us safe.

"Ainsley, answer me!" Evander exclaimed.

Picking my head up carefully, I found that the onslaught had stopped and the ground was now littered with arrows. I turned my gaze toward Evander to see him staring at me with wide, remorseful eyes.

"I'm okay," I told him. "A little cut up, but okay."

A groan of agony ripped through the cavern and I twisted to find Kenji on his back, impaled by an arrow through his stomach.

"Kenji!" Marce screamed as she pushed herself to her feet.

"Marceline, don't!" Evander tried, but it was too late.

Marce rushed for her husband as several arrows rained toward her. One second she was diving for him, and the next, she was being tackled to the ground by Dash as the darts slammed into the place she had been standing a moment prior.

"Let me go!" she demanded, the words breaking on a sob as her stare stayed fixed on Kenji's body slowly rising and falling with each labored breath. Streaks of red painted the dirt, the ground soaking the blood up greedily as if the earth had been starving for it. I closed my thoughts to the images of Felix that tried to rush forward. I couldn't panic. Not now.

"I can't," Dash said, keeping her pinned to the ground. "We'll get to him, I swear, but right now we have to figure out how to get out of here in one piece."

Marce shook her head, not wanting to accept that answer. I couldn't blame her. If it were me, and Van was the one bleeding out, there wouldn't be a person alive who could keep me from him.

"Dashiell, get her to me first," Evander instructed, motioning to the distressed woman beneath him.

Fortunately, they were the closest to the exit, only a handful of feet away. Dash slowly lifted himself off of Marceline, but didn't drop his hold on her arm as he guided her where to safely step. Within minutes, she was next to her king, Van's arms tightly around her as tears streamed down her face for the man she couldn't yet help.

Dash turned around and headed for Ezra next, marking a circle in the dirt with his foot to point out the path the advisor from Venator would need to take. Isla and Declan were next, then Felix and Tallis, and finally me.

I drew in a deep breath as I worked out what circles to step on just as Dash reached me. But rather than hold my hand as he did with the others as they navigated this fucked up maze together, he turned his back to me and crouched down.

"Get on," he said. He had to be joking. There was no way in hell I was doing that, especially when I was as capable as everyone who had made it through. When I didn't move, he twisted his head and looked at me over his shoulder. "If you think I'm taking the chance of you stepping on the wrong spot, you're insane."

"You had no problem with letting everyone else take that risk," I said defensively.

"They aren't you."

When I still didn't move, he redirected his stare across the way to Evander.

"I swear to the Gods Ainsley, if you don't get on his fucking back right now..." my husband warned furiously.

"Fine," I growled, wrapping myself around Dash as he stood and proceeded to effortlessly navigate us to safety.

The moment Dash deposited me on the threshold, he took a deep breath and made his way back out for the last member of our party. He had to have been exhausted and nearly to his baseline with the constant use of his Obscure today, but knowing Dash, he'd take the risk and dip below it if it meant getting Kenji to safety.

I placed a reassuring hand on Marce's shoulder while Van held her as we all watched the scene with bated breath. Dash reached the injured man quickly but seemed to be taking his time with bringing him back.

"What's going on?" Evander demanded as Dash stayed kneeling beside Kenji.

"I'm trying to figure out how best to do this without causing more damage," he answered as he moved, carefully assessing different angles. "There's a lot of blood loss. If I pick him up, I could make it worse."

"And if you don't…" Evander replied, not needing to finish that statement for us to know what he meant.

If Dash didn't, then Kenji would die there.

With a resigned nod to himself, the King of Caelum leaned forward and scooped Kenji into his arms. Blood poured from our advisor as his scream of pain pierced the air, muddled with Marce's fearful cries. Dash moved as fast as he could, but carrying Kenji's weight made him slower and sent him off balance on more than one occasion. I watched in horror as he almost slipped out of the circle twice only to recover a split second before doing so.

Declan, Tallis, and Felix waited at the edge of the threshold with outstretched hands ready to relieve Dash of Kenji's weight. The moment they crossed, the cavern shook again, and the slate that had been blocking the way lifted back up and settled into the wall. The ground vibrated, sending grains of dirt bouncing over the space as it swallowed the arrows whole until the scene looked as untouched as it had been the moment we arrived.

"Fuck this place," Declan said as he held up his hand and conjured a small tornado of wind in his palm.

I dove into myself, finding the doors to my Gifts once again thrumming with life. Even my training suit felt as reinforced as it had before we entered the cavern from hell. Thank the fucking Gods.

"How is he?" Marce croaked as she knelt beside him and took his hand in hers.

"I can't be positive, but I think I've been better," Kenji answered weakly.

She let out a relieved laugh mixed with a cry as she pressed her lips to his pale forehead. He was losing color, and far too quickly.

"Can you help him?" she asked, directing her attention to an exhausted Dash.

He nodded, the movement appearing to take even more from him. "I can try, but with my magic this low, there isn't much I can do. He needs to get to a healer."

Marce accepted Dash's response and moved aside so he could assess the damage. "Do what you can, and I'll clot the wound to buy him more time," I directed as I came over to help.

The King of Caelum pressed his hands to the skin around the puncture and closed his eyes in concentration. His breaths came in heavy pants and his arms shook as he continued to offer more and more of his magic. It was too much.

"I've got it," I told him, replacing his hands with mine and quickly clotting the blood around the wound. "I can prevent his blood from pouring from him, but I can't stop internal damage. So the arrow has to stay until he can get to a Medicus."

Evander stepped forward, holding his hand out for Marce to take. "I'll take the two of you—"

"No," she interrupted, as she repositioned Kenji's head beneath her lap, "You don't leave her." Marceline angled her chin toward me. "She's who you've vowed to look after. Stay with your wife, Van. We'll be fine."

"He's too injured to use his ring," Van argued.

Kenji held up a weak hand and waved him off. "I've got enough strength to at least get us on the other side of this chamber," he joked.

"And I can at least get us back to the cliffs," Marceline added. "After that, if I have to craft a cart and pull him the rest of the way, I will. If that old ass map is correct, there are several Tenebraen camps not far from the entrance we found. We can be at one of them before sunrise if we hurry."

"Marce—"

"Protect your Soul Bonded, Evander."

The King of Tenebrae didn't argue after that. With a quick goodbye from each of us, and a promise to inform us the moment they made it to one of the camps, Kenji and Marce disappeared.

I looked over the seemingly pristine chamber. The ground was perfectly smooth with not a drop of blood to be found. Nothing to indicate the horror we had all gone through minutes prior. How many people had come before us and suffered the same fate only for the events to be erased as if they were too insignificant to be remembered? And what kind of kingdom would go to such lengths to keep others out?

"What now?" Declan asked into the quiet.

Evander's hand found the small of my back as it always did. I tucked myself into his side, needing to feel his presence to ground me. "We keep going," he announced, sliding his fingers between mine. "But this time, let's be more careful. For all we know, every inch of this place is just another trap."

We exited the cavern, staying close to one another just as we had before. The moment we rounded the corner, Onyx and Nova appeared, walking two steps ahead of us. Van called for the wolves and they turned, tilting their head in curiosity as they waited for a command.

"What the hell?" I said under my breath. I scanned the path ahead, but there were no paw prints or tracks indicating they had gone any further than where they stood now. To them, it was as if we were never stopped in the cavern.

"Be on your guard," Evander announced and ordered our wolves to continue leading the way.

We walked for an hour through a damp, twisting passage. Dash's magic was too low to call for his fire, so we spent the entire time in darkness, trusting Onyx and Nova's sense of direction. Eventually, the tunnel widened into another open space, this one resembling a cave more than the circular chamber we had been in earlier.

"We'll set up camp here for the night," Evander declared and dropped his pack to the ground with a heavy thump. Everyone else did the same, sighing with relief to be rid of the extra weight.

I shuffled around the enormous area, appreciating the stalagtites that hung from the ceiling like melting icicles over the cavern's turquoise lake—the same hue as Oli and Marce's eyes. I knelt and scooped a handful, splashing it onto my face and discovering it to be warmer than I had expected given the frigid chill through the air.

"Dash and I will take the first and second watch tonight," Felix announced.

I turned around to find the group huddled around a small fire Dash must have started as Tallis threw sticks he gathered onto it. My brain pricked at me to question why there were pieces of wood in a cave, but I suddenly felt too exhausted to care. I stumbled over the group as Van worked to craft pillows and blankets for everyone.

"Tired, love?" he asked as I curled next to him. He kissed my forehead softly, muttering an order for me to sleep, but I was already drifting off.

I was the last one in the group to wake other than Dash, who was snoring soundly to my left. Everyone else was chatting several feet to the right of the fire, enjoying their rations of food while looking well-rested and clean. My stare shot past them, spying my spare training suit and a towel on a small boulder beside the cavern's lake.

I hurried from my makeshift bed and gave Evander a quick gratitude-filled kiss on the cheek before sinking into the warm water. I sighed at the temperature and relief my aching body instantly felt as I scrubbed the dirt and blood from my flesh. This small moment of peace was exactly what I needed before we dove into whatever torture this place had planned for us today.

As soon as I was sufficiently clean, I quickly dressed and headed for the group. Evander had my plate of food ready for me the moment I stood beside him. Another deserved kiss, this time on his lips.

"How long was I out for?" I asked, taking a bite of the hard cheese.

"Most of the day."

"What? Why didn't you wake me?"

"You needed to rest," he answered and draped his arm over my shoulder as he pulled me into his side. Despite the casual gesture, I could feel how tense he was and tried not to focus on his darkened eyes or how exhausted he looked even though he had a full night of sleep. "We explored a little of the cavern, finding four different tunnels. The day has been spent discussing which to take first."

I nodded and bit into my bread next. "Has Marce—"

"No," Van interjected immediately. I placed the roll down, suddenly feeling sick to my stomach. If she and Kenji didn't make it...

"We've discussed this, Evander," Tallis said, stealing my attention as I looked at him with hopeful eyes. "With no time seeming to pass between us in the cavern and then meeting the wolves in the tunnel, it's possible that things are altered here. There's a chance little more than an hour has elapsed for them outside of this cave."

I reached for Evander's hand and squeezed tightly as I held onto Tallis's theory. "They're fine," I told my husband. "They're going to be fine and we're going to get the hell out of this cave and find Inmuto." He offered a smile—a weak one, but I knew it was all he had in him to muster. I glanced behind me at Dash's sleeping form.

"He's been out since after his first watch ended," Van said, reading where my thoughts had gone.

"And his magic?" I didn't know if Dash had dipped below his baseline yesterday, but I could tell he had to have been close. Given that we still weren't talking, I figured asking anyone besides him was the right course of action.

"Refilling steadily," Tallis answered. I nodded, grateful for his and Felix's Magusier abilities. With both of them with us, Dash's progress would be continually monitored until he was at full strength once again.

As if he could sense us talking about him, Dash released a groan, followed by a mumbled curse as he rose from the ground. He stumbled toward us, dragging a hand through his disheveled hair and looking as cranky as I usually was when first waking up.

"I hate this fucking cave," he said, reaching around his back and removing a jagged rock that had been stuck to him. "What did I miss?"

"Before we dive into that, the fire is almost out, and I didn't want to wake you. Do you mind?" Tallis asked, pointing to the flames that were still burning brightly.

"It's fine," Dash argued.

Tallis's stare dropped to the ground as if he was almost embarrassed to continue. "For us, perhaps, but..." He looked toward the small fire in adoration. "They like it when it's warmer."

I stifled my smile as I spotted the two snoozing wolves on their backs as close to the flames as they could get without getting burned. Dash didn't give it a second thought before conjuring a ball of his magic in his palm and shooting it toward our campfire. Tallis grinned, calmly rushing over to the area and adding more sticks as fuel.

"They seriously are the most adorable creatures ever," Felix said, appearing behind me. Together, we watched the wolves wag their tails as they noticed the size of their fire growing. "Maybe not the black one, though."

I jabbed him in the stomach with my elbow. "Be nice to Onyx, he—" My words were cut off as I noticed something strange rolling over the cavern lake. "Van?" Everyone ceased their chatter, picking up the seriousness in my tone as they followed my line of sight. "What is that?"

Evander took a step closer to the water's edge. "It looks like fog," he replied before abruptly directing his attention toward one of the tunnels. "It's coming from there too." I looked in that direction, noticing an odd flicker of light against the walls.

I checked my sheaths, making sure I had all my daggers in place as I crafted two more to keep in my hands. The ominous fog crept through the space, gliding over our feet before enveloping us in mist that seemed to grow thicker by the second. Just as before in the circular chamber, I felt my Gifts go dormant.

Evander strode forward on his own, sparking a panic in me. I yelled his name, but he didn't stop. Again, I called for him and again he walked faster... until the fog swallowed him completely.

"EVANDER!" I screamed and sprinted after him. His name bounced off the cave walls and slammed back into me. I turned around to demand the others help me find him, but they were gone, too.

I was completely alone.

74

Dashiell

I ran as fast as I could, ignoring the shouts of protest from behind as I chased after Ainsley through a fog that was so dense I could barely see. The logical choice would have been to search together as a group, but the moment she disappeared just as Evander had, my body moved on instinct. It didn't matter that we had spent the last six weeks in a fight barely speaking—I needed to get to her.

Suddenly, the haze seemed to still and everything grew eerily quiet. My steps slowed, my heart a relentless pounding beneath my ribs as I continued my search. The strange candlelight embedded in the walls flickered, sending ominous shadows curling through the fog as soft whispered voices echoed around me. I gripped the dagger at my hip tighter and took one careful step in front of the other as my Obscure lifted to the surface.

The hair on my neck rose as goosebumps pebbled over my skin, every nerve in my body firing off at once telling me something wasn't right. The air was too quiet, too thick, too *strange*, each lungful a blatant warning, but I didn't care. I continued on anyway.

Several minutes passed when a shallow, unstable breath reached my ears, the cadence more familiar than my own. I turned left and then right as my eyes quickly scanned the fog until I saw it: a silhouetted figure crouched against the wall. I rushed over, bending down before Ainsley who was huddled in a ball, her face buried in the arms wrapped tightly across her body.

She flinched and whimpered as I touched her, but the moment she heard my voice, her body relaxed and she looked up at me. "Hey," I whispered. She pushed herself into my arms, forcing me to stumble back as I stood with her. "It's okay," I said. She buried her face in my neck, and I squeezed her tighter as she trembled from fear.

"I got lost, and then there were these voices and..." She trailed off, the emotion in her throat refusing to let her continue. "What happened?"

"I don't know," I answered, pulling her back so I could inspect every inch of her. "Are you hurt?" She shook her head and I breathed a sigh of relief but didn't halt my search. "Where are your daggers?"

She stiffened slightly—a marker of fear—and angled her chin back the way we came. "I lost them when something attacked me." Her chest began to rise and fall at too fast a pace. "I tried to fight, but I couldn't see through the fog. I think I injured whatever it was, though."

I nodded, still looking over her form as I said, "Good. We need to get out of here."

"Wait," she demanded as I tried to pull her along. I stopped, furrowing my brows as I watched her carefully. "I just need a minute before we go back through," she explained, gesturing toward the dense fog. "Before we face whatever the hell lives in there." Her voice was distant as if lost in the memory of an earlier horror.

"Okay," I agreed, and she offered a weak smile. Her hands moved to my sides as if to stabilize herself as she continued to shake from terror.

"Thank you for finding me," she said as she pushed herself closer. Her hands trailed from my sides to my chest and collected a fistful of my shirt as her face rested near mine.

"I always will," I promised as I took a deep breath, inhaling muted jasmine, eucalyptus, and smoke. My eyes fluttered shut to it, picturing all the times I had held Ainsley close and lost myself in her scent.

Her hands moved again, sliding behind my neck and the hair on my nape as she forced my forehead against hers. My throat bobbed as my hands flexed at my sides. We were too close or not close enough. I couldn't tell.

"Dash," she murmured, her breath hot on my skin. I didn't move a muscle as I felt her inch herself up and press her lips to mine in a gentle but demanding kiss.

One second passed, then two, before I pulled back from the embrace. "What are you doing?" I demanded, my voice a broken plea of uncertainty.

"Are you really going to pretend you don't still think about me?" In the faintest of touches, her lips brushed against mine again. With our bodies flush and breaths intermingling, she whispered, "That you don't want me the same way I still want you?" She pressed her mouth to mine, stealing another kiss as her hand raked through my hair with need.

"What about Evander?" I asked, my eyes fluttering open. She relinquished my lips long enough for her gaze to meet mine, her brown eyes sparking with heavy longing.

"He's not you." It was all I needed to hear.

I spun us, slamming her back against the cave wall. A moan of passion slipped from between her lips as I pressed my body against hers to keep her in place. "Dash," she begged, her fingers of one hand digging through my hair while I pinned the other wrist above her head.

"Is this what you want?" I asked, moving my free hand to her waist and sliding up along her ribs. She arched into the touch, her breath a desperate pant as she tried to collide her lips with mine again, but I held her just out of reach.

"Yes." My hand glided up between her breasts until it rested on her collarbone. "Please," she gasped. With a graceful flick of my wrist, I released the dagger hidden between my sleeve and touched the sharp tip of the blade to the flesh beneath her chin. Her wide panicked eyes found mine as I spoke in a low, deadly growl.

"What are you, and what the fuck did you do with Ainsley?"

She shook her head, careful not to pierce her skin with my dagger. "Dash, what are you doing?! It's me—"

"Do *not* fuck with me." I pushed the blade harder, eliciting a sharp inhale from the imposter before me.

"I wouldn't," she argued as a small tear trickled from her eye. "It's the fog—the magic of this place. It's doing something to your mind, Dash. It's me. It's Ainsley. Please." Her hand stroked through my hair as I tightened my grasp on the wrist above her head.

I ground my teeth against the touch but couldn't shake out of her hold. "I'll admit, it was a clever attempt," I said, staring into the eyes that looked so much like Ainsley's. Even the crimson streaks through her irises matched perfectly. But it wasn't her.

"Dash—"

"The scent is wrong," I explained, stepping onto her attempt to argue. Ainsley's floral and winter air aroma was embedded in my blood—a fragrance I would recognize anywhere. "And your daggers are missing."

"I already told you. I lost them when something attacked me," she reasoned, her voice breaking as she tried to tug on my emotions. "And that *something* may very well come back and kill us if we don't—"

"Why not craft new ones?" She was stunned into silence, her eyes darting around me as she tried to come up with an answer. Ainsley and I both knew our Gifts were dormant in the fog, but would this imposter?

"I didn't think of it. My entire focus was on trying not to die," she replied, all bite and none of the sass *my* Ainsley would have delivered the line with. "A fate we very may well succumb to if—"

I yanked her forward just to slam her spine against the cave. Pebbles fell from the ceiling and cracks spidered across the wall from the impact. "You're testing my patience, and I highly recommend refraining from doing so when it comes to *her*."

Her panicked gaze held mine for all of two seconds before the mask melted away, her features falling and a sinister smirk creeping up her lips. "You're a clever thing, aren't you?" she murmured, her voice seductive and serpentine.

"Where is she?"

"Does it matter?" Her hand curved my jaw as long blue nails I hadn't seen manifest trailed up the side of my face in a delicate caress. "We could have such fun, you and I. All those delicious, complicated thoughts." The creature tapped her finger to my temple for emphasis as her hungry stare roved over me. "All that complex desire and pain and passion and fear. I just want another little taste," she begged.

Her mouth opened, and an elongated thin tongue slipped out and dragged up my cheek. I recoiled as she moaned and exerted more pressure on the blade I held against her throat. Warmth, thick and as black as a starless night, spilled down my hand from the small puncture I made in her flesh. She screeched in pain, but I held her in place as her furious eyes—now brown slits—focused back on mine.

"This will be the last time I ask you. Where is she?"

"Gone," she snarled.

Although my heart plummeted at that small word, I knew it wasn't true. If Ainsley was gone, I'd know it down to my marrow. I didn't know *how* I'd know—just that I would. I twisted the imposter's wrist, causing her to shriek from the pain and more blood to spill as she thrashed against me.

"And if she's not already," the creature continued. "She will be soon. My friends are *very* hungry."

Friends. There were more of these *things* lurking about, and Ainsley was in danger—we all were. Fury coursed through me hotter than any fire I could conjure as I prepared myself. I was done wasting time.

"And so am I!" the imposter yelled—and her face transformed. Her skin shifted to a pale grey, lined with black veins that reminded me of shattered glass. Her mouth elongated, stretching open wide to reveal rows upon rows of hundreds of razor-sharp blackened teeth as she lunged forward.

I didn't hesitate, thrusting my blade up and bringing it forward to cleave her jaw in two. At the same time, I released her wrist and grabbed a second dagger to stab through her forehead. The creature fell to the ground, her screams so loud I had to cover my ears against the harsh sound as the cave around us shook. But the moment she hit the dirt, I was on her again, impaling her over and over to ensure the fight was won.

As soon as the air was silent once more and her body ceased moving, I stood, wiped the black blood from my face, and sprinted back into the fog to find Ainsley.

75

Dashiell

I hurried through the cave with a hand pressed to the wall to keep from getting lost. This wasn't happening. There'd be no fucking way we would lose her to the snares of a kingdom that pretended not to exist for eons.

The walls echoed with a resounding cry of pain followed by a wet thump, reverberating in every direction. I quickened my pace, fervently hoping for any sign of her as I diligently searched. The density of the fog increased once more, reinstating the unsettling silence. Through the misty atmosphere, I narrowed my eyes and spotted a shadowed figure in the distance, hunched over. With my sword drawn, I advanced towards the presence.

Slowly, I approached the figure and immediately recognized Ainsley's body, her legs still strapped with daggers in various locations. I gripped my weapon tighter as I moved closer, fully prepared to take down another imposter—possibly one who paid closer attention to detail. But as I inched nearer, the fog gave way, revealing another grey creature crouched over Ainsley with its oily black hair curtained around them.

Rage filled me once more while I watched its blue nails grip the queen's face and its wide mouth rest against her forehead as if sucking away her thoughts. I didn't waste another second and ran for her.

The creature never even looked up as I attacked, too lost in its hunger as I removed its head with a single swing of my blade. The moment Ainsley was free, she sat up and an ear-piercing scream tore from her throat as the inky blood coated her clothes.

Her Obscure ripped from her, shooting out violently in all directions as it thrashed about. I ducked too late as a tendril slammed into my chest, sending me sliding across the dirt a few yards away. Ainsley quickly scrambled to her feet, daggers already in both hands as she faced me, ready to strike again.

"It's okay," I tried, but she bared her teeth in a snarl as she gripped her weapons tighter. "It's me." I raised my hands innocently, dropping the sword and dagger at my feet to show her I meant no harm as I took several steps closer.

"Stop!" she yelled as her Obscure now dangled over her in sharp points, poised and ready to impale me at her command. I did as she requested, careful not to push her too far. "Prove it. Tell me something only you would know."

My eyes darted across her face as I tried to come up with an answer. My response had to be something meaningful, something only the two of us would know if I had any hope of her believing me.

"The first time we had a conversation where you didn't hate me, I told you I liked your hair," I said, the words rushed and coming up all at once. "It wasn't exactly my best line, but you made me nervous. I was *always* nervous around you." She regarded me closely, but I could see a flicker of doubt spark in those brown eyes. "The bracelet I gave you once had a gemstone in the shape of a flame because that's what you resembled to me. A fierce flame."

Ainsley's shoulders relaxed slightly, her grip on her daggers loosening the barest amount. As I tried another step closer, she didn't stop me, although she didn't lower her weapons completely, either.

"The first time we kissed was in the meadow." Another step, another spark of recognition. "The first time I told you I loved you was in the lake. And after the first time we were together, you gave me a handful of raspberries. To be fair, I think I deserved a few more than that, but—"

Her body collided with mine, her arms wrapping around my neck as she buried her face in my chest. "Dash," she breathed, breaking on my name. I kept her tight against me, inhaling her familiar scent and feeling immense relief that I was holding *my* Ainsley this time. "Are you okay?" she demanded, pulling herself back from me before I was ready to let her go, and inspecting every inch of me just as I had done with her imposter.

"I'm fine. You?"

"I think so, but..." She reached to the back of her head and sucked in a sharp breath before revealing her fingers coated in bright red. My hands were immediately on her, moving her hair to the side to get a better view of the injury. An involuntary growl rumbled in the base of my throat as I inspected the small gash in her skull, swearing to every God in the realm that I would destroy—

"I'm fine," she reassured.

It didn't ease my anger. "I'll mend it as soon as we get out of this fog." I looked around, noting that the haze had lifted a fraction more. Perhaps its release was timed, and all we'd have to do was wait it out.

"What was that thing?" Ainsley asked as she stared at the creature that had attacked her.

The ground beneath us shook, the sand shifting as if being drawn to one location—the creature. Dirt spread over its body, covering every inch before it pulled the creature below the surface, leaving nothing but a pool of black blood behind.

Neither of us could comment on what we witnessed before a yell of pain bounced off the cave walls.

"Van!" Ainsley exclaimed and turned to sprint after the sound.

"Ainsley, wait," I demanded, grabbing her wrist. She whirled around and tried to pull out of my hold, but I refused to let her go.

"I need to find him!"

"I'm not saying we won't," I argued. "But we need to do it together. We can't risk getting separated again." She held my stare for a moment, that angry pinch between her brows smoothing until she slowly nodded. I slid my fingers between hers as my other hand held my sword. "Let's go."

⚶

"That's the third time we've passed that," Ainsley said, her fear and irritation mixing to a deadly combination. If we didn't find Evander soon, she was bound to do something reckless.

I glanced to where she pointed, finding streaks of black along the cave wall from the creature I had killed. Its body was nowhere to be found and I couldn't help but wonder if the magic of this place had devoured it just as it had with the one that attacked Ainsley.

"How is this possible?" she demanded, slamming the hilt of her dagger against the stone in frustration.

"I don't know."

We had been going down what felt like a straight tunnel this entire time with no bends or forks, so how were we constantly passing the same markers? Ainsley's Obscure slipped out, snaking effortlessly through the air around us.

"You have to try and relax," I told her. We couldn't reach our Gifts, and the last thing we needed to do was drain the rest of our magic by accessing our Obscures with no plan.

She whirled on me, that fire in her eyes burning brighter as she pointed a dagger in my direction. "They have my husband. Do not tell me to *relax*."

I raised my palms and took a step back. "Okay, maybe that was the wrong word choice," I agreed and gestured for her to lower the blade, "What I meant was that we have to be smart about reserving our magic. Out of the two of us, your Obscure is the only physical manifestation. If Evander is in trouble, we're going to need you as close to full strength as possible when it comes time to access it."

I could see the fight behind her eyes, the struggle she always displayed when trying to calm herself down. Anger had been the emotion she always battled with—the one she was quick to grasp onto whenever control of her surroundings began to slip. Knowing the life she had growing up, I never faulted her for it.

She had been working on her quick temper, that much was clear from her choice to walk away from the sparing ring after Evander and I humiliated her. If she was the same person she had been a year ago, that scenario would have turned out entirely different, more than likely resulting in physical injury and words she'd instantly regret but could never take back. But after catching the tail-end of her training with Brandle last month, I gained a deeper understanding of her struggles.

The realization that she faced a daily battle with her Imperium Gift, as the magic cunningly sought to exploit even the smallest hint of anger, incited my own surge of rage. It was yet another challenge that she should have been spared from. However, it made moments like these that much more impactful. Moments when she chose not to embrace that darkness and instead chose the calm over her chaos.

"This place is fucking with us," she said, lowering the dagger to her side and giving way to reason.

"I know."

"I have to find him."

"And we will, Ainsley. We just have to—" We both jerked our attention away from each other as the fog lifted marginally again, giving way to two figures battling in the distance while a third fell to the ground, the scream of a creature puncturing the surrounding space.

"Evander!" Ainsley yelled and ran for him.

I hurried after her as the King of Tenebrae swung his sword, grunting as he severed the creature's head from its body. Obsidian blood rained down as Evander spun, angling his weapon for the woman who ran for him. He swiped the air between them just as I grabbed her arm and yanked her behind me, my own sword drawn and clashing with my fellow king's.

Evander bellowed again, lunging for me as Ainsley yelled for him to stop, but he was too far gone to listen. He traversed and swung, a dance I had become accustomed to and could predict every step before he took it. Although he was a skilled warrior, he was exhausted, drained, and looked to be injured on his side as crimson blood leaked through the fabric of his shirt.

"Evander stop! It's us!" I tried to no avail as I fought the king, ensuring Ainsley stayed behind me.

"Liar!" he yelled, traversing once more, but I was ready. I lifted my foot, planting a firm kick in his stomach that sent him back several paces and granted me the space I needed to regroup.

"Kaiden!" Ainsley yelled, momentarily hooking her husband's attention. "Kaiden was the name of the boy in your favorite story growing up. You tried to change Onyx's name to his."

Evander's brow pinched as he tried to discern deception versus fact. "Keep going," I whispered.

"While my mother was pregnant, you didn't know what my name would be, so you took it upon yourself to give me one. And it was Love," she continued. Evander's expression shifted as he listened, his stance relaxing and features smoothing from the hard stare he previously wore. "I've always been Love to you."

Ainsley moved slowly from behind me, coming past my shoulder but no farther than that as my hand stayed firmly on her waist to keep her from advancing. As much as it felt wrong to listen to these private memories—like I was intruding on moments that were not meant for anyone but the two of them, just as what I shared with Ainsley was meant only for us—I couldn't risk letting her go and giving them space. Not until Evander relinquished his weapon.

"And when you asked me one morning, just as you had every other, what I wanted to do that day," she continued, moving to the edge of my hold. "I said marry you."

The second Evander's sword fell to the dirt, Ainsley sprinted, throwing herself at him as he gripped her face and crashed his lips to hers. I turned my back to give them privacy as I stood guard, watching the fog for any hint of movement.

"What the hell happened to you?" I heard Ainsley demand.

"It's just a scratch." A tiny rumble reverberated in the space and I suppressed my grin at her attempt at a dissatisfied growl that sounded far more like a gentle purr from an annoyed house cat. "Truly," Evander continued, the amusement in his voice evident.

The sound of a smack resounded through the cave. "Don't you dare run off like that again," she ordered.

"I didn't." I turned at that, meeting Ainsley's curious stare. Evander looked between us, his brows furrowing with confusion. "I was walking just a foot ahead of everyone when the fog rolled in. The next thing I knew, everything went quiet and when I checked behind me, you were gone."

Ainsley's gaze left mine and redirected to her husband. "You didn't hear me calling after you?" He shook his head. "You quickened your pace when the fog thickened and disappeared beyond it. I took off after you the moment you vanished."

"For me, it wasn't like that," he replied, and interlaced his fingers with hers. "You were talking to Felix about Onyx one second and then it went instantly silent the next. As soon as

I noticed you were gone, one of those things charged at me while a second one followed close behind."

The ground trembled beneath my feet, but I didn't have to look over to know the land was swallowing the deceased creatures. The fog thinned again as two screams rang out in the distance—more of these beings dying. Their magic had to be somehow tied to the haze, which was why it only lifted when we took their lives.

"I dodged the first attack, but then it landed a hit and knocked me out," Evander admitted.

"For how long?" I asked.

He shrugged, as he said, "A few seconds, maybe. It trapped me in a vision, but I've had enough training as a Tremo to escape its hold." Ainsley's throat bobbed heavily as she swallowed, and I couldn't help but wonder what horrors the creature had put her mind through before I got to her. "I broke free from the vision and killed the creature right before the second one got to me. And that's when the two of you showed up."

Ainsley's head tilted to the side as she processed his story. "So it's only been a few minutes for you?" Evander nodded and raised an expectant brow. "It's been at least an hour for me."

"And twice as long, for me," I added. The three of us exchanged glances, the unspoken worry of how long it had been for everyone else passing between us. "We need to go."

"Right now," Evander agreed.

Once again, we took off into the fog.

76

Dashiell

It didn't take long before we ran into Declan and Isla, both panting and covered in blood. The Lord of Vorsutos weaved his daggers between his fingers as he and his fiancé studied our group as we did the same.

"Tell me something only I'd know," Evander demanded.

Declan narrowed his eyes, keeping his stance ready as he said, "When you visited me one summer, you broke your arm by jumping out of a tree because you were convinced you could fly. When Olivier found out, we lied about how it happened. One, because you didn't want to look like an idiot, and two, because I didn't want to get in trouble since I encouraged you to do it. Your turn."

Evander lowered his sword while Ainsley and I followed suit. "During another summer I was with you, you took me to my first brothel," he replied. "I could divulge all the shit you got into that night, but I vowed never to do so. However, if you'd like for me to share what happened—"

"Nope; that's good enough for me," Declan interrupted before he sheathed his daggers and embraced the King of Tenebrae. "Now, can we please get the fuck out of here? We've been wandering around for hours."

"You haven't come across the others?" Ainsley inquired, a trickle of worry breaking through the facade of calm. We hadn't found Felix yet, and that was putting her on edge nearly as much as it was me. I had already experienced losing him once and had no plans to ever do it again.

"It's just been us," Isla answered. "As soon as that bitch of a fog came through we lost everyone."

"That seems to be the theme," Van drawled. With an irritated sigh, we all continued our search again.

It was yet another hour before we heard distant yelling that I instantly recognized as my childhood friend. We rushed in the direction, drawing our weapons and covering all angles now that there were so many of us together.

As the screams intensified and the fog gradually dispersed, our visibility improved significantly, save for a slight haze lingering above the ground. As a result, we managed to perceive two figures in the distance, accompanied by creatures near their feet.

I ran for Felix, needing only his annoyed *"You fucking left me, you dick!"* to know it was my best friend and not some imposter. He clasped his arms around me, panting, exasperated, and covered in black blood and innards. Ezra was rising from the ground, looking just as worn as he removed the sword embedded in one of the creature's skulls and sheathed it at his side.

"What the hell were those things?" Jahier's advisor questioned.

We all looked at one another blankly, no one seeming to know the answer. "Did they show you all visions?" Evander asked. Nearly everyone nodded a distant response, and I was suddenly grateful for the encounter I had rather than whatever horror they were given. "They remind me a little bit of wraiths."

I cocked my head in curiosity as I replied, "The creatures from the stories?"

Wraiths were fictional beings in the fairytales told to us as children, often sprinkled through our storybooks. They were never depicted as evil and violent, but rather gentle and kind, only feeding on our various emotions to survive, with fear and anger being the ones that fueled them the most.

In the tales we were told, they would take away the pain and heartache that plagued many, keeping the townspeople happy and content. The victims were always shown a vision of the hurt that was the source, making them relive that horror for only a moment before the wraiths removed it from their thoughts forever. They were saviors and healers of the mind in most stories, nothing like the beings we encountered today.

"The temperament is different," Evander admitted just as the ground swallowed the two creatures Felix and Ezra had slain. "But the sentiment is the same. They fed on us—our fear, our anger, our pain."

"But wraiths aren't real," Isla stated confidently, despite the way her fingers clutched her dagger an infinitesimal amount tighter. "And even if they were, everything we've read about their behavior contradicts what we experienced today."

Evander's shoulders were tense as his head tilted this way and that, contemplating her response. "Perhaps you're right," he said, sweeping his gaze across us. "Or maybe they've just been starved for a *very* long time."

The space dipped into quiet consideration, no one adding to or disputing the King of Tenebrae. Yesterday, I would have argued that those beings were myths, but after all I had seen lately, there wasn't anything I didn't think could be real.

"There's more of them," I added, prompting worried glances from everyone. I pointed the tip of my sword toward the ominous fog. "I noticed it lifts each time we kill one." My gaze traveled over the white mist drifting along the dirt like a warning bell. "And it's still lingering."

Everyone huddled closer on instinct, each person positioning their various weapons at the ready as we all looked over the rolling haze. "Can we just get out of here?" Ezra asked weakly.

"Agreed," Declan contributed. "But let's stay together this time."

The seven of us walked as close as we could to each other with Evander, Ainsley, and me in front while the rest of our party followed closely behind. So close, in fact, that there were often sneers, curses, and grunts of pain from stepping on ankles or bumping into each other.

Finally, after what felt like an eternity, we rounded a corner I was sure had never been there before. The space surrounding us flooded with firelight as Tallis sat no more than a few yards away with Onyx and Nova lying at his feet. The wolves perked up at our approach and the King of Agnitio did the same, his eyes going wide as he took in our state.

"What happened?" he demanded, rising to his feet in a hurry.

"Couldn't bother to stop tending to the fire and come find us?" Evander chastised as his wolves rushed for him and Ainsley. "We're fine," he whispered to Onyx and shooed him away, despite the black one's attempts at inspecting every inch of his owner.

"What do you mean? You've been here the entire time," Tallis explained as he stepped toward us.

"Wait!" I said, throwing a hand up to halt his advance. I could feel Evander's burning stare in my profile, but he didn't argue as he followed my lead, removing a second dagger from his side. "How old is your niece?" Tallis's brow furrowed and he took another step. "Stop!" I demanded again.

"Dashiell, what are you doing?" Tallis asked.

"There's still at least one left," I explained to the group and gestured again to the fog. "Answer the question, Tallis."

The King of Agnitio looked me over before finally saying, "I have several nieces, but if the one you're referring to is Elenora, she was born a year after you at the start of summer and turned twenty-three last month."

I nodded and lowered my sword, but didn't put it away. Tallis advanced then, his stare sweeping across our bloodied clothes. "Now someone please explain to me what happened to you all?"

"After you explain what you meant when you said we were here the entire time," Ainsley replied.

"Exactly that. You were all standing right there holding various conversations. I looked down to tend to the fire and then back up not ten seconds later because your voices instantly went quiet."

"And that's when you saw us like this," she deduced, waving a hand between herself and Ezra directly to her right as the two were the most covered in filth.

He nodded in confirmation and said, "I don't understand."

"Neither do we." Evander dragged a hand through his black hair. "But time and space seemed to be distorted while we were attacked by creatures that resembled wraiths. And according to Dashiell's theory, they're still lurking about."

Evander continued the story of what happened to him while everyone else chimed in to tell their side of the event, but my focus was entirely on the two wolves watching the seven of us covered in filth intently. Nova's ears were flat and ready to pick up on any disturbances, while Onyx's hackles were raised as he slowly studied the crowd. My eyes met his intense gaze and my heart began a thunderous beat as understanding washed over me. I may have trusted the people around me, but I trusted the wolves' instincts more.

I moved toward Ainsley until my hand found the small of her back. She stiffened, a little thrown off by the familiar touch, but as her stare locked onto mine and I applied a small amount of pressure to my hold, she dipped her chin in understanding. Everyone else in our party was too engaged in their retelling of events to notice me usher her toward the edge of the group where I gave Onyx a gentle nod. The King of Tenebrae, however, had picked up on the entire exchange.

My eyes drifted to our target, the only sign I could give. Evander subtly dipped his chin and reached for his dagger, careful not to bring attention to himself. I pulled Ainsley back to further shield her. There was no way I was taking chances with her anymore since the Gods seemed hellbent on her death. First with Tallis's vision, then the onslaught of arrows, and now with these wraith-like creatures.

Evander balled his hand into a fist at his side, keeping his middle and index fingers out as he directed his stare toward his wolves. Onyx and Nova both caught the gesture and watched it intently as their muscles tensed. Their master flicked his fingers forward in the barest of movements, and his wolves leapt at the command with vicious snarls and snapping teeth. Ezra's surprised expression lasted for only a second before it transformed into what we hoped was the last of the creatures.

The wraith tried to flee, making it several steps before Nova's jaws clamped tight around its grey leg and hindered its retreat. It reached back its long blue nails and slashed, hitting Nova on her side and sending her into a pile of rocks. She whimpered at the impact, and Ainsley rushed for her. Onyx lunged, grabbing the wraith's arm between his teeth and thrashing as he yanked until he severed the limb, spraying black blood everywhere.

Evander and Declan both joined the fight, teaming up with Onyx to completely dismember the last remaining creature. The cavern echoed with the sounds of its dying wails, sending a cascade of rocks from above crashing to the ground. With the last of the fog now gone, my magic surged forward in full force and I threw out my hands, suspending a shield over our group as the last of the debris fell.

The moment we were in the clear, I rushed over to Ainsley. Her hands were frantically moving over Nova's fur as she tried to find any traces of blood to clot while her wolf continued to whimper. I pressed my fingers to the animal's body and called for my Medicus Gift, relieved that I could only sense a bruised rib.

"She's fine," I breathed and wiped the beads of sweat from my forehead. I had been using far too much magic the past couple of days and it was wearing me thin, regardless of the amount of rest I received.

"Are you certain?" Ainsley asked, pressing a kiss between Nova's ears.

A growl, low and predatory, rumbled just a few feet away. Both Ainsley and I turned to find Onyx stalking toward us, his teeth bared in a warning.

"Dash, you're positive she's okay?"

"Yeah," I answered, not taking my eyes off the snarling wolf approaching. "It's just a bruised rib. I can fix it in—"

"No," she interrupted, getting to her feet and pulling me up with her. "Back away from her."

"What?"

"Just do it, Dash."

I departed from Nova, and Ainsley joined me, maintaining a safe distance from Onyx as he approached the wounded wolf. He sniffed her before licking her muzzle and face and climbing over her. His darkened gaze swept across the crowd, the black blood still dripping from his maw making him appear even more deadly.

"Like I told you before, she's his Solum. He's not going to think rationally when it comes to her health. His first instinct is to protect her, even from us," Ainsley explained and dropped into a crouch.

"I wasn't going to hurt her."

"I know that. And if it was a serious injury, then we would have figured out how to deal with the situation. But a bruised rib is something the magic of their bond can mend."

She held Onyx's stare, offering a kind smile he didn't seem to recognize. She held her hand out for him to sniff, but he snarled louder.

"Love," Evander warned.

She ignored him and inched closer. "It's just a bruised rib. She's perfectly okay." He snapped his teeth at her, but she didn't so much as flinch while her gaze was locked with his. "Focus, Onyx. Feel her and you'll see. She's okay."

The wolf's stare darted across Ainsley's face as he remained perfectly still. Ainsley nodded encouragingly, urging him to take the time to see that her injury was minor. Eventually, the fur above his eyes lifted as he realized she had been telling the truth.

"She's okay," the Queen of Tenebrae said again as a smile filled her face and she pressed her hand to the top of Onyx's head, scratching him affectionately.

By the time we had bathed and prepared dinner, Onyx had calmed down significantly and allowed everyone to pet Nova. Not me, of course—I was only allowed to look at her, which earned a proud smile from Evander every now and then.

They were both such dicks.

77

Ainsley

I stared out at the expansive cave, wondering if I had made yet another massive mistake. Here I was again, making decisions that had led to injury and death. No matter my intent or how much I thought things through before I acted, I still led others down a path of destruction. Maybe I wasn't meant to rule after all; not if every choice I made cost innocent lives.

My gaze drifted from the cavern lake to the boulder where we had found Ezra's broken body, pale and drained of life. Evander offered to be the one to tell Jahier about his advisor's demise and the wraiths we encountered, but I turned him down. This was my mission, and I would be the one to take responsibility for what happened.

A presence appeared behind me, startling me for only a moment before I relaxed and powerful arms wrapped around my chest. I hooked my hands over his forearms, holding him tight as he rested his chin on the top of my head.

"I'm sorry for being so overbearing. I just can't handle seeing you hurt in any capacity," I admitted.

"I was so angry that afternoon," Dash replied quietly, shifting my hair as he spoke. "But as time went on, the more I thought about it, the more I understood how unfair that was of me." I shook my head, prepared to argue, but he squeezed me tighter in a subtle request to let him finish. "In my mind, the only reason that made sense was that you viewed me as incapable and a liability to not only my kingdom but everyone else's as well. Believing I had failed you again made it all hurt worse."

My fingers pressed into his arms as I shook my head, horrified that his mind had brought him to that conclusion. "Dash, I could never think that about you."

I felt his deep exhale against my back—my declaration stealing the worry from his body. "I know that now," he replied and tightened his grip.

He tucked me further under his chin as he held me, silently working out in his mind what he wanted to say before he voiced it. The quiet didn't bother me. I just missed being in the presence of my friend.

"After learning about Tallis's vision, I felt completely helpless. I'd been worried about you on other occasions before, but it occurred to me *why* this time felt so different. I knew you had Evander, Felix, and your entire family. They'd look after you, protect you, throw themselves in front of harm's way if it meant sparing you. But with this... There was nothing any of us could do." He swallowed hard and drew in a deep breath. "I thought the night of the orchard was the worst of my life, but I had never felt more helpless or scared than in that library the other day. And if I was worried knowing you had all those people in your corner, I couldn't imagine how you felt knowing no one was in mine."

"Still, Dash, I should have gone about things differently and not used your insecurities against you. I was desperate, but it didn't make it right. I can't promise I won't act that way again," I admitted, twisting in his arms to face him, "But I can vow to try."

I thought back to the origin of our fight and the night I spent in Caelum. The two of us stretched the hours thin as we each shared the things we had gone through. I remembered how lost he said he was—how alone—and my heart ached all over again.

"Can you do something for me?" I asked tentatively, unsure if he would grant my request or state that I crossed another line. "Tell me when you're struggling. Don't keep it in."

"I can do that," he whispered.

I nodded, relaxing in his arms. "Can I ask for one more thing?"

"You just did."

I smiled at the callback to a joke we shared long ago. "Talk to me. If you're angry, yell at me, fight with me, but just don't shut me out again."

These past two months had been torture, and I felt as if I were going through the loss of him all over again, though this time it was worse because I had to see him. I had to hear his conversations with Felix or him laughing with Elenora and know he wanted nothing to do with me.

"I can do that, too," he replied, a hint of regret coating the words. "And I'll try to be more understanding of how you feel. If roles were reversed, I know I'd be going out of my mind wondering if you were okay."

A quiet calm in the midst of all the chaos blanketed over us as we stared out at the turquoise water. A sense of peace finally settled, overshadowing my present fears and doubts.

"Do you want Felix every summer?"

"And at least one holiday a year, preferably winter solstice," he said without missing a beat.

"That's mine."

"We can trade off every year."

"Fine," I said with a smile and squeezed him just a little tighter.

We were quiet for a long while as I rested my cheek against his chest, both of us watching the way the rocks hanging from the ceiling dropped beads of water into the lake, causing miniature ripples to form.

"You should get some sleep," he said as he loosened his hold just barely. "You've been standing here for the past twenty minutes, staring at nothing, and I feel you trembling. It's okay to break after what we've been through."

"I can't, Dash. Not in front of everyone. Not after I was the one who brought them all here."

Dash's eyes searched mine as he processed my words, nodding to himself as if he understood where I was coming from.

"You're right; you can't with them," he agreed before redirecting his stare, "But you can with *him*." He angled his chin toward the man whose gaze was firmly locked onto us as he watched intently from near the fire.

My heart cracked slightly as I took in his state—his darkened eyes with purpling beneath, his wild hair, his tense posture, and the tendrils of ink that drifted over his exposed patches of skin. He was more on edge than I had seen in a long time. I offered a weak smile he didn't return.

"He doesn't seem to be doing all that well, either," Dash pointed out. Another silent moment passed as I watched the man I loved struggle to remain calm and focused. "Go," my friend ordered. "He needs you just as much as you do him."

"I have the first watch tonight," I replied absentmindedly, my stare unable to shift to anything besides Van's grey irises now nearly swallowed by black pupils.

"I can take the shift."

"You had it last night and you need sleep, too."

"I'm fine."

"Dash—"

"Ainsley, I'm fine, trust me," he interrupted as he dipped his face in my view to snag my attention from my husband. "You vowed to try, remember?"

I shook my head as I replied, "Can I take it back?"

A slight curve of his lips had my own tugging at the corners. "Nope," he said as he released his embrace and took a step back. "Now go."

I nodded, but couldn't force myself to retreat, our conversation not feeling entirely finished. My focus slid back to Evander as I whispered the worries that had been festering in my mind. "I don't want to fail. I don't want to be weak. And more than anything, I don't want to let him down."

The King of Caelum slid his fingers between mine and tugged on them lightly to get my attention. Reluctantly, I peeled my eyes away from Van to look at him.

"You have to let yourself feel the losses. You have to go through the pain and the guilt and the heartbreak because it makes you that much stronger—that much more determined to never feel it again," he said, the words fluid and precise as if he were reciting them from memory. "I don't think it's possible for you to ever disappoint him, Ains."

Dash pulled me to him and embraced me one last time before instructing me to get some rest. With a meager nod of acceptance and a grateful smile, I left my friend and headed for Evander.

He didn't say a word as I sat beside him and grabbed two pillows and blankets from the several he had already crafted for the group. After setting up our makeshift bed behind us, I pulled him onto it with me, covering us both with the second blanket as our heads hit the pillow.

"Do you have enough magic for a shield?" I murmured as our traveling party's quiet conversations filled the open cavern. With a shallow nod, he released his shadows to curtain around us, offering the privacy we needed. The moment we were concealed by darkness, my face crumpled and my breaths came in shaky gasps.

Evander pulled me tight against him, his own breathing just as erratic as we both let go of our masks and allowed the pain and fear and worry to consume us. Dash was right—we needed each other and that sacred safe space to freely break.

My fingers dug into his arms as he held me, and I took several long sips of air before I met his frantic gaze. "I'm terrified that I made the wrong choice and it's going to cost us even more. I'm scared that I let you down and that I'm too inexperienced to lead," I told him, my voice breaking with every word. My eyes screwed shut and the tears fell as I made my last painful confession. "And I'm scared to die."

Evander's grip on me tightened, but he remained silent. There was no gentle reassurance, no soft caresses, or tender kisses. He knew it wasn't what I wanted—what *neither* of us wanted.

"Your turn," I whispered.

His quivering inhale had my eyes fluttering open to meet his. The sight of his fallen features, glassy stare, and the tattoo that erratically swirled over his flesh intensified my emotions. Our joint pain blended so thoroughly that all we felt was agony through the Soul Bond.

"I'm trying so hard to keep it all together," he croaked as a trickle of tears spilled from his eyes. "But every step we take I think '*Is this it? Is this the moment I lose her?,*' I can't focus on anything but Tallis's vision—on hearing my name on your lips before you die." His chest rose and fell faster against mine as his control further slipped to the depths. I pushed even closer and pressed my forehead to his as I held his face. "I can't lose you. Not again. I can't," he said through a sob.

My trembling lips found his, offering the only solace I could, though I knew it wasn't enough. There was nothing either of us could offer the other in the way of words. Nothing that could take the pain and the fear. But we could have *this*.

We stayed like that for minutes, hours, a lifetime. Until we drifted away into a dreamless sleep, our bodies too exhausted to let our minds have their way with us. And though we were safe for the time being, it didn't matter. There would be no outrunning our fate.

And we both knew it.

78

Dashiell

In the stillness of the night, while everyone slumbered, I savored the symphony of the crackling fire, its melodic sounds providing comfort as I stood guard over the cavern. I've never been bothered by the task of taking watch. I found solace in the tranquil moments where my thoughts were my only companions. It was time I could spend regrouping, planning, healing.

"What do you want?" I whispered, not bothering to look at the black wolf who crept up behind me.

I was still pissed at him for ensuring I was the only one who didn't get to show Nova any affection... Even though it was obvious she preferred me the most out of the present company, excluding her masters.

My lips tugged in a cocky smirk as I remembered how much Felix hated that. He always swore it was because I was constantly giving her treats and not because she truly liked me. So one afternoon, we decided to test that theory.

We sat Nova in the center of a field and Felix and I stood at the edge in separate directions. On three, we both called her name. She immediately came to me. Felix argued that it was because I was louder, so during the next attempt, I stayed silent. Again, she ran to me. He then tried to say it was only because she thought I had food on me, so he worked it into the final round.

Felix helped up a large chicken breast to Nova's face, allowing her to sniff and lick at it before he slowly backed away, dangling it like bait. I wasn't allowed to have any food on me, nor was I allowed to touch her or even call her name. Nova's stare tracked Felix's offering the entire time he spent backing away to the edge of the field, but when she was commanded to move, she still chose me. I refused to let him forget it.

Onyx grumbled low, and I peered over my shoulder to find him sitting there, appearing less than thrilled as Nova sat behind him with perked ears and a wagging tail. The black wolf moved slowly to come before me, his intense gaze serious as his Solum followed and lay at my feet. She rolled to her side and Onyx released a deep growl, the sound less menacing than it usually was.

I looked between them with pinched brows until I realized what was going on. He wanted me to check her ribs. Nodding, I knelt and slowly pressed my hands to her fur, ignoring the consistent rumbling in the base of Onyx's throat—a not-so-gentle reminder that he was there and watching my every move.

My Medicus Gift flowed through her, that bright warmth trailing over each nerve, bone, muscle, and organ to be safe. "She's perfectly fine. Your magic healed her," I told Onyx. He snorted in a way that sounded like *'Of course it fucking did, dumbass.'*

Nova rolled again and jumped up to lick my hand. To my surprise, Onyx didn't stop her, but I still decided not to push my luck, offering her only the briefest of ear scratches before pulling my hand away.

"You should still get some more rest, though," I told her.

Rather than listen and go back to her spot near her masters, she bounded forward with full energy and turned expectantly toward me. I arched a confused brow at her as she wiggled in place, her paws tapping excitedly on the ground as if she were ready to go on an adventure.

As I tried to discern her behavior, something dark and familiar brushed along my leg. My stare dropped to find a wisp of shadow, lacking structure yet somehow corporeal, as it wrapped around me. I trailed my eyes along the tendril until landing on its source—Ainsley, still fast asleep, though her breathing appeared less rhythmic than it had the last time I checked on her.

She and Evander had been engulfed in shadows for hours, the darkness only dissipating late into the night. By the time they could be seen, they were both sound asleep while holding each other close. I had checked on her nearly every half hour since then, more than grateful to see her face free from any tension or sign of nightmares.

Her Obscure climbed higher, wrapping around my wrist and pulling me to my feet. It tugged me in Nova's direction but I kept my stance rooted to the ground. I didn't know what it wanted, but I couldn't leave.

"I'm on watch," I explained as if the shadow could hear me. "I can't go with you."

It tugged again and I spun my wrist, trying to break free from its hold, but Ainsley's magic was too strong. My feet carved a path in the dirt as the Obscure dragged me forward against my will until I reached Nova who looked more than pleased.

"But..." I tried again, turning my head to find Onyx now in my spot, standing guard over the rest of the camp. Apparently, I didn't have a say.

We didn't go far—just right of the part of the lake we designated for bathing. I stood there now that Ainsley's magic felt confident enough to let me free, and looked out at the bright water as I tried to figure out why it brought me here.

"I don't understand," I admitted quietly.

Nova appeared at my side, taking my hand gently between her teeth and guiding me to the lake's edge. Once she let go, she playfully pounced in the water, sending out wild ripples of vibrant colors. I stared in awe as bright greens, yellows, pinks, and purples collided together like spilled ink before transforming back into turquoise when the liquid settled once again. The lake was one body of water, yet for some reason, the areas we had been in before didn't produce the same kaleidoscope of colors.

Although the distance to our camp was minimal, this particular area had seen little exploration apart from our search for Ezra, where we discovered him just a short distance away. I hadn't witnessed anyone entering the water or returning after burying his body, however, Ainsley must have, considering her discovery of the lake's unique colors.

Nova pounced again, splashing around wildly before nudging me forward. Smiling, I shook off her attempt. "I'm fine, but thanks."

Ainsley's Obscure slammed into my back, shoving me face-first into the shallow water. Drenched, I stood and whirled on the magic, ready to... to what? It wasn't as if it was a physical form I could just attack. The tendrils would easily evade or dissipate upon contact, leaving my attempts pointless.

"I hate you," I told it. The point of the wisp moved left, then right. I cocked my head as I studied it. "Can you understand me?" It dropped to the ground and began scrawling delicate letters into the dirt.

My magic can't, but you're not exactly being quiet right now.

An amused smile curved my lips. "Sorry."

The tendril swept through the dirt and erased its earlier message before starting again.

Are you going to make me push you again or are you going to get in?

I rolled my eyes, glad she couldn't see it. "Given the situation we're in, I don't really think there's time to have a casual swim."

Again she erased and wrote another message.

I found the time to have my moment. You should have yours, too.

"You should be sleeping right now instead of giving advice," I deflected.

I'll go back to sleep as soon as you take it. It's really good advice.

"Fine," I conceded. There was never any point in arguing with her anyway. I stripped off my shirt and reached for my pants, stopping before I shifted them too far. "Wait, can you see me?" She had guided me to the area and even shoved me in the water, so that had to mean she could, right?

The tendril moved over the ground, forming new words.

No. My Obscure can't see or hear. I can only feel whatever the magic is touching.

I nodded to myself and finished undressing before taking a tentative step forward. "Are you sure?" As much as I wanted to swim beneath the surface and lose myself in the way it felt to be swallowed by the water, I didn't feel secure in leaving everyone while they were asleep and vulnerable.

Onyx will guard us just as Nova is there to guard you. We'll be fine. Go enjoy the lake, Dash.

The darkness drifted back toward the sleeping figures in the distance, leaving me with just my thoughts and Nova... who was currently trying to bite the swirling colors. I bent down, giving her a kiss between the ears before I finally dove into the water.

I groaned beneath the surface at the feel of the liquid over my flesh and the way it called to my magic. My Gifts were always strongest when near a source, and water had always been my favorite.

I always admired its versatility, evolving into a million different variations of itself. It could be strong and deadly with its unwavering brutal waves. But also calm and serene and welcoming. Bending, molding, changing, but never tamed—never controlled. Growing up, it was a freedom that I envied. And now it was one I tried desperately to emulate.

I swam for the surface, breaching just long enough to suck down a lungful of air before descending once more. Diving deeper, I let my eyes open to watch the array of pastel colors shift beneath my hands as I sliced them through the water, smiling like an easily amused child. It had been so long since I felt this carefree and light with none of the pressures of being king weighing on my shoulders.

The war, the losses, and the struggles all faded to the back of my mind as I enjoyed myself in the quiet depths of the lake, the worries drifting away on the gentle undercurrent. But not Ainsley's fate. That was a concern that would forever stay present in the forefront until we found a solution.

I flipped and spun beneath the surface as I casually explored the vast depths of the cavern, allowing the bright hues to light my way the farther down I went. As I drifted around a large rock pillar that jutted up from the lake's floor, I spied a dark opening against the far wall of the cave. With my intrigue sparked, I kicked for the surface.

When I came back up, my eyes automatically scanned the area, searching for the grey wolf. I found her sitting stoically, facing the opposite way as she guarded me. "Nova," I whispered. Her ear twitched in my direction before she looked at me over her shoulder. "I want to check something out down here—" A warning sound rumbled in her throat before I could finish. Clearly, she didn't like that idea. "Give me five minutes. If I'm not back by then, you can wake the others." She huffed in frustration but turned back around, nonetheless.

I filled my lungs once more with air and dove down. I swam as hard and as fast as I could, but the hole was too deep and the pressure of the water was making my head feel as if it would combust. There was no way I could reach it just by swimming.

So I called for my magic.

The lake parted around me, creating an air pocket for my body as I manipulated the water to bring me to the hole. The pressure increased the further down I moved, but my Gift was able to handle the weight as it kept me protected in my own personal bubble. Felix was going to be pissed that I did this without him.

When we were kids, he used to make me create an orb of air at the bottom of the lake in Caelum that we would sit in for hours. Sometimes we'd talk and share stories, and other times, we'd huddle together and quietly watch the fish swim around us from every angle. I made a mental note to take him to the lake's floor the next time he visited my kingdom.

My five minutes were almost up by the time I reached my destination. I could spare only a few quick seconds before I needed to ascend to show Nova I was still alive and well. Carefully, I pushed as much of the water aside as I could, revealing that the hole was a long tunnel... with a bright light at the end.

The second I made it back onto land, I ran for the group, making it all of two steps before turning around and grabbing my pants to quickly shove on. I was sure the last thing anyone would have wanted after waking up in the middle of the night would be my dick in their face.

Nova sprinted at my side the short distance before splitting off and heading for Onyx as I ran for Ainsley. She and Evander both shot awake at my loud approach, their shadows curling around their hands alert and ready to attack.

"What's going on?" Ainsley demanded the moment she realized it was only me.

I looked between her and Evander as a smile curved my lips.

"I think I found something."

79

Dashiell

I stood at the edge of the lake as everyone gathered to my back, fully dressed and ready to investigate more of the unknown. As soon as I relayed my mysterious findings to the group, it was decided we would all go as one to further explore rather than leave anyone behind. If this place taught us anything, it was that we were far stronger together than apart.

With my hands outstretched before me, I called to my magic, urging the lake to part for us. I wasn't at full strength and hadn't been since we left Ainsley's house, so the task was more difficult than usual. Regardless, I pushed myself harder.

The water split apart, creating a long path of solid ground that led to the tunnel. Two towering walls of cascading colors flanked the walkway, the hues seeming to glow as the water rippled, spraying mist over the path.

The hair at the back of my neck rose as a foreboding feeling sank to the pit of my stomach. I pivoted my head, looking past our traveling party and sweeping my gaze over the massive cavern.

"Is everything okay?" Ainsley asked, and I caught in my periphery her turning to follow my stare.

"I don't know. Something doesn't feel right," I admitted, that unease growing stronger by the second. "We should hurry," I told them as my arms shook from exertion. If something more ominous than the wraiths or the arrow-lined cavern was on its way, I didn't want us to stick around to meet it. Evander sucked in a sharp whistle and his wolves bound forward to lead us at a brisk pace.

We hurried across the floor of the lake to the dark hole in the wall up ahead. I was grateful when we made it there quickly, as I spent the entire time checking behind me for any signs of vile creatures waiting for their chance to attack.

"Pair off," Evander commanded as he and Tallis entered the tunnel behind the wolves. The passageway was just wide enough for two people to stand side by side and only provided a few inches of clearance above our heads.

The moment everyone was in the tunnel, I dropped my arms, letting the lake collide in a violent mix of hues. Keeping the path we were on free from water required far less magic than manipulating an entire lake, though I still felt the effects of my power draining.

"How far do you think this goes?" Ainsley asked, dropping to the back of the group to stand at my side.

"I'd wager a guess, but given how fucked up this whole place has been since we entered, I'd probably be wrong," Declan replied. I offered a weak laugh as everyone else chipped in with various levels of agreement.

Ainsley firmly took hold of my arm and draped it over her shoulder, offering assistance in bearing my weight. It was in no way needed, but I didn't push her away. After being at odds with her for so long, it was nice to have her close. And given our heart-to-heart earlier, I knew this would calm her anxiety over me being hurt.

"Well," Evander said, his attention focused on the long expanse of the tunnel and the bright light at the end, "There's only one way to find out." He whistled again, commanding Onyx and Nova to lead the way, though we went at a much more cautious pace.

"You're exhausted," Ainsley said as we walked. There was no point in denying a fact that was obvious.

"I've been using more than I ever have. I'm not used to it."

"I'm sorry that you have to."

I glanced down to find her looking up at me, her brown eyes wide and worried. Doing my best to shrug, I said, "It's fine. It just proves that my magic is far superior to any of yours."

She rolled her eyes at my playful smirk and faced forward again. "Just promise me you'll give yourself time to replenish."

I nodded and dove into myself, checking my magic levels. Although I was low, I could sense my power refilling. Even with the constant use of having to keep water from rushing into the tunnel, my magic was slowly replenishing itself. In the nearly sixteen years I had access to my Gift, my levels had never increased while my magic was actively in use.

I hummed, musing over the discovery and capturing Ainsley's attention. "The more rapidly you use it, the more you train it to fill at a quicker pace," she answered as if knowing exactly what I had sensed. "That's why Van traverses so much. It drains him the quickest, but his magic has been conditioned to compensate for that usage."

Her reasoning made sense and would explain why I had never experienced anything like it before. Until recently, I had reached for my Gifts only when the occasion called for it, but with the constant training we'd been doing, my magic was rarely ever put away for long.

Smiling, I nudged her with my hip, forcing her to meet my gaze.

"What?" she asked curiously.

"Not long ago, I was putting on displays of magic for you, and now here you are, teaching *me* about it."

Her lips spread into that amused grin that always stole my breath and sent my heart racing at a speed I never wanted to slow down. "It's because I'm better than you now." It was my turn to roll my eyes and face forward as we continued the journey.

For the next two hours we walked, taking sporadic breaks to stretch, eat, and theorize about what could be at the end of the tunnel that seemed to never end. No matter how far we went, the light stayed the same distance away, never appearing larger or brighter.

"Maybe it's another trick," Isla suggested as we trudged along. "This place has been nothing but one after the other."

"I wouldn't doubt it, but there's nothing that can be done about that now," Tallis replied from beside Evander at the front.

No one offered anything else as we continued.

"If I have to split Solstice between you both, does that mean I get two celebrations?" Felix asked excitedly.

"No," I replied through a yawn as I forced my feet to take another step. We had been walking for most of the day, if not well into what should now be night.

"But that means I have to miss the holiday with one of you and I don't want that." He redirected his attention to a half-awake Ainsley in Evander's arms just ahead. "Don't make me choose," he begged.

"I agree, love. It's not fair to keep him from his childhood friend on such an important holiday," Evander added. Felix perked up at Evander's contribution, not understanding the obvious direction the King of Tenebrae was taking the conversation. "So Dashiell should host him every year. In fact, why doesn't Felix move back, and then he can visit Tenebrae on rare occasions?"

Ainsley sleepily rolled her eyes and settled her cheek on Evander's shoulder as she looked back at us. "Fine, Felix. Two Solstices, but I get you on the actual holiday."

"We agreed to trade off every year," I objected.

"I don't recall that," she lied.

"Bullshit. We both know that—" I cut myself off after an unexpected sound reached my ears—one that no one else seemed to pick up on.

I stopped my advance, dropping my gaze to the ground and the small dark puddle my boot was now standing in. Ainsley ordered everyone else to stop, but I barely heard it as I knelt to observe a wet patch no larger in size than my palm.

"What's wrong?" Evander asked.

"There's a puddle," I answered and met his stare. "How?" Evander's brow pinched as he tried to figure out what I was asking. "How is there a puddle when I'm controlling the water?"

A spark of understanding and curiosity danced in his eyes as he crouched and pressed his fingers to the liquid. "It looks and feels like water," he announced, inspecting the drops that trickled down his hand. "But you're saying it's not?"

Was that what I was saying?

"All I know is that I can't control it," I answered as my gaze drifted back to the mysterious puddle. My magic was still in control of the water that had once filled the tunnel, but I couldn't reach out to this.

My attention quickly shifted from the ceiling to the walls as I attempted to ascertain the source of the small puddle. However, there were no visible cracks or leaks present. I dug my fingers into the ground surrounding the liquid and pushed aside the dirt to expand the hole. The puddle filled even more, the source of the water coming from below ground.

"Wait!" Ainsley yelled, her finger pointing to the water. "There was something there."

"What do you mean?" I asked, my focus sliding between her and the water.

"I don't know. There was a flash of blue and then white when you were digging. It was brief, but it was there."

Without a moment of hesitation, Evander dropped to the ground and we both began shoving aside the dirt, revealing patches of cerulean blue and bright white swirls.

"It's the sky!" Ainsley exclaimed as we worked.

Evander jumped up to peer down at the same angle, a curse slipping from between his teeth as he realized what she had. "What the hell?" he breathed.

"Is it another tunnel?" Felix questioned.

The King of Tenebrae's stare collided with mine. "There's only one way to find out," he repeated, arching his brow in challenge.

"I guess so," I replied with a shrug.

He smirked and slipped off his bag, letting it slam to the ground before dropping next to me once again and shoving his hands into the earth.

"Ready?" he asked when the hole was big enough to fit the two of us at the same time. I nodded as I stretched out my limbs. Evander turned his attention to the rest of the group as he said, "We'll go first, then—"

"I'm going with you," Ainsley interrupted, throwing her pack to the ground.

"Nope," Evander and I said in unison. That was absolutely not happening. We had no idea where this hole led to or what would be waiting for us on the other side. With me not being able to control the water, neither of us were comfortable putting her at risk until we had those answers.

"As I was saying," he continued, "Dashiell and I will go first, then come back and let you all know what we found. If we haven't returned in twenty minutes, don't come after us."

"Ains, I'll need you to use your Obscure to create a barrier and protect everyone. I don't know if I'll lose my grip on the water the moment I pass through," I told her.

After a moment, she reluctantly nodded and her darkness spilled around the group, stretching to the ceiling as it formed a solid cage to keep everyone safe. The tightness in her jaw told me she was pissed at having to stay behind, but given her compliance, she knew it was necessary for the survival of everyone here.

"How long can you hold your breath?" I asked Evander.

He bobbed his head from side to side as he contemplated. "Maybe two minutes." Not as long as me, but still longer than I thought.

"If it's nothing but water, we'll swim for one minute and then head back." He nodded his agreement.

"Ready?" Evander asked again as he rolled his neck. "Unless you're too scared."

I snorted as I did the same. "Just try to keep up," I instructed.

With a sly smile from each of us, we inhaled a deep breath and dove into the hole.

80
Dashiell

The liquid around us felt like water, yet not. It was fluid and shapeless but slightly denser, frustrating my magic as it tried and failed to manipulate it to its will. Although we dove down, we were somehow now swimming upward toward the bright blue expanse of sky clearly visible from beneath the surface. Unlike the light in the tunnel, the blue overhead shone brighter the further we swam.

We were still in the depths but close enough to the surface that we could reach it before our designated time to head back. I turned toward Evander as I swam and gave him a quick thumbs-up in question. He replied with the same, and we kicked even harder.

I breached the surface a solid two seconds before Evander and sucked down a victorious gulp of fresh air. His answering scowl the moment he appeared almost made dying several times over the past few days worth it. He rolled his eyes at my smug-as-fuck grin and together, we looked over our surroundings.

The sky that had been visible before was now shrouded by thick cloud cover as light grey mist danced around the surface of the water, concealing everything from sight but a piece of land several yards away. With a curious glance in each other's direction, we both nodded and swam for it.

The mud and grass squished beneath my boots as Evander and I surveyed the area, unable to see more than a few feet in front of us thanks to the dense fog. Luckily for us, it wasn't the kind of fog that made us unable to access our Gifts.

"I'm going to get the others," I announced after ten minutes of exploration.

"I'll keep watch on the shore," Evander agreed.

I dove back in and swam fast for the tunnel where the rest of our friends were waiting.

"How long has it been?" I asked as I emerged from the hole and crawled onto the solid ground of the tunnel.

"About fifteen minutes," Ainsley answered as she helped me to my feet, her stare instantly darting to the hole in search of the man who hadn't come.

"He's at the surface keeping watch," I reassured.

"You found land?" Tallis said.

I nodded and then quickly explained what we had discovered on the other side. Declan and Isla volunteered to go next after we decided to travel in pairs. I led the way, noticing the blue sky was visible again, but just like the last time, the moment we breached the surface, it disappeared completely.

After depositing the Lord of Vorsutos and his fiancé with Evander, I went back down for the second pairing. Tallis and Felix stepped forward, and though I tried to demand Ainsley be in the next group, she refused to release her Obscure until everyone else was safely out. She declared she would go last along with Onyx and Nova.

With a grunt of irritation, I left her once more.

"Are you finally ready?" I asked, nearly out of breath from the constant trips back and forth. Gods, I was fucking exhausted.

"Yup." She called her wolves to her side as she knelt at the hole.

"Make sure to take a deep breath. It's a long swim," I warned.

"How long?"

"About a minute." Her worried stare met mine. "I'll be at your side the whole time and will pull you the entire way if I need to," I told her, knowing she wasn't a strong swimmer.

She let out a shaky breath as she nodded and faced the water once more. "Onyx," she commanded, patting the surface of the hole. The black wolf pounced, splashing the water as he landed on it.

On it—not in.

I dipped my hand into the hole, going straight through just as I always had. Ainsley looked at me curiously, but I shook my head, unable to provide an answer. Why were the wolves being kept out?

"I don't understand," Ainsley whispered, sticking her arm down until the water reached her elbow.

Before I could respond, she was yanked beneath the surface.

With her name on my lips, I threw myself into the hole, frantically scanning the area for where she was taken. My eyes landed on her immediately as dark vines curled around her body, dragging her deeper into the depths of the lake.

She thrashed and screamed as she fought against its hold, exerting her energy and wasting her air. She was panicking and would soon drown if she couldn't get free.

I swam as hard as I could, mentally cursing this fucking place for its traps. I unsheathed the dagger I had at my hip as I quickly closed the distance between us, her frightened stare staying on mine as I worked like hell to reach her.

With an outstretched arm, my fingers brushed hers. I swam harder, propelling myself forward until I was able to grab onto her waist. Carefully, I moved down her body, slicing my blade at the plants that held her hostage. But they kept coming back. Each one I cut away, a second and third grew in its place, sliding across her body and refusing to relinquish her to me.

She screamed again as one of the vines traveled to her throat. Ainsley's nails lengthened into deadly points as her Obscure emerged on instinct, allowing her claws to cleave through the hold on her neck. Rather than regrow as they had before, they shrank back and recoiled.

I grabbed her wrist and forced her to cut another vine along her stomach, producing the same reaction. Her magic was fighting them off. Ainsley seemed to understand and continued to claw around her body, removing piece by piece as fast as she could.

Her body twitched, a telltale sign she was out of air.

And she was still trapped.

Ainsley's eyes met mine and her chest convulsed again, her hands drifting away from the last few remaining vines ensnaring her ankles. Without a second thought or moment of hesitation, I slammed my mouth to hers, breathing out and giving her the last bit of air I had left.

I directed her hand to the vines and quickly sawed through them as her Obscure began to flicker. She was out of time.

I worked faster, refusing to let my mind travel anywhere than on my task. I ignored her other hand drifting absently in the water. I ignored the fact that only one claw remained on her finger while the rest returned to normal. And I ignored the fact that she wasn't moving other than the motions I forced her to make as I cut the last vine away.

I didn't look at her face as my arm wrapped around her and swam for the surface. I couldn't. I was too fucking terrified of what I might see.

My lungs burned and my vision spotted, but I didn't stop. I swam and swam and swam… until I couldn't. Until my body convulsed and my legs wouldn't go any further. Until my vision blurred and I began to sink into the depths, clutching the only woman I had ever loved.

This couldn't be her fate. It could be mine—but not hers.

I tried again, willing my limbs and the Gods to just give me this. To just let me save her. To just let me take her place. I fought against my failing body as I forced my arm to move through the water, pushing us up inch by agonizing inch. I jolted, out of air, energy, and time as my lids fluttered closed and I said one last prayer to save her.

The water moved around me and Ainsley was pulled from my arms—the Gods finally answering my call for once. I kept my eyes shut and let the water finally take me, glad to pay this price.

I let my mind drift freely, going to places I regularly frequented and others I swore I'd never return to again. Images of a thrown apple and running through a palace as a child with Felix at my side. A warm afternoon, sitting on the countertop as my mother handed me a bowl of ingredients to stir. Lying in the meadow overlooking the lake days after my best friend had come to live with me. Flashes of laughter, sparring, and sharing our dreams as we spent our days in the comfort of our Sanctuary. And finally, thoughts of bright brown eyes with an even brighter smile. Her captivating laugh and intoxicating scent. The way she fit in my arms and how holding her was the only sliver of peace I had ever truly known.

I was okay with my fate.

I was okay with it because those I loved were safe.

I squeezed my eyes tighter, letting that smile I had fallen for be the last thing I saw as I waited for death to come.

But it didn't.

An arm wrapped around my waist, pulling me up, up, up, until I was shoved to the surface, the air burning as it traveled down and filled my lungs.

"I've got you," Felix said, his voice filled with more fear than I had ever heard from him. His hand slammed into my back and I sputtered, coughing up water as I tried to take another inhale. "Don't you ever fucking do that to me again."

I didn't answer as my eyes scanned the distance, searching fervently for the only thing that mattered at this moment. Agony, worse than I'd ever felt, sliced through my heart as I watched Evander's fist slam down repeatedly against Ainsley's still chest as his screams pierced the air.

I pushed myself forward, swallowing more water than air as I struggled to get to land, unable to take my eyes off of Ainsley's lifeless form, her skin pale grey and her lips a violet hue. No, no, no, no. This wasn't happening. It couldn't be.

I reached the shore and used the little strength I had left to pull myself out of the water. Evander's cries echoed through the land as he kept going, refusing to let up for a second. No one tried to stop him.

I dug my fingers into the cold dirt as I pulled myself along, dragging my body over the ground as I crawled to her.

"Don't you fucking do this to me!" Evander bellowed, his cheeks streaked with tears as he blew into her mouth before slamming his hand down again. This couldn't be it. It wasn't supposed to be how we lost her. Not here—not to this fucking place. It didn't deserve to claim her.

As I finally reached Ainsley, I placed my hand on her chest, careful not to get in the way of Evander as he continued his attempts to revive her. I closed my eyes and called to the little magic I had left. My Unda Gift was useless as I couldn't control whatever substance this was, so I brought my Medicus to the surface. I had never been more grateful that Perceval wasn't my father than at that moment.

My healing magic plunged into her, wrapping around her organs as I closed my eyes to try and save her. My power enveloped her lungs and pushed the strange liquid away until it traveled up her throat and out of her mouth.

"Don't stop, Dashiell," Tallis advised, and I nearly broke at the small undertone of hope beneath the words.

"Evander," I croaked, unable to say any more than that.

"Give him a moment," Tallis instructed.

My head swam with dizziness and my body was past its breaking point as I directed my magic to her heart. I surrounded the organ, massaging it gently as my consciousness began to slip. I threw the last of my magic, of my energy, of everything I had left into healing as much of her heart as I could.

But then the darkness came and swallowed my consciousness whole.

81

Ainsley

I rolled to the side, coughing and vomiting up a liquid that tasted like water but didn't. It scraped like shards of glass along the inside of my throat as it left my body, but I was happy to be rid of it. My lungs burned like fire and my vision danced with black spots as I was pulled against a body I knew as my home.

Evander's warm tears fell into my hair and along my cheek as he cradled me against him, repeating a declaration of love I'd never get sick of hearing. I tried to hug him back but the most I could offer was a weak press of my fingers into his forearms. He didn't seem to mind as he squeezed me tighter in response and planted kisses across every inch of my face.

I opened my mouth to ask what had happened, but only a broken, hoarse noise escaped me as my eyes pricked with tears from the pain of speaking.

"Shhh," Evander said, pulling back just enough so I could meet his eyes. "We don't know what happened to you yet."

My brow furrowed in confusion. Had Dash not told them? I peered around him to find the King of Caelum lying in the grass unconscious as Felix held his hand. I lunged for him, but Evander kept me back, refusing to relinquish his hold on me.

"It's okay," he said at once. "He saved you, but used all of his magic to do so. He's resting now as it refills."

"Which it is," Felix immediately added, stealing away my next question. "It's replenishing slowly, but he's inching toward being back above his baseline." My stomach tightened with knots to know he dipped below it.

"We're going to rest here for a bit to give you both some time to recover," Evander continued. I nodded as I looked around, unable to see past our small group thanks to a thick, white mist.

"So hold off?" Declan clarified as he twirled his fingers and a small breeze encircled us.

"Yes. Although the fog is concealing our surroundings, it's also hiding *us*," Evander pointed out. "Don't remove it until they've rested enough to continue."

I scanned the fog one last time before frantically turning back to Evander as I remembered what had led me here, doing my best to mouth the names of our wolves.

"Here," Evander answered and whistled. Onyx and Nova pushed through the fog a second later, and I released a sigh of relief. "They came running to us a few minutes after Tallis and Felix showed up," he explained, pointing across the space, though I could see nothing but white. "We thought maybe you and Dashiell discovered a different way out, but when you never showed up, we realized something was wrong."

"So Evander and I dove in to go back, and that's when we found you both," Felix added, his eyes never straying from the man sleeping on the grass before him.

I leaned over to take Dash's other hand in mine and opened my mouth to try and mouth more questions, but Van shook his head. "You need to rest. We can continue this conversation after you do so."

He crafted two pillows and handed one to Felix to slide beneath Dash's head. The other, he set next to the King of Caelum before instructing me to lie down. I did so, too exhausted and weak to argue for a change.

Letting my eyes flutter closed, I listened to the group assign first and second watch as everyone else readied themselves for bed. I didn't know what new horrors would be waiting for us when we woke—just that we had to be ready to face whatever it was. We'd come too far to turn back now.

⚜

"I'm fine," I told him, finally able to speak the words after hours of sleep, though they still came out hoarse. Despite instructing me to rest, Evander had woken me up multiple times just to ensure I was still alive and breathing.

"I'm sorry," he whispered, careful not to wake the others.

I smiled at him, shaking off his apology as I nestled closer, burying my face in his neck as one hand stayed gripped on Dash's while Felix still held the other. Dash hadn't so much as moved since he saved me. The only visible sign that he was alive was the slow rise and fall of his chest. But both Tallis and Felix assured me he was recovering and his magic was refilling at a more rapid pace than it had been earlier.

"How long are we going to stay here for?" I asked.

"How much longer do you need?" Evander replied as his lips grazed my temple.

"I think I'm okay."

"Then we'll wake Dash, check with him, and go from there." He slid a careful finger beneath my chin, tilting it upward so our lips met for a soft kiss. "You're not allowed to die on me again."

"Noted," I replied with a smile.

Felix had the honor of gently nudging Dash awake. My stomach was in knots as it took far longer than I would have liked for his eyes to flutter open. When he did, his stare immediately shot to mine and he sat forward as we both lunged for each other.

"You're alive," he said, his hands spearing through my hair as he held me tight. I nodded, fisting the fabric at his back.

"Are you okay?"

"Yeah. Just don't ever do that to me again."

"I'll try not to," I replied through a broken laugh.

We stayed like that for no less than five minutes, refusing to release each other as we relayed the events of what happened to everyone. Dash told most of the story, as I couldn't remember anything past being pulled into the water when the vines first wrapped around my body.

Another few minutes passed until we were all gathered together, ready to continue the nightmare that was Inmuto.

"Go ahead, Declan," Evander commanded.

The Lord of Vorsutos held his hands before him as he closed his eyes and called to his magic. A moment later, a gust of wind whooshed around us, sending my hair whipping wildly across my face. I shielded my eyes from its force as Declan moved his hands in a circular motion, capturing the wind in a ball and then flinging it forward. It slammed through us in all directions, blowing the fog away and finally revealing our surroundings and the bright blue sky overhead.

"Holy shit," Evander said, and I turned to find his back to me as he took in the expansive view.

We were standing on the edge of a land with nothing below us but clouds as far as the eye could see. To the left was another island with tall green mountains and waterfalls that fell over the edge and poured into the abyss below. Looking up, there were more islands floating in the sky, each a slight variation of the last.

Straight in front of us, with no way to get to it, was the largest of the floating pieces of land. It didn't have a mountainous landscape like the others, its terrain appearing to be completely flat with a wide river snaking through and spilling over the side. But the thing that made it entirely different from the other islands that seemed to surround it was the large palace in the center.

"Vorsutos?" Evander breathed, the question directed at his uncle. Had the cave led us to our neighboring continent to the east? I had never ventured there, but if it looked half as enchanting as this place, I could see why Evander loved to visit.

The ground beneath us trembled as a loud screech pierced the sky. I was knocked to my back by a gust of wind as a massive, winged shadow engulfed us. My jaw dropped in awe and terror as I scrambled to my feet and reached for Evander's hand, which was already extended for me as the largest creature I had ever seen rose from the depths and took to the sky.

The Wyvern twisted and redirected its aim for the middle island, its powerful wings beating hard as it flew.

"Definitely *not* Vorsutos," Declan replied.

The ground shook again, and I prepared myself for the sighting of yet another creature I thought only existed in storybooks. Thankfully, there was no Wyvern this time as the land shifted, extending and creating a long walkway that connected our island with the one that held the palace.

We all exchanged curious glances between each other and the mysterious bridge. "Are we supposed to cross it?" Isla asked.

"And have it magically collapse the second we're all on there? Fuck that," Declan answered.

"Agreed," Evander added as he tilted his head while inspecting the path. "The safest option is for me to go. If something happens, I'll just traverse back."

"And what if you can't?" I objected. I didn't like this idea one bit. "What if it takes your power just as the cave had done?"

"It's always hindered our Gifts, not our Obscure," he argued. "It isn't safe for all of us to go at once."

"Yeah," Felix added, drawing out the word slowly. "I really don't think we're going to have a choice on this one."

The strained tone of his voice had me whirling around on high alert.

Felix's hands were raised in innocence as a blade was poised at his throat. We all reached for our weapons on instinct, but the man holding Felix hostage pressed the sword harder, drawing a thin trickle of blood down my friend's neck.

"I wouldn't do that," the man warned before angling his chin to his left, then right. We followed the movement, discovering three more people flanking wide. They had somehow snuck up on us without anyone noticing. "Now walk," he commanded, pointing with his free hand toward the long bridge that connected the two islands.

"Okay," Evander said, slowly backing his way toward the path.

Everyone in our group did the same, not wanting to provoke our visitors and risk Felix's life. We may have outnumbered them, but we didn't know anything about this place or the magic these people held. Until we learned the answers, we needed to play this as clever and safe as possible.

"Don't let go of my hand," Van whispered to me as the two of us stepped forward to be the first on the bridge with Onyx and Nova at our sides.

I nodded, taking a deep breath as I set one foot on the path that would lead us to the kingdom we fought so hard to find.

82

Felix

I wasn't opposed to a blade held at my throat; in fact, I rather enjoyed it so long as Oli was the person at the other end. This man, however, had shaky hands and two left feet, often stumbling a step and nicking me with the sharp edge. I cast a discreet glance at Dash to communicate my unspoken thoughts, and as expected, he understood.

I watched his blue irises get swallowed by black as his Obscure rose to the surface. With a sweeping gaze, he surveyed the men brandishing swords who were guiding us across the lengthy bridge. My Empathi Gift reached out at the same time, penetrating them as easily as if they were nothing but smoke. I carefully examined their emotions and found a consistent sentiment present in each individual.

Our eyes locked momentarily as Dash's Obscure slowly dissipated. His one nod served as confirmation of my suspicions. These men weren't trained fighters, most likely rarely handling a sword given their clumsiness.

And all of them were filled with fear.

I bore the pain of the blade with clenched teeth for the tenth time while my captor tripped over an insignificant pebble. "You don't have to hold it so tight, you know," I told him.

"Shut up," he growled.

"Did they send you because you lost a bet?" Dash inquired, seizing the attention of the men. "It's obvious that none of you can fight. If you could, you wouldn't have had to rely on the fog and those stupid fucking rings to hide you."

The Tectus stone was rapidly becoming my least favorite among the three we had discovered, due to reasons such as this. At least when we returned home and Sirona bound my ruby to me, I would use it for good. Like sneaking up on Dash to find out what was truly going on between him and Elenora. Ainsley would be so impressed by my cleverness, she'd *have* to let Nova sleep in my room for a change.

The men remained silent, however, I could sense the gaze of all other members in our group as they turned their heads. "Or is it because your ruler doesn't want to show their hand?"

Dash continued. Their heart rates accelerated against my magic and I offered a small nod of confirmation to the King of Caelum. "Not a bad decision on your leader's part," he said with a smirk. "No point in showing your strength before it's necessary." The last sentence was spoken louder than the rest—a subtle command to our group to keep our abilities hidden for now.

The remainder of the way was quiet, save for the air I sucked in through my teeth as the man I dubbed 'Roger' pricked me three more times. At least the view was incredible. Numerous islands, adorned with lush vegetation and glistening turquoise waters, were floating at varying altitudes in the atmosphere. The scene was reminiscent of something from a novel.

I tilted my head and closely observed the hovering land masses, intrigued by the mystery of how objects of such size could maintain their suspension in the air. And why were there so many of them? Why not just have one large piece of land instead of several small islands?

"Vorsutos is like this?" I asked loudly, earning a warning glance from Roger.

"Similar, yes. But we only have a handful of isles, and..." Declan said as he leaned to look over the side of the bridge, "We can see what is below." I did the same and my stomach dropped as I was met with nothing but white clouds.

"How high up are we?" I asked.

"Don't answer that," one of the men told Roger.

Rude.

After a few extra minutes, we eventually arrived at the expansive island in the middle, featuring a palace that far exceeded the one in Caelum. The colossal structure grew even taller as we drew nearer, its white stone towers twisting as they extended toward the sky.

We came to a halt in front of a grand arched wooden door, with a height double its width—a remarkable sight considering it could easily accommodate our entire residence in Tenebrae over the threshold. I strained my neck in an attempt—albeit unsuccessful—to catch a glimpse of the uppermost points of the spires vanishing into the clouds overhead. For a space that could accommodate thousands, the lack of noise was unnerving, devoid of any gentle conversations or the familiar sounds of children's laughter. It put me even more on edge.

Roger, at last, withdrew his sword from my neck and brandished it overhead, giving a command to an unseen individual. The wooden doors came to life with a creak, opening wide to grant us passage.

In my mind, I had imagined stepping into a spacious foyer, characterized by its radiant marble and sweeping staircase. Or perhaps even a courtyard that led to smaller buildings that connected the palace together. But much to my astonishment, I found myself in a vast space that closely resembled ancient ruins, creating a jarring contrast with the building's exterior.

The circular room bore similarities to the one we encountered in the cavern, but these walls reached up towards the clear blue sky, as there was no roof present. Ivy gracefully crawled along the grey stone floor and ascended the walls in all directions, creating a green embrace around us. The stone was adorned with meticulously carved arched doorways, revealing unexplored rooms beyond. Positioned at the heart of the area were three individuals—a woman accompanied by two men.

The man positioned to her right had hair of the deepest shade of red, whereas the one to her left exhibited hair of the most striking white color, which was tied back to expose a profound scar that extended across his face, starting above his eyebrow and concluding at his cheek.

The fucking *bear*.

Roger and his companions guided us into the spacious chamber, directing us to halt at a respectable distance from their leaders. With a gesture of approval from the woman, our escorts promptly exited, leaving us alone with the three figures and the attentive men stationed at each arched exit, their gaze focused on us.

The woman was seated on a throne that appeared to be intricately carved from a large boulder, with its back fashioned from a solid slab of stone. She wore muted green robes that matched the color and intensity of her eyes as she tracked each of our movements with a predator's focus.

Ever the diplomat, Tallis stepped forward and dipped his head in a gracious bow as he said, "Hello, I am—"

"I know who you are, King Tallis of Agnitio," the woman announced, settling her gaze on each person as she named them. "And you, King Dashiell of Caelum and King Evander of Tenebrae. I'm also aware you have brought your wife and the Lord of Vorsutos along with you."

"Queen Ainsley of Tenebrae," Evander corrected as he offered that arrogant grin he loved to wear. "Your sources seemed to have forgotten to give you her name."

The woman's smile in return was anything but pleasant. "No, I simply did not deem the information to be worth remembering."

If this initial interaction was any indication, my expectations for this encounter were not optimistic.

"I have never been fond of lengthy introductions," Tallis remarked, attempting to alleviate the escalating tension. Reluctantly, the woman withdrew her intense stare from Evander and directed it back towards the King of Agnitio. "Though you know who we are, I'm embarrassed to say we cannot say the same of you."

"Don't be," she replied, shifting her weight regally on her throne. "It means my efforts aren't for nothing." She turned her attention toward the red-haired man to her right. He met her stare and then shook his head, urging her against whatever idea she had. With a smile, she turned back to us. "I am Wren, Queen of Inmuto."

The man tilted his face towards the ceiling, expressing his annoyance by rolling his eyes and uttering indistinct words that were inaudible to us. It brought to mind all the instances in which we had cautioned Ainsley against certain actions, only for her to disregard our counsel and proceed regardless. Apparently, strong-willed queens were going to be a common theme in Disparya.

"It's nice to finally meet you, Queen Wren," Tallis said.

"I doubt you'll still believe that in a moment," she replied as she stood from her throne, her long blonde curls falling to her thighs. "I know why you are here, of the war you are facing, and what you want," she continued as she stepped down from the dais with both men flanking her sides. "And my answer is no. We will not help you."

Ainsley pushed forward, the fire in her burning hotter as I felt her fury and fear eclipse the room. "You have to!" she demanded, pointing a finger behind her toward the exit. "We came all this way to find you. We lost people. We—"

"This is a conversation between sovereign rulers, *not* their spouses!" Wren snapped, throwing Ainsley into a stunned silence. "You'll do well to remember your place and not speak unless commanded to do so."

I waited for the retort, for the anger, for the claws—for Ainsley to put the Queen of Inmuto in her place. But to my surprise, my best friend just stood there in utter silence as she stared at Wren.

The Queen of Tenebrae's eyes darted around while her mouth struggled to find words. Yet, when her eyes locked with Dash's, her facial expression softened, leading her to redirect her focus onto the other queen. She performed a graceful bow, then fell back into line, positioning herself beside me rather than at the forefront where she rightfully belonged.

I raised a questioning brow that was met with a look that said, *No point in showing your strength before it's necessary.* The corner of my lip curved upwards. I half expected that the two men at the front would come to her defense, which would further provoke Wren. However, thankfully, they seemed to understand that Ainsley's submissive behavior was all an act.

She was biding her time as she lured the queen into a false sense of security just as she had once done with Perceval, playing to her strengths. The last sovereign that underestimated Ainsley earned a sword through his throat, and I had a feeling that doing the same would be the Queen of Inmuto's greatest downfall.

"As I was saying," Wren continued, addressing only the kings before her, "I will not help you. And as far as you finding us... Well, that wasn't supposed to happen. My ancestors had our kingdom hidden from outsiders for eons, putting protections in place to allow only those who descended from Inmuto to enter at will."

'Protections. What a nice way to put the hell we had gone through for days, nearly losing our lives multiple times.

Evander emitted a snort while shaking his head, prepared to express a contemptuous remark. However, before he could, Wren added, "Why else do you think your companions were able to infiltrate so easily?"

The beating of my heart ceased as she directed her gaze toward the two wolves positioned next to my queen. Ainsley became tense as she gazed at them, as if anticipating their transformation into people at any given moment. Even I found myself concerned that the wolf I had been affectionately embracing for months may not be as I had believed.

"Relax," Wren instructed while gesturing dismissively towards Onyx and Nova, who appeared equally as astonished as the rest of the group. "Your pets are not shifters; just decedents of them. It's why they have the characteristics they do. You've never found it odd that they were so cognizant, possessed magic, and maintained an immortal lifespan?"

Not really, no. Our world was full of things we didn't understand and I, like everyone else, assumed that the species of wolf that they were fell into that category.

"Why would your people reproduce in their shifted form? Are children difficult to come by?" Ainsley asked, her eyes still firmly on Nova's as she tried to work out the recent revelation.

"Some people do not agree with the laws of Inmuto," the former bear stated. He adjusted his shoulders and assumed a more upright posture as he spoke to the assembled audience. "The queen and those before her have done everything in their power to keep our people safe, yet for some that wasn't enough. They longed to leave Inmuto and roam the world freely. Because we are not monsters, the sovereigns over the centuries have granted their wish under one condition: they must stay forever in their shifter forms."

I narrowed my gaze at the bear that I had previously ridden. Throughout my years advising King Perceval, I developed the capacity to understand people as effortlessly as one would peruse a book. I developed the ability to dissect their emotions, observe their movements, and analyze the cadence of their speech. *This* man was executing his lines with rehearsed precision—an indicator of an individual who may not have fully embraced the beliefs they were reciting.

"Most chose to remain in Inmuto, but there were others who accepted the terms. Those that did transformed into the animal of their choosing and lived their days amongst others of their kind," Wren explained, her focus on the two wolves as if only speaking to them. "However, they quickly learned that existing in the wild was dangerous and bonded with the people of Disparya to ensure their survival. They offered a life of servitude for protection. Of course, no one knew they were bonding themselves to shifters from a lost kingdom, instead believing they had stumbled upon a superior species of animal thanks to the magic of the Gods and the lands."

She assumed a kneeling position and extended her hand, beckoning the wolves to approach. Onyx and Nova both growled and bared their teeth at the woman as they moved closer to Ainsley's side.

"They're only with you because you offer them safety," Wren explained, rising once again. "It's what they've evolved to seek through the centuries until they could find their way home. They belong here. It's why the cavern spared them from every horror." With a twist of her head, she diverted her attention towards the Lord of Vorsutos. "I *am* surprised it gave *you* such a hard time, though."

"What is that supposed to mean?" Declan questioned.

The Queen of Inmuto's lips lifted into a sly grin. "What do you think?" In the absence of a response from Declan, she raised her palm and summoned a miniature vortex of wind. "The wielders of my kingdom are Shifters, Earth Breakers, and Wind Weavers. This is where your people in Vorsutos hail from."

I summoned my Magusier Gift, sensing the intense pull of my pupils expanding as it emerged. The individuals in the room transformed into silhouettes of different colors, symbolizing their respective magical abilities. I was already acquainted with the blues, reds, blacks, and golds that meandered aimlessly through my friends, however, the profound greens that twirled within Wren were completely unfamiliar to me.

Catching Ainsley's eye, I nodded, confirming Wren's possession of magic just as I saw Tallis give the same subtle sign to Dash and Evander up ahead.

"As I said before, Inmuto is not a part of Disparya, nor has it been for a long time. Not since this land was divided by Gift rather than kingdom—with all eighteen living independently from each other," Wren explained.

"Then who ruled?" Ainsley asked.

In an unexpected turn of events, Wren opted to address her question instead of dismissing it as she had done in the past. "There were no sovereigns or heirs back then. The factions of Gifted governed over themselves as they saw fit."

"So the Gods didn't choose people to possess more than one Gift?"

Wren tilted her head as she looked at Ainsley, a menacing smile curving her lips. "Oh, they did. But those individuals were hunted and slaughtered."

The Queen of Inmuto stepped back until she reached the center of the room. As she motioned her hands, a forceful gust of wind surged through the surroundings, creating a blur of gray and green as it spun around us.

Wren held her hands up again and then pulled them apart as if she were cleaving the open air in two. The wind ceased abruptly, causing me to stumble momentarily as I struggled to regain my balance, while Ainsley brushed her unruly hair away from her face.

The room appeared to be identical to its previous state, save for one notable distinction. Where ivy had once climbed the walls, covering the space in greenery, there were now illustrations in its place. I examined the drawings and observed that the artwork exhibited similarities to what we had come across in the cavern. The stone walls in that place portrayed numerous deities from our world, whereas the illustrations in this location narrated a cohesive story.

"The creators of our world are not kind beings. They are selfish, callous, and drunk on their own power. They didn't give us magic so that we may thrive—they did it so that they could watch us fight." Disgust emanated from the Queen of Inmuto as she spat out her words, each accusation infused with it. "The Gods wanted us to compete with one another to prove that the magic they bestowed on their people was greater than the others. We were meant as nothing more than careless entertainment for them.

"When we didn't give in to their demands—each Gifted content to live their life in peace—the Gods decided to grant more power to certain individuals, hoping it would spark unease. It did, but not in the way they had thought. Rather than who we now call the heir and sovereign leading their Gifted into battle to fight the others, the people turned on them, cutting them down without a second thought. They were terrified of anyone who held that much magic and decided to remove the possible threat before it could escalate."

Despite the differing targets, the sentiment mirrored the actions of the people of Disparya towards the products of Conjoining over the years. Their fear of the unfamiliar and the potential threat that individuals like Ainsley posed overshadowed any logical reasoning, driving them to advocate for their execution. As usual, individuals tend to resort to extreme reactions when faced with something they don't understand.

"For years, those with two or three Gifts given from the Gods ran for their lives, mostly staying hidden, but they were nearly always found. Once killed, a new heir or sovereign emerged in their place, repeating the vicious cycle until one day, they decided to take matters into their own hands. It was the sovereign of the Dark Gifts who led the rebellion. He sought and found the other future rulers in hiding and convinced them to join his cause." Wren continued with a pointed glare at Evander.

The King of Tenebrae nonchalantly shrugged off any comments the queen had to make about his ancestor. I found it impossible not to notice the similarities between the leader's actions and Evander's present mission. Both individuals experienced fear, misunderstanding, and the responsibility of uniting people for a purpose.

"Not everyone agreed with the idea that those with extra power should be feared. In fact, many people of Disparya worshipped them, believing that the Gods had chosen those individuals to love and protect the people in their stead. The future rulers used this devotion to their advantage and together, they created an army to fight on their behalf."

With a gesture, she indicated a specific area of the stone wall adorned with a drawing that extended from its foundation to its summit. Thousands of beings were on their knees bowing, praying, and worshiping the large figure in the middle with swirling symbols around him. I squinted my eyes, attempting to discern the depiction of the Gifts, but the illustration was antiquated and the intricate elements had faded with time. Above the central figure, the Gods were portrayed in the night sky with cheerful expressions as they observed the scene below.

"The Gifted of Inmuto were the only people who did not seek to kill the ones designated by the Gods to hold more power," Wren added, gesturing to another scene that showed people with various symbols living happily together. "We did not fear them, and because of that, we were granted mercy. One evening, the rulers of the Earth Breakers, the Shifters, the Wind Weavers, and the two extra Gifted individuals of Inmuto all met with the leaders of the rebellion army. An agreement was formed that night. No harm would come to our three Gifted factions if we aided the rebellion in the war against the people of Disparya.

"The Shifters unanimously agreed, but the Earth Breakers and Wind Weavers held reservations against the arrangement, not sure they could entirely trust the leaders of the rebellion," she explained. "So the Earth Breakers that decided against the deal fled to the west to a continent now known as Pravus, and the Wind Weavers escaped to the east."

"To Vorsutos," Declan breathed in realization.

"Yes," Wren answered. "But it was a barren land at the time, so once the rebellion army was victorious, the Earth Breakers that stayed to fight traveled to Vorsutos to provide natural resources to help the Wind Weavers thrive. Inmuto's Gifted were the only ones who cared about all factions of power belonging to their people. We helped one another until it was our time to part."

"It's why we have the same floating isles as you," Declan added, mentally doing the math.

The Queen of Inmuto confirmed Declan's theory with a nod and then carried on. "The extra Gifted fought seamlessly, working together in unison to effortlessly blend their magic to enhance each other's strengths, which allowed them to gain a flawless victory," she mused as I observed the drawing. "Per our arrangement, once the war was won, Inmuto was never to be called upon again, granting us the opportunity to live a life of solitude."

My gaze wandered across the narrative depicted by the illustrations. People armed with swords and daggers as they searched for a being hidden within a cave. Figures huddled around a fire under the cover of night as a meeting was held. A battlefield littered with corpses as people fought, wielding both magic and steel. And finally, a drawing of five figures gathered around a table seated in large thrones—the rulers of Disparya. Hovering over each scene were ethereal beings etched into the sky, observing from above with eager anticipation and menacing grins.

The Queen of Inmuto's version of history was vastly different from what we were taught. We had always been told that the Gods possess benevolence, forgiveness, and a desire to witness the prosperity of their creations in the world they had constructed for us. However, the images etched onto the walls of this room revealed an alternate narrative. One that may have been closer to the truth than our previous beliefs.

"Although the rulers of the newly established kingdoms of Tenebrae, Ministro, Agnitio, Venator, and Caelum held true to their word, ensuring no harm came to those of Inmuto, my people were still apprehensive to trust them fully. So we requested an additional deal be struck. We would relinquish our land and rightful claim on Disparya if we could remain hidden, allowed to live out our lives in peace. The new kings willingly took our offer and together the Earth Breakers, Wind Weavers, and Shifters built our palace amongst the skies, concealed from view with no way to reach us that didn't prove treacherous. We have remained hidden all this time... Until now." She shot the words with a glower at Evander.

With a commanding presence, the King of Tenebrae moved forward, taking in the multitude of illustrations that adorned the walls. He shook his head dismissively and redirected his attention to Wren. "It doesn't matter what happened in the past. We need you now or else we won't have a future," he said.

With her fingers interlaced, she subtly glanced at the man to her right and then at the one to her left. But the former bear did not meet his queen's gaze. His stare was firmly planted on the Queen of Tenebrae who was watching him right back.

"So you're just going to continue hiding as your people die?" Evander exclaimed with a finger pointed at the Queen of Inmuto.

"They are not my people!" she fired back with just as much ferocity. "Their lives are not my burden to bear."

"Bullshit! You call yourself a queen, but you're just playing pretend as you lock yourself away in your tower, content to let millions of people perish."

"As I said before, they are not my concern."

"There are *children* among them!"

"Then I suggest you figure something out or else their blood will be on your hands."

Evander retreated a step as he averted his gaze from Wren, scanning the surroundings. His chest heaved quickly while his eyes frantically searched for an answer on what to do.

"Please," he begged, his voice breaking on the small word as his eyes lingered on his wife before turning back to the Queen of Inmuto, "Don't do this. Don't condemn innocents to their death. The people of Disparya need you."

"*My* people need me," she replied with unwavering resolve. "I won't subject them to a war that isn't theirs."

"Without your numbers, we don't stand a chance. We could catch them off guard with your Gifts. We could—"

"I said no."

Evander scrubbed his face in frustration. "What can we do? What can I give you to change your mind?" he asked desperately, grasping at any chance to save his kingdom—to save us all.

"Nothing."

"Allow me to show you what I've seen. Perhaps then you'll understand how dire the situation is," Tallis requested as he extended his hand. A sword sliced through the air, slamming into the ground between the King of Agnitio and the Queen of Inmuto.

"You will not touch her," the red-haired man growled, forcing Tallis to back up a step.

"I meant her no harm."

"You will *not* touch her," the man repeated.

Tallis lowered his hands to his side as he nodded and took another step backward for safe measure. The man still didn't move.

Wren pressed a gentle hand to his shoulder, and his eyes flittered to hers. "It's alright, Drayce," she said in a soothing tone.

"He will not touch you," Drayce instructed again. Although she was *his* ruler, she nodded, accepting his order. Following that demonstration, it was undeniable how they felt about each other. "He can show *me* instead," Drayce added, giving Wren a look that indicated not to fight him on this.

She blew out a frustrated breath but didn't argue. "Fine. Escort him to the courtyard and do it there." Wren looked over the crowd until her eyes landed on Dash and me. "And take the King of Caelum and his friend with you, as well."

Dash snorted as he shook his head. "That's not happening." I offered my best friend an arch of my brow in a request for elaboration. "She wants to weaken our numbers by splitting us up," Dash explained to the group. "So I think I'll stay right here." Settling in, he crossed his arms over his chest. Wren's jaw tightened as she narrowed her green eyes at him, clearly a little more than pissed he had read her motives.

"I wasn't giving you an option," she said through gritted teeth.

Dash gave a nonchalant lift of his shoulder as he said, "Then I guess you'll have to drag me out there by force."

"That can be arranged!" she snapped, and her canines lengthened into sharp points as her magic emerged. Dash assumed a crouched position, preparing himself for any challenges the queen might present, as the blues in his eyes were once again replaced by darkness.

"Wren," Drayce warned, the tone he used causing her teeth to retract to their normal size. I knew we weren't exactly on the best terms, but I wondered if he could show us how to do that with Ainsley to help coax her claws away when she was pissed. "It's fine. I'll take the King of Agnitio alone. Finish what you need to here and we can discuss what we've learned after." I didn't like the way he said the words—like there was an underlying message as dangerous as the traps we had encountered countless times.

With tensions running high, everyone remained motionless as Tallis was escorted out of the room. He cast one final glance in our direction, offering a reassuring nod before vanishing into the corridor.

"You'll be next," Evander warned—a last attempt to convince the Queen of Inmuto to see his side. "And when they come for you, your people won't stand a chance against their numbers. We can help each other."

Wren inhaled deeply before letting it out in a long slow exhale. "I've already given you my answer, King Evander of Tenebrae. I will not do so again."

"So that's it?" he demanded angrily. His tattoos swirled over the exposed patches of skin on his hands and neck as he threw his arms wide. "Why bother giving us a bullshit history lesson just to send us on our way?"

Wren didn't respond.

"She has no intention of letting us leave this room alive," Ainsley said in a tone of realization.

With her head held high, Wren drew a sword from her back. Slates of stone descended with a resounding crash, effectively sealing off every arched entrance and leaving us trapped.

"It's nothing personal," the Queen of Inmuto replied. "But I can't risk the safety of my kingdom now that you know of our existence."

And then she and her men ran at us.

83

Ainsley

Tendrils of speared darkness tore from me in every direction as my Obscure took to life. I slammed it against our adversaries, enjoying the way their bones snapped on impact as my magic slung them across the room.

Not Wren, though. No, for her I wrapped the darkness around her body, feeling the way her muscles tightened as she tried and failed to conjure her magic of shifting. My Obscure was too strong for her power to break through as it constricted her movements.

"What do you think you're doing?" Wren ground out breathlessly as my magic constricted around her.

I cocked my head to the side as a crease formed between my brows. "Remembering my place. Isn't that what you said to do?" I asked innocently.

"You tricked me."

"No. Your own hubris was your misdoing."

Evander's palm found my lower back as he moved to stand stoically at my side. He placed a small encouraging kiss on my temple, which made me want to kill this queen that much more for denying him.

I twisted my hand, spinning Wren to make her face us more fully. "Order your people to help us," I commanded.

"Never."

I gritted my teeth as I squeezed my Obscure around her tighter. She cried out from the pain but didn't give in to my order.

"Love," Evander whispered, placing a gentle hand over the one outstretched. "We can't force her."

"Watch me," I replied.

Evander moved to my front, blocking my view of the cowardly queen. He bent at the knees, meeting my furious stare with those grey eyes I fell in love with.

"It's her choice," he said, reaching a hand to cup my cheek. "She's the one who will have to live with her decision. We did what we came here to do. We did everything that we could. Don't cross a line you can't come back from."

I wanted to scream, to argue, to fight him on this, but I knew it would be no use. Evander wouldn't force the queen's hand. He was a far better person than I was.

I set her down slowly but didn't call my magic back just yet, keeping her in place as I stepped closer and stopped just a foot away. Staring into her muted green eyes, I could see nothing but disdain and contempt for me.

"You're pathetic," I told her. Wren's lip pulled back in a sneer, but she didn't respond. "You can choose not to lift a finger to those in need and stay hidden amongst the clouds, but we're leaving—together and unharmed. If you have an issue with that, we will gladly fight our way out and I will shred your men limb to limb, starting with Drayce."

The low rumblings of a growl lifted from the base of her throat. Her pupils transformed into slits and her canines elongated at the threat. If she tried to hurt what was mine, I would gladly do the same to hers.

"Wren," the bear shifter warned gently, rising to his feet as he clutched his injured rib. "Just let them go. You've seen what her magic can do. Don't risk it."

Wren's gaze moved from each of us before she hesitantly called upon her magic, simultaneously raising the stone blocking the archways and showing us the path to freedom again. The moment I felt her relax, I uncurled my Obscure and pulled it closer to my body, leaving the tendrils to drift around me in case she tried anything again.

"The wolves—"

"Are free to choose where they go," Evander interrupted.

"They belong here!"

Onyx lunged with snapping teeth as Nova stayed protectively in front of Van and me, her hackles raised and ears flat as she snarled at the Queen of Inmuto.

"They disagree," I pointed out. "Try to take them and I'll end your life right now without a second thought. Consequences be—"

I stopped myself as my magic prickled in warning and my stomach twisted. Every nerve in my body was firing off at once, telling me something was *very* wrong. A quick glance at Evander and Dash told me they were experiencing the same odd sensation. Even Wren looked as if she were going to be sick. She stumbled back and the bear shifter caught her before she could fall. A moment later, a horn echoed into the space from the open roof.

"Stay with them, Torben!" Wren commanded before large cream-colored wings spotted with grey burst from her back. She shot into the air, flapping hard until she passed over the walls and disappeared from view.

"What's going on?" I demanded of the shifter.

Torben's brown eyes stayed fixed on the sky above as his features filled with concern. "That horn has never been used," he muttered, lost to himself as his chest began to quickly rise and fall with panic.

"What does it mean?" Evander asked.

Torben's stare wandered to the King of Tenebrae as his face drained of color.

"Intruders."

We pushed through the massive wooden doors, still cracked open from when we first arrived, and spilled onto the lush grass now full of people. We sprinted forward, weaving around the soldiers whose stares were all concentrated on one location—the island across from us. I shoved my way to the front just behind everyone else in our group to find Wren already there at the edge of the land, her wings tucked in tight as she peered straight ahead. My breath caught in my throat as I observed hundreds of people standing on the floating island we had arrived on, armed and ready for battle.

"Close every passageway that leads to the isles. Instruct everyone to remain indoors and ensure no bridges are conjured," Wren said over her shoulder to Torben. My gaze immediately darted to where the bridge we had crossed once was, and I sighed in relief to see it was gone. The shifter pushed past us as he sprinted back the way he came, following his queen's orders.

"Who are they?" Evander questioned.

Wren quirked a brow and threw him a sidelong glance. "I was just about to ask you the same thing."

My attention diverted back to the hundreds of soldiers gathered across the way, looking over them but finding nothing to tell me where they hailed from. They wore no insignias or distinguishing attire. Nothing out of the ordinary except...

"Pravus. I recognize the uniforms from when I traveled there this fall," Dash said through a long exhale as I stayed focused on the sapphire rings adorning their hands.

"You brought them here!" Wren accused, her wings splaying wide as she faced my husband.

"Why would I do that?! They're our enemy too!" Van argued as he pointed across the space.

"Lies! You just want my kingdom for yourselves!"

"Am I interrupting something?" a voice as smooth as silk and as frigid as ice drawled from the other island.

Despite the distance between the two floating isles, his voice carried effortlessly thanks to the magic of our land. My eyes strained as I searched Pravus's soldiers for the source of the question.

"I'd hate to cause discourse this early," he continued. There was movement in the distance, soldiers slowly parting to form a path as the man walked between the ranks. He laughed, the sound sending a chill slithering down my spine. "I'm just kidding," he said, amused. "That's exactly the kind of thing I enjoy."

The front line finally separated, allowing a tall man to pass through. With piercing violet eyes and dark blonde hair that dropped messily over his brow, he swept his gaze over the islands in the sky before drawing out a whistle.

"You've got quite the place here," he said, panning his attention around the space as he assessed the land masses. "It's no wonder you've stayed hidden. I wouldn't want to share it either."

He dropped his stare and raked it over the crowd before him, landing on each of us and lingering far too long on Evander as a grin split his face.

"Ahh, Evander, King of Tenebrae," he announced and performed a dramatic bow before righting himself. He cocked his head to the side, his forehead creasing as he studied Van. "To be honest, I thought you'd be a bit, I don't know... *scarier*," he said, holding up his hands and curling his fingers like claws to emphasize his point.

Evander smirked and shrugged. "And I'd thought you'd be taller, Oberon."

The Lord of Pravus laughed as he nodded. "I like you, Evander. So much, in fact, that I'm going to offer you a place on *my* side of this war. I'll even let you bring your wife." Oberon's eyes flickered to me before offering a wink.

"I would, but we just decorated the house," Evander replied.

"Dammit," Oberon said with a shrug. "Maybe next time."

"Doubtful."

The Lord of Pravus's smile grew, enjoying this little back and forth with Evander far more than he should have.

"Why are you here?" Dash demanded.

"Not a word out of you!" Oberon exclaimed as he pointed a finger at the King of Caelum, dropping his playful demeanor for the first time. "Your father and I had a good thing going until you had to take over and ruin it."

"My bad," Dash replied.

Oberon stared at him for a long moment before waving a dismissive hand. "Oh, don't worry about it," he said reassuringly. "I took my frustrations out on the men you left behind, so we're all good now."

A bolt of lightning speared down between the two islands, illuminating the space in a flash of light as thunder cracked loudly. Dash's fury was palpable as he glared at the Lord of Pravus with the intensity of the sun.

Oberon applauded excitedly at the display before addressing Dash. "Is that a touchy subject?"

"I'll kill you!" he threatened as he charged forward.

"I welcome the challenge," Oberon replied with a laugh as he opened his arms wide.

Felix moved before I could and placed a hand on Dash's chest, pushing him back as he convinced him to calm down.

"Enough with the shit," Van announced as he crossed his arms over his chest. "Tell us what you want."

Oberon clapped his hands and rubbed his palms together enthusiastically. "I'm so glad you asked, Evander," he said. He smirked as his gaze hungrily dragged up and down my husband. "*You.*"

An involuntary growl, low and deadly, emanated from my throat as I gripped the daggers at my thighs, ready to take them out and hurl them at the man across the way.

"Relax; I already said you can come too, sweetheart," he directed at me as he unsheathed a sword at his side. "I'm in need of a new pet, anyway."

Evander's shadows slipped out and traveled to me on instinct—the need to protect his Soul Bonded ingrained in his very being. I reached for my Imperium as I readied myself to end this fight before it started. But Oberon was too far away and his internal defenses too strong, locking even my Empathi Gift out.

"So what do you say, Evander? How about a trade?" Oberon taunted.

"You have nothing I want."

"Don't I?"

My blood chilled as Oberon turned his head to whistle over his shoulder, and I watched with bated breath as the back rows parted again. Oberon swung his sword, playfully slicing through the air and lunging at invisible targets. This was all one big joke to him—one big game he felt he'd already won.

The front line opened, and I gasped in horror as Marce and Kenji were escorted to the edge of the land where Oberon waited. My shadows emerged, whipping wildly along with

Evander's as we beheld two members of our family being shoved to their knees, bound and gagged.

"Let them go!" Evander bellowed as the rest of our group drew their weapons, prepared to fight.

"Woah, woah, woah," Oberon said, raising his hands in a motion for us to stop. "We haven't even started negotiations yet and you're already resorting to violence." He gave a disapproving shake of his head. "Honestly, where are your manners?"

Bile crept up my throat as I stared at his hostages. Kenji looked far worse than he did the last time we saw him and it was obvious by the paleness of his skin and the arrow still protruding from his stomach that they had never made it to the Tenebrean camp. The worst part was that I had no idea how much time had passed since we parted. Had he been suffering only hours, or had it been days?

"Enough with the fucking games! Just tell me what you want."

"I already did—*you*. Well, your magic more specifically." He narrowed his eyes at my husband and tilted his head. "Do that one thing for me. You know... where you're standing in one place but then you disappear." Oberon hastily ran several feet away. "And then poof!" he yelled, jumping to a stop, "You show up somewhere else. What do you call that, by the way?"

"Fuck you."

Oberon snapped his fingers and pointed at Van. "Perfect. Do the *fuck you* for me."

Evander didn't move, his eyes locked on Marce and Kenji as he tried to work out how to save them. I turned to Dash to find his Obscure was already out, assessing every detail of our situation.

"So what do you say, Evander? *You* for *them*," Oberon said as he walked back to his hostages. He stopped behind Kenji and placed a hand on the top of his head. "Better decide quickly, though. This one doesn't look like he'll last much longer."

My heart pounded beneath my ribs as the air grew thick, making each breath I drew in heavy. No, no, no. Van couldn't sacrifice himself... and yet he would. He wouldn't think twice about giving his life if it meant those he loved were kept from harm. I watched in terror-filled anticipation as Evander glanced down at his palm and then back at me. The agony in his eyes was overwhelming, rendering me lost for words as I held onto his stare like a lifeline.

"How about a taste of what we could do together?" Oberon announced, stealing Van's focus away from me.

The Lord of Pravus smiled and tightened his hold on Kenji's head. My friend bellowed in pain as his wife screamed, the sounds of her anguish muffled by the fabric between her teeth.

Shadows poured from Kenji in all directions and drifted up into Oberon's hand, twirling around his fingers before sinking into his skin.

He released Kenji and held his palm up, showing us the darkness now swirling around his hand and crawling down his wrist. "I always loved the way the shadows feel," Oberon mused as he stared at the magic appreciatively. Magic he had stolen. Perceval's declaration from the night I had killed him flashed into my mind, rocking me with a new sense of terror.

That may have been the case once, but not anymore, he had replied when I pointed out he couldn't take my magic unless I gave it willingly.

A prickling sensation spread throughout my hand and ensnared my focus. Dark swirls of a tattoo caressed over my flesh and formed into a delicate script. I narrowed my eyes, tilting my hand to read the note better. *Keep what you possess hidden, or you will lose him.*

I didn't question the warning written in Tallis's hand as I checked my magic, ensuring my Obscure was tightly locked away. If wielding it would risk Evander's life, it wasn't an option.

"The wrong stones," Dash muttered beneath his breath. I turned my attention to him as he spoke to Felix. "Xavier was mistaken. It's not the sapphires we're meant to fear—it's the emeralds." My focus shifted back to Oberon and the shadows twisting over the emerald ring he wore on his left hand. A stone that had the ability to take our magic? But to what extent?

Oberon stretched his fingers, and the darkness spun and flexed as it molded itself into a sharp blade. He tossed the one he had previously held to the ground and admired his new creation, holding it close to his face as he inspected his work.

"Beautiful," he said with a wide smile.

Kenji grunted again as his shadows dripped from Oberon's hands and traveled back into him. Struggling with pain and exhaustion, he teetered on his knees as thin black veins surfaced on his neck, disappearing beneath his training suit.

"Are you sure I can't convince you to join me?" the Lord of Pravus asked Evander again. My husband dropped his stare to his palm one more time, but didn't respond. Oberon sighed dramatically, letting his shoulders slump in disapproval as he shook his head. "Very well," he drawled and grabbed a fistful of Kenji's hair before yanking it back and slicing the blade across his throat.

Blood spilled to the ground as Marceline's muffled screams reached me, the sound drowned out by the pounding in my ears. Oberon pressed his foot into Kenji's back and kicked him over the edge. I didn't realize I had fallen until my knees collided with the dirt.

And I didn't realize Oberon had shoved Marce into the abyss as well until Evander's furious roar shook the ground as he dove over the edge.

84

Ainsley

Before I could throw myself after him, Evander appeared back on the grass through the shadows of his Obscure with Marceline in his arms. She thrashed and screamed Kenji's name as she fought to get free, but Van held her firm as he worked to cut away her bindings.

Oberon clapped as he excitedly yelled, "That was it! Did you all see it?"

Evander pulled away the fabric covering her mouth, letting her agony rip through the air at full force as tears streaked down his own cheeks.

"Everyone, give King Evander a round of applause for giving us that beautiful display of his *fuck you* magic," Oberon commanded. His soldiers did as instructed, clapping loudly as they cheered and hollered. I wanted him to die the most painful death.

"I'm so sorry," Van croaked as he ran his thumbs over Marce's cheeks, not paying Oberon or his antics any mind. She shook her head as the tears cascaded down her reddened face, refusing to accept her husband's fate.

"I have to save him," she pleaded as she tried to push out of Van's hold, but he wouldn't let go.

"You can't," he whispered mournfully.

Marce fought harder, screaming her denial as she punched and kicked and clawed at her king. There was no reaching her in this state after the man she loved had his throat slit before her eyes.

"Felix!" Evander demanded as he wrapped himself tighter around the woman who had raised him, pinning her down with his shadows.

Felix ran forward and knelt, not needing any instructions to understand the task he was summoned for. He placed his hands on Marce and called to his Empathi Gift. Her breathing became labored and her movements sluggish as his magic slowed the rampant pace of her heart.

"It's okay," Evander whispered, smoothing her blonde curls away from her swollen eyes. "We've got you."

Marce's lids fluttered closed as she fell into a deep sleep. Evander rose with her still in his arms as he glared at the man across the open space who wore a brilliant smile.

"Felix, take her inside," the King of Tenebrae instructed. "She needs you right now more than we do." My friend shook his head as his gaze drifted to Dash and then me, not wanting to leave us to fight this battle alone. "Do it for Olivier, Felix." At the mention of the man he loved, his focus landed back on Evander. With a single nod, he extended his arms and relieved my husband of Marce's sleeping form.

As he made his way through the gawking soldiers of Inmuto, I couldn't help but wonder if Evander's request was for Felix to look after Olivier's twin, or if it was because the King of Tenebrae was afraid that Oli would have to bear the same pain as his sister. Regardless of the rationale, I was grateful that Felix was no longer in immediate danger.

"Take them all out," Wren commanded over her shoulder.

"No!" Dash exclaimed, snagging everyone's attention. "There are only a few hundred soldiers over there."

"Which will make the task that much easier."

"Exactly. Oberon isn't stupid. If he wanted to conquer your kingdom he would have brought the force of his army, not just a handful. He's baiting you. He wants to see what you're capable of."

"If he wants to know what will happen should he attack the Kingdom of Inmuto, then I shall happily show him!" Wren yelled and spun to face her soldiers.

Dash worriedly threw his gaze at me, urging me to help stop Wren. But there was nothing I could do. I had just watched Marce's husband die and I wouldn't risk mine by going against Tallis's warning.

"Let the fun begin then," Oberon said as he extended his arms out wide and clenched his fist. The island they were on trembled, sending a thunderous rumbling sound over the open space.

Shocked gasps and murmurs at our back broke out as we witnessed the island bend beneath Oberon's will. The land extended slowly, creating narrow bridges in all directions aimed at the other floating isles. He snapped his fingers and several soldiers pushed forward and buried their hands in the dirt at his feet. They closed their eyes in concentration, and the creeping land bridges widened slightly as they began to pick up speed.

"I'll be seeing you again soon, Evander," Oberon promised as he dropped his arms, sliding his hands into his pockets and backing away. "One way or another, I always get what I want." He bent his fingers in a small wave before disappearing between the ranks of his men.

"GO!" Wren commanded.

Gusts of wind from flapping wings blew over us, knocking me off balance as I shielded myself. Hundreds of creatures took to the skies—some I had read about, like dragons, wyverns, griffins, and phoenixes, while others looked to be a flying combination of multiple animals in one.

Dash bellowed his warning again, but the Queen of Inmuto paid him no mind as she shifted fully into a griffin and joined the wyvern with deep red scales amongst the clouds. The rest of the soldiers on the ground rushed forward, slamming their hands into the dirt to create a barrier of land or raising their arms above their heads as they called to the wind to assist them. But their three Gifts were up against an army that potentially housed all eighteen.

Pravus's soldiers were all products of Conjoining, so each warrior possessed a Gift from two different kingdoms. With the added benefit of the emerald stone that had stolen Kenji's shadows momentarily, it was possible they had even more.

"I say we leave them," Isla spat as we watched a small barrier of dirt get washed away by water one of the Unda from Pravus conjured. "They refused to help us, so why should we waste our energy doing the same?"

"Because we aren't them," Evander fired back. "We aren't going to deny those in need."

A shriek pierced the air, and I looked up to find a golden dragon plummeting to the enemy's island with a spear of ice protruding from its belly. Wren's griffin screeched as her soldier crashed into the land.

Two of the hybrid creatures dove with talons bared. They collided with the shield Pravus's soldiers put in place, clawing and pecking at it before taking flight and swooping down again. The third time they plunged, our enemy was ready and released arrows and ice spears, impaling the two creatures. They shrieked and fell through the shield that opened and swallowed them whole. A bright light flashed and the shifters turned back into their human forms before being dragged away through the crowd. Oberon's men didn't want the shifters dead; they wanted the power their magic held.

Wren finally seemed to heed Dash's warning and ordered her flying soldiers to retreat higher, gaining a safe distance from their enemy.

"I can use my shadows to repel their attacks," Evander announced, turning his frenzied eyes to me. "But we need your Obscure to penetrate their shield and force them to withdraw." Just as I was about to tell him why I couldn't, my name on Tallis's lips reached my ears as he bellowed it. I turned suddenly, finding him sprinting into the fray.

"Go, Ainsley! You can use it now!" he yelled and pointed to one of the twisting towers of the palace with a flat landing jutting out from the side. "You'll need a higher vantage point for this to work, though."

Before I could go, Evander's hand curved around my wrist. He spun me into him, crashing his lips against mine as his fingers fisted in my hair.

"I love you," he breathed. "You can do this."

"I love you," I said back.

And then I sprinted for the building as the fight continued.

My legs burned as I hurried up the spiraling steps. My muscles ached and my lungs stung, but I didn't slow down. I had to reach the landing. After another few minutes of the painful ascent, I threw myself through the open archway and onto a long strip of rock that protruded from the exterior of the palace. The odd structure must have been used by the flying shifters as a place to land and enter the building.

I trailed my gaze over the view, watching the battle play out as the dragon shifters blew fire down on the shield to no avail. The Earth Breakers from Pravus continued their efforts to construct a bridge to the other islands, but the floating land masses were so spread out that they were far from reaching that goal, thank the Gods.

My eyes found Evander as he directed various soldiers to where he needed them to be, taking control of the situation on the ground as Wren continued to lead her army in the air. His head turned as if feeling my stare on him and I nodded once, letting him know I was ready.

With a heavy fall of his chest, he twisted to face our enemy again and lifted his hands to call for his magic. Shadows surged from him in every direction, engulfing our island as the darkness traveled to the edge and spun. Faster and faster the shadows twirled around the land, repelling the arrows and balls of fire I could see Pravus's soldiers hurl our way.

It was my turn.

My eyes closed as I unclasped the lock on my Obscure's cage and threw the door open wide. It burst free from my hands and spine in grand thrashing tendrils as it crawled through the air to my target, eclipsing the light and shrouding the land in darkness.

Unlike with the shifters, when my Obscure met the shield, it did so silently. The magic billowed like smoke and spread like spilled ink as it crept over the force field, ominously searching for a way in. When it found none, I pushed more of my power into it. The tips of the tendrils sharpened into points, scraping down the shield like claws against glass.

I could feel the soldier's magic begin to buckle under the strength of mine, but I still wasn't using enough to smash that barrier apart. My Obscure needed more. I quickly checked my levels, finding myself halfway to my baseline already. It didn't help that I hadn't been at full strength in days, but that was a fact I couldn't change.

My eyes fluttered open and I shot my gaze down below. Evander was deep in concentration as he kept his shadows a spinning vortex around Inmuto's soldiers, protecting them from harm as his magic took hit after hit from our enemy. I wasn't sure how much longer he had in him either, but it couldn't have been much more than me. We needed to end this, and fast.

With one last lingering look at my husband, I inhaled deeply and threw my hands to the sky. I called to my magic—to everything I had left—as I pushed Tallis's vision of my fate from my mind. This had to be done. We needed to get through that shield and I was the only one who could pierce it.

"Don't you fucking dare!" Dash demanded as he emerged from the open archway, out of breath and with his brow dotted with sweat.

"What are you doing here?" I looked back out at the battle. With the advantage his Obscure gave him, he was crucial to this fight.

"Making sure you don't do something stupid—like use up all your magic and die."

I swallowed hard as his stare made a pointed path for the hands I held outstretched toward the sky. He raised an expectant brow, impatiently waiting for me to drop my arms to my sides, but I couldn't.

"I have to—"

"Bullshit," he interrupted. "You're not risking your life for people who tried to take yours. I'm not fucking letting that happen, Ainsley."

"It's not your decision, Dashiell!"

My hands lowered, not to give in to his request, but so I could point a furious finger at him. I stormed forward and Dash's features rightfully flashed with apprehension as he stood his ground.

"I was tasked with breaking through that shield. My Obscure is the only thing that can do it, and it's demanding more from me," I bit out, slamming my finger into his chest. "So I will give more. I will give *everything* that I can if it means saving the innocents of this kingdom."

I spun around and hurried back toward the edge of the landing as Dash's steps pounded after me.

"Fine, but I'm helping."

"No," I told him as I stretched my arms up again. "You're more useful fighting down there."

"I'm more *useful* keeping you alive. If I can use my magic to help ease the burden of yours, then let me."

"Dash—"

"The sooner we break through that shield, the sooner this battle is over," he objected as he took one of my hands in his and interlaced our fingers. "You can keep arguing with me or you can just accept my help. Either way, I'm not leaving."

I stared into his deep teal-blue eyes as he held up our joined hands. His jaw was hard set and his features were tight as he looked at me, silently relaying what I already knew. There would be no changing his mind on this matter.

"Promise me you won't dip below your baseline again," I demanded. He shook his head, ready to deny me, but I spoke before he could utter the words. "If I die, Tenebrae still has a ruler—someone to lead them through this war. Caelum doesn't. You need to think about your kingdom." A muscle in his jaw feathered as his eyes shifted over my face. He didn't want to agree. "Promise me, Dash."

His gaze was filled with reluctance, but he wouldn't back down on this, so neither would I.

"Fine," he spat through gritted teeth.

I nodded once and clutched his hand tighter as I faced straight ahead. My Obscure still slowly crept over the shield, rolling against it like vicious storm clouds. This was it.

"Direct it around our hands," Dash said, angling his chin to our extended arms. I did as requested and allowed a thin tendril of my Obscure to weave over our wrists.

The King of Caelum closed his eyes and inhaled deeply. A breath later, intense heat enveloped our hands and flames sprang to life, devouring the darkness wrapped around our flesh. I gasped as the fire stretched, crawling along the path of my Obscure through the sky. My magic was like fuels to Dash's, feeding his flames so they became brighter, hotter, stronger as they ignited along my trail through the clouds.

His magic used mine to travel across the space, and soon his fire spread over the shield, creating an orb of shadows and flame. My Obscure scraped down the sides of the force field again, this time with a flamed-tipped claw. I felt the puncture immediately. It was a tiny prick, but it was there.

"It needs more!" I yelled, and dove further down.

"Ainsley…" he warned.

I didn't listen. We were so close—*too close* to give up now.

Another rupture, this time accompanied by distant screams. We were almost through. I plummeted further, ignoring my roaring instincts as they begged for me to turn back.

Two more punctures and the hole was now big enough to shove my Obscure into. I threw myself down the final distance, slamming into the floor of my power as I screamed. It felt as though I was being drained of life itself and ripped as the last scraps of my magic drained from my body. I swayed on my feet, my head swimming as I felt Dash's hold on my arm tighten.

The barrier snapped beneath the blend of my Obscure and Dash's fire, shattering the shield completely. I had given it all—used every last drop of myself, but we had done it. My darkness and Dash's light had won.

I told myself it was all worth it as my world went black with Evander's name on my lips.

85

Dashiell

Yeah, there was no way in hell I would be keeping that promise.

I dove with her, going as far down as I could and hitting the very bottom. I relinquished all of myself once again until I had nothing left to give. Until I felt her collapse into my arms. Until everything went black and I lost consciousness.

If she was going to leave this world, she sure as fuck wouldn't be leaving it alone.

86
Felix

"**D**on't move them!" I insisted.

"We need to get her the fuck out of this kingdom and back home where she can recover," Evander argued and gestured with his chin, silently instructing Declan to hold Dash as he carried Ainsley.

"I understand that, but it isn't safe," I replied, throwing my hands up to halt the two men. "Their magic is completely drained right now, which means they aren't self-healing. Moving them too early could worsen any internal injuries they may have."

I briefly looked back to see my two closest friends lying perfectly motionless side by side. Although it drained me quicker, I kept my Magusier Gift out to watch for any sign of their magic sparking back to life. However, instead of the usual swirling colors of their power, only a faint hue of the former presence remained.

"She'll be fine," he replied and moved toward the bed.

"Evander, don't," Tallis objected, maintaining a focused gaze on Ainsley and Dash while furrowing his brow. Evander turned his back to me to face his fellow king as Tallis took a step closer to our injured. His head inclined inquisitively and his pupils dilated, revealing the emergence of his magic. "Felix is right; they're drained without so much as a scrap left. If we were to relocate them before they have had an opportunity to heal, we would likely cause more harm than good," he recited, leading me to ponder whether he had utilized his Seer Gift to foresee their future.

Evander's head pivoted to his wife for a longing moment before he stumbled back a step and redirected his attention to Tallis. It was unclear which aspect shocked him more—the persistent threat to Ainsley's life or the accuracy of my foresight. Tallis's stare, filled with empathy, was already focused on him.

"Are you sure?" Evander questioned.

"I don't care about the potential risks. I want you out of my kingdom *now*," the Queen of Inmuto demanded from the doorway where she had been for the last ten minutes.

The sole reason for Evander's urgency to depart at once was Wren's denial of her healers to us, as she held us solely accountable for the lives lost today. Because they lacked a Medicus unlike the rest of Disparya, Inmuto relied on tonics and their knowledge of anatomy to treat the sick and injured. It wasn't an ideal situation, but it was better than having no medical assistance at all.

Evander ignored the queen as he repeated his question to Tallis in a desperate plea. The King of Agnitio directed one last look at my friends before giving a shallow nod.

"No one touches them until Tallis says it's okay," Evander announced without hesitation.

I snorted as I mumbled to myself. "The advice wasn't good enough when *I* was the one who gave it?"

Evander shifted his gaze towards me, his grey eyes burning with intensity. "Not even close. I trust Tallis to tell me the truth. You, on the other hand—"

Tallis lightly touched Evander's arm in order to shift his focus. Giving me one final contemptuous look, Evander reluctantly averted his gaze and returned to facing the sleeping figures.

"Get. Out. *Now,*" Wren exclaimed sternly as the room trembled under her immense power.

Evander was there one second—and the next, he was slamming the Queen of Inmuto's spine against the stone wall as his shadows whipped around him. Her guards rushed for them, but Onyx and Nova were there with snapping teeth as they forced them back. Everyone, including myself, drew their weapons, ready to take the battle indoors should we need to.

"You can deny us a healer. You can reject our plea for aid. You can refuse to heed our advice," Evander ground out an inch from her face as he held a dagger to her throat. The eyes of the Queen of Inmuto narrowed into slits, and her hands transformed into talons that were enveloped by Evander's shadows. "But you will *not* command me." He exerted more force, pushing her aggressively against the wall, all the while fixated on her furious green eyes. "I will not risk their health to satisfy your ego."

Evander relinquished his hold on her, simultaneously stepping away as his shadows twirled about him in a fierce tempest of darkness. After a moment of consideration, Wren shifted her gaze from him to the rulers who were peacefully asleep.

"As soon as they're awake, I want you gone," she snarled.

"Done," Evander spat.

With tremendous fury, Wren strode out of the room, the ground trembling with each step. As soon as she left, Evander issued a sharp whistle as a command, and Nova leapt onto the bed and positioned herself over Ainsley and Dash's legs. With a terrifying expression, she exposed her teeth to the guards who were still present in the vicinity. Upon exchanging anxious glances, the men wisely chose to exit the room.

"Declan and Isla, go find food for everyone. We need to regain our strength," Evander commanded.

"And if they won't give it to us?" Declan questioned.

"That's why you'll be taking Onyx with you."

My eyes dipped to the menacing black wolf whose ability to intimidate allowed him to effortlessly acquire whatever he desired. Onyx expressed his agreement with a huff and positioned himself next to the Lord of Vorsutos, receiving a quick scratch between his ears from Isla before they departed the room to procure provisions.

"Felix, go check on Marce," Evander instructed next.

"I just came from her room; she was still asleep when I left," I replied and moved to get closer to Ainsley and Dash. My wolf best friend growled and snapped, refusing to permit my approach.

"Check again."

"But—"

"Felix, I don't care where you go as long as it isn't this room for the next ten minutes. I need a word with Tallis," Evander argued as he pinched the bridge of his nose.

A blend of frustration, anger, and hurt emanated from within him before he swiftly regained control and fortified his internal defenses, cautious not to inadvertently release any further emotions. I took a moment to glance at my friends once more, then nodded and left the room.

⚬

"She may not know."

"She does," Tallis interrupted as I squeezed into the room.

"You can't know that—"

The door creaked and the two men shot their stares at me as I entered. Evander appeared considerably more disheveled than he had mere moments ago, with wide and frantic eyes and his hair in disarray.

"Who knows what?" I asked.

"Did you check on Marce again?" Evander asked as he put some distance between him and Tallis, their hushed conversation now over.

Since Kenji's passing hours ago, we had not obtained much information from her. During the few occasions she was conscious, she spoke in fragmented phrases until her grief became overpowering and I had to put her to sleep once more. The most we had gathered was that Marce and Kenji had barely made it out of the cave before they were captured. It seemed that Oberon had somehow caught wind of our plans and when our companions emerged at the entrance, Pravus's forces were already there waiting.

"Yes, and she's still asleep," I replied as I tried to discern their odd behavior. Something was going on—something the two men clearly didn't want me to know. "Now, who knows what?" I tried again.

"The Queen of Inmuto removed the cave that we discovered," Evander explained as his stare drifted to Ainsley. "Both the cave's entrance and the island we swam to have vanished. Once I told Wren that the sapphire rings could bring Oberon anywhere he'd once been, she didn't want to take the risk. As a precautionary step, I expect her to reconstruct the entire kingdom."

"So once we leave we won't be able to come back?" I asked, walking further into the room. Nova's vigilant gaze followed my every move, remaining on high alert to ensure that I maintained a safe distance from her master.

"Given that I possess an Indico stone, I should be capable of detecting any newly created entrance she may construct. However, Tallis believes that Wren is cognizant of the fact that this is how we initially discovered the cave," he stated, his gaze fixed on the King of Agnitio as he spoke.

"I just think we should anticipate the Queen of Inmuto going to whatever lengths to ensure we don't return," Tallis elaborated.

"Good, because the way in can go fuck itself," Declan added as he and Isla entered the room carrying two trays piled high with food. Onyx shoved through everyone before jumping onto the bed and taking up a protective watch with his Solum.

I listened to the gentle chatter and plans about our return home being discussed amongst our group… All while being unable to shake this gnawing feeling that there was still something I was missing.

87

Ainsley

Pieces flooded back to me in a blur of shifting colors and scattered thoughts. Flashes of bright white and wide wings over a blue sky. Green grass strained with crimson and laughter that made my pulse quicken and blood boil. A soft kiss and a declaration of love. A warm hand around mine and a promise to stay. And then black—cold, damp, empty darkness.

Sensations drifted back next. The tingling of my fingers, a soft pillow beneath my head, the sound of songbirds chirping in the distance, and a golden warmth that stretched through me, bringing comfort and safety. A gentle breeze brushed over my skin, carrying a scent that had my eyes fluttering open in search of the source.

Evander was leaning forward in a chair with his forearms over his knees as he stared at the ground. My heart beat rapidly at the sight of him and the fact that he was alive—we both were. As if feeling my eyes on him, he picked his head up and locked his gaze with mine as a small sigh of relief slipped from between his lips.

"What happened?" I whispered, unable to take my stare from the purpling beneath his frenzied eyes or his disheveled appearance.

"You and Dashiell broke through their shield," he replied with a soft smile that didn't reach his eyes. "Most of Pravus's army used their sapphire rings to escape before Dashiell's fire engulfed them, but we found a few charred remains amongst their dead." Evander gestured to my left and I turned to find the King of Caelum sleeping next to me. "You've both been recovering here since the battle ended."

"How long have I been out?" I asked him.

"Two days," Evander answered. I nodded, trying to swallow, but my throat was dry. "Here," he said and reached for my hand to help me sit up. His gentle touch made me realize I had previously been absent of it, and I only just then noticed how far away he had been sitting.

He positioned me straighter before placing a cup of water in my grasp. I took several small sips, letting the cool drink slip down my throat and ease the sore muscles as I tried to string together the events that led me here... or at least why Evander was being standoffish.

"Marce?"

"Asleep," he replied immediately. "She has been nearly this entire time."

The moment of Kenji's death flashed to the forefront of my mind as I remembered his wide eyes and the violent shade of red that spilled from his throat as Oberon's blade sliced across it. I fisted the sheets with my free hand as my stomach rolled with nausea.

Evander's hands slid over mine and he offered a brief, comforting squeeze before attempting to pull away. It wasn't like him to distance himself from me, especially after a traumatic event like what we had just gone through. Something was wrong.

"Talk to me," I whispered, clutching hard and refusing to relinquish his hand.

His eyes closed and he sucked in a heavy breath as he battled to keep his distress at bay. "It's become glaringly apparent that the Gods are hell-bent on taking you from me." His thumb stroked over my knuckles and when his eyes opened again, there was a glassy sheen over the grey.

"So why aren't you holding onto me tighter?"

His forehead creased and his face flashed with the pain of an answer he didn't want to share. His terror and fury were so intense that I could feel it radiating through our Soul Bond, filling me with emotions that weren't my own.

"Fuck the Gods, Van," I said, placing my hand over his warm cheek. "Since when are you going to allow them to take away something that belongs to you?"

His head drooped slightly and his gaze softened as he looked at me, granting me a glimpse of my favorite version of him—that shy, vulnerable side. The one that craved my love, acceptance, and reassurance. The side that was meant only for me.

"Fuck the Gods," he repeated, though with slightly less conviction than I had delivered the line with. With renewed determination, Evander finally moved closer. He cradled my face possessively as he pressed our foreheads together and quietly breathed, "Mine." I grinned against his mouth as his lips molded to mine in a kiss I needed more than air itself.

"Mine," I repeated as I wrapped my arms around his neck and moved my mouth to kiss his cheeks, nose, and forehead.

"Thank the Gods," a voice said from the other side of the room. I broke apart from my embrace with Evander to find Felix rushing toward me, his arms spread wide. Nova growled and lunged, forcing him back and surprising the hell out of me.

"It's okay, girl," Van commented, leaning over to pet her. She dipped her head into his touch before curling back against Onyx who was sound asleep at the foot of the bed. I looked at Van and arched a curious brow at Nova's aggressive behavior.

"The wolves have been standing guard over the two of you as you recover," my husband explained.

"No one has been allowed within breathing distance of either of you without Evander's permission... which he refused to grant me," Felix added with a pointed glare at the king.

With a smirk, Van shrugged and sat back down in his chair after dragging it closer to the bed, to my relief. He interlaced our fingers and brought my hand up to press against his lips as he mouthed *mine* once again.

"Still nothing," Felix said solemnly, stealing my attention. I twisted to find him sitting on the other side of the bed next to Dash.

"What do you mean?" I asked.

"Dashiell's magic hasn't refilled," Van answered. My heart dropped into the pit of my stomach as I shook my head.

"It has," Felix corrected as he leaned forward to take Dash's hand in his. "But it only replenishes a small amount and then stops before draining again. I don't understand why." He scrubbed a hand down his face as he groaned in frustration.

"Maybe his magic is draining because it's mending him," Evander suggested.

My face scrunched in response and I turned to him. "Has he not been seen by a healer?"

Van shook his head, sending shockwaves of anger through me. "The queen refuses to allow us access to one." Wren jumped near the top of my kill list, just below the traitorous former Kings of Disparya and Oberon, but above the geese who refused to let me feed them.

I pushed my Imperium into the sleeping king beside me, diligently checking every organ for signs of internal bleeding. Thankfully, there were none.

"I can't tell if he has any injuries, but his blood is flowing properly and his heart is beating strong," I told them, earning a sigh of relief from Felix. "He promised me he wouldn't dip below his baseline."

"He promised me *first* that he'd keep you safe, so that nullifies your deal," Evander said. "Felix and Tallis will keep monitoring both your and Dash's magic levels until it's safe enough for you to travel."

I rolled my eyes as I grabbed Dash's other hand and called for my tattoo. I felt the jasmine blossom's petals unfurl on my neck as shadows poured over my skin. The ink twisted and stretched as it covered my flesh, appearing on the fingers I spread between Dash's.

"Still not as scary as mine," Evander whispered as his lips brushed along my temple. "I'm going to go get you some food."

"Get some for Dash, too," I replied, keeping my eyes on the King of Caelum.

"I doubt he'll be eating anytime soon," Felix muttered in a surprising instance of pessimism. I wanted to tell him it would be okay—that Dash would wake and everything would go back to how it was, but it was Van who spoke before I could.

"I think he'll be doing that sooner than you realize." He offered a rare smile to my best friend before departing the room.

It was another day before Dash's magic rose above his baseline and stayed there, and one more after that until he finally woke. Evander's moment of truce with Felix had gone as quickly as it came, replaced with the King of Tenebrae boasting about his accurate prediction to much of Felix's annoyance.

"Your levels are nearly full, but rest another hour or so and then we can be on our way," Tallis instructed Dash.

"You too, cupcake," Felix added, his blown-out pupils swallowing his amber irises as he utilized his Magusier Gift. "Your levels have also dropped, so you need to stop using."

I nodded and called back the ink that drifted over my flesh and brought me comfort while I had waited for Dash to recover. My lips quirked in the corner as Van quietly reminded me that my tattoo still wasn't as terrifying as his, while everyone else in our group planned our return home.

Wren seemed to want us to get out of her kingdom just as badly. After Dash woke up, she offered to let us use one of the portals that would bring us closer to home, as she had destroyed the original entrance we discovered. We gladly accepted with the caveat that Drayce be the one to escort us through. It was the smartest way for us to ensure the portal wasn't a trap, as she wouldn't endanger her lover just to fuck us over.

She refused at first, citing her inability to trust *us* not to hurt *him.* But after a long discussion, Drayce had convinced her to go through with the plan.

Shortly after Tallis approved us for travel, the eight of us and our wolves—much to Wren's dismay—followed Drayce through a portal that deposited us in the forest just outside the village near our home.

"This portal will cease to exist after I pass through, so don't bother trying to return," Drayce instructed.

"I'll try really hard not to be disappointed," Declan said with an eye roll as the rest of us turned our backs without a second thought. A moment later, Drayce was gone.

The short walk home was silent, not a single word uttered as we all tried to work through our trauma and the grief we had experienced. I stole a glance at Marce at the back of the group carefully putting one foot in front of the other. Her face was wan and her eyes hollow as her stare stayed focused ahead. Although she was here with us, it was like she wasn't actually present, her mind and body lost to her depression. I faced forward again as I battled knowing that what we had been through was only the beginning.

My fingers moved absently over a plate as I dunked it into the sink of soapy water. It seemed ridiculous to do dishes within an hour of returning home, but I needed to put my hands to work. I needed to focus on something other than Marceline's cries from down the hall, on the way Dash sat beneath the shade of the tree with his forearms draped over his knees and his head hung low, on the way Rosella knelt before him while Elenora clung to his hand as his body shook. I needed to focus on something other than Felix's broken expression as he told Oli what had happened, or the way Jahier stumbled back as I shared Ezra's fate with him. I needed to forget that the moment we stepped through the front door, my husband let his shadows take him.

As I peered out the kitchen window, my eyes suddenly narrowed and my blood ran hot, filling with rage. I pushed away from the sink and stormed for the front door, slamming it loudly behind me. In several quick strides, I was across the field and to the treeline where Torben stood waiting.

"What the fuck do you want?" I spat, letting the venom seep into each word.

The bear shifter watched me with slumped shoulders and a mournful expression. His pity only made my fury intensify. Wordlessly, he bent down and picked up an object he had placed behind the tree he stood next to. My face crumpled and a broken noise escaped me the moment I caught sight of the urn.

"We bury our dead," I told Torben as I took the vase he extended.

"We do, too," he replied solemnly. "But when I found him... the impact from the fall, it..." He swallowed hard and adverted his gaze to rest upon the house behind me. "I just didn't think she should have to see him like that."

Unease settled in my stomach as his implication hovered in between the words. I angled my chin over my shoulder, screwing my eyes shut as the tears fell. Kenji deserved so much more than the brutal end he was given.

"Thank you," I croaked as I wiped the moisture from my cheeks.

The subtle sound of metal clanging echoed, and I twisted my focus back to Torben to find him digging through his bag. Slowly, he withdrew two of Kenji's daggers, the sapphire ring, and a tightly wrapped piece of cloth.

"His belongings," Torben instructed, handing me the items before taking a step back.

I clutched everything to my chest as I shakily sipped on the open air, hating that in just a few moments, I'd have to present these to Marce. I'd have to steal away whatever sliver of hope she was clinging to and confirm he was truly gone.

"I'm so sorry for your loss," the bear shifter said.

"There will be more," I bit out as tears continued to collect on my lashes. "Thousands of innocent people will suffer a fate they didn't deserve if Inmuto doesn't help." Torben scrubbed a hand down his face as he shook his head.

"I can't—"

"I know you want to." My voice cracked with each word, the pain of our future taking me hostage. "You've watched us for months and never told Wren that I was just as much a sovereign as Evander was. You never told her about these." I held up my palm, letting my Obscure free to drift around my fingers.

"I don't know what you mean—"

"In that field, you could have shifted into a bird and escaped us, but you didn't," I argued through my sobs. "You changed into something slower than your bear so we could follow. You knew we were going to take a different path and instead, you took us through the woods so we'd go through that portal that brought us to the cave. You led us to Inmuto. You—"

"You're mistaken, Ainsley," he said, his tone low and careful. "Whatever you *think* you know, you're wrong. I cannot help you."

"Please," I begged, desperate to change his mind. "Please; we can't do this alone. I can't lose anyone else."

Torben's face was full of sorrow and I could feel how conflicted he was. Nonetheless, he shook his head and backed away. "I wish you all the best of luck," he said before disappearing into the woods.

I sank to the ground, holding Kenji's belongings as I cried, letting Torben take with him the last remaining scrap of hope I had been holding onto.

88

Ainsley

"I never told him I loved him," Marce cried. The thin cloth lay unwrapped on the ground as she clutched the diamond ring that hung from a chain Kenji had been wearing around his neck. "I never told him. I never told him. I never—*told him*." She repeated the phrase through her sobs, each sentence coming out more fragmented than the last.

"He knew," Oli promised as he slumped to the ground, cradling his sister in his arms. "Kenji's always known."

Silent tears trailed down my cheeks and my heart shattered as I mourned for the man we lost, for Marce, and for the life they'd never get to share.

"Ainsley?" Tallis said gently as he approached. I angled my face away, quickly wiping the falling tears before I turned to him with a steadying breath. "I know this isn't the ideal time, but do you know where I can find Evander?"

I shook my head as I backed away from the open door to the study, unable to listen to Marceline beg for the Gods to take her too. Her pain was one I didn't ever want to become familiar with.

"Upstairs, I think," I replied as I tried to recall the last time I had seen him. Straining my ears, my immortal hearing picked up the subtle sound of water running in our bedroom.

"I need to speak to him."

This wasn't the time. Evander had just been through hell and lost one of his own, and now Tallis wanted to spring something else on him. "Not now," I supplied. Evander deserved a break—we all did.

The King of Agnitio placed a hand on my wrist to stop me as I shifted to turn away. His brown eyes met mine, imploring me to reconsider. "Please, Ainsley. It's imperative that I see him."

"Tell me first."

The steam of the shower drifted through the bathing room as thick as our shadows, making it difficult to make out anything but Evander's silhouette. His hands were splayed wide on the marbled wall as the water cascaded onto his neck and down his inked back. I stripped off my clothes, watching in silence as his tattoo violently swirled over his flesh in chaotic patterns that wouldn't slow.

Once beneath the water, my fingers slid up his chest as I pressed my cheek to his back, holding him as tight as I could. Evander pushed away from the wall and placed his hands over mine as his breathing became erratic.

"I've got you," I whispered through a sob. His hold on my hands tightened as his chest continued to rise and fall quickly. "I've got you," I repeated, letting my shadows emerge to envelop us and offer as much comfort as I could give.

He turned in my arms and brought his trembling hands up to cup my face as he leaned in close. We shared breaths, every exhale coming out shaky as we pressed our foreheads together, using each other for support while we both silently cried beneath the stream of water. We had lost our soldiers, but never a member of our family—not truly. Not only was it a devastating loss that none of us knew how to deal with, but it also proved for the first time that we weren't invincible. That any of our lives could be forfeit.

"It would have been you," Evander breathed as he pulled back to gaze down at me with reddened eyes. "Tallis sent a warning that if I saved them, you would be the one who died."

I swallowed the thick lump in my throat as I remembered a similar warning I had received from the King of Agnitio that day. My palm still tingled with the message even though the ink had long since drifted away.

"And I couldn't... I—" His voice broke on the explanation and I pressed my fingers into his back, pulling him flush against me.

"It was an impossible choice," I soothed, but Evander shook his head.

"It wasn't. It was the easiest fucking decision I've ever made." He brushed his thumbs over my cheeks as he stared into my eyes. "I'm heartbroken over Kenji's death, but I'm even more terrified to know it isn't over. It's my fault that he died, but if I'm forced to make the same choice again, I will. Losing you isn't an option. It never will be." His grasp around my face tightened as he spoke, not enough to hurt but enough that I knew where his priorities lay. "Do you hate me for that?"

My forehead wrinkled as my lips set into a frown. "Never, Evander," I whispered as I shook my head. How could I, when I had been faced with the same decision and chose as he had? "My Obscure could have saved them, but if I revealed that magic, Tallis said I would have lost you."

He dragged his hands through his black hair, smoothing the wet strands back as a few pieces flopped over his brow. I brushed them away from his face before taking his hand in mine and tugging gently.

"Come on," I whispered as I led him out of the shower.

We took turns drying off one another and changing into fresh clothes, doing our best to take care of each other through our devastation. I crawled beneath the sheets of our bed and pulled Evander against me, running my fingers through his damp hair as his cheek rested over my racing heart.

"Kenji's death isn't your fault."

"If I had just listened to you and not traversed he wouldn't have been impaled. If I had fought Marce and taken them myself—"

"Kenji's death is not your fault," I said again, placing my hand beneath his chin and tilting it up so he was forced to meet my gaze. "It's not your fault, just as Ezra's isn't mine. *They* chose to come knowing the risks—knowing that none of us were exempt from death."

I had allowed myself to feel their losses just as Dash had instructed, and during that agonizing pain of self-doubt and blame, I had to come to terms with the truth. It wasn't my fault, and dwelling on it wouldn't change the past.

"You can't scrutinize what you did and didn't do. Going left instead of right could have spared the people we lost... Or it could have meant that someone else we loved would have taken their place," I continued. Evander's lip wobbled as his eyes misted over again, his grief shattering my heart. "The only way we know for certain that Kenji wouldn't have died during this trip was for him not to come at all. And we both know he would have never stayed behind so long as Marce came."

Evander closed his eyes and a tear slipped free as he nodded. "How am I supposed to look at her now?" he rasped, the words barely audible. "How am I supposed to look at the woman who raised me—the woman who has done *everything* for me—knowing that I sacrificed the love of her life to save mine?"

He pushed away from me and pressed the heels of his palms to his eyes as he fractured into a million pieces. I threw my arms around him, holding him steady as I tried to search for an answer that wouldn't come.

"I don't know," I admitted as I embraced him. "I wish I did, Evander."

Squeezing him tight, I ran my hands over his back, down his arms, and through his hair, trying desperately to give him a shred of peace. It wasn't much, but it was all I could think to offer him. Eventually, his breathing came slower and the heavy sobs settled into gentle shudders.

"We just need to train harder," he said. "Maybe if we—" I stiffened against him as he spoke, giving myself away before I could help it. "What is it?" he asked as he pulled back to look at me.

I twisted, averting my gaze as I prepared myself to disclose another revelation. Taking a deep breath in and blowing it out slowly, I faced him again, unable to keep myself composed as I said, "We're out of time, Evander." He shook his head, denying my claim. "There was another shift in Tallis's vision."

"No—"

"—Oberon's army will be in Tenebrae in two days." His head tipped back to the ceiling as he gulped down the air in deep lungfuls. "Everyone is taking the measures to mobilize their forces."

"We aren't ready," he supplied, the emotion in his throat thick.

"I know," I whispered, grabbing ahold of his face and forcing him to look at me as I crawled onto his lap. "I know." My arms wrapped around his neck and his enveloped my back, holding my body as close to him as he could.

"Did he say anything else?"

"That he needs to speak with you."

Evander shifted beneath me and I constricted my hold on him. "Ainsley, I need to go," he argued.

"Tallis can wait."

"He can't—"

"We just lost a member of our family and now may lose even more in a matter of hours. Tallis can wait ten Gods damn minutes so I can hold my husband," I responded, looking into his charcoal eyes. "He may need you right now, but *I* need you more."

Without a breath of hesitation, Evander pressed his lips to mine as he nodded and raked his fingers through my hair. I kissed him back. I kissed him to erase the pain and the fear and the misery of knowing that our time together could be up. If Tallis's vision of my death proved right, then it two days it would be.

89
Ainsley

I sat on the couch of our library with my head resting on Imogen's shoulder, listening to the crackling symphony of the fire. After he left the sanctuary of our bedroom yesterday, Evander had spent the evening and most of today in the study with Tallis, Dash, Lia, Isla, and Declan. I had drifted in and out of the room throughout the day, but I couldn't take another strategy meeting—not when it had to do with trying to keep me alive, something Evander had been obsessing over for the past twenty-four hours when Tallis told him that his vision of my fate hadn't changed.

So instead of listening to my husband frantically suggest different scenarios during the battle that could change my future, I decided to focus on helping Oli and Cal ensure the palace was stocked and ready for the wounded who would inevitably be brought in. Marce hadn't been seen since yesterday after she received Kenji's ashes and the ring he'd never had a chance to give her. But I knew she was safe in her room thanks to Onyx and Nova slipping in and out of it as they vigilantly kept watch over her.

"Are you happy?" I asked, enjoying the warmth of the flames on my skin as they cast a gentle orange glow over the space.

"What are you going on about now?" Imogen asked.

Calidore, Oli, and Felix sat in chairs on the opposite side of the room, chatting and enjoying their liquor while Imogen and I sat together near the fireplace, appreciating the sizzling comfort of the flames. Elenora, Brandle, and Jahier had chosen to spend the night at the camp with the soldiers to prepare for the battle, whereas Rosella opted to stay at the palace where she would work with Imogen and Marce to take care of the injured who arrived there tomorrow. The absence of everyone made our house quieter than it had been in months.

"You've been through so much because of me," I admitted, remembering that King Perceval had Imogen's entire family killed because she helped me escape Caelum. She shifted her shoulder, forcing me to sit up and look into her hazel eyes. "I know that I'm not your... And you're not technically... but..."

"Ainsley, take a breath," she said gently as I struggled to pull the words from my addled mind.

Throughout yesterday and today, everyone had slowly started to say their goodbyes to one another. Private conversations were held in various rooms that often led to our family members emerging with reddened eyes or tear-streaked cheeks. I had taken the time to have my moments with everyone individually except for Dash, Felix, and Imogen, putting the three of them off for as long as I could. But tomorrow Oberon's forces would arrive, and I was out of time.

I nodded, breathing in deep and letting it out in a long exhale. "You've been the closest thing I've ever had to a mother. And it's okay if you don't see me as..." I took another deep breath as I blinked away the tears that pricked. "But it's what I consider you to be to me. And I just want to know that you're happy. That being here has made the hardships worth it."

Imogen stared at me for a long moment, not saying a single word as her eyes roamed over my face. With a soft smile, she placed her hand on the back of my head and guided me to her shoulder once again. Closing my eyes, I breathed in her cinnamon and honey scent as I nestled closer to her.

"I remember the day you first arrived at the palace," she began, her fingers finding their way into my hair as she gently stroked the strands and rested her head against mine. "I thought to myself, *'Here is someone who has yet to realize her worth.'*" Imogen drew in a long breath as if lost in the memory. "I have watched you struggle and grow and bloom into the most exquisite person—someone who is loving, kind, fierce, and worthy of the title of queen. I am beyond proud of what you have accomplished, but more than that, Ainsley, I am honored to call you my daughter."

I grinned, not bothering to wipe away the tear that fell at her words.

"Even when I'm being dramatic?"

Imogen laughed through the lump I could hear in her throat. "Even then," she said and placed a kiss on the top of my head. "And as for your question about my happiness, my answer is yes. I'm free, I'm with you, and I've been able to find love with two amazing people. One of which your husband has annoyingly kept occupied most of the day."

Rolling my eyes, I grunted my agreement and sat up as my stare wandered to the open door. The hour was getting late, and they had yet to emerge from the study.

"I'll check on them," I volunteered as I slid from the couch and made my way out of the room.

The moment I crossed over the threshold I spotted everyone exiting the study at the opposite end of the hall. Tallis headed for the stairs that led to the bedrooms and Declan and Isla were already halfway to the library where I stood awkwardly waiting beneath the doorframe.

Dash and Evander emerged next, speaking low as the King of Caelum slid something into his right pocket. Their eyes immediately fell on me as if sensing my presence, but they didn't relinquish their discussion until Lia appeared in the corridor a moment later.

With a single nod, Dash backed away from Van and strolled down the hall toward me. Evander's attention was on Lia next as she threw her arms around his neck and pulled him close. I turned and rested my back against the doorframe as I redirected my attention to gaze over the people in the library. Though Lia had been with Evander most of the day, I wasn't sure if he had been able to have a moment with her just as he had with our other family members.

"Hey," Dash whispered as he reached me.

"Hey," I replied with a weak smile. I knew I was running out of time to say what I needed to, but I wasn't ready. I couldn't find the words required to say goodbye to the two men who had meant so much to me. So instead, I angled my chin down and asked, "What's in your pocket?"

Dash followed my stare and then revealed several rolled slips of paper. "Instructions for my council should something happen to me tomorrow," he answered, sliding the transfer paper back into his left pocket. I shoved the last six words of his statement from my mind as I nodded and faced forward again.

Imogen's knee bounced in place as her fingers tapped against the arm of the couch. So much so that Cal left his spot by Oli to sit next to her, placing her fidgeting hand in his as he kissed her temple.

"You're more impatient than Ainsley, you know that, right?" he teased. In true Imogen fashion, she scoffed and rolled her eyes, waving a dismissive hand over his accurate observation.

He kissed her again, this time on the lips, and I turned away to give them privacy for their intimate moment, finding Dash's stare already on me. My pulse quickened as I read in his deep teal-blue eyes what he was about to do.

"Ainsley, our friendship has meant—"

"No, Dash," I interrupted, vehemently shaking my head. "Not right now, not tonight. I can't."

He dropped his mouth to argue just as quickening footsteps echoed off the corridor walls. Lia's arms wrapped around my neck as she hugged me from behind a breath later. I squeezed her hold but swiftly relinquished her the moment I heard Imogen's relieved sigh. Lia kissed my cheek before rushing over to the couch and wedging herself between Cal and Imogen.

They curled against each other, enjoying the simple peace of being together. And as the three of them affectionally held hands and shared tender kisses, I couldn't help but smile. Imogen deserved this.

Her family had been slaughtered and despite that, she stayed under the roof of the king responsible, all so she could look after Dash. So she could protect him, guide him, and ensure he became the man his mother wanted him to be. Imogen was selfless, compassionate, and deserving of the love she had finally found. And as Cal and Lia both gazed at the woman I considered my mother with undying affection, I knew they believed that, too.

"Okay," Dash agreed before pushing off the door and making his way to Felix and Oli.

"How about a game?" Declan suggested as he held up a full bottle of wine. "Well, it's not exactly a *game,* but a way to pass the time. We'll go around and each person will tell the story of their favorite memory."

"Where does the wine come in?" Dash asked as he took the bottle and poured himself a healthy serving.

"It doesn't. But as this may very well be our last night in this world, I figured a drink couldn't hurt."

Evander's presence loomed behind me a split second before his arms encircled my waist and he pulled me back against his chest. His lips found the sensitive skin just below my ear as he kissed softly before whispering, "I've missed you." I hummed my agreement, too entranced by the way his mouth felt on my skin to bother with words. "Would you like to play?" he asked as everyone moved closer to sit in a circle.

I shook my head without hesitation. Although I cherished my family, the only person I desired to be with tonight was my husband.

"Good," he said, as the shadows of his Obscure drifted around us. "Neither do I."

The darkness hadn't yet dissipated as we tore off each other's clothes, our mouths colliding in fervent need. We didn't even make it to the bed—we *couldn't*—as our desire consumed us and we sank to the floor, taking each other in the middle of our room.

90
Ainsley

Tender kisses along my throat, my collarbone, my jaw, and my cheeks beckoned me awake. Our room was still painted in moonlight and the soft violet hue of a pending dawn, though the sun hadn't yet crested over the mountains. The battle was quickly approaching, but it hadn't yet reached us. We still had time; still had this quiet moment between us to savor and cherish and hold on to for as long as possible.

We hadn't slept much after finally making it into bed, finding our time was better spent tangling together beneath the sheets all night. My fingers raked through his black hair and down the muscles of his back as I urged him higher, needing his lips to relinquish my throat and instead claim my mouth. He did as I silently commanded and planted kisses along my flesh until his tongue was moving over mine in a dance we had done a thousand times before. This was what I wanted—not thoughts of war or what and who I stood to lose in a matter of hours. I wanted the desire in his touch, the passion in his kiss, and the fire of our love to erase everything but the here and now.

I widened my legs, and Evander settled between them without missing a beat, his hand dropping low to slide my shirt higher until he was pulling it over my head. The moment I was free from it, I enclosed my teeth around his bottom lip, tugging gently as his body lowered onto mine again. He groaned and angled his knee higher to spread my legs even further apart as he pressed the tip of himself into me. My hips arched on instinct, my body demanding I take more of him, but as he sank fully inside of me, it still wasn't enough. We were as close as two people could physically be, but I still needed *more* of him, of this, of *us*.

My ankles locked around his middle as I urged him deeper, moving in time to each thrust of his hips. His mouth was on mine, his hands were in my hair, and his body was drawing me in and pushing me closer to an edge I wanted nothing more than to cling to.

"I love you," I whispered, but Evander didn't respond. Not with words, anyway.

There was barely any distance between us, but somehow, he still managed to close the invisible gap. Van kissed me harder and my senses were overcome with the taste of him mixed with salt. My hands flew to his cheeks, my fingers brushing over a path of wetness trailing down his flesh, and I swallowed the lump in my throat.

He drove himself deeper as our bodies moved as one, both of us ignoring the steady flow of tears slipping from beneath our lids as we savored each other. This couldn't be our last time. It *wouldn't*. I couldn't find him just to lose him barely a year later. I refused to believe that life could be so cruel.

Shadows unfurled around us as we reveled in our pleasure. We didn't want to rush, and that was evident in our slow and languid movements. This embrace—this *dance*—wasn't like our usual routine, one filled with messy tongues and teeth and burning passion. This was gentle and methodic, tender and sweet. It was pure love. One that only we could ever share.

My magic drifted toward him, penetrating his flesh until it had made its way inside him as it had once done before.

"You've already claimed me, love," he said as his hands moved to cradle my cheeks. I mirrored the movement, and he pulled his face from mine. His glassy grey eyes skewered me, a piercing stab through my heart as I read the pain and fear in his features. Given the way his gaze frantically darted across every inch of my face, I could imagine I didn't look much better.

"Is there a rule that says I can't do it again?" I asked, the words coming out fractured and unintelligible. "You're mine. I should be allowed to do it as many times as I want."

If he understood my broken plea through the sobs, I couldn't be sure, but he nodded just the same and I felt his magic enter me as well. I clung to his darkness and our Soul Bond, breathing it in and letting it consume me until we were one and the same.

"Evander," I croaked, unsure of what I was asking for, but I just knowing I needed *something*.

"I know," he replied, seeming to understand whatever I was after. He shifted his hips, moving our bodies faster as my legs trembled around him and my darkness enveloped his.

My magic was greedy and desperate. His mouth pulled away from mine as he groaned at the feel of me, and his own power surged through my veins hungrily. My back bowed off the bed, arching into his body even more as I whimpered and moaned and clawed at his back. I could barely breathe, barely *think* about anything other than us at this moment. He was mine, and I was his. We were connected by magic, by love, by soul—and there was no future where we didn't exist without the other.

Evander's mouth dropped to my neck, and he licked up the hollow of my throat as his hands gripped me possessively. I could feel how close he was to his release, his arms shaking as he continued to thrust into me over and over again, giving me every inch he had to offer. My spine tingled and my core heated as I matched his movements against me. I gripped his face and pulled it back up to mine, wanting to feel his lips on mine as I came undone beneath him.

"I love you," I said again as tears continued to stream down my cheeks.

"I love you," he finally whispered back. And we both fell into the oblivion of our love. I would not lose him today. We would not lose each other.

We dressed in a silence that was anything but comforting. Evander strapped daggers to the holsters on my thighs and hips as I adjusted the thin but strong armor across his chest, our fingers sometimes lingering longer than necessary, like we couldn't bear to not touch each other.

Once we were donned in our battle gear and armed to the teeth, we stood in the center of our room, both of our gazes drifting over the space as we committed it to memory. Golden sunlight streaked over Evander's face and we both turned to the open window to see the first rays of morning stretch across the horizon. It was time.

"Ready?" he asked, and his throat flexed as he swallowed. I wasn't, but I nodded anyway. Evander took a single step around me and my hand shot out to grab his. "Wait," I said, pulling him back in front of me.

We hadn't said our goodbyes last night the way we had with the rest of our family, and I was sure it was because neither of us were capable of imagining a world where the other didn't exist. But this was war, and that possibility became more of a reality with each passing second. It would truly be a miracle blessed by the Gods if every member of our friends and family made it out alive today. And I would never forgive myself if I didn't tell him what he meant to me one last time.

"I don't want to do this," Evander said with a lump in his throat.

"I know," I replied as I nodded in understanding. I didn't want to either, but Marce's words played in my mind on repeat. *I never told him. I never told him. I never told him.* And I refused to allow myself to say the same. "You don't have to, but I do."

I sucked in a shaky breath as my eyes filled to the brim with unshed tears, and my heart ached with the pain of my pending words. My mouth opened and closed as I tried to form sentences with the thoughts that assaulted me, but nothing seemed to come forward. There was so much and not enough that I needed to tell him, needed to say to ensure he grasped the reality of what he was to me. His fingers wove between mine as a gentle sigh escaped from his lips like words of encouragement. I clutched him tightly as I drew in a deep and steadying breath.

"I was so alone for most of my life," I began, my voice shaking and lips trembling as I spoke, but I had to continue. "And when I came to you, I was broken and hurt and betrayed. I didn't want to believe in good or love or anything that wasn't my own anger, but you wouldn't accept that." A sob tore through my throat, and Evander moved his hands to cradle my face, his thumbs sweeping back and forth to catch the falling tears. "You brought me back to life when I didn't care about living. You showed me what I could be and never once wavered in your beliefs during any of my missteps or stumbles. You were always there, reaching out your hand to help me up and loving me fully."

I closed my eyes as the unrelenting tears poured down my face in a persistent stream. Every inch of my heart ached for this man, and the prospect of our time together being over was a pain I couldn't comprehend. He was my Soul Bonded, my Claimed, my husband, and the love of my life. There was no future for me without him.

"I'm so grateful for you, Evander, and I'm honored to call you mine. We may have only had a short time together, but it was worth every sacrifice, every heartache, every lonely night because it all led me to you," I continued, letting my eyes flutter open to meet his once again. "And if I leave this world today, I'll be waiting for you in the next—albeit impatiently, but still." He breathed a muffled sound of amusement as his fingers squeezed mine. "I love you, Evander, and I will continue to do so with my last breath. You have my heart, my soul, all of me—always."

I pushed onto my toes and pressed my lips to his, tasting our love for one another. It didn't feel like I said enough, yet it would have to be. We were out of time. I settled back to my normal height and offered a weak smile before turning to head out of the room. Evander caught my wrist, halting my advance and I twisted to gaze up at him, reading the conflict in his eyes.

"The only regret I have in this life involves you," he began slowly, the emotion already thick in his throat. "I didn't find you soon enough and because of that, we missed out on those years together. We didn't get to have the inside jokes, the long nights spent talking when we should have been asleep, or you chasing me through the woods because I was being a little shithead and ran away from you. We didn't get the days where we rushed through the palace, causing chaos and destruction, or you creeping into my room in the middle of the night to bait Onyx with cookies so he'd leave me and come to you instead." I released a breathy laugh at his depiction of us as children, wishing so much it had come to fruition.

I could picture us at that age perfectly. Evander with his big bright eyes and messy black hair as he ran through the halls while I chased him, pissed that my legs were too short to keep up. I could see us hiding in an alcove eating the stolen desserts Van had managed to procure as Oli searched high and low for us. I could see him slipping into my room during storms to sleep next to me because I was scared of the thunder. We'd argue and fight like hell, but we'd be inseparable.

"And then when we grew older, you'd find someone you liked. Someone who'd make you smile and laugh, and it would shred me to pieces because I would have undoubtedly fallen first. There isn't a world in which that isn't the case," he continued as his lips lifted in a lopsided grin. "Our past was stolen from us and now it kills me to think our future might be too. I want the life we deserve to share. I want the fights and disagreements just to make up an hour later tangled beneath our sheets. I want the cold winter nights dancing above the village and the warm summer days laying in the grass with you on the clifftop." His voice broke with each declaration, piercing my heart with more pain than I had ever felt before.

"I wish I could say the time we had together was enough—that it made everything we went through while apart worth it—but I'd be lying. I'm selfish when it comes to you, and I want more. This isn't how we're supposed to end," he sobbed, gripping my face tight as he became a blurry silhouette in my vision. "We're supposed to be together. We're supposed to rule our kingdom side by side. We're supposed to fill our house with sacred memories and the sound of our children's laughter. This isn't where we part—it can't be."

I broke, crumpling to the ground as Evander slumped with me, holding me tight against his chest. We cried together, both of us struggling to come to terms with what our future could hold. I was supposed to die in battle with Evander's name and a declaration of love on my lips. Tallis *saw* it, and that vision—to my knowledge—hadn't changed.

Slowly, Evander flicked the tip of my nose up with his. "I will always find you, love. Every time." His lips molded to mine, letting me feel every ounce of devotion and promise in his embrace.

"Ten minutes?" I rasped.

Evander sniffled and nodded. "Ten minutes."

91

Ainsley

The kitchen was silent when we entered as everyone sat or stood next to a plate of untouched food and looked off in various directions. The somber mood was a heavy pressure on my chest that even my internal defenses couldn't keep out. There was no making light of today—no words of wisdom to pull us through the darkness. We all knew what we stood to lose.

I inhaled a trembling breath as I cast a glance over the members of my family, committing their faces to memory. Lia's smile as she kissed Imogen goodbye and Cal's soft golden eyes as he did the same. Felix's knowing glance at Dash as his hand stayed interlaced with Oli's. Marce as she tied back her blonde curls with the wolves sitting stoically at her feet. And Dash's piercing blue eyes as they met mine, silently conveying the words I denied him of last night.

"We should go," Tallis announced.

Evander's hand on me tightened as he nodded shallowly. I didn't bother to wipe the tears as I said goodbye to Imogen for what could have been the final time. And I didn't have it in me to be strong or brave as I drifted back to Evander's side, kissing him gently before his shadows swept all of us away to meet our fate.

Elenora, Brandle, and Jahier had been waiting for us the moment we arrived at the camp. The land bled gold with the promise of sunrise over the hills as small plumes of smoke from various extinguished campfires drifted through the morning air. I didn't know what to expect before a battle, but I didn't anticipate everything being so quiet. It wasn't a comforting silence like what Evander and I often shared in the early hours. It was ominous, heavy, and thick with horror-filled implications.

We met with the generals leading each of our allied kingdom's armies to go over our plan of attack. Even with the forces of Tenebrae, Caelum, Agnitio, and several hundred soldiers from Venator, we didn't compare to the numbers Oberon had on his side according to the reports we had received. Unfortunately, with the sudden change of vision, Vorsutos wouldn't make it to this battle in time. Declan had instead mobilized them to go straight to the Palace of Tenebrae upon arrival so they could assist with the casualties that would be sent there.

"You cannot call for your Obscure," Tallis instructed me beneath his breath while all other rulers focused on the map laid out on a large table.

"I have to," I argued. My magic could cut through our enemies in the blink of an eye. It could be the extra push we needed to claim victory today.

"You must keep that power hidden during the battle. There will be a time to call for it, and you'll know when that is. But do not pull that magic free until then."

"Can you be any more vague?"

His lips twitched as he said, "Probably." I rolled my eyes and blew out a long breath. I didn't like debilitating myself by cutting off an integral part of my being. "I need you to trust me, Ainsley. If you use your Obscure before it's time, there will be catastrophic consequences."

Reluctantly I agreed, putting my trust in his visions.

An hour later we were scattered along the field as our soldiers stood in formation, looking over the vast space as we focused on our enemy in the distance. By the looks of it, Pravus's army was smaller than we had anticipated. The clench of Van's jaw and the hushed curse slipping from Dash's lips told me that wasn't a good thing. I just didn't know why.

"Five minutes," Tallis announced, sending a chill down my spine. Five more minutes to feel afraid, and then I'd shove the fear away.

I gazed up at Evander as he watched me with a patient and loving expression. He tilted his head, directing my focus to the people behind us. "Say what you need to," he instructed, as my eyes landed on Dash and Elenora sharing a quiet conversation across the space.

Van drifted from my side and wandered over to Oli as I waited for the King of Caelum to be finished. If all we had was five minutes, I wasn't going to take it from them. They deserved to have every second they could spend together.

Lia nudged me with her hip and I twisted to find her holding out a small colorful bracelet that looked like it had been made by a child. "Here," she said, extending it in an offering.

I brushed my fingers along the beading but didn't take it. "What is it?"

She rolled her eyes and said, "A bracelet, obviously."

"No shit," I replied with a smirk, "But why are you giving it to me?"

Lia groaned in agitation and grabbed my wrist, forcing the bracelet over my hand. "Tessa made it for me when I brought her to Tenebrae. It was a parting gift meant to keep me safe when she moved to the north with her new family," she explained.

My chest tightened as I remembered the little girl Lia had saved in Ministro—the one she had claimed as her own daughter to spare her from death before rescuing hundreds of children from that same fate.

"I can't take this," I argued and reached to remove the bracelet from my wrist.

Lia's hand curled around mine, halting me from my task. "Imogen said the same thing when I tried to give it to her this morning. Except *she* called me ridiculous and dramatic."

My lips curled upward as I pictured the scene. "She's just scared," I told Lia.

"I know," she replied softly. "So am I."

Her stare drifted to Calidore who was watching us intently, no doubt wanting to spend the last few minutes of his time with her.

"Keep it for the battle. You can return it once it's over," she said, wrapping her arms around me in a tight hug. "You're going to be fine. You're strong, powerful, and capable, Ainsley." She pulled away and flashed a beautiful bright smile as she tucked a loose strand of red hair behind her ear.

I wanted to believe her, but I had gone through too much to pretend everything would magically work out. Naivety was a luxury I could no longer afford.

"Promise me you'll look after him," I instructed.

Her green eyes softened as she watched me, slightly misting over. After a moment of consideration, she extended her hand as she held my gaze. "I promise." I took it, shaking once to solidify the death vow.

Elenora moving away from Dash caught in my periphery and I took that as my cue to leave Lia and head to him. He studied me as I approached, his throat flexing as his knee bounced nervously.

"Me first?" I asked as I finally reached him.

He agreed and ran his thumb over the pads of his fingers the way he always did when he was anxious. Smiling weakly, I took his trembling hands in mine, needing to hold on to him as we did this.

"I've struggled to come up with what to say to you because there are simply no words that could ever encompass what you mean to me, Dash," I said, fighting the way my voice shook as I spoke. "So instead of trying and failing, I'm just going to say *thank you*. Thank you for never giving up on me. For continuing to try, even when I didn't deserve it. Thank you for walks every night, for the birthdays, for the Sanctuary. Thank you for opening your heart and letting me in." I squeezed his hands harder as his eyes misted over and tears collected on my lashes. "Thank you for showing me I was worthy of being loved despite my stubbornness, quick temper, and countless flaws. Before you, I had never known what it was like to feel that wanted," I added, exhaling a long breath.

Dash raised a brow and I nodded, confirming it was his turn.

"I've dreaded having this conversation," he admitted. I offered him a warm smile that said, *me too.* "With everyone else, I've said my piece, but with you, I draw a blank. There's so much that I want to tell you, but every time I try, I lose the words. So please bear with me as I fumble around trying to find them."

I squeezed his hands in a gentle gesture of encouragement as I stared into the blue eyes that had always captivated me wholly.

"You were my first love," he began slowly. "I never knew those feelings could be so intense and could alter my very being so completely. Every day you enamor me, inspire me, and drive me to be a better version of myself—to be the *best* version of myself. You've taught me to question, to fight, and to possess an unbelievable amount of patience." I laughed through my tears as my smile stretched from ear to ear. Dash slid his thumb back and forth over my knuckles as he gazed down at me, his throat flexing as he swallowed hard. "And you've taught me how to love someone deeply the right way."

I closed my eyes, tilting my face to the sky as I tried to shake off the pain. There wasn't much more of this I could take—of the goodbyes, of the fear, of the death. It was all more than any of us should have had to experience.

"Now it's *my* turn to thank *you*," he told me before inhaling a steadying breath. "Thank you for allowing me into your life. For offering me your heart and your friendship. And for forgiving me when I betrayed them both. I couldn't imagine a life with you not in it."

I threw my arms around him and buried my face in his neck. He constricted his grip on me and I prayed to the Gods this wouldn't be the last time he held me like this.

"I love you, Dashiell."

I didn't bother to wipe the tears that fell. He deserved to know how much this goodbye was destroying me. He deserved to know how much he meant.

"I love you, Ainsley," he replied through a broken rasp.

"I'm trying really hard not to be offended that I wasn't invited to this," Felix croaked.

Without letting me go, Dash lifted out one arm in invitation and Felix collided with us a moment later. Our bodies moved on instinct and they positioned me in the center like they always did when the three of us held each other. I breathed in their scents, holding on to the fragrance and the feelings of peace, serenity, and home they always brought me.

"Two more minutes," Tallis announced, sending my heart into a thunderous race as I wiggled free.

I smoothed back my hair before turning to Felix with wet eyes.

"We already said goodbye to each other once, and I refuse to have to do it again," I instructed. There wasn't anything more I could add that I hadn't said the night I thought he died in my arms.

Felix grinned sadly but nodded as he replied, "Agreed. Once was more than enough." We embraced, kissing each other on the cheek before separating.

I threw another yearning stare over the two boys that meant the world to me—my first love and my best friend. "I love you both," I told them as I backed away, giving them the chance to be alone together one last time before all hell broke loose.

92
Dashiell

"We said we'd never do this," Felix reminded, dragging my attention away from the third member of our trio as she headed for her husband.

My lips lifted in the corner as I remembered that very conversation when we were only thirteen. "We claimed that saying goodbye meant we were accepting defeat and we were too good for that."

Felix grinned broadly as he nodded, his amber eyes distant as if he were recalling it all, too. "Exactly."

I blew out a long breath as I stared at the person who had been my best friend since we were eight years old. The person who didn't share my blood but was my brother in every way that mattered. The person who knew me better than anyone in the world and loved me through every fault and mistake I had made.

"Perfect, because then I won't have to tell you that you've been the one constant light in my life. Or that I'm grateful every day for that fucking apple you threw at me when I met you," I told him with a weak grin. "Or that you've been the best brother and friend I could have ever asked for." The words were fragmented versions of their former selves, barely distinguishable through the emotion constricting my throat.

Felix nodded as tears ran down his cheeks. "Thank the Gods, because that means I won't have to tell you that you've always been my home, Dash. Or that I'm the luckiest bastard in the world to be able to call you my brother." He moved closer and pulled me into a tight embrace. "Or that every day I become more proud of the man and king you are," he said through his cries.

I fisted my hands in the fabric at his back, unable to loosen my grip on him even if I wanted to.

"We wouldn't want that," I said as I sniffled.

"Definitely not."

We both let out a broken laugh as we held each other.

"I love you, Felix."

"I love you, too, Dash."

We didn't let go until Tallis announced it was time.

"There's something I'll need you to do for me," I instructed, keeping my voice low as I pulled away. My hand slid into my right pocket as I took a deep breath. "I can't tell you what it is right now, but when I call for you, I need you to come."

He regarded me for only a moment before nodding. "Okay."

The air was quiet when Evander, Tallis, Jahier, Ainsley, and I stepped to the front line while Oberon, Arden, and Harbin moved to theirs, each of our sides protected by a shield that shimmered in the early morning light. Though we were still a safe distance across the open field from each other, we could easily carry a conversation.

"Good morning King Evander and friends," the Lord of Pravus began as he brought a cup of what looked to be coffee to his lips. The fucking prick. "Did everyone have a peaceful night's sleep?"

No one on our side spoke as we glared at the man who had killed one of our own so brutally. Oberon groaned in frustration as he gestured a hand over us and turned to address King Harbin of Ministro to his left.

"See, this is what I was telling you about. They're incredibly rude. Here I am, just trying to ensure they were well rested before the festivities and—"

"Fuck off," I bit out, already over his games.

"And that one right there is the worst," Oberon continued as he pointed to me and leaned in closer to Harbin. "Always so snappy. You know, I still haven't even received A WRITTEN LETTER OF APOLOGY FROM HIM," he yelled, directing his stare toward me, "for backing out of the arrangement I had made with Caelum. The amount of stress I had to—"

"Do you ever shut up?" Evander chimed in dramatically.

Oberon smiled wide, this time leaning over to Arden as he said, "And that one's my favorite."

He brought his cup back to his lips and took another long drink, sighing loudly after he swallowed. He tossed the empty mug over his shoulder and shoved his hands in his pocket as he gave the King of Tenebrae his undivided attention.

"Did you give any more thought to my offer?" Oberon asked hopefully. "Say the word and we can make a trade."

"You have nothing I want," Evander said just as he had before.

Oberon nodded, dramatically bobbing his head up and down in understanding. "Right, right, because I killed the last one. How's the blonde doing by the way?"

My hand instinctively reached out, snagging Ainsley's wrist as she tried to charge forward with a growl. Evander's shadows spilled around him, but thankfully, he didn't give in to the bait. I now understood why Tallis had instructed Evander to keep Marce away from the battle and assign her to help Imogen and Rosella instead. If Evander was having difficulty controlling himself, then there was no telling how Kenji's widow would have handled seeing her husband's murderer.

"How about this," Oberon offered as he tapped a finger to his chin. "You come with me, and I'll let the rest of you live."

"Or... and hear me out," Evander started, "I kill you, and the rest of us live."

Oberon bellowed with laughter as he placed his hands on King Arden of Venator's shoulders and shook enthusiastically. "I fucking love this one," he said, gesturing to the King of Tenebrae. "I think he'll make a great addition to the team. What do you say, Evander?"

Evander shrugged, his arms firmly crossed over his chest. "My wife says I'm not allowed to play with you."

Oberon chuckled and shook his head. "You sure? We've cornered you on your land and our numbers exceed yours. Some would say it's wise to strike a deal before the bloodshed begins and you lose even more than you already have." Evander didn't respond—none of us did. We weren't entirely prepared for the surprise battle, but we weren't going to give up either. "Fine," Oberon said through a sigh and began backing away. "Let the fun begin, then." He offered a salute before turning around completely and walking through his ranks with the two former Kings of Disparya at his side.

We waited until the three had disappeared from view before the five of us retreated to the top of the hill where the rest of our army and friends stood impatiently.

"What now?" Jahier asked as we all put one heavy foot in front of the other.

Evander cleared his throat and took a deep breath before he replied. "Now we fight. War is a string of battles, each more brutal than the last. Pace yourselves. Remember what you've learned in training and be smart about the risks you take. Today doesn't mark the only fight ahead of us."

I slid my hand into my right pocket as I inhaled a steadying breath and counted to fifty.

The battle played out as anticipated, starting slow and organized as the front ranks pushed forward to meet each other. Eventually, as numbers dwindled and fear began to take root, the fight turned messy and chaotic—a recipe for disaster and bloodshed. The number of soldiers Pravus, Ministro, and Venator possessed should have been enough to end this battle before it truly began, but the field only held perhaps less than half of what we had expected. Though it gave us a fighting chance here today, it only meant that our enemy was causing destruction in another part of Disparya. And since the strength of our forces was here, our enemy would go virtually unchallenged.

I swallowed the implication that our kingdoms were being stolen from under us as I swung my sword, slicing a Ministrian soldier in two. I was exhausted and weak from the hours spent alternating between magic and steel, but I didn't give up. My gaze quickly scanned over the field as I checked on Ainsley and Felix, both of whom were holding their own in battle. Still, I lingered close.

The months of intense training had sharpened my senses and honed my abilities more than I had ever thought possible. Switching between my Gifts and a sword had become like second nature and I used less magic than I previously would have prior to the lessons.

Occasionally, my back found Evander's, and just as we had in Caelum, we fought in unison, timing the use of our Gifts perfectly to one another. Other times, I fought near Ainsley. During our sparring sessions, she had always held her own, but for some reason, she wasn't utilizing her Obscure—magic that she had constantly relied on.

If she wasn't calling for the power that could rip people apart, I knew it had to be for a reason. Rather than question her about it, I chose to help by playing to her strengths. Her skill with a dagger was outmatched amongst our group, but I stayed close to compensate for her lack of speed. And while I surpassed others in close combat, Ainsley took care of the approaching soldiers, striking them down with her daggers before they reached me.

I wiped away the warm rush of crimson that streaked across my face from the fatal blow I dealt and conjured a ball of water in my hands to combat the fire that had been thrown at me by one of Pravus's soldiers. The moment his element had been washed away, my heart rate slowed without my permission as a soft light flooded through me, urging my body to relax. I reached for the dagger at my hip and flung it at my enemy, taking him down for good. Having to fight products of Conjoining when you weren't sure what two Gifts they possessed was proving to be annoying as fuck.

I panted, trying to catch my breath as I surveyed the chaos. The field was soaked with scarlet and lost futures. Hundreds of dead lay still as the living fought amongst them, stepping over their bodies as they swung and evaded. This battle was a bloodbath—one we were barely surviving.

My gaze swept left, catching sight of three heads exploding from a snap of Brandle's fingers as he utilized his Imperium Gift and then quickly relied on his blade to fight two more off. I could practically hear Ainsley demand him to teach her how to do that the second the battle was over and we returned home. The mere thought of the Queen of Tenebrae had my eyes searching the area until I found her ten feet away, wrapping her shadows around her enemy to pin him in place as she stabbed a dagger through his eye.

With a final deep breath, I conjured my fire in one hand and gripped my sword in the other. Before I could take a single step, Evander's gaze found mine. I raised a brow in question but he shook his head and refocused on his task of turning the five men surrounding him into shriveled grey husks thanks to his fear-inducing magic. With a nod of hope to myself, I rejoined the fray.

We all gave everything we could to our fight, pushing the fears from our minds and focusing solely on our task. Although we were severely outnumbered by both soldiers and magic, we fought valiantly. It wouldn't be an easy victory, but we still had a chance. At least we thought we did.

Until a bellow of agony ruptured through the land.

My stomach bottomed out and the breath was stolen from my lungs as I watched Calidore sink to the ground covered in crimson. But it wasn't his blood that soaked through his clothes. It belonged to the woman he clutched in his arms, her red hair spilling onto the grass around them.

93

Ainsley

I screamed my fury as I sprinted for Lia, my sword slicing through the air and dismembering anyone that came in my way. But we were surrounded by the enemy and the more I cleared the area, the more people flooded into it, obstructing my view until I was surrounded by uniforms that weren't our own.

I fought the best I could, weaving and ducking and diving as I evaded each attack, effortlessly switching between my shadows, my Imperium, and my blade. But they wouldn't stop coming.

Darkness swirled around me and a heartbeat later, I was standing high upon the hill behind our protective shield as Evander's Obscure drifted away.

"Lia," I rasped through a sob, my voice hoarse from all of the commands I had yelled throughout the morning of battle.

"I know," Evander whispered, pulling me close as we both stared into the distance where Cal's shadows had enveloped them, protecting them from the onslaught of weapons that banged against the dark shield.

Evander stepped back from me and disappeared before materializing again with Calidore and Lia, her body pale and lifeless. I shoved my Imperium Gift into her, biting back the gasp of horror as I felt her shredded heart beneath the touch of my magic. I tried to shove her blood back into the still organ, but the damage was too extensive.

Dash appeared a breath later, slamming his hands to the wound on her chest as he called for his Medicus Gift. The warm, bright magic pulsed over mine as it frantically searched for a way to repair Lia's broken body, but it was no use. She was already gone and there was no bringing her back. I brushed my magic over his in comfort as he leaned back and pulled his hands away from Lia with a solemn shake of his head.

My fingers absentmindedly drifted to the bracelet around my wrist as I pushed myself to my feet. We had lost another.

Felix and Oli rushed over, sinking to the ground as they mourned for the beautiful woman who had sacrificed so much until the very end. My heart shattered as their cries muddled with

Cal's. I stood there as still as a statue as I wept, thinking over the times I had spent with her. The nights of laughter and sage advice. The way she never pried before I was ready, but was always there whenever I needed her.

That loving smile and bright light in her eyes were forever extinguished, left only to distant memories. I turned and emptied my stomach. Lia deserved more. Cal and Imogen deserved more.

I looked back over the field below at the countless sea of colors that littered the blood-soaked earth. King Harbin emerged from between the ranks for the first time since the fighting commenced. He shoved his way along the dead, stopping a short distance away from several soldiers too engaged in combat to notice him. Harbin closed his hands and extended his arms wide as his chest rose and fell heavily.

Evander tensed and slid his fingers between mine as we moved away from Lia's body to get a better view of the king. My head tilted as I watched him while my stomach tightened with anxious anticipation.

The ground trembled, sending shockwaves of power rumbling through the earth as Harbin closed his fist, grunting loudly.

"No," Evander breathed.

Just as I was going to inquire what he meant, movement across the field snagged my attention. I narrowed my eyes as I studied the scene, noting the slight twitching among the fallen. Harbin's eyes flew open and with a menacing smirk, he slammed his hands together, sending a visible wave of power through the land.

The dead soldiers from every kingdom pushed themselves up from the ground and faced us, ready for their orders.

"Oh Gods," I whispered as I staggered back. "His Obscure can control the dead."

"Not all of them," Dash added from somewhere behind us. I scanned the ground, noticing that several still remained lifeless in the grass. "It has limitations just as all of ours do." Dash's observation didn't make me feel any better.

King Harbin snapped his fingers and the dead fell to the earth once again, void of any movement. He smiled again and backed away through the crowd. The display was meant as a warning and a promise of what was to come. We couldn't survive it—not today at least.

"Van," I said as I peered up at him. But my husband's gaze was focused on an altercation to the right.

I leaned around him to follow his stare to watch an enemy soldier plunge his sword through the eye of one of ours. Evander's focus shifted straight ahead a second before one of Tallis's men was beheaded.

"Van," I tried again, but he turned his attention somewhere else as if he hadn't heard me.

His wide frenzied eyes found another fight, this time two of Pravus's soldiers stabbing one of Jahier's through the heart. Again and again Evander twisted, landing on a death blow seconds before it occurred like he had already seen it coming.

We were wasting time standing around when we should have been getting our soldiers out. We may have lost this battle, but if we didn't retreat now, we'd lose the entire war. We needed time to regroup, collect ourselves, and plan now that we knew what King Harbin's Obscure was capable of.

"Evander, look at me," I instructed, grabbing his face and forcing his wild eyes to meet mine. "We can't win here today. We have to go." He shook his head as I read the panic in every crease of his brow.

I turned my stare away from him, watching more of our soldiers get cut down by our enemy. We weren't going to last more than an hour if we didn't get out of here. Oberon could claim the victory today, but it would be his last.

"FALL BACK!" I yelled over the land. Echos of my command rang out over the space as the soldiers on our side ran for the safety of our shield.

"Love," Evander croaked as his hands tightened on my waist. His breaths came in anxious gulps as the panic consumed him. I crushed my lips to his, trying desperately to ease his mind and keep him grounded. We couldn't afford for him to get lost in his fear—not right now.

"I love you," I whispered, offering him the words that always brought me comfort.

"I... love you," he repeated slowly.

I released his face as I stared back over the crowd of retreating soldiers while others still fought. "FALL BACK! GET TO THE SHIELD *NOW*!" I directed, waving my arms around as I beckoned our men to us. We didn't have much time left.

My gaze traveled up to Evander, but his stare was focused on something behind me as he gave a gentle nod.

An order.

I twisted my head to peer over my shoulder just as strong arms wrapped around me, holding me in place. I faced forward again, not understanding what was happening only to see that Evander was gone.

Shadows drifted on the wind before me as he reappeared across the field... walking to our enemies.

"*NO!*" I screamed as I kicked and thrashed against my captor.

"I'm so sorry," Dash whispered as something sharp pierced my neck, sending a burst of cold into my veins.

The wolf venom spread through me, wrapping around my magic and covering each Gift's door in a thick layer of ice. Even my Obscure was unreachable.

I fought harder, kicking and clawing at the arms that held me. I had to get free. I had to reach Van.

"Felix!" Dash yelled.

A moment later, my friend's hands were on me. I could feel my heart slow and my eyes become heavy as I watched Evander inch closer to the enemy's barrier. This wasn't happening. I wouldn't let it.

I needed magic to help him so I did the only thing I could think of. I shoved as much as I could of myself into Dash and took his. He grunted in pain as I slipped through his defenses and pierced his raw power. I grabbed onto it and pulled it into me.

I took and took and took until the ice covering my doors melted and I had access to my magic once again. My claws sank into Felix next, earning a whine from his as I ripped his Empathi Gift from my body and shoved it away.

"Ainsley, no—" Dash tried, but it was too late. My Obscure tore from me in all directions, slamming against the two men that held me and knocking them to the ground.

I didn't look back as I took off through the field, sprinting as fast as I could as Evander finally crossed behind enemy lines. No, no, no, no, *no*.

I ran harder, my darkness whipping behind me in a violent storm of black and slicing through anyone that came too close. This wasn't going to happen.

This isn't where we part—it can't be.

Evander's words from this morning clung to the corners of my mind. It can't be, it can't be, it can't be.

We're supposed to be together.

It can't be.

We're supposed to rule our kingdom side by side.

It can't be.

We're supposed to fill our house with sacred memories.

It can't be.

And the sound of our children's laughter.

This isn't where we part—it can't be.

I shoved my power forward and my Obscure surged to the shield up ahead. It slammed into the barricade and crept over it like a billowing violent storm as I kept running. I jumped over bodies and weaved through swinging swords. I dodged punches and spheres of fire that rained over me. I pushed through allies and enemies alike as I forced myself to go faster.

It can't be.

My body crashed into the shield in a thunderous collision as I screamed my rage, my eyes never leaving the man watching me as Oberon stood at his side. No, no, no, no, no. My fingers turned black as they lengthened into sharp points. I kicked and scratched and clawed at the shield, fighting like hell to break through and get to him.

My husband, my Claimed, my Soul Bonded.

This isn't where we part—it can't be.

My chest ached with the pending agony and his broken stare. His pain, my pain. Everything muddled and mix together in a violent cacophony of chaos, unable to tell through my screams where I ended and he began.

This isn't where we part—it can't be.

My claws continued to scrape down the barrier as Oberon's expression filled with a surprised delight and hunger. Warmth splashed across my face as a metallic tang spread over my tongue, but I didn't stop. I kept clawing, banging, smashing my hands against that shield as hard as I could.

This isn't where we part—it can't be.

Tears streamed from Evander's reddened eyes as he watched me fight my way to him, but he remained still.

"Please!" I begged, unsure if he could hear my desperation. "Please don't go. Don't leave me!"

I banged my fist against the shield with each word, the pain of my broken heart a crushing weight in my chest that I knew he could feel.

I love you, he mouthed.

I slammed my fists harder.

This isn't where we part—it can't be.

Oberon leaned in close to Evander as his hungry eyes raked over me and the darkness that drifted all around. He whispered something and Evander's eyes went wide with fear as Oberon shoved a needle into his neck.

"NO!" I screamed again.

Oberon bent his fingers in a small wave and the shield disappeared.

Along with everyone else.

My knees hit the dirt as my eyes frantically scanned the now empty space in front of me. The only sign anyone had been there were the bodies they didn't bother to take with them. My breaths became labored as I gulped on the air, giving into my panic.

Gone. Evander was gone.

I tipped my head back as my screams cleaved the sky. Let the Gods feel my fury, my rage, my vengeance. My Obscure thrashed around me wildly and I could feel it slice through flesh and bone, unable to tell if I was hurting friend or foe. But I couldn't stop.

Everything hurt.

This isn't where we part—it can't be.

But it was.

I closed my eyes and my palms pressed to the warm, wet grass as I emptied my stomach in between my sobs. This wasn't happening. It couldn't be. This was just a nightmare I'd wake from at any moment and see that Evander was still here, sleeping at my side in our bed.

Someone scooped me up from the ground and I swayed in their arms as they walked, not caring if the enemy had taken me.

"Why?" I croaked.

"Because losing you was never an option," Declan answered, holding me tighter against him as my world went black.

94

Ainsley

"How are you feeling?" Sirona asked.

I didn't respond as my stare stayed fixed on Cal and Imogen and the body they sat next to, neatly wrapped in fabric. The battle had ended only hours ago, and yet it felt like a lifetime had passed since I watched Evander disappear before my eyes.

"I'll set the bones once your magic replenishes a bit more. It'll help with healing them faster," Sirona explained. I glanced down at the hands wrapped in cloth as I sat quietly on one of the beds in the Medicus facility at the palace. Apparently, I had broken every single finger as I tried to smash through Oberon's shield. "You should take the tonic," she added and gestured to the vial on the table to my left. "It'll help with the pain."

I snorted bitterly. She had to be fucking kidding me. As if there was anything in this world that would ease the suffering of Evander being taken from me.

"I meant the pain in your hands," she amended softly, knowing where my mind had gone.

I didn't care. The injury was nothing compared to the agony of my shredded heart.

"Where will you bury her?" I asked, needing to divert my attention away from the healer before I snapped.

Cal let out a heavy breath as his sorrowful eyes turned to me. "North. It's where she always wanted to settle," he answered with a nod. "I'll bury her by the sea."

I closed my eyes for a moment, replaying Lia's words to Cal all those months ago. *And when this war is over, you and I will move to our house by the sea, just as you've been promising me for centuries.'*

"She'd like that," I said through my tears. Imogen's forehead pressed to Lia's body as she shuddered, breaking over the love she had finally found only to have it ripped from her months later. Cal pulled Imogen to his chest, cradling her as they both cried.

"I know we can't leave right now, so I'll see if Tallis can preserve—"

"No," I interrupted him with a shake of my head as I looked over my fallen friend—the first one I had made in Tenebrae. "Lia deserves to rest. She's earned it."

"Are you sure?" he questioned. I could hear the conflict in his voice. The desire to serve his kingdom and the need to take care of the woman he had loved for centuries.

"Take her to the sea, Cal." He nodded and smiled through his tears. "If you want to stay there for a while, you can."

"I can't," he corrected. "I need to be put to use. If I'm not, I'll just think about all the ways I failed her."

"You didn't," Imogen interrupted, pushing back to gaze at him.

"All Lia wanted was to live a simple life, and I didn't give that to her."

Imogen's hands cupped his face as she held his stare. "All Lia wanted was *you*, Calidore. It didn't matter where she was, she just needed to be with *you*. Don't you dare believe that you failed her."

She pressed her lips to his, kissing him softly as she held him close. I turned away, envious of what they had together and what I had lost.

This isn't where we part—it can't be.

With a deep breath, I collected myself and turned to Sirona who was organizing supplies across the private room.

"Let them in," I instructed her.

With a dip of her chin, she strolled over to the door and opened it wide, revealing several sets of anxious eyes who had been waiting in the hall since I was brought here over an hour ago.

"What of the missing enemy soldiers?" I asked immediately—a clear sign we wouldn't be discussing anything other than business.

Everyone exchanged curious glances before Tallis stepped forward first. "They attacked various strongholds in Caelum and Agnitio. Reports say they now occupy the western coast of Caelum."

I turned to Dash next. "Your plans?"

He shook his head as his arms crossed over his chest. I could see it in his eyes that he wanted to discuss what happened on the battlefield, but I was barely holding myself together as I looked at him.

"My kingdom is too large to keep control of with all of my forces scattered. I've ordered an evacuation of that coast with instructions to head east. It'll be easier to maintain the protection of half the land for now," he answered.

I nodded and twisted to look at Jahier. He cleared his throat before standing up straighter. "Fortunately, several of my father's soldiers have defected to our side. Tallis's people are interrogating them now to ensure we don't walk into a trap."

The first good news thus far.

Declan stepped forward without having to be called upon. "My soldiers should be here within two days. They are at your disposal. Place them where you see fit."

I drew a deep breath and clicked open the door to my Imperium, letting the rage and chaos fill me until it was all I knew. They took what belonged to me and I would stop at nothing to get him back. I turned to Cal to find his eyes already on me. He nodded as I raised my brow in question. "Imogen and I will be back in one week."

"When you return, I'll need you to take over my throne," I replied. He bowed his head without hesitation as the rest of the room broke out in concerned whispers.

"I can lead the armies," Marce announced from the threshold where her back was casually pressed against the doorframe. As she looked over Lia's body, there was a fire in her eyes that hadn't been there before. "Do what you need to, Your Majesty," she added. "I'll take care of our army in your absence."

"What absence?" Felix asked as he stepped forward cautiously. I dropped my focus to my wounded hands, unable to look at him.

"Olivier," I called as I unwrapped the cloth and let the fabric fall to the floor, revealing my fingers at odd angles. "I'll need you with me."

My Obscure came forth, crawling around my injuries and snapping the bones loudly into place. I ignored the protests of everyone in the room as I watched my fingers straighten before turning black and lengthening into claws. I was right—that pain was nothing compared to losing Evander.

Oli was already at my side as I jumped down from the table and strolled for the door.

"Where are you going?" Felix tried again.

My heart pounded in my ears and the bloodlust grew thick in my veins. I didn't stop as I called out the answer.

"To rip the world apart."